pp 80 - 94

The Storie

》》》》》》》》》 《《《《《《《《《《

Heinrich Böll

THE STORIES OF
Heinrich Böll

TRANSLATED FROM THE GERMAN BY

LEILA VENNEWITZ

NORTHWESTERN UNIVERSITY PRESS

EVANSTON, ILLINOIS

》》》》》》》》》》 《《《《《《《《《《《

Northwestern University Press

Evanston, Illinois 60208-4210

Originally published in German under the title *Gesammelte Erzählungen*.
Copyright © 1981, 1994 by Verlag Kiepenheuer & Witsch, Köln. Translation
copyright © 1986 by Leila Vennewitz and the Estate of Heinrich Böll. First pub-
lished in the United States in 1986 by Alfred A. Knopf, Inc., New York.
Northwestern University Press edition published 1995 by permission of Verlag
Kiepenheuer & Witsch and Leila Vennewitz. All rights reserved.

Second printing 2000

Printed in the United States of America

ISBN 0-8101-1207-8

The paper used in this publication meets the minimum requirements of the
American National Standard for Information Sciences—Permanence of Paper
for Printed Library Materials, ANSI Z39.48-1984.

Contents

Contents

[handwritten annotation: Look up /see Ribick / peu tree (online?)]

The Stories of Heinrich Böll

Breaking the News

D o you know those dreadful little places where you keep wondering why the railroad ever built a station there; where infinity seems to have congealed over a handful of dirty houses and a dilapidated factory, with fields on all sides condemned to eternal sterility; where you are suddenly aware that they are without hope because there is not a tree, not even a steeple, in sight? The man with the red cap—at last, at last, he gives the signal for the train to pull out—vanishes beneath a signboard bearing an imposing name, and you feel he is paid just to sleep twelve hours a day under a blanket of boredom. A gray horizon is draped over bleak fields cultivated by no one.

Yet I was not the only person to get out: an old woman carrying a large brown-paper parcel stepped down from the next compartment, but by the time I had emerged from the grimy little station she had disappeared as if swallowed up by the ground, and for a moment I was at a loss, not knowing whom to ask for directions. The scattering of brick houses with their dead windows and yellowish-green curtains defied all idea of human habitation, and at right angles to this token street ran a black wall that seemed on the point of collapse. I walked toward this grim-looking wall, afraid to knock at one of the houses of the dead. Then I turned the corner, and next to the grubby, barely legible sign saying "Inn," I read the words "Main Street" in clear, neat white lettering on a blue ground. A few more houses forming a crooked façade, crumbling plaster, and on the opposite side, long and windowless, the dingy factory wall like a barricade to the land of desolation. Following my instinct I turned left, but here the place suddenly came to an end; the wall continued for another ten yards or so, then came a leaden-gray field with a barely visible shimmer of green; somewhere the field merged with the gray, limitless horizon, and I had the terrible feeling that I was standing at the end of the world on the brink of a bottomless abyss, as if condemned to be dragged down into that silent, sinister, irresistible undertow of utter hopelessness.

On my left was a small, squat cottage, the kind workmen build in their spare time; I swayed, stumbled, toward it. Passing through a pitiful little gate with a leafless briar rose growing above it, I saw the number, and knew I had come to the right house.

The faded green shutters, their paint long washed away by the rain, were firmly closed, as if glued tight; the low roof—I could reach the gutter with my hand—had been patched with rusty corrugated sheets. The silence was absolute: it was the hour when twilight pauses for breath before welling up, gray and inexorable, over the edge of the horizon. I hesitated for a moment or two at the front door, wishing I had died in '45 when . . . instead of standing here about to enter this house. Just as I was going to raise my hand to knock, I heard a cooing sound, a woman's laugh, from inside; that mysterious, indefinable laugh that, depending on our mood, can either soothe us or wring our hearts. Only a woman who was not alone could laugh like that; again I hesitated, and again the burning, rending desire rose up in me to plunge into the gray infinity of the falling twilight that now hung over the broad fields and was beckoning, beckoning me . . . and with my last ounce of strength I pounded on the door.

First silence, then whispers—and footsteps, soft, slippered footsteps; the door opened, and I saw a fair, pink-cheeked woman who immediately put me in mind of that kind of indescribable radiance that illumines the farthest corners of a shadowy Rembrandt. Golden-red she glowed like a lamp before my eyes in this eternity of gray and black.

With a low cry she stepped back, holding the door open with trembling hands, but when I had taken off my army cap and said, hoarsely, "Good evening," the rigid lines of fear slackened in that strangely shapeless face, and she smiled uneasily and said, "Yes." In the background a muscular male figure loomed up and melted into the obscurity of the narrow passage. "I'd like to see Frau Brink," I said in a low voice. "Yes," the woman repeated tonelessly, and nervously pushed open a door. The male figure disappeared in the gloom. I entered a small room, crammed with shabby furniture, where the odor of bad food and excellent cigars seemed to have settled permanently. Her white hand went up to the switch: now that the light fell on her she seemed pale and amorphous, almost corpselike, only her fair, reddish hair was alive and warm. Her hands still trembling, she clutched her dark-red dress to her heavy breasts although it was closely buttoned—almost as if she were afraid I might stab her. The look in her watery blue eyes was wary, alarmed, as if, certain that some terrible sentence was awaiting her, she were facing a judge. Even the cheap sentimental prints seemed to have been stuck on the walls like indictments.

"Don't be alarmed," I said, my voice tense, and instantly I knew that was the worst way I could possibly have chosen to begin, but before I could go on she said, in a strangely composed voice: "I know all about it, he's dead . . . dead." I could only nod. I reached into my pocket to hand over his few belongings, but in the passage a furious voice shouted "Gitta!" She looked at me in despair, then flung open the door and called out shrilly: "For God's sake, can't you wait five minutes?" and banged the door shut again, and I could picture the man slinking off into a corner. Her eyes looked up defiantly, almost triumphantly, into mine.

I slowly placed the wedding ring, the watch, and the paybook with the well-thumbed photographs on the green plush tablecloth. Suddenly she started to sob, wild, terrible cries like an animal's. The outlines of her face dissolved, became soft and shapeless like a slug, and shining teardrops gushed out between her short fleshy fingers. She collapsed onto the sofa, leaning on the table with her right hand while with her left she fingered the pathetic little objects. Memory seemed to be lacerating her with a thousand swords. I knew then that the war would never be over, never, as long as somewhere a wound it had inflicted was still bleeding.

I threw aside everything—disgust, fear, and desolation—like a contemptible burden and placed my hand on the plump, heaving shoulder, and as she turned her astonished face toward me I saw for the first time a resemblance to that photo of a pretty, smiling girl that I had had to look at so many hundreds of times, in '45 when . . .

"Where was it—please sit down—on the Russian front?" I could see she was liable to burst into tears again at any moment.

"No, in the West, in the prisoner-of-war camp—there were more than a hundred thousand of us. . . ."

"And when?" Her gaze was wide and alert and extraordinarily alive, her whole face tense and young—as if her life depended on my reply. "In July '45," I said quietly.

She seemed to reflect for a moment, then she smiled—a pure and innocent smile, and I guessed why she was smiling.

Suddenly I felt as if the house were threatening to collapse about my ears, and I got up. Without a word she opened the door, she wanted to hold it open for me but I waited obstinately until she had gone ahead; and when she gave me her pudgy little hand she said, with a dry sob, "I knew it, I knew it, when I saw him off—it's almost three years ago now—when I saw him off at the station," and then she added almost in a whisper, "Don't despise me."

I felt a spasm of pain at these words—good God, surely I didn't look like a judge? And before she could stop me I had kissed her small, soft hand: it was the first time in my life I had ever kissed a woman's hand.

Outside darkness had fallen and, as if still under the spell of fear, I paused for a moment by the closed door. Then I heard her sobbing inside, loud, wild sobs, she was leaning against the front door with only the thickness of the wood between us, and at that moment I did indeed long for the house to collapse about her and bury her.

Then, slowly and very, very carefully—for I was afraid of sinking any moment into an abyss—I groped my way back to the station. Lights were twinkling in the houses of the dead, the tiny place seemed to have grown in all directions. I could even see small lamps beyond the black wall that seemed to be illuminating vast expanses of yard. Dusk had become dense and heavy, foggy, vaporous, and impenetrable.

In the drafty little waiting room there was only an elderly couple standing close together, shivering, in one corner. I waited a long time, my hands in my pockets, my cap pulled down over my ears, for there was a cold draft blowing in from the tracks, and night was falling lower, lower, like an enormous weight.

"If only there were a little more bread, and a bit of tobacco," muttered the man behind me. And I kept leaning forward to peer along the parallel lines of tracks as they converged in the distance between dim lights.

Suddenly the door was flung open, and the man with the red cap, his face a picture of eager devotion to duty, shouted out, as if he had to make his voice carry across the waiting room of a great railroad station: "Train for Cologne—ninety-five minutes late!"

At that moment I felt as if I had been taken prisoner for the rest of my life.

My Pal with the
Long Hair

IT WAS a funny thing: exactly five minutes before the raid started I had
a feeling something was wrong. . . . I looked warily round, then strolled
along the Rhine toward the station, and it didn't surprise me at all to see
the jeeps come dashing up full of red capped military police who proceeded to surround the block, cordon it off, and begin their search. It all
happened incredibly fast. I stood just outside the cordon and calmly lit a
cigarette. Everything was done so quietly. Quantities of cigarettes landed
on the ground. Too bad, I thought . . . instinctively making a rough
calculation as to the cash that must be lying around there. The truck rapidly
filled up with the ones they had nabbed. Franz was among them . . . he
gestured to me from a distance in a resigned kind of way, as much as to
say: Just my luck. One of the policemen turned round to look at me, so
I left. But slowly, very slowly. Hell, let them pick me up too, I couldn't
care less.

I was in no mood to go back to my room, so I continued my stroll
toward the station. I flicked a pebble aside with my stick. The sun was
warm, and a cool, soft breeze blew from the Rhine.

At the station buffet I gave Fritz, the waiter, the two hundred
cigarettes and stuffed the money into my hip pocket. I had no more to sell
now, just a packet for myself. In spite of the crowds jamming the place,
I managed to find a seat and ordered a bowl of soup and some bread. Again
I saw Fritz signaling me from across the room, but I didn't feel like getting
up, so he came hurrying across to me, with little Mausbach, the contact
man, in tow. They both seemed pretty excited. "Man, are you ever a cool
customer!" muttered Fritz and, shaking his head, he went off, leaving the
field to little Mausbach.

Mausbach was all out of breath. "For God's sake, man," he stammered, "beat it! They've searched your room and found the dope. . . . Oh
my God!" He was almost choking. I patted him reassuringly on the
shoulder and gave him twenty marks. "That's OK," I said, and off he
trotted. But I suddenly had an idea and called him back. "Listen, Heini,"

7

I said, "d'you suppose you could find a safe place for my books and overcoat? They're in my room. I'll come by again in a couple of weeks, OK? You can keep the rest of my things." He nodded. I could trust him. I knew that.

Too bad, I thought again—eight thousand marks down the drain. Nowhere, nowhere could a fellow feel safe.

A few inquisitive glances came my way as I slowly sat down again and nonchalantly reached for my pocket. Then the buzzing of the crowds closed over me, and I knew that nowhere else could I have been as marvelously alone with my thoughts as here, surrounded by all these swarms of people milling around in the station buffet.

All at once I was aware that my gaze, as it more or less automatically circled the room without taking anything in, invariably halted at the same spot, as if attracted to it by some magnetic spell. Each time, as my gaze casually toured the room, there was that spot where my eye was caught for a second before sliding hastily over it. I awoke as if from a deep sleep and, now with seeing eyes, looked in that direction.

Two tables away from me sat a girl wearing a light-colored coat, a tan beret on her dark hair, reading a newspaper. I could see very little of her: her shoulders hunching slightly forward, a tiny portion of her nose, and her slender, motionless hands. And I could see her legs too, beautiful legs, slim and . . . yes, clean. I don't know how long I stared at her; from time to time I caught sight of the narrow oval of her face as she turned a page. Suddenly she raised her head and for a moment looked me straight in the face with her large gray eyes, grave and detached, then resumed her reading.

That brief glance found its mark.

Patiently, yet conscious of my beating heart, I kept my eyes fixed on her until she finally finished the paper, leaned her arms on the table and, with a strangely despairing gesture, took a sip from her glass of beer.

Now I could see her whole face. A pale face, very pale, a small, fine-drawn mouth, and a straight, patrician nose . . . but her eyes, those huge, grave, gray eyes! Like a mourning veil her black hair hung down in dark waves to her shoulders.

I don't know how long I stared at her, whether it was twenty minutes, an hour, or longer. Each time she ran her eyes over my face, her glance became more uneasy, more brief, but her face showed none of the indignation girls usually show on such occasions. Uneasiness, yes . . . and fear.

God knows I didn't want to make her uneasy or afraid, but I couldn't take my eyes off her.

At last she got up abruptly, slung a worn haversack over her shoulder, and quickly left the buffet. I followed her. Without turning round she went up the steps toward the barrier. I kept her firmly, firmly within my line of vision as, with barely a pause, I hurriedly bought a platform ticket. She had a good head start on me, and I had to tuck my stick under my arm and try to run a little. I very nearly lost her in the dimly lit underpass leading up to the platform. I found her up at the top leaning against the remains of a bombed-out platform shelter. She was staring fixedly at the tracks. Not *once* did she turn round.

A chill wind from the Rhine was blowing right into the station. Evening came. A lot of people with packs and rucksacks, boxes and suitcases, stood about on the platform with harassed expressions. They turned their heads in dismay to where the wind was blowing from, and shivered. Ahead of them, dark blue and tranquil, yawned the great semicircle of the sky, punctured by the iron latticework of the station roof.

I limped slowly up and down, now and then glancing toward the girl to make sure she hadn't disappeared. But she was still there, still leaning straight-legged against the ruined wall, her eyes fixed on the flat, black trough in which the shining rails were embedded.

At last the train backed slowly into the station. While I was looking toward the engine, the girl had jumped onto the moving train and disappeared into a compartment. I lost sight of her for several minutes among all the knots of people jostling their way into the compartments, but before long I glimpsed the tan beret in the last car. I got in and sat down right opposite her, so close that our knees were almost touching. When she looked at me, very gravely and quietly, her brows slightly puckered, the expression in her great gray eyes told me that she knew I had been following her the whole time. Again and again my eyes fastened helplessly on her face as the train sped into the oncoming evening. My lips refused to utter a word. The fields sank from view, and the villages gradually became shrouded in the night. I felt cold. Where was I going to sleep tonight, I thought . . . where would I ever be able to breathe easily again? Ah, if I could only bury my face in that black hair. That was all I asked, I asked for nothing more. . . . I lit a cigarette. She cast a fleeting but oddly alert glance at the package. I merely held it out to her, saying huskily, "Help yourself," and felt as if my heart were going to jump out of my throat. She hesitated for a fraction of a second, and in spite of the darkness I saw her momentarily blush. Then she took one. She pulled deeply and hungrily on the cigarette as she smoked.

"You are very generous." Her voice was dark-toned and brusque. A few minutes later I heard the conductor in the next compartment, and as if at a signal we instantly threw ourselves back into our corners and pretended to be asleep. But I could see through my half-open lids that she was laughing. I watched the conductor as he shone his glaring flashlight onto the tickets and checked them. And the next moment the light was shining right into my face. I could feel from the way the light wavered that he was hesitating. Then the light fell on her. How pale she was, and how sad the white surface of her forehead.

A stout woman sitting beside me pulled at the conductor's sleeve and whispered something in his ear. I caught the words: "American cigarettes . . . black market . . . no ticket," to which the conductor responded by giving me a spiteful jab in the ribs.

There was silence in the compartment as I asked her quietly where she was going. She named a town. I bought two tickets for the place and paid the fine. The silence of the other passengers, after the conductor had gone, was icy and scornful. But her voice was strange, warm and yet mocking, as she asked, "So you're going there too?"

"Oh, I might as well get off there. I have friends there. I've got no permanent home. . . ."

"I see" was all she said. She leaned back in her corner, and in the close darkness I could only glimpse her face whenever a light outside rushed by.

It was pitch-dark by the time we got out. Dark and warm. And when we emerged from the station, the small town was already fast asleep. The little houses slept safe and sound beneath the gentle trees. "I'll go with you," I said hoarsely. "It's so dark you can't see a thing."

But suddenly she stopped. It was under a streetlight. She fixed me with a long, wide-eyed stare and said in a strained voice, "If only I knew where I was going." Her face moved slightly, like a scarf stirred by a breeze. No, we did not kiss. . . . We walked slowly out through the town and eventually crawled into a haystack. I had no friends here, of course: I was as much a stranger in this silent town as in any other. When it got chilly toward morning, I crept close beside her, and she covered me with part of her thin, skimpy coat. And so we warmed each other with our breath and our blood.

We have been together ever since—in these hard times.

The Man with
the Knives

Jupp HELD the knife by the tip of the blade, letting it joggle idly up and down; it was a long, tapering bread knife, obviously razor-sharp. With a sudden flick of the wrist he tossed the knife into the air. Up it went, whirring like a propeller; the shining blade glittered like a golden fish in a sheaf of lingering sunbeams, struck the ceiling, lost its spin, and plunged down straight at Jupp's head. In a flash Jupp had placed a wooden block on his head; the knife scored into the wood and remained embedded there, gently swaying. Jupp removed the block from his head, withdrew the knife, and flung it with a gesture of annoyance at the door, where it stuck, quivering, in the frame until it gradually stopped vibrating and fell to the floor. . . .

"It makes me sick," said Jupp quietly. "I've been working on the logical assumption that people who've paid for their tickets really want to see a show where life and limb are at stake—like at the Roman circuses —they want to be convinced of at least the possibility of bloodshed, know what I mean?"

He picked up the knife and tossed it neatly against the top crossbar of the window, with such force that the panes rattled and threatened to fall out of the crumbling putty. This throw—confident and unerring— took me back to those hours of semidarkness in the past when he had thrown his pocketknife against the dugout post, from bottom to top and down again.

"I'll do anything," he went on, "to give the customers a thrill. I'll even cut off my ears, only it's hard to find anyone to stick them back on again. Here, I want to show you something."

He opened the door for me, and we went out into the hallway. A few shreds of wallpaper still clung to the walls where the glue was too stubborn for them to be ripped off and used for lighting the stove. After passing through a moldering bathroom, we emerged onto a kind of terrace, its concrete floor cracked and moss-covered.

Jupp pointed upward.

"The higher the knife goes, of course, the greater the effect. But I need some resistance up there for the thing to strike against and lose momentum so that it can come hurtling down straight at my useless skull. Look!" He pointed up to where the iron girders of a ruined balcony stuck out into the air.

"This is where I used to practice. For a whole year. Watch!" He sent the knife soaring upward. It rose with marvelous symmetry and evenness, seeming to climb as smoothly and effortlessly as a bird; then it struck one of the girders, shot down with breathtaking speed, and crashed into the wooden block. The impact itself must have been terrific. Jupp didn't bat an eyelid. The knife had buried itself a couple of inches in the wood.

"But that's fantastic!" I cried. "It's absolutely sensational, they'll have to like it—what an act!"

Jupp nonchalantly withdrew the knife from the wood, grasped it by the handle, and made a thrust in the air.

"Oh, they like it all right. They pay me twelve marks a night, and between the main acts they let me play around a bit with the knife. But the act's not elaborate enough. A man, a knife, a block of wood, don't you see? I ought to have a half-naked girl so I can send the knife spinning a hair's breadth past her nose. That'd make the crowd go wild. But try and find that kind of a girl!"

He went ahead as we returned to his room. He placed the knife carefully on the table, the wooden block beside it, and rubbed his hands. We sat down on the crate beside the stove and were silent. Taking some bread out of my pocket, I said, "Be my guest."

"Thanks, I will, but let me make some coffee. Then you can come along and watch my performance."

He put some more wood in the stove and set the pot over the opening. "It's infuriating," he said. "Maybe I look too serious, a bit like a sergeant still, eh?"

"Nonsense, you never were a sergeant. D'you smile when they clap?"

"Of course—and bow too."

"I couldn't. I couldn't smile in a cemetery."

"That's a great mistake: a cemetery's the very place *to* smile."

"I don't get it."

"Because they aren't dead. They're none of them dead, see?"

"I see, all right, but I don't believe it."

"There's still a bit of the lieutenant about you after all. Well, in that case it just takes longer, of course. The point is, I'm only too glad if they enjoy it. They're burned out inside; I give them a bit of a thrill and get paid for it. Perhaps one of them, just one, will go home and not forget me. 'That man with the knife, for Christ's sake, he wasn't scared, and I'm scared all the time, for Christ's sake,' maybe that's what he'll say because they're all scared, all the time. They trail their fear behind them like a heavy shadow, and it makes me happy if they can forget about it and laugh a little. Isn't that reason enough to smile?"

I said nothing, my eyes on the water, waiting for it to boil. Jupp poured the boiling water onto the coffee in the brown enamel pot, and we took turns drinking from the pot and shared my bread. Outside, the mild dusk began to fall, flowing into the room like soft gray milk.

"What are *you* doing these days, by the way?" asked Jupp.

"Nothing . . . just getting by."

"A hard way to make a living."

"Right—for this loaf of bread I had to collect a hundred bricks and clean them. Casual labor."

"Hm . . . Want to see another of my tricks?"

In response to my nod he stood up, switched on the light, and went over to the wall, where he pushed aside a kind of rug, disclosing the rough outline of a man drawn in charcoal on the reddish color-wash: a strange lump protruded from what was supposed to be the head, probably signifying a hat. On closer inspection I saw that the man had been drawn on a skillfully camouflaged door. I watched expectantly as Jupp proceeded to pull out a handsome little brown leather suitcase from under the miserable affair that served as his bed and put it on the table. Before opening it, he came over and placed four cigarette butts in front of me. "Roll those into two thin ones," he said.

I moved my seat so that I could watch him as well as get a bit more of the gentle warmth from the stove. While I was carefully pulling the butts apart on the bread paper spread over my knees, Jupp had snapped open the lock of the suitcase and pulled out an odd-looking object: one of those flannel bags consisting of a series of pockets in which our mothers used to keep their table silver. He deftly untied the ribbon and let the bundle unroll across the table to reveal a dozen wood-handled knives, the kind that, in the days when our mothers danced the waltz, were known as "hunting cutlery."

I divided the tobacco shreds scrupulously in half onto the two cigarette papers and rolled them. "Here," I said.

"Here," Jupp said too, and "Thanks," bringing over the flannel bag for me to look at.

"This is all I managed to salvage from my parents' belongings. Almost everything was burned or lost in the rubble, and the rest stolen. When I got back from POW camp I was really on my beam ends, didn't own a thing in the world—until one day a dignified old lady, a friend of my mother's, tracked me down and brought along this nice suitcase. A few days before my mother was killed in an air raid she had left it with the old lady to be looked after, and it had survived. Funny, isn't it? But of course we know that when people panic they try to save the strangest things. Never the essential ones. So then at least I was the owner of the contents of this suitcase: the brown enamel pot, twelve forks, twelve knives and twelve spoons, and the long bread knife. I sold the spoons and forks, living off the proceeds for a year, and practiced with the knives, thirteen of them. Watch. . . ."

I passed him the spill I had used to light my cigarette. Jupp stuck his cigarette to his lower lip, fastened the ribbon of the flannel bag to a button on the shoulder of his jacket, and let the flannel unroll along his arm like some exotic panoply of war. Then with incredible speed he whisked the knives out of their pockets, and before I could follow his movements he had thrown all twelve like lightning against the dim human outline, which reminded me of those sinister, shambling figures that came lurching at us toward the end of the war from every billboard, every corner, harbingers of defeat and destruction. Two knives were sticking out of the man's hat, two over each shoulder, and the others, three a side, along the dangling arms. . . .

"Fantastic!" I cried. "Fantastic! But you've got your act right there, with a bit of dramatizing."

"All I need is a man, better still a girl. But I know I'll never find anyone," he said with a sigh, plucking the knives out of the door and slipping them carefully back into their pockets. "The girls are too scared and the men want too much money. Can't blame them, of course; it's a risky business."

Once again he flung the knives back at the door in such a way as to split the entire black figure accurately down the middle with dazzling symmetry. The thirteenth knife, the big one, stuck like a deadly arrow just where the man's heart should have been.

Jupp took a final puff of the thin, tobacco-filled roll of paper and threw the scant remains behind the stove.

"Let's go," he said, "it's time we were off." He stuck his head out the window, muttered something about "damned rain," and added: "It's a few minutes to eight, I'm on at eight-thirty."

While he was packing the knives away in the suitcase I stood with my face by the open window. Decaying villas seemed to be whimpering softly in the rain, and from behind a wall of swaying poplars came the screech of the streetcar. But nowhere could I see a clock.

"How d'you know what time it is?"

"Instinct—that's part of my training."

I gaped at him. First he helped me on with my coat and then put on his windbreaker. My shoulder is slightly paralyzed and I can't move my arms beyond a certain radius, just far enough to clean bricks. We put on our caps and went out into the dingy corridor, and I was glad to hear at least some voices in the house, laughter, and a subdued murmuring.

"It's like this," said Jupp as we went down the stairs. "What I've tried to do is trace certain cosmic laws. Watch." He put the suitcase down on a stair and spread his arms, an Icarus poised for flight in the way the ancient Greeks used to show him. His matter-of-fact expression assumed a strangely cool and dreamlike quality, something between obsession and detachment, something magical, that I found quite spine-chilling. "Like this," he said softly. "I simply reach out into the atmosphere, I feel my hands getting longer and longer, reaching out into a dimension governed by different laws, they push through a ceiling, and beyond are strange, spell-binding tensions—I just take hold of them, that's all . . . and then I seize their laws, snatch them away, part thief, part lover, and carry them off." He clenched his fists, drawing them close to his body. "Let's go," he said, and his expression was its usual matter-of-fact self. I followed him in a daze. . . .

Outside, a chill rain was falling softly and steadily. We turned up our collars and withdrew shivering into ourselves. The mist of twilight was surging through the streets, already tinged with the bluish darkness of night. In several basements among the bombed-out villas a meager light was burning under the towering black weight of a great ruin. The street gradually became a muddy path where to left and right, in the opaque twilight, shacks loomed up in the scrawny gardens like junks afloat in a shallow backwater. We crossed the streetcar tracks, plunged into the maze of narrow streets on the city's outskirts, where among piles of rubble and garbage a few houses still stand intact in the dirt, until we emerged suddenly into a busy street. The tide of the crowds carried us along for a bit, until we turned a corner into a dark side street where a garish illuminated sign saying "The Seven Mills" was reflected in the glistening asphalt.

The foyer of the vaudeville theater was empty. The performance had already begun, and the buzzing of the audience penetrated the shabby red drapes.

With a laugh Jupp pointed to a photograph in a display case, where he was shown in cowboy costume between two coyly smiling dancers whose breasts were hung with sparkling tinsel. Beneath was the caption: "The Man with the Knives."

"Come on," said Jupp, and before I grasped what was happening I found myself being dragged through a half-hidden door. We climbed a poorly lit staircase, narrow and winding, the smell of sweat and greasepaint indicating the nearness of the stage. Jupp was ahead—suddenly he halted in a turn of the stairs, put down the suitcase, and, gripping me by the shoulders, asked in a hushed voice, "Are you game?"

I had been expecting this question for so long that when it came its suddenness startled me. I must have looked nonplussed, for after a pause he said, "Well?"

I still hesitated, and suddenly we heard a great roar of laughter that seemed to come pouring out of the narrow passage and engulf us like a tidal wave; it was so overwhelming that I jumped and involuntarily shuddered.

"I'm scared," I whispered.

"So am I. Don't you trust me?"

"Sure I do . . . but . . . let's go," I said hoarsely, pushing past him and adding, with the courage born of despair, "I've nothing to lose."

We emerged onto a narrow corridor with a number of rough ply-wood cubicles right and left. A few oddly garbed figures were scurrying about, and through an opening in the flimsy wings I could see a clown on the stage, his enormous mouth wide open; once again the roar of the crowd's laughter engulfed us, but Jupp pulled me through a door and shut it behind us. I looked around. The cubicle was tiny, practically bare. On the wall was a mirror, Jupp's cowboy costume hung on the single nail, and on a rickety chair lay an old deck of cards. Jupp moved with nervous haste; he took my wet coat from me, flung the cowboy suit onto the chair, hung up my coat, then his windbreaker. Over the top of the partition I could see an electric clock on a fake red Doric column, showing twenty-five after eight.

"Five minutes," muttered Jupp, slipping into his costume. "Shall we rehearse it?"

Just then someone knocked on the cubicle door and called, "You're on!"

Jupp buttoned up his shirt and stuck a ten-gallon hat on his head. With a forced laugh I cried, "D'you expect a condemned man to rehearse his own hanging?"

Jupp snatched up the suitcase and dragged me through the door. Outside stood a bald-headed man watching the clown going through his final motions on the stage. Jupp whispered something to the man that I didn't catch, the man glanced up with a start, looked at me, looked at Jupp, and shook his head vehemently. And again Jupp whispered something to him.

I couldn't have cared less. Let them impale me alive. I had a crippled shoulder, I had just finished a thin cigarette, tomorrow I would get three-quarters of a loaf for seventy-five bricks. But tomorrow. . . . The applause almost blew down the wings. The clown, his face tired and contorted, staggered toward us through the opening in the wings, stood there for a few seconds looking morose, and then went back onto the stage, where he smiled graciously and bowed. The orchestra played a fanfare. Jupp was still whispering to the bald-headed man. Three times the clown came back into the wings and three times he went out onto the stage and bowed, smiling.

Then the orchestra struck up a march and, suitcase in hand, Jupp strode smartly out onto the stage. His appearance was greeted with subdued clapping. Weary-eyed I watched Jupp fasten the playing cards onto nails that were already in place and then impale each card with a knife, one by one, precisely in the center. The applause became more animated, but not enthusiastic. Then, to a muffled roll of drums, he performed his trick with the bread knife and the block of wood, and underneath all my indifference I was aware that the act really was a bit thin. Across from me, on the other side of the stage, a few scantily dressed girls stood watching. . . . And suddenly the bald-headed man seized me by the shoulder, dragged me onto the stage, greeted Jupp with a grandiose sweep of the arm and, in the spurious voice of a policeman, said, "Good evening, Herr Borgalevsky."

"Good evening, Herr Erdmenger," replied Jupp, likewise in ceremonious tones.

"I've brought you a horsethief, a proper scoundrel, Herr Bor- galevsky, for you to tickle a bit with your shiny knives before we hang him . . . a real scoundrel. . . ." I found his voice totally ridiculous, pathetically artificial, like paper flowers or the cheapest kind of greasepaint. I glanced at the audience, and from that moment on, faced by that glim- mering, slavering, hydra-headed monster crouching there in the dark ready to spring, I simply switched off.

I didn't give a damn, I was dazzled by the glare of the spotlight, and in my threadbare suit and shabby shoes I probably made a pretty convinc- ing horsethief.

"Oh, leave him here with me, Herr Erdmenger. I know how to deal with him."

"Splendid, let him have it, and don't spare the knives."

Jupp took hold of me by the collar while the grinning Erdmenger swaggered off the stage. Someone threw a rope onto the stage, and Jupp proceeded to tie me by the feet to a cardboard column that had a fake door, painted blue, propped up behind it. I was aware of something like an ecstasy of insensibility. To my right I heard the eerie stirring of the tense audience, and I realized Jupp had been right in speaking of its bloodlust. Its thirst quivered on the sickly, stale air, and the orchestra, with its facile drum roll, its muffled lasciviousness, heightened the effect of grisly tragicomedy in which real blood would flow, stage blood that had been paid for. . . . I stared straight ahead, letting my body sag, the rope being so firmly tied that it held me upright. The drum roll became softer and softer as Jupp calmly pulled his knives out of the playing cards and slipped them back into their pockets, from time to time casting melodramatic glances my way as if to size me up. Then, having packed away all his knives, he turned to the audience and in the same odiously stagy voice announced, "Ladies and gentlemen, I am now about to outline this young man with knives, but I wish to demonstrate to you that I do not throw blunt knives." He produced a piece of string, and with perfect sangfroid removed one knife after another from its pocket, touched the string with each, cutting it into twelve pieces, and then replaced the knives one by one in their pockets.

While all this was going on I looked far beyond him, far beyond the wings, far beyond the half-naked girls, into another life, it seemed. . . .

The tension in the audience was electrifying. Jupp came over to me, pretended to adjust the rope, and said softly into my ear, "Don't move a muscle, and trust me. . . ."

This added delay nearly broke the tension, it was threatening to peter out, but he suddenly stretched out his arms, letting his hands flutter like hovering birds, and his face assumed that look of magical concentration that I had marveled at on the stairs. He appeared to be casting a spell over the audience too with this sorcerer's pose. I seemed to hear a strange, unearthly groan and realized that this was a warning signal for me.

Withdrawing my gaze from limitless horizons, I looked at Jupp, now standing opposite me so that our eyes were on a level; he raised his hand, moving it slowly toward a pocket, and again I realized that this was a signal for me. I stood completely still and closed my eyes. . . .

It was a glorious feeling, lasting maybe two seconds, I'm not sure. Listening to the swish of the knives and the short sharp hiss of air as they plunged into the fake blue door, I felt as if I were walking along a very narrow plank over a bottomless abyss. I walked with perfect confidence, yet felt all the thrill of danger. I was afraid, yet absolutely certain that I would not fall; I was not counting, yet I opened my eyes at the very moment when the last knife pierced the door beside my right hand. . . .

A storm of applause jerked me bolt upright. I opened my eyes properly to find myself looking into Jupp's white face: he had rushed over to me and was untying the rope with trembling hands. Then he pulled me into the center of the stage, right up to the very edge. He bowed, and I bowed; as the applause swelled he pointed to me and I to him; then he smiled at me, I smiled at him, and we both bowed smiling to the audience.

Back in the cubicle, not a word was said. Jupp threw the perforated playing cards onto the chair, took my coat off the nail and helped me on with it. Then he hung his cowboy costume back on the nail, pulled on his windbreaker, and we put on our caps. As I opened the door the little bald-headed man rushed up to us shouting, "I'm raising you to forty marks!" He handed Jupp some cash. I realized then that Jupp was my boss, and I smiled; he looked at me too and smiled.

Jupp took my arm, and side by side we walked down the narrow, poorly lit stairs that smelled of stale greasepaint. When we reached the foyer Jupp said with a laugh, "Now let's go and buy some cigarettes and bread. . . ."

But it was not till an hour later that I realized I now had a proper profession, a profession where all I needed to do was stand still and dream a little. For twelve or twenty seconds. I was the man who has knives thrown at him. . . .

Reunion
on the Avenue

Sometimes, when it got really quiet, when the hoarse growl of the machine guns had died down and that hideous harsh sound of grenade launchers had ceased, when over the lines there hovered an indefinable something that our fathers might have called peace: during those hours we would interrupt our lice picking or our shallow sleep, and Lieutenant Hecker's long hands would finger the catch of the ammunition case that was let into the wall of our dugout and known to us as our bar. He would tug at the leather strap, making the prong of the clasp snap out of its hole and disclose our property in all its glory: on the left the Lieutenant's bottle, on the right mine, and in the middle, jointly owned, our most treasured possession, saved up for the hours when it got really quiet. . . .

Between the gray-white bottles of potato schnapps stood two bottles of genuine French cognac, the finest we had ever tasted. In some manner that defied explanation, passing through untold opportunities for pilfering and the very heart of the jungle of corruption, genuine Hennessy would turn up at intervals in our front-line dugouts, where we were fighting dirt, lice, and despair. The youngsters, with the craving of pallid children for sweet things, shuddered at the mere mention of schnapps, so we gave them chocolate and candy in exchange for their share of this golden elixir, and seldom, I imagine, was any barter concluded with greater satisfaction to both parties.

"Come on," Hecker used to say, after buttoning on a clean collar—if one was available—and running his hand voluptuously over his freshly shaved chin. I would slowly get to my feet and emerge from the shadowy depths of our dugout, lethargically brush the wisps of straw from my uniform, and confine myself to the only ritual for which I could still summon enough energy: comb my hair, and slowly, with a dedication bordering on the unnatural, wash my hands in Hecker's shaving water—some coffee dregs in a tin can. Meanwhile Hecker, patiently waiting for me to clean my nails, would first set up an ammunition case between us as a kind of table, then take out his handkerchief and wipe our two schnapps glasses: thick, solid affairs that we guarded as carefully as our tobacco. By the time he had dug the big pack of cigarettes out from the inner recesses of his pocket, I had completed my preparations.

It was usually in the afternoon, we had pushed aside the blanket hanging in front of our dugout, and sometimes a bit of modest sunshine warmed our feet. . . .

Our eyes met, we touched glasses, drank, and smoked. Our silence had a quality of solemn rapture. The only evidence of the enemy was the sound of a sniper's bullet striking the ground, with scrupulous punctuality and at regular intervals, just in front of the beams shoring up the earth bank at the entrance to our dugout. With a small, rather endearing "flup," the bullet would whir into the crumbling earth. It often reminded me of the modest, barely audible scurrying of a field mouse across a path on a quiet afternoon. There was something soothing about this sound, for it reassured us that this delectable hour now about to begin was not a dream, not an illusion, but part of our real life.

Only after the fourth or fifth glass would we start to talk. Beneath the exhausted rubble of our hearts, this miraculous potion awakened something strangely precious that our fathers might have called nostalgia.

About the war, the present, we had said all we had to say. Too often and too intimately had we seen the bared teeth in its hideous face, too often had its nauseating breath set our hearts quivering as we listened on dark nights to the wounded pleading in two languages between the lines. We loathed it too deeply to be able to believe in the cant sent up like soap bubbles by the riffraff on both sides to invest it with the virtues of a "mission."

Nor could the future serve as a topic. The future was a black tunnel full of sharp corners that we were going to bump into, and we lived in dread of it, for the appalling existence we led as soldiers who had to wish for the war to be lost had hollowed out our hearts.

We talked about the past; about those meager rudiments of what our fathers might have called life. About that all too brief span of human memories caught between the rotting corpse of the Weimar Republic and that bloated monster of a state whose pay we had to pocket.

"Picture a little café," said Hecker, "under some trees, maybe, in the fall. The smell of moisture and decaying leaves in the air, and you're translating a poem by Verlaine. You're wearing very light shoes, and later, when dusk falls in opaque clouds, you scuff your way home—know what I mean? You scuff your feet through the wet leaves and look into the faces of the girls coming toward you. . . ." He filled our glasses, his hands as quiet as those of a kindly doctor operating on a child, we touched glasses and drank. . . . "Maybe one of the girls smiles at you, you smile back, and you both go on your way without turning round. That little smile you exchanged will never die, never, I tell you. . . . It may be your signal of recognition when you meet again in another life . . . an absurd little smile. . . ."

A marvelously youthful light came into his eyes, he looked at me and laughed, and I smiled too, grasped the bottle and poured. We drank three or four glasses, one after another, and no tobacco ever tasted finer than the one that blended with the exquisite aroma of the cognac.

At intervals the sniper's bullet would remind us that time was dripping remorselessly away; and behind our pleasure and our enjoyment of the hour there was again that inexorable threat to our existence that could wipe us out with a bursting shell, a sentry's warning cry, or a command to attack or retreat. We began to drink faster, our conversation grew more distraught, the gentle contentment in our eyes was joined by passion and hatred; and when, as was inevitable, the bottom of the bottle became visible, Hecker would become unutterably sad, his eyes would turn toward me like blurred disks, and in a low, almost incoherent voice he would begin whispering: "That girl, you know, lived at the end of an avenue, and the last time I was on leave. . . ."

That was the signal for me to cut him short. "Lieutenant," I would say, coldly and severely, "be quiet, d'you hear?" He had told me himself, "When I start talking about a girl who lived at the end of an avenue, it's time for you to tell me to shut up, d'you understand? You must, you must!"

And I obeyed this command, although it went against the grain, for when I reminded him, Hecker would stop in his tracks, the light in his eyes would go out, they would become hard and sober, and around his mouth the old creases of bitterness would reappear. . . .

On that particular day, however, the one I am talking about, everything was unusual. We had been issued underwear, brand-new underwear, and a fresh supply of cognac. I had shaved and even gone so far as to wash my feet in the tin can; in fact, I practically took a bath, for they had even sent us new socks, socks with white borders that were still really white.

Hecker was leaning back on our pallet, smoking and watching me wash. It was absolutely silent outside, but this silence was evil and numbing, a threatening silence, and I could tell from Hecker's hands when he lit a fresh cigarette from the old one that he was on edge and afraid: we were all afraid, everyone who was still human was afraid.

Suddenly we heard the faint scurrying sound the sniper's bullet always made in the earth bank, and with this gentle sound the silence ceased to be unnerving. With one breath we both laughed out loud; Hecker jumped to his feet, stamped around a bit, and shouted like a child, "Hooray, hooray, now let's get drunk, drunk in honor of our friend who always fires at the same place and always at the wrong place!"

He unfastened the catch, slapped me on the shoulder, and waited patiently until I had pulled my boots on again and seated myself in readiness for our drinking session. Hecker spread a clean handkerchief over the case and drew two light-brown cigars of impressive length from his breast pocket.

"You can't beat that," he said as he laughed, "cognac and a good cigar!" We touched glasses, drank, and smoked with slow, rapturous enjoyment.

"How about you talking for a change?" cried Hecker. "Come on, tell me something about yourself," he said, giving me a serious look. "You know something? You've never told me a thing, you've always let me rattle on."

"There's not much to tell," I observed in a low voice, and then I looked at him, poured some more cognac, waited, and then we drank together, and it was marvelous to feel the cool, superbly warming drink flowing into us in a stream of dark gold. "You see," I began diffidently, "I'm younger than you and a bit older. I was hopeless in school, so I had to quit and learn a trade, they apprenticed me to a cabinetmaker. That was pretty hard to take at first, but in time, after a year or so, I began to enjoy the work. There's something tremendously satisfying about working with wood. You make yourself a drawing on some nice white paper, get your wood ready, clean, fine-grained planks, and then you plane them with loving care while the smell of wood rises into your nostrils. I believe I would have made quite a good cabinetmaker, but at nineteen I was called up, and I've never recovered from the first shock I got after passing through the barracks gates, not even now, after six years, that's why I don't talk much . . . with you fellows it's a bit different. . . ." I blushed, it was the longest speech I had ever made in my life.

Hecker looked at me reflectively. "I see," he said. "I like the sound of that: cabinetmaker."

"But haven't you ever had a girl?" he suddenly resumed, raising his voice, and I knew at once that I would soon have to cut him short again. "Never ever? Haven't you ever leaned your head on a soft shoulder and smelled her hair . . . never?" This time it was he who refilled our glasses, and with these two drinks the bottle was empty. Hecker glanced round with a look of terrible sadness. "No walls here to smash a bottle against, eh? Wait a minute," he shouted suddenly with a wild laugh, "our friend must have something too, let's have him smash it."

He stepped forward and placed the bottle on the spot where the sniper's bullets always struck the earth, and before I could stop him he had taken the next bottle out of our bar, opened it, and filled our glasses. We touched glasses, and at the same moment a gentle "ping" sounded from outside on the bank: we looked up in alarm and saw how for an instant the bottle stood steady, almost rigid, but the next instant its top half slid off, leaving the bottom half still standing. The chunk of broken glass rolled into the ditch almost to our feet, and all I remember is being frightened, frightened from the moment the bottle was shattered. . . .

At the same time I was seized by a profound indifference while I helped Hecker empty the second bottle as fast as he filled our glasses. Yes, fear and at the same time indifference. Hecker was frightened too, I could tell; our agonized eyes avoided each other, and that day I couldn't summon the strength to interrupt him when he started talking about the girl. . . .

"You know," he said urgently, looking beyond me, "she lived at the end of an avenue, and the last time I was on leave it was in the fall, real fall weather, late afternoon, and I can't begin to describe how beautiful the avenue was." A wild, rapturous, yet somehow frenzied happiness leaped into his eyes, and if only for the sake of that happiness I was glad I had not interrupted him; as he went on talking he worked his hands like a person trying to give shape to something without knowing how, and I could feel him searching for the right expressions to describe the avenue to me. I filled our glasses, we drank up, I filled them again, we tossed them back. . . .

"The avenue," he said huskily, almost stammering, "the avenue was all golden—I'm not kidding, it really was, black trees with gold, and a grayish blue shimmer in the gold—I was in ecstasy as I walked slowly along under the trees as far as that house, I felt as if that fantastic beauty had spun a web around me, and I drank in the intoxicating transience of our human happiness. Do you know what I mean? That magical certainty moved me inexpressibly . . . and . . . and . . ."

Hecker was silent for a while, evidently searching for words again; I poured out some more cognac, we touched glasses, and drank: at that precise instant the bottom half of the bottle on the bank was shattered too, and with maddening deliberation the pieces of glass rolled one after another into the ditch.

I was startled to see Hecker jump to his feet, lean down, and thrust the blanket aside. I held on to his sleeve, and I knew now why I had been frightened all along. "Let go!" he shouted. "Let go . . . I'm going—I'm going to the avenue. . . ." Outside, I stood next to him, holding the bottle. "I'm going," whispered Hecker, "I'm going all the way along it, right to the end where the house is! There's a brown iron gate in front of it, and she lives upstairs, and . . ." I ducked hurriedly as a bullet whistled past me into the bank, landing just where the bottle had stood.

Hecker was whispering incoherent, rambling words, on his face a look of serene happiness, mild and gentle now, and there might still have been time to call him back as he had ordered me to. From his ramblings I could distinguish only the same words, repeated over and over, "I'm going—don't try to stop me, I'm going to the house where my girl lives. . . ."

I felt a real coward, crouching there on the ground holding the bottle of cognac, and guilty at being sober, cruelly sober, while Hecker wore an expression of unutterably sweet, serene drunkenness. He was staring straight ahead at the enemy lines between black sunflower stalks and shelled farmhouses; I watched him narrowly as he smoked a cigarette.

"Lieutenant," I called softly, holding out the bottle, "come and have a drink," and when I tried to stand up I realized I was drunk too, and I cursed myself to the very depths of my being for not having called him back soon enough, for now it was obviously too late. He hadn't heard me call, and just as I was about to open my mouth to call him again, at least to entice him back out of danger with the bottle, I heard the clear, high-pitched "ping" of an exploding bullet. With appalling suddenness Hecker turned round, gave me one brief and blissful smile, placed his cigarette on the bank, and collapsed, falling slowly, slowly backward. An icy hand gripped my heart, the bottle slid from my grasp, and I watched in shock and dismay as the cognac, gently gurgling, flowed out and formed a little puddle. Once again it was very quiet, and the silence was menacing. . . .

At last I found the courage to raise my eyes and look into Hecker's face: his cheeks had caved in, his eyes were black and rigid, yet his face still bore a hint of that smile which had blossomed there as he whispered those frenzied words. I knew he was dead. But all of a sudden I started shouting, shouting like a madman. I leaned over the bank, oblivious to all caution, and shouted to the next dugout, "Heini! Help! Heini, Hecker's dead!" and without waiting for an answer I sank sobbing to the ground, seized by unspeakable horror, for Hecker's head had raised itself a little, barely perceptibly, but visibly, and blood was welling out of it and a ghastly yellowish-white substance that could only be his brains; it flowed on and on, and frozen with terror I could only think: Where can all this blood be coming from, just from his head? The whole floor of our dugout was covered with blood, the clayey soil didn't absorb it, and the blood reached the spot where I knelt beside the empty bottle. . . .

I was alone in the world with Hecker's blood, for Heini didn't answer and the gentle swish of the sniper's bullet was no longer audible. . . .

Suddenly, however, the silence was rent by an explosion, I scrambled to my feet, and at the same moment something struck me in the back, although strangely enough I felt no pain. I sank forward with my head on Hecker's chest, and while noise sprang to life around me, the frantic barking of the machine gun from Heini's dugout and the sickening impact of the grenade launchers that we called pipe organs, I became quite calm: for mingling with Hecker's dark blood that still covered the bottom of the dugout was a lighter, miraculously light blood that I knew was warm and my own; and I sank down and down until I found myself, smiling happily, at the entrance to that avenue which Hecker hadn't known how to describe, because the trees were bare, solitude and desolation were nesting among wan shadows, and hope died in my heart, while far off, at an immense distance, I could see Hecker's beckoning figure outlined against a soft golden light. . . .

Broommakers

OUR MATH teacher was as good-natured as he was hot-tempered. He used to come charging into the classroom—hands in pockets—spew his cigarette butt into the cuspidor to the left of the wastepaper basket, take the dais by storm and, standing by his desk, call out my name as he asked some question or other to which I never knew the answer, no matter what it was.

After I had floundered my way to a halt, he would walk over to me, very slowly, accompanied by the tittering of the whole class, and cuff me over the head—my long-suffering head—in his rough good-natured way, muttering, "You boneheaded broommaker, you."

It became a kind of ritual, the thought of which made me tremble throughout my school days, the more so since my knowledge of science, far from growing with increased demands, seemed to diminish. But, having duly cuffed me, he would leave me in peace, leave me to my meandering daydreams, for to try and teach me math was a completely hopeless proposition. I dragged my F after me all through those years like the heavy ball chained to a convict's feet.

What impressed me about him was that he never had a book or notes with him, not even a slip of paper: he performed his occult arts with casual ease, tossing stupendous formulas onto the blackboard with something of a tightrope walker's absolute mastery. The one thing he could not draw was circles. He was too impatient. He would wind a string around a long piece of chalk, pick the imaginary center, and swing the chalk round with such gusto that it would snap and, with a whining screech, go bounding across the blackboard—dash–dot, dot–dash. He never managed to make the beginning and end meet, and the result was an unsightly gaping outline, truly an unacknowledged symbol of Creation rent asunder. And that sound of the squeaking, screeching, chattering chalk piled further agony on my already tortured brain: I would stir from my daydreams, look up, and the minute he caught sight of me he would rush over, pull me up by the ears, and order me to draw his circles for him. For this was an art, springing from some slumbering, innate law within me, that I mastered to near perfection. What an exquisite feeling it was, to play with the chalk for half a second. It was a minor ecstasy, the world around me would drop away, and I was filled with a profound happiness that made up for all the agony . . . but even from this sweet oblivion I would be roused by a rough, although this time respectful, tug at my hair, and with the laughter of the entire class in my ears I would slink back to my seat like a whipped dog, incapable now of reentering my dreamworld, to wait in perpetual agony for the bell to ring. . . .

It was a long time since those early days, a long time since my dreams had become more disturbing, a long time since he had dropped the *du* when calling me "a boneheaded broommaker," and there were long months of torment during which there were no circles to be drawn and I was condemned to hopeless attempts to clamber over the brittle girders of algebraical bridges, still dragging my F behind me, the familiar ritual still being performed. But then when we had to volunteer for officer training a brief test was improvised, simple but nonetheless a test, and my expression of utter wretchedness as I faced the stern examining board may have softened the math teacher's heart, for he was so skillful in putting words into my mouth that I actually passed. Later on, however, as we shook hands with the teachers on leaving, he advised me to forego the use of my mathematical knowledge and to be sure to avoid joining a technical unit. "Infantry," he whispered, "join the infantry, that's the place for all . . . broommakers," and for the last time, with a gesture that concealed his affection, he made as if to cuff me over the head—my now well-seasoned head.

SCARCELY TWO months later, at the Odessa airfield, I was sitting crouched over my pack, in deep mud, watching a real broommaker, the first I had ever seen.

Winter had come early, and over the nearby city the sky hung gray and comfortless between the horizons. Dingy tall buildings were visible among outlying gardens and black fences. In the distance, where the Black Sea must be, the sky was even darker, almost blue-black, as if twilight and evening came from the east. Somewhere in the background the trundling monsters were being refueled alongside cavernous hangars, after which they trundled back and, standing there in horrible complacency, were loaded up with men, gray, tired, despairing soldiers whose eyes were devoid of all emotion but fear—for the Crimea had long since been encircled. . . .

Our platoon must have been one of the last; no one spoke, and in spite of our long greatcoats we were shivering. Some of the men were eating in desperation, others were smoking, and because this was prohibited they covered their pipes with their palms and blew the smoke out in slow, thin puffs.

I had plenty of time to watch the broommaker as he sat a little way off beside a garden fence. He was wearing one of those rakish-looking Russian hats, and in his bearded face the short stocky brown pipe was as broad and long as his nose. But there were peace and simplicity in his quietly working hands as they picked up the bunches of furze twigs, cut them, tied them with wire, and fastened the finished bundles in the holes of the broom handle.

I had turned over onto my stomach, lying almost flat on my pack, and all I saw was the looming silhouette of this quiet, humble man, working steadily and unhurriedly away at his brooms. Never in my life have I envied anyone as much as that broommaker, neither the top student, nor Schimski the math brain, nor the best football player on the school team, nor even Hegenbach, whose brother had the Knight's Cross; not one of those had I ever envied as I envied that broommaker, sitting by a fence on the outskirts of Odessa and serenely smoking his pipe.

I longed secretly to catch the man's eye, for I fancied it would be comforting to look directly into that face, but I was suddenly jerked up by my coat, shouted at, and jammed into the droning aircraft, and once we had taken off and were flying high above the distracting jumble of gardens and roads and churches, it would have been impossible to try to make out the broommaker.

First I squatted on my pack, but then I slipped down behind it onto the floor and, stupefied by the oppressive silence of my fellow victims, was listening to the unearthly drone of the aircraft, while the constant vibration began to make my head quiver as it leaned against the metal wall. The darkness of the narrow fuselage was relieved only by a somewhat lighter darkness up front, where the pilot sat, and this pale reflection threw an eerie light on the mute, dim figures squatting left and right and all around me on their packs.

But suddenly a strange noise tore across the sky, so real and familiar that I sat bolt upright: it was as if the hand of a giant math teacher were drawing a massive hunk of chalk in an arc across the limitless expanse of dark sky, and the noise exactly matched the familiar one I had heard two months before, the same leap and chatter of protesting chalk.

Arc after arc was drawn across the sky by the hand of the colossus, but now, instead of being only white and dark gray, it was red on blue and purple on black, and the flashing streaks faded without completing their circles, chattered, screeched, and died away.

I suffered not for the terrified, frenzied groans of my fellow victims, or the shouting of the lieutenant vainly ordering the men to be quiet and stay where they were, or even the agonized face of the pilot. I suffered merely for those eternally uncompleted circles that flared up over the sky, in a fury of haste and hate, and never ever returned to their starting point, those botched circles whose ends never met to achieve the perfect beauty of the circle. They tormented me along with the chattering, screeching, leaping wrath of the giant hand, the hand I dreaded would grab me by the hair and cuff me brutally over the head.

Then came the real shock. I suddenly realized that this sky-splitting fury was in fact a noise: close to my head I heard a strange hiss as of a baleful, swiftly descending hand, felt a moist, hot pain, jumped up with a cry, and reached out toward the sky where just then another searing yellow flash blazed up; with my right hand I held on tight to this flailing yellow snake, letting it spin its angry circle, confident that I would be able to complete the circle, for this was the one and only art I had been born to master. So I held it, guided it, the flailing, raging, jerking, chattering snake, held on to it while my breath came hot and my twitching mouth hurt and the moist pain in my head seemed to increase, and as I brought the points together, drawing the glorious round arc of the circle and gazing at it with pride, the spaces between the dots and dashes closed and an immense, hissing short circuit filled the entire circle with light and fire until the whole sky was burning, and the abrupt momentum of the plunging aircraft rent the world in two. All I could see was light and fire, and the mutilated tail of the machine, a jagged tail like the black stump of a broom fit to carry a witch riding off to her sabbath. . . .

My Expensive Leg

T HEY'RE GIVING me a chance now. They sent me a postcard telling me to come down to the Department, and I went. They were very nice to me at the Department. They took out my file card and said, "Hm." I also said, "Hm."

"Which leg?" asked the official.

"The right."

"The whole leg?"

"The whole leg."

"Hm," he went again. He proceeded to shuffle through various papers. I was allowed to sit down.

Finally the man found what seemed to be the right paper. He said, "I think I have something here for you. Very nice too. A job you can sit down at. Shoeshine stand in a public convenience on Republic Square. How about that?"

"I can't shine shoes; that's one thing people have always noticed about me, my inability to shine shoes."

"You can learn," he said. "One can learn anything. A German can do anything. You can take a free course if you like."

"Hm," I went.

"You'll take the job?"

"No," I said, "I won't. I want a higher pension."

"You must be out of your mind," he replied, his tone mild and good-humored.

"I'm not out of my mind, no one can give me back my leg, I'm not even allowed to sell cigarettes any more, they're already making that difficult for me."

The man leaned all the way back in his chair and drew a deep breath. "My dear fellow," he said, launching into a lecture, "your leg's a damned expensive leg. I see that you're twenty-nine years of age, your heart is sound, in fact apart from your leg you're as fit as a fiddle. You'll live to be seventy. Figure it out for yourself, seventy marks a month, twelve times a year, that's forty-one times twelve times seventy. Figure it out for yourself, not counting interest, and don't imagine your leg's unique. What's more, you're not the only one who'll probably live to a ripe old age. And then you want a higher pension! I'm sorry, but you must be out of your mind."

"I think, sir," I said, also leaning back and drawing a deep breath, "I think that you grossly underestimate my leg. My leg is much more expensive, it is a very expensive leg indeed. It so happens that my head is as sound as my heart. Let me explain."

"I'm a very busy man."

"I'll explain!" I said. "You will see that my leg has saved the lives of a great number of people who today are drawing nice fat pensions.

"What happened was this: I was lying all by myself somewhere up front. My job was to spot them when they came so that the others would have time to clear out. The staffs in the rear were packing up, and while they didn't want to clear out too soon they also didn't want to leave it too long. At first there were two of us, but they shot the other fellow, he's not costing you a cent now. It's true he was married, but his wife is in good health and able to work, you don't need to worry. He was a real bargain. He'd only been a soldier for a month, all he cost was a postcard and a few bread rations. There's a good soldier for you, at least he let himself be killed off. But now there I was, all by myself, scared stiff, and it was cold, and I wanted to clear out too, in fact I was just going to clear out when . . ."

"I'm really very busy," said the man, beginning to search for a pencil.

"No, listen," I said, "this is where it gets interesting. Just as I was going to clear out, this business of my leg happened. And because I had to go on lying there anyway, I thought I might as well pass the word, so I passed the word, and they all took off, one after another, in descending order of rank, first the divisional staff, then the regimental, then the battalion, and so on, one after another. The silly part was, you see, they were in such a hurry they forgot to take me along! It was really too silly for words, because if I hadn't lost my leg they would all be dead, the general, the colonel, the major, and so on down, and you wouldn't have to pay them any pensions. Now just figure out what my leg is costing you. The general is fifty-two, the colonel forty-eight, and the major fifty, all of them hale and hearty, their heads as well as their hearts, and with the military life they lead they'll live to be at least eighty, like Hindenburg. Figure it out for yourself: a hundred and sixty times twelve times thirty, we'll call it an average of thirty, shall we? My leg's become a damned expensive leg, one of the most expensive legs I can think of, d'you see what I mean?"

"You really must be out of your mind," said the man.

"No," I replied, "I'm not. Unfortunately my heart is as sound as my head, and it's a pity I wasn't killed too, a couple of minutes before that business of my leg happened. We would have saved a lot of money."

"Are you going to take that job?" asked the man.

"No," I said, and left.

And Where
Were You, Adam?

I

FIRST CAME a face, large, yellow, tragic, moving past their lines; that was
the general. The general looked tired. The face with puffy blue shadows
under the malaria-yellow eyes, the slack, thin-lipped mouth of a man
dogged by bad luck, moved hurriedly past the thousand men. The general
started off at the right-hand corner of the dusty hollow square, looked
sadly into each face, rounded the corners carelessly, with no dash or
precision, and it was there for all to see: his chest bore plenty of medals,
it sparkled with silver and gold, but his neck was empty, no decoration
hung there. And although they knew that the Knight's Cross around a
general's neck didn't mean a lot, it was discouraging to see him without
even that much. That skinny yellow neck, unadorned, was a reminder of
lost battles, bungled retreats, of rebukes, the unpleasant, scathing rebukes
exchanged among senior officers, of sarcastic telephone conversations,
transferred chiefs of staff, and a tired, elderly man who seemed without
hope as he took off his tunic in the evening and, with his thin legs, his
malaria-racked body, sat down on the edge of his bed to drink schnapps.
Each of the three times three hundred and thirty-three men into whose
faces he looked was aware of a strange feeling: sorrow, pity, fear, and a
secret fury. Fury at this war, which had already gone on far too long, far
too long for a general's neck to be still without its rightful decoration. The
general raised his hand to his shabby cap—at least he saluted smartly—and
on reaching the left-hand corner of the hollow square he made a somewhat
brisker turn, walked to the middle of the open side, and stood still while
the swarm of officers grouped itself around him, casually yet methodically;
and it was embarrassing to see him standing there, with no decoration

around his neck, while the Knight's Crosses of others, lower in rank, could be seen sparkling in the sun.

For a moment it looked as if he were going to say something, but he merely touched his cap again in an abrupt salute and turned so unexpectedly on his heel that the startled swarm of officers stepped back to let him pass. And everyone watched the short, spare figure get into the car, the officers saluted once again, and a swirling white cloud of dust announced that the general was driving west, where the sun was already quite low on the horizon, not far from those flat white roofs over there where the front did not exist.

Then they marched, three times one hundred and eleven men, to another part of the city, southward, past cafés of scruffy elegance, past movie houses and churches, through slums where dogs and chickens lay dozing in doorways, with slatternly, pretty, white-breasted women leaning on window sills, where from dirty taverns came the monotonous, strangely stirring sound of drinking men singing. Streetcars screeched by at reckless speed—and then they came to a district where all was quiet. Here were villas surrounded by green gardens, army vehicles stood parked in front of stone gateways, and they marched through one of these stone gateways, entered meticulously tended grounds, and once again formed a hollow square, a smaller one this time, three times one hundred and eleven men.

Their packs were set down behind them, in rows, rifles were stacked, and when the men were standing at attention again, tired and hungry, thirsty, fuming and fed up with this damned war, when they were standing at attention again a thin, aristocratic face moved past their lines: that was the colonel, pale, hard-eyed, with tight lips and a long nose. They all took it for granted that the collar under this face should be adorned with the Knight's Cross. But this face was not to their liking either. The colonel took the corners at right angles, with a slow, firm tread, without omitting a single pair of eyes, and when he finally swung into the open side, a few officers in his wake, they all knew he was about to say something, and they all had the same thought, how thirsty they were, how badly they needed something to drink and eat, or to sleep or smoke a cigarette.

"Fellow soldiers!" came the high-pitched, clear voice. "Fellow soldiers, I bid you welcome! I haven't much to say to you, just this: it's up to us to chase those spineless creatures right back to their steppes. Understand?"

The voice paused, and the silence during this pause was embarrassing, almost deathly, and they all saw that by now the sun was red, dark red, and the deathly red reflection seemed to be caught in the Knight's Cross at the colonel's neck, concentrated in those four shining bars of the cross, and they saw for the first time that the cross was surmounted with oak-leaves, which they called cabbage.

The colonel wore cabbage at his neck.

"Do you understand?" shouted the taut voice, cracking now.

"Yessir," a few of the men called out, but the voices were hoarse, tired, listless.

"Do you understand, I say!" the voice shouted again, now so strident that it seemed to soar into the sky, swiftly, far too swiftly, like some demented lark trying to pluck a star with its beak.

"Yessir," a few more called out, but not many, and those who did were also tired, hoarse, listless, and nothing in this man's voice could quench their thirst, satisfy their hunger, their craving for a cigarette.

The colonel lashed the air furiously with his cane, they heard something that sounded like "rabble," and he strode rapidly off to the rear, followed by his adjutant, a tall young first lieutenant, who was much too tall, and much too young, for them not to feel sorry for him.

The sun still hung over the horizon, just above the rooftops, a glowing iron egg that seemed to be rolling down over the flat white roofs, and the sky was burned gray, almost white; the sparse leaves hung limply from the trees as they marched on, eastward now at last, through the suburbs, past shacks, over cobbles, past the huts of rag-and-bone men, past a totally incongruous group of modern, dirty apartment blocks, past garbage dumps, through gardens where rotting melons lay on the ground and overripe tomatoes hung from tall stalks, covered with dust, stalks that were much too tall and had an unfamiliar look about them. The cornfields looked odd too, with their thick corncobs being pecked at by flocks of black birds that flew up lethargically at the approach of the men's weary tread, clouds of birds that hovered undecidedly in the air, then settled down to resume their pecking.

Now there were only three times thirty-five men, a weary, dust-coated platoon, with sore feet and sweating faces, led by a first lieutenant whose face plainly showed that he was fed to the teeth. As soon as he took command, they knew what kind of man he was. All he had done was look at them and, tired as they were, and thirsty, thirsty, they could read it in his eyes. "It's a lot of shit," said his expression, "just a lot of shit, but we can't do a thing about it." And then came his voice, with studied indifference, contemptuous of all regulation commands: "Let's go."

Next they halted at a grimy school standing among half-withered trees. The foul black puddles, with flies buzzing and darting above them, looked as if they had been standing there for months between rough cobbles and a chalk-scribbled urinal that gave out a nauseating stench, acrid and unmistakable.

"Halt," said the first lieutenant. He went into the schoolhouse, and his walk, elegant and languid, was that of a man who was fed to the teeth.

This time there was no need to form a hollow square, and the captain who walked past them did not even salute; he wore no belt, a straw was stuck between his teeth, and from the look of his plump face with its black eyebrows he appeared to be easygoing. He merely nodded, went "Hm," stopped in front of them, and said: "We haven't got much time, boys. I'll send along the sergeant major and have you assigned to your companies right away." But they had already looked past his round healthy face and seen the ammunition trucks standing ready loaded, and on the ledges of the soiled open windows lay piles of battle packs, neat olive-drab bundles, beside them the belts and the rest of the gear, haversacks, cartridge pouches, spades, gas masks.

When they set off they were only eight times three men, and they marched back through the cornfields as far as the ugly modern apartment blocks, then turned east again until they reached the sparse woods in the midst of which stood a few houses that looked something like an artist's colony: flat-roofed bungalow affairs with picture windows. There were wicker chairs in the gardens, and when the men halted and about-faced they saw that the sun was behind the roofs now, that its glow filled the whole dome of the sky with a red that was just a shade too pale, like badly painted blood—and behind them, in the east, it was already deep twilight and warm. Soldiers were squatting in the shadow outside the bungalows, there were some rifle-pyramids, ten or so, and they noticed that the men had already buckled on their belts: the steel helmets hooked to their belts shone with a ruddy gleam.

The first lieutenant, coming out now from one of the bungalows, did not walk past them at all. He stopped at once in front of them, and they saw he had only one decoration, a little black one that wasn't really a decoration at all, an insignificant medal stamped out of black tin, a sign that he had shed blood for the Fatherland. The lieutenant's face was tired and sad, and now when he looked at them he looked first at their decorations, then into their faces, and said, "Good," and after a brief pause, with a glance at his watch, "You're tired, I realize that, but it can't be helped —we have to leave in fifteen minutes."

Then he looked at the sergeant major beside him and said, "No point in taking down particulars—just collect the paybooks and put them in with the baggage. Assign the men quickly so they've time for a drink of water. And don't forget to fill up your canteens while you're about it!" he called to the three times eight men.

The sergeant major standing beside him looked irritable and conceited. He had four times as many decorations as the lieutenant, and with a nod he shouted, "Come on now, let's have those paybooks!"

He placed the pile on a wobbly garden table and began sorting them, and while the paybooks were being counted and divided up the men all had the same thought: the journey had been tiring, a bloody bore, but it hadn't been serious. And the general, the colonel, the captain, even the first lieutenant, were all far away, they couldn't do anything to them now. But these fellows here, they owned them, this sergeant major who saluted and clicked his heels the way they all used to four years ago, and that bull of a sergeant who at this point emerged from the rear, threw away his cigarette, and adjusted his belt—these were the fellows who owned them, until they were captured or lay around somewhere wounded—or dead.

Of the thousand men only one was left, and he stood facing the sergeant major, looking helplessly around because there was no one beside, behind, or in front of him; and when he looked at the sergeant major again he realized he was thirsty, very thirsty, and that of those fifteen minutes at least eight had already gone by.

The sergeant major had picked up his paybook from the table and opened it; he looked at the first page, raised his eyes, and asked, "Feinhals?"

"Yessir."

"And you're an architect—you can draw?"

"Yessir."

"Headquarters platoon, we can use him, sir," said the sergeant major, turning to the first lieutenant.

"Good," said the first lieutenant, looking over toward the city, and Feinhals followed his gaze, and now he could see what was evidently fascinating the officer: the sun was lying on the ground, at the end of a street, between two houses; it looked very odd, just lying there on the ground like a flattened, shining apple between two dirty Rumanian houses at the edge of town, an apple growing dimmer by the second, almost as if lying in its own shadow.

"Good," repeated the first lieutenant, and Feinhals didn't know whether he really meant the sun or was just saying the word mechanically. It occurred to Feinhals that he had been on the move for four years now, and four years ago the postcard had said he was being called up for a few weeks' maneuvers. But suddenly the war had started.

"Go and get yourself a drink," the sergeant major told Feinhals.

Feinhals ran over to join the others and found the water supply right away: a rusted iron pipe with a leaky garden faucet among some scrawny pine trees, and the water ran out in a stream no thicker than half the size of a little finger, but even worse was the fact that about ten men were standing there, shoving, cursing, and pushing away each other's mess bowls.

The sight of the trickling water drove Feinhals almost frantic. He grabbed the mess bowl from his haversack, forced his way through the others, and suddenly felt a surge of boundless strength. He squeezed his mess bowl in between the others, between all those shifting metal apertures, no longer knowing which was his; his eyes followed his arm, saw that his was the one with the darker enamel; he thrust it forward, and felt something that made him tremble: it was getting heavy. He was past knowing which was more wonderful: to drink, or to feel his mess bowl getting heavier. Suddenly, feeling his hands lose their strength, he jerked it back, his very veins trembling with weakness, and while behind him voices shouted, "Fall in—let's go!" he sat down, held the mess bowl between his knees because he lacked the strength to lift it, and bent over it like a dog over its bowl, his shaking fingers pressing it gently down so that the lower edge dipped and the water level touched his lips, and when he actually felt his upper lip getting wet and he began to sip, the word danced before his eyes in a kaleidoscope of colors, "Water, terwa, aterw," with insane clarity he saw it written in his mind's eye: water. Strength flowed back into his hands, he could lift the bowl and drink.

Someone jerked him upright and gave him a shove, and he saw the company lined up, headed by the first lieutenant, who was shouting, "Let's go, let's go!" and he swung his rifle over his shoulder and slipped into the space up front indicated by a wave of the sergeant major's hand.

Off they marched, into the darkness, and he moved without wanting to: what he really wanted was to drop, but he marched on, without wanting to, the weight of his body forcing him to straighten his knees, and when he straightened his knees his sore feet propelled themselves forward, carrying along great slabs of pain that were much too big for his feet; his feet were too small for this pain; and when he propelled his feet forward the whole bulk of his backside, shoulders, arms, and head started moving again, forcing him to straighten his knees, and when he straightened his knees his sore feet propelled themselves forward. . . .

Three hours later he was lying exhausted somewhere on sparse steppe grass, his eyes following a vague shape that was crawling away in the gray darkness; the shape had brought him two greasy pieces of paper, some bread, a roll of lemon drops, and six cigarettes, and it had said, "D'you know the password?"

"No."

"Victory. That's the password: victory."

And he repeated softly, "Victory. That's the password: victory," and the word tasted like tepid water on his tongue.

He peeled the paper off the roll and stuck a lemon drop in his mouth; when he felt the thin, acid, synthetic flavor in his mouth, the saliva came pouring out of his glands, and he washed down the first wave of this sweet-tasting bitterness—and at that moment he heard the shells: they had been rumbling around for hours over some distant line, and now they were flying across it, sputtering, hissing, rattling like badly nailed crates, and bursting behind them. The second lot landed not far ahead of them: fountains of sand showed up like disintegrating mushrooms against the bright darkness of the eastern sky, and he noticed that it was dark now behind him and a bit lighter in front. The third lot he never heard: right in amongst them, sledgehammers seemed to be smashing up plywood sheets, crashing, splintering, close, dangerous. Dust and powder fumes were drifting along near the ground, and when he had thrown himself over and lay pressed against the earth, his head thrust into a hollow in the mound he had heaped up, he heard the command being passed along, "Get set to advance!" Coming from the right, the whisper hissed past them like a burning fuse, quiet and dangerous, and as he was about to adjust his battle pack, to tighten it, there was a crash right next to him, and it felt as if someone had knocked away his hand and was tugging violently at his upper arm. His whole left arm was bathed in moist warmth, and he raised his face from the ground and shouted, "I've been hit!" but didn't even hear himself shouting, all he heard was a quiet voice saying, "Horse Droppings."

Far, far away, as if separated from him by thick panes of glass, very close and yet far away, "Horse Droppings," said the voice; quiet, well-bred, far away, subdued, "Horse Droppings, Captain Bauer speaking, yessir." Not a sound, then came the voice, "I can hear you, Colonel." Pause, not a sound, only a kind of bubbling in the distance, a gentle hissing and sputtering as if something were boiling over. Then he realized he had closed his eyes, so he opened them: he saw the captain's head, and now he could also hear the voice more distinctly; the head was framed in a dark, dirty window opening, and the captain's face was tired, unshaven and ill-tempered, his eyes were screwed tight, and he said three times in succession, with barely a pause between each: "Yes, Colonel"—"Yes, Colonel"—"Yes, Colonel."

Then the captain put on his steel helmet, and his broad, good-natured face and dark head looked quite ridiculous now as he said to someone beside him, "Hell—there's a breakthrough at Horse Droppings 3, Sharpshooter 4, I'll have to go forward." Another voice shouted into the building, "Dispatch rider, report to the captain," and it carried on like an echo, reverberating around inside the building and getting fainter and fainter, "Dispatch rider, report to the captain—dispatch rider, report to the captain!"

Next he heard the rattle of a motor and followed the dry rasping sound as it came closer; he saw the motorcycle slowly turn a corner, slackening speed until it stopped in front of him, throbbing, covered with dust, and the driver, his face tired and apathetic, remained seated on the pulsing machine and shouted toward the window, "Motorcycle for the captain reporting!" And the captain came out, walking slowly, legs wide apart, a cigar in his mouth, the steel helmet giving him the look of a sinister squat mushroom. He climbed without enthusiasm into the sidecar, said "Let's go," and the machine bounced and rattled off, at high speed, veiled in dust, in the direction of the seething confusion up front.

Feinhals wondered if he had ever been so happy in his life. He felt almost no pain; his left arm, lying beside him like a tight bundle, stiff and bloody, damp and unfamiliar, felt faintly uncomfortable, that was all. Everything else was all right; he could raise each leg separately, wriggle his feet in his boots, lift his head, and he could smoke as he lay there, facing him was the sun as it hung a hand's breadth above the gray cloud of dust in the east. All noise was somehow remote and subdued, his head felt as if wrapped in a layer of cotton, and it occurred to him that he had had nothing to eat for almost twenty-four hours except an acid, synthetic lemon drop, and nothing to drink except a little water, rusty and tepid and tasting of sand.

When he felt himself being lifted up and carried away, he closed his eyes again, but he could see it all, it was so familiar, it had all happened to him somewhere else: they carried him past the exhaust fumes of a throbbing vehicle into the hot, gasoline-reeking interior, the stretcher scraped against the metal rails, and then the engine started up and the noise outside retreated farther and farther, almost imperceptibly, just as the evening before it had come imperceptibly closer. A few isolated shells burst in the suburbs, regularly, quietly, and just as he felt himself dropping off to sleep he thought: How nice, it was all over so quickly this time, so quickly. . . . All it had meant was a little thirst, sore feet, and a little fear.

When the ambulance stopped with a jerk, he awoke from his half-sleep. Doors were flung open, once again the stretchers scraped against the metal rails, and he was carried into a cool white corridor where it was very quiet. The stretchers stood in rows like lounge chairs on a narrow deck, and next to him he saw a head of thick black hair, lying quietly, and on the stretcher beyond that a bald head, moving restlessly from side to side, and up at the end, on the first stretcher, a white head, heavily bandaged, completely covered, ugly and much too narrow, and from this bundle of gauze came a voice, piercing, shrill, clear, harsh as it rose to the ceiling, helpless yet insolent, the voice of the colonel, and the voice cried, "Champagne!"

"Piss," said the bald head calmly, "drink your own piss." Someone behind laughed, quietly and cautiously.

"Champagne," cried the voice in fury, "chilled champagne!"

"Shut up," said the bald head calmly, "why don't you shut up?"

"Champagne," whimpered the voice, "I want some champagne"; and the white head sank back, it was lying flat now, and from between thick layers of gauze rose a thin pointed nose, and the voice became even shriller and shouted: "A girl—get me a girl. . . ."

"Do it to yourself," retorted the bald head.

At last the white head was carried through a door, and there was silence.

In the silence they could hear only the isolated shells bursting in distant parts of the city, muffled far-off explosions thrumming softly away at the edge of the war. And when the white head of the colonel, now lying silently on one side, was carried out and the bald head was carried in, the sound of a car could be heard approaching outside: the muted sound of a whining engine came closer, quickly and almost threateningly, and now it was so close it seemed about to ram the cool white building. Then suddenly silence fell, outside a voice shouted something, and when they turned their heads, startled out of their peaceful, dozing weariness, they saw the general walking slowly past the stretchers and wordlessly placing packs of cigarettes on the men's laps. The silence became more and more oppressive the nearer the little man's footsteps approached from behind, and at last Feinhals saw the general's face quite close: yellow, large and sad, with snow-white eyebrows, dark traces of dust around the thin mouth, and written in this face was the message that this battle, too, had been lost.

II

HE HEARD a voice saying "Bressen—Bressen, look at me," and he knew this was the voice of Kleewitz, the divisional medical officer, who must have been sent here to find out when he would be going back. But he wouldn't be going back, he never wanted to be reminded again of that regiment—and he didn't look at Kleewitz. He looked fixedly at the picture hanging way over to the right, almost in the dark corner: a flock of sheep, painted gray and green, and in the middle of them a shepherd in a blue cloak playing a flute.

He thought about things no one else on earth would have dreamed of, things he liked thinking about, repulsive though they were. He wasn't sure whether he heard Kleewitz's voice; he did hear it, of course, but he didn't want to admit it, and he looked at the shepherd playing his flute instead of turning his head and saying, "Kleewitz, how nice of you to come."

Next he heard the shuffle of papers, and he assumed they were studying his medical history. He looked at the back of the shepherd's neck and recalled how for a time he had been a nodder at a hotel, in a very high-class restaurant. At noon, when the local businessmen came for lunch, he would walk through the restaurant, very erect, and bow, and it was funny how quickly and accurately he had grasped the required nuances: whether he gave a short bow or a deep one, whether he merely nodded and, if so, how he nodded, and sometimes he would just move his head very briefly, more of an opening and closing of his eyes really, that gave the impression he was moving his head. He found status differences so easy to recognize—like army ranks, that hierarchy of braided and flat, starred and unstarred, shoulder loops, all the way down to the great mass of people with their more or less undecorated shoulders.

In this restaurant the scale of bowing was relatively simple: it was all a matter of bankroll, of the size of the bill. He wasn't even especially obliging, he almost never smiled, and his face—despite his efforts to look as impassive as possible—his face never lost that expression of severity and vigilance. A feeling crept over everyone he looked at, not so much of being honored as of being guilty; all felt themselves observed, inspected, and he soon discovered that there were certain people who became confused, so confused that they unthinkingly applied their knives to their potatoes the moment his glance rested on them and who nervously fingered their wallets as soon as he had passed. The only thing that surprised him was that they kept coming back, even this kind. Back they came and submitted to being nodded at, to that uncomfortable scrutiny that goes with a high-class restaurant. His thin, aristocratic face and a knack of wearing clothes well brought him in quite a decent income; besides, he ate there for nothing. But while he tried to assume a certain air of haughtiness, he was in fact often quite nervous. There were days when he could feel the sweat gathering and breaking out all over his body so that he could hardly breathe. And the owner was a coarse fellow, good-natured, vain about his success but awkward in manner; late at night, when the place was gradually emptying and he could think about going home, the owner would sometimes dig his stubby fingers into the cigar box and, despite his protests, stuff three or four cigars into the top pocket of Bressen's jacket. "Go on," the owner would mumble with his diffident smile, "take them—they're good cigars." And he would take them. He smoked them in the evening with Velten, with whom he shared a small furnished apartment, and Velten never failed to be surprised at the quality of the cigars. "Bressen," Velten would say, "I must say, Bressen, you smoke an excellent weed." He would make no comment and no pretense at refusing when Velten brought home an especially good bottle. Velten traveled for a wine merchant, and when business was good he would take home a bottle of champagne.

"Champagne," he said out loud to himself, "chilled champagne."

"That's all he ever says," said the ward medical officer standing beside him.

"Are you referring to the colonel?" asked Kleewitz coldly.

"That's right, Colonel Bressen. The only thing the colonel ever says: Champagne—chilled champagne. And sometimes he talks about women —girls."

He had loathed having to take his meals at the restaurant. In a grubby back room off a worn tablecloth, served by the ungracious cook who paid absolutely no attention to his fondness for desserts—and in his nose, throat, and mouth that sickening stale reek of cooking, greasy and disgusting—and that constant coming and going of the owner, the way he would plump himself down beside him for a few seconds, cigar in mouth, pour himself a schnapps, and sit there silently knocking back the stuff.

Later on he had given lessons in social etiquette. The town he lived in was very suitable for this kind of instruction, containing as it did a great many rich people who didn't even know that fish was eaten differently from meat, who had literally eaten with their fingers all their lives, and who now had cars, villas, and women—people who could no longer bear to be the kind of people they really were. He taught them how to perform adequately on the slippery ice of social obligations; he went to their homes, discussed menus, taught them how to handle servants, and stayed for dinner —he had to teach them every gesture, watch them like a hawk, correct them, and he tried to show them how to open a bottle of champagne without assistance.

"Champagne," he said out loud to himself, "chilled champagne."

"Oh, for God's sake," cried Kleewitz, "Bressen, look at me!" But he had no intention of looking at Kleewitz; he never wanted to be reminded of it again, the regiment that had disintegrated in his hands like dry tinder; Horse Droppings, Sharpshooter, Sugarloaf—under the command of his staff known as Hunting Lodge—all finished! And shortly after that he heard Kleewitz leave.

He was glad to be able to detach his gaze at last from the flock of sheep and the stupid shepherd; it was hanging a bit too far over to the right and he was getting a crick in his neck. The second picture hung almost directly opposite him, and he was compelled to look at it, although that one didn't appeal to him either: it showed Crown Prince Michael talking to a Rumanian peasant, flanked by Marshal Antonescu and the queen. The stance of the Rumanian peasant was alarming. He was standing with his feet too close and too firmly together, and he seemed about to tip forward and throw the gift in his hands at the young king's feet. Bressen couldn't quite make out what the gift was—salt or bread or a hunk of goat cheese —but the young king was smiling at the peasant. Bressen had long ceased to see these things; he was thankful to have found a spot to stare at without worrying about getting a crick in his neck.

What had amazed him so during those etiquette lessons—what he hadn't known and had long tried to ignore—was that such things could actually be learned, this little performance: how to handle a knife and fork correctly. It often shocked him to see these fellows and their womenfolk treating him after three months with formal courtesy, as if he were a competent instructor of limited scope, and smile as they handed him a check. There were some, of course, who never made it—their fingers were too clumsy, they were incapable of cutting the rind off a piece of cheese without picking up the whole slice, or of holding a wineglass properly by the stem—and then there was a third category who never learned but who couldn't have cared less—as well as those he never met but heard about, who considered it a waste of time to consult him.

His sole consolation during this period was the opportunity for an occasional affair with their wives—there was no risk attached to these little adventures, which didn't disappoint him although they seemed to put the women off him. He had many affairs during this time—with all kinds of women—but not a single one had ever come to him or gone out with him a second time, although he usually ordered champagne.

"Champagne," he said out loud to himself, "chilled champagne."

He said it when he was alone too—it felt better that way—and for a moment he thought about the war, this war, just for an instant, until he heard two more people entering the room. He went on staring at that indefinable hunk that the Rumanian peasant was holding out to young

King Michael—and for a moment he caught a glimpse, between himself and the picture, of the pink hand of the senior medical officer as the latter leaned over and took the chart down from its hook.

"Champagne," said Bressen in a loud voice, "champagne and a girl."

"Colonel Bressen," said the senior medical officer, urgently but softly. "Colonel Bressen!" There was a brief silence, and the senior medical officer said to the person beside him, "Mark his tag 'Home Hospitalization,' and transfer him to Vienna—needless to say the division will be very sorry to have to get along without Colonel Bressen, but . . ."

"Right, sir," said the ward medical officer. Bressen heard nothing more, although they must be standing beside him because he had not heard the door. Then came the rustling of those damned papers again, they must be rereading his medical history. Not a word was said.

Later on certain people had recalled that there were things he really could teach and which there was some point in teaching: the new army regulations, already familiar to him because he received the new issues regularly. He was put in charge of training the Stahlhelm and Youth Groups in his area, and he clearly remembered this honor having coincided with that period in his life when he had discovered an inordinate craving for sweet things and a decline in his interest in affairs with women. His notion of keeping a horse had proved a good one, although it meant scrimping a bit, for now on maneuver days he could ride out onto the heath early in the morning, hold discussions with subordinates, go through the drill plan—and best of all he could get to know the men in a way that was hardly possible while they were on duty: veterans and strangely clear-headed yet naïve young men who now and again had gone so far as to risk openly contradicting him. What saddened him was a certain amount of official secrecy that prevented him from riding back to town at the head of the troops—but while on duty it was almost like the old days: he was thoroughly familiar with combat duty at battalion level, and he had no cause to find fault with the new regulations, which had made good use of wartime experience without aiming at anything in the way of an actual revolution in methods. The things he had always encouraged and considered of prime importance were: route marches, standing at attention, about-turns executed with maximum precision—and those were red-letter days when he felt sufficiently strong and confident to risk something that even in peacetime and with well-disciplined troops had been risky: battalion maneuvers.

But the secrecy was soon dropped, before long there were daily maneuvers, and it didn't feel very different when one day he was made a real major again, in command of a real battalion.

For a moment he was not sure whether he was actually turning or whether this turning was already one of those things beyond the edge of his consciousness, but turning he was, and he was aware that he was turning, and it was depressing to find that so far nothing had occurred beyond the edge of his consciousness: he was being turned. They had lifted him up and swung him carefully out of his bed onto a stretcher. At first his head fell back, for a moment he was staring at the ceiling, but then a pillow was pushed under his head and his gaze fell precisely on the third picture hanging in his room. This was a picture he had never seen, it hung near the door, and at first he was glad to be able to look at it, since otherwise he would have had to look straight at the two doctors, between whom the picture was now hanging. The senior medical officer seemed to have left the room. The ward medical officer was talking to another, younger medical officer he had never seen before; he saw the short, plump ward MO read some passages from his medical history to his colleague in a low voice and explain something to him. Bressen couldn't understand what they were saying, not because he couldn't hear—it bothered him very much that so far he had not been able to close his ears—no, it was just that they were too far away and whispering. From the corridor he could hear everything: people calling out, cries of the wounded, and the throbbing hum of motors outside. He saw the back of the stretcher bearer standing in front of him, and now the one standing behind him said, "Let's go."

"The bags," said the front stretcher bearer. "Major," he called across to the ward MO, "someone'll have to carry out those bags."

"Get hold of a few fellows."

The two stretcher bearers went out into the corridor.

Without moving his head, Bressen carefully studied the third picture between the two doctors' heads: this picture was incredible, he couldn't understand how it had ever got here. He didn't know whether they were in a school or a convent, but as for there being Catholics in Rumania, he had never heard of such a thing. In Germany there were some, he had heard about those—but in Rumania! And now here was a picture of the Virgin Mary. It annoyed him to be forced to look at this picture, but he had no option, he was forced to stare at her, that woman in the sky-blue cloak whose face he found disconcertingly grave; she stood poised on a globe, looking up to Heaven, which consisted of snow-white clouds, and around her hands was twisted a string of brown wooden beads. He gently shook his head and thought: What a repulsive picture, and suddenly he noticed the two doctors watching him. They looked at him, then at the picture, followed his gaze, and slowly returned to him. It wasn't easy to stare between those two heads—those four eyes that were looking into his—at the picture which he found so repulsive. He couldn't think of anything to take his mind off it; he tried to let his thoughts slip back to those years which a moment ago had been so easy to recall, years when he felt that the things which had once been his world were slowly becoming a world again: the association with staff officers, barracks gossip, adjutants, orderlies. He found himself unable to think about them. He was hemmed in by those eight inches left free by the two heads, and in those eight inches hung the picture—but it was a relief to see this space become larger because now they were approaching him, separating, and standing one on either side of him.

Now he couldn't see them at all, just their white smocks at the periphery of his vision. He heard exactly what they were saying.

"So you don't think it has anything to do with this injury?"

"Definitely not," said the ward MO; he opened the medical history again, papers rustled. "Definitely not. It's only a trifling scalp wound—very minor. Healed in five days. Nothing—not a trace of the usual symptoms of concussion, not a thing. I can only assume it was shock—or . . ." He broke off.

"What were you going to say?"

"I'm not going to stick my neck out."

"Go on—tell me."

It was annoying that both the doctors should remain silent, they seemed to be exchanging some kind of signals—then the younger one burst out laughing. Bressen hadn't heard a word spoken. Then both doctors laughed. He was glad when the two soldiers came in accompanied by a third with his arm in a sling.

"Feinhals," the ward medical officer told him, "take the brief case out to the ambulance. The heavy bags will be sent on later," he called to the stretcher bearers.

"Are you serious?" asked the other doctor.

"Absolutely."

Bressen felt himself being lifted up and carried off; the picture of the Virgin slipped away to his left, the wall came closer, then the window frame outside in the corridor, again he was swung—he looked into the long corridor, one more swing, and he closed his eyes: outside the sun was dazzlingly bright. He was relieved when the ambulance door closed behind him.

III

THERE WERE a great many sergeants in the German army—with enough stars to decorate the sky of some thick-witted underworld—and a great many sergeants called Schneider, and of these quite a number who had been christened Alois, but at this particular time only one of these sergeants called Alois Schneider was stationed in the Hungarian village of Szokarhely; Szokarhely was a compact little place, half village, half resort. It was summer.

Schneider's office was a narrow room papered in yellow; on the door outside hung a pink cardboard sign on which was printed in black India ink: "Discharges, Sgt. Schneider."

The desk was so placed that Schneider sat with his back to the window, and when he had nothing to do he would get up, turn around, and look out onto the narrow dusty road leading on the left to the village, and on the right, between cornfields and apricot orchards, out into the puszta.

Schneider had almost nothing to do. Only a few seriously wounded men still remained in the hospital; all those fit to be moved had been loaded into ambulances and taken away—and the rest, the walking wounded, had been discharged, loaded onto trucks, and taken to the redeployment center at the front. Schneider could look out of the window for hours on end: outside, the air was close, muggy, and the best remedy for this climate was pale-yellow apricot schnapps mixed with soda water. The schnapps was mildly tart, as well as cheap, pure, and good, and it was very pleasant to sit by the window, look out at the sky or onto the road, and get drunk. Intoxication was a long time coming, Schneider had to fight hard for it; it was necessary—even in the morning—to consume a considerable quantity of schnapps in order to reach a state in which boredom and futility became bearable. Schneider had a system: in the first glass he took only a dash of schnapps, in the second a bit more, the third was 50:50, the fourth he drank neat, the fifth 50:50 again, the sixth was as strong as the second, and the seventh as weak as the first. He drank only seven glasses—by about ten-thirty he was through with this ritual and had reached a state he called raging soberness, a cold fire consumed him, and he was armed to cope with the boredom and futility of the day. The first discharge cases usually turned up shortly before eleven, most of them around eleven-fifteen, and that still gave him almost an hour to look out onto the road, where from time to time a cart, drawn by lean horses and churning up a lot of dust, would race past on its way to the village; or he could catch flies, conduct ingenious dialogues with imaginary superiors—sarcastic, terse—or maybe sort out the rubber stamps on his desk, straighten the papers.

ABOUT THIS TIME—around ten-thirty—Schmitz was standing in the room containing the two patients on whom he had operated that morning: on the left, Lieutenant Moll, aged twenty-one, looking like an old woman, his peaked face seemed to be grinning under the anesthetic. Clouds of flies swarmed over the bandages on his hands, squatted drowsily on the blood-soaked gauze around his head. Schmitz fanned them away—it was hope-less, he shook his head and drew the white sheet as far as he could over the sleeping man's head. He began pulling on the clean white smock he wore on his rounds, buttoned it slowly, and looked at the other patient, Captain Bauer, who seemed to be gradually coming out of the anesthetic, mumbling indistinctly, his eyes closed; he tried to move but couldn't, he was strapped down, even his head had been firmly tied to the bars at the head of the bed—only his lips moved, and now and again it looked for a moment as if he were about to open his eyelids—and he would start mumbling again. Schmitz dug his hands into the pockets of his smock and waited—the room was shadowy, the air fetid, there was a slight smell of cow dung, and even with closed doors and windows there were swarms of flies; at one time cattle had been kept in the basement beneath.

The captain's sporadic, inarticulate mumbling appeared to be taking shape; now he was opening his mouth at regular intervals and seemed to be uttering one single word, which Schmitz could not understand—an oddly fascinating mixture of E and O and throaty sounds—then all of a sudden the captain opened his eyes. "Bauer," cried Schmitz, but he knew it was no use. He stepped closer and waved his hands in front of the captain's eyes—there was no reflex. Schmitz held his hand close to the captain's eyes, so close that he could feel the man's eyebrows on his palm: nothing—the captain merely went on repeating his incomprehensible word at regular intervals. He was looking inside himself, and no one knew what was inside. Suddenly he uttered the word very distinctly, sharply articulated as if he had learned it by heart—then again. Schmitz held his ear close to the captain's mouth. "Byelyogorshe," said the captain. Schmitz listened intently, he had never heard the word and had no idea what it meant, but he liked the sound of it, it was beautiful, he thought—mysterious and beautiful. Outside all was quiet—he could hear the cap-tain's breathing, he looked into his eyes and with bated breath waited each time for the word: "Byelyogorshe." Schmitz looked at his watch, following the second hand—how slowly that tiny finger seemed to crawl across the watch face—fifty seconds: "Byelyogorshe." It seemed to take forever for the next fifty seconds to pass. Outside, trucks were driving into the courtyard. Someone called out in the corridor. Schmitz remembered that the senior MO had sent a message asking him to do his rounds for him, another truck drove into the yard. "Byelyogorshe," said the captain; Schmitz waited once more—the door opened, a sergeant appeared, Schmitz signaled impatiently to him to keep quiet, stared at the little second hand, and sighed as it touched the thirty. "Byelyogorshe," said the captain.

"What is it?" Schmitz asked the sergeant.

"Time to make the rounds," said the sergeant.

"I'm coming," said Schmitz. He pulled his sleeve down over his watch when the second hand came to twenty and the captain's lips had just closed—he stared at the man's mouth, waited, and drew back his sleeve when the lips began to move. "Byelyogorshe": the second hand stood exactly at ten.

Schmitz walked slowly out of the room.

THAT DAY there were no discharge cases. Schneider waited until eleven-fifteen, then went out to get some cigarettes. In the corridor he stopped by the window. Outside, the senior MO's car was being washed. Thursday, Schneider thought. Thursday was the day for washing the senior MO's car.

The building was in the form of a square open toward the rear, toward the railway. In the north wing was Surgery, in the center Administration and X-ray, in the south wing kitchen and staff quarters, and at the far end a suite of six rooms occupied by the administrator. This complex had once housed an agricultural college. At the rear, in the large grounds running straight across the open side, were shower rooms, stables, and model plantations, neatly defined beds containing all kinds of plants. The grounds and orchards went all the way down to the railway, and sometimes the administrator's wife could be seen riding there with her small son, a six-year-old straddling a pony and yelling. The administrator's wife was young and pretty, and whenever she had been playing with her son at the end of the grounds she would call in at the administration office and complain about the unexploded shell lying down there by the cesspool, in her view extremely dangerous. She was invariably assured that something would be done about it, but nothing ever was.

Schneider stood by the window watching the senior MO's driver painstakingly performing his duties; although he had been driving and looking after this car for two years, he was obeying the rules and had spread the lube chart out on a crate, had put on his fatigues, and stood surrounded by pails and oilcans. The senior MO's car was upholstered in red leather, and very low-slung. Thursday, thought Schneider, Thursday again. In the calendar of routines, Thursday was the day for washing the senior MO's car. He greeted the fair-haired nurse hurrying past him and walked a few steps to the canteen door, but the door was locked.

TWO TRUCKS drove into the yard and parked well away from the MO's car. Schneider continued to look out of the window: at that moment the girl who brought the fruit drove into the yard. She held the reins herself, seated on an upturned crate, and drove her little cart carefully between the vehicles toward the kitchen. Her name was Szarka, and every Wednesday she brought fruit and vegetables from one of the nearby villages. People came with fruit and vegetables every day, the paymaster had a number of suppliers, but on Wednesdays only Szarka came. Schneider was quite sure about this: many a time he had interrupted his work on a Wednesday about ten-thirty, gone over to the window, and stood there waiting until the dust cloud stirred up by her little cart at the side of the avenue leading to the station came in sight, and he always waited until she came closer, until he could make out the little horse through the dust cloud, then the cartwheels, and finally the girl with the pretty oval face and the smile around her mouth. Schneider lighted his last cigarette and sat down on the window sill. Today I'm going to speak to her, he thought, and at the same instant he thought of how every Wednesday he thought: Today I'm going to speak to her, and that he never had. But today he would for sure. There was something about Szarka that he had felt only in the women here, in these girls from the puszta, girls who were always shown in movies as hot-blooded, capering ninnies. Szarka was cool, cool and of an almost impalpable tenderness; she behaved tenderly toward her horse, toward the fruit in her baskets: apricots and tomatoes, plums and pears, cucumbers and paprikas. Her gaily painted little cart slipped in between the greasy oilcans and crates, stopped at the kitchen, and she tapped her whip on the window.

Generally at this hour of the day all was quiet indoors. The MO was making his rounds, spreading a mood of anxious solemnity, everything was tidy, and an indefinable tension could be felt in the corridors. But today there was a restless hubbub, everywhere doors were being banged, people were calling out. Schneider was somehow aware of this at the edge of his consciousness; he smoked his last cigarette and watched Szarka negotiating with the mess sergeant. Normally she negotiated with the paymaster, who tried to pinch her behind—but Pratzki, the mess sergeant, was a slightly built, practical fellow, a bit high-strung, who was an excellent cook and reputed to have no use for women. Szarka seemed to be urging him, gesticulating, mostly the gesture for paying, but the cook merely shrugged his shoulders and pointed to the main building, to the very spot where Schneider was sitting. The girl turned and looked almost straight at Schneider; he jumped off the window sill and heard his name being called in the corridor: "Schneider, Schneider!" There was a moment's silence, and again someone shouted, "Sergeant Schneider!" Schneider gave one more glance outside: Szarka took her little horse by the bridle and led it toward the main building; the MO's driver was standing in a large puddle folding up his lube chart. Schneider walked slowly toward the office, thinking of many things before he reached it. that he must speak to the girl today, whatever happened, that the MO's car couldn't be washed on a Wednesday —and that it was out of the question for Szarka to come on a Thursday.

He was met by the retinue accompanying the medical officer on his rounds. It emerged from the big ward, now almost empty; white smocks, a few nurses, the ward sergeant, the orderlies, a mute procession led not by the senior MO but by Schmitz, a noncommissioned medical officer, a man who was seldom heard to speak. Schmitz was short and plump and nondescript-looking, but his eyes were cool and gray, and sometimes, when he lowered the lids for an instant, he seemed about to say something, but he never did. The retinue dispersed as Schneider reached the office; he saw Schmitz approaching, held open the door for him, and the two men walked into the room together.

The sergeant major had his ear to the receiver. His broad face wore a look of annoyance. He was just saying, "No, sir," then the senior MO's voice was audible through the receiver, the sergeant major looked at Schneider and the noncommissioned MO, gestured to the latter to take a seat, and smiled as he looked at Schneider. Then he said, "Yes, sir; very well, sir," and replaced the receiver.

"What's up?" asked Schmitz. "I take it we're getting out of here." He opened the newspaper lying in front of him, flipped it shut again immediately, and looked over the shoulder of Feinhals, who was sitting beside him. Schmitz regarded the sergeant major coolly. He had seen that Feinhals was preparing a map of the surrounding area. "Szokarhely Base" was printed across the top.

"Yes," said the sergeant major, "we've orders to redeploy." He was trying to remain calm, but there was a nasty glint in his eyes as he looked at Schneider. And his hands were trembling. He glanced at the crates, painted army-gray, stacked along the walls; with their lids open they could be used as lockers or desks. He still did not offer Schneider a chair.

"Give me a cigarette, Feinhals, till I can get some more," said Schneider. Feinhals got up, opened the blue pack, and held it out to Schneider. Schmitz took one too. Schneider stood leaning against the wall, smoking.

"I know," he said into the silence. "I'll be with the rear unit. It used to be the advance unit."

The sergeant major flushed. The sound of a typewriter came from the next room. The telephone rang, the sergeant major lifted the receiver, gave his name, and said, "Very well, sir—I'll have them sent over for signature."

He replaced the receiver. "Feinhals," he said, "go over and see if the order of the day is ready." Schmitz and Schneider exchanged glances. Schmitz looked at the desk and opened the newspaper again. "High Treason Trial Begins," he read. He flipped the paper shut again immediately.

Feinhals returned with the clerk from the next room. The clerk was a pale, fair-haired noncom with fingers stained from smoking.

"Otten," Schneider called out to him, "will you be opening up the canteen again?"

"Just a moment, if you don't mind," said the sergeant major, furious. "I've got more important things to do right now." He drummed on the desk with his fingers while the clerk sorted the sets of paper. He turned the typed sheets face down and pulled out the carbons. There were three sets, each consisting of two typed pages and four carbon copies. The typed sheets appeared to contain nothing but names. Schneider thought about the girl. Probably she was with the paymaster now, getting her money. He stepped closer to the window to get a better view of the gate.

"Don't forget," he said to Otten, "to leave us some cigarettes."

"Shut up!" shouted the sergeant major.

He handed the papers to Feinhals, saying, "Take these over to the senior MO for signature." Feinhals clipped them together and left the room.

The sergeant major turned to Schmitz and Schneider, but Schneider was looking out of the window. It was almost noon, and the road was empty; opposite was a large field where a market was held on Wednesdays: the littered stalls stood abandoned in the sunshine. So it *is* Wednesday, he thought, turning toward the sergeant major, who had a carbon copy of the order of the day in his hand. Feinhals had returned and was standing by the door.

". . . will remain here," the sergeant major was saying. "Feinhals has a sketch map of the place. This time everything's to be done in battle order. A formality, as you know, Schneider," he added. "You'd better round up a few men and have the weapons brought in from the infectious ward. The other wards have already been notified."

"Weapons?" asked Schneider. "Is that a formality too?"

The sergeant major flushed again. Schmitz took another cigarette from Feinhals's pack. "I'd like to see the list of wounded. Will the senior MO be leading the advance unit?"

"Yes," said the sergeant major, "he's the one that drew up the list."

"I'd like to see it," said Schmitz.

Once more the sergeant major flushed. Then he reached into the drawer and handed Schmitz the list. Schmitz read it through carefully, saying each name quietly over to himself; there was silence in the room, no one said anything, they were all looking at the man reading the list. Outside in the corridor there was a commotion. They all jumped as Schmitz suddenly cried out, "Lieutenant Moll and Captain Bauer, for Christ's sake!" He flung the list onto the desk and looked at the sergeant major. "Any medical student knows that no patient is fit to travel an hour and a half after a serious operation." He picked up the list from the desk and rapped the paper with his fingers. "I might just as well put a bullet through their heads as load them into an ambulance." He looked at Schneider, then at Feinhals, then at the sergeant major and Otten. "They must have known yesterday that we were clearing out today—why wasn't the operation postponed, eh?"

"Orders only arrived this morning, an hour ago," said the sergeant major.

"Orders! Orders!" exclaimed Schmitz. He threw the list onto the desk, saying to Schneider, "Come on, let's get out of here." When they were outside he said, "You weren't listening just then—I'm in charge of the rear unit—we'll talk about it later." He walked rapidly toward the senior MO's office, and Schneider strolled away to his room.

He paused at each window on the way, looking out to make sure Szarka's cart was still standing in front of the gate. By now the courtyard was jammed with trucks and ambulances, and in the middle stood the MO's car. They had already begun loading, and Schneider noticed that outside the kitchen the baskets of fruit were also being loaded, and the MO's driver was lugging a gray metal trunk across the yard.

The corridors were crowded. In his room Schneider walked quickly to the locker, poured the rest of the apricot schnapps into a glass, and added some soda water, and as he drank it he could hear the first motor starting up outside. Glass in hand, he went out into the corridor and stood by the window: he had heard right away that the first motor to start up was the MO's; it was a good motor, Schneider knew nothing about such things, but he could tell by the sound that it was a good motor. Just then the MO crossed the courtyard, he wasn't carrying any baggage, and his field cap was slightly askew. He looked pretty much as usual; only his face, otherwise rather distinguished, pale, with faint pinkish overtones, was scarlet. The MO was a good-looking man, tall and spare, an excellent horseman who mounted his horse every morning at six, whip in hand, and rode off into the puszta at a steady canter, a dwindling figure vanishing into that flat landscape that seemed to consist only of horizon. But now his face was scarlet, and only once had Schneider seen the MO's face scarlet, and that was when Schmitz had carried out with success an operation that the MO had not wanted to tackle. Now Schmitz was walking beside the MO; Schmitz was quite calm, whereas the MO was waving his arms . . . but now Schneider had seen the girl coming toward him along the corridor. She seemed to be confused by all the commotion and looking for someone who was not involved in the general exodus. She said something in Hungarian that he did not understand, then he pointed to his room and beckoned her over. Outside, the first vehicle, the MO's, was moving off, and the column slowly followed. . . .

Evidently the girl took him for a deputy of the paymaster's. She did not sit down on the chair he offered, and when he perched on the edge of the desk she continued to stand facing him, trying to make him understand what she wanted and gesturing vigorously as she spoke. It was a relief to be able to look at her without having to listen to her, for it was hopeless to try and understand what she was saying. But he let her talk just so that he could look at her. She seemed rather thin, perhaps she was too young, very young, much younger than he had thought—her breasts were small, the beauty of her small face was perfect, and he waited almost breathlessly for the moments when her long eyelashes lay on the brown cheeks—very brief moments in which her small mouth remained closed, round and red, the lips slightly too narrow. He studied her very carefully and had to admit that he was a bit disappointed—but she was charming, and all of a sudden he raised his hands defensively and shook his head. She stopped speaking at once, looking at him suspiciously; he said softly, "I'd like to kiss you, do you understand?" By this time he no longer knew whether he really did want to kiss her, and it embarrassed him to see her blush, to see the color slowly spreading over that dark skin, and he realized she hadn't understood a single word but knew what he meant. She took a step back as he slowly approached her, and he could see from the scared look in her eyes and from the thin neck with its wildly pulsing vein that she was three months too young. He stopped, shook his head, and said in a low voice: "Forgive me—forget it—understand?" But the look in her eyes became more scared than ever, and he was afraid she was going to scream. This time she seemed to understand even less. With a sigh he stepped up to her, took hold of her small hands, and as he lifted them to his mouth he saw they were dirty, they smelled of earth and leather, leeks and onions, and he brushed them with his lips and tried to smile. She looked at him in growing bewilderment, until he patted her on the shoulder, saying, "Come along, we'll go and see you get your money." Not until he held up his hand and made the unmistakable gesture of paying did she give a little smile and follow him out into the corridor.

In the corridor they ran into Schmitz and Otten.

"Where are you going?" asked Schmitz.

"To see the paymaster," said Schneider. "The girl wants her money."

"The paymaster's gone," said Schmitz. "He left yesterday evening, for Szolnok; from there he's going to join up with the advance unit." He lowered his lids for a moment, then looked at the men. No one said a word. The girl glanced from one to the other. "Otten," said Schmitz, "round up the rear unit, I need a few men for unloading, no one seemed to think of leaving any food for us."

"And the girl?" asked Schneider.

Schmitz shrugged his shoulders. "I can't give her any money."

"Should she come back tomorrow morning?"

Schmitz looked at the girl. She smiled at him.

"No," he said, "it had better be this afternoon."

Otten ran along the corridor, shouting, "Rear unit fall in!"

Schmitz went out into the courtyard and stood beside the truck, while Schneider accompanied the girl to her cart. He tried to explain to her that she should come back in the afternoon, but she kept vigorously shaking her head until he realized she was not going to leave without her money. He continued to stand beside her, watched her climb onto the cart, turn her crate up, and take out a brown-paper parcel. Then she hung the feedbag over the horse's nose and unwrapped the parcel: part of a loaf of bread, a large flat meat patty, and a leek. Her wine was in a squat green bottle. She was smiling at him now, and suddenly, in the midst of chewing, she said "Nagyvárad," and struck the air several times with her fist, horizontally away from her body, making a solemn face as she did so. Schneider imagined she was demonstrating a fistfight which someone had lost, or maybe—he thought—she was trying to show that she felt she had been cheated. He didn't know what "Nagyvárad" meant. Hungarian was a very difficult language, it didn't even have a word for tobacco.

The girl shook her head. "Nagyvárad, Nagyvárad," she repeated vehemently several times, striking the air again with her fist, horizontally away from her chest. She shook her head and laughed, chewing hard, and took a quick gulp of wine. "Oh!" she went, "Nagyvárad—Russ," again the boxing gesture, this time prolonged and in a wide arc: "Russ—Russ." She pointed to the southeast and imitated the noise of tanks approaching: "Bru-bru-bru. . . ."

Suddenly Schneider nodded, and she laughed out loud, but broke off in the middle and assumed a very grave expression. Schneider realized that Nagyvárad must be a town, and the boxing gesture was now quite clear. He looked across to the men standing by the truck and unloading. Schmitz was standing up front beside the driver and signing something. Schneider called out to him, "When you have a moment, sir, would you mind coming over here?" Schmitz nodded.

The girl had finished her meal. She carefully wrapped up the bread and the remains of the leek and stuck the cork back in the bottle.

"Would you like some water for the horse?" asked Schneider. She looked at him questioningly.

"Water," he said, "for the horse." He leaned slightly forward and tried to imitate a horse drinking.

"Oh," she cried, "oh, yo!" Her eyes held a strange look, of curiosity somehow, curiosity and tenderness.

Across the yard the truck moved off, and Schmitz walked over.

Their eyes followed the truck; outside, another column stood waiting for the entrance to become free.

"What is it?" asked Schmitz.

"She's talking about a breakthrough near a town beginning with Nagy."

Schmitz nodded. "Nagyvárad," he said, "I know."

"You know?"

"I heard it last night over the radio."

"Is it far from here?"

Schmitz looked thoughtfully at the long column of trucks driving into the yard. "Far," he said with a sigh, "far doesn't mean a thing in this war—must be about sixty miles. Maybe we should give the girl her money in cigarettes—right now."

Schneider looked at Schmitz and felt himself blushing. "Hold on a minute," he said, "I'd like her to stay for a bit."

"Suit yourself," said Schmitz, walking slowly off toward the south wing.

As he entered the patients' room, the captain said in a low, hollow tone: "Byelyogorshe." Schmitz knew it was pointless to look at his watch; that rhythm was more precise than any watch could ever be, and while he sat on the edge of the bed, the medical history in his hand, almost lulled to sleep by that ever-recurring word, he tried to figure out how such a rhythm could come about—what mechanism, what clockwork, in that appallingly patched-up, sliced-up skull, was releasing that monotonous litany? And what happened in those fifty seconds when the man said nothing, merely breathed? Schmitz knew almost nothing about him: born March 1895 in Wuppertal; rank: captain; service: army; civilian occupation: businessman; religion: Lutheran; residence, troop unit, wounds, illnesses, type of injury. Nor was there anything particularly striking about this man's life: his school record was not good, he had been a very mediocre student, somewhat unreliable; he had only had to repeat a year once, and on graduating he had even had a B in geography, English, and Phys. Ed. He had had no love for the war; without wanting to, he had been made a lieutenant in 1915. He drank a bit, but not excessively—and later, when he was married, he could never bring himself to deceive his wife, however simple and enticing it might sometimes have been to arrange an affair. He just couldn't bring himself to do it.

Schmitz knew that everything in the medical history was virtually irrelevant as long as he didn't know why the man said "Byelyogorshe" and what it meant to him—and Schmitz knew that he would never know, yet he would have happily sat there forever, waiting for that word.

Outside it was very quiet. He listened tensely and expectantly to the silence into which from time to time that word dropped. But the silence was stronger, oppressively strong, and slowly, almost reluctantly, Schmitz got up and went out of the room.

AFTER SCHMITZ had left them, the girl looked at Schneider and seemed embarrassed. She made a hurried gesture of drinking. "Oh, of course," he said, "the water." He went toward the building to get some water. At the entrance he had to jump back: an elegant red car drove past him, quietly but a little too fast and, carefully avoiding the parked ambulances, swung toward the rear, where the administrator had his quarters.

On coming back with the pail of water, Schneider had to jump aside again. Horns were sounding, the column was getting under way. In the first truck sat the sergeant major, the others followed slowly. The sergeant major did not look at Schneider. Schneider let the long line of trucks pass and stepped into the courtyard, now oppressively empty and quiet. He set the pail down in front of the horse and looked at the girl; she pointed to

Schmitz, just then emerging from the south wing. Schmitz walked past them out through the entrance, and they slowly followed. They stood side by side watching the column move off in the direction of the station. "The two from the infectious ward actually did bring along some weapons," Schmitz said quietly.

"Ah yes," exclaimed Schneider, "I'd forgotten about that."

Schmitz shook his head. "We won't be needing them—on the contrary. Come on, let's go." He paused beside the girl. "I think we'd better give her the cigarettes now, eh? Just in case?"

Schneider nodded. "Didn't they leave us a truck? How are we supposed to get away?"

"One truck's supposed to be coming back," said Schmitz. "The MO promised me."

The two men exchanged glances.

"There come some refugees," said Schmitz, pointing toward the village: a weary group was approaching. The refugees trudged slowly past without looking at them. They were tired and sad and did not look at either the soldiers or the girl.

"They've come a long way," said Schmitz. "Look how tired the horses are. It's useless to run away; at that speed they'll never escape the war."

A car horn blew behind them, sharp and impatient, insolent. They moved slowly apart, Schneider toward the girl. The administrator's car was pushing its way out; it was forced to stop, almost hitting a refugee cart. They could see the occupants quite distinctly, they were sitting right in front of their noses, it was like being in the front row at the movies, painfully close to the screen. In front, at the wheel, sat the administrator, his sharp, rather weak profile motionless; beside him on the seat was a pile of suitcases and blankets, firmly fastened with ropes so they would not topple over on him during the drive. Behind him sat his wife, her beautiful profile as motionless as his; both seemed bent on looking neither right nor left. She was holding the baby on her lap, their six-year-old boy was beside her. He was the only one looking out; his lively face was pressed to the glass, and he smiled at the soldiers. It was two minutes before the car could go on—the horses were tired, and somewhere further along the trek had stalled. They could see the man at the wheel grow tense: he was sweating, he blinked rapidly, and his wife whispered something to him from the back seat. There was scarcely a sound, only the refugees calling out wearily along the trek, and a child crying; but suddenly from the courtyard behind them came shouts, hoarse yells, and they looked back. At that instant a stone struck the car, but it only smacked into the folded tent; the second stone knocked a dent in the saucepan tied to the top as if for a family outing. The man who was yelling and running up to them was the janitor; he occupied two rooms in the bathhouse at the far end of the grounds. He was quite close now, standing right in the entrance, but he had run out of stones. As he bent down, cursing, the snag in the trek sorted itself out, and the car, hooting imperiously, got under way. A flowerpot swished through the air but landed only where a second ago the car had been standing, on the swept pavement of blue chips. The clay pot shattered, the fragments rolled apart, forming an oddly symmetrical circle around the lump of soil, which first seemed to retain its shape but then suddenly crumbled apart, releasing the roots of a geranium whose blossoms, red and innocent, remained upright in the center.

The janitor stood between the soldiers. He was not cursing now, he was weeping, the tears clearly visible on his grimy cheeks, and his posture was both touching and horrifying: leaning forward, fists clenched, his grubby old jacket flapping about his hollow chest. He jumped when a woman's voice screamed behind him in the courtyard, then he turned and walked slowly back, weeping. Szarka followed him, drawing away when Schneider put out his hand toward her. She took hold of her horse, led it outside, climbed onto the cart, and picked up the reins.

"I'll go and get the cigarettes," cried Schmitz. "Don't let her leave —I'll be right back." Schneider held the horse firmly by the bridle, the girl brought the whip down on his hand; it hurt, but he hung on. He looked back and was surprised to see Schmitz running. He wouldn't have thought Schmitz would ever run. The girl raised her whip again, but instead of bringing it down on his hand she placed it beside her on the seat, and Schneider was amazed to see her suddenly smile: it was the smile he had often seen on her, tender and cool, and he went up to the cart and carefully lifted her down from her upturned crate. She called out something to the horse, and when Schneider put his arms around her, he saw that she was still a bit nervous, but she did not resist, she just looked uneasily about her. It was dark in the entrance; Schneider kissed her carefully on the cheeks, on the nose, and pushed back her smooth black hair to kiss the nape of her neck. He was startled to hear Schmitz throw the cigarettes into the cart. The girl's head shot up, her eyes went to the red packages. Schmitz did not look at Schneider but turned on his heel and went back into the courtyard. The girl was blushing, she looked at Schneider but deliberately past his eyes, and all at once she called out to the horse, a crisp, short word, and jerked the reins. Schneider moved aside. He waited until she was fifty paces away, then called her name into the silence—she hesitated, did not turn around, raised the whip over her head in a farewell gesture, and drove on. Schneider walked slowly back into the courtyard.

The seven men of the rear unit were sitting over a meal outside what had been the kitchen; there was a pail of soup on the table in the courtyard, and beside it thick slices of bread and meat. Schneider heard muffled blows coming from inside the building. He raised his eyebrows at the men.

"The janitor's breaking down the door to the administrator's quarters," said Feinhals, adding a moment later, "At least he might have left the door open; there's no point in destroying it."

Schmitz entered the building with four soldiers to collect all the material for loading. Schneider stayed behind with Feinhals and Otten.

"I've been given a nice job," said Otten.

Feinhals was drinking red schnapps out of an enamel mug; he passed a few packs of cigarettes to Schneider. "Thanks," said Schneider.

"I've been given the job," said Otten, "of throwing the machine gun and the machine pistol and the rest of the junk into the cesspool, down there where the dud shell's lying. You can give me a hand, Feinhals."

"OK," said Feinhals. With his soup spoon he was slowly drawing patterns on the table from a soup puddle that ran broad and brown from the center to the edge.

"Let's go then," said Otten.

Shortly after this Schneider fell asleep, bent over the lid of his mess bowl. His cigarette went on burning. It was lying at the edge of the table; the fine ash ate its way slowly out of the cigarette paper, the burning tip crept on, burning a narrow black trail in the table as far as the edge of the cigarette, and four minutes later only a slender gray stick of ash was left, stuck to the table. This little gray stick lay there a long time, almost an hour, until Schneider woke up and brushed it off with his arm without ever having seen it. He woke up just as the truck was driving into the yard. Almost simultaneously with the sound of the truck they heard the first tanks. Schneider leaped to his feet. The others, who were standing around smoking, were on the point of laughing, but stopped short of it: that distant rumble spoke for itself.

"How about that," said Schmitz, "the truck really did turn up. Feinhals, go up into the attic, maybe you can see something from there."

Feinhals walked over to the south wing. The janitor was leaning on a window sill in the administrator's quarters, watching the men. His wife could be heard moving about inside, there was a faint tinkle, she appeared to be counting glasses.

"Let's load the stuff," said Schmitz. The driver gestured impatiently;

he looked very tired. "Balls," he said, "climb in and leave the crap behind."
He picked up a pack from the table, ripped it open, and lit a cigarette.

"Start loading," said Schmitz. "We've got to wait anyway till Feinhals gets back."

The driver shrugged his shoulders, sat down at the table, and ladled
some soup from the pail into Schneider's mess bowl.

The rest of the men loaded the truck with everything that had been
left behind in the building: a few beds, an officer's barrack box, his name
printed on it in black paint, "Lt. Greck," a stove, and a pile of soldiers'
packs, knapsacks, kit bags, and a few rifles; then a pile of underwear:
bundled shirts, underpants, socks, and some fur-lined vests.

Feinhals called down from the attic, "I can't see a thing. There's a
row of poplars in the village blocking my view. Can you hear them? I
can, quite clearly."

"Yes," called Schmitz, "we can hear them. Come on down."

"OK," said Feinhals. His head vanished from the skylight.

"Someone ought to go down to the railroad embankment," said
Schmitz, "he'd be sure to see them from there."

"It's no use," said the truck driver, "they're not in sight yet."

"How can you tell?"

"By listening. I can hear they're not in sight yet. Besides, they're
coming from two directions."

He pointed toward the southwest, and his gesture seemed to conjure
up the rumble over there too: he was right, they could hear it now.

"Hell," said Schmitz. "What do we do now?"

"Get going," said the driver. He stepped aside and, shaking his head,
looked on as the others finished off the job of loading the table onto the
truck, as well as the bench he had been sitting on.

Feinhals came out of the building. "One of the patients is yelling,"
he said.

"I'll go," said Schmitz. "You fellows get going."

They stood there, hesitating. Then they slowly followed him, all
except the driver. Schmitz turned around, saying quietly, "Get going, I tell
you, I have to stay behind anyway, with the patients." Again they hesitated, then promptly followed him again.

"Damn it all," Schmitz called back to them, "get going, I tell you.
You need to get a head start on this damned plain."

This time they halted and did not follow. Only Schneider walked
slowly after him as he disappeared into the building. The rest moved
slowly toward the truck. Feinhals hesitated a moment. It was a brief pause,

then he entered the building and came face to face with Schneider.

"D'you need something?" Schneider asked. "Everything's already on the truck."

"Unload some bread, and some margarine—and cigarettes." The door to the sickroom opened. Feinhals looked in and exclaimed, "My God, the captain."

"D'you know him?" asked Schmitz.

"Yes," said Feinhals, "I once spent half a day in his battalion."

"Where?"

"I don't know what the place was called."

"Get out of here, you two," cried Schmitz, "and quit fooling around."

Feinhals said, "Be seeing you," and left.

"What made you stay behind?" asked Schmitz, but he did not seem to expect a reply, and Schneider gave none. They both stood listening to the noise of the departing truck, the motor sounding hollow as the truck drove through the entrance; then it was outside on the road to the station —and even beyond the station they could still hear it, until it gradually became very faint.

The rumbling of the tanks had stopped. They heard firing.

"Heavy flak," said Schmitz. "We really should go down to the embankment."

"I'll go," said Schneider. Inside the room the captain said "Byelyogorshe." He said it almost without emphasis, yet with a certain pleasure. His face was dark, with a dense black growth of beard, his head was firmly bandaged. Schneider looked at Schmitz. "Hopeless," he said. "If he gets better, comes through this, well. . . ." He shrugged his shoulders.

"Byelyogorshe," said the captain. Then he started to cry. He cried soundlessly, without the least alteration in his expression, but even through his tears he said, "Byelyogorshe."

"There's a court-martial proceeding against him," said Schmitz. "He was thrown off a motorcycle and wasn't wearing a steel helmet. He was a captain."

"I'll just run down to the embankment," said Schneider, "maybe I can see something from there. If any more troops come back, I'll join them . . . so . . ."

Schmitz nodded.

"Byelyogorshe," said the captain.

When Schneider came out into the courtyard, he saw that at the far end the janitor had run up a flag in the administrator's quarters, a pathetic red rag with a clumsy yellow sickle and white hammer stitched to it. Now the rumbling in the southeast was also becoming more distinct again. The firing seemed to have ceased. He walked slowly past the planted beds, only stopping when he reached the cesspool. Beside the cesspool lay the dud shell. It had been lying there for months. Months ago, SS units that had been dug in along the railroad tracks had been fighting Hungarian rebels holed up in the school, but it had been only a very brief skirmish: the traces of firing had almost disappeared from the façade. Only the dud had remained where it was, a rusty piece of iron, the length of an arm and tapering to a round point, scarcely noticeable. It looked almost like a piece of rotting wood. In the high grass it was hardly visible, but the administrator's wife had made numerous protests against its existence, and reports had been submitted that never received a reply.

Schneider's pace slackened a little while he had to pass the dud. In the grass he saw the footprints of Otten and Feinhals, who had thrown the machine gun into the cesspool, but the surface of the cesspool was smooth again, a green, greasy smoothness. Schneider continued on past the beds, through the tree farm, across the meadow, and climbed up onto the railroad embankment. Those four or five feet seemed to raise him to an immense height above the ground. He looked beyond the village out onto the broad plain to the left of the tracks and saw nothing. But the sound had become more distinct. He listened carefully for any firing. Nothing. The rumbling came from exactly the same direction as the tracks. Schneider sat down and waited. The village was absolutely silent; it lay there as if dead, with its trees, the little houses, the square church tower. It looked very small because to the left of the embankment there was not a single house. Schneider began to smoke.

INDOORS, SCHMITZ was sitting beside the man who said "Byelyogorshe." Over and over again. His tears had dried up. The man stared straight ahead with his dark eyes and repeated "Byelyogorshe," like a beautiful melody, Schmitz thought—anyway, he could have listened forever to this one word. The other patient was asleep.

The man who kept saying "Byelyogorshe" was called Bauer, Captain Bauer. He had previously been a textile agent, and before that a student, but before he became a student he had been a lieutenant, for almost four years, and later, as a textile agent, things had not been easy for him. It all depended on whether people had money, and people hardly ever did have money. At least, not the people who might have bought his sweaters. Expensive sweaters always sold well, so did cheap ones, but his particular line, the medium-priced range, were always very hard to sell. . . . He hadn't

managed to pick up an agency for cheap sweaters, or for expensive ones
—those were the good agencies, and good agencies went to the people who
didn't need them. Fifteen years he had spent as an agent for those slow-
selling sweaters; the first twelve years had been a loathsome, never-ending,
horrible struggle, chasing from store to store, from building to building,
the kind of life that wore a man down. It had put years on his wife. When
he first met her she had been twenty-three and he twenty-six—he was still
a student, fond of a drink, while she was a slender, fair-haired girl who
couldn't drink any wine at all. But she had never uttered a cross word to
him, a quiet woman who had held her tongue even when he sacrificed his
university career to sell sweaters. He had often been surprised himself at
his own stamina—to have been selling those sweaters for twelve years!—
and at his wife's calm acceptance of everything. Then for three years things
had gone a bit better, and suddenly, after fifteen years, the whole situation
had changed: he acquired the agency for both the expensive and the cheap
sweaters and kept the agency for the medium-priced range. Business had
been booming, and now others were doing the legwork for him. He could
spend all his time at home, telephoning and signing; he had a warehouseman, a bookkeeper, and a stenographer. Now he had money, but now his
wife—who was never really well and had had five miscarriages in quick
succession—had cancer. It had finally been confirmed. And besides, these
halcyon days had lasted only four months—until the war broke out.

"Byelyogorshe," said the captain.

Schmitz looked at him; he would have liked to know what the man
was thinking about. He felt an ungovernable curiosity to know the whole
man, that large and rather hollow face, deathly pale under its stubble, those
staring eyes that seemed to say "Byelyogorshe"—for now his mouth barely
moved. Then the man started crying again, his tears running soundlessly
down his cheeks. He was no hero, and it had been pretty rough to have
the lieutenant colonel shout into the phone telling him to find out what
his bunch were doing, that something was wrong at Horse Droppings, and
to have to drive up to the front line with that steel helmet on his head,
knowing what a fool he looked in it. He was no hero, he had never said
he was, in fact he knew he wasn't. And when he was close to the front
line he had taken off the steel helmet because he didn't want to look like
a fool when he got to the front and had to start shouting. He held the steel
helmet in his hand and thought: What the hell, why not take a chance,
and the closer he got to that stupid mess up front, the less scared he was.
Hell, they all knew there wasn't a thing he could do, that anyone could
do, because they had too few guns and no tanks. So why start shouting
like an idiot? Every officer knew that too many tanks and too many guns

had been ordered back to cover staff quarters. Shit, he thought, unaware that he was being brave. And then he was thrown off the machine and his whole skull was ripped open, and the only thing left inside him was the word "Byelyogorshe." That was all. It seemed to be enough to keep him talking for the whole of the rest of his life, it was a world for him, a world that no one knew or ever would know.

He had no idea, of course, that a court-martial had been instituted against him on grounds of self-mutilation because he had removed his steel helmet while under fire and, what was more, while on a motorcycle. He had no idea of this—and he never would have. The drawing up of the paper bearing his name and serial number, and all the other documents, had been so much wasted effort—he would never find out about them, they would never reach him now. He merely said, every fifty seconds, "Byelyogorshe."

Schmitz never took his eyes off him. He would willingly have gone out of his mind himself to know what was going on inside this man's mind. And at the same time he envied him.

He jumped when Schneider opened the door. "What is it?" asked Schmitz. "They're coming," said Schneider. "They're here. No more of our troops managed to get through."

Schmitz had heard nothing. Now he heard them. They were there. To the left they were already in the village. Now he understood what the driver had meant: "I can hear they're not in sight yet." Now you could hear they were in sight—clearly in sight.

"The flag," said Schmitz, "we should have hung out the flag with the red cross—it would have been worth a try."

"We still can."

"Here it is," said Schmitz. He pulled it out from under his pack on the table. Schneider took it.

"Coming?" he asked.

They left. Schneider stuck his head out the window and pulled it back in again immediately. His face was white.

"They're right there," he said, "by the embankment."

"I'll go and meet them," said Schmitz.

Schneider shook his head. He raised the flag high above his head and went out through the door. He swung round to the right and made straight for the embankment. It was very quiet, even the tanks were quiet as they stood parked at the edge of the village. The school was the last building before the station. It was in that direction that their gun barrels were pointing, but Schneider didn't see them. He didn't see the tanks at all, he saw nothing. He felt ridiculous, holding the flag like that in front of himself as if he were in a parade, and he could feel that his blood was fear. Just plain fear. He walked stiffly, straight ahead, almost like a puppet, holding the flag in front of himself. He walked slowly until he stumbled. That woke him up. He had stumbled over a wire connecting the vinestocks in a model plantation. Now he saw everything. There were two tanks, they were parked behind the embankment, and the one in front was slowly veering its turret to aim at him. Then, when he had passed the trees, he saw there were more. They were standing behind and beside one another in formation across the field, and the red stars painted on them seemed repulsive and very alien to him. He had never seen them before. Next came the cesspool. Now he had only to pass the beds, cross the tree farm, climb up the embankment—but at the cesspool he hesitated; he was suddenly scared again, worse than before. Before he hadn't realized; he had thought his blood was turning to ice, he hadn't realized it was fear. Now his blood was like fire, and he saw nothing but red—nothing else—gigantic red stars that struck terror into him. Just then he stepped on the dud, and the dud exploded.

At first nothing happened. In the silence the explosion was staggeringly loud. The Russians knew only that the shell had not come from them, and that the man with the flag had suddenly vanished in a cloud of dust. Shortly after that they started pounding away at the building in a frenzy. They swung all their gun barrels around, redeployed themselves for firing, fired first into the south wing, then into the central building and the north wing, where the janitor's tiny flag hung limply from the window. It fell into the dirt that crumbled down from the building—and finally they fired again into the south wing, this time long and furiously; they had not fired their guns for a long time, and they sawed through the thin façade until the building toppled forward. It was not until later that they noticed there had not been a single shot from the other side.

IV

ONLY TWO big patches of color were left: one green, a cucumber vendor's great mound, the other pinkish-yellow, apricots. In the middle of the market square stood the swingboats. They were there permanently. Their colors had faded, their blue and red as dingy and dirty as the colors of a venerable old ship anchored in the harbor and patiently waiting to be scrapped. The swingboats hung down stiffly, not one was moving, and smoke curled up from the chimney of the trailer parked alongside them.

The patches of color were slowly breaking up: the dark and light greens of the intertwined mosaic of cucumbers dwindled rapidly; Greck could see from a long way off that two people were busy breaking it up. The apricots took longer, much longer: a woman, all by herself, was picking the apricots up one by one and carefully placing them in baskets. Cucumbers were evidently not as fragile as apricots. Greck slowed his pace. Deny it, he thought, simply deny everything. That's the only thing to do if they find out. The only thing. Life was worth a denial, after all. But they wouldn't find out, he was sure of that. It did surprise him, though, to find that there were so many Jews still around here.

The paving between the low trees and little houses was uneven, but he did not notice it. He was pretty scared, and he had the feeling: The faster I get away from there, the less chance there is of attracting attention, and most likely I won't have to deny anything. But I must hurry. He was walking faster again now, hurrying along. He had almost reached the square; the cart with the cucumbers was already passing him, and beyond it there was still that woman painstakingly packing away her apricots. Her pile had not yet been reduced by half.

Greck saw the swingboats. Never in his life had he gone for a ride on a swingboat. Such pleasures had not been for him; they were forbidden in his family, first because he was never really well, and then because that was no way to behave, in public, swinging through the air like some silly monkey. And he had never done anything that was forbidden—today had been the first time, and right off something so terrible, almost the worst thing you could do, something that automatically cost you your life.

Greck could feel the panic in his throat, and he lurched quickly, reeling in the sunshine, across the empty square toward the swingboats. Smoke was puffing more vigorously now from the trailer's chimney. They must have put some more coal on, he thought: no, wood. He didn't know what they put on stoves in Hungary. And he didn't care. He knocked on the trailer door: a man appeared, naked to the waist, he was blond, unshaven, and big-boned, his face had something almost Dutch about it; only the nose was strikingly narrow, and he had very dark eyes.

"What is it?" he asked in German. Greck could feel the sweat trickling into his mouth; he licked his lips, wiped the palm of his hand across his face, and said, "The swings, I'd like to go for a ride."

The man in the doorway screwed up his eyes, then nodded. He ran his tongue over his teeth. Behind him appeared his wife; she was in her petticoat, sweat was dripping down her face, and the dark-red shoulder straps were sweat-stained. In one hand she was holding a wooden spoon, in the other arm a child. The child was dirty. The woman was very dark, somber, Greck thought. There was definitely something sinister about these people. Perhaps tyes, then nodded. He ran his tongue over his teeth. Behind him appeared his wife; she was in her petticoat, sweat was dripping down her face, and the dark-red shoulder straps were sweat-stained. In one hand she was holding a wooden spoon, in the other arm a child. The child was dirty. The woman was very dark, somber, Greck thought. There was definitely something sinister about these people. Perhaps they were suspicious of him. Greck no longer wanted a ride on the swingboats, but the man, whose tongue had finally settled down, said, "Well, if you really want to—in this heat—at midday."

He came down the steps; Greck moved aside and followed him the few paces to the swingboats.

"How much?" he asked feebly. They'll think I'm nuts, he thought. The sweat was driving him crazy. He wiped his sleeve across his face and climbed the wooden steps to the iron framework. The man released a brake, one of the swingboats in the middle swayed gently to and fro.

"I guess," said the man, "you'd better not go too high, or I'll have to stay here and watch. It's the law."

Greck found his German repulsive. It was an odd mixture of softness and impudence, as if he were uttering an entirely foreign language with German words.

"I won't," Greck said. "You can go. . . . How much?"

The man shrugged his shoulders. "Give me one pengö," he said. Greck gave him his last pengö and carefully climbed in.

The little boat was wider than he had thought. He felt quite safe and began to use the technique he had so often been able to watch but not use. He held on to the iron stanchions, unclasped his fingers to wipe off the sweat, then straightened his knee, bent it, straightened it, and was amazed to feel the swingboat move. It was very simple, all you had to do was make sure the bending of your knee did not interfere with the rhythmic movement set up by the swing: you had to increase the rhythm by throwing your weight back, with straight legs, as the boat swung forward, and by letting yourself fall forward as the boat swung back. Greck saw that the man was still standing beside him, and he shouted, "What's the matter? You don't have to stay." The man shook his head, and Greck ceased to pay attention to him. All of a sudden he knew he had been missing something vital in his life: riding a swingboat. It was glorious. The sweat dried on his forehead, and the gentle coolness of the rocking motion even dried the sweat on his body: the air blew through him, fresh and exquisite, with every swing, and furthermore the world was changed. One minute it consisted merely of a few dirty planks with broad grooves running along them, and on the downward swing he had the whole sky to himself. "Watch out!" cried the man down below, "hold tight!" Greck could feel the man putting on the brake: a gentle jolt that severely hampered his swinging.

"Leave me alone!" he shouted. But the man shook his head. Greck quickly swung himself up again. This was the glorious part: to stand parallel to the earth as the little boat swung back—to see those dirty planks that signified the world—and then, plunging forward again, to kick your feet into the sky, to see it overhead as if you were lying in a meadow, only this way you were closer to the sky, infinitely closer. Everything in between was insignificant. On his left the woman was carefully packing away her apricots; her pile never seemed to get any less. On the right stood that fat blond fellow who had to obey the law and slow him down; a few chickens waddled across his field of vision, over there was a road. His cap flew off his head.

Deny it, he thought, as he calmed down, simply deny it; they won't believe it if I deny it. I don't do things like that. No one would believe I could do a thing like that. I've got a good reputation. I know they don't think much of me because I've got chronic indigestion, but they like me in their way, and no one would believe I could do a thing like that. He was both proud and timid, and it was a glorious feeling to find he had the courage to go on this swingboat. He would write to his mother about it. No, better not. Mama didn't understand about things like that. Whatever life may bring, always behave with dignity! was her motto. She would never understand how her son, an attorney, Lieutenant Greck, could take a ride in a swingboat, in the middle of a broiling hot day in a dirty Hungarian market square, in full view of anyone—anyone at all—who happened to be passing by. No, no—he could picture her shaking her head, a woman without humor; he knew that and it was no use trying to fight it. And that other thing: oh God! Although he didn't want to, he couldn't help thinking about it, how he had undressed in the Jewish tailor's back room: a stuffy little hole with scraps of patching material lying around, half-finished suits with buckram tacked onto them, and a repulsively large bowl of cucumber salad with drowning flies floating around in it—he could feel fluid rising into his mouth, and he knew he was turning pale, disgusting fluid in his mouth—but he could still see himself, taking off his pants and revealing his second pair, taking the money, and the toothless old man's grin following him as he hurried out of the shop.

Suddenly the world began to spin around him. "Stop!" he yelled, "stop!" The man down below jammed on the brake, he felt it, the hard rhythmic jolting. Then the swing came to a standstill; he knew he looked ridiculous and pathetic, and he carefully stepped out, walked behind the framework, and spat: his stomach had settled down but he still had that disgusting taste in his mouth. He felt giddy, sat down on a step, and closed his eyes; the rhythm of the ride was still in his eyes, he could feel his eyeballs twitching, he had to spit again. It took quite a while for the movement of his eyeballs to calm down.

He rose and picked up his cap from the ground. The man was standing beside him, looked at him impassively; then his wife appeared. Greck was surprised to see how small she was. A tiny, swarthy little thing with a gaunt face. She was holding a mug. The blond fellow took the mug from her and held it out to Greck. "Drink," he said without emotion. Greck shook his head. "Drink," said the man, "it will do you good."

Greck took the mug; the stuff tasted very bitter, but it helped. The couple smiled, they smiled mechanically because they were used to smiling at this kind of thing, not because they cared for him or pitied him.

"Thanks very much," he said. He felt in his pocket for coins, there were none left, only that terrible great hundred-pengö bill, and he shrugged his shoulders helplessly. He could feel himself flushing. "OK," said the man, "that's OK." *"Heil Hitler,"* said Greck. The man merely nodded.

Greck did not look back. The sweat was beginning to flow again. It seemed to come boiling out of his pores. Across the square was a tavern. He longed for a wash.

Inside the tavern the air was oddly chilly yet stuffy. The room was almost empty. Greck noticed that the man standing behind the bar looked first at his medals. The man's gaze was cool, not unfriendly, but cool. In the corner to the left sat a young couple with dirty dishes on the table in front of them and a carafe of wine, there was a beer bottle on the table too. Greck sat down in the corner to the right so he could look out on the street. He felt a sense of relief. His watch showed one o'clock, and he didn't have to be back until six. The man came out from behind the bar and walked slowly over to him. Greck wondered what he should drink. He really didn't want anything. Just a wash. He wasn't one for alcohol; besides, it didn't agree with him. Not for nothing had his mother warned him against it, just as she had against riding swingboats. Once again the innkeeper, now facing him, looked first at the left side of his chest.

"Afternoon," said the man. "What can I get you?"

"Some coffee," said Greck, "d'you have any coffee?" The man nodded. The nod said everything: it said that the glance to the left side of Greck's chest and the word "coffee" had told everything. "And a schnapps," said Greck. But it seemed to be too late.

"What kind?" asked the man.

"Apricot," said Greck.

The fellow went off. He was fat. His pants made fat rolls across his backside, and he was wearing slippers. Sloppy—like everything else here, thought Greck. He looked across at the young lovers. Swarms of flies were perched on the dirty plates with remains of food, chop bones, little mounds of vegetables, and wilted lettuce in earthenware bowls. Disgusting, thought Greck.

A soldier came in, looked nervously around, saluted Greck across the room, and walked over to the bar. The soldier had no medals at all. And yet there was a warmth in the innkeeper's eyes that annoyed Greck. Maybe, he thought, because I'm an officer they expect me to have more medals, splendid gold and silver affairs, these knuckleheads here in Hungary. Maybe I look as though I ought to be wearing medals: I'm tall and slim, blond. Hell, he thought, what a revolting business. He looked out the window.

The woman with the apricots was almost through now, and all of a sudden he knew what he really wanted to eat: some fruit. Oh, that would do him good! His mother had always given him plenty of fruit when it was in season and cheap, and it had done him a lot of good. Fruit was cheap here, and he had money, and wanted to eat some fruit. He hesitated at the thought of the money; his thoughts hesitated. Sweat broke out heavily again. Nothing would happen, and if something did: deny it, deny it, just deny everything. Nobody was going to believe some dirty Jew that he, Greck, had sold him his pants. Nobody would believe it if he denied it, and even if they identified the pants as his, he could say they had been stolen or something. But nobody was going to go to all that trouble. And anyway, why should they find out in his particular case? The affair had opened his eyes in a flash: everyone sold something, damn it all. Everyone. He knew now what happened to the gasoline that the tanks were short of, what became of the warm winter clothing—and they were his own pants, after all, that he had sold, the ones that had been made for him, at his own expense, at Grunk's, the tailor in Coelsde.

Where were all those pengös supposed to come from? Nobody's pay was enough for the kind of extravagances that cocky little lieutenant managed to afford, the one who shared his room and ate cream pastries in the afternoon and drank real whisky in the evening, had all the women he wanted, and turned up his nose at anything but a particular brand of cigarette that by this time cost a lot of money.

What the hell, he thought, I've been a fool, I've been a fool all along. Always respectable and law-abiding, while everyone else—everyone else has been having himself a good time. What the hell.

The innkeeper brought the coffee and the apricot schnapps. "Anything to eat?" he asked.

"No, thanks," said Greck.

The coffee smelled unfamiliar. He tried it: it was mild, with an odd mildness. Some quite pleasant substitute. The schnapps was sharp and burning but felt good. He sipped it slowly, drop by drop. That was it: he must take alcohol like medicine, that was it.

The apricot patch outside on the square had gone. Greck jumped up and ran to the door. "Just a minute," he called to the innkeeper.

The old woman was slowly driving her cart across the square; now she was level with the swingboats, and she speeded up her horse to a comfortable trot. Greck stopped her as she turned into the street. She pulled in the reins. He looked at her face: a broad-boned, elderly woman with handsome features, her face suntanned and sturdy. Greck went up to the cart.

"Fruit," he said, "give me some apricots, please." She looked at him with a smile. Somehow her smile had no warmth. Then she glanced at her baskets and asked, "Bag?" Greck shook his head. Her voice was warm and deep. He watched while she climbed around her seat onto the cart; her legs were surprisingly sturdy. Noticeably so. Greck's mouth watered at the sight of the fruit: it was magnificent. He thought of home. Apricots, he thought, those times when Mama had been able to get apricots! And here, here they got taken back from market. Cucumbers too. He took an apricot from the cart and ate it: it was tart yet at the same time sweet, already a shade too soft and warm, but he enjoyed it. "Very good," he said.

The woman smiled at him again. She took some loose pieces of paper and deftly made a kind of bag into which she very carefully laid the apricots. The way she looked at him struck him as odd. "Enough?" she asked. He nodded. She folded over the ends of paper, tucked them in, and handed him the package. He took his hundred-pengö bill out of his pocket. "Here," he said. Her eyes opened wide, and she said, "Oh, oh," then shook her head. But she took the bill, and for an instant she held on to his hand, clasping it up by the wrist although there was no need to, up by the wrist, for the merest second; then she took the bill, stuck it between her lips, and rummaged around under her skirt to pull out her purse. "No," cried Greck, "no, no, put it away." He looked anxiously around. That great red bill was horribly conspicuous. The street was busy, even a streetcar was passing. "Put it away," he cried, "put it away!" He tore it out of her mouth. She bit her lip, whether with anger or amusement he couldn't tell.

Furious, he dug out a second apricot, sank his teeth into it, and waited. The sweat was standing in thick beads on his forehead. He was having a hard time holding the apricots together in the loose bag. It seemed to him that the old woman was deliberately taking her time—he even considered running away, but she would probably set up a terrible hue and cry and everyone would come running. The Hungarians were allies, not enemies. He sighed and waited. Across the street a soldier emerged from the tavern, not the one who had just gone in. This one had medals on his chest: three—as well as insignia on his sleeve. He saluted Greck, and Greck nodded in response. Again a streetcar passed, on the other side this time, people walked by, many people, and behind him, behind that dilapidated board fence, the swingboat calliope softly began to drone. The old woman smoothed out one bill after another until it looked as though her purse held no more. Then came the coins. Patiently she stacked up little nickel piles beside her on the seat. Then she carefully took the bill from him and handed him first the bills, then the nickel piles. "Ninety-eight," she said. He turned to go, but she suddenly laid her hand on his forearm: her hand was broad and warm and quite dry, and her face came closer. "Girl?" she asked in a whisper, smiling at him. "Pretty girl, eh?"

"No, no," he said hastily, "thanks all the same."

She darted her hand under her skirt, drew out a scrap of paper, and quickly passed it to him. "There," she said. "There." He added it to the bills, she gave a flick to the reins, and he walked back across the street carefully carrying his loose package.

The table in front of the young couple had still not been cleared. He couldn't understand these people: flies clustered in hordes on the plates, the rims of the glasses, and this young man was gesturing animatedly as he spoke in a low insistent voice to the girl. The innkeeper came toward Greck. "Can I have a wash?" asked Greck. The innkeeper stared at him. "A wash," said Greck impatiently. "A wash, for God's sake." Infuriated at the man's obtuseness, he rubbed his hands together. The innkeeper gave a sudden nod, turned, and beckoned Greck to follow him.

Greck followed, paused to let the innkeeper hold back the dark-green curtain for him—the fellow's expression seemed to have changed. It looked as if he were asking something. They walked along a short narrow passage, and the innkeeper opened a door. "Here you are," he said. Greck went in. The cleanliness of the washroom surprised him. The washbasins were neatly cemented to the wall, the doors were painted white. Beside the washbasin hung a towel. The innkeeper brought a cake of green army soap. "Here you are," he repeated. Greck felt at a loss. The innkeeper left. Greck sniffed the towel, it seemed clean. Then he quickly removed his tunic, washed his neck and face all over, and ran water over his arms. He hesitated a moment, then put on his tunic again and slowly washed his hands. The soldier he had seen before came in, the one with no medals. Greck stepped aside so the soldier could get to the urinal. He buttoned his tunic, picked up the soap, and left. At the bar he gave the innkeeper the soap, said "Thanks," and sat down again.

The innkeeper's expression was stony. Greck wondered what was keeping the soldier. The young couple in the corner had gone. The table had still not been cleared, a jumble of dirty dishes. Greck drank the rest of his cold coffee and sipped the apricot schnapps. Then he began to eat his fruit.

He felt an insane craving for this juicy, fleshy stuff and ate six apricots in quick succession—and suddenly he felt nauseated: the apricots were too warm. He took another sip of schnapps; the schnapps was also too warm. The innkeeper stood behind the bar, smoking and somnolent. Another soldier came in. The innkeeper seemed to know him, and the two men whispered together. The soldier drank beer; he had one medal, the Cross of Merit. The soldier who had just been to the toilet came back, paid at the bar, and left. At the door he saluted. Greck returned the salute, and then the soldier who had just arrived went to the toilet. Outside, the swingboat calliope was droning away. The sound, wild yet sluggish, filled Greck with melancholy. He would never forget that ride. Too bad it had turned his stomach. Outside, things had begun to liven up a bit: across the square there was an ice-cream parlor, people were crowding in front of it. The tobacco shop next door to it was empty. The soiled green curtain in the corner was pushed aside, and out came a girl. At once the innkeeper's eyes went to Greck. The girl looked at him too. He could only just make her out; she seemed to be wearing a red dress, in that dense, greenish light the color looked nondescript, and the only thing he could see clearly was her heavily made-up face, very white, the mouth painted startlingly red. He could not see the expression on her face, he thought she was smiling a little, but he could be wrong; he could hardly see her. She was holding some money, holding the bill out straight, like a child, the way she would have held a flower or a stick. The innkeeper gave her a bottle of wine and some cigarettes, without switching his gaze from Greck. He did not look at the girl at all, not a word passed between them.

Greck took the crumpled bills from his pocket and picked out the scrap of paper the old woman had given him. He placed it on the table and put the money back in his pocket. He was acutely conscious of the innkeeper's gaze and looked up. There was no doubt about it now, the girl was smiling at him; there she stood, holding the green bottle, her fingers curved around a few loose cigarettes, little white sticks that matched her face. All he was aware of in the darkness were her startling white face, the dark mouth, and the piercingly white cigarettes in her hand. She gave a brief smile, then moved aside the curtain and left.

The innkeeper was now gazing fixedly at Greck. His expression was stony, with something menacing about it. Greck was scared of him. That's how murderers look, he thought, and he would have welcomed the chance to leave quickly. Outside, the calliope was droning away, the streetcar squealed past, and sadness filled him, an alien and solemn sadness. The repulsive apricots, soft and warm, lay in front of him on the table, and flies were sticking to his cup. He did not wave them away. All at once he got up and called, "The bill, please," raising his voice to give himself courage. The innkeeper hurried over. Greck took some money from his pocket. He watched the flies now slowly gathering on the apricots, black sticky dots on that repulsive pink; the thought of having eaten them almost turned his stomach.

"Three pengös," said the innkeeper. Greck handed him the money. The innkeeper glanced at the schnapps glass, still half full, then at Greck's chest, at the scrap of paper lying on the table, and he picked it up at the very instant Greck reached for it. The innkeeper grinned, his big fat pale face looked repulsive. The innkeeper read the address on the paper: it was his own. He grinned, more hideously than ever. Sweat broke out over Greck's body again.

"Do you still need this paper?" asked the innkeeper.

"No," said Greck. "Good-bye." It occurred to him he had to say *"Heil Hitler,"* and in the doorway he added *"Heil Hitler!"* The innkeeper did not respond. Turning round, Greck saw the man toss the remains of the schnapps onto the floor. The apricots shone warm and pink, like rose-pink wounds in a dark body. . . . Greck was glad to be out on the street, and he hurried off. He was ashamed to go back to the hospital before his leave was up, the cocky little lieutenant would laugh at him. But what he really wanted was to go back right now and lie down on his bed. He felt like having a decent meal, but when he actually thought of food he remembered the apricots, repulsively pink, and his nausea increased. He thought of the woman he had gone to at noon, straight from the hospital. Her mechanical kisses on his neck suddenly hurt, and he knew why he had found the apricots so repulsive: they were the same color as her underwear, she had sweated a bit, and her body had been warm. It was a stupid idea to go to a woman in the middle of the day in this heat. But he had been following the advice of his father, who had told him he must be sure and have a woman at least once a month. This woman hadn't been bad, a sturdy little person who would probably have been delightful in the evening. She had taken the last of his money off him and known right away what he was up to as soon as she saw he was wearing two pairs of pants. She had laughed and given him the name of the Jewish tailor where he could sell them.

He slowed down. He felt sick to his stomach. He knew it: he should have had a proper meal. Now it was too late, he wouldn't be able to eat a thing. Everything disgusted him: the woman, the dirty Jew, even the swingboats, though that had been a novelty, but they disgusted him too, and the fruit, the innkeeper, the soldier—the lot. He had liked the girl. He had liked her very much. But it wouldn't do to have a woman twice in one day. She had looked very lovely, standing there in the dark in that green corner with her white face, but close up she was sure to be sweaty and smelly too. These girls probably couldn't help being sweaty, they didn't have the money to smell nice in the middle of the day in this heat.

He was passing a restaurant. Chairs stood on the street among tubs of stiff green plants. He sat down in a corner and ordered some soda water. "With ice," he called after the waiter. The waiter nodded. A couple at the next table were talking Rumanian.

Greck was now thirty-three and had been suffering from chronic indigestion ever since he was sixteen. Fortunately, his father was a doctor, not a good doctor but the only one in the small town, and they were reasonably well off. But his mother was thrifty. In the summer they used to go to health resorts, or south to the Alps, and often to the coast, and during the winter, when they stayed home, they ate poorly. The only time they ate well was when guests came, but they had few guests. In their small town the center for all social gatherings was the inn, and he was not allowed to go with his parents to the inn. When guests came, wine was served, but by the time he reached the age when he could have drunk wine, he was already suffering from chronic indigestion. They had always eaten a lot of potato salad. He didn't know exactly how often it had actually been, whether three or four times a week, but some days he had the feeling that as a boy he had eaten nothing but potato salad. A doctor once told him, years later, that his symptoms almost bordered on those of malnutrition, and that potato salad was poison to his system.

Word soon got around his home town that he was sick, and indeed, you could see he was, and the girls more or less ignored him. His father wasn't that well off, not enough to compensate for his ill health. In school he didn't shine either. On finishing high school, in 1931, he was allowed to choose a graduation gift, and he chose a trip. He soon got off the train, in Hagen took a room in a hotel, and spent the evening feverishly roaming the town, but he couldn't find a prostitute in Hagen, and left the next day for Frankfurt, where he stayed a week. At the end of a week he had run out of money and took the train home. On the train he thought he would die. At home he was received with shocked surprise; he had had enough money for a three-week trip. His father looked at him, his mother wept, and there was a terrible scene with his old man, who forced him to take off his clothes and be examined. It was a Saturday afternoon, he had never forgotten it; outside, all was quiet in those clean streets, so medieval and idyllic, warm and deep, the bells rang for a long, long time, and he stood facing his father and had to submit to having his body tapped by the old man's fingers. In the surgery. He hated that fat face and the breath that always smelled slightly of beer, and he made up his mind to commit suicide. His father's hands kept tapping his body, that gray head of thick hair moving for a long time below his chest. "You're crazy," said his father on finally raising his head, and he grinned softly. "You're crazy. A woman once or twice a month is plenty for you." He knew his old man was right.

That evening he sat with Mama drinking weak tea. She didn't say a word, but all at once she began to cry. He laid aside the newspaper and went to his room.

Two weeks later he went to Marburg, to the university. He followed his father's advice to the letter, much as he hated him. After five years he graduated in law. In 1937 he did his first tour of military duty, in 1938 his second, and in 1939, after he'd spent two years in the district attorney's office, the war broke out, and he was sent to the front as a second lieutenant. He disliked the war. The war made new demands on him. It was no longer enough to be a qualified attorney, to have a good position with chances of promotion. Now they all looked at his chest when he came home. His chest was but meagerly decorated. In her letters Mama told him to take care of himself and at the same time made hints that felt like pinpricks.

"The Beckers' boy Hugo has been home on leave. He has the Iron Cross, First Class. Not bad for a boy who never got through high school, who couldn't even make it as a butcher's apprentice. I hear they're even going to make him an officer. Sounds incredible to me. Wesendonk has been badly wounded, they say he's going to lose his leg." Even that was something, to lose a leg.

He told the waiter to bring him some more soda water. The soda water made him feel better. It was ice-cold. He longed to be able to wipe out everything he had done, that silly business with the Jew, and that stupid idea of buying a bit of fruit on a busy street with a hundred-pengö bill. The thought of that scene made him sweat again. Suddenly he felt his stomach beginning to rebel. He kept his seat and looked around for the toilet. Everyone in the restaurant was sitting quietly chatting. Not a soul moved. He looked anxiously around until his eyes fell on a green curtain beside the counter; he got slowly to his feet and walked stiffly toward the green curtain. On the way he had to salute, a captain was sitting there with a woman; his salute was brief and smart, and he was glad to reach the green curtain.

By four o'clock he was already back at the hospital. The cocky little lieutenant was sitting there with his bags packed. He was wearing his black tank uniform, numerous decorations shone on his chest. Greck knew exactly which ones they were. There were five of them. The lieutenant was drinking wine and eating slices of bread and meat. He called to Greck as he entered, "Your barrack box has arrived."

"Good," said Greck. He walked over to his bed and dragged the box by the handle over to the window.

"By the way," said the lieutenant, "they had to leave your battalion commander behind at Szokarhely. Schmitz stayed with him. He wasn't fit to be moved, that captain of yours."

"Too bad," said Greck. He began to open his box. "I'd leave it shut if I were you," said the lieutenant, "we have to move on, the lot of us, you too."

"Me too?"

"That's right," the lieutenant laughed, then his childlike face became solemn. "They're soon going to be organizing stomach commandos."

Greck could feel his stomach protesting again. He breathed heavily at the sight of the meat lying there right in front of his eyes in all its clarity. Those gritty specks of fat in the canned meat looked to him like fly eggs. He walked rapidly to the window to get some air. Outside, a cart was driving by loaded with apricots. Greck vomited—he felt an incredible sense of relief.

"Bon appétit!" cried the little lieutenant.

V

FEINHALS HAD gone into town to buy pins, cardboard, and India ink, but all he had managed to get was the cardboard, deep-pink cardboard, the kind the sergeant major liked for making placards. On his way back from town, it started to rain. The rain was warm. Feinhals tried to push the thick roll under his tunic, but the roll was too long and too thick, and when he noticed the wrapping paper beginning to get wet at the edges and the pink of the cardboard coming through, he walked faster. At a street corner, he had to wait. Tanks were clumsily rounding the curve, slowly swinging first their gun barrels and then their rear ends as they continued on toward the southeast. People stood quietly watching the tanks. Feinhals walked on. The rain was coming down solidly now, dripping from the trees, and when he turned into the street leading to his clearing station, there were already large puddles on the black ground.

On the door hung the big white sign on which he had printed in pale-red pencil: "Hospital Clearing Station—Szentgyörgy." Soon a better sign would hang there, sturdy, deep pink, printed in script with India ink. Plain for all to see. At this hour there was no one about. Feinhals rang the bell, inside the porter pressed the switch for the latch; he nodded to the porter as he passed his little cubicle, and entered the corridor. In the corridor a machine pistol and a rifle were hanging on coat hooks. Beside each door was a little glass peephole with a thermometer hanging behind it. Everything was clean, and it was very peaceful, and Feinhals walked very quietly. Behind the first door he could hear the sergeant major on the telephone. In the corridor hung photographs of schoolmistresses and a large colored view of Szentgyörgy.

Feinhals turned to the right, went out through a door, and was in the schoolyard. The schoolyard was surrounded by big trees, and beyond its walls clustered tall buildings. Feinhals looked at a window on the fourth floor: the window was open. He walked quickly back into the building and up the stairs.

On the landings hung the photographs of former graduating classes. A whole row of big brown-and-gilt frames surrounding waist-length photos of girls: thick oval pieces of cardboard, each with a picture of a girl. The first frame showed the class of '18; 1918 seemed to have been the first graduating year. The girls were wearing stiff white blouses and smiling sadly. Feinhals had looked at them often, every day for almost a week. Surrounded by the girls' pictures was one of a very dark, severe-looking lady wearing pince-nez; she must be the headmistress. From 1918 to 1932 it was the same lady—in those fourteen years she did not seem to have changed. It was always the same photo; most likely she always took the same one to the photographer and had him stick it in the center. Feinhals paused in front of the class of '28. Here his eyes were drawn to a girl because of her figure: her name was Maria Kartök, she wore her hair in bangs low on her forehead, almost to her eyebrows, and her face was confident and pretty. Feinhals smiled. He had now reached the second landing and walked on up to the class of '32. He had also graduated in 1932. He looked at each girl in turn, they must have been nineteen at the time, his own age then, and now they were thirty-two: in this class there was another girl wearing bangs, only halfway down her forehead, and her face

was confident and of a certain severe tenderness. Her name was Ilona
Kartök and she was very like her sister, only she seemed slighter and less
vain. The stiff blouse suited her well, and she was the only girl in the frame
who was not smiling. Feinhals stood there for a few seconds, smiled again,
and continued slowly on up to the fourth floor. He was sweating but had
no free hand to take off his cap, so he walked on.

At one end of the landing a statue of the Virgin Mary stood in a niche
in the wall. It was made of plaster, a vase of fresh flowers had been placed
in front of it; that morning there had been tulips in the vase, now there
were yellow and red roses, tight, barely opened buds. Feinhals halted and
looked along the corridor. Seen as a whole, that corridor full of girls'
pictures looked monotonous: all those girls looked like butterflies, innumerable butterflies with slightly darker heads, preserved and collected in
large frames. It seemed to be always the same ones, only the large, dark,
center one changed from time to time. It changed in 1932, in 1940, and
in 1944. Way up on the left, at the end of the third landing, hung the year
of '44, girls in stiff white blouses, smiling and unhappy, and in the middle
a dark elderly lady who was also smiling and also seemed unhappy. As he
passed, Feinhals glanced at the year of '42; there was a Kartök in that one
too, called Szorna, but there was nothing striking about her: she wore her
hair like all the others, her face was round and touching. When he got to
the top, to the corridor that was as silent as the rest of the house, he heard
trucks driving up outside. He threw his stuff on the window sill, opened
a window, and looked out. The sergeant major was standing down on the
street facing a column of trucks, their motors still running. Soldiers with
bandages jumped down onto the road, and at the rear, from a large red
furniture van, came a whole group of soldiers with their packs. The street
quickly filled up. The sergeant major shouted, "Here—over here—everyone into the corridor—and wait there." A straggling gray procession
moved slowly in through the doors. Across the street, windows were flung
open, heads looked out, and people gathered at the corner.

Some of the women were crying.

Feinhals shut the window. The building was still quiet—the first
sounds were just rising faintly from the corridor below; he walked slowly
to the end of the corridor, where he kicked once at a door, and a woman's
voice inside said, "Yes?" He felt himself blushing as he pressed down the
latch with his elbow. He did not see her right away; the room was full
of stuffed animals, wide shelves held rolled maps, and neatly galvanized
glass-topped cases displaying rock specimens, and on the wall hung a
colored print of embroidery samples and a numbered series of illustrations
showing all the stages of infant care.

"Hello there," cried Feinhals.

"Yes?" she called. He went toward the window where a narrow aisle opened up between cabinets and map stands. She was sitting at a little table. Her face was rounder than downstairs in the picture, the severity seemed to have grown softer and the tenderness more pronounced. She was shy yet amused when he said "Good afternoon," and she nodded to him. He threw the big paper roll on the window sill, then the parcel he had been carrying in his left hand, tossed his cap down beside them, and wiped the sweat off his face.

"I need your help, Ilona," he said. "I'd appreciate it if you could let me have some India ink."

She stood up, closing the book lying in front of her.

"India ink," she said. "India ink, I don't know what that is."

"I thought you were a teacher!"

She laughed.

"India ink," he said, "is a kind of drawing ink. Well, then—d'you know what a lettering pen is?"

"I can imagine," she said with a smile. "A pen for writing fancy lettering—yes, I know what that is."

"D'you think you could lend me one?"

"I believe so." She gestured toward the cupboard behind him, but he saw that she would never come out from the corner behind the table.

He had discovered her three days earlier in this room and had spent hours with her every day, but she had never come close: she seemed scared of him. She was very devout, very innocent and intelligent, he had already had long talks with her, and he could feel that she was drawn to him— but she had never come close, close enough for him to suddenly put his arms around her and kiss her. He had had long talks with her, hung around her for hours, and a few times they had discussed religion, but he would have liked to kiss her; only she never came close.

He frowned and shrugged his shoulders. "Just one word," he said hoarsely. "You've only to say one word, and I'll never come into your room again."

Her expression became serious. She lowered her lids, pursed her lips, looked up again: "I don't know," she said softly, "whether I'd like that —besides, it wouldn't make any difference, would it?"

"No," he said. She nodded.

He walked back to the aisle leading to the door and said, "I don't understand how anyone can become a teacher in a school they've gone to for nine years."

"Why not?" she said. "I always liked school, and I still do."

"Isn't there any school now?"

"Oh yes—we've combined with another one."

"And it's your job to stay here and keep an eye on things, I know. Very smart of your headmistress to leave the prettiest teacher behind in the building," he saw her blush, "as well as the most reliable, I know. . . ." He glanced around at the teaching aids. "D'you have a map of Europe in here?"

"Of course," she said.

"And some pins?" She looked at him in surprise and nodded.

"Be a nice girl," he said, "and let me have the map of Europe and a few pins." He unbuttoned his left pocket, fished out a small wax-paper envelope, and shook the contents carefully into his hand: little red cardboard flags; he picked one up and showed it to her. "Come on," he cried, "we're going to play General Staff, it's a great game." He saw her hesitate. "Come on," he cried, "I promise I won't touch you."

She came slowly out and walked over to the rack that held the maps. He looked down into the yard as she passed him, then turned around and helped her set up the stand she was dragging out from somewhere. She fastened in the map, undid the cord, and slowly cranked up the stand. He stood beside her holding the little red flags. "Good God," he muttered, "are we like animals, that all you girls are so scared of us?"

"Yes," she said in a low voice, looking at him; he could tell she was still scared. "Like wolves," she said, breathing hard. "Wolves that are liable to start talking about love any minute. Disturbing kind of people. Please," she said very softly, "don't do that."

"Don't do what?"

"Talk about love," she said very softly.

"Not for the present, I promise." He was peering at the map and did not notice the sidelong smile she gave him.

"The pins, please," he said without turning his head. He stood impatiently facing the map, staring at the brightly colored, irregular shapes, and passed his hand over them. The main front from East Prussia's eastern corner ran down almost dead straight as far as Nagyvárad, except in the middle, near Lvov, where there was a bulge, but no one had any exact information.

He glanced impatiently across at her; she was rummaging in the big drawer of a heavy walnut closet: towels, sheets, diapers, a large naked doll —then she hurried back, holding out a big tin full of pins. His fingers groped around in it, hastily picking out the ones with red or blue heads. She watched closely as he inserted the pins in the little cardboard flags and carefully stuck them into the map.

They looked at each other; outside in the corridor there was noise, doors banging, boots tramping, the voices of the sergeant major and soldiers.

"What's happening?" she asked in alarm.

"Nothing," he said calmly. "The first patients have arrived."

He planted a flag down at the bottom where there was a large dot —Nagyvárad—ran his hand gently across Yugoslavia, and carefully stuck a flag on Belgrade, then farther along on Rome, and was surprised to see how close Paris was to the German frontier. With his left hand resting on Paris, he slowly ran his right hand all the way across to Stalingrad. The distance between Stalingrad and Nagyvárad was greater than between Paris and Nagyvárad. He shrugged his shoulders and carefully stuck little flags in the spaces between the marked points.

"Oh," she cried—he turned to her, she looked tense, excited; her face seemed to have narrowed, it was smooth and brown, and on those pretty cheeks the down was visible almost up to her dark eyes. She still wore bangs, but shorter than downstairs in the picture. She was breathing hard. "Isn't it a great game?" he asked softly.

"Yes," she said, "terrible—it's all so—you say it—so—like a relief map."

"Three-dimensional, you mean," he said.

"That's it!" she cried. "It's all three-dimensional—it's like looking into a room."

The noise in the corridor had died down, the doors seemed to be closed, but Feinhals suddenly heard his name quite clearly. "Feinhals," shouted the sergeant major. "Where the hell are you?"

Ilona looked at him with raised eyebrows.

"Are they calling you?"

"Yes."

"You'd better go," she said in a low voice. "Please, I don't want them to find you here."

"How long will you be here?"

"Till seven."

"Wait for me—I'll be back."

She nodded, her cheeks fiery red, and stood facing him until he stepped aside to let her into her corner.

"There's some cake in that parcel on the window sill," he said. "It's for you." He opened the door, looked out, and hurried into the corridor.

He walked slowly downstairs, although he could hear the sergeant major calling "Feinhals" on the third-floor corridor. He smiled at Szorna as he passed the class of '42, but the light was already fading and he could not make out Ilona's face; the big frame hung in the middle of the wall, and the shadows were closing in. And at the bottom of the stairs stood the sergeant major, who shouted, "For Christ's sake, where the hell have you been? I've been looking for you for an hour."

"I had to go into town, remember? I bought some cardboard for the placards."

"I know, I know, but you've been back half an hour. Let's go." He took Feinhals by the arm and walked down to the lower floor with him. The sound of singing came from the rooms, and the Russian nurses were hurrying along the corridor with trays.

The sergeant major had been very easy on Feinhals ever since the latter had returned from Szokarhely; he was easy on everyone and at the same time very much on edge since being given the job of organizing a hospital clearing station. The sergeant major was worried about things Feinhals could not know of. During the last few weeks something had happened in this army of which Feinhals could not be aware and the consequences of which he could not judge. But the sergeant major lived on these things, by them and them only, and the fact that they were no longer working worried him very much. Until recently, the possibility of a transfer or an unwelcome posting had been relatively remote; every order was circumvented before it even got to the unit. The authority that drew up the order was the first to circumvent it, and confidential phone calls informed the units to which the order was transmitted of the means of circumventing it—and as orders and regulations became more and more threatening, so the means of bypassing them became more and more simple, and in fact no one acted on them except to secure the removal of undesirable people. As a last resort: a medical examination or a phone call—and things went back to normal.

But all this had changed. Phone calls were no good now, because the people you had been used to talking to no longer existed, or existed someplace where they couldn't be reached—and the ones you did talk to now didn't know you and had no incentive to help you because they knew you in turn wouldn't be able to help them. The threads were confused or tangled, and the only thing left to do was to save your own skin from one day to the next. Until now the war had taken place over the telephone, but now the war had begun to dominate the telephone. Authorities, code names, superior officers changed every day, and it might happen that you were assigned to a division which the next day consisted only of a general, three staff officers, and a few clerks. . . .

On reaching the bottom the sergeant major let go of Feinhals's arm and opened the door himself. Otten was sitting at the table smoking. The table had a distinct black scorch mark from a cigarette. Otten was reading a newspaper.

"Well, it's about time," he said, laying aside the paper.

The sergeant major looked at Feinhals, Feinhals looked at Otten.

"I can't do a thing about it," said the sergeant major with a shrug. "I have to transfer all those under forty who aren't on the permanent staff or who no longer qualify as patients. Honestly—I can't do a thing about it. You'll have to go."

"Where to?" asked Feinhals.

"To the redeployment center at the front—and what's more, 'forthwith,' " said Otten. He passed the marching orders to Feinhals. Feinhals read them through.

" 'Forthwith,' " said Feinhals. " 'Forthwith'—nothing sensible ever happened 'forthwith.' " The marching orders still in his hand, he said, "Do we both have to appear on the same marching orders—I mean, together . . . ?"

The sergeant major gave him a close look. "What d'you mean? Now, don't go making a fool of yourself," he said in a low voice.

"What's the time?" asked Feinhals.

"Just on seven," said Otten. He stood up, he had already buckled on his belt and placed his pack on the table.

The sergeant major sat down at the table, pulled open the drawer, and looked at Otten. "Suit yourselves," he said. "Once you fellows are on your way, it's no longer up to me." He shrugged his shoulders.

"OK, then, I'll make out one for each of you."

"I'll get my stuff," said Feinhals.

When he saw Ilona upstairs, he stopped in the corridor and watched her shut the door, then rattle the latch and nod. She had on her hat and coat and was carrying the parcel of cake. She was wearing a green coat and a brown beret, and he thought she looked even prettier than in her red sleeveless jacket. She was short, a shade too buxom maybe, but when he saw her face, the line of her neck, he felt something he had never felt before at the sight of a woman: he loved her and wanted to possess her. She gave the latch one more rattle, to make sure the door was really locked, and then walked slowly along the corridor. He watched her tensely and noticed that she smiled yet was startled to find him suddenly in front of her.

"I thought you were going to wait for me," he said.

"I'd forgotten I had to leave in a hurry. I was going to leave a message downstairs that I'd be back in an hour."

"Did you really mean to come back?"

"Yes," she said. She looked at him and smiled.

"I'll come with you," he said. "Wait for me. I'll only be a minute."

"You can't come with me. Don't." She shook her head wearily. "I promise I'll be back."

"Where are you going?"

She was silent, glanced around, but the corridor was empty; it was dinnertime, and subdued noises came from the rooms. Then she looked at him again. "To the ghetto," she said. "I have to go to the ghetto with my mother." She looked at him expectantly, but he merely asked, "What are you going to do there?"

"It's being evacuated today. Our relatives are there. We're taking some things to them. The cake too." She looked at the parcel she was carrying, and held it out to him. "You don't mind my giving it away, do you?"

"Your relatives," he said, taking her arm. "Come on—let's go." He walked down the stairs beside her, grasping her arm.

"Your relatives are Jews? Your mother?"

She nodded. "And me," she said, "all of us." She stopped. "Just a moment." She freed her arm, took the flowers out of the vase in front of the Virgin Mary's statue, and carefully removed the faded ones. "Will you promise to put fresh water in the vase? I won't be here tomorrow. I have to be at school. Promise—and maybe some flowers too?"

"I can't. I have to leave tonight. Otherwise . . ."

"Otherwise you would?"

He nodded. "I'd do anything to please you."

"Only to please me?" she said.

He smiled. "I don't know—I'd do it anyway, I think, but it would never have occurred to me to do it. Just a minute!" he exclaimed.

They had reached the third-floor corridor. He ran along it to his room and quickly stuffed a few oddments into his bag. Then he put on his belt and ran out. She had walked slowly on ahead, and he caught up with her in front of the photos of the class of '32. She looked thoughtful.

"What is it?" he asked.

"Nothing," she said softly. "I would so much like to be sentimental —I can't. This picture doesn't move me, it means absolutely nothing to me. Let's go."

She promised to wait for him by the entrance, and he ran quickly into the office to pick up his marching orders. Otten had already left. The sergeant major grasped Feinhals by the sleeve. "Don't go making a fool of yourself," he said, "and good luck."

"Thanks," said Feinhals, and hurried out of the building.

She was waiting for him at the street corner. He took her arm and walked slowly beside her into town. It had stopped raining, but the air was still moist, with a sweet smell, and they walked along very quiet side streets that ran almost parallel to the main streets but were very quiet, past small houses with little low trees in front of them.

"How come you don't live in the ghetto?" he asked.

"Because of my father. He was an officer in the last war and got a lot of medals and lost both legs. But yesterday he sent his medals back to the garrison commander, and his artificial legs—a big brown-paper parcel. Please, let me go on alone now," she urged.

"Why?"

"I want to walk home alone."

"I'll go with you."

"It's no use. You'll be seen, someone from my family will see you," she looked at him, "and then they won't let me come any more."

"You'll be back?"

"Yes," she said quietly. "For sure. I promise."

"Give me a kiss," he said.

She blushed and stood still. The street was empty and silent. Over the wall beside them hung branches of faded pink hawthorn.

"Why should we kiss?" she asked in a low voice; she looked at him sadly, and he was afraid she was going to cry. "I'm scared of love."

"Why?" he asked softly.

"Because there's no such thing—or only for a few moments."

"We won't have much more than a few moments," he said softly. He set his bag down on the ground, took the parcel from her, and put his arms around her. He kissed her on the neck, behind the ears, and felt her mouth on his cheek. "Don't go away," he whispered in her ear, "don't go away. It's not right to go away when there's a war on. Stay here." She shook her head. "I can't," she said, "my mother gets scared to death if I'm late." She kissed him once more on the cheek and was surprised to find she didn't mind—she liked it very much. "Here," she said. She turned his head as it rested against her shoulder and kissed him on the corner of the mouth. She now felt really glad that she would soon be with him again.

She kissed him once more on the corner of the mouth and looked at him for a moment. She used to think it must be wonderful to have a husband and children; she had always thought of both of them at the same time, but now she wasn't thinking of children—no, she hadn't been thinking of children when she kissed him and realized she would see him again soon. It made her sad, yet the thought pleased her. "There!" she whispered, "I really must go. . . ."

He looked over her shoulder along the street; it was empty and silent, and the noise from the next street seemed very remote. The little trees had been carefully pollarded. Ilona's hand was groping for his neck, and he could tell that this hand was very small, firm, and slender. "Stay here," he said, "or let me go with you. Never mind what happens. It won't work out—you don't know what war is—you don't know the people who make it. It's not right to separate even for a minute unless you have to."

"I have to," she said. "Try to understand."

"Then let me go with you."

"No, no," she pleaded. "I can't do that to my father, don't you understand?"

"I understand," he said, kissing her neck. "I understand everything, much too much. But I love you, and I want you to stay. Please stay."

She freed herself, looked at him, and said, "Don't ask me to. Please."

"I won't," he said softly. "Off you go. Where shall I wait?"

"Walk on a bit with me, I'll show you a little café where you can wait."

He tried to walk slowly, but she pulled him along, and he was surprised when they suddenly crossed a busy street. She pointed to a little narrow building, saying, "Wait there for me."

"Will you be back?"

"Yes," she said with a smile, "I promise—as soon as I can. I love you."

She threw her arms around his neck and kissed him on the mouth. Then she hurried off; he didn't want to watch her go so he walked toward the little café.

As he entered, he felt very miserable, very empty, as if he had missed something. He knew there was no point in waiting, yet at the same time he knew he had to wait. He must give God this chance of making everything turn out as it should, as it might have, although there was no doubt in his mind that everything had already turned out differently: she wouldn't be back. Something would happen to prevent her from coming back—perhaps it was asking too much to love a Jewish girl while this war was on and to hope she would come back. He didn't even know her address, and he must go through the motions of hope by waiting for her here, although he had no hope. He might have run after her, maybe, and forced her to stay—but you couldn't force people, you could only kill people, that was the only thing you could force on them. You couldn't force anyone to live, or to love, it was useless; the only thing that had any real power over them was death. And now he had to wait, although he knew it was useless. Moreover, he knew he would wait for longer than an hour, longer than tonight, because this was the only thing that linked them together: this little café her finger had pointed out, and the only certainty was that she had not lied. She would come, right away and very quickly, as quickly as she could, if she had the power to decide. . . .

From the clock over the counter he saw it was twenty to eight. He didn't feel like anything to eat or drink so he ordered some soda water when the proprietress came over, and when he saw she was disappointed, he ordered a carafe of wine. Near the door sat a Hungarian soldier with his girl, and in the middle a fat fellow with a sallow face and a pitch-black cigar in his mouth. He quickly finished the carafe of wine so as to reassure the proprietress, and ordered another. The woman gave him a friendly smile, she was middle-aged, thin and blonde.

There were moments when he even thought she would come. Then he imagined where he would go with her: they would take a room somewhere, and before they went through the bedroom door he would tell her she was his wife. The room was dark, the bed in it old and brown and wide; there was a religious picture hanging on the wall, and a chest of drawers with a blue china basin containing lukewarm water, and the window looked out onto an orchard. That room existed, he knew it did, he had only to go into town and look for it and he would find it, that room, wherever it was he would find it, that very room, in a cheap hotel, in an inn, in a pension; that room existed, the room which for one moment had been destined to receive them tonight—but they would never enter that room. With painful clarity he saw the soiled rug beside the bed and the little window opening onto the orchard, the brown paint had peeled off the window frame; it was a lovely room with its big, brown, wide bed they had almost lain in together. But now that room would stay empty.

All the same, there were moments when he believed it wasn't decided yet. If she hadn't been Jewish—it was very hard to love a Jewish girl while this war was on, but he did love her, he loved her very much, enough to want to sleep with her and talk to her, for hours and very often and over and over again—and he knew there weren't many women you could sleep with and talk to for hours. With her it would have been possible—a lot of things would have been possible with her.

He ordered another carafe of wine. He had not yet opened the bottle of soda water. The fellow with the pitch-black cigar left, and now he was alone in the café with the middle-aged blonde proprietress, who had a skinny neck, and the Hungarian soldier with his girl. He drank some wine and tried to think of something else. He thought about his home, but he had hardly ever been there. Since leaving school he had hardly been home at all; besides, at home he was scared—the little town lay between railroad and river, in a great loop, as it were; the roads leading to it and through it were treeless, asphalted, and in summer there was only the musty, airless shade of the fruit trees. It didn't cool off even in the evening. He had usually gone home in the fall and helped with the harvest because he enjoyed that: those great orchards full of fruit, great trucks full, so many trucks full of pears and apples and plums being driven along the Rhine to the cities. Home was beautiful in the fall, and he got along well with his mother and dad, and it made no difference to him when his sister got married to some fruit grower or other—but home was beautiful in the fall. In winter the little place lay once again flat and deserted between river and railroad in the cold, and the heavy, cloying smell from the jam factory would drift in thick clouds across the plain and take your breath away. No, he was always glad to get away again. His job was building houses and schools, factories and apartment houses for a large firm, and army barracks. . . .

But there was no point in trying to think about these things. Now he had to think of having forgotten to ask Ilona for her address—just in case. But he could get it from the building superintendent at the school, or from her headmistress, and there was no reason, after all, why he couldn't make inquiries, look for her, talk to her, perhaps go and see her. But all that belonged to those pointless things you had to do to give God a chance, you just had to do them, and sometimes it turned out that there was some point to them after all. The moment you admitted there might be some point to them, that they might come off—the moment you had to admit that, you were lost. And you had to keep on doing them. Search and wait—that was all there was to hope for, and that was terrible. He didn't know what they did with the Hungarian Jews. He had heard there had been a dispute over this between the Hungarian and German governments, but you could never tell what the Germans would do. And he had forgotten to ask Ilona for her address. The most important thing to do in wartime, exchange addresses, was the one thing they had forgotten, and for her it was still more important to have an address. But this was all pointless: she would never come back.

He preferred thinking about the room they would have shared together. . . .

He saw it was close on nine: the hour had long since passed. The clock hand moved very slowly while you were looking at it, but as soon as you took your eyes off it, even for a moment, it seemed to jump. It was nine o'clock, and he had been waiting here for almost an hour and a half; he had to go on waiting, or he could hurry over to the school and ask the building superintendent for her address, and go there. He ordered another carafe of wine and saw that the proprietress was satisfied.

At five after nine the military police checked the café, an officer with a corporal, and at first they merely glanced inside and turned to leave— he saw them very distinctly because he had begun to stare at the door. There was something wonderful about staring at the door: the door was hope, but all he saw was this officer in his steel helmet and the corporal behind him, just looking in and then turning to leave, until the officer caught sight of him and walked slowly over to him. He knew the game was up: these people had the only effective means, they had death at their beck and call, death obeyed them instantly. And to be dead meant not to be able to do anything in this world any more, and he still had plans for doing something in this world: he wanted to wait for Ilona, to look for her and to love her—even though he knew it was pointless, he wanted to, because there was just a chance it might work out. These men in their steel helmets held death in the palm of their hand, death was in their little pistols, their unsmiling faces, and even if these two men didn't want to call upon death, there were thousands standing behind them who were only too glad to give death a chance, with gallows and machine pistols—death was at their beck and call. The officer looked at him, said nothing, just held out his hand. The officer was tired, couldn't have cared less, really; he did his job mechanically, probably it bored him, but he did it, and he did it consistently and seriously. Feinhals handed over his paybook and marching orders. The corporal made a sign to Feinhals to stand up. With a shrug Feinhals stood up. He noticed that the proprietress was trembling and the Hungarian soldier looked alarmed.

"Come along," said the officer quietly.

"I haven't paid yet," said Feinhals.

"Pay at the counter."

Feinhals buckled on his belt, picked up his bag, and walked between the two men to the counter. The proprietress took the money, and the corporal went ahead and opened the door. Feinhals went out. He knew they couldn't do anything to him; still, he might have been scared, yet he wasn't. Outside it was dark, lights were showing in stores and restaurants, and everything looked very nice and summery. On the street outside the café stood a large red furniture van: the door at the back had been opened, part of it had been let down and rested on the rough paving like a ramp. People were standing about on the street and watching uneasily: in front of the opening stood a guard holding a machine pistol.

"Get in," said the officer. Feinhals climbed up the ramp into the van; in the darkness he saw a lot of heads, weapons—but no one inside said a word. When he was all the way in, he noticed the van was full.

VI

T HE RED furniture van drove slowly through the town; it was securely locked, the padded doors bolted, and on its sides was painted in black lettering "Göros Bros., Budapest. Forwarding Agents." The van did not stop again. Through the opening in the roof a man's head looked out, carefully noting the surroundings, from time to time bending down apparently to call out something. The man saw lighted cafés, ice-cream parlors, people in summer clothes, but suddenly his eye was caught by a green furniture van that was trying vainly to overtake them on the wide boulevard. The driver of the green van was a man in army uniform, beside him sat a second man in army uniform holding a machine pistol on his knees, but the opening in the roof of the green van had been secured with barbed wire. The driver of the green van honked impatiently behind the red van as the latter lumbered through the town. Not until they reached a major intersection and the street widened and opened out could the green van overtake; it nipped quickly past, and the man looking out of the opening noticed that the green van turned into a wide street evidently going north whereas the red van drove south, almost due south. The face of the man in the opening grew more and more serious. He was short and slight, and his face had a wizened look, and when the red van had driven on a bit farther, he bent his head and shouted down into the van, "I'm pretty sure we're driving out of town, the houses aren't so close together now." From below came a muffled murmur in reply, and the red van was driving faster now, faster than one would have given it credit for. The road was empty and dark, and between the close branches of the trees the air hung moist and heavy and sweet, and the man in the roof opening bent down and shouted, "No more houses, highway now—going south."

The howls from below grew louder, but the van drove even faster. The man in the opening was tired, he had a long train trip behind him, and he was standing on the shoulders of two men of different heights, which made him even more tired, and he was ready to quit, but he was the shortest and slightest of the men in the van, and they had picked him to see what was going on outside.

Now came a long stretch where he saw nothing. A very long stretch, it seemed to him—and when the men down below pulled at his leg and wanted to know what was going on, he said nothing was going on, all he could see was the trees bordering the highway and the dark fields. Then he saw two soldiers with a motorcycle standing by the roadside, the soldiers were shining their flashlight back and forth across a map. They glanced up as the big furniture van passed. Then the man in the opening saw nothing again for a while, until they passed a stationary tank column. One tank seemed to have broken down, someone was lying on his stomach underneath it and someone else was shining a carbide lamp over it. Farmhouses slid past them very quickly, dark farmhouses, and a truck column overtook them on the left, driving very fast; soldiers were sitting on the trucks. From behind the trucks came a small gray car flying a commandant's pennant. The commandant's car was driving even faster than the trucks. Some soldiers, infantrymen, were sitting hunched up beside a barn; some were lying on the ground smoking. Next they went through a village, and shortly after the village the man in the opening heard firing for the first time. It was a heavy battery located to the right of the road; great barrels pointed steep and black into the dark-blue sky. Bloody fire flashed from the gun muzzles, casting a soft ruddy sheen on the wall of a barn. The man recoiled, he had never heard firing before, and he was scared. He was a sick man, a very sick man, with some chronic stomach ailment, his name was Sergeant Finck, and he was the commissary at a big hospital near Linz, on the Danube, and he had had misgivings ever since the head of the hospital had sent him to Hungary to pick up some genuine Tokay wine, Tokay and liqueurs and as much champagne as he could lay hands on. Imagine going to Hungary for champagne. Still: he, Finck, was the only man at the hospital who could be trusted to tell a genuine Tokay from a phony one, and, after all, in Tokay there must be some genuine Tokay wine. The old man, Colonel Ginzler, was very partial to genuine Tokay, but it was probably mostly because of his drinking pal and skat companion, that Colonel Bressen whom you involuntarily called von Bressen because he looked so distinguished with his narrow unsmiling face and the unusual decoration around his neck. Finck owned an inn back home, and he knew people, and he knew the old man was just showing off, sending him off like that to pick up fifty bottles of genuine Tokay—some bet or other which that colonel had probably goaded him into.

Finck had been to Tokay, where he had picked up fifty bottles of Tokay wine, and genuine at that, much to his surprise—he was an innkeeper, an innkeeper in a wine town, he had his own vineyards too, and he knew his wines. And he didn't trust the Tokay he had bought as genuine in Tokay, a suitcase and a wicker basket full. He had managed to bring along the suitcase, it was down there in the van, but he hadn't been able to bring the wicker basket. There had been no time at Szentgyörgy, they had been herded straight from the train into the furniture van; it had been no good protesting, saying he was ill, the whole platform had been cordoned off, it was no good even trying, they were marched straight into the furniture van parked outside the station. Some of the men started to mutiny and shout, but the guards seemed to be deaf and dumb.

Finck was nervous about his Tokay—the old man was touchy about wine and even touchier about what he called his honor. He was pretty certain to have given that colonel his word or some such thing that he would drink Tokay with him on Sunday. Most likely he had even named the hour. But now it was Thursday, probably Friday morning—it must be getting on for midnight at least—and now they were driving south, quite fast, and there wasn't the faintest chance of being able to deliver the wine on Sunday. Finck was scared, scared of the old man and scared of the colonel. He didn't like that colonel. He knew something about him that he never had and never could tell anyone, because no one would believe it, something disgusting that Finck wouldn't have thought possible. Finck had seen it for himself, quite distinctly—and he knew how important it was for him that the colonel shouldn't know he had seen it. He had to go along to the colonel's room several times a day, with something to eat or drink or some books. And the colonel was someone you handled with great care. One evening he had gone into the colonel's room without knocking, and there in the semidarkness he had seen it, that ghastly expression on the elderly white face—it took Finck's appetite away for the rest of that evening. When a young fellow was caught doing something like that back home they poured cold water over him right away, and it worked. . . .

Down below, the men were pulling at his leg again, and he shouted down to them that he had seen cannon, cannon firing, and the yelling down below grew louder. The flashes from the gun muzzles they had driven past were fading away behind them, and the sound of the shells being fired, which at first had seemed horribly close, now seemed as far away as the sound of the shells landing, while the van was steadily approaching the area where the shells were landing. They drove past more tanks, stationary columns; then came more guns, these seemed to be smaller, they were standing next to a draw well, and the flames from their muzzles lit up the sinister gallows-outline of the well in sharp flashes. Again there was nothing for a while, until they passed some more columns, then nothing again—and then Finck heard the firing of machine guns. The van was heading straight for the area toward which the machine guns were firing.

And suddenly they stopped in a village. Finck clambered down inside and got out with the others. In the village all was confusion; there were trucks standing around all over the place, people yelling, soldiers running across the road, and the firing of the machine guns grew louder and louder. Feinhals walked behind the little sergeant who had been standing in the roof opening and was now carrying his heavy suitcase; he was so short and walked so doubled up that the butt of his rifle dragged along the ground. Feinhals fastened his bag to the carrying strap and took a stride forward to catch up with the little sergeant. "I'll give you a hand," he said. "What have you got in there anyway?"

"Wine," said the little man, gasping. "Wine for our hospital adminis-trator."

"Leave it here, for God's sake," said Feinhals. "How can you lug a suitcase full of wine up to the front?"

The little man shook his head obstinately. He was so exhausted he could hardly walk, his knees were wobbling, and he shook his head sadly and nodded his thanks as Feinhals reached for the handle. The suitcase seemed fantastically heavy to Feinhals.

The machine gun on the right had stopped firing, the tanks were firing into the village now. From behind them came the crash of splitting timbers, and a gentle reflection from a fire threw a soft light over the muddy, rutted road.

"Throw the thing away, man," said Feinhals. "You must be out of your mind."

The sergeant did not answer; he seemed to grip the handle even tighter. Behind them another house started burning.

Suddenly the second lieutenant walking ahead of them halted and called out, "Get close to the house!" They ran right up to the wall of the house in front of which they had stopped. The little sergeant lurched against it and sat down on his suitcase. Now the machine gun on the left had also stopped firing. The officer went indoors and came out at once with a first lieutenant. Feinhals recognized him. They had to line up, and Feinhals knew the first lieutenant was trying to make out their decorations in the reddish twilight: on his own chest he now had one more, a proper one now, at least the ribbon for it, adorning his chest in black, white, and red. Thank God, thought Feinhals, he had that medal at least. The first lieutenant looked at them for a moment, smiling, then said, "Very nice," smiled again, and repeated, "Very nice, eh?" to the second lieutenant standing behind him. But the second lieutenant said nothing. They could see him distinctly now. He was short and pale, no longer very young, it seemed, and his face was grimy and unsmiling. He didn't have a single medal on his chest.

"Brecht," the first lieutenant told him, "take two men as reinforcement. And some bazookas. We'll send the others to Undolf—four, I guess. I'll keep the rest here."

"Two," said Brecht. "Yessir, two men, and some bazookas."

"Right," said the first lieutenant. "You know where to find those things?"

"Yessir."

"Report back in half an hour, please."

"Yessir," said the second lieutenant.

Feinhals and Finck were the first in line, and the second lieutenant tapped them on the chest, saying, "Come along," then turned on his heel and marched off. They had to hurry to keep up with him. The little sergeant snatched up his suitcase, Feinhals helped him, and they hurried off as fast as they could behind the little second lieutenant. Beyond the house they turned to the right into a narrow lane that seemed to lead out into the country between hedges and meadows. Ahead of them all was quiet, but behind them that tank was still firing regularly into the village, and the small battery, the last one they had driven past, was still firing to the right, roughly in the direction in which they were heading.

Feinhals suddenly dropped to the ground and shouted to the others, "Watch out!" There was a tinkle as they let go of the suitcase, and the second lieutenant up front also dropped to the ground. From up ahead, from the direction in which they had been marching, grenade launchers were firing into the village, they were firing in rapid succession now, there seemed to be a great many of them; splinters whizzed through the air, smacked against house walls, bigger fragments droned past them not far away.

"Get up," shouted the second lieutenant. "Carry on."

"Hold it!" cried Feinhals. He had heard that brittle clack again, a delicate, almost cheerful sound, and he was scared. There was a great crash as the grenade struck Finck's suitcase—the lid of the suitcase flew off with a fierce hiss and hit a tree twenty yards away, broken glass tore through the air like a swarm of demented birds, Feinhals could feel the wine splashing onto the back of his neck. He ducked in alarm: he hadn't heard these being fired, but there was an explosion ahead of them, on the field above a low earth bank. A haystack standing out black against the reddish background fell apart and started to smolder; it began to glow in the middle like tinder, then blazed up as it burst into flames.

The second lieutenant came crawling back down the hollow. "What the hell's going on here?" he whispered to Feinhals.

"He had wine in the suitcase," whispered Feinhals. "Hey there," he called softly across to Finck—a dark lump lying crouched beside the suitcase. Nothing stirred. "Hell," said the second lieutenant under his breath, "surely he's not. . . ."

Feinhals crawled the two paces over to Finck, bumped his head against Finck's foot, propped himself up on his elbows, and pulled himself closer. The light from the burning haystack did not reach this hollow, it was dark in this shallow depression while the field at the side of the lane was already bathed in reddish light. "Hey there," said Feinhals quietly. He smelled the strong sweet fumes from a wine puddle, drew back his hands because he had thrust them into broken glass, and, beginning with the shoes, groped carefully up the man's legs, surprised to find how short this sergeant was; his legs were short, his body skinny. "Hey there," he called softly, "hey there, pal," but Finck did not answer. The second lieutenant had crawled over and said, "What's up?" Feinhals groped farther along until he touched blood—that wasn't wine—he drew back his hand and said quietly, "I think he's dead. A big wound in the back, soaked with blood; d'you have a flashlight?"

"Perhaps we could . . ."

"Or lift him up there onto the field . . ."

"Wine," said the second lieutenant, "a suitcase full of wine . . . what did he want that for?"

"For a commissariat, I think."

Finck was not heavy. They carried him, walking doubled up, across the path, rolled him over the grass bank until he was lying flat, dark and flat in the light. His back was black with blood. Feinhals turned him over carefully—he saw the face for the first time; it was frail, very frail, thin, still slightly damp with sweat, the thick black hair clinging to the forehead.

"My God," said Feinhals.

"What is it?"

"He got one right in the chest. A splinter as big as your fist."

"In the chest?"

"That's right—he must have been kneeling over his suitcase."

"Contrary to regulations," said the second lieutenant, but his own joke seemed to turn sour on him. "Get his paybook and identity tag. . . ."

Feinhals carefully unbuttoned the blood-soaked tunic, felt for the neck until his fingers closed on a bloodied piece of metal. He found the paybook right away too; it was in the left-hand breast pocket and seemed clean.

"Hell," the second lieutenant said behind him, "the suitcase is heavy —it still is." He had dragged it across the path and was also pulling Finck's rifle along by its strap. "Did you get the things?"

"Yes," said Feinhals.

"Let's get out of here." The second lieutenant dragged the suitcase along by one corner until the hollow came to an end and the ground was flat again, then he whispered to Feinhals, "Get behind that wall on the left," and crawled ahead. "Push the suitcase after me." Feinhals pushed the suitcase after him and crawled slowly up the little rise. Behind the wall, which ran at right angles to their path, they could stand upright, and now they looked at each other. The glow from the burning haystack was bright enough for them to see one another distinctly, and they stared at each other for a moment. "What's your name?" asked the officer.

"Feinhals."

"Mine's Brecht," said the second lieutenant. He smiled awkwardly. "I must admit I've got a hell of a thirst." He bent down over the suitcase, drew it onto the strip of thick grass, and carefully tipped out the contents. There was a gentle clinking and burbling. "Look at that," he said, picking up a small, undamaged bottle. "Tokay." The label was smeared with blood and wet with wine. Feinhals watched the officer carefully push aside the broken glass—five or six bottles seemed to be still intact. Brecht got out his pocketknife and opened one. He drank. "Marvelous," he said as he put down the bottle. "Want some?"

"Thanks," said Feinhals. He took the bottle and drank a mouthful; he found it too sweet, handed the bottle back, and repeated, "Thanks."

The grenade launchers were firing again into the village, farther away now, and suddenly a machine gun fired quite close in front of them. "Thank God," said Brecht. "I was beginning to think those had gone too."

He finished the bottle and let it roll down into the hollow. "We have to get past this wall on the left."

The haystack was in full blaze now, but at the very bottom only a glow was left. Sparks showered.

"You look pretty sensible," said the officer.

Feinhals was silent.

"What I mean is," said Brecht as he started to open the second bottle, "what I mean is, sensible enough to know that this war's a load of shit."

Feinhals was silent.

"By that I mean," went on Brecht, "that when you win a war it isn't a load of shit, and this war—so it seems to me—is a very, very bad war."

"Yes," said Feinhals. "It's a very, very bad war." The heavy firing of the machine gun at such close quarters was getting on his nerves.

"Where's the machine gun?" he asked quietly.

"Over there, where this wall comes to an end—it's a farm—we're in front of it now—the machine gun's behind it. . . ."

The machine gun fired a few more short sharp rounds, then stopped. Next a Russian machine gun fired, then they heard rifle shots, and again the German and Russian machine guns fired together. And suddenly there was silence.

"Shit," said Brecht.

The haystack began to collapse, the flames were no longer beating so high, there was a gentle crackling, and darkness fell lower. The second lieutenant held out a bottle to Feinhals. Feinhals shook his head. "No, thanks, it's too sweet for me," he said.

"Have you been with the infantry long?" asked Brecht.

"Yes," said Feinhals, "four years."

"My God," said Brecht. "The stupid thing is that I don't know much about the infantry—practically speaking, that is, and I'd be a fool to say I did. I've had two years' training as a night fighter—just finished it—and my training cost the government a few nice single-family homes, all so that I can get blown to pieces in the infantry and lay down my life to get to Valhalla. What a load of shit, eh?" He took another drink. Feinhals was silent.

"What does one do, actually, when the enemy is superior?" the second lieutenant persevered. "Two days ago we were fifteen miles away, and we kept hearing we weren't going to budge. But we did budge. I know the rules too well. The rules say: The German soldier does not yield, he would rather be killed—something like that, but I'm not blind and I'm not deaf. I ask you," he said solemnly, "what do we do?"

"Clear out, I guess," said Feinhals.

"Great," said the second lieutenant. "Clear out. Great—clear out." He laughed softly. "There's something missing in our fine Prussian regulations: there's no provision for retreat in our training, that's why we have to be so smart when we do retreat. I believe our regulations are the only ones that say nothing about retreat, only 'delaying tactics,' and these jokers aren't going to let themselves be delayed any longer. Let's go," he said. He stuffed two bottles into his pockets. "Off to this lovely war again. My God," he added, "the poor bugger lugged that wine all the way here— the poor bugger. . . ."

Feinhals followed slowly. As they turned the corner of the wall, they heard men running toward them. The footsteps were clearly audible, close now. The second lieutenant jumped back behind the wall, tucked his machine pistol under his arm, and whispered to Feinhals: "Here's your chance to earn eighteen pfennigs' worth of tin for your chest." But Feinhals noticed he was trembling. "Hell," whispered the second lieutenant, "this is serious, this is war."

The footsteps came closer, the men were no longer running.

"Don't worry," said Feinhals quietly, "those aren't Russians."

Brecht was silent.

"I wonder why they were running—and making all that racket. . . ."

Brecht was silent.

"They're your men," said Feinhals. The footsteps sounded quite close now.

Although they could tell from the silhouettes that the men wearing steel helmets and rounding the corner were Germans, the second lieutenant called softly, "Halt, password." The men were startled; Feinhals saw them hesitate and flinch. "Shit," said one of them. "The password's shit."

"Tannenberg," said another voice.

"What the hell are you doing here?" said Brecht. "Get in behind that wall. One of you stand at the corner and listen."

Feinhals was surprised to see how many there were. He tried to count them in the dark, there seemed to be six or seven. They sat down on the grassy strip. "That's wine," said the second lieutenant; he groped for the bottles and passed them across. "Split it up between you."

"Prinz," he said, "Corporal Prinz, what's going on?"

Prinz was the one standing at the corner. Feinhals saw his medals glinting in the dark as he turned.

"Lieutenant," said Prinz, "this is just nonsense. They've already overtaken us left and right, and surely you're not trying to tell me that here of all places, right next to this dirty farm, here of all places where our machine gun happens to be standing, the front is supposed to be held. Lieutenant, the front is several hundred miles wide and has been slipping for quite a while now—and I don't believe these hundred and fifty yards have been destined to produce a Knight's Cross—it's time we cleared out; if we don't we'll be caught in the middle, and not a soul's going to give a damn. . . ."

"The front's got to be held somewhere. Are you all there?"

"Yes," said Prinz, "we're all here—and I don't think a front can be held by convalescents and men just back from sick leave. Incidentally, young Genzki's been wounded—he got a bullet through his arm. Genzki," he called softly, "where are you?"

A slight figure detached itself from the wall.

"All right," said the second lieutenant, "you can go back. Feinhals, you go with him, the first-aid post is right where your bus stopped. Report to the old man that I've moved the machine gun back thirty yards—and bring some bazookas back with you. Send another man along with them, Prinz."

"Wecke," said Prinz, "you go. Did you come with the furniture van too?" he asked Feinhals.

"Yes."

"So did we."

"Go on," said the second lieutenant, "get a move on; hand in the paybook to the old man. . . ."

"Someone killed?" asked Prinz.

"Yes," said the second lieutenant impatiently. "Go on, get a move on."

Feinhals walked slowly to the village with the two men. Now several tanks were firing into it from the south and east. Ahead of them, where the main road entered the village to the left, they heard deafening explosions, men yelling, and they stood still for a moment and exchanged glances.

"Great," said the short fellow with the wounded arm.

They hurried on, but when they emerged from the hollow a voice called, "Password?"

"Tannenberg," they growled.

"Brecht? Combat unit Brecht?"

"Yes," called Feinhals.

"Go back! Everyone back into the village; assemble on the main road!"

"Run back to the others," Wecke told Feinhals. "You go."

Feinhals ran down the hollow, up the other side, and called from halfway up, "Hey, Lieutenant Brecht!"

"What is it?"

"We've all got to go back—back to the village—and assemble on the main road."

They all walked slowly back together.

The red furniture van had almost filled up again. Feinhals slowly climbed the ramp, sat down just inside, leaned back, and tried to sleep. The deafening explosions seemed somewhat ridiculous to him now that he could hear it was German tanks trying to keep the road open. They were banging away much too much, there was altogether more banging in this war than necessary, but no doubt it was all part of this war. Everyone was in now except for a major handing out decorations and the few men to whom he was handing them. A corporal, a sergeant, and three privates were standing facing the little gray-haired major, who, his head bare, was hurriedly presenting the crosses and documents. From time to time he would call, "First Lieutenant Greck—First Lieutenant Greck!" Finally he shouted, "Brecht, where's Lieutenant Brecht?" From the depths of the van Brecht called, "Here, sir!" moved slowly forward, touched his hand to his cap, and, standing on the ramp, reported, "Second Lieutenant Brecht, Major."

"Where's your company commander?" asked the major. Although not furious, the major did look annoyed. The soldiers he had decorated walked slowly up the ramp and squeezed past Brecht into the van.

The major stood all by himself on the village street holding an Iron Cross First Class, and Brecht, his face expressing complete blankness, said, "No idea, Major. A few minutes ago Lieutenant Greck ordered me to lead the company to the assembly point, he had to," Brecht stopped and wavered, "Lieutenant Greck was suffering from severe indigestion. . . ."

"Greck!" shouted the major in the direction of the village. "Greck!" He turned away, shaking his head, and said to Brecht: "Your company fought very well indeed—but we have to get out. . . ."

A second German tank banged away from the street in front of them toward the right, and the small battery behind seemed to have veered round; it was firing in the same direction as the tanks. In the village many houses were burning now—and the church, which stood in the center of the village and was taller than any of the houses, was filled with a ruddy glow. The motor of the furniture van began to throb. The major stood irresolutely at the roadside and shouted to the van driver, "Get started."

Feinhals opened the paybook and read, "Finck, Gustav, sergeant; civilian occupation: innkeeper; place of residence: Heidesheim. . . ."

Heidesheim, thought Feinhals, with a shock. Heidesheim was two miles from his home, and he knew the inn with the sign, painted brown, "Finck's Wineshop & Hotel, estab. 1710." He had often driven past but never gone in—then the door was slammed in his face, and the red furniture van drove off.

Again and again Greck tried to stand up and run to the end of the village where they were waiting for him, but he couldn't. As soon as he straightened himself, a griping pain like a corkscrew in his stomach forced him to double up, and he felt the urge to defecate—he was squatting beside the low wall surrounding the cesspool, his stool came in driblets, barely a tablespoonful at a time, while the pressure in his racked abdomen was enormous; he could not sit properly, the only bearable position was squatting, completely doubled up, and getting some slight relief when the stool left his bowels in small quantities—at such moments his hopes would rise, hopes that the cramps might be over, but they were only over for that moment. This griping pain was so paralyzing that he couldn't walk, he couldn't even have crawled slowly; the only way he could have propelled himself would have been to tip forward and drag himself painfully along by his hands, but even then he wouldn't have got there in time. It was another three hundred yards to the departure point, and now and again through the noise of the firing he would hear Major Krenz calling his name —but by this time he hardly cared: he had stomach cramps, intense, violent stomach cramps. He held on to the wall, his naked bottom shivering, and in his bowels that grinding pain would form and re-form, like some slowly accumulating explosive that surely must be devastating in effect but, when it did come, was always minimal, kept accumulating, kept promising to bring final release while never releasing more than a tiny morsel of stool. . . .

Tears ran down his face; he no longer thought of anything connected with the war, although all around him shells were bursting and he could distinctly hear the trucks driving away from the village. Even the tanks withdrew onto the highway and moved off, firing, toward the town; he could hear it all, very graphically, and in his mind's eye he had a clear picture of the village being surrounded. But the pain in his stomach was bigger, closer, more important, monstrous. He thought about this pain that wouldn't let up, that paralyzed him—and in a frenzied, grinning procession, all the doctors he had ever consulted for his agonizing condition passed in front of him, headed by his repulsive father. They surrounded him, those useless creatures who had never had the guts to tell him straight out that his illness was due simply to constant malnutrition in his youth.

A shell landed in the cesspool, a wave splashed over him, soaking him with that disgusting liquid; he could taste it on his lips, and he sobbed more bitterly than ever, until he noticed that the farmhouse was in the tanks' direct line of fire. Shells were whining right past his ears, over his head, incredibly hard round balls that caused a great rush of air. Glass tinkled behind him, timbers shattered, and inside the house a woman screamed, chunks of plaster and splinters of wood flew all around him. He tipped forward, ducked behind the wall surrounding the cesspool, and carefully buttoned his pants. Although his bowels were still convulsively releasing tiny amounts of that terrible pain, he crawled slowly down the steep little stone path to get away from the immediate vicinity of the farmhouse. His pants were fastened, but he could crawl no farther, the pain was paralyzing him. He lay where he was, and for a few seconds his whole life spun round him—a kaleidoscope of unspeakably monotonous pain and humiliation. Only his tears seemed important and real to him as they flowed freely down his face into the muck, that muck he had tasted on his lips—straw, excrement, mud, and hay. He was still sobbing when a shell hit the center beam of a barn roof, and the great wooden structure with its bales of pressed straw collapsed and buried him.

VII

THE GREEN furniture van had an excellent engine. The two men up front in the cab, who took turns driving, did not talk much, but when they did, they spoke almost exclusively about the engine. "Isn't she a beaut," they would say from time to time, shaking their heads in amazement and listening spellbound to that powerful, dark, regular throbbing with never a false or disquieting note to it. The night was warm and dark, and the road, as they drove steadily northward, was sometimes choked with army vehicles or horse-drawn carts, and every now and again they had to jam on the brakes because they suddenly came face to face with marching columns and almost drove into that strange formless mass of dark figures whose faces were lit up by their headlights. The roads were narrow, too narrow to allow furniture vans, tanks, and marching columns to pass, but the farther north they drove the emptier became the road, and for a long time there was nothing to stop them driving the green van as fast as it would go; the cones of their headlights lit up trees and houses, sometimes, in a curve, shooting into a field and making the tall corn or tomato plants stand out sharp and clear. Finally the road became quite empty, the men were yawning now, and they stopped somewhere in a village on a side road for a rest; they opened their packs, gulped the hot, very strong coffee from their canteens, opened flat round cans of chocolate, and calmly made themselves sandwiches, opening their cans of butter, sniffing the contents, and spreading the butter thickly on the bread before covering it with slabs of sausage, the sausage red and ingrained with peppercorns. The men took their time over their meal. Their gray, tired faces revived, and one—the man now sitting on the left and the first to finish—lit a cigarette and drew a letter from his pocket; he unfolded it and took a snapshot out of the folds: it showed a charming little girl playing with a rabbit in a meadow. Holding the picture out to the man beside him, he said, "How d'you like that—cute, eh? My kid," he laughed, "a home-leave kid." The other man went on chewing as he answered, staring at the picture and mumbling, "Cute—home-leave kid, eh? How old is she?"

"Three."

"Haven't you got a picture of your wife?"

"Sure." The man on the left took out his wallet—but suddenly paused, saying, "Listen to that, they must have gone nuts." From the interior of the green van came a deep, angry mumbling and the shrill screams of a woman.

"Go and make them shut up," said the man behind the wheel.

The other man opened the cab door and looked out onto the village street. It was warm and dark outside, and the houses were unlit; there was a smell of manure, a very strong smell of cow dung, and in one of the houses a dog barked. The man got out, cursing under his breath at the deep soft mud of the village street, and walked slowly around the van. From outside, the mumbling was only faintly audible, more like a gentle buzzing inside a box, but now two dogs were barking in the village, then three, and suddenly a light went on in a window somewhere, and a man's silhouette became visible. The driver—his name was Schröder—couldn't be bothered to open the heavy padded doors at the rear, it didn't seem worth the effort, so he took his machine pistol and banged the steel butt a few times against the side of the van; there was silence at once. Then Schröder jumped up onto the tire to see if the barbed wire was still securely in place over the closed opening in the roof. The barbed wire was still securely in place.

He climbed back into the cab. Plorin had finished his meal; he was drinking coffee now and smoking, and the picture of the three-year-old girl with the rabbit was lying in front of him. "Cute kid all right," he said, raising his head for a moment. "You're not saying anything—don't you have a picture of your wife?"

"Sure." Schröder took out his wallet again, opened it, and removed a well-thumbed snapshot: it was of a woman, short, grown a little stout, wearing a fur coat. The woman was smiling inanely, her face was rather haggard and tired, and the black shoes with the heels that were much too high looked as though they hurt. Her thick hair, heavy and brownish, had been permed. "Good-looking girl," said Plorin. "Let's get going."

"Right," said Schröder, "start her up." He gave another glance outside; by this time a lot of dogs were barking in the village, and a lot of windows showed lights, and people were calling out to each other in the darkness.

"Let's go," he said, slamming the door. "Start her up."

Plorin turned the key in the ignition, the motor started at once; he let it idle for a few seconds, then pressed down the gas pedal, and the green furniture van maneuvered itself slowly onto the highway. "She's a beaut all right," said Plorin, "a real beaut."

The noise of the engine filled the whole cab, their ears were full of the steady hum, but after a short distance that deep murmur from the inside of the van became audible again. "Let's have a song," Plorin said to Schröder.

Schröder sang. He sang lustily, lifting up his voice, not very beautifully and not altogether accurately, but with real feeling. The emotional parts he sang with special fervor, and in some parts his voice was so emotional it sounded as if he were about to cry, but he did not cry. One song he seemed especially fond of was "Heidemarie," it was clearly his favorite. For a whole hour he sang at the top of his voice, and after an hour the two men changed places, and now Plorin sang.

"Good thing the old man can't hear us singing," said Plorin with a laugh. Schröder laughed too, and Plorin resumed his singing. He sang almost the same songs as Schröder, but he seemed to like "Gray Columns on the March" best, this was the one he sang most often; he sang it slowly, he sang it fast, and the especially moving parts, the ones stressing the misery and nobility of a hero's life, he sang very slowly and dramatically and sometimes several times in a row. Schröder, now at the wheel, stared fixedly at the road, driving the van at top speed, and softly whistled an accompaniment. They heard nothing more now from the inside of the green van.

It was getting chilly up front; they wrapped blankets around their legs, and from time to time, as they drove, they gulped coffee from their flasks. They had stopped singing, but inside the green van it was silent. Everything was silent, for that matter. Outside, everything was asleep; the highway was empty and wet—it must have been raining here—and the villages they drove through looked dead. They were caught briefly by the headlights in the darkness, a house or two, sometimes a church on the main road—for an instant they would leap up out of the darkness and then were left behind.

About four in the morning they stopped for a second breather. They were both tired by this time, their faces gray and drawn and grimy, and they hardly spoke; the hour's drive still ahead of them seemed endless. They made only a brief halt by the roadside, wiped their faces with schnapps, listlessly ate up their sandwiches, and swilled down the rest of the coffee. They finished the chocolate from their flat cans and lit cigarettes. Somewhat refreshed they drove on, and Schröder, now at the wheel again, whistled softly to himself, while Plorin, wrapped in a blanket, slept. Not a sound came from the inside of the green van.

A light rain started to fall, and dawn was breaking as they turned off the main road, wound their way through the narrow streets of a village out into the open country, and began driving slowly through a forest. Ground mist was rising, and when the van emerged from the forest there was a meadow, with army huts on it, then another little forest and a meadow, and the van stopped and impatiently sounded its horn in front of a big gate consisting of beams and barbed wire. The gate was flanked by a black-white-and-red sentrybox and a tall watchtower on which a man in a steel helmet was standing beside a machine gun. The gate was opened by the sentry, who grinned as he looked into the cab, and the green van drove slowly into the fenced enclosure.

The driver nudged his neighbor. "We're here," he said. They opened the cab doors and got out with their packs.

Birds were twittering in the forest; the sun came up in the east and shone on the green trees. Soft mist covered everything.

Schröder and Plorin walked wearily toward a hut behind the watchtower. As they climbed the few steps to the door, they saw a whole column of trucks parked on the camp road ready to leave. It was quiet in the camp; nothing moved but the smoke that came pouring out of the crematorium chimney.

The SS lieutenant was sitting crouched over a table and had fallen asleep. As he woke up with a start, the two men gave him a tired grin, saying, "Here we are."

He got up, stretched, and said with a yawn, "That's good." He sleepily lit a cigarette, ran his fingers through his hair, put on a cap, straightened his belt, and glanced into the mirror as he flicked the grains of sleep from the corners of his eyes. "How many are there?" he asked.

"Sixty-seven," said Schröder, tossing a sheaf of papers onto the table.

"Is that the lot?"

"Yes—that's the lot," said Schröder. "What's new?"

"We're clearing out—tonight."

"Is that definite?"

"Yes—it's getting too hot around here."

"Where to?"

"Toward 'Greater Germany—Subdivision Austria'!" The SS lieutenant laughed. "Go and get some sleep," he said. "It's going to be another tough night; we're off tonight at seven sharp."

"And the camp?" asked Plorin.

The SS lieutenant took off his cap, carefully combed his hair, and with his right hand arranged his forelock. He was a handsome fellow, brown-haired and slim. He sighed.

"The camp," he said, "there's no more camp now—by tonight there'll be no more camp. It's empty."

"Empty?" asked Plorin; he had sat down and was slowly rubbing his sleeve along his machine pistol, which had got damp.

"Empty," repeated the SS lieutenant; he grinned faintly, shrugged his shoulders. "The camp's empty, I tell you—isn't that enough?"

"Have they been taken away?" asked Schröder, already at the door.

"Damn it all," said the SS lieutenant, "leave me alone, can't you? I said empty, not taken away—except for the choir." He grinned. "We all know the old man's crazy about his choir. Mark my words, he'll be taking that along again. . . ."

"Hm," said each of the two men, and then again, "Hm. . . ." And Schröder added, "The old man's completely nuts about his singing." All three laughed.

"OK, then, we'll be off now," said Plorin. "I'll leave the van where it is, I'm all in."

"Never mind the van," said the SS lieutenant. "Willi can drive it away."

"OK, then—we're off." The two drivers left.

The SS lieutenant nodded, walked to the window, and looked out at the green furniture van parked on the camp road, just where the waiting column began. The camp was quite silent. It was another hour before the green van was opened, when SS Captain Filskeit arrived at the camp. Filskeit had black hair, he was of medium height, and his pale and intelligent face radiated an aura of chastity. He was strict, a stickler for order, and would tolerate no deviation. His actions were governed solely by regulations. When the sentry saluted, he nodded, glanced at the green furniture van, and stepped into the guardroom. The SS lieutenant saluted.

"How many?" asked Filskeit.

"Sixty-seven, sir."

"Good," said Filskeit. "I'll expect them in an hour for choir practice." He nodded casually, left the guardroom, and walked across the camp ground. The camp was square, a quadrangle consisting of four times four huts with a small gap on the south side for the gate. At the corners were watchtowers. In the center were the cookhouse, the latrine hut; in one corner of the camp, next to the southeast watchtower, was the bath hut, and next to the bath hut, the crematorium. The camp was completely silent except for one of the sentries—the one on the northeast watchtower—who was singing something softly to himself; apart from that the silence was unbroken. Wispy blue smoke was rising from the cookhouse, and from the crematorium came dense black smoke, fortunately drifting south; the crematorium had been belching dense clouds of smoke for a long time. Filskeit gave a quick look around, nodded, and went to his office, which was next to the kitchen. He threw his cap on the table and nodded in satisfaction: everything was in order. He might have smiled at the thought, but Filskeit never smiled. To him life was very serious, his army career even more so, but the most serious thing of all was art.

SS Captain Filskeit loved art, music. Some people found his pale, intelligent face handsome, but the angular, oversized chin dragged down the finer part of his face and gave his intelligent features an expression of brutality that was as shocking as it was surprising.

Filskeit had once studied music, but he loved music too much to be able to summon that grain of realism that the professional must have, so he went to work for a bank and remained a passionate amateur of music. His hobby was choral singing.

He was a hardworking and ambitious individual, very reliable, and he soon advanced to the post of department head in the bank. But his real passion was music, choral singing. At first all-male choirs.

At one time, in the distant past, he had been choirmaster of the Concordia Choral Society, he had been twenty-eight, but that was fifteen years ago—and, although a layman, he had been elected choirmaster. It would have been impossible to find a professional musician who would have furthered the society's aims more passionately or more meticulously. It was fascinating to watch his pale, faintly twitching face and his slender hands as he conducted. The members were afraid of him because he was so meticulous, no wrong note escaped his hearing, he flew into a rage whenever someone was guilty of sloppiness, and there had come a time when these decent, worthy singers had enough of his strictness, his tireless energy, and chose another choirmaster. At the same time he had been conductor of the church choir in his parish, although the liturgy did not appeal to him. But in those days he had seized every opportunity of getting his hands on a choir. The parish priest was popularly known as "the saint," a gentle, rather foolish man who could sometimes look very severe: white-haired and old, he knew nothing about music. But he invariably attended choir practice, and sometimes he would smile gently, and Filskeit hated that smile: it was the smile of love, a compassionate, poignant love. And sometimes the priest's face would take on a look of severity, and Filskeit could feel his aversion to the liturgy mounting simultaneously with his hatred of that smile. That smile of "the saint" seemed to say: Futile —futile—but I love you. He did not want to be loved, and his hatred of those anthems and that priest's smile steadily increased, and when the Concordia dismissed him, he left the church choir. He would often think of that smile, that elusive severity, and that "Jewish" look of love, as he called it, which seemed to him both down-to-earth and loving, and his breast was devoured by hate and torment. . . .

His successor was a schoolteacher who enjoyed his beer and a good cigar and liked listening to dirty stories. Filskeit had loathed all these things: he neither smoked nor drank, and he was not interested in women.

Not long after, attracted by the idea of racism, corresponding as it did to his secret ideals, he joined the Hitler Youth, where he rapidly advanced to the position of regional choirmaster, organized choirs, including "speaking choirs," and discovered his real love: mixed choral singing. At home—he had an austerely furnished barrack-like room in a Düsseldorf suburb—he devoted his time to choral literature and to every work on racism that he could get hold of. The result of this long and intensive study was an article of his own, which he entitled "The Interrelationship of Choir and Race." He submitted it to a state music academy which returned it to him with the addition of some sarcastic marginal notes. It was not until later that Filskeit found out that the head of this academy was a Jew called Neumann.

In 1933 he gave up banking for good in order to devote himself entirely to his musical assignments within the Party. His article was approved by a music school and, after some condensing, printed in a professional journal. He held the rank of unit leader in the Hitler Youth but his duties also embraced the SA and the SS, his specialty being speaking choirs, male choirs, and mixed choral singing. His qualities of leadership were undisputed. When war broke out he resisted being classified as indispensable, applied several times for admission to the SS Death's Head units, and was rejected twice because he had black hair, was too short, and patently belonged to the stocky, "pyknic" type. No one knew that he often stood for hours in despair in front of the mirror at home and saw what it was impossible not to see: he was not a member of that race which he so ardently admired and to which Lohengrin had belonged.

But the third time he applied, the Death's Head units accepted him because of the excellent references he submitted from all the Party organizations.

During the early war years he suffered greatly as a result of his musical reputation: instead of being sent to the front, he was assigned to training courses, later becoming a course director and then a director of a course for course directors; he directed the choral training of whole SS armies, and one of his supreme achievements was a choir of legionaries which, while representing thirteen different countries and eighteen different languages, sang a chorus from *Tannhäuser* in perfect vocal harmony. Later he was awarded the Cross of Merit First Class, one of the rarest military decorations; but not until he volunteered for the twentieth time for military service was he assigned to a military training course and finally got to the front: in 1943 he was given a small concentration camp in Germany, and at last, in 1944, was made commandant of a ghetto in Hungary. Later, when that ghetto had to be evacuated because the Russians were getting close, he was given this little camp in the north.

It was a matter of pride with him to carry out all orders to the letter. He had quickly discovered the enormous latent fund of musical talent among the prisoners—he was surprised to find this among Jews—and he applied the selective principle by ordering each new arrival to undergo a singing test and by recording each one's vocal capacity on an index card, with marks ranging from zero to ten. Very few were given ten—those were assigned immediately to the camp choir—and those who got zero had little prospect of remaining alive for more than two days. When required to supply batches of prisoners for removal, he chose them in such a way as to retain a nucleus of good male and female voices so that his choir always remained complete. This choir, which he conducted with a strictness harking back to the days of the Concordia Choral Society, was his pride and joy. With this choir he could have beaten any competition, but unfortunately the only audience it ever had were the dying prisoners and the guard personnel.

But orders were even more sacred to him than music, and he had recently received a number of orders that had weakened his choir: the ghettos and camps in Hungary were being evacuated, and because the large camps to which he had formerly sent Jews no longer existed, and his small camp had no railroad connection, he had to kill them all in his camp. But even now there were still sufficient work parties—for cookhouse and crematorium and bath hut—to preserve at least the very best of the voices.

Filskeit did not like killing. He had never killed anyone himself, and that was one of his frustrations: he was incapable of it. He realized that it was necessary, and admired the orders, which he saw were strictly carried out; the important thing, after all, was not whether one liked carrying out orders but to realize their necessity, to respect them, and to see that they were carried out. . . .

Filskeit went to the window and looked out. Two trucks had driven up behind the green furniture van, the drivers had just got down and were walking wearily up the steps to the guardroom.

SS Lieutenant Blauert came through the gate with five men and opened the big heavy padded doors of the furniture van. The people inside screamed—the daylight hurt their eyes—their screams were long and piercing, and the ones who jumped down staggered to where Blauert pointed.

The first was a dark-haired young woman wearing a green coat; she was dirty, and her dress seemed to be torn; she was anxiously trying to keep her coat closed with her hands, and a girl of twelve or thirteen was clinging to her arm. Neither had any baggage.

The people who staggered out of the van lined up on the assembly square, and Filskeit counted them under his breath as he watched the roll call proceed: there were sixty-one men, women, and children, varying greatly in dress, behavior, and age. Nothing more emerged from the green van—six had apparently died. The green van moved slowly off and halted by the crematorium. Filskeit nodded in satisfaction: six corpses were unloaded and hauled off into the building.

The baggage of the van's occupants was stacked up in front of the guardroom. The two trucks were also unloaded. Filskeit counted the rows of five as they slowly filled up: twenty-nine rows of five. SS Lieutenant Blauert shouted through the megaphone, "Attention, everyone! You are at present in a transit camp. You will not remain here long. You will proceed one by one to the prisoners' registration section, then to the office of the camp commandant, to whom you will submit for a personal test. This will be followed by a bath and delousing, after which there will be hot coffee for all. Anyone offering the slightest resistance will be instantly shot." He pointed to the watchtowers, whose machine guns had now been swiveled round to aim at the assembly square, and to the five men standing behind him with cocked machine pistols.

Filskeit paced impatiently up and down behind his window. He had noticed a few fair-haired Jews. There were many fair-haired Jews in Hungary. He liked them even less than the dark ones, although there were specimens among them that might have embellished any illustrated work on the Nordic race.

He watched the first woman, the one in the green coat and the torn dress, enter the registration hut, and he sat down, placing his cocked pistol beside him on the table. In a few minutes she would be here to sing for him.

FOR TEN hours Ilona had been waiting for fear. But fear did not come. In these ten hours she had had to experience and submit to many things: disgust and horror, hunger and thirst, gasping for air, despair when the light struck her, and a strangely cool kind of happiness when, for minutes or quarters of an hour, she managed to be alone—but she had waited in vain for fear. Fear did not come. This world in which she had been living for ten hours was spectral, as spectral as reality—as spectral as the things she had heard about. But hearing about them had frightened her more than now finding herself in the midst of them. She had very few desires left: one of these desires was to be alone so that she could really pray.

She had pictured her life quite differently. Up to now its course had been orderly, satisfying, according to plan, pretty well exactly as she had pictured it—even when her plans had turned out to be mistaken—but this was something she had not expected. She had counted on being spared this.

If all went well, she would be dead in half an hour. She was lucky, she was the first. She knew very well what kind of bath huts those were that that creature had spoken of, she knew she had to face ten minutes of death throes, but even this, because it still seemed so remote, did not frighten her. In the van, too, she had had to endure many things that touched her personally but did not penetrate. Someone had tried to rape her, a fellow whose sexual craving she had smelled in the dark and whom she now tried in vain to identify. Someone else had shielded her from him, an elderly man who had whispered to her later that he had been arrested because of a pair of pants, because of one pair of pants that he had bought from an officer; but now she couldn't recognize that man either. The other fellow had felt for her breasts in the dark, torn her dress, and kissed the nape of her neck—but luckily the other man had come between them. Even the cake had been knocked out of her hand, the little parcel, the only thing she had taken with her—it had fallen to the floor, and in the dark, groping around on the floor, she had managed to get hold of only a few broken pieces ingrained with grit and icing. She had eaten them with Maria —some of the cake had been squashed in her coat pocket—but hours later, when she drew small sticky lumps out of her pocket, they tasted wonderful; she gave some to the child and ate some herself, and it tasted wonderful, this squashed gritty cake which she scraped to the last crumb from her pocket. Some people had committed suicide, they bled to death almost without a sound, emitting odd gasps and groans in the corner, until those next to them slipped in the flowing blood and screamed hysterically. But they stopped screaming when the guard banged on the side of the van. It had sounded ominous and terrible, that banging, it couldn't have been done by a human being, they had long ceased to be among human beings. . . .

She was also waiting in vain for remorse; it had been senseless to leave that soldier, whom she liked very much, whose name she did not even know, absolutely senseless. Her parents' apartment was already empty; the only person she found there was her sister's confused and terrified child, young Maria, who had come home from school and found the apartment empty. Her parents and grandparents had already gone—neighbors told her they had been picked up at midday. And it had been senseless for her and Maria to run to the ghetto to look for her parents and grandparents: as always, they reached the ghetto by way of the back room of a hairdresser's and ran through the empty streets, arriving just in time to be shoved into that furniture van which had been standing there, waiting to leave, and in which they hoped to find their relatives. They found neither parents nor grandparents; they were not in that van. Ilona was amazed that none of the neighbors had thought of hurrying over to the school to warn her, but even Maria had not thought of it. Still, it would probably have made no difference if someone had warned her. . . . In the van someone had stuck a lighted cigarette between her lips, later she found out it had been the man who was picked up because of the pants. It was the first cigarette she had ever smoked, and she found it very refreshing and very soothing. She did not know her benefactor's name, none of them revealed their identity, neither that panting, lecherous fellow nor her benefactor, and when a match flared up all the faces looked alike: terrible faces full of fear and hatred.

But there had also been long stretches when she could pray. At the convent she had learned by heart all the prayers, all the litanies, and long sections of the liturgy for high holidays, and she was glad now that she knew them. Praying filled her with a cool serenity. She did not pray to be given something, or to be spared something, not for a quick painless death or for her life; she simply prayed, and she was glad when she could lean against the padded rear door and that at least her back was alone. At first she had stood the other way around, with her back to the press of bodies, and when she became tired and started to droop, tipping over backward, her body must have aroused that raging lust in the man she fell against, a lust that frightened but did not offend her—almost the opposite, she had a feeling of being somehow part of him, of this stranger. . . .

She was glad to be standing free, at least with her back alone against the padding intended for the protection of good furniture. She held Maria close to her body and was glad the child was asleep. She tried to pray as devoutly as she always did but found she couldn't; all she could manage was a cool rational meditation. She had pictured her life quite differently: she had passed her teacher-training finals at twenty-three, then she had entered the convent—her relatives were disappointed but approved her decision. She had spent a whole year at the convent, it had been a very happy time, and if she had actually become a nun, she would now be a teaching sister in Argentina, in some very beautiful convent no doubt; but she had not become a nun, because the desire to marry and have children was so strong in her that even after a year it had not been subdued—and she had gone back into the world. She became a very successful teacher, and she enjoyed it; she loved her two subjects, German and Music, and was fond of the children, she could hardly imagine anything more beautiful than a children's choir. She was very successful with the children's choir she organized at school, and the choral works sung by the children, those Latin choral works which they rehearsed for feast days, had a truly angelic neutrality—it was a free and inward joy from which the children sang, sang words they did not understand and which were beautiful. Life seemed beautiful to her—for long periods, almost always. What troubled her was this desire for tenderness and children, it troubled her because she found nobody; there were many men who became interested in her, some even confessed their love, and she let some of them kiss her, but she was waiting for something she could not have described, she did not call it love—there were many kinds of love—she would have preferred to call it surprise, and she had believed she was experiencing this sense of surprise when the soldier whose name she did not know stood beside her facing the map and stuck in the little flags. She knew he was in love with her. The last two days he had been spending hours chatting with her, and she found him very nice, although his uniform worried and alarmed her a little, but suddenly, in those few minutes while she stood next to him and he seemed to have forgotten her, his grave, poignant face, and his hands as they explored the map of Europe, had surprised her, she had a sense of joy and could have sung. He was the first man whose kiss she had ever returned. . . .

She walked slowly up the steps to the hut, pulling Maria along; she glanced up astonished when the guard jabbed the muzzle of his machine pistol into her side and shouted, "Faster—faster." She walked faster. Inside sat three clerks at tables; big stacks of index cards lay in front of them, the cards as big as cigar-box lids. She was pushed toward the first table, Maria toward the second, and toward the third table came an old man, in rags and unshaven, who gave her a fleeting smile. She smiled back; that must be her benefactor.

She gave her name, her occupation, her date of birth, and her religion, and was surprised when the clerk asked her age. "Twenty-three," she said.

Another half hour, she thought. Maybe she would still have a chance to be alone for a bit after all. She was astonished at the casual atmosphere in this place given over to the administration of death. Everything was done mechanically, somewhat irritably, impatiently: these people were doing their job with the same lack of enthusiasm they would have brought to any other clerical work, they were merely doing their duty, a duty which they found tiresome but did anyway. No one did anything to her; she was still waiting for fear, the fear she had been dreading. She had been very scared when she left the convent, very scared as she walked to the streetcar carrying her suitcase, clasping her money in her moist fingers. The world had seemed alien and ugly, this world to which she had longed to return so as to have a husband and children—a series of joys which she could not find in the convent and which now, walking to the streetcar, she no longer hoped to find; but she was very ashamed, ashamed of this fear. . . .

As she walked over to the second hut, she scanned the rows of waiting people for familiar faces but found none. She went up the steps; when she hesitated at the door, the guard waved her impatiently inside, and she went in, pulling Maria along: that seemed to be the wrong thing to do, and she had her second encounter with brutality when the guard wrenched the child from her and, when the child struggled, pulled her by the hair. She heard Maria scream, and walked into the room holding her registration card. There was only one man in the room, and he was in the uniform of an officer; he was wearing a very impressive, narrow silver decoration in the shape of a cross on his chest. His face looked pale and haggard, and when he raised his head to look at her, she was shocked at his massive chin, which almost disfigured him. He mutely held out his hand, she gave him the card and waited. Still no fear. The man read the card, looked at her, and said quietly, "Sing something."

She hesitated. "Go on," he said impatiently, "sing something—never mind what. . . ."

She looked at him and opened her mouth. She sang the All Saints' Litany in a version which she had recently discovered and set aside to practice with the children. While she sang, she watched the man very intently, and suddenly she knew what fear was when he stood up and looked at her.

She continued to sing while the face in front of her became contorted like some horrible growth in a state of convulsion. She sang beautifully, and she did not know she was smiling, despite the slowly mounting fear now caught in her throat and waiting to be spewed out. . . .

As soon as she started to sing, silence fell, outside as well. Filskeit stared at her. She was beautiful—a woman—he had never had a woman —his life had been spent in stifling chastity—much of it, when he was alone, in front of the mirror, in which he vainly sought beauty and nobility and racial perfection—here it was, beauty and nobility and racial perfection, combined with something that completely paralyzed him: faith. He did not realize he was letting her sing on, even beyond the antiphony—perhaps he was dreaming—and in her gaze, although he saw she was trembling—in her gaze was something almost like love—or was it scorn —"*Fili, Redemptor mundi, Deus,*" she sang—he had never heard a woman sing like that.

"*Spiritus Sancte, Deus*"—her voice was powerful, warm, and of incredible clarity. He must be dreaming—now she would sing: *Sancta Trinitas, unus Deus*—he still remembered it—and she sang it:

"*Sancta Trinitas*"—Catholic Jews? he thought—I must be going mad. He ran to the window and flung it open: outside they were all standing there, listening, not a soul moved. Filskeit could feel himself twitching, he tried to shout, but from his throat came only a hoarse toneless rasp, and from outside came that breathless hush while the woman went on singing:

"*Sancta Dei Genitrix*" . . . With trembling fingers he picked up his pistol, turned around, and fired blindly at the woman, who slumped to the floor and began to scream. Now he had found his voice again, once hers had stopped singing. "Wipe them out!" he screamed. "Wipe out the whole damn lot—and the choir too—bring out the choir—bring it outside—" He emptied the entire magazine into the woman, who was lying on the floor and in her agony spewing out her fear. . . .

Outside, the slaughter began.

VIII

THE WIDOW Suchan had been watching the war for the past three years. It had all begun with the arrival of German soldiers and army vehicles, and cavalry; they had crossed the bridge that dusty autumn and headed toward the passes leading over to the Polish side. It had had the genuine look of war, grimy soldiers, weary officers and horses, motorcycles chasing back and forth, a whole afternoon of war, with a few intermissions: a fine spectacle, you might say. The soldiers had marched across the bridge, with the trucks driving up ahead and motorcycles fore and aft, and the widow Suchan had never seen them again.

After that things had quieted down a bit, except for a German army truck turning up now and again; it would drive across the bridge and disappear into the forest, and she could hear the sound of its engine for a long time in the silence as it drove up the mountain on the other side, laboriously wheezing, groaning, with a few intermissions—for a long time

—until it had evidently disappeared over the ridge. She pictured the trucks driving past her native village, where she had spent her childhood, the summers on the pastures and the winters at the spinning wheel—very high up, all by herself in summertime on those barren stony meadows. She had often leaned over the ridge for hours to see if anything was moving up or down the road. But in those days there were no cars here yet; occasionally there would be a cart, usually it was Gypsies or Jews going across to the Polish side. It was not until much later, long after she had left, that the railroad had been built crossing the bridge near Szarny and running along the very same valley she used to look down on from those upland pastures. She had not been up there for a long time, almost ten years, and she listened for the trucks as long as she could—and she could still hear them even after they had vanished over the ridge and were driving along the mountain road, and maybe now it was her nephew's boys who were looking down at the German army vehicles toiling along.

But they did not come often. The truck came regularly every two months, and between times there were not many vehicles—occasionally one carrying soldiers who stopped in for a beer before having to drive up into the mountains, and in the evening it would come down carrying the other soldiers who stopped in for a beer before driving down into the plain. But there were not many soldiers up there; the truck came only three times altogether, for, six months after the war had passed by her on its way into the mountains, the bridge leading behind her house across the river was blown up. It happened at night, and she would never forget the blast and the shriek she let out, the neighbors calling from across the street, and the steady screaming of her daughter Maria, who was then twenty-eight and getting more and more peculiar. The windowpanes were smashed, the cows lowed in the stable, and the dog barked the whole night through. When daylight came, they saw what had happened: the bridge had gone, the concrete piers were still standing, catwalk, roadway, railings, had all been neatly blown away, and the rusty girders lay down below in the river, sticking out here and there. That very morning a German officer had arrived with five soldiers; they searched all of Berczaba, first her house, every room, the stables, and even Maria's bed, with Maria still in it—she had been lying there whimpering in her room since the blast during the night. Next they went through the Temanns' house across the street: every room, every bale of hay and straw in the barn; and even Brachy's house was searched although no one had lived in it for three years and it was slowly falling to pieces. The Brachys had gone to work in Bratislava, and so far no one had turned up who wanted to buy the house and farm.

The Germans had been furious, but they hadn't found a thing. They had hauled out the boat from her shed and rowed across the river to Tzenkoshik, the little village that lay just where the road started to climb: you could see the church spire beyond the forest from her attic window. But in Tzenkoshik they hadn't found a thing either, nor in Tesarzy—although, of course, they probably didn't know that the two Svortchik boys had disappeared after the bridge was blown up.

To her mind, it was ridiculous to blow up the bridge: the German truck crossed it only about every two months, and between times, very occasionally, a car would turn up carrying soldiers, and the bridge served no one but the farmers who owned pastureland and forests on the other side. It certainly couldn't matter to the Germans if once every two months they had to make half an hour's detour as far as Szarny, only three miles away, where the railroad bridge crossed the river.

It took a few days for her to grasp what the destruction of the bridge meant to her. At first a lot of inquisitive people had shown up, they would have a schnapps or a beer at her place and want to be told the whole story, but then Berczaba became quiet, very quiet; the farmers and hired hands who had to go into the forest or up to the pastures on the other side stopped coming, so did the people who used to drive to Tzenkoshik on Sundays, the couples out for a stroll in the woods, and even the soldiers, and the only thing she sold in two weeks was a beer to Temann from across the street, that skinflint who made his own schnapps. It was very depressing to think that in future all she was going to sell was a glass of beer to that stingy Temann—everyone knew how stingy he was.

But this very quiet period lasted only three weeks. One day a gray, high-speed little army car arrived with three officers who inspected the ruined bridge, paced up and down the bank for half an hour, field glasses in hand, stared out over the countryside, first from the Temanns', then went up into her attic and stared out over the countryside from up there, and drove off, without having so much as a single schnapps at her place.

And two days later a slow cloud of dust moved from Tesarzy toward Berczaba: it was some tired soldiers, seven of them plus a corporal, who tried to explain that they were to live, sleep, and eat at her place. At first she was scared, but then she realized what a good thing it was for her, and she hurried upstairs to Maria, who was still in bed.

The soldiers seemed in no hurry, they waited patiently—men, no longer young, who filled their pipes, drank beer, unloaded their packs, and made themselves comfortable. They waited patiently until she had emptied out three little rooms upstairs: the hired hand's room, empty for the past three years because she could no longer afford hired help; the little room which her husband had once said was for visitors or guests, but there were never any visitors, and guests never came; and her bedroom, the one she had shared with her husband. She herself moved in with Maria, into the latter's room. Later, when she came downstairs, the corporal began to explain that the village council would have to pay her a lot of kronen for this, and that she was to cook for the soldiers and would be paid for this too.

The soldiers were the best customers she had ever had. Those eight men consumed more in a month than all the people together who used to cross the bridge separately. The soldiers appeared to have plenty of money and any amount of time. Their duties seemed ridiculous to her: two of them always had to cover a certain route together—along the riverbank, then across in the boat, back again, along another stretch of riverbank— they were relieved every two hours; and up in the attic sat one man who scanned the countryside through his field glasses and was relieved every three hours. They made themselves comfortable up there in the attic, they had widened the dormer window by removing a few tiles, covering it with a sheet of metal at night, and there they sat all day long in an old armchair, with cushions on it, that stood perched on a table. There one of the men would sit all day long, staring up into the mountains, into the forest, at the riverbank, sometimes also back toward Tesarzy, and the others loafed around and were bored. She was horrified when she found out how much the soldiers got paid for this, and their families at home got paid too. One of them was a schoolteacher, and he worked out for her exactly how much his wife got, but it was so much that she couldn't believe it. It was too much, what that schoolteacher's wife got paid for her husband to lounge around here, eat goulash, vegetables, and potatoes, drink coffee, eat bread and sausage—they even got tobacco every day. When he wasn't eating, he was lounging around in her bar leisurely drinking his beer and reading, he read all the time, he seemed to have a whole pack full of books, and when he wasn't eating or reading, he was lounging up there in the attic with his field glasses, of no use to anyone, staring at the forests and meadows or watching the farmers in the fields. This soldier was very nice to her, his name was Becker; but she didn't care for him because all he did was read, just drink beer and read and lounge around the place.

But that was all a long time ago. Those first soldiers hadn't stayed long, four months, then others had come who had stayed for six months, then others again for almost a year, and then they were relieved regularly every six months, and some would come back who had been there before, and they all did the same thing, for three years: loaf around, drink beer, play cards, and lounge about up there in the attic or over in the meadow, and stroll uselessly around in the forest with their rifles on their backs. She was paid a lot of money for housing the soldiers and cooking for them. Others came too; the bar had become a living room for the soldiers.

The sergeant who had been quartered with her for the past four months was called Peter, she didn't know his surname; he was heavy-set, walked like a farmer, even had a mustache, and the sight of him often reminded her of her husband, Wenzel Suchan, who had not returned from another war: soldiers had crossed the bridge then too, covered with dust, on foot and on horseback, with mud-caked baggage trains, soldiers who never came back—it was years before they came back, and she couldn't tell whether they were the same ones who had gone up the other side so long ago. She had been young, twenty-two, a pretty woman, when Wenzel Suchan brought her down from the mountain and made her his wife: she felt very rich, very lucky, to be the wife of an innkeeper who kept a hired hand to work in the fields, and a horse, and she loved the twenty-six-year-old Wenzel Suchan with his deliberate walk and his mustache. Wenzel had been a corporal with a rifle brigade in Bratislava, and shortly after the unfamiliar, dusty soldiers had made their way through the forest up the hill, past her native village, Wenzel Suchan had gone to Bratislava again, as a corporal with a rifle brigade, and they had sent him south to a country called Rumania, to the mountains; from there he had written her three postcards saying he was fine, and on the last postcard he told her he had been made a sergeant. After that she heard nothing for four weeks, then she got a letter from Vienna saying he had been killed.

Soon after that Maria was born, Maria who was now pregnant by that sergeant called Peter who looked like Wenzel Suchan. In her memory Wenzel lived on as a young man, twenty-six years old, and this sergeant who was called Peter and was forty-five—seven years younger than herself —seemed very old to her. Many a night she had lain awake waiting for Maria, and Maria had not come until dawn, slipping barefoot into the room and getting quickly into bed just before the cocks began to crow. Many a night she had waited and prayed, and she had put many more flowers before the Virgin Mary's picture downstairs than she used to, but Maria had become pregnant, and the sergeant came to see her, embarrassed, awkward as a peasant, and explained that he would marry Maria when the war was over.

Well, there was nothing she could do about it, and she continued to put lots of flowers before the Virgin Mary's picture downstairs in the passageway, and waited. Things became quiet in Berczaba, much quieter it seemed to her, although nothing had changed: the soldiers lounged around in the bar, wrote letters, played cards, drank schnapps and beer, and some of them had started up a trade in things that were not obtainable here:

pocketknives, razor blades, scissors—wonderful scissors—and socks. They took money for them, or exchanged the money for butter and eggs, because they had more leisure than money to spend on drinks during this leisure. Now there was another one who read all day and even had a whole case of books driven over by truck from Tesarzy station. He was a professor, he also spent half the day in the attic staring through his field glasses at the mountains, into the forest, at the riverbank, and sometimes back toward Tesarzy, or watching the farmers at work in the fields, and he also told her his wife received money, large sums of money, so and so many thousand kronen a month—and she didn't believe him either, it was too much, a crazy sum, he must be lying, his wife couldn't be paid all that for her husband to sit around here reading books and writing half the day and often half the night, and then a few hours a day sitting up there in the attic with the field glasses. One of the men used to sketch. In fine weather he would sit outdoors by the river, sketching the mountains there was such a fine view of from here, the river, the remains of the bridge. He sketched her too a few times, and she admired the pictures very much and hung one of them in the bar.

They had been stationed here for three years now, these soldiers, always eight men, doing nothing. They strolled along the river, crossed over in her boat, strolled through the woods as far as Tzenkoshik, came back, crossed the river again, walked past along the bank, then partway down to Tesarzy, and were relieved. They ate well, slept a lot, and had plenty of money, and she often thought that maybe Wenzel Suchan had been taken away, all those years ago, to do nothing in another country— Wenzel, whom she badly needed, who could work and liked to work. They had most likely taken him away to do nothing in that country called Rumania, to wait around doing nothing until he was killed by a bullet. But these soldiers under her roof didn't get hit by bullets: as long as they had been here they had only fired their rifles a few times. Each time there was great excitement, and each time it had turned out to be a mistake— usually they had shot at game that was moving in the forest and hadn't halted when challenged, but even that didn't happen very often, only four or five times in these three years, and once they had shot at a woman who had come down the river at night from Tzenkoshik and then run through the forest to get a doctor in Tesarzy for her child, they had shot at this woman too, but luckily they hadn't hit her, and afterward they had helped her into the boat and even rowed her across—and the professor, who hadn't gone to bed yet and was sitting in the bar reading and writing, the professor had gone with her to Tesarzy. But in these three years they hadn't found a single partisan. Everybody knew there were none left here now that the Svortchik boys had gone; even in Szarny, where the big railroad bridge was, no partisans were ever seen. . . .

Although she was making money from the war, it was bitter for her to imagine that Wenzel Suchan had probably done nothing in that country called Rumania, that he hadn't been able to do anything. Most likely that's what war meant, men doing nothing and going to other countries so no one could see them at it. Anyway, she found it both disgusting and ridiculous to watch these men doing nothing for three years but steal time, and getting well paid to shoot once a year, at night, by mistake, at game or some poor woman who was trying to fetch a doctor for her child; disgusting and ridiculous for these men to have to loaf around while she had so much to do she didn't know which way to turn. She had to cook, look after the cows and pigs and chickens, and many of the soldiers even paid her to clean their boots, darn their socks, and wash their underclothes; she had so much to do that she had to take on a hired hand again, a man from Tesarzy, for Maria had been doing nothing ever since she got pregnant. She treated this sergeant as if he were her husband: slept in his room, got him his breakfast, kept his clothes clean, and sometimes scolded him.

But one day, after almost exactly three years, a very high-ranking officer turned up, with red stripes down his pants and a gold-braided collar —she heard later that he was a real general—this high-ranking officer arrived with a few others in a very fast car from Tesarzy. His face was all yellow, he looked sad, and in front of her house he bawled out Sergeant Peter because Peter hadn't been wearing his belt and pistol when he came out to report—and the officer stood there, furious, and waited. She saw him stamping his foot, his face seemed to shrink and get even yellower, and he barked at another officer standing beside him and saluting with a trembling hand, a gray-haired, tired-looking man of over sixty whom she knew because sometimes he would ride down from Tesarzy on his bicycle and chat in a very nice friendly way with the sergeant and the soldiers in the bar—and then later, wheeling his bicycle and accompanied by the professor, walk slowly back to Tesarzy. At last Peter came out, wearing his belt and pistol, and walked with the men to the river. They crossed over in the boat, walked through the forest, returned, and stood for a long time beside the bridge. Then they went up into the attic, and finally the officers drove off again, and Peter stood outside the house with two soldiers; they raised their arms in salute and stayed that way for a long time, until the car was almost back in Tesarzy. Then Peter went into the house again, furious, threw his cap onto the table, and the only thing he said to Maria was "Looks like they're going to rebuild the bridge."

And two days later another vehicle, a truck, came dashing up from Tesarzy, and out of this truck jumped seven young soldiers and a young officer who strode into the house and spent half an hour with the sergeant in his room. Maria tried to join in this conversation, walking right into the room, but the young officer waved her out, and she went in again, and again the young officer impatiently waved her out; she stayed at the top of the stairs, crying, and had to look on while the old soldiers collected their packs and the young ones moved into their rooms. She waited for half an hour, crying, flew into a rage when the professor patted her on the shoulder, and clung shrieking and sobbing to Peter when he finally came out of the room carrying his pack and with a very red face tried to calm her down, to comfort her—she clung to him until he had climbed into the truck. Then, still weeping, she stood on the steps and watched the truck dash off toward Tesarzy. She knew he would never be back, although he had promised her he would. . . .

FEINHALS ARRIVED in Berczaba two days before the rebuilding of the bridge began. The tiny hamlet consisted of a tavern and two houses, one of which was abandoned and falling into decay, and when he got out with the others, the whole place was enveloped in the bitter smoke from the potato fires smoldering in the fields. It was quiet and peaceful, nowhere any sign of war. . . .

It was only during the return trip in the red furniture van that he was found to have a splinter in his leg, a glass splinter, as the operation revealed, a minute fragment of a bottle of Tokay, and there had been an odd and embarrassing negotiation because he might have been in line for the silver medal for wounds except that the senior medical officer did not award silver medals for wounds caused by glass splinters, and for a few days the suspicion of self-mutilation hung over him, until Lieutenant Brecht, whom he named as a witness, sent in his report. The wound healed quickly, although he drank a lot of schnapps, and after a month he was sent to some redeployment center that packed him off to Berczaba. He waited downstairs in the tavern until the room Gress had chosen for them became free. He drank some wine, thought about Ilona, and heard the noise in the house made by the men getting ready to leave. The old soldiers were hunting for their belongings; the landlady stood behind the counter dourly taking in the scene, a middle-aged woman, quite pretty, still quite pretty, and in the passageway beyond her another woman was bawling her head off.

Then he heard the woman wailing and sobbing more lustily than ever, and heard the truck take off for the village they had just come from. Gress appeared and took him up to his room. The room was low, the plaster flaking off in places, black beams supported the ceiling, and it smelled stuffy; the air outside was close, and the window gave onto a garden: a grassy plot with old fruit trees, flowerbeds along the sides, stables, and at the end, outside a shed, a boat on blocks, its paint peeling off. It was quiet outside. To the left across the hedge he could see the bridge, rusty iron girders stuck out of the water, and the concrete piers were overgrown with moss. The little river seemed to be some forty or fifty yards wide.

So now he was sharing a room with Gress. He had met him yesterday at the redeployment center and decided not to say one word more than necessary to him. Gress had four decorations on his chest, and he liked telling tales—never stopped, in fact—about the Polish, Rumanian, French, and Russian girls he claimed to have left behind, all with broken hearts. Feinhals didn't feel like listening, it was a nuisance as well as a bore, embarrassing too, and Gress seemed to be one of those men who believed people would listen to them because they had decorations on their chest, more decorations than most.

Feinhals himself had only one decoration, a single medal, and he was a born listener because he never said anything, or hardly ever, and asked for no explanations. He was glad to learn that he and Gress were to take turns manning the observation post: this would mean he would be rid of him during the daytime at least. . . . He lay down on the bed the minute Gress announced his intention of breaking the heart of a Slovak girl, any Slovak girl.

He was tired, and every night when he lay down to sleep somewhere, he hoped to dream about Ilona, but he never did. He would recapture every word he had exchanged with her, think about her very hard, but when he fell asleep she did not come. Often he felt, before falling asleep, that he needed only to turn over to feel her arm, but she was not there beside him, she was a long way away, and it was useless to turn over. He was a long time falling asleep because he was thinking so hard about her and imagining the room that had been intended to receive them—and when he did drop off, he slept badly, and in the morning he had forgotten what he had dreamed about. He had not dreamed about Ilona.

He prayed in bed at night too, and thought about the talks he used to have with her before they had to leave; she had invariably blushed, and she seemed embarrassed by his presence in the room, among stuffed animals, rock specimens, maps, and health charts. But maybe it had only embarrassed her to talk about religion—she had always gone fiery red—it seemed to distress her to state her beliefs, and she stated her belief in faith, hope, and charity, and was shocked when he said he couldn't go to church because the faces and sermons of most priests were more than he could stand. "We have to pray to console God," she had said. . . .

He never thought she would let herself be kissed, but he had kissed her, and she him, and he knew she would have gone with him to that room he now saw so often in his mind's eye: none too clean, water still standing in the bluish wash basin, the wide brown bed, and the view into the neglected orchard where windfalls lay decaying under the trees. He always pictured himself lying in bed with her and talking, but he never dreamed about it. . . .

Next morning the regular routine began. He sat perched up there in the armchair on the wobbly table, in the fusty attic of this house, looking with the field glasses out through the dormer window into the mountains, into the forest, scanning the riverbank and sometimes back toward the hamlet they had driven over from in the truck. He couldn't find any partisans—maybe the farmers in the fields were partisans, only you couldn't tell this with field glasses. It was so quiet that it hurt, and he felt as though he had been perched up here for years, and he raised the field glasses, adjusting the screw, and looked out across the forest, past the yellow church spire, into the mountains. The air was very clear, and way up there among craggy rocks he could see a herd of goats; the animals were scattered like tiny white hard-edged cloudlets, very white against that gray, soft-green background, and he could feel himself capturing the silence through the field glasses, and the loneliness too. The animals moved very slowly, very seldom—as if they were being pulled along on short strings. With the field glasses he could see them as he would have done with the naked eye at two or three miles; they seemed very far away, infinitely far away, silent and lonely, those animals; he could not see the goatherd. It was a shock to put down the glasses and find he could no longer see them, not a trace of them, although he gazed intently beyond the church spire up at the mountain. Not even their whiteness was visible; they must be a long way off. He picked up the glasses again and looked at the white goats, whose loneliness he could feel—but the sound of commands being given down in the garden startled him, and he lowered the glasses, looked first without them into the garden and watched the men drilling. Lieutenant Mück himself was in command. Feinhals lifted the glasses to his eyes, adjusted the lenses, and studied Mück closely; he had known him only two days, but he had already seen that Mück took matters seriously. His fine, dark profile was like a mask, deadly serious, the hands behind his back did not move, and the muscles of the thin neck twitched. Mück did not look well, his complexion was pasty, almost gray, the lips were bloodless and barely moved when they uttered "Left turn," "Right turn," and "About turn." At the moment Feinhals could see only Mück's profile, that deadly serious, rigid half of his face, the lips that barely moved, the sorrowful left eye that seemed to be looking not at the drilling soldiers but far away, somewhere—maybe back into the past. Then he looked at Gress: his face was swollen, he looked in some way upset.

When—again without the glasses—he looked down into the garden where the soldiers were doing left turns, right turns, and about turns on that lush, wonderful expanse of grass, he saw a woman hanging out the washing on a line strung between the stables. It must be the daughter who had been crying and carrying on in the passageway yesterday. She looked grave, somber—so somber that she was not pretty but beautiful, a fine-drawn, very dark face with tightly pressed lips. She did not even glance at the four soldiers and the lieutenant.

When he went up to the attic next morning, just before eight, he felt as if he had been there for months, years almost. The silence and loneliness seemed quite natural: the gentle mooing of the cows in the stable and the smell of the potato fires still hanging in the air, a few fires were still smoldering, and when he adjusted the glasses, aiming them at a point far off in the distance in line with the tip of the yellow church spire, all he captured in the lenses was loneliness. Up there it was empty—a gray, soft-green surface dotted with black rocks. . . .

Mück had gone with the four soldiers to the riverbank to practice sighting. The sound of his brief, sad commands came softly across, too faint to disturb the silence—they enhanced it almost; and downstairs in the kitchen the young woman was singing a halting Slovak folk song. The old woman had gone into the field with the hired hand to dig potatoes. Across the street in the other farmhouse it was quiet too. Although he scanned the mountains for quite a time, his eyes saw nothing but silent, lonely expanses, steep rocks, except to the right where a train's white vapor came puffing out of the forest and quickly drifted apart; through the field glasses the vapor looked like dust settling over the treetops. There was not a sound to be heard except for Mück's brief commands at the riverbank and the young woman's haunting song from downstairs. . . .

Then they returned from the riverbank, and he could hear them singing. It was sad to hear those four men singing, a pathetic, ragged, very thin quartet singing "Gray Columns on the March." He could also hear Mück's "left, right—left, right"; Mück seemed to be desperately battling the loneliness, but it was no use. The silence was stronger than his commands, stronger than the singing.

As they halted outside the house, he heard the first truck arriving from the hamlet they had left the day before yesterday. He quickly trained his glasses on the road: a cloud of dust was rapidly approaching, he could make out the cab and something large and bulky showing above the roof.

"What's up?" they called to him from the street.

"A truck," he said, keeping the lenses on the approaching vehicle, and at that moment he heard the young woman come out of the house. She spoke to the soldiers and called something up to him. He could not make out what she was saying, but he called down, "The driver's a civilian; there's a Brownshirt sitting next to him, seems to be someone from the Party; on the back of the truck there's a cement mixer!"

"A cement mixer?" they called up.

"Yes!" he said.

Now those down below could also make out the cab of the truck; and the man in brown, and the cement mixer, and they could see another truck approaching from the village, a smaller cloud of dust, then another and another, a whole column heading from the village toward the remains of the bridge. By the time the first truck halted just before the approach to the bridge, the second truck was already so close that they could make out the cab and the load of that one too: hut prefabs. But now they all ran up to the first truck, including Maria, all except the lieutenant, as the truck door opened and a man in brown jumped out. The man was bareheaded, suntanned, with a frank, attractive face. "*Heil Hitler,* boys," he shouted, "is this Berczaba?"

"Yes," said the soldiers. They took their hands uncertainly out of their pockets. The man had a major's shoulder loops on his brown tunic. They did not know how to address him.

He called into the cab, "We're here, switch off the motor!" Looking beyond the soldiers at the lieutenant, he paused for a moment, advanced a few steps. The lieutenant also advanced a few steps; then the man stopped and waited, and Lieutenant Mück walked the rest of the way quite fast until he stood facing the man in brown. First Mück's hand went to his cap, then his arm went up for the *Heil Hitler* salute, and he said, "Mück!" and the man in brown also raised his arm, then held his hand out to Mück, shook hands, and said, "I'm Deussen—in charge of construction—we're going to rebuild the bridge here."

The lieutenant looked at the soldiers, the soldiers looked at Maria, Maria ran into the house, and Deussen bounced jauntily away to direct the approaching vehicles.

Deussen went about everything with great determination, great vigor, but with something obliging and friendly in his manner. He asked the widow Suchan to show him the kitchen, smiled, pursed his lips, said nothing, went across to the abandoned house, inspected it very thoroughly, and when he emerged he was smiling, and within minutes two trucks loaded with prefabs were on their way back to Tesarzy. He set up his own quarters at the Temanns', appeared shortly thereafter leaning on the window sill smoking and watching the unloading of the trucks. There was another young man in brown with the trucks, wearing a sergeant's shoulder patches. Now and again Deussen would call something out to him from the window. Meanwhile all the trucks had arrived, ten of them, and the place was a hive of workmen, iron girders, beams, sacks of cement, and an hour later a little motorboat came down the river from Szarny. A third man in brown got out of the boat, and two pretty, suntanned Slovak women who were greeted gaily by the workmen.

Feinhals watched it all very closely. First the big kitchen stove was carried into the dilapidated house, then the following were unloaded: complete iron railings, rivets, screws, creosoted beams, survey instruments, and kitchen supplies. By eleven the Slovak women were already peeling potatoes, and by noon all the stuff had been unloaded, even a shed for the cement had been assembled, and three more trucks arrived from the village to strew gravel on the approach to the bridge. When he went downstairs for lunch, Gress having relieved him, he saw that a sign had been nailed over the bar entrance saying "Canteen."

For the next few days he continued to watch the building activities very closely and was astonished at the precision with which everything had been planned: nothing was done needlessly, no material lay farther away than necessary from the point at which it was to be used. Feinhals had been on many construction sites in his time, and in charge of several construction jobs, but he was astonished to see how neatly and deftly this one was carried out. After only three days the bridge piers had been carefully filled with concrete, and while they were still pouring the last pier the erection of the heavy iron girders was already under way on the first one. By the fourth day a catwalk across the bridge had already been completed, and after a week he saw trucks driving up on the other side of the river carrying bridge sections, heavy vehicles that Deussen used simultaneously as ramp and base for erecting the final girder sections. Now that the catwalk was finished, everything went much faster, and Feinhals spent less time looking up to the mountains or into the forest. He observed the building of the bridge very closely, and even when he had to drill with the other men he usually watched the workmen: he loved this work.

In the evenings, when dusk was falling and the attic observation post was not manned, he would sit in the garden listening to a young Russian called Stalin—Stalin Gadlenko—playing the balalaika. Indoors there was singing, drinking, even dancing, although dancing was prohibited, but Deussen seemed to close his eyes to all that. He was in very good spirits: he had been given two weeks to build the bridge, and if the work continued at this rate, he would be through in twelve days. He saved a lot of gas because he could buy all the cooking supplies from Temann and the widow Suchan without sending a truck out all over the countryside, and he saw to it that the workmen were issued cigarettes, were well fed, and felt at ease; he knew this was better than exerting authority which, although it induced fear, actually inhibited the work. He had already built a number of bridges, most of which had meanwhile been blown up again; but for a time at least they had served their purpose, and he had never had any trouble meeting his deadlines.

The widow Suchan was pleased: the bridge would be there again, it would still be there even when the war was over, and if it was there the soldiers would probably stay and people from the villages would start coming back too. The workmen also seemed content. Every third day a snappy little light-brown car would drive down from Tesarzy and screech to a halt outside the tavern, and from the car would emerge a man in brown who looked old and tired and wore a captain's shoulder loops, and the workmen were rounded up and paid; they were paid plenty, enough to be able to buy socks from the soldiers, and shirts, and to spend the evening drinking and dancing with the pretty Slovak women who worked in the kitchen.

On the tenth day Feinhals saw that the bridge was finished: the railing was in place, the framework for the roadway completed, and he watched cement and girders being loaded and driven away, as well as the shed that had housed the cement. Half the workmen went back too, and one of the kitchen women, and Berczaba quieted down somewhat. All that was left now were fifteen workmen, Deussen and the young man in brown with the sergeant's shoulder patches, and one woman in the kitchen, at whom Feinhals looked very often. She spent the whole morning sitting by the window peeling potatoes, singing to herself, and she would pound the meat and clean the vegetables and was very pretty. When she smiled, he felt a pang, and through the field glasses he could plainly see her mouth on the other side of the street, and her fine dark eyebrows and white teeth. She always sang softly to herself—and that evening he went into the bar and danced with her. He danced a lot with her, and he saw her dark eyes close up, felt her firm white arms under his hands, and was rather disappointed to find that she smelled of cooking—it was close and smoky in the bar. She was the only woman, except for Maria, who sat at the counter and didn't dance. That night he dreamed about this Slovak woman whose name he didn't know; he had a very vivid dream about her, although after getting into bed he had again thought for a long time and very hard about Ilona.

Next day he didn't look across at her through his field glasses, although he could hear her singing, softly humming; he looked up to the mountains and was pleased to be able to pick out a herd of goats again, now they were to the right of the church spire, white specks moving jerkily against a gray, soft-green background.

Suddenly he put down the field glasses: he had heard a shot, the echo of a distant explosion coming down from the mountains. There it was again, very distinct, not loud, very far away. The workmen on the bridge paused, the Slovak woman broke off her singing, and Lieutenant Mück came running up to the attic in a state of agitation, wrenched the field glasses out of his hands, and looked up to the mountains. He looked up to the mountains for a very long time, but there were no more explosions, and Mück handed the glasses back to him, murmuring, "Keep watching now—keep watching," and ran back into the yard where he was supervising the men cleaning their weapons.

That afternoon seemed quieter than previous ones, although the sounds remained the same: the workmen on the bridge sawing creosoted beams, joining and screwing them together; the voice of the old woman scolding her daughter downstairs in the kitchen and getting no reply; and the gentle humming of the Slovak woman sitting by the open window as she prepared supper for the workmen—big yellow potatoes were frying in the pan, and an earthenware bowl of tomatoes shone in the dusk. Feinhals trained his glasses on the mountains, on the forest, scanned the riverbank; all was quiet on the other side, nothing moved. The two sentries had disappeared into the forest, and he aimed the glasses at the workmen on the bridge. They were already halfway through their work, the black, solid beams of the roadway were gradually meeting, and when he swung the glasses around, he could look down on the road at all the remaining material being loaded: tools and girders, beds, chairs, and the kitchen stove, and soon after that the truck with eight workmen aboard drove off toward Tesarzy. The Slovak woman leaned on the window sill and waved them good-bye, the place seemed quieter, even the motorboat went off up the river in the late afternoon, and in the roadway over the bridge there was only one bit missing—three or four beams. There was a gap of about six feet when the men knocked off work. Feinhals saw them leave their tools lying on the bridge. The truck returned from Tesarzy, stopped outside the kitchen, and unloaded a small basket of fruit and a few bottles, and shortly before Feinhals was relieved, there came again the echo of muffled explosions from above: it resounded from the mountains like stage thunder, artificially multiplied, reverberating, dying away, three times—four times —then there was silence. And again Lieutenant Mück came running upstairs and looked through the field glasses, his face twitching. Swinging them from left to right he scanned the rocks, the ridges, put down the glasses with a shake of his head, wrote a message on a piece of paper, and within a few minutes Gress was pedaling off to Tesarzy on Deussen's bicycle.

After Gress had left, Feinhals distinctly heard sounds of a machine-gun duel from the mountains. The hard, hollow rasp of a Russian machine gun contrasting with the high-pitched, nervous barking of a German one that grated like a frenzied hornet—the shots came so fast they seemed to skid. The skirmish was brief; only a few rounds were exchanged; then hand grenades burst, three or four, and again the noise was multiplied. Over and over again, until they died away, they sent their echo down into the plain. Somehow it seemed ridiculous to Feinhals: the war, wherever it showed up, was associated with completely unnecessary noise. This time Mück didn't come upstairs, he stood on the bridge and stared at the mountains; one more isolated shot came from above, from a rifle apparently, the echo sounding as thin as the noise of a rolling stone; then all was quiet until dusk fell. Feinhals replaced the sheet of metal on the roof and slowly went downstairs.

Gress was not back yet, and down in the bar Mück was anxiously holding forth about increased alertness for the night. There he stood, his face deadly serious, his fingers fumbling nervously with his two decorations; he had hung his loaded machine pistol around his neck and his steel helmet from his belt.

Before Gress got back, a gray car arrived from Tesarzy and out of it got a stout, red-faced captain and a spare, stern-looking first lieutenant, both of whom walked across the bridge with Mück. Feinhals stood in front of the house and watched them. It looked as though the three figures had disappeared for good, but they soon came back; the car turned. Across the street Deussen was looking out of the window, and on the ground floor of the workmen's quarters the men were sitting in the semidarkness around a rough table, tomatoes and potatoes on their plates. In the corner of the room stood the Slovak woman, one hand on hip, in the other a cigarette —the flourish of her arm as she brought the cigarette to her lips seemed to Feinhals a shade too elaborate. Then, as the motor of the gray car started up, she came closer, leaned on the window sill smoking her cigarette, and smiled at Feinhals. He looked intently at her face, forgetting to salute the two departing officers: the woman was wearing a dark bodice, and the white of her breast shone heartshaped below her brown face. Mück walked past Feinhals on his way into the house and said, "Bring the machine gun over here." Feinhals now saw that where the officers' car had been parked, a black, slender machine gun was lying on the road beside some ammunition cases. He slowly crossed the road and brought back the machine gun, then crossed over a second time and brought back the ammunition cases. The Slovak woman was still leaning on the window sill; she flicked off the glowing end of her cigarette and stuck the rest into her apron pocket. She was still looking at Feinhals but no longer smiling—she looked sad, her mouth was a poignant pale red. Then all at once she pursed her lips a little, turned, and began to clear the table. The workmen came out of the house and walked toward the bridge.

They were still working on it when Feinhals walked across the bridge half an hour later with the machine gun. They were putting the last beam in place in the dark. Deussen himself screwed in the very last rivet. He had one of the men hold a carbide lamp for him, and to Feinhals it looked as though he were holding the spanner like the handle of a barrel organ, as though he were boring into a great dark box that produced no sound. Feinhals put down the machine gun, said "Just a moment" to Gress, and went back once more. He had heard the motor being started up in the truck standing outside the workmen's quarters; he walked back to the ramp and watched the rest of the household objects being loaded. There was not much left: a stove, a few chairs, a basket of potatoes, crockery, and the workmen's own things. The workmen walked back from the bridge and all got into the truck. They were carrying bottles of schnapps and drinking from them. The last person to get in was the Slovak woman. She was wearing a red kerchief around her head and had very little to carry: a bundle wrapped up in a blue cloth. Feinhals hesitated a moment as he watched her get in the truck, then walked quickly back. Deussen was the last to come off the bridge; he was holding the spanner and went slowly into Temann's house.

They spent half the night crouching there with the brand-new machine gun behind the little wall that bordered the ramp, listening into the night. The silence was unbroken. Now and again the patrol emerged from the forest; they would exchange a few desultory words and then go on crouching there mutely, their eyes fixed on the narrow road leading into the forest. But nothing came. Up in the mountains the silence was unbroken too. Just before midnight, when they were relieved, they went indoors and fell asleep at once. It was almost morning when they heard a noise and got up. Gress waited to put on his boots, but Feinhals stood barefoot at the window and looked across to the other side: a crowd of people were standing over there, arguing with the lieutenant, who evidently did not want to let them cross the bridge. They had apparently come down from the mountains and from the village whose church spire was visible beyond the forest, a long file of people with carts and bundles that seemed to extend even beyond the point where the forest began. Their shrill voices were full of fear, and Feinhals saw the widow Suchan, in slippers, throw a coat over her shoulders and walk across the bridge. She stopped beside the lieutenant and talked for a long time to the crowd, then started to argue with the lieutenant. Deussen arrived too; he walked slowly across, cigarette between his lips, and also spoke to the lieutenant, then to the landlady, then to the crowd—until at last the file of refugees on the other side started to move in the direction of Szarny. There were many carts piled high with children and crates, chickens in baskets, a long file that could proceed only at a snail's pace. Deussen returned with the landlady and, shaking his head, tried to explain something to her.

Feinhals dressed slowly and lay down again on the bed. He tried to sleep, but Gress was fussing about as he shaved and whistling softly to himself, and a few minutes later they heard two vehicles approaching. At first it sounded as though they were driving side by side, then one seemed to overtake the other; one was hardly audible yet as the other drove up to the door. Feinhals got up and went downstairs: it was the brown car that had sometimes brought the captain with the workmen's pay. He was standing across the street outside Temann's house, and just then Deussen walked toward the bridge with a man in brown who was also wearing a major's shoulder loops. But now the second car arrived too. This car was gray and caked with dirt and mud-splashed, and there seemed to be something wrong with it; it drew up in front of the tavern, and a cheery little lieutenant jumped out and called to Feinhals, "Start packing, it's getting sticky here. Where's the old man?" Feinhals noticed that the little lieutenant was wearing a sapper's shoulder patches. He pointed toward the bridge, saying, "Over there."

"Thanks," said the lieutenant. He called to the soldier in the car, "Get everything ready," and ran quickly toward the bridge. Feinhals followed. The man in the brown uniform with the major's shoulder loops inspected the bridge minutely, had Deussen show him everything, nodded appreciatively, even shook his head appreciatively, and walked slowly back with Deussen. Deussen emerged at once from Temann's house with his pack, spanner in hand, and the brown car drove quickly off.

Mück returned with the two machine gunners, the sapper lieutenant, and an artillery noncom without a weapon, dirty and harassed in appearance: sweat was running down the man's face, he had no pack either, not even a cap, and kept pointing excitedly into the forest, and beyond the forest up into the mountains. Now Feinhals could hear: vehicles were coming slowly down the road. The little sapper lieutenant ran over to his car shouting, "Hurry, hurry!" The soldier came running up with gray metal boxes, brown cardboard packages, and a bundle of wires. The lieutenant looked at his watch. "Seven," he said, "we've got ten minutes." He glanced at Mück. "It's to be blown up at exactly ten past. The counterattack's been called off."

Feinhals slowly mounted the stairs, collected his things in his room, picked up his rifle, placed everything outside the door of the house, and walked back inside. The two women, still not dressed, ran distractedly along the passages, snatching random objects from the rooms and screaming at one another. Feinhals looked at the Virgin Mary: the flowers had wilted. He carefully picked out the wilted stalks, rearranged the remaining fresh flowers, and looked at his watch. It was eight minutes past, and across on the other side the sound of the approaching vehicles could be heard more clearly now, they must have already passed the village and be in the forest. Outside, everyone stood ready to leave. Lieutenant Mück had a message pad in his hand and was taking down the particulars of the harassed artillery noncom, who was sitting exhausted on the bench.

"Schniewind," said the noncom, "Arthur Schniewind . . . we're with 912." Mück nodded and slipped the message pad into his leather satchel. At that moment the little sapper lieutenant came running back with the soldier, shouting, "Take cover—take cover!" They all threw themselves onto the road, as close as they could to the house, the front of which stood at an angle to the bridge ramp. The sapper lieutenant looked at his watch —then the bridge blew up. There was not much of a crash, nothing whizzed through the air; there was a rending sound, then an explosion like a few hand grenades, and they heard the heavy roadway smacking into the water. They waited another moment or two until the little lieutenant said, "That's it." They stood up and looked at the bridge: the concrete piers were still standing, the catwalk and roadway had been neatly blown away, only across on the other side one section of the railing still hung in the air.

The approaching vehicles sounded quite close by now, then suddenly there was silence: they must have stopped in the forest.

The little sapper lieutenant had got into his car and, cranking down a window, called out to Mück, "What are you waiting for? You've got no orders to wait here."

He saluted briefly and drove off in his dirty little car.

"Fall in!" shouted Lieutenant Mück. They lined up on the road, Mück stood there and looked at the two houses, but in the two houses nothing stirred. All they could hear was a woman weeping, but it sounded like the old woman.

"Forward march!" shouted Mück, "forward march, march at ease." He strode ahead, deadly serious and sad—he seemed to be gazing somewhere far away, or back into the past, somewhere.

IX

FEINHALS WAS surprised at the size of Finck's premises. All he had seen from the front was this narrow old building with the sign saying "Finck's Wineshop & Hotel, estab. 1710," some rather dilapidated-looking steps leading into the bar, a window on the left, two on the right of the door, and, next to the farthest window on the right the entrance to the courtyard, which was like every other winegrower's entrance: a sagging gateway, painted green, just wide enough for a cart to drive through.

But now, on opening the front door, he found himself looking through the passage into a large, neatly paved courtyard, its four sides formed by sturdy buildings. Around the second floor ran a balcony enclosed by a wooden railing, and through another gateway a second courtyard was visible, with sheds in it, and on the right a single-story building, obviously a reception hall. He took it all in carefully, listened, and paused suddenly at the sight of the two American sentries: they were guarding the second gateway, walking past each other like caged animals who have discovered a certain rhythm that enables them to pass. One was wearing glasses and his lips moved continuously; and the other was smoking a cigarette; they had pushed their steel helmets to the back of their heads and looked pretty tired.

Feinhals tried the latch of the left-hand door, onto which someone had stuck a piece of paper marked "Private," then the latch of the right-hand door, which bore a sign saying "Bar." Both doors were locked. He stood there waiting while he watched the sentries steadily pacing up and down. In the silence there was only the occasional shot to be heard; the opposing sides seemed to be exchanging shells like balls not meant to be taken seriously, just a token that the war was still on; they rose like alarm signals that burst somewhere, exploded, and announced in the silence, "War, this is war. Look out: war!" Their echo was only faintly audible. But after listening for a few minutes to this harmless noise, Feinhals realized he had been mistaken: the shells were coming from the American side only, none from the German side. It was not an exchange of fire, it was a purely one-sided discharge of explosions occurring at regular intervals and producing a multiple, slightly menacing echo on the other side of the little river.

Feinhals stepped forward, slowly, into the dark corner of the passage, where it led on the left into the cellar and on the right to a little door with a cardboard notice nailed to it saying "Kitchen." He knocked at the kitchen door, heard a faint "Come in, please," and pressed down the latch. Four faces looked at him, and he was shocked by the resemblance of two of the faces to that lifeless, exhausted face that he had seen, dimly lit by the ruddy reflection from the fire, on that far-off grassy slope outside a Hungarian village. The old man by the window smoking a pipe resembled that face very much; he was thin and old, with a tired wisdom in his eyes. The second face whose resemblance startled him was that of a boy of about six, playing with a toy wagon as he squatted on the floor and raised his eyes to him. The child also was thin, he also looked old, tired, and wise; his dark eyes looked at Feinhals, then the boy lowered his incurious gaze and listlessly pushed the wagon across the floor.

The two women sat at the table peeling potatoes. One was old, but her healthy face was broad and brown, and it was clear that she had been a handsome woman. The one beside her looked faded and aging, although she was obviously younger than she appeared: she looked tired and dispirited, the movements of her hands were apathetic. Wisps of blond hair fell over her pale forehead, whereas the older woman wore her hair combed tightly back.

"Good morning," said Feinhals.

"Good morning," they replied.

Feinhals closed the door behind him and hesitated, he cleared his throat and could feel the sweat breaking out on him, a fine sweat that made his shirt cling to his armpits and back. The younger of the two women sitting at the table looked at him, and he noticed she had the same delicate white hands as the boy, who was squatting on the floor and calmly guiding his wagon around some chipped tiles. In the small room there was a stale smell of innumerable meals. Frying pans and saucepans hung all around the walls.

The two women glanced at the man by the window who was looking out into the courtyard. He pointed to a chair, saying, "Please sit down."

Feinhals sat down beside the older woman and said, "My name's Feinhals—I'm from Weidesheim—I'm trying to get home."

Both the women looked up, the old man showed more interest. "Feinhals," he said, "from Weidesheim. Jacob Feinhals's son?"

"Yes. How are things in Weidesheim?"

The old man shrugged his shoulders, puffed out a cloud of smoke, and said, "Not too bad—they're waiting for the Americans to occupy the place, but they haven't done so yet. They've been here for three weeks, but they won't go the mile and a half to Weidesheim. The Germans aren't there either, it's a no-man's-land, nobody's interested in it, the location's not good. . . ."

"You can hear the Germans firing into it sometimes," the young woman said, "but not very often."

"That's right, you can hear them," said the old man; he looked keenly at Feinhals. "Where have you come from now?"

"From the other side—I waited over there for three weeks, for the Americans to come."

"Directly across from here?"

"No—farther south—near Grinzheim."

"Grinzheim, eh? That's where you crossed over?"

"Yes, last night."

"And changed into civilian clothes?"

Feinhals shook his head. "No," he said, "I was wearing civilians over there—they're discharging a good many soldiers now."

The old man laughed softly and looked at the young woman. "D'you hear that, Trude," he said, "they're discharging a good many soldiers now. Oh, what can one do but laugh. . . ."

The women had finished peeling potatoes; the young woman picked up the bowl, went to the sink in the corner, and shook the potatoes into a sieve. She turned on the water and began listlessly washing the potatoes.

The older woman touched Feinhals's arm. He turned toward her.

"Are they discharging very many?" she asked.

"Yes, they are," said Feinhals. "Some units are discharging everyone—on condition that they assemble in the Ruhr. But I didn't go to the Ruhr."

The woman at the sink began to cry. She cried soundlessly, barely moving her thin shoulders.

"Or cry," said the old man by the window, "laugh or cry." He looked at Feinhals. "Her husband was killed—my son." He pointed his pipe at the woman standing at the sink, crying as she slowly and carefully washed the potatoes. "In Hungary," said the old man, "last fall."

"He was supposed to be discharged last summer," said the old woman sitting next to Feinhals. "They were just about to do so several times; he was a sick man, very sick, but I suppose they didn't want to let him go. He was running the canteen." She shook her head, and her eyes went to the younger woman at the sink. The younger woman shook the washed potatoes carefully into a clean saucepan and filled it with water. She was still crying, very quietly, almost without a sound, and she placed the pan on the stove and went over to the corner to get her handkerchief from the pocket of a smock.

Feinhals knew his expression must have changed. He had not often thought of Finck, only now and again and for brief moments, but now it all came back to him so vividly that the scene was clearer in his mind's eye than when he had seen it in reality: that incredibly heavy suitcase the shell had suddenly exploded into, the way the suitcase lid had whirled up and how the wine had splashed in the dark onto the path and the back of his neck, how the broken glass had tinkled—and how small and skinny the man had felt as his hand had groped along the body until it reached the great bloody wound and he had drawn back his hand. . . .

He watched the child playing on the floor. With his thin white fingers he calmly pulled the wagon around the chipped tiles—little pieces of kindling lay there being loaded, unloaded, loaded, unloaded. The boy looked very frail and had the same listless movements as his mother, now seated at the table holding her handkerchief to her face. Feinhals looked around the room in distress and wondered whether he ought to tell them, but he lowered his head again and decided to tell them later. He would tell the old man about it. Right now he didn't want to talk about it; in any case, it didn't seem to occur to them to wonder how Finck had got from his field hospital all the way to Hungary. The old woman touched his arm again. "What is it?" she asked quietly. "Are you hungry? Don't you feel well?"

"No, I'm all right," said Feinhals, "thanks very much." With her penetrating gaze still on him he repeated, "No, I'm all right, really, thanks just the same."

"How about a glass of wine," asked the old man from the window, "or a schnapps?"

"Yes," said Feinhals, "a schnapps would be fine."

"Trude," said the old man, "get the gentleman a schnapps."

The young woman stood up and went into the next room. "We're rather cramped," the old woman told Feinhals. "All we have is this kitchen and the bar, but we hear they're moving on soon; they've got a lot of tanks here, and the prisoners are going to be taken away."

"Do you have prisoners here in the house?"

"Yes," said the old man, "there are some over there in the hall. They're all high-ranking officers being interrogated here. As soon as they've been interrogated, they get taken away. One of them's even a general. Look, over there!"

Feinhals went to the window, and the old man pointed past the sentries and through the gateway into the second courtyard, to the windows of the hall that were covered with barbed wire.

"There," said the old man, "another of them's being taken off for interrogation."

Feinhals recognized the general at once: he looked better, more relaxed, and he was wearing the Knight's Cross at his neck now; he even seemed to be smiling gently as he walked quietly and docilely ahead of the two sentries, who had the barrels of their machine pistols trained on him. Almost all the yellow had left the general's face, and he no longer looked tired either; his face was harmonious, quiet, cultivated, and humane, that very gentle smile made his face beautiful. He passed through the gateway, walked calmly across the yard, and preceded the two sentries up the steps.

"That was the general," said Finck. "They've got colonels in there too, and majors, all staff officers, close to thirty of them."

The young woman returned from the bar carrying glasses and the bottle of schnapps. She placed one glass on the window sill in front of Finck and the other on the table in front of Feinhals's place. Feinhals remained standing at the window. From there he could see out across the second courtyard as far as the street leading past the rear of the building. Two sentries with machine pistols were standing there too, and across the street from where the sentries stood Feinhals now recognized the window of the coffin shop, and he knew this was the street where the high school was. The coffin was still in the window: polished black with silver fittings and a black cloth with silver tassels. Maybe it was the same coffin that had been there thirteen years ago, when he had gone to high school.

"Prost," said the old man, raising his glass.

Feinhals went quickly to the table, picked up his glass, said "Thanks" to the young woman and *"Prost"* to the old man, and drank. The schnapps was good. "When d'you imagine would be a good time for me to try and get home?"

"You have to be sure and get through at a place where there are no Americans—by the Kerpel would be best—do you know the Kerpel?"

"Yes," said Feinhals. "Aren't there any there?"

"No, none. People often come across to get bread at night—women, they all come through the Kerpel. . . ."

"During the day they do sometimes fire into it," said the young woman.

"Yes," said the old man, "during the day they do sometimes fire into it. . . ."

"Thanks," said Feinhals, "thanks very much," and finished his schnapps.

The old man stood up. "I'm driving up the hill," he said. "You'd better come along. From up there you have a good view of everything, even your father's house. . . ."

"Right," said Feinhals, "I'll come along."

He looked at the women seated at the table cleaning vegetables, carefully removing the leaves from two cabbages, inspecting the leaves, shredding them, and throwing them into a sieve.

The child looked up, suddenly abandoning the wagon, and asked, "May I come too?"

"Yes," said Finck, "come along." He put his pipe down on the window sill.

"Now it's the next one's turn," he called. "Look."

Feinhals hurried to the window: the colonel was dragging his feet now, his gaunt face looked ill, and his collar, with the decorations dangling from it, was much too big for him. He hardly raised his knees, his arms hung limp. "A disgrace," muttered Finck, "a disgrace." He took his hat from the peg and put it on.

"Good-bye," said Feinhals.

"Good-bye," said the women.

"We'll be back for dinner," said Finck.

PRIVATE BERCHEM did not like the war. He had been a waiter and bartender in a nightclub, and until the end of 1944 he had managed to avoid being called up, and during the war he had learned a lot of things in this nightclub, things that had been confirmed for him once and for all in nearly fifteen hundred war-nights. He had always known that most men can't take as much alcohol as they think, and that most men spend a great part of their lives persuading themselves that they are real devils when it comes to drinking, and that they also try to convince the women they bring along of the same thing. But there were very few men who really knew how to drink, whom it was a pleasure to watch drinking. And even in wartime there were still precious few of those around.

Most people made the mistake of assuming that a piece of shiny metal on the chest or at the neck could change the man who wore it. They seemed to believe that a stupid fellow could become intelligent and a weakling strong if at some prominent spot on his uniform he were hung with a decoration, which he might very possibly have earned. But Berchem had realized this wasn't so: if it *was* possible to change a man by way of a decoration, then it could only be for the worse. But most of these men he had seen only one night, and he hadn't known them before, and all he knew was that most of them couldn't take alcohol, although they all thought they could and told convincing tales of how much they had drunk at one session at such and such a time and at such and such a place. It wasn't a pretty sight when they got drunk, and this nightclub, where he had spent fifteen hundred war-nights as a waiter, was not very closely checked for black-market goods: after all, there had to be someplace where heroes could get something to drink and smoke and eat, and his boss was twenty-eight, as fit as a fiddle, and even by December 1944 he still hadn't joined up. Nor was the boss bothered by the bombs, although they were gradually destroying the whole town. The boss had a villa out in the country, among trees, it even had an air-raid shelter, and sometimes he got a kick out of inviting a few heroes, the ones who were the best company, to a private drinking party, and he would load them into his car and entertain them in his villa outside the town.

Throughout fifteen hundred war-nights Berchem had kept a careful eye on what went on, and he had often had to listen too, although he found that boring. He didn't know how many assaults and encirclements he was familiar with from hearsay. For a time he had considered writing it all down, but there were too many assaults, too many encirclements, and there were too many heroes who wore no decorations and felt obliged to tell you that actually they deserved them because—he had listened to so many of these "because" stories, and he was fed up with the war. But some told the truth when they were drunk, and he also heard the truth from many heroes and barmaids from France and Poland, Hungary and Rumania. He had always got along well with barmaids. Most of them could handle their liquor, and he had a soft spot for women you could have a drink with.

But now he was lying in a barn in a place called Auelberg, with a pair of field glasses, an exercise book and a few pencils, and a wristwatch, and it was his job to write down everything he observed in a place called Weidesheim a hundred and fifty yards away on the other side of the little river. There was not much to see in Weidesheim: half the front of the place consisted of the wall of the jam factory, and the jam factory had closed down. Sometimes people crossed the street, once in a while; they would go off in the direction of Heidesheim and were soon out of sight in the narrow lanes. People climbed up to their vineyards and their orchards, and he could see them working up there, beyond Weidesheim, but he did not have to write anything down in his exercise book that happened beyond Weidesheim. The cannon for which he was acting as observer here got only seven shells a day, and these shells had to be fired somehow or other, otherwise the cannon wouldn't get any at all, and the seven shells weren't enough for a duel with the Americans who were occupying Heidesheim —it was useless, in fact forbidden, to fire at the Americans, because they returned every shot with a hundred of their own, they were very touchy. So no purpose was achieved by Berchem entering in his little book: "10:30 American vehicle from Heidesheim stopped at house next to entrance to jam factory. Car parked in front of jam factory. Returned 11:15." This car came every day and parked for nearly an hour a hundred and fifty yards away from him, but it was useless for him to enter it in his book: this car was never fired at. Every day an American soldier would get out of the car, remain in the house almost always for an hour, and then drive off again.

Berchem's first gunnery officer had been a lieutenant called Gracht, and he was said to be a clergyman. Berchem had not had much to do with clergymen, but he found this one very nice. Gracht had always directed his seven shells into the mouth of the river, which was to the left of Heidesheim, a sandy, swampy little delta known to the local inhabitants as the Kerpel, where only reeds grew. His shells certainly wouldn't harm anyone there, and Berchem had thereupon begun to enter in his little book, several times a day: "Noticeable activity at river mouth." The lieutenant had made no comment and continued to direct his seven shells into the swamp. But two days ago the command up there had changed; now it was a sergeant major called Schniewind, who took his seven shells very seriously. Schniewind also did not fire at the American car that was always parked outside the jam factory, what he had his eye on was the white flags: obviously the inhabitants of Weidesheim were still counting daily on the Americans occupying their village, but the Americans did not occupy the village. Its position was very unfavorable, in a loop, very exposed, whereas Heidesheim was hardly exposed at all, and the Americans were clearly not planning to advance. At other points they had already marched a hundred and twenty miles into Germany, they had almost reached the center of the country, but here in Heidesheim they had been stationary for the last three weeks, and for every shell that struck Heidesheim they had returned more than a hundred, but nobody was firing at Heidesheim now. The seven shells were intended for Weidesheim and its environs, and Sergeant Major Schniewind had decided to punish the people of Weidesheim for their lack of patriotic feeling. A white flag was something he could not stomach.

Nevertheless, that day Berchem entered in his little book as usual: "9:00 a.m. noticeable activity at river mouth." And he made the same entry at 10:15—and again at 11:45 he wrote: "American vehicle from H. to W. jam factory." At noon he left his post for a few minutes to go and pick up his lunch. As he was about to climb down the ladder, Schniewind called to him from below, "Hold on up there for a moment." Berchem crawled back to the barn window and picked up the field glasses. Schniewind took the glasses from him, threw himself on his stomach in the prescribed combat-ready position, and squinted through the lenses. Berchem looked sidelong at him: Schniewind was one of those people who can't take alcohol but persuade themselves and manage to convince others that they can take a great deal. There was something not quite genuine about the keenness with which he lay there on his stomach staring at the desolate, lifeless village of Weidesheim, and Berchem noticed that the star on his shoulder patch was still quite new, like the piece of braid encircling his shoulder patch with a perfect horseshoe. Schniewind passed the field glasses back to Berchem, saying, "The bastards, those goddamn bastards with their white flags—give me your book." Berchem handed it to him. Schniewind leafed through it. "What a load of crap," he said. "I can't think what you fellows imagine is going on in that swampy river mouth of yours, there's nothing but frogs there. Give me those." He snatched the field glasses from Berchem and trained them on the river mouth. Berchem noticed a slight trace of saliva around Schniewind's mouth and a very fine thread of saliva hanging down. "Nothing," muttered Schniewind, "not a single solitary thing in that river mouth—nothing's moving—what crap." He ripped a page from the exercise book, took a pencil stub from his pocket, and, still looking out the window, wrote something on the paper. "Bastards," he muttered, "those bastards." Whereupon he turned away, without saluting, and climbed down the ladder. Berchem followed him one minute later to go pick up his lunch.

FROM UP here, looking down from the vineyard, there was a good view over the whole area, and Feinhals realized why Weidesheim had not been occupied by either Germans or Americans: it wasn't worth it. Fifteen houses, and a jam factory that had closed down. The railroad station was at Heidesheim, and across the river, Auelberg station was occupied by Germans: Weidesheim lay in a dead loop. Between Weidesheim and the hills, in a hollow, lay Heidesheim, and he could see solid rows of parked tanks on every open space of any size: in the schoolyard, alongside the church, in the market square, and on the big parking lot by the Hotel zum Stern—wherever you looked, tanks and vehicles that were not even camouflaged. In the valley the trees were already in blossom, slopes and meadows were covered with blossoming treetops, white, pink, and blue-white, and the air was mild: it was spring. From up here he could see the

Finck premises lying like a fissure, the two square courtyards between the narrow streets; he could even make out the four sentries, and in the yard of the coffin shop he saw a man working at a big creamy-yellow box, slightly slanting, that was evidently to be a coffin—the freshly planed wood stood out clearly, shining pinkish-yellow, and the carpenter's wife was sitting on a bench in the sun, near her husband, cleaning vegetables.

The streets were busy with women shoppers and soldiers, and just then a crowd of schoolchildren came out of the school building at the end of the village. But in Weidesheim the silence was complete. The houses looked as if they were hiding among the great treetops, but he knew every house in the place, and saw at first glance that the Berg and Hoppenrath houses were damaged but that his father's was undamaged; there it stood, broad and yellow beside the main road with its comfortable façade, and the white flag hanging from his parents' bedroom on the second floor was extra large, larger than the white flags he could see hanging from the windows of other houses. The linden trees were already green. But not a soul was in sight, and the white flags hung stiff and dead in the windless air. The big courtyard of the jam factory was empty too, rusty pails lay around untidily in heaps, the sheds had been locked. Suddenly he saw an American car approaching from Heidesheim station and driving quite fast through meadows and orchards toward Weidesheim. Now and again the car would vanish beneath the white treetops, then reappear, finally emerging onto the main street of Weidesheim and pulling up at the entrance to the jam factory.

"For God's sake," Feinhals said quietly to Finck, pointing to the car. "What's that?"

Finck, sitting beside him on the bench outside the toolshed, calmly shook his head. "Nothing," he said, "nothing of any importance; that's Fräulein Merzbach's lover—he drives over every day."

"An American?"

"Of course," said Finck. "She's scared to come to him over here because sometimes the Germans fire into the village—so he goes to her."

Feinhals smiled. He knew Fräulein Merzbach well. She was a few years younger than himself, and at the time he left home, she had been fourteen, a skinny, restless teenager who played the piano much too much and badly—he could recall many a Sunday afternoon when she had been playing downstairs in the living room of the manager's apartment while he sat reading in the garden next door, and when her playing stopped her thin pale face would appear at the window, and she would look out into the gardens, sad and discontented. Then for a few minutes it would be quiet, until she went back to the piano to continue her playing. She must be twenty-seven now, and somehow he was pleased that she had a lover.

He thought about how he would soon be down there, at home, right next door to the Merzbachs, and that at noon tomorrow he would probably see this American. Maybe he could speak to him, and maybe there would be a chance of getting hold of some papers through him—he was sure to be an officer. It wasn't likely Fräulein Merzbach would have a private for a lover.

He also thought about his little apartment in town, which he knew no longer existed. The people there had written him that the house was no longer standing, and he tried to imagine it, but he couldn't imagine it, although he had seen many houses that no longer existed. But that his apartment should no longer exist was something he couldn't imagine. He hadn't even gone there when he was granted leave to check the damage; he couldn't see why he should go there just to see that there was nothing left. The last time he had been there, in 1943, the house had still been standing; he had nailed cardboard across the broken windows and had gone to the nightclub a few doors away. There he had sat for three hours, until his train left, and he had chatted for a while with the waiter, who was very nice, a quiet, matter-of-fact type, still young, who had sold him cigarettes for forty pfennigs and a bottle of French cognac for sixty-five marks. That was cheap, and the waiter had even told him his name—he had forgotten it now—and had recommended a woman whose attraction lay in her apparently genuine German respectability. Her name was Grete, and everyone called her Ma, and the waiter had said she was a very nice person to have a drink with and a chat. He had spent three hours chatting with Grete, who really did seem to be respectable; she told him about her old home in Schleswig-Holstein and tried to cheer him up about the war. It had really been very nice at that nightclub, although after midnight a few drunk officers and men had insisted on doing the goose step.

He was glad to be going home and to be able to stay there now. He would stay a long time, doing nothing until he could see what was what. There would certainly be plenty of work after the war, but he didn't intend to work much. He didn't feel like it—he didn't want to do anything, maybe help a bit with the harvest, without getting involved, like the summer vacationers who don't mind putting their hand to a pitchfork once in a while. Maybe later on he would start rebuilding a few houses in the neighborhood, if he could get the contracts. His gaze swept over Heidesheim: much of it had been destroyed, a whole row of houses next to the station as well as the station itself. A freight train was still standing there, its engine shot to pieces beside the tracks; lumber was being loaded from one freight car onto an American truck, and the fresh planks stood out as clearly as the coffin in the carpenter's garden that had been lighter and brighter than the blossoms on the trees, its creamy yellow shining brightly up at him. . . .

He wondered which way to go. Finck had explained that American sentries were posted along the railroad tracks, where they had dug themselves in, and they didn't bother individuals going out to work in the fields. But if he wanted to make quite sure, he could crawl through the canal in which the silted-up river was caught for a few hundred yards; you could duck as you went through it, and many people who for some reason or other wanted to get to the other side had used it—and at the end of the canal was the dense underbrush of the Kerpel reaching all the way to the gardens of Weidesheim. Once he was in the gardens, nobody could see him, and there he knew every step of the way. Or he might carry a hoe or a spade on his shoulder. Finck assured him that many people came across every day from Weidesheim to work in the vineyards and orchards.

All he wanted was peace and quiet: to lie at home in bed, to know that no one could bother him, to think about Ilona, perhaps to dream about her. Later on he would start working, sooner or later—but first he wanted to sleep as long as he liked and be spoiled by his mother; she would be very happy if he came to stay for a long time. And most likely there would be tobacco or cigarettes at home, and at last he would have a chance to catch up on his reading. Fräulein Merzbach could almost certainly play the piano better by this time. He realized how happy he had been in those days, when he could sit in the garden reading and having to listen to Fräulein Merzbach play the piano badly; he had been happy, although he hadn't known it at the time. Now he knew it. Once he had dreamed of building houses such as nobody had ever built, but later he had built houses that were almost exactly the same as the ones other people built. He had become a very mediocre architect, and he knew it, but still it was nice to understand one's craft and build simple, good houses that sometimes turned out to be quite pleasing when they were finished. The important thing was not to take oneself too seriously—that was all. The way home seemed very long now, although it couldn't be much more than half an hour; he felt very tired and lazy, and he would have liked to drive the rest of the way very quickly by car, drive home, get into bed, and go to sleep. It seemed such an effort to have to walk the route he soon must walk: right through the American front line. There might be trouble, and he didn't want any more trouble; he was tired, and it all seemed such an effort.

He removed his cap and folded his hands when the noonday bell struck. Finck and the little boy did the same; and the carpenter down there in the yard, working away at the coffin, put down his tool, and his wife laid aside the vegetable basket and stood with folded hands in the yard. People no longer seemed ashamed of praying in public, and he found it somehow repugnant, in himself too. At one time he used to pray—Ilona had prayed too, a very devout, intelligent woman, who was even beautiful, and so intelligent that she couldn't be confounded in her faith even by the priests. Now as he prayed he caught himself praying for something, as a matter of habit almost, although there was nothing he wanted: Ilona was dead, what was there to pray for? But he prayed for her return—from somewhere or other, for his safe homecoming, although this was now almost accomplished. He suspected all these people of praying for something, for the fulfillment of some wish or other, but Ilona had told him, "We have to pray to console God," she had read that somewhere and found it worth remembering, and as he stood there with folded hands he made up his mind that he would only pray properly when he could cease to pray for anything. When that happened he would go to church too, although he found it hard to bear the faces of most priests and their sermons, but he would do it to console God—maybe to console God for the faces and sermons of the priests. He smiled, unclasped his hands, and put on his cap. . . . "Look," said Finck, "now they're being taken away." He pointed down toward Heidesheim, and Feinhals saw that a truck was standing outside the coffinmaker's house, a truck that was slowly filling up with officers from Finck's little reception hall: even from up here their decorations stood out clearly. Then the truck disappeared rapidly along the tree-lined road toward the west, to where the war was over. . . .

"People are saying they'll be advancing soon," said Finck. "D'you see all the tanks?"

"I hope they take Weidesheim pretty soon," said Feinhals.

Finck nodded. "It won't be long now—will you come over and see us?"

"Yes," said Feinhals, "I'll come and see you often."

"I'd like that very much," said Finck. "Have some tobacco?"

"Thanks," said Feinhals; he filled a pipe, Finck held out a match, and for a while they gazed down onto the blossoming plain, Finck's hand resting on his grandson's head.

"I'll be off now," said Feinhals suddenly. "I must go, I want to get home. . . ."

"Go ahead," said Finck, "it's quite all right, there's no danger."

Feinhals shook hands with him. "Thank you very much," he said and looked at him. "Thank you very much—I hope I can come over and see you soon." He shook hands with the boy too, and the child looked at him thoughtfully and a bit suspiciously out of his dark, narrow-lidded eyes.

"You'd better take along the hoe," said Finck.

"Thanks, I will," said Feinhals, taking the hoe from Finck.

For a while as he walked down the hill it seemed as if he were heading straight for the coffin being made down there in the yard, he was walking straight for it, he watched the yellow shining box grow bigger and more distinct, as if through the lenses of field glasses, until he swung to the right past the village; there he was swallowed up by the stream of schoolchildren just leaving the school, he stayed among a group of children as far as the town gate and was alone as he quietly crossed the road to the underpass. He didn't want to crawl through the canal, it was too much of an effort. To walk through the trackless, marshy Kerpel was also too much of an effort—and besides, it would just make him conspicuous if he entered the village first from the right and then from the left. He took the direct path that led across meadows and orchards and was completely calm when a hundred yards ahead he saw someone walking along carrying a hoe.

The Americans had posted only a couple of sentries at the underpass. The two men had taken off their steel helmets and were smoking as they stared with bored expressions at the blossoming gardens between Heidesheim and Weidesheim; they paid no attention to Feinhals, they had been here for three weeks now, and for the last two weeks nothing had been fired at Heidesheim. Feinhals walked calmly past them, nodded, they casually nodded back.

Only ten more minutes now: straight through the gardens, then around to the left between the Heusers and the Hoppenraths, down the main road a bit, and he would be home. He might meet someone he knew on the way, but he met no one; it was perfectly quiet except for the distant sounds of rumbling trucks, but at this hour no one seemed to think of firing. Right now there were not even the regular sounds of shells exploding that had seemed like warning signals.

He thought with a certain bitterness of Ilona: somehow he felt she had shirked things, she was dead, and to die was perhaps the easiest—she should have been with him now, and he felt she might have been with him. But she seemed to have known that it was better not to become very old and build one's life on a love that was real only for a few moments while there was another, everlasting love. She seemed to have known many things, more than he did, and he felt cheated because he would soon be home, where he would live, read, not work too hard if he could avoid it, and pray, to console God, not to ask Him for something He couldn't give, because He loved you: money or success, or something that helped you to muddle along through life. Most people muddled along through life somehow, he would have to too, for he wouldn't be building houses that could only be built by him—any mediocre architect could build them. . . .

He smiled as he passed the Hoppenraths' garden: they still hadn't sprayed their trees with that white stuff his father claimed was indispensable. He was always having rows with old Hoppenrath about it, but old Hoppenrath still hadn't got that white stuff on his trees. It wasn't far now to his parents' house—on the left was the Heusers' house, on the right the Hoppenraths', and he had only to walk through this narrow lane, then to the left down the main road a bit. The Heusers had the white stuff on their trees. He smiled. He distinctly heard the shell being fired from the other side, and he threw himself to the ground—instantly—and tried to go on smiling, but he couldn't help flinching when the shell landed in the Hoppenraths' garden. It burst in a treetop, and a gentle dense rain of white blossoms fell onto the grass. The second shell seemed to land farther along, more toward the Bäumers' house, almost directly opposite his father's, the third and fourth landed at the same level but more to the left, they sounded as if they were of medium caliber. He got slowly to his feet as the fifth also fell over there—and then there was nothing more. He listened for a while, heard no more firing, and quickly walked on. Dogs were barking all over the village, and he could hear the chickens and ducks frantically flapping their wings in Heuser's barn—from some barns came the muffled lowing of cows too, and he thought: Pointless, how pointless. But maybe they were firing at the American car, which he hadn't heard driving back yet; no, as he turned the corner of the main road he saw the car had already left—the street was quite empty—and the muffled lowing of the cows and the barking of the dogs accompanied him for the few steps he still had to take.

The white flag hanging from his father's house was the only one in the whole street, and he now saw that it was very large—it must be one of his mother's huge tablecloths, the kind she took out of the closet on special occasions. He smiled again, but suddenly threw himself to the ground and knew it was too late. Pointless, he thought, how utterly pointless. The sixth shell struck the gable of his parents' house. Stones fell, plaster crumbled onto the street, and he heard his mother scream down in the basement. He crawled quickly toward the house, heard the seventh shell being fired, and screamed even before it landed, he screamed very loud, for several seconds, and suddenly he knew that dying was not that easy—he screamed at the top of his voice until the shell struck him, and he rolled in death onto the threshold of the house. The flagpole had snapped, and the white cloth fell over him.

Children Are
Civilians Too

"No, you can't," said the sentry gruffly.

"Why?" I asked.

"Because it's against the rules."

"Why is it against the rules?"

"Because it is, chum, that's what; patients aren't allowed outside."

"But," I said with pride, "I'm one of the wounded."

The sentry gave me a scornful look. "I guess this is the first time you've been wounded, or you'd know that the wounded are patients too. Go on, get back in."

But I persisted. "Have a heart," I said, "I only want to buy cakes from that little girl."

I pointed outside to where a pretty little Russian girl was standing in the whirling snow peddling cakes.

"Get back inside, I tell you!"

The snow was falling softly into the huge puddles on the black schoolyard; the little girl stood there patiently, calling out over and over again, "Khakes . . . khakes . . ."

"My God," I told the sentry, "my mouth's watering, why don't you just let the child come inside?"

"Civilians aren't allowed inside."

"Good God, man," I said, "the child's just a child."

He gave me another scornful look. "I suppose children aren't civilians, eh?"

It was intolerable, the empty, dark street was wrapped in powdery snow, and the child stood there all alone, calling out "Khakes . . ." although no one passed.

I started to walk out anyway, but the sentry grabbed me by the sleeve and shouted furiously, "Get back, or I'll call the sergeant!"

"You're a damn fool," I snapped back at him.

"That's right," said the sentry with satisfaction. "Anyone who still has a sense of duty is considered a damn fool by you fellows."

I stood for another half minute in the whirling snow, watching the white flakes turn to mud; the whole schoolyard was full of puddles, and dotted about lay little white islands like icing sugar. Suddenly I saw the little girl wink at me and walk off in apparent unconcern down the street. I followed along the inner side of the wall.

"Damn it all," I thought, "am I really a patient?" And then I noticed a hole in the wall next to the urinal, and on the other side of the hole stood the little girl with the cakes. The sentry couldn't see us here. May the Führer bless your sense of duty, I thought.

The cakes looked marvelous: macaroons and cream slices, buttermilk twists and nut squares gleaming with oil. "How much?" I asked the child.

She smiled, lifted the basket toward me, and said in her piping voice, "Two marks fyifty each."

"All the same price?"

"Yes," she nodded.

The snow fell on her fine blond hair, powdering her with fleeting silver dust; her smile was utterly bewitching. The dismal street behind her was empty, and the world seemed dead. . . .

I took a buttermilk twist and bit into it. It was delicious, there was marzipan in it. Aha, I thought, that's why these cost as much as the others.

The little girl was smiling.

"Good?" she asked. "Good?"

I nodded. I didn't mind the cold, I had a thick bandage round my head that made me look very romantic. I tried a cream slice and let the delectable stuff melt slowly in my mouth. And again my mouth watered. . . .

"Here," I whispered, "I'll take the lot, how many are there?"

She began counting, carefully, with a delicate, rather dirty little forefinger, while I devoured a nut square. It was very quiet, it seemed almost as if there were a soft, gentle weaving of snowflakes in the air. She counted very slowly, made one or two mistakes, and I stood there quite still, eating two more cakes. Then she raised her eyes to me suddenly, at such a startling angle that her pupils slanted upward and the whites of her eyes were the thin blue of skim milk. She twittered something at me in Russian, but I shrugged my shoulders with a smile, whereupon she bent down and with her dirty little finger wrote a 45 in the snow; I added my five, saying, "Let me have the basket too, will you?"

She nodded, carefully handing me the basket through the hole, and I passed a couple of hundred-mark bills through to her. We had money to burn; the Russians were paying seven hundred marks for a coat, and for three months we had seen nothing but mud and blood, a few whores, and money.

"Come back tomorrow, OK?" I whispered, but she was no longer listening. Quick as a wink she had slipped away, and when I stuck my head sadly through the gap in the wall, she had vanished, and I saw only the silent Russian street, dismal and empty; the snow seemed to be gradually entombing the flat-roofed houses. I stood there for a long time, like a sad-eyed animal looking out through a fence, and it was only when I felt my neck getting stiff that I pulled my head back inside the prison.

For the first time I noticed the revolting urinal stench from the corner, and all the nice little cakes were covered with a light sugar-icing of snow. With a sigh I picked up the basket and walked toward the building; I did not feel cold, I had that romantic-looking bandage round my head and could have stood for another hour in the snow. I left because I had to go someplace. A fellow has to go someplace, doesn't he? You can't stand around and let yourself be buried in snow. You have to go someplace, even when you're wounded in a strange, black, very dark country. . . .

At the Bridge

THEY HAVE patched up my legs and given me a job I can do sitting down: I count the people crossing the new bridge. They get such a kick out of it, documenting their efficiency with figures; that senseless nothing made up of a few numbers goes to their heads, and all day long, all day long, my soundless mouth ticks away like clockwork, piling number on number, just so I can present them each evening with the triumph of a figure.

They beam delightedly when I hand over the result of my day's labors, the higher the figure the broader their smiles, and they have every reason to hug themselves when they climb into bed, for many thousands of pedestrians cross their new bridge every day. . . .

But their statistics are wrong. I am sorry, but they are wrong. I am an untrustworthy soul, although I have no trouble giving an impression of sterling integrity.

Secretly it gives me pleasure to do them out of one pedestrian every so often, and then again, when I feel sorry for them, to throw in a few extra. I hold their happiness in the palm of my hand. When I am mad at the world, when I have smoked all my cigarettes, I just give them the average, sometimes less than the average; and when my spirits soar, when I am in a good mood, I pour out my generosity in a five-digit number. It makes them so happy! They positively snatch the sheet from my hand, their eyes light up, and they pat me on the back. How blissfully ignorant they are! And then they start multiplying, dividing, working out percentages, God knows what all. They figure out how many people crossed the bridge per minute today, and how many will have crossed the bridge in ten years. They are in love with the future-perfect tense, the future-perfect is their specialty—and yet I can't help being sorry that the whole thing is a fallacy.

When my little sweetheart crosses the bridge—which she does twice a day—my heart simply stops beating. The tireless ticking of my heart just comes to a halt until she has turned into the avenue and disappeared. And all the people who pass by during that time don't get counted. Those two minutes are mine, all mine, and nobody is going to take them away from me. And when she returns every evening from her ice-cream parlor, when she walks along on the far side, past my soundless mouth which must count, count, then my heart stops beating again, and I don't resume counting until she is out of sight. And all those who are lucky enough to file past my unseeing eyes during those minutes will not be immortalized in statistics: shadow-men and shadow-women, creatures of no account, they are barred from the parade of future-perfect statistics.

Needless to say, I love her. But she hasn't the slightest idea, and I would rather she didn't find out. I don't want her to suspect what havoc she wreaks in all those calculations, I want her to walk serenely off to her ice-cream parlor, unsuspecting and innocent with her long brown hair and slender feet, and to get lots of tips. I love her. It must surely be obvious that I love her.

Not long ago they checked up on me. My partner, who sits across the street and has to count the cars, gave me plenty of warning, and that day I was a lynx-eyed devil. I counted like crazy, no speedometer could do better. The chief statistician, no less, posted himself across the street for an hour, and then compared his tally with mine. I was only one short. My little sweetheart had walked past, and as long as I live I won't allow that adorable child to be whisked off into the future-perfect tense; they're not going to take my little sweetheart and multiply her and divide her and turn her into a meaningless percentage. It made my heart bleed to have to go on counting without turning round to watch her, and I am certainly grateful to my partner across the street who has to count the cars. It might have cost me my job, my very existence.

The chief statistician clapped me on the shoulder and said I was a good fellow, trustworthy and loyal. "To be out one in one hour," he said, "really makes no odds. We allow for a certain margin of error anyway. I'm going to apply for your transfer to horse-drawn vehicles."

Horse-drawn vehicles are, of course, a piece of cake. There's nothing to it. There are never more than a couple of dozen horse-drawn vehicles a day, and to tick over the next number in your brain once every half hour —what a cinch!

Horse-drawn vehicles would be terrific. Between four and eight they are not allowed across the bridge at all, and I could walk to the ice-cream parlor, feast my eyes on her or maybe walk her partway home, my little uncounted sweetheart. . . .

In the Darkness

"LIGHT THE candle," said a voice.

There was no sound, only that exasperating, aimless rustle of someone trying to get to sleep.

"Light the candle, I say," came the voice again, on a sharper note this time.

The sounds at last became distinguishable as someone moving, throwing aside the blanket, and sitting up; this was apparent from the breathing, which now came from above. The straw rustled too.

"Well?" said the voice.

"The lieutenant said we weren't to light the candle except on orders, in an emergency," said a younger, diffident voice.

"Light the candle, I say, you little pipsqueak," the older voice shouted back.

He sat up now too, their heads were on the same level in the dark, their breathing was parallel.

The one who had first spoken irritably followed the movements of the other, who had tucked the candle away somewhere in his pack. His breathing relaxed when he eventually heard the sound of the matchbox.

The match flared up and there was light: a sparse yellow light.

Their eyes met. Invariably, as soon as there was enough light, their eyes met. Yet they knew one another so well, much too well. They almost hated each other, so familiar was each to each; they knew one another's very smell, the smell of every pore, so to speak, but still their eyes met, those of the older man and the younger. The younger one was pale and slight with a nondescript face, and the older one was pale and slight and unshaven with a nondescript face.

"Now, listen," said the older man, calmer now, "when are you ever going to learn that you don't do everything the lieutenants tell you?"

"He'll . . ." the younger one tried to begin.

"He won't do a thing," said the older one, in a sharper tone again and lighting a cigarette from the candle. "He'll keep his trap shut, and if he doesn't, and I don't happen to be around, then tell him to wait till I get back, it was me who lit the candle, understand? Do you understand?"

"Yessir."

"To hell with that Yessir crap, just Yes when you're talking to me. And undo your belt," he was shouting again now, "take that damn crappy belt off when you go to sleep."

The younger man looked at him nervously and took off his belt, placing it beside him in the straw.

"Roll your coat up into a pillow. That's right. OK . . . and now go to sleep, I'll wake you when it's time for you to die. . . ."

The younger man rolled onto his side and tried to sleep. All that was visible was the young brown hair, matted and untidy, a very thin neck, and the empty shoulders of his uniform tunic. The candle flickered gently, letting its meager light swing back and forth in the dark dugout like a great yellow butterfly uncertain where to settle.

The older man stayed as he was, knees drawn up, puffing out cigarette smoke at the ground in front of him. The ground was dark brown, here and there white blade marks showed where the spade had cut through a root or, a little closer to the surface, a tuber. The roof consisted of a few planks with a groundsheet thrown over them, and in the spaces between the planks the groundsheet sagged a little because the earth lying on top of it was heavy, heavy and wet. Outside, it was raining. The soft swish of steadily falling water sounded indescribably persistent, and the older man, still staring fixedly at the ground, now noticed a thin trickle of water oozing into the dugout under the roof. The tiny stream backed up slightly on encountering some loose earth, then flowed on past the obstacle until it reached the next one, which was the man's feet, and the ever-growing tide flowed all around the man's feet until his black boots lay in the water just like a peninsula. The man spat his cigarette butt into the puddle and lit another from the candle. In doing so he took the candle down from the edge of the dugout and placed it beside him on an ammunition case. The half where the younger man was lying was almost in darkness, reached now by the swaying light in brief spasms only, and these gradually subsided.

"Go to sleep, damn you," said the older man. "D'you hear? Go to sleep!"

"Yessir . . . yes," came the faint voice, obviously wider awake than before, when it had been dark.

"Hold on," said the older man, less harshly again. "A couple more cigarettes and then I'll put it out, and at least we'll drown in the dark."

He went on smoking, sometimes turning his head to the left, where the boy was lying, but he spat the second butt into the steadily growing puddle, lit the third, and still he could tell from the breathing beside him that the kid couldn't sleep.

He then took the spade, thrust it into the soft earth, and made a little mud wall behind the blanket forming the entrance. Behind this wall he heaped up a second layer of earth. With a spadeful of earth he covered the puddle at his feet. Outside, there was no sound save the gentle swish of the rain; little by little, the earth lying on top of the groundsheet had evidently become saturated, for water was now beginning to drip from above too.

"Oh shit," muttered the older man. "Are you asleep?"

"No."

The man spat the third cigarette butt over the mud wall and blew out the candle. He pulled up his blanket again, worked his feet into a comfortable position, and lay back with a sigh. It was quite silent and quite dark, and again the only sound was that aimless rustle of someone trying to get to sleep, and the swish of the rain, very gentle.

"Willi's been wounded," the boy's voice said suddenly, after a few minutes' silence. The voice was more awake than ever, in fact not even sleepy.

"What d'you mean?" asked the man in reply.

"Just that—wounded," came the younger voice, with something like triumph in it, pleased that it knew some important piece of news which the older voice obviously knew nothing about. "Wounded while he was shitting."

"You're nuts," said the man; then he gave another sigh and went on, "That's what I call a real break; I never heard of such luck. One day you come back from leave and the next day you get wounded while you're shitting. Is it serious?"

"No," said the boy with a laugh, "though actually it's not minor either. A bullet fracture, but in the arm."

"A bullet fracture in the arm! You come back from leave and while you're shitting you get wounded, a bullet fracture in the arm! What a break. . . . How did it happen?"

"When they went for water last evening," came the younger voice, quite animated now. "When they went for water, they were going down the hill at the back, carrying their water cans, and Willi told Sergeant Schubert, 'I've got to shit, Sergeant!' 'Nothing doing,' said the sergeant. But Willi couldn't hold on any longer so he just ran off, pulled down his pants, and bang! A grenade. And they actually had to pull up his pants for him. His left arm was wounded, and his right arm was holding it, so he ran off like that to get it bandaged, with his pants around his ankles.

They all laughed, everyone laughed, even Sergeant Schubert laughed." He added the last few words almost apologetically, as if to excuse his own laughter, because he was laughing now. . . .

But the older man wasn't laughing.

"Light!" he said with an oath. "Here, give me the matches, let's have some light!" He struck a match, cursing as it flared up. "At least I want some light, even if I don't get wounded. At least let's have some light, the least they can do is give us enough candles if they want to play war. Light! Light!" He was shouting again as he lit another cigarette.

The younger voice had sat up again and was poking around with a spoon in a greasy can held on his knees.

And there they sat, crouching side by side, without a word, in the yellow light.

The man smoked aggressively, and the boy was already looking somewhat greasy: his childish face smeared, bread crumbs sticking to his matted hair around most of his hairline.

The boy then proceeded to scrape out the grease can with a piece of bread.

All of a sudden there was silence: the rain had stopped. Neither of them moved, they looked at each other, the man with the cigarette in his hand, the boy holding the bread in his trembling fingers. It was uncannily quiet, they took a few breaths, and then heard rain still dripping somewhere from the groundsheet.

"Hell," said the older man. "D'you suppose the sentry's still there? I can't hear a thing."

The boy put the bread into his mouth and threw the can into the straw beside him.

"I don't know," said the boy. "They're going to let us know when it's our turn to relieve."

The older man got up quickly. He blew out the light, jammed on his steel helmet, and thrust aside the blanket. What came through the opening was not light. Just cool damp darkness. The man pinched out his cigarette and stuck his head outside.

"Hell," he muttered outside, "not a thing. Hey!" he called softly. Then his dark head reappeared inside, and he asked, "Where's the next dugout?"

The boy groped his way to his feet and stood next to the other man in the opening.

"Quiet!" said the man suddenly, in a sharp, low tone. "Something's crawling around out there."

They peered ahead. It was true: in the silent darkness there was a sound of someone crawling, and all of a sudden an unearthly snapping sound that made them both jump. It sounded as if someone had flung a live cat against the wall: the sound of breaking bones.

"Hell," muttered the older man, "there's something funny going on. Where's the sentry?"

"Over there," said the boy, groping in the dark for the other man's hand and lifting it toward the right. "Over there," he repeated. "That's where the dugout is too."

"Wait here," said the older man, "and better get your rifle, just in case."

Once again they heard that sickening snapping sound, then silence, and someone crawling.

The older man crept forward through the mud, occasionally halting and quietly listening, until after a few yards he finally heard a muffled voice; then he saw a faint gleam of light from the ground, felt around till he found the entrance, and called, "Hey, chum!"

The voice stopped, the light went out, a blanket was pushed aside, and a man's dark head came up out of the ground.

"What's up?"

"Where's the sentry?"

"Over there—right here."

"Where?"

"Hey there, Neuer! . . . Hey there!"

No answer: the crawling sound had stopped, all sound had stopped, there was only darkness out there, silent darkness. "God damn it, that's queer," said the voice of the man who had come up out of the ground. "Hey there! . . . That's funny, he was standing right here by the dugout, only a few feet away." He pulled himself up over the edge and stood beside the man who had called him.

"There was someone crawling around out there," said the man who had come across from the other dugout. "I know there was. The bastard's quiet now."

"Better have a look," said the man who had come up out of the ground. "Shall we take a look?"

"Hm, there certainly ought to be a sentry here."

"You fellows are next."

"I know, but . . ."

"Ssh!"

Once again they could hear someone crawling out there, perhaps twenty feet away.

"God damn it," said the man who had come up out of the ground, "you're right."

"Maybe someone still alive from last night, trying to crawl away."

"Or new ones."

"But what about the sentry, for God's sake?"

"Shall we go?"

"OK."

Both men instantly dropped to the ground and started to move forward, crawling through the mud. From down there, from a worm's-eye view, everything looked different. Every minutest elevation in the soil became a mountain range behind which, far off, something strange was visible: a slightly lighter darkness, the sky. Pistol in hand, they crawled on, yard by yard through the mud.

"God damn it," whispered the man who had come up out of the ground, "a Russki from last night."

His companion also soon bumped into a corpse, a mute, leaden bundle. Suddenly they were silent, holding their breath: there was that cracking sound again, quite close, as if someone had been given a terrific wallop on the jaw. Then they heard someone panting.

"Hey," called the man who had come up out of the ground, "who's there?"

The call silenced all sound, the very air seemed to hold its breath, until a quavering voice spoke, "It's me. . . ."

"God damn it, what the hell are you doing out there, you old asshole, driving us all nuts?" shouted the man who had come up out of the ground.

"I'm looking for something," came the voice again.

The two men had got to their feet and now walked over to the spot where the voice was coming from the ground.

"I'm looking for a pair of shoes," said the voice, but now they were standing next to him. Their eyes had become accustomed to the dark, and they could see corpses lying all around, ten or a dozen, lying there like logs, black and motionless, and the sentry was squatting beside one of these logs, fumbling around its feet.

"Your job's to stick to your post," said the man who had come up out of the ground.

The other man, the one who had summoned him out of the ground, dropped like a stone and bent over the dead man's face. The man who had been squatting suddenly covered his face with his hands and began whimpering like a cowed animal.

"Oh no," said the man who had summoned the other out of the ground, adding in an undertone, "I guess you need teeth too, eh? Gold teeth, eh?"

"What's that?" asked the man who had come up out of the ground, while at his feet the cringing figure whimpered louder than ever.

"Oh no," said the first man again, and the weight of the world seemed to be lying on his breast.

"Teeth?" asked the man who had come up out of the ground, whereupon he threw himself down beside the cringing figure and ripped a cloth bag from his hand.

"Oh no!" the cringing figure cried too, and every extremity of human terror was expressed in this cry.

The man who had summoned the other out of the ground turned away, for the man who had come up out of the ground had placed his pistol against the cringing figure's head, and he pressed the trigger.

"Teeth," he muttered, as the sound of the shot died away. "Gold teeth."

They walked slowly back, stepping very carefully as long as they were in the area where the dead lay.

"You fellows are on now," said the man who had come up out of the ground, before vanishing into the ground again.

"Right," was all the other man said, and he too crawled slowly back through the mud before vanishing into the ground again.

He could tell at once that the boy was still awake; there was that aimless rustle of someone trying to get to sleep.

"Light the candle," he said quietly.

The yellow flame leaped up again, feebly illumining the little hole.

"What happened?" asked the boy in alarm, catching sight of the older man's face.

"The sentry's gone; you'll have to replace him."

"Yes," said the youngster. "Give me the watch, will you, so I can wake the others."

"Here."

The older man squatted down on his straw and lit a cigarette, watching thoughtfully as the boy buckled on his belt, pulled on his coat, defused a hand grenade, and then wearily checked his machine pistol for ammunition.

"Right," said the boy finally. "So long, now."

"So long," said the man, and he blew out the candle and lay in total darkness all alone in the ground. . . .

The Train
Was on Time

As they walked through the dark underpass, they could hear the train rumbling up to the platform overhead, and the resounding voice came smoothly over the loudspeaker: "The troop train now arriving from Paris will depart for Przemyśl via . . ."

Then they had climbed the steps to the platform and were standing by the leave train from which beaming soldiers were emerging, weighed down with huge packages. The platform quickly emptied, it was the usual scene. At some of the windows stood girls or women or a very silent, grim-faced father . . . and the resounding voice was telling people to hurry. The train was on time.

"Why don't you get on?" the chaplain asked the soldier anxiously.

"Get on?" asked the soldier, amazed. "Why, I might want to hurl myself under the wheels, I might want to desert . . . eh? What's the hurry? I might go crazy, I've a perfect right to, I've a perfect right to go crazy. I don't want to die, that's what's so horrible—that I don't want to die." His voice was cold and hard, as if the words were pouring from his lips like ice. "Don't say any more! I'll get on all right, there's always a spot somewhere . . . yes . . . yes, don't mind me, pray for me!" He grasped his pack, boarded the train through the nearest door, let down the window from inside, and leaned out, while overhead the resounding voice hung like a cloud of mucus: "The train is now leaving. . . ."

"I don't want to die!" he shouted. "I don't want to die, but the terrible thing is that I'm going to die—soon!" The black figure on that cold gray platform retreated farther and farther into the distance . . . farther and farther, until the station was swallowed up by night.

Now and again what appears to be a casually spoken word will suddenly acquire a cabalistic significance. It becomes charged and strangely swift, races ahead of the speaker, is destined to throw open a chamber in the uncertain confines of the future and to return to him with the deadly accuracy of a boomerang. Out of the small talk of unreflecting speech, usually from among those halting, colorless good-byes exchanged beside trains on their way to death, it falls back on the speaker like a leaden wave, and he becomes aware of the force, both frightening and intoxicating, of the workings of fate. To lovers and soldiers, to men marked for death and to those filled with the cosmic force of life, this power is sometimes given, without warning; a sudden revelation is conferred on them, a bounty and a burden . . . and the word sinks, sinks down inside them.

As Andreas was slowly groping his way back into the center of the car, the word "soon" entered him like a bullet, painlessly and almost imperceptibly penetrating flesh, tissue, cells, nerves, until at some point it caught, like a barbed hook, exploded, and ripped open a savage wound, making blood pour out . . . life, pain. . . .

Soon, he thought, and felt himself turning pale. At the same time he did all the usual things, almost unconsciously. He struck a match, lighting up the heaps of sitting, stretched-out, sleeping soldiers who lay around, across, under, and on top of their luggage. The smell of stale tobacco smoke was mixed with the smell of stale sweat and that strangely gritty dirt that clings to all soldiers in the mass. The flame of the dying matchstick flared up with a final hiss, and in that last glow he saw, over by the narrowing corridor, a small empty space. He carefully picked his way toward it, his bundle tucked under one arm, his cap in his hand.

Soon, he thought, and the shock of fear lay deep, deep. Fear and absolute certainty. Never again, he thought, never again will I see this station, never again the face of my friend, the man I abused right up to the last moment . . . never again. Soon! He reached the empty space, set his pack carefully on the floor in order not to wake the sleeping men around him, and sat down on it so he could lean back against a compartment door. Then he tried to arrange his legs as comfortably as possible; he stretched the left one carefully past the face of one sleeping soldier, and placed the right one across a piece of luggage that was shielding the back of another. In the compartment behind him a match flared up, and someone began to smoke silently in the dark. By turning slightly to one side he could see the glowing tip of the cigarette; and sometimes, when the unknown man drew on it, the reflection spread over an unfamiliar soldier's face, gray and tired, with bitter creases in it, starkly and terribly sober.

Soon, he thought. The rattle of the train, it was all so familiar. The smell, the desire to smoke, the feeling he had to smoke. The last thing he wanted to do was sleep. The somber outlines of the city moved past the window. Somewhere in the distance searchlights were raking the sky, like long spectral fingers parting the blue cloak of the night . . . from far away came the firing of antiaircraft guns . . . and those darkened, mute, somber houses. When would this Soon be? The blood flowed out of his heart, flowed back into his heart, circling, circling, life was circling, and all this pulse beat said was: Soon! He could no longer say, no longer even think: I don't want to die. As often as he tried to form the sentence, he thought: I'm going to die . . . soon.

Behind him a second gray face now showed up in the glow of a cigarette, and he could hear a subdued, weary murmuring. The two unknown men were talking.

"Dresden," said one voice.

"Dortmund," the other.

The murmuring continued, became more animated. Then another voice swore, and the murmuring subsided again; it petered out, and again there was only one cigarette behind him. It was the second cigarette, and finally this one went out too, and again there was this gray darkness behind and beside him, and facing him the black night with the countless houses, all mute, all black. Only in the distance those silent, uncannily long, spectral fingers of the searchlights, still groping across the sky. It seemed as if the faces belonging to those fingers must be grinning, eerily grinning, cynically grinning like the faces of usurers and swindlers. "We'll get you," said the thin-lipped, gaping mouths belonging to those fingers. "We'll get you, we'll grope all night long." Maybe they were looking for a bedbug, a tiny bug in the cloak of the night, those fingers, and they would find the bug. . . .

Soon. Soon. Soon. Soon. When is Soon? What a terrible word: Soon. Soon can mean in one second, Soon can mean in one year. Soon is a terrible word. This Soon compresses the future, shrinks it, offers no certainty, no certainty whatever, it stands for absolute uncertainty. Soon is nothing and Soon is a lot. Soon is everything. Soon is death. . . .

Soon I shall be dead. I shall die, soon. You have said so yourself, and someone inside you and someone outside you has told you that this Soon will be fulfilled. One thing is sure, this Soon will be in wartime. That's a certainty, that's a fact.

How much longer will the war go on?

It can last for another year before everything finally collapses in the East, and if the Americans in the West don't attack, or the British, then it will go on for another two years before the Russians reach the Atlantic. They will attack, though. But all in all it will last another year at the very least, the war won't be over before the end of 1944. The way this whole apparatus is built up, it's too obedient, too cowardly, too docile. So I may still have anything from one second to one year. How many seconds are there in a year? Soon I'm going to die, before the war is over. I shan't ever know peacetime again. No more peacetime. There'll be no more of anything, no music . . . no flowers . . . no poetry . . . no more human joy; soon I'm going to die.

This Soon is like a thunderclap. This little word is like the spark that sets off the thunderstorm, and suddenly, for the thousandth part of a second, the whole world is bright beneath this word.

The smell of bodies is the same as ever. The smell of dirt and dust and boot polish. Funny, wherever there are soldiers there's dirt. The spectral fingers had found the bug. . . .

He lit a fresh cigarette. I'll try to picture the future, he thought. Maybe it's an illusion, this Soon, maybe I'm overtired, maybe it's tension or nerves. He tried to imagine what he would do when the war was over. He would . . . he would . . . But there was a wall he couldn't get over, a totally black wall. He couldn't imagine anything. Of course he could force himself to complete the sentence in his mind: I'll go to university . . . I'll take a room somewhere . . . with books, cigarettes . . . go to university . . . music . . . poetry . . . flowers. But even as he forced himself to complete the sentence in his mind, he knew it wouldn't happen. None of it would happen. Those aren't dreams, those are pale, colorless thoughts devoid of weight, blood, all human substance. The future has no face now, it is cut off somewhere; and the more he thought about it, the more he realized how close he was to this Soon. Soon I'm going to die, that's a certainty that lies between one year and one second. There are no more dreams. . . .

Soon. Maybe two months. He tried to imagine it in terms of time, to discover whether the wall rose this side of the next two months, that wall he would not be going beyond. Two months, that meant the end of November. But he couldn't grasp it in terms of time. Two months: an image that has no power. He might just as well say: three months or four months or six, the image evokes no echo. January, he thought. But the wall isn't there at all. A strange, unquiet hope awakens: May, he thought with a sudden leap ahead. Nothing. The wall is silent. There's no wall anywhere. There's nothing. This Soon . . . this Soon is only a frightening bogey. November, he thought. Nothing! A fierce, terrible joy springs to life. January: January of next year, a year and a half away—a year and a half of life! Nothing! No wall!

He sighed with relief and went on thinking, his thoughts now racing across time as over light, very low hurdles. January, May, December! Nothing! And suddenly he was aware that he was groping in a void. The place where the wall rose up couldn't be grasped in terms of time. Time was irrelevant. Time had ceased to exist. And yet hope still remained. He had leaped so splendidly over the months. Years . . .

Soon I'm going to die, and he felt like a swimmer who knows he is near the shore and finds himself suddenly flung back into the tide by the surf. Soon! That's where the wall is, the wall beyond which he will cease to exist, will cease to be on this earth.

Krakow, he thought suddenly, and his heart missed a beat as if an artery had twisted itself into a knot, blocking off the blood. He is on the right track—Krakow! Nothing! Farther. Przemyśl! Nothing! Lvov! Nothing! Then he starts racing: Cernăuți, Jassy, Kishinev, Nikopol! But at the last name he already senses that this is only make-believe, make-believe like the thought: I'll go to the university. Never again, never again will he see Nikopol! Back to Jassy. No, he won't see Jassy again either. He won't see Cernăuți again. Lvov! Lvov he'll see again, Lvov he'll reach alive! I'm mad, he thought, I'm out of my mind, this means I'll die between Lvov and Cernăuți! What a crazy idea. . . . He forced himself to switch off his thoughts and started smoking again and staring into the face of the night. I'm hysterical, I'm crazy, I've been smoking too much, talking, talking for nights on end, days on end, with no sleep, no food, just smoking, it's enough to make anyone lose his mind. . . .

I must have something to eat, he thought, something to drink. Food and drink keep body and soul together. This damn smoking all the time! He started fumbling with his pack, but while he peered toward his feet in the dark, trying to find the buckle, and then began rummaging around in his pack where sandwiches and underwear, tobacco, cigarettes, and a bottle of schnapps all lay in a heap, he became aware of a leaden, implacable fatigue that clogged his veins. . . . He fell asleep . . . his hands on the open pack, one leg—the left—next to a face he had never seen, one leg—the right—across someone's luggage, and with his tired and by now dirty hands resting on his pack he fell asleep, his head on his chest. . . .

He was awakened by someone treading on his fingers. A stab of pain, he opened his eyes; someone had passed by in a hurry, bumped him in the back and trodden on his hands. He saw it was daylight and heard another resounding voice hospitably announcing a station name, and he realized it was Dortmund. The man who had spent the night behind him smoking and murmuring was getting out, cursing as he barged along the corridor; for that unknown gray face, this was home. Dortmund. The man next to him, the one whose luggage his right leg had been resting on, was awake and sat up on the cold floor of the corridor, rubbing his eyes. The man on the left, whose face his left foot was resting against, was still asleep. Dortmund. Girls carrying steaming pots of coffee were hurrying up and down the platform. The same as ever. Women were standing around weeping; girls being kissed, fathers . . . it was all so familiar: he must be crazy.

But, to tell the truth, all he knew was that the instant he opened his eyes he knew that Soon was still there. Deep within him the little barb had drawn blood, it had caught and would never let go now. This Soon had grabbed him like a hook, and he was going to squirm on it, squirm until he was between Lvov and Cernăuți. . . .

Like lightning, in the millionth part of a second it took him to wake up, came the hope that this Soon would have disappeared, like the night, a bogey in the wake of endless talking and endless smoking. But it was still there, implacably there. . . .

He sat up, his eye fell on his pack, still half open, and he stuffed back a shirt that had slipped out. The man on his right had let down a window and was holding out a mug into which a thin, tired girl was pouring coffee. The smell of the coffee was horrible, thin steam that made him feel queasy; it was the smell of barracks, of army cookhouses, a smell that had spread all over Europe—and that was meant to spread all over the world. And yet (so deep are the roots of habit) and yet he also held out his mug for the girl to fill; the gray coffee that was as gray as a uniform. He could smell the stale exhalation from the girl; she must have slept in her clothes, gone from train to train during the night, lugging coffee, lugging coffee. . . .

She smelled penetratingly of that vile coffee. Perhaps she slept right up close to the coffeepot as it stood on a stove to keep hot, slept until the next train arrived. Her skin was gray and rough like dirty milk, and wisps of her scanty, pale-black hair crept out from under a little cap, but her eyes were soft and sad, and when she bent over to fill his mug, he saw the charming nape of her neck. What a pretty girl, he thought: everyone will think she's ugly, and she's pretty, she's beautiful . . . she has delicate little fingers too. . . . I could spend hours watching her pour my coffee; if only the mug had a hole, if only she would pour and pour, I would see her soft eyes and that charming nape, and if only that resounding voice would shut up. Everything bad comes from those resounding voices; those resounding voices started the war, and those resounding voices regulate the worst war of all, the war at railroad stations.

To hell with all resounding voices!

The man in the red cap was waiting obediently for the resounding voice that had to say its piece, then the train got under way, lighter by a few heroes, richer by a few heroes. It was daylight but still early: seven o'clock. Never again, never ever again will I pass through Dortmund. How strange, a city like Dortmund; I've passed through it often and have never been in the town itself. Never ever will I know what Dortmund is like, and never ever again will I see this girl with the coffeepot. Never again; soon I'm going to die, between Lvov and Cernăuți. My life is now nothing but a specific number of miles, a section of railway line. But that's odd, there's no front between Lvov and Cernăuți, and not many partisans either. Or has there been some glorious great cave-in along the front overnight? Is the war suddenly, quite suddenly, over? Will peace come before this Soon? Some kind of disaster? Maybe the divine beast is dead, assassinated at last, or the Russians have launched an attack on all fronts and swept everything before them as far as between Lvov and Cernăuți, and capitulation. . . .

There was no escape; the sleeping men had woken up, they were beginning to eat, drink, chat. . . .

He leaned against the open window and let the chill morning wind beat against his face. I'll get drunk, he thought, I'll knock back a whole bottle, then I won't know a thing, then I'll be safe at least as far as Breslau. He bent down, hurriedly opened his pack, but an invisible hand restrained him from grasping the bottle. He took out a sandwich and quietly and slowly began to chew. How terrible, to have to eat just before one's death. Soon I'm going to die, yet I still have to eat. Slices of bread and sausage, air-raid sandwiches packed for him by his friend the chaplain, a whole package of sandwiches with plenty of sausage in them, and the terrible thing was that they tasted so good.

He leaned against the open window, quietly eating and chewing, from time to time reaching down into his open pack for another sandwich. Between mouthfuls he sipped the lukewarm coffee.

It was terrible to look into the drab houses where the slaves were getting ready to march off to their factories. House after house, house after house, and everywhere lived people who suffered, who laughed, people who ate and drank and begat new human beings, people who tomorrow might be dead; the place was teeming with human life. Old women and children, men, and soldiers too. Soldiers were standing at windows, one here, one there, and each man knew when he would be on the train again, traveling back to hell. . . .

"Hey there, bud," said a husky voice behind him, "want to join us in a little game?" He swung round. "Yes!" he said without thinking, at the same time catching sight of a deck of cards in a soldier's hand: the soldier, who was grinning at him, needed a shave. I said Yes, he thought, so he nodded and followed the soldier. The corridor was deserted except for two men who had taken themselves off with their luggage to the vestibule, where one of them, a tall fellow with blond hair and slack features, was sitting on the floor, grinning.

"Find anybody?"

"Yes," said the unshaven soldier in his husky voice.

Soon I'm going to die, thought Andreas, squatting down on his pack, which he had brought along. Each time he put down the pack his steel helmet rattled, and now the sight of the steel helmet reminded him that he had forgotten his rifle. My rifle, he thought, it's standing propped up in Paul's closet behind his raincoat. He smiled. "That's right, buddy," said the blond fellow. "Forget your troubles and join the game."

The two men had made themselves very snug. They were sitting by a door, but the door was barricaded, the handle tightly secured with wire, and luggage had been stacked up in front of it. The unshaven soldier took a pair of pliers out of his pocket—he was wearing regular blue work pants —he took out the pliers, fished out a roll of wire from somewhere under the luggage, and began to wind fresh wire still more tightly around the door handle.

"That's right, buddy," said the blond fellow. "They can kiss our arses till we get to Przemyśl. You're going that far, aren't you? I see you are," he said when Andreas nodded.

Andreas soon realized they were drunk; the unshaven soldier had a whole battery of bottles in his carton, and he passed the bottles around. First they played blackjack. The train rattled, daylight grew stronger, and they stopped at stations with resounding voices and stations without resounding voices. It filled up and emptied, filled up and emptied, and all the time the three men stayed in their corner playing cards.

Sometimes, at a station, someone outside would rattle furiously at the locked door and swear, but they would only laugh and go on with their game and throw the empty bottles out of the window. Andreas didn't think about the game at all; these games of chance were so wonderfully simple there was no need to think, your mind could be somewhere else. . . .

Paul would be up by now, if he had slept at all. Maybe there had been another air-raid alarm and he hadn't had any sleep. If he had slept, then it could only have been for a few hours. He must have got home at four. Now it was almost ten. So he had slept till eight, then got up, washed, read Mass, prayed for me. He prayed for me to be happy because I had denied human happiness.

"Pass!" he said. Marvelous—you just said "Pass!" and had time to think. . . .

Then he would have gone home and smoked cigarette butts in his pipe, had a bite to eat, some air-raid sandwiches, and gone off again. Someplace or other. Maybe to a girl having an illegitimate baby by a soldier, maybe to a mother, or maybe to the black market to buy a few cigarettes.

"Flush," he said.

He had won again. The money in his pocket made quite a packet now.

"You're a lucky bastard," said the soldier who needed a shave. "Drink up, my friends!" He passed the bottle around again, he was sweating, and beneath the mask of coarse joviality his face was very sad and preoccupied. He shuffled the cards. . . . A good thing I don't have to shuffle them. I need one more minute to think about Paul, to concentrate on Paul, tired and pale; now he's walking through the ruins and praying, all the time. I gave him hell, you should never give anyone hell, not even a sergeant. . . .

"Three of a kind," he said, "and a pair." He had won again.

The other men laughed; they didn't care about the money, all they wanted was to kill time. What a laborious, frightful business it was, this killing time, over and over again that little second hand racing invisibly beyond the horizon, over and over again you threw a heavy dark sack over it, in the certain knowledge that the little hand went racing on, relentlessly on and on. . . .

"Nordhausen!" proclaimed a resounding voice. "Nordhausen!" The voice announced the name of the station just as he was shuffling the cards. "Troop train now departing for Przemyśl via . . ." and then it said, "All aboard and close the doors!" How normal it all was. He slowly dealt the cards. It was already close on eleven. They were still drinking schnapps; the schnapps was good. He made a few complimentary remarks about the schnapps to the soldier who needed a shave. The train had filled up again. They had very little room now, and quite a few of the men were looking at them. It had become uncomfortable, and it was impossible to avoid overhearing the men's chatter.

"Pass," he said. The blond fellow and the unshaven soldier were sparring good-naturedly for the kitty. They knew they were both bluffing, but they both laughed: the point was to see who could bluff best.

"Practically speaking," said a North German voice behind him, "practically speaking we've already won the war!"

"Hm," came another voice.

"As if the Führer could lose a war!" said a third voice. "It's crazy to say such a thing anyway: winning a war! Anyone who talks about winning a war must already be considering the possibility of losing one. Once we start a war, that war is won."

"The Crimea's already cut off," said a fourth voice. "The Russians have closed it off at Perekop."

"That's where I'm being sent," said a faint voice, "to the Crimea. . . ."

"Only by plane, though," came the confident voice of the war winner. "It's great by plane. . . ."

"The Tommies won't risk it."

The silence of those who said nothing was terrible. It was the silence of those who don't forget, of those who know they are done for.

The blond fellow had shuffled, and the unshaven soldier opened with fifty marks.

Andreas saw he was holding a royal flush.

"And fifty," he said, laughing.

"I'm in," said the unshaven soldier.

"Raise twenty."

"I'm in."

Needless to say, the unshaven soldier lost.

"Two hundred and forty marks," said a voice behind them, accompanied, as the sound of the voice indicated, by a shake of the head. It had been quiet for a minute while they had been battling for the kitty. Then the chatter started up again.

"Have a drink," said the unshaven soldier.

"This door business is crazy, I tell you!"

"What door?"

"They've barricaded the door, those bastards, those scabs!"

"Shut up!"

A station without a resounding voice. God bless stations without resounding voices. The buzzing chatter of the other men went on, they had forgotten about the door and the two hundred and forty marks, and Andreas gradually began to realize he was a bit drunk.

"Shouldn't we have a break?" he said. "I'd like a bite to eat."

"No!" shouted the unshaven soldier. "Not on your life. We'll carry on till we get to Przemyśl! No!" His voice was filled with a terrible fear. The blond fellow yawned and began muttering. "No," shouted the unshaven soldier. . . .

They went on playing.

"The 42 MG is all we need to win the war. The others have nothing like it. . . ."

"The Führer knows what he's doing!"

But the silence of those who said nothing, nothing at all, was terrible. It was the silence of those who knew they were all done for.

At times the train got so full they could hardly hold their cards. All three were drunk by now, but very clear in the head. Then the train would empty again, there were loud voices, resounding and unresounding. Railroad stations. The day wore on to afternoon. From time to time they would pause for a snack, then go on playing, go on drinking. The schnapps was excellent.

"Well, it's French, after all," said the soldier who needed a shave. He seemed to need one more than ever now. His face was pallid under the black stubble. His eyes were red, he hardly ever won, but he appeared to have a vast supply of money. Now the blond fellow was winning often. They were playing chemin-de-fer, the train being empty again; then they played rummy, and suddenly the cards fell from the unshaven soldier's hand; he slumped forward and began to snore horribly. The blond fellow straightened him, gently arranging him so that he could sleep propped up. They put something over his feet, and Andreas returned his winnings to the man's pocket.

How gently and tenderly the blond fellow treats his friend! I'd never have expected it of that slob.

I wonder what Paul's doing now?

They got to their feet and stretched, shook crumbs and dirt from their laps, and cigarette ash, and flung the last empty bottle out of the window.

They were traveling through an empty countryside, to the left and right glorious gardens, gentle hills, smiling clouds—an autumn afternoon. Soon, soon I'm going to die. Between Lvov and Cernăuți. During the card game he had tried to pray, but he kept having to think about it; he had tried again to form sentences in the future and realized they had no force. He had tried again to grasp it in terms of time—it was make-believe, idle make-believe! But he had only to think of the word "Przemyśl" to know he was on the right track. Lvov! His heart missed a beat. Cernăuți! Nothing . . . it must be somewhere in between . . . he couldn't visualize it, he had no mental picture of the map. "D'you have a map?" he asked the blond fellow, who was looking out of the window.

"No," he said amiably, "but he does!" He pointed to the soldier who needed a shave. "He has a map. How restless he is. He's got something on his mind. That's a fellow with something terrible on his mind, I tell you. . . ."

Andreas said nothing and looked over the man's shoulder through the window. "Radebeul!" said a resounding Saxon voice. A decent voice, a good voice, a German voice, a voice that might just as well be saying: The next ten thousand into the slaughterhouse, please. . . .

It was wonderful outside, still almost like summer, September weather. Soon I'm going to die, I'll never see that tree again, that russet tree over there by the green house. I'll never see that girl wheeling her bike again, the girl in the yellow dress with the black hair. These things the train's racing past, I'll never see any of them again. . . .

The blond fellow was asleep now too, he had sat down on the floor beside his pal, and in sleep they had sunk against one another; the snores of one were harsh and loud, of the other soft and whistling. The corridor was deserted except for now and again someone going to the john, and occasionally someone would say, "There's room inside, you know, buddy." But it was much nicer in the corridor, in the corridor you were more alone, and now that both the others were asleep he was quite alone; it had been a terrific idea to secure the door with wire.

Everything the train's leaving behind I'm leaving behind too, once and for all, he thought. I'll never see any more of this again, never again this segment of sky full of soft gray-blue clouds, never again this little fly, a very young one, perched on the window frame and flying off now, off to somewhere in Radebeul; that little fly will stay in Radebeul, I guess . . . stay behind under this segment of sky, that little fly will never keep me company between Lvov and Cernăuți. The fly is on its way to Radebeul, maybe it's flying into some kitchen heavy with the odor of potatoes boiled in their jackets and the acrid smell of cheap vinegar, where they're making potato salad for some soldier who's now free to suffer for three weeks through the alleged joys of home leave . . . that's all I'll ever see, he thought, for at that moment the train swung in a great loop and was coming into Dresden.

At Dresden the platform was very full, and at Dresden many men got out. The window faced a whole cluster of soldiers headed by a stout, red-faced young lieutenant. The soldiers were all dressed up in brand-new uniforms, the lieutenant was also in his brand-new hand-me-downs for the doomed; even the decorations on his chest were as new as freshly cast lead soldiers, they looked like complete fakes. The lieutenant grasped the door handle and rattled it.

"Open up there!" he shouted at Andreas.

"The door's closed, it won't open," Andreas shouted back.

"Don't shout at me, open up, open up at once!"

Andreas shut his mouth and glowered at the lieutenant. I'm soon going to die, he thought, and he's shouting at me. His gaze went beyond the lieutenant; the soldiers standing with the lieutenant grinned behind his back. At least the faces of these men were not new, they had old, gray, knowing faces, only their uniforms were new, and even their decorations seemed old and worn. Only the lieutenant was new from top to toe, he even had a brand-new face. His cheeks became redder still, and his blue eyes went a bit red too. Now he lowered his voice, and it was so soft, with such a soft threat in it, that Andreas had to laugh. "Are you going to open the door?" he asked. Rage was exploding from his shiny buttons. "Look at me at least!" he roared at Andreas. But Andreas did not look at him. I'm going to die soon, he thought; all these people standing around on the platform, I'll never see any of them again, not one. And he wouldn't smell that smell again either, that smell of dust and railroad smoke, here at his window saturated with the smell of the lieutenant's brand-new uniform that smelled of synthetic wool.

"I'll have you arrested," roared the lieutenant. "I'll report you to the military police!"

Luckily the blond fellow had woken up. He came to the window, sleepy-eyed, stood impeccably at attention, and said to the lieutenant, "Regret to report, sir, that the door was sealed off on the station side on account of its being defective: to prevent accidents." He delivered this in the regulation manner, briskly and submissively; it was marvelous the way he spoke, like a clock striking twelve. The lieutenant let out one more furious sigh. "Why didn't you say so?" he yelled at Andreas.

"Regret to report further, sir, that my companion is deaf, stone deaf," the blond fellow rattled off. "Head wound." The soldiers behind the lieutenant laughed, and the lieutenant turned beet-red, swung round, and went on to look for space somewhere else. The bevy of men followed him. "Stupid bastard," muttered the blond fellow after him.

I could get out here, thought Andreas as he watched the lively bustle on the platform. I could get out here, go off someplace, anyplace, on and on, till they caught me and put me up against a wall, and I wouldn't die between Lvov and Cernăuţi, I would be shot in some little village in Saxony or die like a dog in a concentration camp. But I'm standing here by the window and I feel as if I were made of lead. I can't move, I feel paralyzed, this train is part of me and I'm part of the train, this train that has to carry me to my appointed end, and the strange part about it is that I have absolutely no desire to get out here and stroll along the banks of the Elbe under those nice trees. I long for Poland, I long for that horizon as intensely, as fiercely and ardently, as only a lover can long for his beloved. If only the train would move, if only it would get going! Why is it standing here, why is it standing so long in this godforsaken Saxony, why has the resounding voice been silent for so long? I'm bursting with impatience. I'm not scared, that's the strange thing, I'm not scared, just indescribably curious and restless. And yet I don't want to die. I want to live, theoretically life is beautiful, theoretically life is glorious, and I don't want to get out, it's funny to think I could get out. I need only walk along the corridor, leave my useless pack behind and clear out, anywhere, stroll under the trees with their fall coloring, and I go on standing here as if I were made of lead; I want to stay on this train, I have a terrible longing for the gray drabness of Poland and for that unknown stretch between Lvov and Cernăuți where I have to die.

Shortly after Dresden the unshaven soldier woke too. His face was ashen under the stubble, and his eyes sadder than ever. Without a word he opened a can and began eating the meat inside, spearing lumps of it onto his fork; with it he ate some bread. His hands were dirty, and from time to time scraps of meat would fall to the floor, the floor where he would be sleeping again tonight, with its litter of cigarette butts and that accumulation of impersonal grime which every soldier seems to attract like a magnet. The blond fellow was eating too.

Andreas stood at the window and saw nothing; it was light outside and the sunshine still mild, but he saw nothing. His thoughts were seething as the train sped by the pleasant garden suburbs around Dresden. He waited impatiently for his unshaven friend to finish his meal so that he could ask him for the map. He had no idea what it was like between Lvov and Cernăuți. Nikopol he could imagine, even Lvov and Przemyśl . . . Odessa and Nikolayev . . . and Kerch, but Cernăuți was only a name; it made him think of Jews and onions, of gray streets with flat-roofed houses, wide streets, and traces of administration buildings of the old Austrian Empire, neglected gardens around crumbling imperial façades that might now be sheltering hospitals or first-aid posts; and those boulevards of Eastern Europe with their brooding charm, their squat trees, cropped to prevent the flat-roofed houses from being crushed by treetops. No treetops. . . .

That's what Cernăuți would be like, but what came first, what came between Lvov and Cernăuți, was something he couldn't picture at all. It must be Galicia, Lvov being the capital of Galicia. And somewhere there was Volhynia—all dark, somber names smelling of pogroms and vast gloomy estates where brooding women dreamed of adultery since they had begun to find their blubber-necked husbands repulsive. . . .

Galicia, a dark word, a terrible word, and yet a splendid word. It sounded something like a knife cutting very quietly . . . Galicia. . . .

Lvov is all right, Lvov he can visualize. Splendid and gloomy and without lightness, those cities, with bloody pasts and untamed back streets, silent and untamed.

The soldier who needed a shave threw his can out of the window, returned the loaf, from which he had been biting off mouthfuls, to his pack, and lit a cigarette. His face was sad, sad, full of remorse somehow, as if he were ashamed of the orgy of cards and boozing; he joined Andreas at the window, leaning his elbows on it, and Andreas sensed that he wanted to talk.

"Look at that, a factory," he said, "a chair factory."

"Yes," said Andreas. He saw nothing, nor did he want to see anything, only the map. "Might I," he made a great effort, "might I have a look at the map?"

"What map?" Andreas felt a deep stab of fear and knew he turned pale. Supposing this fellow didn't have any map?

"The map of Poland," he stammered, "the map of where we're going."

"Oh, that one," said the man. He bent down at once, fumbled in his pack, and handed Andreas the folded map.

It was horrible to have the man leaning over the map with him. Andreas could smell the canned meat on his breath, which was still not quite free of the odor of digested, partially acidulated schnapps. He could smell the sweat and grime and was too wrought up to see anything; then he saw the man's finger, a thick, red, dirty, yet very good-natured finger, and the man said, "That's where I have to go." Andreas read the name of the place: "Kolomyya." Strange, now that he looked closer he could see that Lvov was not far at all from this Kolomyya . . . he went back . . . Stanislav, Lvov . . . Lvov . . . Stanislav, Kolomyya, Cernăuţi. Strange, he thought; Stanislav, Kolomyya . . . these names evoked no definite echo. That voice inside him, that wakeful, sensitive voice, oscillated and trembled like a compass needle that cannot settle. Kolomyya, shall I get as far as Kolomyya? Nothing definite . . . a strange wavering of the ever-vibrating needle . . . Stanislav? The same quivering. Nikopol! he thought suddenly. Nothing.

"Yes," said the man, "that's where my unit is. Repair depot. I'm lucky." But it sounded as if he really meant: I'm having a terrible time.

Funny, thought Andreas. I had imagined there would be a plain in that area, a green patch with a few black dots, but the map is whitish-yellow there. Foothills of the Carpathians, he thought suddenly, and in his mind's eye he instantly saw his school, all of it, the corridors and the bust of Cicero and the narrow playground squeezed in between tenements, and in summertime the women leaning out of the windows in their bras, and the janitor's room downstairs where you could get a mug of cocoa, and the big storeroom, dry as a bone, where they used to go for a quick smoke during recess. Foothills of the Carpathians. . . .

Now the man's finger was lying farther to the southeast. "Kherson," he said, "that's where we were last, and now we're moving farther back, probably as far as Lvov or right into the Hungarian Carpathians. The front's collapsing in Nikopol—I guess you heard that on the news, eh? They're wading through the mud, a retreat through mud! Must be a madhouse, all the vehicles get stuck, and when three happen to get stuck one behind the other everything on the road behind them has had it, there's no going back and no going forward, and they blow up the lot . . . they blow up the lot, and everyone has to foot-slog it, the generals too, I hope. But I bet they get flown out. . . . They ought to go on foot, on foot like the Führer's beloved infantry. Are you with the infantry?"

"Yes," said Andreas. He had not taken in much. His gaze was resting almost tenderly on this section of the map, it was yellowish-white with only four black dots, one big fat one: Lvov, and one slightly smaller: Cernăuţi, and two very little ones: Kolomyya and Stanislav.

"Let me keep the map," he said huskily, "let me keep it," without looking at the other man. He could not bear to part with the map, and he trembled at the thought that the man might say no. Many people are like that, an object suddenly becomes valuable to them because someone else would like to have it. An object that the very next moment they might throw away becomes precious and valuable and they wouldn't dream of selling it, just because someone else would like to own it and use it.

Many people are like that, but the unshaven soldier wasn't.

"Sure," he said, surprised, "it's not worth anything. Twenty pfennigs. Besides, it's an old one. Where're you heading for, anyway?"

"Nikopol," said Andreas, and again he was aware of that appalling void as he uttered the word, he felt as if he had cheated his companion. He dared not look at him.

"Well, by the time you get down there, Nikopol will be gone; maybe Kishinev—that's as far as you'll get."

"Think so?" Andreas asked. Kishinev didn't mean anything to him either.

"Sure. Maybe even Kolomyya." The man laughed. "How long will it take you to get down there? Let's see. Tomorrow morning Breslau. Tomorrow night Przemyśl. Thursday, Friday night, maybe sooner. Then Lvov. Let's see, Saturday evening I'll be in Kolomyya; you'll need a few days longer, another week if you're smart—in a week they'll have left Nikopol, in a week Nikopol will be gone for good as far as we're concerned."

Saturday, Andreas thought. Saturday feels quite safe, no emptiness there. Saturday I'll still be alive. He hadn't dared think that close. Now he understood why his heart had been silent when he thought in months, let alone years. That had been a leap, far far beyond the goal, a shot in the void that had no echo, into the no-man's-land that no longer existed for him. It's quite close, the end is staggeringly close. Saturday. A fierce, exquisite, painful vibration. Saturday I'll still be alive, all of Saturday.

Three more days. But by Saturday evening this fellow plans to be in Kolomyya, so I should be in Cernăuţi by late Saturday night, and it isn't going to be in Cernăuţi but between Lvov and Cernăuţi, and not Saturday. Sunday, he thought suddenly. Nothing—not much—a gentle, very, very sad and uncertain feeling. On Sunday morning I'm going to die between Lvov and Cernăuţi.

Now for the first time he looked at his unshaven friend. He was shocked by his face, chalk-white under the black stubble. And there was fear in the eyes. Yet he's going to a repair depot and not to the front, thought Andreas. Why this fear, why this sorrow? This was more than just a hangover. Now he looked the man straight in the eye, and he was even more shocked by that yawning abyss of despair. This was more than just fear and emptiness, something ghastly was draining him, and he knew why the man had to drink, had to drink, to pour something, anything, into that abyss. . . .

"The funny part is," the man burst out hoarsely, "the funny part is that I'm on leave. Till next Wednesday, a whole week. But I just cleared out. My wife is . . . my wife," he was choking on something terrible between a sob and rage. "My wife, you see," he said, "has got someone else. Yes," he laughed abruptly, "that's right, she's got someone else, my friend. Funny thing, you go all over Europe, sleep with a French girl here and a Rumanian whore there, and in Kiev you chase the Russian girls; and when you go on leave and stop over in someplace like Warsaw or Krakow, you can't resist the pretty Polish girls either. It's impossible . . . and . . . and . . . and"—again he choked down that horrible mass of something between a sob and rage as if it were offal—"and then you get home, no warning of course, after fifteen months, and there's a guy lying on your sofa, a man, a Russian, that's right, a Russian's lying on your sofa, the phonograph's playing a tango, and your wife's sitting at the table wearing red pajamas and mixing something . . . yes, that's how it was, exactly. God knows I sent home enough schnapps and liqueurs . . . from France, Hungary, Russia. The guy's so scared he half swallows his cigarette, and your wife screams like an animal . . . I tell you, like an animal!" A shudder passed over his massive shoulders. "Like an animal, I tell you, that's all I know." Andreas looked back in alarm, just one brief glance. But the blond fellow couldn't hear anything. He was calmly sitting there, quite calmly, almost comfortably, and spreading scarlet jam from an immaculate glass jar onto white bread. He spread the jam neatly and calmly, taking bites like a civil servant, almost like a chief inspector. Maybe the blond fellow was an inspector. The unshaven soldier was silent, and something made him shiver. Nobody could have heard what he said. The train had torn away his words . . . they had flown away, flown off inaudibly with the rush of air . . . maybe they had flown back to Dresden . . . to Rade-beul . . . where the little fly was perched somewhere and the girl in the yellow dress was leaning against her bicycle . . . still leaning . . . still leaning. . . .

"Yes," said the unshaven soldier, speaking rapidly, almost impersonally, as if he wanted to reel off a tape he had begun. "I cleared out, simply cleared out. On the way there I had put on my work pants, I wanted to save my new black Panzer ones with the creases in them for my leave. I had been looking forward to seeing my wife . . . God, I was looking forward to it . . . not only to . . . not only to that. No, no!" He shouted, "It's something quite different, the thing you look forward to. It's at home, it's your wife, see? What you do with the other women is nothing, you've forgotten it after an hour . . . and now, now a Russian's sitting there, a tall guy, I could see that much, and the way he was lying there and smoking . . . nowhere else in the world can a man lounge around and smoke that way. Besides, I could tell by his nose he was a Russian . . . you can always tell by their noses. . . ."

I must pray more, Andreas thought, I've hardly prayed since I left home. His companion fell silent again, looking out into the gentle country-side with the sunlight lying over it like a golden shimmer. The blond fellow was still sitting there, he drank some coffee from a flask; now he was eating white bread and butter, the butter was in a brand-new container; he was eating very methodically, very neatly. I must pray more, Andreas thought, and just as he was about to begin, the unshaven soldier started up again. "Yes, I cleared out. By the next train, and took the whole lot back with me. Booze and meat and money, all that money I'd taken along, everything was for her, don't you see? Why else would I have lugged all that stuff along? Just for her. What I need now is a drink . . . where can a fellow get some booze now, I've been racking my brains; these people are daft here, they don't have any black market here. . . ."

"I've got some schnapps," said Andreas. "D'you want some?"

"Schnapps . . . God, man, schnapps!"

Andreas smiled. "I'll let you have the schnapps in exchange for the map, OK?" His companion hugged him. His face was almost happy. Andreas bent over his pack and dug out a bottle of schnapps. For a moment he thought: I'll ration him; I won't give him the second bottle till he needs it or till he wakes up from the stupor he's going to drink himself into. But then he rummaged in the pack again and brought out the second bottle.

"There you are," he said. "You drink it, I don't want any!"

Soon I'm going to die, he was thinking . . . soon, soon, and this

Soon was no longer quite so blurred; he had already groped his way up
to this Soon, circled it and sniffed it, and already he knew that he was
going to die during the night of Saturday to Sunday, between Lvov and
Cernăuți . . . in Galicia. Down there was eastern Galicia, where he would
be quite close to Bukovina and Volhynia. Those names were like unfamiliar drinks. Bukovina—that sounded like a sturdy plum schnapps, and
Volhynia—that sounded like a very thick, swampy beer, like the beer he
had once drunk in Budapest, a real soupy beer.

He glanced back once more through the glass pane and saw the
unshaven soldier lifting the bottle to his mouth, and the blond fellow shake
his head when the other man offered it to him. Then he looked out again
but saw nothing—only that Polish horizon, away in the distance beyond
an endless plain, that intoxicating, wide horizon that he would see when
the hour came. . . .

It's a good thing I'm not alone, he thought. Nobody could go
through this alone, and he was glad he had agreed to join in the game and
had met these two fellows. That one who needed a shave, he had liked him
from the start; and the blond fellow, well, he didn't seem as effete as he
looked. Or maybe he really was effete, but he was a human being. It is
not good for a man to be alone. It would be terribly difficult to be alone
with the others now filling up the corridor again, those fellows nattering
about nothing but leave and heroism, promotions and decorations, food
and tobacco and women, women, all those women who had been madly
in love with every man jack of them. . . . No girl will cry over me, he
thought; how strange. How sad. If only somewhere a girl would think of
me! Even if she was unhappy. God is with those who are unhappy.
Unhappiness is life, pain is life. It would be nice if somewhere a girl were
thinking of me and crying over me . . . I would pull her after me
. . . I would drag her along behind me by her tears, she shouldn't wait for
me forever and ever. There's no such girl. A strange thought. No girl I've
kissed. It's just possible, though not probable, that there is one girl who
still thinks of me; but she can't be thinking of me. For a tenth of a second
our eyes held each other's, maybe even less than a tenth of a second, and
I can't forget her eyes. For three and a half years I've had to think about
them and haven't been able to forget them. Only a tenth of a second or
less, and I don't know her name, I don't know a thing about her, her eyes
are all I know, very gentle, almost pale, sad eyes the color of sand dark
with rain; unhappy eyes, much that was animal in them and all that was
human, and never, never forgotten, not for a single day in three and a half
years, and I don't know her name, I don't know where she lives. Three
and a half years! I don't know whether she was tall or short, I didn't even

see her hands. If I had at least seen her hands! Only her face, and not even that clearly; dark hair, maybe black, maybe brown, a slender, long face, not pretty, not smooth, but the eyes, almost slanting, like dark sand, full of sorrow, and those eyes belong to me, only to me, and those eyes rested on me and smiled for a tenth of a second. . . . There was just a wall and beyond that a house, and on the wall rested two elbows, and between those elbows rested that face, rested those eyes in some French hamlet near Amiens, beneath the scorching summer sky burned gray by the heat. There was a country road ahead of me running uphill between scrawny trees, and on the right was a wall running alongside, and behind us lay Amiens steaming as if in a cauldron; smoke hung over the town, and the murky smoke of battle smoldering like a thunderstorm; on the left motorcycles drove by with hysterical officers, tanks rumbled past on their broad tracks and showered us with dust, and somewhere up front cannon were roaring. The road going uphill suddenly made me feel giddy, it tilted before my eyes, and the wall charging madly up the hill beside the road suddenly tipped over, it simply tipped over, and I fell over with the wall, as if my life were the life of the wall. The whole world turned upside down, and all I saw of it was a plane crashing, but the plane didn't crash from above downward, from sky to ground, it crashed from ground to sky, and now I saw that the sky was the ground, I was lying on the gray-blue, pitilessly hot surface of the sky. Then someone tipped brandy over my face, rubbed me, tipped some brandy down my throat, and I could raise my eyes and above me I saw the wall, that wall, that wall made of bricks with gaps in between, and on that wall rested two pointed elbows, and between the elbows I saw those eyes for a tenth of a second. Just at that moment the lieutenant shouted, "Keep going! Keep going! Get up!" And someone grabbed me by the collar and thrust me into the road, and the road pulled me away, and once again I was crammed into the column and couldn't turn around, couldn't even turn around. . . .

Is it such a disgrace, then, to long to know what forehead belonged to those eyes, what mouth and what breast and what hands? Would it have been asking too much to be allowed to know what heart belonged to them, a girl's heart perhaps; to be allowed to kiss that mouth belonging to those eyes, just once, before I got thrust into the next hamlet where all of a sudden they knocked my leg out from under me? It was summer, and the harvest stood golden in the fields, thin blades, some of them scorched black, that had been eaten up by the summer, and I hated nothing so much as to die a hero's death in a field of corn, it reminded me too much of a poem, and I didn't care to die like in a poem, to die a hero's death like a propaganda picture for this dirty war . . . and even so it was like some patriotic poem, to be lying in a field of corn, bleeding and wounded and cursing, and perhaps to have to die there, five minutes away from those eyes.

But only the bone was broken. I was a hero, wounded on the fields of France, not far from Amiens, not far from the wall that charged madly up the hill, and a mere five minutes from that face, of which I had been allowed to see only the eyes. . . .

For only a tenth of a second was I allowed to see my only love, who was perhaps no more than an apparition, and now I must die, between Lvov and Cernăuţi, facing the wide Polish horizon.

And didn't I promise them, those eyes, to pray for them every day, every day, and today is almost over? It's already getting dark, and yesterday I gave her only a passing thought while I was playing cards, the girl whose name I don't know and whose mouth I never kissed. . . .

It shocked Andreas to find he was suddenly hungry. It was Thursday evening, and on Sunday he was going to die, and he was hungry, he was so hungry his head ached; he was so hungry he was exhausted. It was very quiet in the corridor, and not so crowded now. He sat down beside the unshaven soldier, who promptly made room for him, and all three men were silent. Even the blond fellow was silent: he had a harmonica between his lips and was playing it on the closed side. It was a little harmonica, and he slid the closed side gently back and forth across his lips, and you could tell from his expression that he was hearing the tunes in his head. The unshaven soldier was drinking, drinking systematically and silently at regular intervals, and his eyes were beginning to glisten. Andreas finished the last package of air-raid sandwiches. They had got a bit dry, but his hunger welcomed them eagerly, and they tasted marvelous; he ate six whole sandwiches and asked the blond fellow for the flask of coffee. The sandwiches were really delicious, they tasted wonderful, and afterward he felt disgracefully relaxed, shockingly content. He was very glad the other two weren't talking, and the regular rattle of the train, of which they could feel the least movement, was rather soothing. Now I'll pray, he thought, I'll say all the prayers I know by heart, and a few more as well. First he said the Credo, then a Paternoster and Ave Maria, de Profundis . . . ut pupillam oculi—Come Holy Ghost; then the Credo again because it was so wonderfully complete; then the Good Friday intercession because it was so wonderfully all-embracing, it even included the unbelieving Jews. That made him think of Cernăuţi, and he said a special prayer for the Jews of Cernăuţi and for the Jews of Lvov, and no doubt there were Jews in Stanislav too, and in Kolomyya . . . then another Paternoster, and then a prayer of his own. It was a great place to pray, sitting beside those two silent men, one soundlessly and intently playing the wrong side of his harmonica, the other steadily drinking schnapps. . . .

Outside it had got dark, and he prayed a long time for the eyes, a terribly long time, much longer than for all the others. And for the unshaven soldier too, and the blond fellow, and for the one who had said yesterday: Practically speaking, practically speaking, we've already won the war, especially for him.

"Breslau," said the unshaven soldier suddenly, and his voice had a strangely heavy, almost metallic sound, as if he were beginning to get a bit drunk again. "Breslau, we must soon be getting into Breslau. . . ."

Andreas now recited the poem to himself: "Once there was a belfry-man, in Breslau Town of old . . ." To his mind it was a magnificent poem, and he greatly regretted not knowing quite all of it by heart. No, he thought, I'm not going to die right away. I shall die on Sunday morning or during the night, between Lvov and Cernăuți, facing that immense Polish horizon.

After that he said the poem "Archibald Douglas" over to himself, thought about the sorrowful eyes, and fell asleep with a smile. . . .

Waking up was always terrible. The night before, someone had stepped on his fingers, and tonight he had a terrible dream: he was sitting somewhere on a wet, very cold plain and had no legs, no legs at all, he was sitting on the stumps of his thighs, and the sky over this plain was black and lowering, and this sky was slowly sinking onto the plain, getting closer and closer, closer and closer, the sky was sinking very slowly, and he couldn't run away, and he couldn't scream because he knew it was no use screaming. The futility of it paralyzed him. Where would there be a soul hereabouts to hear his screams? Yet he couldn't let himself be crushed by that descending sky. He didn't even know whether the plain was grass, wet grass, or just earth or only mud . . . he couldn't move, he refused to hop forward on his hands like a lame bird, and where to, anyway? The horizon was endless, endless, wherever he looked, and the sky was sinking, and then suddenly something very cold and wet splashed onto his head, and for a millionth of a second he thought the black sky was only rain and that it would open now, that was what he thought in the millionth of a second, and he tried to scream . . . but he awoke and instantly saw that the unshaven soldier was standing over him, the bottle raised to his mouth, and knew that a drop from the bottle had splashed onto his forehead. . . .

It all came back to him right away. Sunday morning . . . now it was Friday. Two more days. It all came back. The blond fellow was asleep, the unshaven soldier was drinking in fierce gulps, and it was cold in the compartment; there was a draft under the door, and the prayers had expired, and the thought of the eyes no longer aroused that poignant bliss, just sorrow and loneliness. It all came back, and in the morning everything looked different, everything was glamourless and everything was futile, and it would be wonderful, too wonderful for words, if in the morning this Soon could expire too, this Soon that had now become quite definite, quite certain. But this Soon was there, it was always there right away, as if it had been waiting to pounce; ever since he had uttered the word, it had lain on him like second sight. For two days now it had been as close to him, as inseparably linked to him as his soul, his heart. This Soon was just as strong and sure in the morning. Sunday morning. . . .

The unshaven soldier had also noticed that Andreas was awake. He was still standing over him, drinking from the bottle. In the dim gray light it was frightening, that bulky outline, leaning forward as if to pounce, the bottle at his lips, and the glittering eyes, and the strange, menacing gurgle from the bottle.

"Where are we?" Andreas asked in a hoarse whisper. He was scared; it was cold and still almost totally dark.

"Not far from Przemyśl now," said the man. "Want a drink?"

"Yes." The schnapps tasted good. It ran into him like sharp fire, driving his blood around as fire under a kettle brings water to the boil. The schnapps tasted good, it warmed him. He handed the bottle back.

"Go on, have another drink," said the man roughly. "I got myself some more in Kraków."

"No."

The man sat down beside him, and it felt good to know there was someone there who wasn't asleep, when you were awake and utterly miserable. Everyone was asleep; the blond fellow was snoring again, soft whistling sounds coming from his corner, and the others, the terribly silent and the terribly talkative, they were all asleep. The air in the corridor was foul—sour and grimy, full of sweat and steam.

Suddenly he realized they were already in Poland. His heart stood still for a moment, missed another beat as if the artery had suddenly knotted, blocking off the blood. Never again will I be in Germany, Germany's gone. The train left Germany while I was asleep. Somewhere there was a line, an invisible line across a field or right through the middle of a village, and that was the border, and the train passed callously over it, and I was no longer in Germany, and no one woke me so I could have one more look out into the night and at least see a piece of the night that hung over Germany. Of course no one knows I shan't see it again, no one knows I'm going to die, no one on the train. Never again will I see the Rhine. The Rhine! The Rhine! Never again! This train is simply taking me along, carting me off to Przemyśl, and there's Poland, hopeless hapless Poland, and I'll never see the Rhine, never smell it again, that exquisite tang of water and seaweed that coats and clings to every stone along the banks of the Rhine. Never again the avenues along the Rhine, the gardens behind the villas, and the boats, so bright and clean and gay, and the bridges, those splendid bridges, spare and elegant, leaping over the water like great slender animals.

"Pass me the bottle again," he said huskily. His companion handed it to him, and he drank long and deep of that fire, that liquid fire that burns out the bleak misery of the heart. Then he lit a cigarette, and he wished his friend would say something. But first he wanted to pray, just because he felt so miserable, that was why he wanted to pray. He said the same prayers as the evening before, but this time he prayed first for the eyes, so he wouldn't forget them. The eyes were always with him, but not always with the same clarity. Sometimes they submerged for months and were only there in the sense that his lips were there and his feet, which were always with him and of which he was only occasionally aware, only when they hurt; and sometimes, at irregular intervals, often after months, the eyes would surface like some new burning pain, and on days like that he prayed in the evening for the eyes. Today, he had to pray for the eyes in the morning. He also prayed again for the Jews of Cernăuți, and for the Jews of Stanislav and Kolomyya; there were Jews all over Galicia— Galicia, the word was like a snake with tiny feet and shaped like a knife, a snake with glittering eyes, gliding smoothly over the ground and slicing, slicing the ground in two. Galicia . . . a dark, beautiful word, filled with anguish, and in this country I am going to die.

There was a lot of blood in that word, blood made to flow by the knife. Bukovina, he thought, that's a good solid word, I shan't die there, I shall die in Galicia, in eastern Galicia. I must have a look, when it gets light, and see where the province of Bukovina begins. I won't see it any more now; I'm getting closer and closer. Cernăuți is already in Bukovina, I won't see that.

"Kolomyya," he asked his companion, "is that in Galicia?"

"Don't know. Poland, I think."

Every border has a terrible finality. There's a line, and that's it. And the train goes across it just as it would go across a dead body, or a live body. And hope is dead, the hope of being sent back once more to France and finding the eyes again and the lips belonging to the eyes, and the heart and the breast, a woman's breast that must belong to those eyes. That hope is quite dead, completely cut off. Forever and ever those eyes will only be eyes, they will never surround themselves again with body and clothes and hair, no hands, no human hands, no woman's hands that might one day caress you. That hope had always been there, for after all it was a human being, a living human being, to which those eyes belonged, a girl or a woman. But not now. Now there were only eyes, no lips now, never again a mouth, a heart, never again to feel a living heart under a soft skin beating against your hand, never again . . . never . . . never. Sunday morning, between Lvov and Kolomyya. Cernăuţi was far away now, as far as Nikopol and Kishinev. That Soon had narrowed down even more; it was very narrow now. Two days, Lvov, Kolomyya. He knew he might get barely as far as Kolomyya, but certainly no farther. No heart, no mouth, only eyes, only the soul, that unhappy, lovely soul that had no body; wedged between two elbows like a witch pinned to her stake before they burn her. . . .

The border had cut off a lot of things. Paul was finally gone too. Only memory, hope, and dream. "We live on hope," Paul had once said. As if one were to say, "We live on credit." We have no security . . . nothing . . . only eyes, and don't know whether three and a half years of prayer have coaxed those eyes over to the place we may hope to reach. . . .

Yes, later on he did limp up that hill, from the hospital in Amiens, and nothing was the same. The road was not gray as it ran up the hill, it was just an ordinary road. The hill carried the road on its back, and the wall had no intention of swaying and charging; the wall just stood there. And there was the house, which he hadn't recognized, only the wall, he had recognized that, a wall made of bricks with gaps in them where bricks had been left out to make a kind of pattern. A Frenchman was standing there, a real lower-middle-class type, his pipe between his teeth, his eyes full of that truly French derision—ponderous, bourgeois—and the man had known nothing. He knew only that they had all gone, fled, and that the Germans had looted everything although a banner had been strung right across the road saying "Looting Punishable by Death." No, no eyes, only the man's wife, an obese matron who kept her hand tucked in the top of her dress, a face rather like a rabbit's. No child, no daughter, no sister, no sister-in-law, nothing! Just poky rooms full of kitsch and stale air, and the couple's derisive looks as they watched him searching helplessly, agonizingly.

That glass cabinet: the Germans had smashed it up. And burned holes in the carpet with their cigarette butts, and slept on the couch with their whores and messed it all up. He spat with contempt. But that had all happened later, not during the battle while Amiens was smoking, much later, after the pilot had crashed in the wheatfield over there, where you could see the tail of the aircraft sticking in the earth. The pipe pointed out of the window . . . yes, there it was, sticking in the earth, the tail with the emblem, and on the French steel helmet on the grave right next to it the sun was glinting. It was all real, as real as the smell from the kitchen of the roast in the oven, and the smashed glass cabinet and, down there in the valley, the cathedral in Amiens. "A fine example of French Gothic architecture . . ."

No eyes. Nothing, nothing at all.

"Maybe," said the man, "maybe it was a whore." But the man pitied him. It was a miracle that this bourgeois little man could feel pity, pity for a German soldier who belonged to the same army as the ones who had stolen his knives and forks and his clocks, and had slept on his couch with their whores, messing it all up, ruining it.

The pain was so overpowering that he just stood there in the doorway, looking at the spot on the road where he had passed out; the pain was so great that he didn't feel it. The man shook his head. Perhaps he had never seen such unhappy eyes as those of this soldier leaning heavily on his cane.

"*Peut-être,*" he said before Andreas left, "*peut-être une folle,* a madwoman from the asylum over there." He gestured toward the wall, where red-roofed buildings showed among fine tall trees. "A mental asylum. During the battle they all ran away, you see, and they all had to be rounded up again, a tough job. . . ."

"Thanks . . . thanks." On up the hill toward the asylum. The wall began close by, but there was no gate. It was a long, long walk up the hot hill until he reached a gate, and he knew in advance, he knew there would be no one left. A sentry in a steel helmet stood at the gate, and there were no more lunatics, only some sick and wounded and a VD treatment center.

"A big VD center," said the sentry. "Did you pick up something too, bud?"

Andreas looked across to the big field where the aircraft's tail with the emblem was sticking in the earth and the steel helmet was glinting in the sun.

"It's so cheap here, that's the trouble," said the sentry, who was bored. "You can have it for fifty pfennigs." He laughed. "Fifty pfennigs!"

"That's right," said Andreas . . . Forty million, he thought, France has forty million inhabitants, that's too many. You can't search among all those, I must wait . . . I must look into every pair of eyes I meet. He didn't feel like walking on another three minutes and having a look at the field where he had been wounded. For it wasn't the same field, everything was different. It wasn't the same road, or the same wall, they had all forgotten;

the road had forgotten too, just as people forget, and the wall had forgotten that once it had collapsed with fear and he with it. And the tail of the aircraft over there was a dream, a dream with a French emblem. Why go look at the field? Why walk those extra three minutes and recall with hate and pain the patriotic poem that he had remembered against his will? Why torment his tired legs any further?

"Now," said the soldier who needed a shave, "now we're getting close to Przemyśl." "Pass me the bottle again," said Andreas. He took another swig.

It was still cold, but dawn was softly breaking, and soon the horizon would be visible, that Polish horizon. Dark houses and a plain full of shadows, and the sky above it always threatening to collapse because there was nothing to hold it up. Perhaps this was already Galicia, perhaps this plain rising out of the dusk, drab and gray and full of sorrow and blood, perhaps this plain was already Galicia . . . Galicia . . . eastern Galicia. . . .

"You've had a good long sleep," said the soldier who needed a shave. "From seven to five. It's five o'clock already. Kraków to Tarnów . . . all gone; I didn't sleep a wink. That's how long we've already been in Poland. Kraków to Tarnów, and now Przemyśl. . . ."

What a fantastic difference between Przemyśl and the Rhine. I've slept for ten hours, and now I'm hungry again, and I've got forty-eight hours to live. Forty-eight hours have already gone by. For forty-eight hours this Soon has been suspended inside me: Soon I'm going to die. At first it was certain, but far off; certain, but unclear; it's been getting steadily narrower and narrower, already it's narrowed down to a few miles of road and two days away, and every turn of these wheels brings me closer. Every turn of the wheels tears a piece off my life, off an unhappy life. These wheels are grinding away my life, whittling away my life with their stupid rhythm; they rattle across Polish soil as heedlessly as they rattled along by the Rhine, and they are the same wheels. Maybe Paul caught sight of the wheel that's under this door, this oily, dirt-encrusted train wheel that's come all the way from Paris, maybe even from Le Havre. From Paris, the Gare Montparnasse . . . Soon they'll be sitting in wicker chairs under awnings and drinking wine in the autumn breeze, swallowing that sweet dust of Paris and sipping absinthe or Pernod, nonchalantly flicking their cigarette butts into the gutter that runs under that soft sky, that ever-mocking sky. There are only five million people in Paris, and many streets, many alleys, and many, many houses, and from not one of the windows do those eyes look out; even five million are too many. . . .

All at once the soldier who needed a shave began speaking very rapidly. It was lighter now, and the first of the sleeping men began to stir, to turn over in their sleep, and it seemed as if he must speak before they were fully awake. He wanted to speak into the night, into a listening ear in the night. . . .

"The terrible part is that I shall never see her again, I know I won't," he said in a low voice, "and I don't know what'll become of her. It's three days now since I left, three days. What's she been doing in those three days? I don't believe that Russian is still with her—because she screamed like an animal, like an animal facing the barrel of a hunter's gun. There's no one with her. She's waiting. God, I wouldn't want to be a woman. Always waiting . . . waiting . . . waiting . . . waiting."

The unshaven soldier screamed softly, but it was a scream all right, a terribly soft scream. "She's waiting . . . she can't live without me. There's no one with her, and no one will ever go to her now. She's waiting only for me, and I love her. Now she's as innocent as a girl that's never thought of kissing, and that innocence is all for me. That ghastly, terrible shock has completely cleansed her, I know it has . . . and no one, no one on earth can help her but me, no one, and here I am on a train heading for Przemyśl . . . I'm going to Lvov . . . to Kolomyya . . . and never again will I cross the German border. That's something no one would ever be able to understand, why I don't take the next train back to her—why don't I? No one would ever be able to understand that. But I'm scared of that innocence . . . and I love her very much, and I'm going to die, and all she'll ever get from me now will be an official letter saying: Fallen for Greater Germany. . . ." He took a long, deep drink.

"How slowly the train's going, buddy, don't you think? I want to get away, far away . . . and quickly, and I don't know why I don't change trains and go back, I've still got time. I wish the train would go faster, much faster. . . ."

Some of the men had woken and were blinking morosely into the false light rising from the plain. . . .

"I'm scared," whispered the unshaven soldier into Andreas's ear, "I'm scared, that's what, scared of dying but even more scared of going back, going back to her . . . that's why I'd rather die. . . . Maybe I'll write to her. . . ."

The men who had woken up were combing back their hair, lighting cigarettes, and looking contemptuously out the windows, where dark huts stood among what seemed to be barren fields. There were no people in this country . . . somewhere over there were some hills . . . everything was gray . . . Polish horizon. . . .

The unshaven soldier was silent. There was hardly any life left in him.

He had not been able to sleep all night; the spark in him had gone out, and his eyes were like blind mirrors, his cheeks yellow and cavernous, and what had been the need for a shave was now a beard, a reddish-black beard below the thick hair on his forehead.

"Those are precisely the advantages of the 37 antitank weapon," came a clipped voice. "Those are precisely the advantages . . . mobility . . . mobility. . . ." "And no louder than a knock at the door," said an equally clipped voice with a laugh.

"Not really?" "Yes, he got the Knight's Cross for that . . . and all we did was shit in our pants. . . ."

"They ought to listen to the Führer, that's what I say. Get rid of the aristocrats. Von Kruseiten, he was called. What a name. A damned know-it-all. . . ." Lucky fellow, that one with the beard, asleep now when the nattering starts up and able to stay awake when everything's quiet. I must be grateful, I've still got two more nights, thought Andreas . . . two long, long nights. I'd like to be alone then. If they knew I'd prayed for the Jews in Černăuţi and Stanislav and Kolomyya, they'd arrest me on the spot or stick me in the madhouse. . . . 37 antitank weapon.

The blond fellow rubbed his narrow, hideously filmy eyes for a very long time. There was something scaly in the corners of them, something disgusting, but it didn't stop him offering Andreas bread, white bread and jam. And he still had some coffee in the flask. It felt good to eat; Andreas realized he was very hungry again. It was almost a craving, and he could no longer control his eyes as they embraced the great loaf of bread. That white bread was unbelievably good.

"Yes," sighed the blond fellow, "my mother baked it for me just before I left." Later on, Andreas sat for a long time in the john, smoking. The john was the only place where you could be really alone: the only place in the whole world, in the whole of Hitler's great-and-glorious army. It was good to sit there and smoke, and he felt he had once again got the better of his depression. Depression was only a bogey that haunted you just after you woke up; here he was alone, and he had everything. When he wasn't alone, he had nothing. Here he had everything, Paul and the eyes of the girl he loved . . . the blond fellow and the man who needed a shave, and the one who had said: Practically speaking, practically speaking, we've already won the war; and the one who had just said: Those are precisely the advantages of the 37 antitank weapon—they were all there, and the prayers were alive too, very close and warm, and it felt good to be alone. When you were alone you didn't feel so lonely any more. This evening, he thought, I'll pray for a long time again, this evening in Lvov. Lvov is the springboard . . . between Lvov and Kolomyya. . . . The train was getting closer and closer to the goal, and the wheels that had rumbled through Paris, the Gare Montparnasse, maybe through Le Havre or Abbeville, were going as far as Przemyśl . . . till they got quite close to the springboard. . . .

It was full daylight now, but the sun didn't seem to be coming through today; somewhere in the thick gray mass of clouds hung a pale spot with a soft gray light streaming from it that lit up the forests, distant hills . . . villages and the dark-clad figures who shaded their eyes to follow the train out of sight. Galicia . . . Galicia. . . . He stayed in the john until the deafening thumping and swearing on the other side of the door drove him out.

The train arrived in Przemyśl on time. It was almost pleasant there. They waited until everyone had left the train, then woke up the man with the beard. The platform was already empty. The sun had come through and was beating down on dusty piles of rock and sand. The man with the beard knew at once what to do.

"Yes," was all he said. Then he stood up and cut the wire so they could get out right there. Andreas had the least luggage, just his pack, which was very light now that the heavy air-raid sandwiches had all been eaten. He had only a shirt and a pair of socks and some writing paper and his flask, which was always empty, and his steel helmet, since he had left his rifle behind in Paul's clothes closet, where it stood propped up behind the raincoat.

The blond fellow had a Luftwaffe rucksack and a suitcase, and the bearded soldier had two cartons and a knapsack; both men also had pistols. Stepping out into the sunshine, they saw for the first time that the bearded soldier was a sergeant. The dull braid showed up now against his gray collar. The platform was deserted; the place looked like a freight yard. To the right lay army huts, hut after hut, delousing huts, cookhouse huts, recreation huts, dormitory huts, and no doubt a brothel hut where everything was guaranteed fully sanitary. Huts wherever you looked; but they walked to the left, way over to the left, where there was a dead, overgrown track and an overgrown loading ramp by a fir tree. There they lay down, and in the sunshine behind the army huts they could see the old towers of Przemyśl on the river San.

The bearded soldier did not sit down. He merely set his baggage on the ground and said, "I'll go and pick up our rations and find out when the train leaves for Lvov, eh? You fellows try to get some sleep." He took their leave passes and disappeared very slowly down the platform. He ambled along at a terribly slow, maddeningly slow, pace, and they saw that his blue work pants were soiled, full of stains and torn places as if from barbed wire; he walked very slowly, with almost a rolling gait, and from a distance he might have been taken for a sailor.

It was noon, very hot, and the shade of the fir tree was already drenched with heat, a dry shade without gentleness. The blond fellow had spread out his blanket, and they lay with their heads on their packs, looking toward the city across the hot steaming roofs of all those army huts. At some point the bearded soldier vanished between two huts, walking as if he didn't care where he was going. . . .

Alongside another platform stood a train about to leave for Germany. The locomotive already had steam up, and bareheaded soldiers were looking out of the windows. Why don't I get on, thought Andreas; it's really very odd. Why don't I find a seat in that train and go back to the Rhine? Why don't I buy myself a leave pass in this country where you can buy anything, and go back to Paris, the Gare Montparnasse, and comb the streets, one by one, hunt through every house and look for one little tender gesture from the hands that must belong to those eyes? Five million, that's one eighth, why shouldn't she be among them? Why don't I go to Amiens, to the house with the pierced brick wall, and put a bullet through my head at the spot where her gaze, very close and tender, true and deep, rested in my soul for a quarter of a second? But these thoughts were as leaden as his legs. It felt great to stretch your legs; your legs got longer and longer, and he felt as though he could stretch them all the way to Przemyśl.

They lay there smoking, sluggish and weary as only men can be who have been sleeping and sitting in a cramped railroad car.

The sun had made a wide arc by the time Andreas awoke. The bearded soldier still was not back. The blond fellow was awake and smoking.

The train for Germany had left, but already there was another train for Germany standing there, and from the large delousing hut on the other side emerged gray figures with their parcels and knapsacks, rifles slung around their necks, bound for Germany. One of them started running, then three ran, then ten, then they were all running, bumping into one another, knocking parcels out of hands . . . and the whole gray weary wretched column of men was running because one of them had begun to panic. . . .

"Where did you put the map?" asked the blond fellow. These were the first words spoken by either of them in a long while.

Andreas pulled the map out of his tunic pocket, unfolded it, and sat up, spreading it out on his knees. His eyes went to where Galicia was, but the blond fellow's finger was lying much farther to the south and east; it was a long, shapely finger, with fine hair on it, a finger that not even the dirt had deprived of any of its good breeding.

"There," he said, "that's where I'm heading. With any luck it'll take me another ten days." His finger with its flat, still glossy, blue-sheened nail filled the whole bay between Odessa and the Crimea. The edge of the nail lay beside Nikolayev.

"Nikolayev?" Andreas asked.

"No." The blond fellow winced, and his nail slid lower down, and Andreas noticed that he was staring at the map but seeing nothing and thinking of something else. "No," said the blond fellow. "Ochakov. I'm with the antiaircraft; before that we were in Anapa, in the Kuban, you know, but we got out of there. And now it's Ochakov."

Suddenly the two men looked at one another. For the first time in the forty-eight hours they had been cooped up together, they looked at one another. They had played cards together by the hour, drunk and eaten and slept leaning against each other, but now for the first time they looked at one another. A strangely repellent, whitish-gray, slimy film coated the blond fellow's eyes. To Andreas it looked as though the man's gaze were piercing the faint first scab that closes over a festering wound. Now all at once he realized what that repulsive aura was which emanated from this man who at one time, when his eyes were still clear, must have been handsome, fair and slender with well-bred hands. So that's it, thought Andreas.

"Yes," said the blond fellow very quietly, "that's it," as if he realized what Andreas was thinking. He went on speaking, his voice quiet, uncannily quiet. "That's it. He seduced me, that sergeant major. I'm totally corrupted now, rotten to the core, life holds no more pleasure for me, not even eating, it just looked as if I enjoyed that, I eat automatically, I drink automatically, I sleep automatically. It's not my fault: they corrupted me!" he cried, then his voice subsided again.

"For six weeks we lay in a gun emplacement, way up along the Sivash . . . not a house in sight . . . not even a broken wall. Marshes, water . . . willow shrubs . . . and the Russians flew over it when they wanted to attack our planes flying from Odessa to the Crimea. For six weeks we lay there. Words can't describe it. We were just one cannon with six men and the sergeant major. Not a living soul for miles. Our food supplies were trucked in as far as the edge of the marsh, and we had to pick them up from there and carry across log-walks to our emplacement; the rations were always for two weeks, no shortage of grub. Eating was the only break in the monotony, that and catching fish and chasing mosquitoes —those fantastic swarms of mosquitoes, I don't know why we didn't go out of our minds. The sergeant major was like an animal. Filth poured from his mouth all day long, those first few days, and his eating habits were foul. Meat and fat, hardly any bread." A terrible sigh was wrenched from his breast. "Any man who doesn't eat bread is a hopeless case, I tell you. Yes. . . ." Terrible silence, while the sun stood golden and warm and fair over Przemyśl.

"My God," he groaned, "so he seduced us, what else is there to say? We were all like that—except one. He refused. He was an old fellow, married and with a family; in the evening he used often to show us snapshots of his kids, and weep . . . that was before. He refused, he would hit out, threaten us . . . he was stronger than the five of us put together; and one night when he was alone on sentry duty, the sergeant major shot him. He crept out and put a bullet through him—from behind. With the man's own pistol; then he yanked us out of our bunks and we had to help him throw the body into the marshes. Corpses are heavy . . . I'm telling you, the bodies of dead men weigh a ton. Corpses are heavier than the whole world; the six of us could scarcely carry him. It was dark and raining, and I thought: This is what hell must be like. And the sergeant major sent in a report that the old fellow had mutinied and threatened him with his weapon, and he took along the old fellow's pistol as proof—there was one bullet missing from it, of course. And they sent his wife a letter saying he had fallen for Greater Germany in the Sivash marshes . . . yes; and a week later the first food truck arrived with a telegram for me saying our factory had been destroyed and I was to go on leave; and I didn't even go back to the emplacement, I just took off!" There was a fierce joy in his voice—"I just took off! He must have hit the roof! And they first interrogated me in the office about the old fellow, and I gave them exactly the same story as the sergeant major's. And then I was off . . . off! From the battery to the section in Ochakov, then Odessa, and then I took off. . . ." Terrible silence, while the sun still shone, fair and warm and gentle; Andreas felt an appalling nausea. That's the worst, he thought, that's the worst. . . .

"After that I never enjoyed anything again, and I never will. I'm scared to look at a woman. The whole time I was home I just lay around in a kind of stupor, crying away like some idiot child, and my mother thought I had some awful disease. But how could I tell her about it? It was something you can't tell anyone. . . ."

How crazy for the sun to shine like that, Andreas thought, and a dreadful nausea lay like poison in his blood. He reached for the blond fellow's hand, but the man shrank back in horror. "No," he cried, "don't!" He threw himself onto his stomach, hid his head in his arms, and sobbed.

It sounded as if the ground would burst open, and above his sobbing the sky was smiling, above the army huts, above all those huts and above the towers of Przemyśl on the river San. . . .

"Let me die," he sobbed. "I just want to die, then it'll be all over. Let me die. . . ." His words were stifled by a choking sound, and now Andreas could hear him crying, crying real tears, wet tears.

Andreas saw no more. A torrent of blood and dirt and slime had poured over him; he prayed, prayed desperately, as a drowning man shouts who is struggling all alone out in the middle of a lake and can see no shore and no rescuer. . . .

That's wonderful, he thought, crying is wonderful, crying is good for you, crying, crying, what wretched creature has never cried? I should cry too, that's what I should do. The sergeant cried, and the blond fellow cried, and I haven't cried for three and a half years, not one tear since I walked back down that hill into Amiens and was too lazy to walk those extra three minutes as far as the field where I had been wounded.

The second train had left too; the station was empty now. Funny, thought Andreas, even if I wanted to, I couldn't go back now. I could never leave these two fellows alone. Besides, I don't want to go back, I never want to go back. . . .

The station with all its various tracks was deserted now. A heat haze danced between the rails, and somewhere back there by the entrance a group of Poles were working, shoveling ballast onto the tracks, and coming along the platform was an odd figure wearing the pants of the unshaven soldier. From way off you could see it was no longer the bearded, fierce, desperate fellow who had been cooped up in the train and drinking to drown his sorrows. This was a different person; only the pants were still those of the unshaven soldier. His face was all smooth and pink, his cap at a slight angle, and in his eyes, as he came closer, could be seen something of the real sergeant, a mixture of indifference, mockery, cynicism, and militarism. Those eyes seemed to have done with dreaming, the unshaven soldier was now shaved and washed, his hair was combed, his hands were clean, and it was just as well to know that his name was Willi, for it was impossible to think of him any more as the unshaven soldier, you had to think of him as Willi. The blond fellow was still lying on his blanket, his face on his folded arms, and from his heavy breathing you couldn't tell whether he was sleeping, groaning, or crying.

"Is he asleep?" Willi asked.

"Yes."

Willi unpacked the rations and arranged everything neatly in two piles. "Three days' supply," he said. For each man there was a whole loaf of bread and a large sausage, its wrapping paper wet with the moisture oozing from it. For each man there was slightly less than half a pound of butter, eighteen cigarettes, and three rolls of fruit drops.

"Nothing for you?" Andreas asked.

Willi looked at him in surprise, almost offended. "But I've still got my ration cards for sixteen days!" Strange to think that all that hadn't been a dream, all those things Willi had talked about during the night. It had been the truth; it had been the same person as this man facing him now, smoothly shaven, the quiet eyes holding no more than a modicum of pain; the same person who was now standing in the shade of the fir tree and, very carefully, so as not to spoil the creases, pulling on the pants of his black Panzer uniform. Brand-new pants that suited him down to the ground. He now looked every inch a sergeant.

"There's some beer here too," said Willi. He unpacked three bottles of beer, and they set up Willi's carton between them as a table and began to eat. The blond fellow did not stir; he lay there on his face as many a dead man lies on the battlefield. Willi had some Polish bacon, white bread, and onions. The beer was excellent; it was even cool.

"These Polish barbers," said Willi, "they're tremendous. For six marks, everything included, they make a new man of you, they even shampoo your hair! Just tremendous, and can they ever cut hair!" He took off his peaked cap and pointed to the well-contoured back of his head. "That's what I call a haircut." Andreas was still looking at him in amazement. In Willi's eyes there was now something sentimental, some sergeant-like sentimentality. It was very pleasant eating like this as if at a proper table, well away from those army huts.

"You fellows," said Willi, chewing and clearly enjoying his beer, "you fellows should go and have a wash, or get yourselves washed, makes you feel like a new man. You get rid of everything, all that dirt. And then the shave! You could use one." He glanced at Andreas's chin. "You could certainly use one. I tell you, it's tremendous, you don't feel tired any more, you . . . you"—he was groping for the right word—"all I can say is, you feel like a new man. You've still got time, our train doesn't leave for two hours. We'll be in Lvov this evening. From Lvov we take the civilian express, the courier train, the one that goes direct from Warsaw to Bucharest. It's a terrific train, I always take it. All you need is to get your pass stamped, and we'll see to that"—he guffawed—"we'll see to that, but I'm not letting on how!"

But surely we won't need twenty-four hours to get from Lvov to that place where it's going to happen, thought Andreas. Something's wrong there. We won't be leaving Lvov as early as five tomorrow morning. The sandwiches tasted marvelous. He spread the butter thickly on the bread and ate it with chunks of the juicy sausage. That's really strange, he thought, this is Sunday's butter and maybe even part of Monday's, I'm eating butter I'm no longer entitled to. I'm not even entitled to Sunday's butter. Rations are calculated from noon to noon, and starting Sunday noon, I'm not entitled to any more butter. Perhaps they'll court-martial me . . . they'll lay my body on a desk before a tribunal and say: He ate Sunday's butter and even part of Monday's, he robbed the great-and-glorious German Wehrmacht. He knew he was going to die, but that didn't stop him from eating the butter and bread and sausage and candy, or from smoking the cigarettes. We can't enter that anywhere, there's no place to enter rations for the dead. We're not heathens, after all, who place food in graves for their dead. We are positive Christians, and he has robbed the positive Christian, glorious Greater German Wehrmacht. We must find him guilty. . . .

"In Lvov," Willi said, laughing, "that's where I'll get that rubber stamp, in Lvov. You can get anything in Lvov. I know my way around there."

Andreas had only to say one word, only to ask, and he would have found out how and where one obtained the rubber stamp in Lvov. Willi was just itching to tell him. But Andreas didn't care about finding out. It was fine with him if they got the stamp. The civilian express was fine with him. It was wonderful to travel by civilian train. They weren't for soldiers only, for men only. It was terrible to be always among men, men were so womanish. But in that train there would be women . . . Polish women . . . Rumanian women . . . German women . . . women spies . . . diplomats' wives. It was nice to ride on a train with women . . . as far as . . . as . . . where he was going to die. What would happen? Partisans? There were partisans all over the place, but why would partisans attack a train carrying civilians? There were plenty of leave trains carrying whole regiments of soldiers with weapons, luggage, food, clothing, money, and ammunition.

Willi was disappointed that Andreas did not ask where he could get hold of the stamp in Lvov. He wanted so badly to talk about Lvov. "Lvov," he cried with a laugh. And since Andreas still did not ask, he launched out anyway, "In Lvov, you know, we always sold the cars."

"Always?" Andreas was listening now. "You always sold them?"

"I mean, when we had one to sell. We're a repair depot, see, and often there's a wreck left over, often it's a wreck that's not really a wreck at all. You just have to say it's scrap, that's all. And the superintendent has to close both eyes because he's been going to bed all the time with that Jewish girl from Cernăuți. But it isn't scrap at all, that car, see? You can take two or three and make a terrific car out of them, the Russians are terrific at that. And in Lvov they'll give you forty thousand marks for it. Divided by four. Me and three men from my column. It's damn dangerous, of course, you're taking a hell of a risk." He sighed heavily. "You sweat blood, I can tell you. You never know whether the fellow you're dealing with mightn't be from the Gestapo, you can never tell, not till it's all over. For two whole weeks you sweat blood. If after two weeks there's been no report and none of the bunch have been arrested, that means you've come out on top again. Forty thousand marks." He took a drink of beer with obvious enjoyment.

"When I think of all that stuff lying in the mud around Nikopol. It's worth millions, I tell you, millions! And not a damn soul gets a thing out of it, only the Russians. You know," he lit a cigarette, savoring it, "now and again we could sell something that wasn't so dangerous. One day a spare part, another day a motor or some tires. Clothing too. They're keen as hell to get hold of clothing. Coats, now—they'll fetch a thousand marks, a good coat will. Back home, you know, I've built myself a little house, a nice little house with a workshop . . . for . . . for . . . What did you say?" he asked abruptly. But Andreas had said nothing; he shot Willi a quick glance and saw that his eye had darkened, he was frowning, and that he hurriedly finished his beer. Even without the beard, the old face was there again . . . the sun was still shining golden above the towers of Przemyśl on the river San, and the blond fellow was stirring. It was obvious he had only been pretending to be asleep. Now he was pretending to wake up. He stretched his limbs very deliberately, turned over, and opened his eyes, but he didn't know that the traces of tears in his grimy face were still plainly visible. There were proper furrows, furrows in the grime as on the face of a very little girl who has had her sandwich pinched on the playground. He didn't know this; maybe he had even forgotten that he had been crying. His eyes were red-rimmed and unsightly; he really did look as if he might have venereal disease. . . .

"Aaah," he yawned, "I'm glad there's some grub." His beer had got a bit tepid, but he gulped it down thirstily and began to eat while the other two smoked and very slowly, without the least hurry, drank vodka, crystal-clear, wonderful vodka unpacked by Willi.

"Yes," said Willi with a laugh, but he broke off so abruptly that the other two looked at him in alarm. Willi blushed, looked at the ground, and took a big gulp of vodka.

"What was that?" Andreas asked quietly. "What were you going to say?"

Willi spoke in a very low voice. "I was going to say that I'm now drinking up our mortgage, literally our mortgage. You see, there was a mortgage on the house my wife owned when we got married, a small one of four thousand, and I had been meaning to pay it off now . . . but come on, let's drink. *Prost!*"

The blond fellow also didn't feel like going into town to some barber, or to a washroom in one of those army huts. They tucked towels and soap under their arms, and off they went.

"And make sure your boots are nice and clean too, boys!" Willi called after them. His own boots were indeed shining with fresh polish.

Somewhere down at the end of a track there was a big water pump for the locomotives. It dripped constantly, slowly; a steady trickle of water flowed from it, and the sand all around was one large puddle. It was true, it did feel good to have a wash. If only the soap would lather properly. Andreas took his shaving soap. I shan't be needing it any more, he thought. Although it's enough for three months, of course, and it was only "issued" to me a month ago, but I shan't be needing it any more, and the partisans can have what's left. The partisans need soap too, Poles love shaving. Shaving and shoeshining are their specialties. But just as they were about to start shaving, they saw Willi in the distance calling and waving, and his gestures were so emphatic, so dramatic, you might say, that they packed up their things and dried themselves off as they ran back.

"Boys!" called Willi. "There's a leave train for Kovel just come in, it's running late. We'll be in Lvov in four hours—you can get a shave in Lvov. . . ." They slipped their tunics and coats back on again, put on their caps, and carried their luggage over to the platform where the delayed train for Kovel was standing. Not many got out at Przemyśl, but Willi found a compartment from which a whole group of Panzer soldiers emerged, young fellows, boys in new uniforms that filled the air with the smell of army stores. A whole corridor became empty, and they quickly boarded the train before the ones who had stayed on it had a chance to spread themselves out with their luggage.

"Four o'clock!" cried Willi triumphantly. "That means we'll be in Lvov by ten at the very latest. That's great. Couldn't have made better time, this glorious delayed train! A whole night to ourselves, a whole night!"

They quickly installed themselves in such a way that they could at least sit back to back.

As he sat there, Andreas finally managed to dry his wet ears properly; then he took everything out of his pack and neatly rearranged all the things he had hastily stuffed into it. Now there were a soiled shirt and soiled underpants and a pair of clean socks, the remains of the sausage, the remains of the butter in its container, Monday's sausage and half Monday's butter and Sunday's and Monday's candy, and cigarettes, to which he was even entitled, and even some bread left over from Sunday noon; and his prayer book, he had lugged his prayer book around all through the war and never used it. He always said his prayers just as they came to him, but he could never go on a trip without it. How strange, he thought, how strange it all is, and he lit a cigarette, one to which he was still entitled, a Saturday cigarette, for the ration period from Friday noon to Saturday noon. . . .

The blond fellow was playing his harmonica, and the two of them smoked in silence while the train got under way. The blond fellow was playing properly now, improvising, it seemed; soft, moving, amorphous forms that made you think of swampland.

That's it, thought Andreas, the Sivash marshes, I wonder what they're doing there now beside their cannon. He shuddered. Maybe they've killed each other off, maybe they've finished off the sergeant major, maybe they've been relieved. Let's hope they've been relieved. Tonight I'll say a prayer for the men beside the cannon in the Sivash marshes, and also for the man who fell for Greater Germany because he didn't want, because he didn't want . . . to get that way; that's truly a hero's death. His bones are lying somewhere up there in a marsh in the Crimea, no one knows where his grave is, no one's going to dig him up and take him to a heroes' cemetery, no one's ever going to think of it again, and one day he'll rise again, way up there out of the Sivash marshes, the father of two kids with a wife living in Germany, and the local Nazi leader, with a terribly sad expression, took her the letter, in Bremen or in Cologne, or in Leverkusen, maybe his wife lives in Leverkusen. He will rise again, way up there out of the Sivash marshes, and it will be revealed that he did not fall for Greater Germany at all, nor because he mutinied and attacked the sergeant major, but because he didn't want to get that way.

They were both startled when the blond fellow abruptly broke off playing; they had been swathed, wreathed about, in those soft gentle misty melodies, and now the web was torn. "Look," said the blond fellow, pointing to the arm of a soldier standing by the window and smoking a pipe, "that's what we used to make back home. Funny thing, you see so few of them, yet we used to make thousands." They didn't know what he was talking about. The blond fellow looked confused, and he blushed as he faced their puzzled eyes. "Crimea badges," he said impatiently. "We used to make lots of Crimea badges. Now they're making Kuban badges, they'll soon be handing those out. We used to make the medals for blowing up tanks too, and years ago the Sudeten medals with the tiny shield showing Hradshin Castle. In '38." They continued to look at him as if he were talking Greek, their eyes were still puzzled, and he reddened still further.

"For God's sake," he almost shouted, "we had a factory back home!"

"Oh," said the two others.

"Yes, a patriotic-flag factory."

"A flag factory?" Willi asked.

"Yes, that's what they called it, of course we made flags too. Truckloads of flags, I'm telling you, years ago . . . let's see . . . in '33, I think it was. Of course, that's when it must have been. But mostly we made medals and trophies and badges for clubs, you know the sort of thing, little shields saying: 'Club Champion 1934,' or some such thing. And badges for athletic clubs, and swastika pins, and those little enamel flags to pin on. Red-white-and-blue, or the French vertical blue-white-and-red. We exported a lot. But since the war we've only made for ourselves. Wound badges too, huge quantities of those. Black, silver, and gold. But black, huge quantities of black. We made a lot of money. And old medals from World War One, we made those too, and combat badges, and the little ribbons you wear with civilian dress. Yes . . ." He sighed, broke off, glanced once more at the Crimea badge of the soldier who was leaning on the window and still smoking his pipe, and then he started to play again. Slowly, slowly the light began to fade . . . and suddenly, without transition, twilight was there, welling up stronger and darker until evening swiftly came, and you could sense the cool night on the threshold. The blond fellow went on playing his swampy melodies that wafted dreamily into them like drugs . . . Sivash, Andreas thought, I must pray for the men beside the cannon in the Sivash marshes before I go to sleep. He realized he was beginning to doze off again, his last night but one. He prayed . . . prayed . . . but the words got mixed up, everything became blurred. . . . Willi's wife in her red pajamas . . . the eyes . . . the smug little Frenchman . . . the blond fellow, and the one who had said: Practically speaking, practically speaking, we've already won the war.

THIS TIME he woke up because the train stopped for a long time. At a railroad station it was different; you turned over with a yawn and could feel the impatience in the wheels, and you knew the train would soon be under way. But this time the train stopped for so long that the wheels seemed frozen to the rails. The train was at a standstill. Not at a station, not on a siding. Half asleep, Andreas groped his way to his feet and saw everyone crowding around the windows. He felt rather forlorn, all by himself like that in the dark corridor, especially since he couldn't spot Willi and the blond fellow right away. They must be up front by the windows. It was dark outside and cold, and he guessed it was at least one or two in the morning. He heard railroad cars rumbling past outside, and he heard soldiers singing in them—their stale, stupid, fatuous songs that were so deeply buried in their guts that they had worn a groove like a tune in a record, and as soon as they opened their mouths they sang, sang those songs: "Heidemarie" and "Jolly Huntsman." . . . He had sung them too sometimes, without knowing or wanting to, those songs that had been sunk into them, buried in them, drilled into them so as to kill their thoughts. These were the songs they were now shouting into the dark, somber, sorrowful Polish night, and it seemed to Andreas that far off, somewhere far away he would be able to hear an echo, beyond the somber, invisible horizon, a mocking, diminutive, and very distinct echo . . . "Jolly Huntsman" . . . "Jolly Huntsman" . . . "Heidemarie." A lot of cars must have passed, then no more, and everyone left the windows and went back to their places. Including Willi and the blond fellow.

"The SS," said Willi. "They're being thrown in around Cherkassy. There's another pocket there or something. Pickpockets!"

"They'll manage it somehow," said a voice.

Willi sat down beside Andreas and said it was two o'clock. "Shit, we'll miss the train at Lvov if we don't get moving right away. It's still another two hours. We'll have to leave Sunday morning. . . ."

"But we'll be starting up any minute," said the blond fellow, who was standing at the window again.

"Maybe," said Willi, "but then we won't have any time in Lvov. Half an hour is the craps for Lvov. Lvov!" He laughed.

"Me?" they suddenly heard the blond fellow call.

"Yes, you!" shouted a voice outside. "Get ready to take up your post." Grumbling, the blond fellow came back, and outside someone in a steel helmet stood on the step and stuck his face in through the train window. It was a heavy, thick skull, and they saw dark eyes and an official-looking forehead, the blond fellow having lit a match to find his belt and steel helmet.

"Any noncoms in there?" shouted the voice under the steel helmet. It was a voice that could only shout. No one spoke up. "Are there any noncoms in there, I said!"

No one spoke up. Willi gave Andreas a derisive nudge.

"Don't make me come and look for myself; if I find a noncom in there, it's going to be tough for him!"

For a further second nobody spoke up, although Andreas could see that the place was swarming with noncoms. Suddenly someone quite near Andreas said, "Here!"

"Fast asleep, eh?" shouted the voice under the steel helmet.

"Yessir!" said the voice, and Andreas now saw it was the man with the Crimea badge.

A few of the men laughed.

"What's your name?" shouted the voice under the steel helmet.

"Corporal Schneider."

"You'll be in charge for as long as we stop here, understand?"

"Yessir!"

"Good. You there"—he pointed to the blond fellow—"what's your name?"

"Private Siebental."

"OK: Private Siebental will stand guard outside this car until four o'clock. If we're still here by then, have him relieved. Also, place a sentry outside the car on the other side and have him relieved too if necessary. There may be partisans in the area."

"Yessir!"

The face under the steel helmet vanished, muttering to itself, "Corporal Schneider."

Andreas was trembling. I hope to God I don't have to stand guard, he thought. I'm sitting right next to him, and he'll grab my sleeve and put me on duty. Corporal Schneider had switched on his flashlight and was shining it along the corridor. First he shone it on the collars of those who were lying down and pretending to be asleep; then he grabbed one of them by the collar, saying with a laugh, "Come on, take your gun and stand out there, and don't blame me!"

The one who had been picked swore as he got ready. I hope to God they don't find out I've no rifle, no weapon at all, that my rifle's standing propped up in Paul's closet behind his raincoat. What's Paul going to do with the rifle anyway? A chaplain with a rifle, the Gestapo'll just love that. He can't report it, because then he'd have to give my name and he would worry that they might write to my platoon. How awful that on top of everything else I had to leave my rifle behind at Paul's. . . .

"Come on, man, it's only till we get going again," said the corporal to the soldier who was cursing as he groped his way to the door and flung it open. It seemed strange that the train didn't move on; a quarter of an hour passed; they were too tense to sleep. Maybe there really were partisans in the area, and it was no joke being attacked in a train. Maybe it would be the same tomorrow night. Strange . . . strange. Maybe that's how it would be between Lvov and . . . no, not even Kolomyya. Twenty-four hours to go, twenty-four or at most twenty-six. It's already Saturday, it's actually Saturday. How utterly thoughtless I've been . . . I've known since Wednesday . . . and I've done nothing, I know it with absolute certainty, and I've hardly prayed any more than usual. I played cards. I drank. I ate and really enjoyed my food, and I slept. I slept too much, and time has leaped forward, time always leaps forward, and now here I am only twenty-four hours away from it. I've done nothing. After all, when you know you're going to die you have all kinds of things to settle, to regret, prayers to say, many prayers to say, and I've prayed hardly any more than I usually do. And yet I know for sure. I know for sure. Saturday morning. Sunday morning. Literally one more day. I must pray, pray. . . .

"Got a drink? It's lousy cold out here." The blond fellow stuck his head in through the window, and under the steel helmet his effete greyhound-head looked terrible. Willi held the bottle to the man's mouth and let him have a long drink. He also held the bottle out to Andreas.

"No," said Andreas.

"There's a train coming." It was the blond fellow's voice again. Everyone dashed to the window. It was half an hour behind the first train, and it was another of those, another troop train, with more songs, more "Jolly Huntsman" . . . "Jolly Huntsman" and "Heidemarie" in that dark, sorrowful Polish night . . . "Jolly Huntsman." A train like that took a long time to pass, with baggage car and cookhouse car and the cars for the soldiers, and all the time "Jolly Huntsman" and "Today it's Germany that's ours, tomorrow all the world . . . all the world . . . all the world. . . ."

"More SS troops," said Willi, "and all going to Cherkassy. The crap there seems to be collapsing too." He said this in an undertone, since eager and optimistic voices next to him were saying they would manage it somehow.

Softly "Jolly Huntsman" died away in the night, the song growing dim in the direction of Lvov, like a subdued, very soft whimpering, and once again there was the dark, sorrowful Polish night. . . .

"Let's hope there won't be another seventeen of these trains," muttered Willi. He offered Andreas the bottle again, but again Andreas refused. It's high time for me to say my prayers, he thought. This is the last night of my life but one, and I'm not going to spend it sleeping or napping. I'm not going to defile it with drink or waste it. I must say my prayers now, and above all repent. There's always so much to repent; even in an unhappy life like mine there are a lot of things to repent. That time in France when

I drank a whole bottle of cherry brandy on a broiling hot day, like an animal; I keeled over like an animal, it nearly finished me. A whole bottle of cherry brandy when it was ninety in the shade, on a treeless street in some French hamlet. Because I was almost passing out with thirst and had nothing else to drink. It was ghastly, and it took me a week to get rid of my headache. And I had a row with Paul, I always insulted him by calling him a damn parson, I was always talking about damn parsons. It's terrible, when you've got to die, to think you've insulted someone. I used to talk back to my teachers at school too, and I wrote "Shit" on the bust of Cicero; it was stupid, I was just a kid, but I knew it was wrong and silly, I did it anyway because I knew the other kids would laugh, that was the only reason I did it, because I wanted the others to laugh at a joke of mine. Out of vanity. Not because I really thought Cicero was shit; if I had done it for that reason it wouldn't have been as bad, but I did it for a joke. One should never do anything for a joke. And I used to make fun of Lieutenant Schreckmüller, of that sad, pale little fellow; the lieutenant's shoulder patches lay so heavily on his shoulders, so heavily, and you could tell he was marked for death. I used to make fun of him too, because I couldn't resist being known as a wit, as a sarcastic old trooper. That was worse than anything, maybe, and I don't know if God can forgive that. I made fun of him, of the way he looked like a Hitler Youth kid, and he was marked for death, I could tell from his face, and he was killed; he was shot down during the first attack in the Carpathians, and his body rolled down a slope, it was horrible the way it rolled down, and as the body rolled over it got covered with dirt; it was horrible, and to tell the truth it looked kind of ridiculous, that body rolling down, faster and faster, faster and faster, till it bounced onto the floor of the valley. . . .

And in Paris I abused a whore. In the middle of the night; that was awful. It was cold, and she accosted me—she practically assaulted me— and I could see from her fingers and the tip of her nose that she was chilled to the marrow, shivering with hunger. I felt quite sick when she said, "Come on, dearie," and I pushed her away, although she was shivering and ugly and all alone on that great wide street, and she might have been glad if I had lain beside her in her pitiful bed and just warmed her up a bit. And I actually pushed her away into the gutter and spat out abuse after her. If I only knew what became of her that night. Perhaps she drowned herself in the Seine because she was too ugly to get a nibble from anyone that night, and the terrible part is that I wouldn't have treated her so badly if she had been pretty. . . . If she had been pretty I might not have been so disgusted by her profession and she wouldn't have been pushed into the gutter and I might have been quite glad to warm up beside her and do some other things too. God knows what would have happened if she had been pretty. It's a terrible thing to maltreat a person because that person seems ugly to you. There are no ugly people. That poor soul, God forgive me twenty-four hours before my death for having pushed away that poor, ugly, shivering whore, at night, on that wide empty Paris street where there wasn't one single customer left for her, no one but me. God forgive me for everything, you can't undo what's done, nothing can ever be undone, and the pathetic whimpering of that poor girl will haunt that Paris street forever and ever and accuse me, and the wretched doglike eyes of that Lieutenant Schreckmüller, whose childish shoulders were not nearly strong enough for the weight of his shoulder patches. . . .

If I could only cry. I can't even cry over all these things. I feel heartsick and contrite and terrible, but I can't cry over them. Everyone else can cry, even the blond fellow, everyone but me. God grant me the power to cry. . . .

There must be a lot of other things I can't think of right now. That can't be all by a long way. There were the people I despised and loathed *is this* and mentally abused, for instance, like the man who said: Practically *meta-* speaking, practically speaking, we've already won the war; I hated that man *fictional?* too, but I forced myself to pray for him because he was such a fool. I still have to pray for the one who just said: They'll manage it somehow, and for all the ones who sang "Jolly Huntsman" with such gusto.

I hated the lot of them, all those fellows who just went by in the train singing "Jolly Huntsman" . . . and "Heidemarie" . . . and "A Soldier's Life Is a Splendid Life" . . . and "Today it's Germany that's ours, tomorrow all the world." I hated the lot of them, the whole lot, all those fellows who lay squashed up against me in the train and in barracks. God, those barracks. . . .

"That's it!" shouted a voice outside. "Everyone back on the train!" The blond fellow got on and the man from the other side, and the train whistled and moved off. "Thank God for that," said Willi. But it was too late anyway. It was three-thirty, and it would take them at least another two hours to get to Lvov, and the courier train, the civilian express from Warsaw to Bucharest, left at five.

"So much the better," said Willi. "That gives us a whole day in Lvov." He laughed again. He wanted so badly to tell them some more about Lvov. You could hear it in his voice, but nobody reacted, nobody asked him to go on. They were tired, it was three-thirty and cold, the dark Polish sky hung over them, and those two battalions or regiments that were being thrown into the Cherkassy pocket had set them thinking. No one spoke, although none of them were asleep. Only the rattle of the train lulled them to sleep, killed their thoughts, sucked the thinking out of their heads, that regular clickety-clack, clickety-clack, it put them to sleep. They were all poor, gray, hungry, misguided, and deluded children, and their cradle was the trains, the leave trains that went clickety-clack and lulled them to sleep.

The blond fellow seemed to be genuinely asleep now. He had got very cold outside, and the fug here in the corridor must have actually seemed quite warm and put him to sleep. Only Willi was awake, Willi who had once been the soldier in need of a shave. From time to time he could be heard reaching for his bottle of vodka and gulping the stuff down, swearing at intervals under his breath, and from time to time he would strike a match and smoke, and then he would light up Andreas's face and see that he was wide awake. But he said nothing. And it was odd that he should say nothing. . . .

Andreas wanted to pray, he wanted desperately to pray; first, all the prayers he had always said, and then a few more of his own, and then he wanted to say over the names, to begin to say over the names, of all the people he had to pray for, but then he thought that was crazy, to say all those names. You would have to include everybody, the whole world. You would have to say two billion names . . . forty million, he thought . . . no, two billion names it would have to be. You'd simply have to say: Everyone. But that wasn't enough, he had at least to begin to say the names of the people he had to pray for. First the ones you had hurt, the ones you were indebted to. He began with his school, then with the labor service, then the barracks and the war and all the people whose names occurred to him along the way. His uncle, he had hated him too because he had always spoken so glowingly of the army, of the happiest days of his life. He thought about his parents, whom he had never known. Paul. Paul would be getting up soon and saying Mass. It will be the third he's said since I left, thought Andreas, perhaps he understood when I called out: I'm going to die . . . soon. Perhaps Paul understood and will say a Mass for me Sunday morning, an hour before or after I've died. I hope Paul thinks about the others, about the soldiers who are like the blond fellow, and the ones who are like Willi, and the ones who say: Practically speaking, practically speaking, we've already won the war; and the ones who day and night sing "Jolly Huntsman" and "Heidemarie," and "A Soldier's Life Is a Splendid Life," and "Ah, the Sunshine of Mexico." On this cold, miserable morning under the dark, sorrowful Galician sky, he didn't think of the eyes at all. Now we must be in Galicia, he thought, quite close to Lvov, since Lvov is the capital of Galicia. Now I must be just about in the center of the net where I'm going to be caught. There's only one more province: Galicia, and I'm in Galicia. As long as I live I shall never see anything but Galicia. It has narrowed down very much, that Soon. To twenty-four hours and a few miles. Not many miles now to Lvov, maybe forty, and beyond Lvov at most another forty. My life's already been narrowed down to eighty miles in Galicia, in Galicia . . . like a knife on invisible snake's feet, a knife creeping along, softly creeping along, a softly creeping knife. Galicia. How will it happen, I wonder? Will I be shot or stabbed . . . or trampled to death . . . or will I simply be crushed to death in a crushed railroad car? There are such an infinite number of ways to die. You can also be shot by a sergeant major for refusing to do what the blond fellow did; you can die any way you like, and the letter will always say: He fell for Greater Germany. And I must be sure to pray for the men with the cannon down there in the Sivash marshes . . . must be sure . . . must be sure . . . clickety-clack . . . must be sure . . . clickety-clack . . . must be sure men with cannon . . . in the Sivash marshes . . . clickety-clack. . . .

IT WAS terrible to find he had finally fallen asleep after all. And now they were in Lvov. It was a big station, black iron girders and grimy white signboards, and there it was, in black and white, between the platforms: Lvov. This was the springboard. It was almost incredible how quickly you could get from the Rhine to Lvov. Lvov, there it was in black and white, irrevocably: Lvov. Capital of Galicia. Another forty miles less. The net was quite small now. Forty miles, maybe even less, maybe only five. Beyond Lvov, between Lvov and Cernăuţi, that could mean a mile beyond Lvov. Again this was as elastic as the Soon that he thought he had managed to narrow down. . . .

"Boy, can you ever sleep!" said Willi, now cheerfully collecting his belongings. "Can you ever sleep! I never saw anything like it. The train stopped twice. You nearly had to do sentry duty, but I told the corporal you were sick and he let you go on sleeping. Time to get up!" The car was empty, and the blond fellow was already standing outside with his Luftwaffe rucksack and his suitcase.

It felt very odd to be walking along a platform in the main station of Lvov. . . .

It was eleven o'clock, almost midday, and Andreas felt famished. But the thought of the sausage disgusted him. Butter and bread and something hot! It's ages since I had a hot meal; I'd like something hot to eat. Funny, he thought, as he followed Willi and the blond fellow, my first thought in Lvov is that I'd like a hot meal. Fourteen or fifteen hours before your death, you feel you've got to have a hot meal. He laughed, and this made the other two turn around and look at him in surprise, but he avoided their eyes and blushed. There was the barrier, there stood a sentry in a steel helmet, as at every station in Europe, and the sentry said to Andreas, because he was the last of the three, "Waiting room to the left, for the use of enlisted men too."

Once past the barrier Willi became almost aggressive. There he stood, in the middle of the station, lit a cigarette, and mimicked in a loud voice, "Waiting room for the use of enlisted men to the left! That's what they'd like, to herd us cattle into the barn they've fixed up for us." They looked at him in alarm, but he laughed. "Just leave it to me, boys. Lvov's right up my alley. Waiting room for the use of enlisted men! There are bars in this place, restaurants," he clicked his tongue, "as good as any in Europe," and he repeated sarcastically, "as any in Europe."

His face was already beginning to look somewhat unshaven again; he seemed to have a tremendously strong growth of beard. It was the same face as before, very sad and desperate.

Without a word he preceded the others through the exit, crossed, still without a word, a big crowded square, and very quickly they found themselves in a dark narrow side street; a car was standing at the corner, a ramshackle old taxi, and, as in a dream, it turned out Willi knew the driver. "Stani," he shouted, and again as in a dream a sleepy-eyed, grubby old Pole hoisted himself in the driver's seat and recognized Willi with a grin. Willi mentioned some Polish name, and the next moment they were sitting in the taxi with their luggage, driving through Lvov. The streets were the same as in any big city anywhere in the world. Wide, elegant streets, streets that had seen better days, sad streets with faded yellow façades and looking dead and deserted. People, people, and Stani drove very fast, as in a dream: all Lvov seemed to belong to Willi. They drove along a wide avenue, an avenue like anywhere else in the world yet definitely a Polish avenue, and Stani came to a stop. He was given a bill —fifty marks, as Andreas saw—and with a grin Stani helped them set their luggage on the sidewalk; it was all done in a few seconds, and in another few seconds they found themselves striding through a neglected front garden and entering a very long, musty hallway of a house whose façade seemed to be crumbling away. A house dating from the days of the old Hapsburg Empire. Andreas instantly recognized its aura of former Austrian imperial grandeur; perhaps a high-ranking officer had lived here, long ago, in the days of the waltz, or a senior civil servant. This was an old Austrian mansion; they could be found everywhere, all through the Balkans, in

Hungary and Yugoslavia, and of course in Galicia too. All this flashed through his mind in the brief second it took to enter the long, dark, musty hallway.

But then, with a happy smile, Willi opened a soiled white door, very high and wide, and there was a restaurant with comfortable chairs, and attractively set tables with flowers on them—autumn flowers, thought Andreas, the kind you see on graves, and he thought: This will be my last meal before my execution. Willi led them over to an alcove that could be curtained off, and there were more comfortable chairs and an attractively set table, and it was all like a dream. Wasn't I standing a minute ago under a signboard with letters on it in black and white: Lvov?

Waiter! A smart Polish waiter wearing shiny shoes, shaved to perfection and grinning; only his jacket was a bit soiled. They all grin here, thought Andreas. The waiter's jacket was a bit soiled, but never mind, his shoes were like a grand duke's and he was shaved like a god . . . highly polished black shoes. . . .

"Georg," said Willi, "these gentlemen would like a wash and a shave." It sounded like an order. No, it was an order. Andreas had to laugh as he followed the grinning waiter. He felt as if he had been invited to the home of a genteel grandmother or a genteel uncle, and Uncle had said: Unshaven or unwashed children may not come to the table. . . .

The washroom was spacious, clean. Georg brought hot water. "Perhaps the gentlemen would like some toilet soap, excellent quality, fifteen marks."

"Bring it," said Andreas with a laugh. "Papa will pay for everything."

Georg brought the soap and repeated with a grin, "Papa will pay." The blond fellow had a wash too; they stripped to the waist, soaped themselves, dried themselves voluptuously, their arms and all over their yellowish-white, unaired soldiers' skin. It's lucky I brought along my socks, thought Andreas, I'll wash my feet too, and I can put on my clean socks. Socks must be very expensive here, and why should I leave the socks in my pack? I'm sure the partisans have socks. He washed his feet and laughed at the blond fellow, who looked very astonished. The blond fellow really was in a daze.

It feels great to have a smooth chin again, as smooth as a Pole's, and I'm only sorry that tomorrow morning I'll have stubble on it again, thought Andreas. The blond fellow did not need to shave, he had only a trace of down on his upper lip. Andreas wondered for the first time how old the blond fellow might be, as he drew on his nice clean shirt, with a proper civilian collar so he could leave off that stupid army neckband;

a blue shirt that had once been quite dark but was now sky-blue. He buttoned it up and drew on his tunic, his shabby gray tunic with the wound badge. Perhaps the badge was made in this fellow's patriotic-flag factory, he thought. Oh yes, he had meant to figure out the blond fellow's age. He has no beard, of course, but Paul had no beard either, and Paul is twenty-six. This fellow might be seventeen or he might be forty; he has a strange face; I expect he's twenty. Besides, he's already a private first class, he must have been serving for more than a year or almost two. Twenty —twenty-one, Andreas figured. All right. Tunic on, collar done up, it really felt great to be clean.

No, thanks, they could find their way back to the alcove alone. By this time a few officers, whom they had to salute, were sitting in the restaurant. That was awful, having to salute, saluting was terrible, and it was a relief to be back in the shelter of the alcove.

"That's how I like to see you, boys," said Willi. Willi was drinking wine and smoking a cigar. The table had already been set with various plates, forks, knives, and spoons.

Georg waited on them silently. First came a soup. Bouillon, Andreas thought. He prayed softly, a long prayer; the others had already begun their soup, and he was still praying, and it was odd that they did not comment.

After the soup came some sort of potato salad, just a tiny portion. With it an apéritif. Like in France. Then came a series of meat dishes. First some meat patties, then something very peculiar-looking. "And what is this?" Willi asked majestically, but he laughed as he said it.

"That?" Georg grinned. "That's pork heart . . . very good pork heart. . . ." Then came a cutlet, a good juicy cutlet. A real "last meal," thought Andreas, just right for a condemned man, and he was shocked to find how good it all tasted. It's disgraceful, he thought. I ought to be praying, praying, spending the whole day somewhere on my knees, and here I am eating pork heart. . . . It's disgraceful. Next came vegetables, the first vegetables, peas. Then finally some potatoes. And then more meat, something resembling a goulash, a very tasty goulash. More vegetables, and a salad. Finally something green. And wine with everything; Willi poured, very majestically, laughing as he did so.

"We'll blow the whole mortgage today. Long live the Lvov mortgage!" They drank a toast to the Lvov mortgage.

A whole series of desserts. Like in France, Andreas thought. First some creamy pudding, with real eggs in it. Then a piece of cake with hot vanilla sauce. With this they had more wine, poured by Willi, a very sweet wine. Then came something very small, a tiny object lying on a white plate. It was something with chocolate icing, puff pastry with chocolate icing and cream inside, real cream. Pity it's so small, thought Andreas. No one said a word, the blond fellow was still in a daze, it was frightening to see his face, he kept his mouth open and chewed and ate and drank. And finally there actually came some cheese. Why, damn it all, exactly like in France, cheese and bread, and that was it. Cheese closes the stomach, thought Andreas; they drank white wine with it, white wine from France . . . Sauternes. . . .

My God, hadn't he drunk Sauternes in Le Tréport on a terrace overlooking the sea, Sauternes, delicious as milk, fire, and honey, Sauternes in Le Tréport on a terrace overlooking the sea on a summer evening, and hadn't those beloved eyes been with him that evening, almost as close as all those years ago in Amiens? Sauternes in Le Tréport. It was the same wine. He had a good memory for tastes. Sauternes in Le Tréport, and she had been close to him with mouth and hair and her eyes, the wine makes all this possible, and it's good to eat bread and cheese with white wine. . . .

"Well, boys," said Willi, in the best of spirits, "did you enjoy your meal?" Yes, they had really enjoyed it; they felt very content.

They had not overeaten. You must drink wine with your meal, it's wonderful. Andreas prayed. . . . You must say grace after a meal, and he prayed for a long time—while the others leaned back in their chairs and smoked, Andreas propped his elbows on the table and prayed. . . .

Life is beautiful, he thought, it was beautiful. Twelve hours before my death I have to find out that life is beautiful, and it's too late. I've been ungrateful, I've denied the existence of human happiness. And life was beautiful. He turned red with humiliation, red with fear, red with remorse. I really did deny the existence of human happiness, and life was beautiful. I've had an unhappy life . . . a wasted life, as they say. I've suffered every instant from this ghastly uniform, and they've nattered my ears off, and they made me shed blood on their battlefields, real blood it was, three times I was wounded on the field of so-called honor, outside Amiens, and down at Tiraspol, and then in Nikopol—and I've seen nothing but dirt and blood and shit and smelled nothing but filth . . . and misery . . . heard nothing but obscenities, and for a mere tenth of a second I was allowed to know true human love, the love of man and woman, which surely must be beautiful, for a mere tenth of a second, and twelve hours or eleven hours before my death I have to find out that life was beautiful. I drank Sauternes . . . on a terrace above Le Tréport by the sea, and in Cayeux, in Cayeux I also drank Sauternes, also on a summer evening, and my beloved was with me . . . and in Paris I used to spend hours at those sidewalk cafés soaking up some other glorious golden wine. I know for sure my beloved was with me, and I didn't need to comb through forty million people to find happiness. I thought I had forgotten nothing, I had forgotten everything . . . everything . . . and this meal was wonderful. . . . The pork heart and the cheese, and the wine that gave me the power to remember that life is beautiful. . . . Twelve hours, or eleven hours, to go. . . .

Last of all, he thought once more about the Jews of Cernăuți, then he remembered the Jews of Lvov, and the Jews of Stanislav and Kolomyya, the cannon down there in the Sivash marshes. And the man who had said: Those are precisely the advantages of the 37 antitank weapon. . . . And that poor ugly shivering whore in Paris whom he had pushed away in the night . . .

"Come on, buddy, have another drink!" said Willi roughly, and Andreas raised his head and drank. There was still some wine left, the bottle was standing in the ice bucket; he emptied his glass and Willi refilled it.

All this is happening in Lvov, everything I'm doing here, he thought, in a mansion of the old Hapsburg Empire, in an old dilapidated imperial mansion, in one of the great rooms of this house where they used to entertain on a grand scale, give glamorous balls where they danced the waltz, at least—he counted under his breath—at least twenty-eight years ago, no, twenty-nine, twenty-nine years ago there was no war yet. Twenty-nine years ago all this was still Austria . . . then it was Poland . . . then it was Russia . . . and now, now it's all Greater Germany. They used to have balls . . . they danced the waltz, wonderful waltzes, and they would smile at one another and dance . . . and outdoors, in the big garden that must be behind the house, in that big garden they would kiss, the lieutenants and the girls . . . and maybe the majors and the wives, and the host, he must have been a colonel or a general and he pretended not to see what was going on . . . or maybe he was a very senior civil servant or some such thing . . . maybe. . . .

"Come on, buddy, have another drink!" Yes, he'd like some more wine. Time is running out, he thought, I wonder what time it is. It was eleven, or eleven-fifteen, when we left the station, by now it must be two or three o'clock . . . twelve more hours, no, more than that. The train doesn't leave till five, and then I've got till . . . soon. That Soon was all blurred again now. Forty miles beyond Lvov, it won't be more than that. Forty miles, that'll be an hour and a half by train, that would make it six-thirty, it'll be light by then. All of a sudden, just as he was raising his glass to his lips, he knew it would never be light again. Thirty miles . . . an hour or three-quarters of an hour before the first hint of dawn. No, it'll still be dark, there'll be no dawn! That's it! That's it exactly! Five forty-five, and tomorrow is already Sunday, and tomorrow Paul begins his new week, and all this week Paul has the six o'clock Mass. I shall die as Paul is mounting the steps to the altar. That's absolutely certain, when he starts reciting the antiphons without an altar boy. He once told me that you can't count on altar boys nowadays. When Paul is reciting the antiphons between Lvov and . . . he must look and see which place is thirty miles beyond Lvov. He must get hold of the map. He glanced up and saw that the blond fellow was still dozing in his chair; he was tired, he had had sentry duty. Willi was awake and smiling happily, Willi was drunk, and the map was in the other man's pocket. But there was plenty of time. More than twelve hours, fifteen hours to go. . . . In these fifteen hours he had to see to a lot of things. Say my prayers, say my prayers, no more sleep . . . whatever happens, no more sleep, and I'm glad I'm so sure now. Willi also knows he's going to die, and the blond fellow is ready to die too, their lives are over; it will soon be full, the hourglass is nearly full, and death has only a few, a very few, more grains of sand to add.

"Well, boys," said Willi, "sorry, but it's time we were moving. Nice here. Wasn't it?" He nudged the blond fellow, who woke up. He was still dreaming, his face was all dreams, and his eyes no longer had that nasty, slimy look; there was something childlike about them, and that might have been because he had had a real dream, had been genuinely happy. Happiness washes away many things, just as suffering washes away many things.

"Because now," said Willi, "now we have to go to the rubber-stamp place. But I'm not giving anything away yet!" He was rather hurt that nobody asked him; he beckoned to Georg and paid something over four hundred marks. The tip was a princely one. "And a taxi," said Willi. They picked up their luggage, buckled their belts, put on their caps, and went out past the officers, past the civilians, and past the ones in the brown uniforms. And there was much amazement in the eyes of the officers and of the ones in the brown uniforms. And it was just like in every bar in Europe, in French bars, Hungarian, Rumanian, Russian, and Yugoslav bars, and Czechoslovakian and Dutch and Belgian and Norwegian and Italian and Luxembourg bars: the same buckling of belts and putting on of caps and saluting at the door, as if one were leaving a temple inhabited by very stern gods.

And they left the imperial mansion, the imperial driveway, and Andreas cast one more glance at that crumbling façade, the waltz façade, before they got into the taxi and were off.

"Now," said Willi, "now we're going to the rubber-stamp place. They open at five."

"May I have another look at the map?" Andreas asked the blond fellow, but before the latter could pull the map out of his Luftwaffe pack they were stopping again. They had driven only a short distance along the wide, brooding imperial avenue. Beyond lay open country and a few villas, and the house they had stopped at was a Polish house. The roof was flattish, the façade a dirty yellow, and the narrow, tall windows were closed with shutters reminiscent of France, shutters with very narrow slits, very flimsy-looking, painted gray. It was a Polish house, this rubber-stamp place, and something told Andreas immediately that it was a brothel. The whole ground floor was hidden by a thick beech hedge, and as they walked through the front garden he saw that the ground-floor windows were not shuttered. . . .

He saw russet-colored curtains, dirty russet-colored, almost dark brown with a touch of red. "You can get any stamp in the world here," said Willi with a laugh. "You just have to know the ropes and be firm." They stood with their luggage outside the front door after Willi had pulled the bell, and it was some time before they heard any sound in the silent, mysterious house. Andreas was sure they were being watched. They were watched for a long time, so long that Willi began to get uneasy. "Damn it all," he said peevishly, "they don't have to hide anything from me. They hide everything suspicious, see, when someone they don't know comes to the door." But at that moment the door opened, and an oldish woman came toward Willi with outstretched arms and a fulsome smile.

"I almost didn't recognize you," she said in welcoming tones. "Come in! And these," she said, indicating Andreas and the other man, "these are two young friends of yours," she shook her head disapprovingly, "two very, very young friends for our house."

All three men went inside and set down their luggage in an alcove in the hall.

"We need our passes stamped for the train tomorrow morning at five, the courier train—you know the one I mean."

The woman looked doubtfully at the two younger men. She was a bit nervous. Her graying hair was a wig, you could tell. Her narrow, sharp-featured face with the gray, indeterminate eyes was made up, very discreetly made up. She was wearing a smart dress patterned in red and black, closed at the neck so as not to show her skin, that faded neck-skin, like the skin of a fowl. She ought to wear a high closed collar, Andreas thought, a general's collar.

"Very well," said the woman, with some hesitation, "and . . . anything else?"

"Maybe a drink, and I'd like a girl—how about you fellows?"

"No," said Andreas, "no girl."

The blond fellow flushed and was sweating with fear. It must be terrible for him, Andreas thought; maybe it would help him to have a girl.

Suddenly Andreas heard music. It was a snatch of music, the merest shred. Somewhere a door had been opened to a room where there must be a radio, and in the half second that the door was open he heard a few snatches of music, like someone searching along a radio panel for the right station . . . jazz . . . marching songs . . . a resounding voice and a bit of Schubert . . . Schubert . . . Schubert. . . . Now the door was shut again, but Andreas felt as if someone had thrust a knife into his heart and opened a secret floodgate: he turned pale, swayed, and leaned against the wall. Music . . . a snatch of Schubert . . . I'd give ten years of my life to hear a whole Schubert song again, but all I've got is twelve and three-quarter hours, it must be five o'clock by now.

"How about you?" asked the oldish woman, whose mouth was horrible. He could see that now: it was a narrow, cramped slot of a mouth, a mouth that was only interested in money, a moneybox mouth. "How about you," asked the woman, alarmed, "don't you want anything?"

"Music," stammered Andreas, "do you sell music here too?" She looked at him in bewilderment, hesitated. No doubt there was nothing she had not sold. Rubber stamps and girls and pistols—that mouth was a mouth that dealt in everything—but she didn't know whether it was possible to sell music.

"I . . ." she said, embarrassed, "music . . . but of course." It's always a good idea to start with yes. You can always say no later. If you say no right off, your chances of doing business are nil.

Andreas had straightened up again. "Will you sell me some music?"

"Not without a girl," smiled the woman.

Andreas threw Willi an agonized look. He didn't know what it would cost, music *and* a girl, and strangely enough Willi understood that look at once. "Remember the mortgage, my lad," he cried. "Long live the Lvov mortgage! It's all ours!"

"All right," Andreas said to the woman, "I'll take some music and a girl." The door was opened by three girls who stood laughing in the hall, they had been listening to the negotiations, two were brunettes and one was a redhead. The redhead, who had recognized Willi and flung her arms around his neck, called out to the oldish woman, "Why don't you sell him the 'opera singer'?" The two brunettes laughed, and one of them appropriated the blond fellow and laid a hand on his arm. He gave a sob at her touch, buckled at the knees like a straw, and the brunette had to grab him and hold on to him, whispering, "Don't be scared, sweetie, there's no need to be scared!"

Actually, it was a good thing the blond fellow was sobbing. Andreas wanted to weep too; the waters behind the floodgate were pressing forward to where the wall had been pierced. At last I'll be able to cry, but I'm not going to cry in front of this slot of a mouth that's only interested in money. Maybe I'll cry when I'm with the "opera singer."

"That's right," said the remaining brunette pertly. "If he wants music, send him the opera singer." She turned away, and Andreas, still leaning against the wall, could hear the door being opened again, and again his ear caught a snatch of music, but it wasn't Schubert . . . it was something by Liszt . . . Liszt was beautiful too . . . and Liszt could make me cry, he thought; I haven't cried for three and a half years.

The blond fellow was leaning against his brunette like a child, his head resting on her breast; he was weeping, and this weeping was good. No more Sivash marshes in these tears, no more terror, and yet much pain, much pain. And the redhead, who had a good-natured face, said to Willi, whose arm was clasped around her waist, "Buy him the opera singer, he's a sweetie, I think he's a real sweetie with his music." She blew Andreas a kiss. "He's young and a real sweetheart, you old rascal, and you must buy him the opera singer and a piano. . . ."

"The mortgage, the whole Lvov mortgage is ours!" Willi shouted.

The oldish woman led Andreas up the stairs and along a corridor, past many closed doors, into a room furnished with some easy chairs, a couch, and a piano.

"This is a little bar for special occasions," she said. "The price is six hundred a night, and the opera singer—that's a nickname, of course—the opera singer costs two hundred and fifty a night, not including refreshments."

Andreas staggered over to one of the armchairs, nodded, waved her away, and was glad to see the woman go. He heard her call out in the corridor, "Olina . . . Olina. . . ."

I ought to have rented just the piano, thought Andreas, just the piano, but then he shuddered at the idea of being in this house at all. In despair he dashed to the window and flung back the curtain. Outside it was still light. Why this artificial darkness? It's the last day I'll ever see, why draw the curtains over it? The sun was still above a hill and shining with gentle warmth into gardens lying behind handsome villas, shining on the roofs of the villas. It's time they harvested the apples, Andreas thought, it's the end of September, the apples must be ripe here too. In Cherkassy another pocket has been closed, and the pickpockets will manage it somehow.

Everything's being managed, everything's being managed, and here I sit by a window in a brothel, in the "rubber-stamp house," with only twelve more hours to live, twelve and a half hours, and I ought to be praying, praying, on my knees, but I'm powerless against this floodgate that's been opened, pierced open by the dagger that was thrust into me downstairs in the hall: music. And it's just as well I'm not going to spend the whole night alone with this piano. I'd go crazy, a piano especially. A piano. It's a good thing Olina is coming, the "opera singer." The map! I forgot the map, he thought. I forgot to ask the blond fellow for it; I just have to know what lies thirty miles beyond Lvov . . . I just have to . . . it can't be Stanislav, not even Stanislav, I won't even get as far as Stanislav. Between Lvov and Cernăuţi . . . how certain I was at first about Cernăuţi! At first I would have been ready to bet I'd get to see Cernăuţi, a suburb of Cernăuţi . . . only another thirty miles now . . . another twelve hours. . . .

He swung round in alarm at a very soft sound, as of a cat slipping into the room. The opera singer was standing by the door, which she had closed softly behind her. She was small and very slight, with fine, delicate features, and her golden, very beautiful hair was tied loosely back on the crown of her head. There were red slippers on her feet, and she wore a pale-green dress. As soon as their eyes met, her hand went to her shoulder, as though to undo her dress then and there. . . .

"No!" cried Andreas, and instantly regretted letting fly at her like that. I've already bawled out one of them, he thought, and I'll never be able to wipe that out. The opera singer looked at him, less offended than surprised. The strange note of anguish in his voice had caught her ear. "No," said Andreas more gently, "don't."

He moved toward her, stepped back, sat down, stood up again, and added, "Is it all right to call you by your first name?"

"Yes," she said, very low. "My name is Olina."

"I know," he said. "Mine's Andreas."

She sat down in the armchair he gestured toward and gave him a puzzled, almost apprehensive look. He walked to the door and turned the key in the lock. Sitting beside her, he studied her profile. She had a finely drawn nose, neither round nor pointed, a Fragonard nose, he thought, and a Fragonard mouth too. She looked wanton in a way, but she could just as easily be innocent, as innocently wanton as those Fragonard shepherdesses, but she had a Polish face; the nape of her neck was Polish, supple, elemental.

He was glad he had brought cigarettes. But he was out of matches. She quickly got up, opened a closet that was crammed with bottles and boxes, and took out some matches. Before handing them to him she wrote something down on a sheet of paper lying in the closet. "I have to note down everything," she said, her voice still low, "even these."

They smoked and looked out into the golden countryside with the gardens of Lvov behind the villas.

"You used to be an opera singer?" asked Andreas.

"No," she said, "they just call me that because I studied music. They think if you've studied music you must be an opera singer."

"So you can't sing?"

"Oh yes I can, but I didn't study singing, I just sing . . . like that, you know."

"And what did you study?"

"The piano," she said quietly, "I wanted to be a pianist."

How strange, thought Andreas, I wanted to be a pianist too. A stab of pain constricted his heart. I wanted to be a pianist, it was the dream of my life. I could play quite nicely, really, quite well, but school hung around my neck like a leaden weight. School prevented me. First I had to finish school. Everyone in Germany first has to finish school. You can't do a thing without a high-school diploma. First I had to finish school, and by the time I'd done that it was 1939, and I had to join the labor service, and by the time I was through with that the war had started; that was four and a half years ago and I haven't touched a piano since. I wanted to be a pianist. I dreamed about it, just as much as other people dream of becoming school principals. But I wanted to be a pianist, and I loved the piano more than anything else in the world, but nothing came of it. First school, then labor service, and by that time they'd started a war, the bastards. . . . The pain was suffocating him, and he had never felt as wretched in his life. It'll do me good to suffer. Perhaps that'll help me to be forgiven for sitting here in a brothel in Lvov beside the opera singer who costs two hundred and fifty for a whole night without matches and without piano, the piano that costs six hundred. Perhaps I'll be forgiven for all that because this pain is numbing me, paralyzing me, because she said the words "pianist" and "piano." It's excruciating, this pain, it's like an acrid poison in my throat and it's sliding farther and farther down, through my gullet and into my stomach, and spreading all through my body. Half an hour ago I was still happy because I'd drunk Sauternes, because I remembered the terrace above Le Tréport where the eyes had been very close to me, and where I played the piano to them, to those eyes, in my imagination, and now I'm consumed with agony, sitting in this brothel beside this lovely girl whom the entire great-and-glorious German Wehrmacht would envy me. And I'm glad I'm suffering, I'm glad I'm almost passing out with pain, I'm happy to be suffering, suffering so excruciatingly, because then I may hope to be forgiven everything, forgiven for not praying, praying, praying, not spending my last twelve hours on my knees praying. But where could I kneel? Nowhere on earth could I kneel in peace. I'll tell Olina to keep watch at the door, and I'll get Willi to pay six hundred marks for the piano, and two hundred and fifty marks for the beautiful opera singer without matches, and I'll buy Olina a bottle of wine so she won't get bored. . . .

"What's the matter?" Olina asked. There was surprise in her gentle voice since he had cried no.

He looked at her, and it was wonderful to see her eyes. Gray, very gentle, sad eyes. He must give her an answer.

"Nothing," he said; and then suddenly he asked, and it was a tremendous effort to force the few words out of his mouth through the poison of his pain, "Did you finish your music studies?"

"No," she said shortly, and he saw it would be cruel to question her. She tossed her cigarette into the large metal ashtray that she had placed on the floor between their two armchairs, and asked, her voice low and gentle again, "Shall I tell you about it?"

"Yes," he said, not daring to look at her, for those gray eyes, that were perfectly calm, scared him.

"All right." But she did not begin. She was looking at the floor; he was aware when she raised her head, and then she asked suddenly, "How old are you?"

"In February I would be twenty-four," he said quietly.

"In February you would be twenty-four. 'Would be' . . . won't you be?"

He looked at her, astonished. What a sensitive ear she had! And all at once he knew he would tell her about it, her alone. She was the only person who was to know everything, that he was going to die, tomorrow morning, just before six, or just after six, in . . .

"Oh well," he said, "it's just a manner of speaking. What's the place called," he asked suddenly, "that lies thirty miles beyond Lvov toward . . . toward Cernăuţi?"

Her astonishment was growing. "Stry," she said.

Stry? What a strange name, Andreas thought, I must have overlooked it on the map. For God's sake, I must pray for the Jews of Stry too. Let's hope there are still some Jews in Stry . . . Stry . . . so that's where it will be, he would die just this side of Stry . . . not even Stanislav, not even Kolomyya, and a long, long way this side of Cernăuţi. Stry! That was it! Maybe it wasn't even on that map of Willi's. . . .

"So you'll be twenty-four in February," said Olina. "Funny, so will

I." He looked at her. She smiled. "So will I," she repeated. "I was born February 12, 1920."

They looked at each other for a long time, a very long time, and their eyes sank into one another's, and then Olina leaned toward him, and because the chairs were too far apart she rose, moved toward him, and made as if to put her arms around him, but he turned aside. "No," he said quietly, "not that, don't be angry with me, later . . . I'll explain . . . My . . . my birthday's February 15."

She lit another cigarette, he was glad he hadn't offended her. She was smiling. She was thinking, after all he's hired the room and me for the whole night. And it's only six o'clock, not even quite six. . . .

"You were going to tell me about it," said Andreas.

"Yes," she said. "We're the same age. I like that. I'm three days older than you. I expect I'm your sister. . . ." She laughed. "Maybe I really am your sister."

"Please, tell me about it."

"I am," she said, "I am telling you. In Warsaw I studied at the Conservatory of Music. You wanted to hear about my studies, didn't you?"

"Yes!"

"Do you know Warsaw?"

"No."

"Well then. Here we go. Warsaw is a big city, a beautiful city, and the Conservatory was in a house like this one. Only the garden was bigger, much bigger. During recess we could stroll in that lovely big garden and flirt. They told me I was very talented. I took piano. I would rather have played only the harpsichord at first, but no one taught that, so I had to take piano. For my audition I had to play a short, simple little Beethoven sonata. That was tricky. It's so easy to make a mess of those simple little things, or one plays them too emotionally. It's very difficult to play those simple things. It was Beethoven, you know, but a very early Beethoven, almost classical in style, almost like Haydn. A very subtle piece for an audition, d'you see?"

"Yes," said Andreas, and he could sense that soon he was going to cry.

"Good. I passed, with a Very Good. I studied and played till . . . let's see . . . till the war started. That's right, it was the fall of '39—two years. I learned a lot and flirted a lot. I always did like kissing and all that, you know. I could play Liszt quite well by that time, and Tchaikovsky. But I could never really play Bach properly. I would have liked to play Bach. And I could play Chopin quite well too. Fine. Then came the war.

... Oh yes, and there was a garden behind the Conservatory, a wonderful garden, with benches and arbors, and sometimes we had parties, and there would be music and dancing in the garden. Once we had a Mozart evening, a wonderful Mozart evening. . . . Mozart was another one I could already play quite well. Well, then came the war!"

She broke off abruptly, and Andreas turned questioning eyes on her. She looked angry. The hair seemed to bristle above that Fragonard forehead.

"For God's sake," she burst out, "do what the others all do with me. This is ridiculous!"

"No," said Andreas, "you have to tell me."

"That," she said frowning, "is something you can't pay for."

"Yes I can," he said. "I'll pay in the same coin. I'll tell you my story too. Everything. . . ."

But she was silent. She stared at the floor and was silent. He studied her out of the corner of his eye and thought: She does look like a tart after all. There's sex in every fiber of that pretty face, and she's not an innocent shepherdess, she's a very wanton shepherdess. It gave him a pang to find that she was a tart after all: the dream had been very lovely. She might be standing anywhere in the Gare Montparnasse. And it did him good to feel that pain again. For a time it had completely gone. He loved listening to her gentle voice telling him about the Conservatory. . . .

"It's boring," she said suddenly. She spoke with complete indifference.

"Let's have some wine," said Andreas.

She rose, walked briskly to the closet, and in a businesslike voice asked, "What would you like to drink?" She looked into the closet. "There's some red wine and some white, Moselle, I think."

"All right," he said, "let's have some Moselle."

She brought over the bottle, pushed a little table up to their chairs, handed him the corkscrew, and set out glasses while he opened the bottle. He watched her, then poured the wine, they raised their glasses, and he smiled into her angry eyes.

"Let's drink to the year of our birth," he said, "1920."

She smiled against her will. "All right, but I'm not going to tell you any more."

"Shall I tell you my story?"

"No," she said. "All you fellows can talk about is the war. I've been listening to that for two years now. Always the war. As soon as you've finished . . . you begin talking about the war. It's boring."

"What would you like to do, then?"

"I'd like to seduce you. You're a virgin, aren't you?"

"Yes," said Andreas, and was taken aback at the way she promptly jumped up. "I knew it," she cried, "I knew it!" He saw her eager, flushed face, the eyes flashing at him, and thought: Funny, I've never seen any woman I've desired less than this one, and she's beautiful, and I could have her right now. Oh yes, sometimes a thrill has gone through me, without my trying or wanting it, and for that split second I've known that it must be truly wonderful to possess a woman. But there's never been one I desired as little as this one. I'll tell her about it, I'll tell her everything. . . .

"Olina," he said, pointing to the piano, "Olina, play the little Beethoven sonata."

"Promise you'll . . . promise you'll make love to me."

"No," he said quietly. "Come and sit here." He made her sit beside him in the armchair, and she looked at him without saying a word.

"Now, listen," he said. "I'm going to tell you my story."

He looked out of the window and saw that the sun had gone down and that only a very little light remained over the gardens. Very soon there would be no more sunlight outside in the gardens, and never again, never again would the sun shine, never again would he see a single ray of sunshine. The last night was beginning, and the last day had passed like all the others, wasted and meaningless. He had prayed a bit and drunk some wine and now he was in a brothel. He waited until it was dark. He had no idea how long it took, he had forgotten the girl, forgotten the wine, the whole house, and all he saw was a last little bit of the forest, whose treetops caught a few final glints from the setting sun, a few tiny glints from the sun. Some reddish gleams, exquisite, indescribably beautiful on those treetops. A tiny crown of light, the last light he would ever see. Now it was gone . . . no, there was still a bit, a tiny little bit on the tallest of the trees, the one that reached up the highest and could still catch something of the golden reflection that would remain for only half a second . . . until it was all gone. It's still there, he thought, holding his breath . . . still a particle of light up there on the treetop . . . an absurd little shimmer of sunlight, and no one in the world but me is watching it. Still there . . . still there, it was like a smile that faded very slowly . . . still there, and now it was gone! The light has gone out, the lantern has vanished, and I shall never see it again. . . .

"Olina," he said softly, and he felt he could speak now, and he knew he would win her because it was dark. A woman can only be won in the dark. Funny, he thought, I wonder if that's really true. He had the feeling that Olina belonged to him now, had surrendered to him. "Olina," he said softly, "tomorrow morning I must die. That's right," he said calmly, looking at her shocked face, "don't be scared! Tomorrow morning I must die. You're the first and only person I've told. I am certain. I must die. A moment ago the sun went down. Just this side of Stry I shall die. . . ."

She jumped to her feet and looked at him in horror. "You're mad," she whispered, white-faced.

"No," he said, "I'm not mad, that's how it is, you must believe me. You must believe that I'm not mad, that tomorrow morning I shall die, and now you must play me the little Beethoven sonata."

She stared at him, aghast, and murmured, "But . . . but that's impossible."

"I'm absolutely certain and you have told me the last thing I needed to know, Stry, that's it. What a terrible name, Stry. What kind of a word is that, Stry? Why must I die just this side of Stry? Why did it have first to be between Lvov and Cernăuți . . . then Kolomyya . . . then Stanislav . . . then Stry? The moment you said Stry, I knew that was the place. Wait!" he called, as she rushed to the door and stood staring at him with terrified eyes.

"You must stay with me," he said, "you must stay with me. I'm a human being, and I can't stand it alone. Stay with me, Olina. I'm not mad. Don't scream." He held his hand over her mouth. "My God, what can I do to prove to you I'm not mad? What can I do? Tell me what I can do to prove to you I'm not mad."

But she was too frightened to hear what he was saying. She merely stared at him with her terrified eyes, and all at once he realized what a dreadful profession she had. If he were really mad, she would now be standing there helpless. They send her to a room, and two hundred and fifty marks are paid for her because she is the "opera singer," a very valuable little doll, and she has to go to that room like a soldier going to the front. She has to go, even though she is the opera singer, a very valuable little doll. A terrible life. They send her to a room and she has no idea who is inside. An old man, a young one, an ugly man or a handsome one, bestial or innocent. She has no idea and goes to the room, and now there she is, frightened, just frightened, too frightened to hear what he is saying. It is truly a sin to go to a brothel, he thought. They send girls to a room, just like that. . . . He gently stroked the hand he was restraining her by, and strangely enough the fear in her eyes began to recede. He went on stroking it, and felt as if he were stroking a child. I've never desired a woman as little as this one. A child . . . and suddenly he saw that poor grubby little girl in a suburb of Berlin, playing among prefabs where there were some scrawny gardens, and the other kids had taken her doll and thrown it into a puddle . . . and then run away. And he had bent down and pulled the doll out of the puddle; it was dripping with dirty water, a dangling, frayed, cheap ragdoll, and he had to stroke the child for a long time and try and console her for her poor doll's having got wet . . . a child. . . .

"You're all right now, aren't you?" he said. She nodded, and there were tears in her eyes. He led her gently back to the chair. The dusk had become heavy and sad.

She sat down obediently, keeping her still somewhat nervous gaze on him. He poured her some wine. She drank. Then she sighed deeply. "God, how you scared me," she said, and thirstily gulped down the rest of her wine.

"Olina," he said, "you're twenty-three now. Just ask yourself whether you're going to be twenty-five, will you?" he urged her. "Say to yourself: I am twenty-five years old. That's February 1945, Olina. Try, think hard." She closed her eyes, and he saw from her lips that she was saying something under her breath that in Polish must mean: February 1945.

"No," she said, as if waking up, and she shook her head. "There's nothing there, as if it didn't exist—how odd."

"You see?" he said. "And when I think: Sunday noon, tomorrow noon, that doesn't exist for me. That's the way it is. I'm not mad." He saw her close her eyes again and say something under her breath. . . .

"It's odd," she said softly, "but February 1944 doesn't exist either. . . . Oh, for heaven's sake," she broke out, "why won't you make love? Why won't you dance with me?" She moved swiftly to the piano and sat down. And then she played: "I'm dancing with you into heaven, the seventh heaven of love. . . ."

Andreas smiled. "Come on, play the Beethoven sonata . . . play a . . ."

But again she was playing "I'm dancing with you into heaven, the seventh heaven of love." She played it very softly, as softly as dusk was now sinking into the room through the open curtains. She played the sentimental tune unsentimentally, which was strange. The notes sounded crisp, almost staccato, very soft, almost as if suddenly she were turning this brothel piano into a harpsichord. Harpsichord, thought Andreas, that's the right instrument for her, she ought to play the harpsichord. . . .

The popular tune she was now playing was no longer the same, yet it was the same. What a lovely tune it is, thought Andreas. It's fantastic, what she can make of it. Perhaps she studied composition too, and she's turning this trivial tune into a sonata hovering in the dusk. Now and again, at intervals, she would play the original melody again, pure and clear, unsentimentally: "I'm dancing with you into heaven, the seventh heaven of love." Now and again, between the gentle, playful waves, she allowed the theme to rear up like a granite cliff.

It was almost dark now, it was getting chilly, but he didn't care; the music sounded so beautiful that he wasn't going to get up and close the window; even if subzero air were to come in through the window from the gardens of Lvov, he wasn't going to get up. . . . Maybe I'm dreaming it's 1943 and I'm sitting here in a Lvov brothel wearing the gray tunic of Hitler's army; maybe I'm dreaming, maybe I was born in the seventeenth century or the eighteenth, and I'm sitting in my mistress's drawing room, and she's playing the harpsichord, just for me, all the music in the world just for me . . . in a château somewhere in France, or a little schloss in western Germany, and I'm listening to the harpsichord in an eighteenth-century drawing room, played by someone who loves me, who is playing just for me, just for me. The whole world is mine, here in the dusk; very soon the candles will be lit, we won't call a servant . . . no, no servant . . . I shall light the candles with a paper spill, and I shall light the paper spill with my paybook from the fire in the hearth. No, there's no fire burning in the hearth. I shall light the fire myself, the air from the garden, from the grounds of the château, is damp and cool; I shall kneel by the hearth, tenderly place the kindling in layers, crumple each page of my paybook, and light the fire with the matches she noted down. Those matches will be paid for with the Lvov mortgage. I shall kneel at her feet, for she will be waiting with tender impatience for the fire to be lit in the hearth. Her feet have grown cold at the harpsichord; she has sat at the open window in this damp, cool air for a long, long time, playing for me, my sister, she has been playing so beautifully that I wouldn't get up to close the window . . . and I shall make a lovely bright fire, and we won't need any servants, no indeed, no servants! Just as well the door is locked. . . .

Nineteen forty-three. A terrible century; what awful clothes the men will be wearing; they will glorify war and wear dirt-colored clothes in the war, while we never glorified war, war was an honest craft at which now and again a man got cheated of his rightful wages; and we wore cheerful clothes when we worked at this craft, just as a doctor wears cheerful clothes and a mayor . . . and a prostitute. But those people will be wearing horrible clothes and will glorify war and fight wars for their national honor: a terrible century; 1943. . . .

We have all night, all night. Dusk has only just fallen in the garden, the door is locked, and nothing can disturb us; the whole château is ours; wine and candles and a harpsichord! Eight hundred and fifty marks without the matches; millions lying around Nikopol! Nikopol! Nothing! . . . Kishinev? Nothing! . . . Cernăuți? Nothing! . . . Kolomyya? Nothing! . . . Stanislav? Nothing! Stry . . . Stry . . . that terrible name that is like a streak, a bloody streak across my throat! In Stry I'm going to be murdered. Every death is a murder, every death in war is a murder for which someone is responsible. In Stry!

"I'm dancing with you into heaven, the seventh heaven of love!"

It was not a dream at all, a dream ending with the last note of that melodic paraphrase; it merely tore the frail web that had been cast over him, and now for the first time, by the open window, in the cool of the dusk, he realized he had been crying. He had neither known it nor felt it, but his face was wet, and Olina's hands, soft and very small, were drying his face; the rivulets had run down his face and collected in the closed collar of his tunic; she undid the hook and dried his neck with her handkerchief. She dried his cheeks and around his eyes, and he was grateful that she said nothing. . . .

A strangely sober joy filled him. The girl switched on the light, closed the window with averted face, and it was possible she had been crying too. This chaste happiness is something I have never known, he thought, as she crossed to the closet. I've always only desired, I've desired an unknown body, and I've desired that soul too, but here I desire nothing. . . . How strange that I have to find this out in a Lvov brothel, on the last evening of my life, on the threshold of the last night of my earthly existence that is to come to an end tomorrow morning in Stry with a bloody streak. . . .

"Lie down," said Olina. She indicated the little sofa, and he noticed that she had switched on an electric kettle in that mysterious closet.

"I'll make some coffee," she said, "and until it's ready I'll go on with my story."

He lay down, and she sat beside him. They smoked, the ashtray lying conveniently on a stool so they could both reach it. He barely needed to stretch out his hand.

"I needn't tell you," she began quietly, "that you mustn't ever speak to anyone about it. Even if you . . . if you were not to die, you would never betray my secret. I know that. I had to swear by God and all the saints and by our beloved Poland that I would never tell a soul, but if I tell you it's as if I were telling myself, and I can't keep anything from you any more than I can keep anything from myself!" She stood up and poured the bubbling water very slowly and tenderly into a small coffeepot. Each time she paused for a few seconds she would smile at him before continuing to pour, very slowly, and now he could see she had been crying too. Then she filled the cups that were standing beside the ashtray.

"The war broke out in 1939. In Warsaw my parents were buried under the ruins of our big house, and there I was, all alone in the garden of the Conservatory, where I had been flirting, and the director was taken away because he was a Jew. Well, I just didn't feel like going on with the piano. The Germans had somehow or other raped us all, every single one of us." She drank some coffee; he took a sip too. She smiled at him.

"It's funny that you're a German and I don't hate you." She fell silent again, smiling, and he thought, It's remarkable how quickly she's surrendered. When she went to the piano she wanted to seduce me, and the first time she played "I'm dancing with you into heaven, the seventh heaven of love," it was still far from clear. While she was playing she cried. . . .

"All Poland," she went on, "is a resistance movement. You people have no idea. No one suspects how big it is. There is hardly a single unpatriotic Pole. When one of you Germans sells his pistol anywhere in Warsaw or Kraków, he should realize that in doing so he's selling as many of his comrades' lives as there is ammunition in that pistol. When anywhere, anywhere at all," she went on passionately, "a general or a lance corporal sleeps with a girl and so much as tells her they didn't get any rations near Kiev or Kishinev or some such place, or that they retreated only two miles, he never suspects that this is jotted down, and that this gladdens the girl's heart more than the twenty or two hundred and fifty zlotys she's been paid for her seeming surrender. It's so easy to be a spy among you people that I soon got disgusted with it. All one had to do was get on with it. I don't understand it."

She shook her head and gave him a look almost of contempt. "I don't understand it. You're the most garrulous people in the world, and sentimental down to your fingertips. Which army are you with?"

He told her the number.

"No," she said, "he was from a different one. A general who used to come and see me here sometimes. He talked like a sentimental schoolboy who's had a bit too much to drink. 'My boys,' he would groan, 'my poor boys!' And a little later on, the old lecher would be babbling away to me about all kinds of things that were vitally important. He's got a lot of his poor boys on his conscience . . . and he told me a lot of things. And then . . . then," she hesitated, "then I'd be like ice. . . ."

"And were there some you loved?" asked Andreas. Funny, he thought, that it should hurt to know there were some she might have loved.

"Yes," she said, "there were some I really loved—not many." She looked at him, and he saw she was crying again. He took her hand, sat up, and poured some coffee with his free hand.

"Soldiers," she said softly. "Yes. There were some soldiers I loved . . . and I knew it made no difference that they were Germans, whom actually I ought to have hated. You know, when I gave myself to them, I felt I was no longer part of the terrible game we're all playing, the game I had an especially big part in. The game of sending others to their death, men one didn't know. You see," she whispered, "some fellow, a lance corporal or a general, tells me something here, and I pass on the information—machinery is set in motion, and somewhere men die because I passed on that information, do you see what I mean?" She looked at him out of frantic eyes. "Do you see what I mean? Or take yourself: You tell some fellow at the station, 'Take that train, bud, rather than that one'—and that's the very train the partisans attack, and your buddy dies because you told him, 'Take that train.' That's why it was so wonderful just to give oneself to them, just abandon oneself, and forget everything else. I asked them nothing for our mosaic and told them nothing. I had to love them. And what's so terrible is that afterwards they're always sad. . . ."

"Mosaic," asked Andreas huskily, "what's that?"

"The whole espionage system is a mosaic. Everything's assembled and numbered, every smallest scrap we get hold of, until the picture's complete. It slowly fills out . . . and many of these mosaics make up the whole picture . . . of you people . . . of your war . . . your army. . . .

"You know," she went on, looking at him very seriously, "the terrible part is that it's all so senseless. Everywhere it's only the innocent who are murdered. Everywhere. By us too. Somehow I've always known that"—she looked away from him—"but, you know, what frightens me is that I didn't grasp it fully till I walked into this room and saw you. Your shoulders, the back of your neck, there in the golden sunshine." She pointed to the window where the two chairs were.

"I know that now. When they sent me here, when Madame told me, 'There's someone waiting for you in the bar. I don't think you'll get much out of him but at least he pays well'—as soon as she said that, I thought: I'll get something out of him, all right. Or it's someone I can love. Not one of the victims, because there are only victims and executioners. And when I saw you standing over there by the window, your shoulders, the back of your neck, your stooping young figure as if you were thousands of years old, it came to me for the first time that we also only murder the innocent . . . only the innocent. . . ."

The soundlessness of that crying was terrible. Andreas rose, stroked the nape of her neck in passing, and went to the piano. Her eyes followed him in astonishment. Her tears dried up at once. She watched him as he sat there, on the piano stool, staring at the keys, his hands spread apprehensively, and across his forehead there was a terrible furrow, an anguished furrow.

He's forgotten me, she thought, he's forgotten me, how awful it is that they always forget us at the very moment when they are really themselves. He's not thinking about me any more, he'll never think about me any more. Tomorrow morning he will die in Stry . . . and he'll waste no more thoughts on me.

He is the first and only one I've loved. The first. He is absolutely alone now. He is unbelievably sad and alone. That furrow across his forehead, it cuts him in two, his face is pale with terror, and he has spread his hands as if he had to grasp some dreadful animal. . . . If he could only play, if he could only play, he would be with me again. The first note will give him back to me. To me, to me, he belongs to me . . . he is my brother, I am three days older than he is. If he could only play. There's some monstrous cramp inside him, spreading his hands, turning him deathly pale, making him fearfully unhappy. There's nothing left of all I wanted to give him with my playing . . . with my story, there's nothing of all that with him now. It's all gone; he's alone now with his pain.

And indeed, when all at once he attacked the keys with a fierce rage in his face, he raised his eyes, and his eyes went straight to her. He smiled at her, and she had never seen such a happy face as that face of his above the black surface of the piano in the soft yellow lamplight. Oh, how I love him, she thought. How happy he is, he's mine, here in this room till morning. . . .

She had imagined he would play something crazy, some wild piece by Tchaikovsky or Liszt, or one of those glorious lilting Chopin pieces, because he had attacked the keys like a madman.

No, he played a sonatina by Beethoven. A delicate little piece, very tricky, and for a second she was afraid he would "mess it up." But he played very beautifully, very carefully, perhaps a shade too carefully, as if he did not trust his own strength. How tenderly he played, and she had never seen such a happy face as that soldier's face above the polished surface of the piano. He played the sonatina a little uncertainly, but purely, more purely than she had ever heard it, very clear and clean.

She hoped he would go on playing. It was wonderful; she had lain down on the sofa, where he had been lying, and she saw the cigarette gradually burning away in the ashtray. She longed to draw on it but dared not move; the slightest movement might destroy that music; and the best part of all was that very happy soldier's face above the black, shining surface of the piano. . . .

"No," he said with a laugh as he got to his feet, "there's not much left. It's no use. The fact is, you have to have studied, and I never did." He bent over her and dried her tears, and he was glad she had cried. "No," he said softly, "stay where you are. I was going to tell you my story too, remember?"

"Yes," she whispered. "Tell me, and give me some wine."

This is happiness, he thought, as he went to the closet. This is bliss, although I've just discovered that I'm no good at the piano. There's been no miracle. I haven't suddenly become a pianist. It's done with now, and yet I'm happy. He looked into the closet and asked over his shoulder, "Which would you like?"

"Red," she said with a smile, "a red one now."

He took a less slender bottle out of the closet, then he saw the sheet of paper and the pencil and studied the paper. At the top was something in Polish: that would be the matches; then came *"Mosel"* in German, and in front of that a Polish word no doubt meaning bottle. What charming handwriting she has, he thought, pretty, feminine handwriting, and under *"Mosel"* he wrote *"Bordeaux,"* and below the Polish word for bottle he made a ditto mark. "Did you really put it down?" she asked, smiling, as he poured the wine.

"Yes."

"You wouldn't even cheat a madame?"

"Yes, I would," he said, and he suddenly remembered Dresden station, and the taste of Dresden station, painfully distinct, was in his mouth, and he saw the fat, red-faced lieutenant. "Yes, I would; I once tricked a lieutenant." He told her the story. She laughed. "But that isn't so bad."

"Yes it is," he said, "it's very bad. I shouldn't have done that, I should have called out after him, 'I'm not deaf.' I said nothing, because I have to die soon and because he yelled at me like that . . . because I was full of pain. Besides, I was too lazy. Yes," he said softly, "I actually was too lazy to do it because it was so wonderful to have the taste of life in my mouth. I wanted to get it clear, I remember exactly, I thought: You must never let someone feel humiliated on your account, even if it's a brand-new lieutenant, not even if he has brand-new medals on his chest. You must never let that happen, I thought, and I can still see him walking off, embarrassed and smarting, crimson in the face, followed by his grinning flock of subordinates. I can see his fat arms and his pathetic shoulders. When I think of those pathetic, stupid shoulders of his, I almost have to weep. But I was too lazy, just too lazy, to open my mouth. It wasn't even fear, just plain laziness. God, I thought, how beautiful life is after all, all these people milling about on the platform. One's going to his wife, the other to his girl, and that woman's going to her son, and it's autumn, how wonderful, and that couple over there going toward the barrier, this evening or tonight they'll be kissing under the soft trees down by the Elbe." He sighed. "I'll tell you all the people I've cheated!"

"Oh no," she said, "don't. Tell me something nice . . . and pour me some more!" She laughed. "Who could you ever have cheated?"

"I'll tell you the truth. Everything I've stolen and all the people I've cheated. . . ." He poured more wine, they raised their glasses, and in that second while they looked at each other, smiling, over the rims of their glasses, he drew her lovely face deep within himself. I mustn't lose it, he thought, I must never lose it, she is mine.

I love him, she thought, I love him. . . .

"My father," he said quietly, "my father died from the effects of a serious wound that plagued him for three years after the war. I was a year old when he died. And my mother soon followed him. That's all I know about it. I learned about all this one day when I had to be told that the woman I had always thought of as my mother wasn't my mother at all. I grew up with an aunt, a sister of my mother's who had married an attorney. He made good money, but we were always terribly poor. He drank. I took it so much for granted that a man should come to the breakfast table with a thick head and in a foul temper that later on, when I got to know other men, fathers of my friends, it seemed to me they weren't men at all. That there were men who weren't stewed every evening, and who didn't make hysterical scenes every morning at breakfast, was something I couldn't conceive. A 'thing which was not,' as Swift's Houyhnhnms say. I thought we were born to be yelled at, that women were born to be yelled at, to grapple with bailiffs, to fight terrible pitched battles with shopkeepers and go off and open a new account somewhere else. My aunt was a genius—she was a genius at opening new accounts. When things were at their blackest she would become very quiet, take an aspirin, and dash off, and by the time she came back she had money. And I thought she was my mother; and I thought that fat bloated monster with burst blood vessels all over his cheeks was my respected begetter. His eyes had a yellowish tinge, and his breath reeked of beer, he stank like stale yeast. I thought he was my father. We lived in a very grand villa, with a maid and all that, and often my aunt didn't even have small change for a short streetcar ride. And my uncle was a famous attorney. Isn't that boring?" he asked abruptly, getting up to refill the glasses.

"No," she whispered, "no, go on." It took him only two seconds carefully to refill the slender glasses that stood on the coffee table, yet she took in his hands and the pale, narrow face and thought: I wonder what he looked like all those years ago, when he was five or six years old, or thirteen, sitting at that breakfast table. She had no trouble picturing that fat, drunken fellow grumbling about the jam because all he really wanted was some sausage. When they have a hangover, all they ever want is sausage. And the woman, frail perhaps, and that pale little fellow sitting there, very timid, almost too scared to eat or cough although the heavy cigar smoke caught at his throat; he would have liked to cough and didn't dare because that drunken fat monster would fly into a rage, because that famous attorney would lose control of himself at the sound of that child's cough. . . .

"Your aunt," she said, "what did she look like? Tell me exactly what your aunt looked like!"

"My aunt was very small and frail."

"Was she like your mother?"

"Yes, she was very much like my mother, to judge by the photographs. Later on, when I was older and knew about a lot of things, I used to think: How terrible it must be when he . . . when he embraces her, that hulking great fellow with his breath and the burst blood vessels all over his distended cheeks and his nose; she's forced to see them right up close, and those great yellow bleary eyes and everything. That picture haunted me for months, once I had thought of it. And all the time I thought it was my father, and I would torment myself all night long with the question: Why do they marry men like that? And . . ."

"And you cheated her too, your aunt, didn't you?"

"Yes," he said. He was silent for a moment and looked past her eyes. "That was terrible. You know, when he was seriously ill at one time—liver, kidneys, heart, his insides were all shot, of course—he was in hospital, and we took a taxi there one Sunday morning because he was to have an operation. It was a glorious sunny day, and I was absolutely miserable. And my aunt cried terribly, and she kept whispering to me, begging me to pray for him to get well. She kept whispering this to me, and I had to promise her. And I didn't do it. I was nine, and by that time I knew he wasn't my father, and I didn't pray for him to get well. I just couldn't. I didn't pray for him not to get well—no, I stopped short at that idea. But as to praying for him to get well: no, that I didn't do. I couldn't help thinking all the time how wonderful it would be if . . . yes, I did think that. The house all to ourselves, and no more scenes or anything . . . and yet I had promised my aunt to pray for him. I couldn't do it. The only thing I could think was: Why on earth do they marry men like that?"

"Because they love them," Olina interrupted.

"Yes," he said in surprise, "you know, don't you? She did love him, she had loved him, and she still loved him. At the time, of course, as a young attorney, he had looked different; there was a photo of him taken just after he passed his finals. Wearing one of those godawful student's caps. Remember—1907? He looked different then, but only on the outside."

"How do you mean?"

"Just that—only on the outside. To me his eyes looked exactly the same. Only his stomach wasn't that fat yet. But to me he looked dreadful even as a young man in that photo. I would have seen him the way he was going to look at forty-five, I wouldn't have married him. And she still loved him, although he was a wreck, although he tormented her, wasn't even faithful to her. She loved him absolutely and unconditionally. I can't understand it. . . ."

"You can't understand it?" He looked at her again in surprise. She was sitting up now, had swung her legs down, her face was close to his.

"You can't understand it?" she asked passionately.

"No," he said, astonished.

"Then you don't know what love is. Yes." She looked at him, and suddenly he was afraid of that solemn, wholly altered face. "Yes," she repeated. "Unconditionally! Love is always unconditional, you see. Haven't you," she murmured, "haven't you ever loved a woman?"

He quickly closed his eyes. Again that deep, thrusting stab of pain. That too, he thought, I have to tell her about that too. There must be no secrets between us, and I had been hoping I could keep that, that memory of an unknown face, hoping I could keep that gift to myself and take it with me. His eyes remained closed, and there was silence. He was trembling in his anguish. No, he thought, let me keep it. That's my own most private possession, and for three and a half years it's been all I've had to live on . . . just that tenth of a second on the hill outside Amiens. Why did she have to thrust so deeply and unerringly into me? Why did she have to open up that carefully protected scar with one word, a word that pierces me like a probe, the probe of an unerring surgeon. . . .

So that's it, she thought. He loves someone else. He's trembling, he's spreading his hands and closing his eyes, and I've hurt him. The ones you love are the ones you're bound to hurt the most, that's the law of love. His pain is too great for tears. Some pain is so great that tears are powerless, she thought. Oh, why aren't I that other woman he loves? Why can't I transpose this soul and this body? There's nothing, nothing of myself that I want to keep, I would surrender my whole self to have only . . . only the eyes of that other woman. This last night before his death, the last night for me too because when he's gone I shall have ceased to care about anything . . . oh, if only I could have her eyelashes, give my whole self in exchange for her eyelashes. . . .

"Yes," he said softly. His voice was without emotion, the voice of someone on the brink of death. "Yes, I loved her so much I would have sold my soul to feel her mouth for just one second. I've only just realized this—now that you ask me. And perhaps that's why I was never to know her. I would have committed murder just to see the hem of her dress as she turned a corner. Just something, something real. And I prayed, I prayed for her every day. All lies and all self-deception, because I believed I loved only her soul. Only her soul! And I would have sold all those thousands of prayers for one single kiss from her lips. I've only just realized this." He rose suddenly to his feet, and she was glad his voice was human again, a human voice that suffered and lived. Again the thought came to her that he was alone now, that he was no longer thinking of her, he was alone again.

"Yes," he said into the room, "I believed it was only her soul that I loved. But what is a soul without a body, what is a human soul without a body? I couldn't desire her soul so passionately, with all the insane passion I was capable of, without longing for her just to smile at me at least once, once. God"—he slashed the air with his hand—"always the hope, and nothing but the hope, that that soul might become flesh," he cried, "only the insane burden of hope! What's the time?" He turned on her and, although he spoke roughly and brusquely as if she were a servant girl, she was glad to see that at least he had not forgotten her presence. "Forgive me," he added swiftly, grasping her hand, but she had already forgiven him, she had forgiven him before it happened. She glanced at the clock and smiled. "Eleven." And she was filled with a great happiness, only eleven. Not yet midnight, not even midnight, how glorious, how lovely, how wonderful. She was as gay as a carefree child, jumped up and danced across the room: I'm dancing with you into heaven, the seventh heaven of love. . . .

He watched her, thinking: It's strange, really, that I can't be angry with her. Here I am, half dead with pain, deathly sick, and she's dancing, although she has shared my pain, and I can't be angry, I can't . . .

"You know what?" she asked, suddenly pausing. "We must have something to eat, that's what we need."

"No," he said, appalled. "No."

"Why not?"

"Because then you'd have to leave me. No, no," he cried out in anguish, "you mustn't leave me for a single second. Without you . . . without you . . . without you I can't go on living!"

"What?" she asked, without knowing which word her lips were forming, for a delirious hope had sprung up within her.

"That's right," he said softly, "you mustn't go away."

No, she thought, that's not it after all. I'm not the one he loves. And aloud she said, "I don't have to go away! There's food too in the closet."

How miraculous, that somewhere in a drawer of that closet there should be cookies, and cheese wrapped in silver foil. What a glorious meal, cookies and cheese and wine. He didn't like his cigarette. The tobacco was dry, and it had a kind of foul army taste.

"Give me a cigar," he said, and needless to say there was a cigar there too. A whole box of cigars good enough for a major, all for the Lvov mortgage. It felt good to stand there on the soft carpet, watching Olina arrange the little snack on the coffee table with gentle, loving hands. When she had finished, she suddenly turned to him and looked at him with a smile, "You couldn't go on living without me?"

"No," he said, and his heart was so heavy he couldn't laugh; and he thought: I ought to add now: Because I love you, and that would be true and it would not be true. If I said it I would have to kiss her, and that would be a lie, everything would be a lie, and yet I could say with a clear conscience: I love you, but I would have to give a long, long explanation, an explanation that I don't know myself yet. Always those eyes of hers, very gentle and loving and happy, the opposite of the eyes I desired . . . still desire . . . and he repeated, looking straight into her eyes, "I couldn't go on living without you," and now he was smiling. . . .

At the very moment when they were raising their glasses to drink a toast to their birthdays or their wasted lives, at that very moment their hands began to tremble violently; they put down their glasses and looked at one another in dismay: there had been a knock at the door. . . .

Andreas held back Olina's arm and slowly stood up. He strode to the door, taking only three seconds to reach it. So this is the end, he thought. They're taking her away from me, they don't want her to stay with me till morning. Time is still alive, and the world is turning. Willi and the blond fellow are each in bed with a girl somewhere in this house, that old woman is downstairs lying in wait for her money; the slot of her mouth always open, slightly open. What shall I do when I'm alone? I shan't even be able to pray, to go down on my knees. I can't live without her, because I do love her. They mustn't do that. . . .

"Yes," he asked softly.

"Olina," came the madame's voice. "I have to speak to Olina."

Andreas looked around, pale, aghast. I'll give up the five hours if only I can spend just one more half hour with her. They can have her then. But

I want to spend one more half hour with her, and look at her, just look at her; maybe she'll play the piano again. Even if it's only "I'm dancing with you into heaven. . . ."

Olina smiled at him, and he knew from that smile that she would stay with him, whatever happened. And yet he was scared, and he knew now, as Olina quietly unlocked the door, that he did not want to part with this fear for her. That he loved this fear too. "Leave your hand in mine, at least," he whispered as she was going out, and she left her hand in his, and he heard her outside beginning to talk to the madame in hurried, heated Polish. The two women were locked in combat. The moneybox was doing battle with Olina. He anxiously scanned her eyes when she came back without closing the door. He did not let go of her hand. She had turned pale too, and he could see that her confidence was no longer very great. . . .

"The general's turned up. He's offering two thousand. He's furious. He must be raising the roof down there. D'you have any money left? We have to make up the difference, otherwise. . . ."

"Yes," he said; he hastily turned out his pockets, which still contained money he had won from Willi at cards. Olina twittered something in Polish through the door. "Hurry," she whispered. She counted the bills. "Three hundred, right? I haven't a thing! Not a thing!" she said frantically. "Yes I have—here's a ring, that's five hundred. It's not worth more than that. Eight hundred."

"My coat," said Andreas, "here it is."

Olina went to the door with the three hundred, the ring, and the coat. She was even less confident on her return.

"She reckons the coat's worth four, only four—no more. And the ring six, thank God for that, six. Thirteen hundred. Don't you have anything else? Hurry!" she whispered. "If he gets impatient and comes upstairs, we're sunk."

"My paybook," he said.

"Yes, let me have it. A genuine paybook is worth a lot."

"And my watch."

"Yes," she laughed nervously, "the watch. You still have a watch. Is it running?"

"No," he said.

Olina went to the door with the paybook and the watch. More excited Polish whispering. Andreas ran after her. "Here's a sweater," he called through the door, "a hand, a leg. Can't you use a human leg, a wonderful, superb human leg . . . a leg from an almost-innocent? Can't you use that? To make up the difference. Are you still short?" His voice was quite matter-of-fact, not excited, and he kept Olina's hand in his.

"No," came the madame's voice from outside. "But your boots. Your boots would make up the difference."

It's hard work, taking off one's boots. But he managed, just as he had managed to pull them on quickly when the Russians came roaring up to the position. He took off his boots and passed them out by way of Olina's small hand.

And the door was shut again. Olina stood before him, her face quivering. "I have nothing," she wept. "My clothes belong to the old woman. So does my body, and my soul—she doesn't want my soul. Only the devil wants souls, and humans are worse than the devil. Forgive me," she wept, "I have nothing."

Andreas drew her toward him and softly stroked her face. "Come," he whispered, "come, I'll make love to you. . . ." But she raised her face and smiled. "No," she whispered, "no, never mind, it's not important."

Again footsteps approached along the corridor, those confident, unswerving footsteps, but strangely enough they were no longer afraid. They exchanged smiles.

"Olina," the voice called outside the door.

More Polish twittering. Olina smiled at him over her shoulder. "When do you have to leave?"

"At four."

She closed the door without locking it, came back, and said, "At four the general's car is coming to pick me up."

Her trembling hands had spilled wine over the cheese, so she cleared it away, gathered up the soiled tablecloth, and rearranged the things. The cigar had not gone out, thought Andreas, who was watching her. The world had nearly come to an end, but the cigar had not gone, and her hands were quieter than ever. "Coming?"

Yes, he sat down opposite her, laid aside the cigar, and for a few minutes they looked past one another, in silence and almost blushing, because they were both terribly ashamed at the knowledge that they were praying, that they were both praying, here in this brothel, on this couch. . . .

"It's midnight now," she said as they began eating. It's Sunday now, thought Andreas, Sunday, and he abruptly set down his glass and the cookie he had just begun; a frightful cramp paralyzed his jaws and hands and seemed even to blind his eyes; I don't want to die, he thought and, without realizing it, he stammered, like a weeping child, "I . . . I don't want to die."

I must be mad to think I can smell paint so vividly . . . I was barely seven at the time they painted the garden fence: it was the first day of school holidays, and Uncle Hans was away, it had rained in the night, and now the sun was shining in that moist garden . . . it was so wonderful . . . so beautiful, and as I lay in bed I could distinctly smell the garden and the paint, for the painters had already started painting the fence green. I was allowed to stay in bed a while because school was out, Uncle Hans was away, and I was to get hot chocolate for breakfast, Aunt Marianne had promised me the night before because she had just opened a new account . . . whenever we opened a new account, a brand-new one, we began by buying something special. And that paint, I can smell it as plainly as anything, but I must be mad . . . there can't possibly be a smell of green paint here. That pale face across from me, that's Olina, a Polish prostitute and spy . . . nothing here in this room can smell so cruelly of paint and conjure up that day in my childhood so vividly. "I don't want to die," stammered his mouth. "I don't want to leave all this behind . . . no one can force me to get onto that train going to . . . Stry, no one on earth. My God, maybe it would be a mercy if I did lose my mind. But don't let me lose it! No, no! Even though it hurts like hell to smell that green paint now, let me rather savor this pain than go mad . . . and Aunt Marianne's voice telling me I can stay in bed a while, since Uncle Hans is away. . . ."

"What's that?" he asked, startled. Olina had risen, without his noticing it; she was sitting at the piano, and her lips were quivering in her pale face.

"Rain," she said softly, and it seemed to cost her an unspeakable effort to open her mouth, she hardly had the strength to nod toward the window.

Yes, that soft rushing sound that roused him with the power of a sudden burst of organ music . . . that was rain . . . it was raining in the brothel garden . . . and on the treetops where he had seen the sun for the last time. "No!" he cried as Olina touched the keys, "no," but then he felt the tears, and he knew he had never cried before in his life . . . these tears were life, a raging torrent formed from countless streams . . . all flowing together and welling up into one agonizing outburst . . . the green paint that smelled of holidays . . . and the terrible corpse of Uncle Hans laid out in its coffin in the study, shrouded in the heavy air of candles . . . many, many evenings with Paul and the hours of exquisite torment spent trying to play the piano . . . school and war, war . . . war, and the unknown face he had desired, had . . . and in that blinding wet torrent there floated, like a quivering disk, pale and agonizing, the sole reality: Olina's face.

All this because of a few bars of Schubert, making it possible for me to cry as I have never cried in my life, to cry as maybe I only cried when

I was born, when that dazzling light threatened to cut me in two. Suddenly a chord struck his ear, a chord that shook him to the depths of his being. It was Bach, yet she had never been able to play Bach. . . .

It was like a tower that was spiraling upward from within, piling level upon level. The tower grew and pulled him with it, as if it had been hurled up from the bowels of the earth by a gushing spring that was fiercely shooting its way past the gloom of centuries into the light, into the light. An aching happiness filled him as, against his will yet knowingly and consciously, he was borne upward on level after level of that pure, upthrusting tower; as if borne on a cloud of fantasy, wreathed in what seemed a weightless, poignant felicity, he was yet made to experience all the effort and all the pain of the climber; this was spirit, this was clarity, little remained of human aberration; a fantastically clean, clear playing of compelling force. It was Bach, yet she had never been able to play Bach . . . perhaps she wasn't playing at all . . . perhaps it was the angels . . . the angels of clarity, singing in towers each more ethereal and radiant than the last . . . light, light, oh God . . . that light. . . .

"Stop!" he cried out, and Olina's hands recoiled from the keys as if his voice had torn them away. . . .

He rubbed his aching forehead, and he saw that the girl sitting there in the soft lamplight was not only startled by his voice: she was exhausted, she was weary, infinitely weary, the towers she had had to climb with her frail hands had been unimaginably high. She was just tired. The corners of her mouth twitched like those of a child that is too tired even to cry; her hair had loosened . . . she was pale, and deep shadows encircled her eyes.

Andreas moved toward her, took her in his arms, and laid her on the sofa. She closed her eyes and sighed. Gently, very gently she shook her head as if to say: Just let me rest . . . all I want is to rest a little. . . . Peace, and it was good to see her fall asleep; her face sank to one side.

Andreas rested his head in his hands on the little table and was also aware of an infinite weariness. It's Sunday, he thought, one o'clock in the morning, three more hours to go, and I must not sleep, I will not sleep, I shall not sleep; and he looked at her ardently and tenderly. That pure, gentle, small, wan girlish face, now faintly smiling in the bliss of sleep. I must not sleep, thought Andreas, yet he could feel his weariness bearing relentlessly down on him. I must not sleep. God, don't let me fall asleep, let me look at her face. . . . I needed to come to this brothel in Lvov, I needed to come here to find out that there is such a thing as love without desire, the way I love Olina . . . I must not fall asleep, I must look at that mouth . . . that forehead and those exhausted, golden, delicate wisps of hair over her face and the dark shadows of indescribable exhaustion around her eyes. She played Bach, to the very limits of human capacity. I must not fall asleep . . . it's cold . . . the cruel hostility of the morning is already waiting behind the dark curtains of the night. It's cold, and I have nothing to cover her with . . . I've sold my coat, and we made a mess of the tablecloth . . . it's lying around somewhere stained with wine. My tunic, I could put my tunic over her . . . I could cover the open neck of her dress with my tunic, but even as he thought this he simply felt too tired to get up and take off his tunic . . . I can't even lift my arm, and I must not fall asleep; I've still got so many things to do, so many things to do. Just let me rest here a bit with my arms on the table, then I'll get up and put my tunic over her, and I'll pray, pray, kneel by this couch that has seen so many sins, kneel by that pure face from which I had to learn that there is such a thing as love without desire . . . I must not fall asleep . . . no, no, I must not fall asleep. . . .

His awakening gaze was like a bird that suddenly dies high up in the air in flight and plunges, plunges into the infinity of despair; but Olina's smiling eyes caught him as he fell. He had been desperately afraid that it was too late . . . too late to hurry to the appointed place. Too late to hurry to the only rendezvous that mattered. Her smiling gaze caught him, and she answered the unspoken yet anguished question, saying softly, "It's three-thirty . . . don't worry!" And only now did he feel her light hand resting on his head.

Her face lay on the same level as his, and he hardly needed to move his head to kiss her. It's a pity, he thought, that I don't desire her, a pity that it's no sacrifice for me not to desire her, no sacrifice not to kiss her and not to long to sink down into that seemingly sullied womb. . . .

And he touched her lips with his, and there was nothing. They exchanged smiles of amazement. There was nothing. It was like an ineffectual bullet bouncing off armor of which they themselves were not aware.

"Come on," she said softly, "I'd better see you get something for your feet, hadn't I?"

"No," said Andreas, "don't leave me, you mustn't leave me for a single second. Never mind the shoes. I can just as well die in my socks, lots of men have died in their socks. Fled in panic when they were suddenly confronted by the Russians, and died wounded in the back, facing Germany, wounded in the back, the worst disgrace that could befall the Spartans. Many died like that. Never mind the shoes, I'm so tired. . . ."

"No," she said, glancing at her watch. "I could have given up my watch, and you would have kept your boots. One always thinks one has no more to give, and I honestly had forgotten my watch. I'll trade my watch for your boots, we won't be needing it any more . . . or anything else."

"Or anything else," he repeated under his breath, and he raised his eyes and looked around the room, and for the first time he saw how pitiful it was, the ancient wallpaper and meager furniture: old armchairs over there by the window, and a dingy couch.

"Yes," Olina murmured, "I'm going to get you away. Don't look so scared!" She smiled, her eyes close to his white, tired face. "That car of the general's is a gift from heaven. Just trust me and believe me: no matter where I take you, it will be life. Do you believe me?" Andreas nodded in bewilderment, and she repeated, her face close to his as if in solemn entreaty, "No matter where I take you, it will be life. Trust me!" She clasped his head. "There are tiny little places in the Carpathians where no one will ever find us. A few houses, a little chapel, no partisans even. I used to go to one; I would try to say a few prayers and play on the priest's old baby grand. D'you hear?" She sought his eyes, but his gaze was still roaming the soiled wallpaper against which bottles had been smashed and sticky fingers had been wiped. "We'll have music, d'you hear?"

"Yes," he groaned. "But the others, those other two. I can't leave them now. It's impossible."

"That's out!"

"And the driver," he asked, "what did you intend doing with the driver?" They stood face to face, and there was something like hostility between their eyes. Olina tried to smile. "Starting today," she said softly, "starting today, I'm not going to hand over any more innocent men to the executioner. You must trust me! It wouldn't have been too difficult just with you. Simply have the driver stop somewhere, and then we'd run away . . . disappear! Free, just disappear! But with your two friends it won't work."

"All right, then, you'll have to leave me. No," he raised his arm to silence her. "I'm simply telling you there's to be no bargaining. It's either —or. You must understand, you must," he said, looking deep into her serious eyes, "because you loved them, some of them, didn't you? You must understand."

Slowly, heavily, Olina's head drooped. Andreas did not realize this was a nod until she said, "All right, I'll try. . . ."

While Olina, her hand on the door, waited for him, he cast one more look around that dirty little Polish bar, then followed her out into the ill-lit corridor. But the room, the bar, was palatial compared with that corridor in the early morning. That mocking, chill, dingy half-light in a brothel corridor at four in the morning. Those doors, like doors in a barracks, all alike. All equally shabby. And that dreary, dreary squalor.

"In here," said Olina. She pushed open one of the doors and there was her room, scantily furnished with the necessities of her trade: a bed, a small table and two chairs, and a wash basin on a spindly, three-legged stand, next to the stand a pitcher, and a small closet against the wall. Only the bare necessities, like in a barracks. . . .

It was all so unreal, sitting on the bed and watching Olina wash her hands, take her shoes out of the closet, remove her red slippers, and put on her shoes. Oh yes, there was a mirror too, for her to refurbish her beauty. Those traces of tears must be wiped away and fresh powder put on, there being nothing ghastlier than a red-eyed whore. Lipstick and eyebrow pencil had to be reapplied, nails cleaned, and all this was carried out as deftly as a soldier preparing for the alert.

"You must trust me," she said in a chatty, matter-of-fact tone. "I'm going to get you away, d'you hear? It won't be easy if you insist on taking along the other two, but it can be done. A lot can be done. . . ."

Don't let me go out of my mind, Andreas prayed, don't let me go out of my mind in this brutal attempt to grasp reality. The whole thing is impossible—this room in a brothel, shabby and faded in the gray dawn, full of revolting smells, and that girl over there by the mirror, crooning softly, crooning to me, while her fingers skillfully touch up the red on her lips. This is impossible, and this tired heart of mine that wishes for nothing, and these limp senses of mine that desire nothing, neither to smoke nor eat nor drink, and my soul that is deprived of all longing and wants only to sleep, to sleep . . .

Maybe I'm already dead. Who can grasp all this, these bedclothes I automatically pushed aside, the way one always does if one has to sit down on a bed, these sheets that are not dirty and yet not clean, these horribly mysterious sheets, not dirty and not clean . . . and that girl over there by the mirror, busy coloring her eyebrows, black, fine-drawn eyebrows on a pale forehead.

" 'A-hunting and fishing we will go, as in the good old days!' D'you know that one?" asked Olina with a smile. "It's a German poem. 'Archibald Douglas.' It's about a man who was exiled from his native land. And we Poles, we have been exiled *into* our native land, into the midst of one's native land; no one knows what that means. Born 1920. 'A-hunting and fishing we will go, as in the good old days.' Listen!" She was actually crooning that old ballad, and it seemed to Andreas that now the limit had been reached, a gray cold morning in a Polish brothel, and a ballad, set to music by Löwe, being crooned for his benefit. . . .

"Olina!" came that level voice again outside the door.

"Yes?"

"The bill. Hand it out to me, please. And get ready to leave, the car's at the door. . . ."

So this is the reality, the girl handing out the bill through the door, with tapering fingers, a bill on which everything had been written down, beginning with the matches, which he still had in his pocket, those matches he had been given yesterday evening at six. That's how fantastically fast time goes, this time we cannot grasp, and I've done nothing, nothing, in that time, and there's nothing I can do but follow this refurbished beauty down the stairs to settle the account.

"THESE POLISH tarts," said Willi, "simply terrific! That's what I call passion, eh?"

"Yes."

The room downstairs was just as meagerly furnished. A few rickety chairs, a bench, a threadbare carpet that looked like frayed paper, and Willi was smoking. He was completely unshaven and was searching his luggage for more cigarettes.

"You were certainly the most expensive, my lad. My bill wasn't much less either. But this young friend of ours, he cost almost nothing. Hey there!" He dug the blond fellow, who was still asleep, in the ribs. "A hundred and forty-six marks." He snorted with laughter. "It seems he actually did sleep with the girl, literally slept. There were two hundred marks left over, so I slid them under the door of his girl's room, as a tip, see? Because she made him happy so cheaply. D'you happen to have a cigarette left?"

"Yes."

"Thanks."

What an incredibly long time Olina was taking to settle the account, over there in the madame's office, at four in the morning. That was an hour when the whole world slept. Even in the girls' rooms all was quiet, and downstairs in the big reception room it was quite dark. The door from which the music had come was dark, and one could see and smell that dark room. The only sound was the discreet engine purring away outside. Olina was behind that reddish door, and it was all reality. It had to be reality. . . .

"So you think this general's whore-car will take us too?"

"Yes!"

"Hm. A Maybach, I can tell by the engine. Neat job. Mind if I go ahead and speak to the driver? He's sure to be a noncom."

Willi shouldered his luggage and opened the door, and there it really was, the night, the gray-veiled night and the dim headlights of a waiting car out there by the entrance. As coldly and inescapably real as all war-nights, full of cold menace, full of horrible mockery; out there in the dirty holes . . . in the cellars . . . in the many, many towns cowering in fear . . . summoned up, those appalling nights that at four in the morning have achieved their most deadly power, those ghastly, indescribably terrible war-nights. One of these was there outside the door, a night full of terror, a night with no home, not even the smallest, smallest warm corner to hide in . . . those nights that had been summoned up by the resounding voices. . . .

So she really believes she can rescue me. Andreas smiled. She believes it is possible to slip through the fine mesh of this net. This child believes there is such a thing as escape . . . she believes she will find ways to avoid Stry. That word has been cradled within me since my birth. It has lain deep, deep down, unacknowledged and unawakened; it was with me when I was still a child, and maybe a dark shudder rippled through me, many years ago in school, when we learned about the foothills of the Carpathians and I read the words Galicia and Lvov and Stry on the map, in the middle of that yellow-white patch. And I've forgotten that shudder. Maybe, often and often, the barb of death and summons was cast into me without ever catching in anything down there, and only that tiny little word had been set up and saved up for it, and finally the barb caught. . . .

Stry . . . that tiny little word, terrible and bloody, has surfaced and expanded into an ominous cloud that now overshadows everything. And she believes she will find ways of avoiding Stry. . . .

Besides, her promise doesn't attract me. I'm not attracted by that little village in the Carpathians where she proposes to play on the priest's piano. I'm not attracted by that seeming security . . . all we have is promises and pledges and a dark uncertain horizon over which we have to plunge to find security. . . .

At last the door opened, and Andreas was surprised by the rigid pallor of Olina's face. She had put on a fur coat, a charming little cap was perched on her beautiful loose hair, and there was no watch on her wrist, for he was wearing his boots again. The account had been settled. The old woman was smiling so mysteriously. Her hands were folded across her desiccated body, and after the soldiers had picked up their luggage and Andreas was opening the door, she smiled and uttered a single word. "Stry," she said. Olina did not hear it: she was already outside.

"I too," said Olina in a low voice as they sat side by side in the car,

"I too am condemned. I too have betrayed my country because I spent all last night with you instead of sounding out the general." She took his hand and smiled at him. "But don't forget what I told you: No matter where I take you, it will be life. Right?"

"Right," said Andreas. The whole night ran through his memory like a smooth thread being reeled off, yet there was one knot that left him no peace. Stry, the old woman had said, and how can she know that Stry . . . he hadn't said anything about it to her, and still less would Olina have mentioned that word. . . .

So this is supposed to be reality: a discreetly purring car with its subdued headlights illuminating the nameless road. Trees, and now and again houses, all saturated with gray darkness. In front of him those two necks, encircled by sergeants' braid almost identical, solid German necks, and the cigarette smoke drifting back from the driver's seat. Beside him the blond fellow, sleeping like a child worn out by playing, and on the right the steady gentle contact with Olina's fur coat and the smooth thread of the memory of that lovely night sliding by, faster and faster, and always stopping short at that strange knot, at the place where the old woman had said: Stry. . . .

Andreas leaned forward to look at the softly lit clock on the dashboard, and he saw it was six o'clock, just on six. An icy shock ran through him, and he thought: God, God, what have I done with my time, I've done nothing, I've never done anything, I must pray, pray for them all, and at this very moment Paul is walking up the altar steps at home and beginning to recite: *Introibo*. And on his own lips too the word began to form: *Introibo*.

But now an invisible giant hand passed over the softly gliding car, a terrible, silent stirring of the air, and into this silence came Willi's dry voice, asking, "Where are you taking us, bud?" "To Stry!" said a disembodied voice.

And then the car was slashed by two raging knives that rasped with savage hatred, one from the front, the other from behind, tearing into that metal body which reared and turned, filled with the shriek of fear of its occupants. . . .

In the silence that followed there was no sound but the passionate devouring of the flames.

My God, thought Andreas, are they *all* dead? . . . And my legs . . . my arms, is only my head left? . . . Is no one there? . . . I'm lying on this bare road, on my breast lies the weight of the world, so heavily that I can find no words to pray. . . .

Am I crying? he thought suddenly, for he could feel something moist running down his cheeks: no, something was dripping onto his cheeks; and in that ashen morning light, which was still without the yellow mildness of the sun, he saw that Olina's hand was hanging down over his head from a fragment of the car, and that blood was dripping onto his face from her hands, and he was past knowing that now he was really beginning to cry. . . .

Candles
for the Madonna

M Y STAY here was a brief one. I had an appointment in the late
afternoon with the representative of a firm that was toying with
the idea of taking over a product which has been causing us something of
a headache: candles. We put all our money into the manufacture of
tremendous stocks on the assumption that the electricity shortage would
continue indefinitely. We have worked very hard, been thrifty and honest,
and when I say "we" I mean my wife and myself. We are producers,
wholesalers, retailers; we combine every stage in the holy estate of commerce: we are agents, workmen, traveling salesmen, manufacturers.

But we put our money on the wrong horse. There is not much
demand for candles these days. Electricity rationing has been abolished,
even most basements now have electric light again; and at the very moment
when our hard work, our efforts, all our struggles, seemed about to bear
fruit—the production of a large quantity of candles—at that precise
moment the demand dried up.

Our attempts to do business with those religious enterprises dealing
in what are known as devotional supplies came to nothing. These firms had
hoarded candles in abundance—better ones than ours, incidentally, the
fancy kind, with green, red, blue, and yellow ribbons, embroidered with
little golden stars, winding around them, like Aesculapius' snake—and
enhancing both their reverent and aesthetic appeal. They also come in
various lengths and sizes, whereas ours are all identical and of simple
design: about ten inches long, smooth, yellow, quite plain, their only asset
the beauty of simplicity.

We were forced to admit that we had miscalculated; compared with
the splendid products displayed by the devotional-supply houses, our
candles look humble indeed, and nobody buys anything humble-looking.
Nor has our willingness to reduce our price resulted in any increase in sales.
On the other hand, of course, we lack the money to plan new designs, let
alone manufacture them, since the income we derive from the limited sale
of the stock we have produced is barely enough to cover our living

expenses and steadily mounting costs. I have, for instance, to make longer and longer trips in order to call on genuinely or apparently interested parties, I have to keep on reducing our price, and we know we have no alternative but to unload the substantial stocks still on our hands and find some other means of making a living.

I had come to this town in response to a letter from a wholesaler who had intimated that he would take a considerable quantity off my hands at an acceptable price. I was foolish enough to believe him, came all the way here, and was now calling on this fellow. He had a magnificent apartment, luxurious, spacious, furnished in great style, and the large office where he received me was crammed with samples of all the various products that make money for his type of business. Arranged on long shelves were plaster saints, statuettes of Joseph, Virgin Marys, bleeding Sacred Hearts, mild-eyed, fair-haired penitents whose plaster pedestals bore the name, in a variety of languages and embossed lettering (choice of gold or red), Madeleine, Maddalena, Magdalena, Magdalene; Nativity scenes (complete or sectional), oxen, asses, Infant Jesuses in wax or plaster, shepherds, and angels of all ages: tots, youths, children, graybeards; plaster palm leaves adorned with gold or silver Hallelujahs, holy-water stoups of stainless steel, plaster, copper, pottery, some in good taste, some in bad.

The man himself—a jovial, red-faced fellow—asked me to sit down, affected some initial interest, and offered me a cigar. He wanted to know how we happened to get into this particular branch of manufacturing, and after I had explained that we had inherited nothing from the war but a huge pile of stearin which my wife had salvaged from four blazing trucks in front of our bombed-out house and which no one had since claimed as their property, after I had smoked about a quarter of my cigar, he suddenly said, without any preamble, "I'm sorry I had you come here, but I've changed my mind." Perhaps my sudden loss of color did strike him as odd after all. "Yes," he went on, "I really am sorry about it, but after considering all the angles I've come to the conclusion that your product won't sell. It won't sell! Believe me, I know! Sorry!" He smiled, shrugged his shoulders, and held out his hand. I put down the half-smoked cigar and left.

By this time it was dark, and I was a total stranger in the town. Although, in spite of everything, I was aware of a certain relief, I had the terrible feeling that I was not only poor, deceived, the victim of a misguided idea, but also ridiculous. It would seem that I was unfit for the so-called battle of life, for the career of manufacturer and dealer. Our candles would not sell even for a pittance, they weren't good enough to hold their own in the field of devotionalist competition, and we probably wouldn't even be able to give them away, whereas other, inferior candles were being bought. I would never discover the secret of business success, although, with my wife, I had hit upon the secret of making candles.

I lugged my heavy sample case to the streetcar stop and waited a long time. The darkness was soft and clear, it was summer. Streetlights were on at the crossings, people were strolling about in the evening, it was quiet; I was standing beside a big circular traffic island fringed by dark, empty office buildings. Behind me was a little park; I heard the sound of running water, and on turning round I saw a great marble woman standing there, with thin jets of water spouting from her rigid breasts into a copper basin. I felt chilly and realized I was tired. At last the streetcar arrived; soft music poured from brightly lit cafés, but the station was in an empty, quiet part of town. All I could glean from the big blackboard there was the departure time of a train which would get me only halfway home and which, if I took it, would cost me a whole night of waiting room, grime, and a bowl of repulsive soup at the station in a little place with no hotel. I turned away, went outside again, and counted my money by the light of a gas lamp: nine marks, return ticket, and a few pfennigs. Some cars were standing there that looked as if they had been waiting there forever, and little trees, cropped like new recruits. Dear little trees, I thought, nice little trees, obedient little trees. Doctors' white nameplates showed up against a few unlighted houses, and through a café window I looked in on a gathering of empty chairs for whose benefit a writhing violinist was producing sobs that might have moved stones but hardly a human being. At last, in a lane skirting the bulk of a dark church, I came upon a painted green sign: "Rooms." I stepped inside.

Behind me I could hear the streetcar on its return trip to the better-lit, more populated part of town. The hall was empty, and I turned to the right into a little room containing four tables and twelve chairs; to the left, bottles of beer and lemonade stood in metal display stands on a built-in counter. Everything looked clean and plain. Green hessian, divided by narrow strips of brown wood, had been tacked to the walls with rosette-shaped copper nails. The chairs were green too, upholstered in some soft, velvety material. Pale-yellow curtains had been drawn closely across the windows, and behind the counter a serving hatch opened into a kitchen. I put down my suitcase, drew a chair toward me, and sat down. I was very tired.

How quiet it was here, even quieter than the station which, strangely enough, was some distance from the business center, a gloomy, cavernous place filled with the muffled sounds of an invisible bustle: bustle behind closed wickets, bustle behind wooden barriers.

I was hungry too, and I found the utter futility of this journey very depressing. I was glad of the few minutes to myself in this quiet, unpretentious room. I would have liked to smoke but found I had no cigarettes, and now I regretted having abandoned the cigar in the wholesale devotionalist's office. Although I might well be depressed at having gone on yet another wild-goose chase, I was aware of a growing sense of relief that I couldn't quite define or account for, but perhaps in my heart I rejoiced at my final expulsion from the devotional-supply trade.

I had not been idle after the war. I had helped clear away ruins, remove rubble, scrape bricks clean, build walls, haul sand, shift lime; I had submitted applications—many, many applications—thumbed through books, carefully watched over my pile of stearin. On my own, with no help from those who might have given me the benefit of their experience, I had found out how to make candles, beautiful, simple, good-quality candles, tinted a soft yellow that gave them the luster of melting beeswax. I had done everything to get on my feet, as they say: to find some way of earning a living, and although I ought to have been sad, the very futility of my efforts was now filling me with a joy such as I had never known.

I had not been ungenerous. I had given away candles to people living in cramped unlighted holes, and whenever there had been a chance of profiteering, I had avoided it. I had gone hungry and devoted myself single-mindedly toward this method of making a living; but although I might have expected a reward for what one might call my integrity, I almost rejoiced to find myself evidently unworthy of any reward.

The thought also crossed my mind that perhaps we would have done better after all to manufacture shoe polish, as someone had advised us, to mix other ingredients with the basic material, to get hold of some formulas, acquire a stock of cardboard containers, and fill them up.

In the midst of my musings the landlady entered the room, a slight, elderly woman. Her dress was green, the green of the beer and lemonade bottles on the counter. "Good evening," she said pleasantly. I returned her greeting, and she asked, "What can I do for you?"

"I would like a room, if you have one."

"Certainly," she said. "What price had you in mind?"

"The cheapest."

"That would be three marks fifty."

"Fine," I said, relieved. "And perhaps something to eat?"

"Certainly."

"Bread, some cheese and butter, and"—I ran my eyes over the bottles on the counter—"perhaps some wine."

"Certainly," she said, "a bottle?"

"No, no! A glass and—how much will that come to?"

She had gone behind the counter and was already pushing back the hook to open the serving hatch, but she paused to ask, "All together?"

"Yes please, all together."

She reached under the counter, took out pad and pencil, and again it was very quiet while she slowly wrote and added up. Despite the reserve in her manner, her whole presence, as she stood there, radiated a reassuring kindness. And she endeared herself to me still further by apparently making several mistakes in her addition. She slowly wrote down the items, frowned as she added them up, shook her head, crossed them out, rewrote everything, added up again, this time without frowning, and in gray pencil wrote the result at the bottom, finally saying in her soft voice, "Six-twenty —no, six, I beg your pardon."

I smiled. "That's fine. And have you any cigars?"

"Certainly." She reached under the counter again and held out a box. I took two and thanked her. The woman quietly gave the order through to the kitchen and left the room.

Scarcely had she gone when the door opened and in walked a young man, of slight build, unshaven, wearing a light-colored raincoat; behind him was a girl in a brown coat, hatless. The couple approached quietly, almost diffidently, and with a brief "Good evening" turned toward the counter. The boy was carrying the girl's shabby leather bag, and although he was obviously at pains to appear undaunted and to display the bravado of a man who regularly spends the night with his girl in a hotel, I could see his lower lip trembling and tiny beads of sweat on the stubble of his beard. The couple stood there like customers awaiting their turn in a store. The fact that they were hatless and that the bag was their only luggage made them look like refugees who had arrived at some transit camp. The girl was beautiful, her skin alive, warm, and slightly flushed, and her heavy brown hair hanging loosely over her shoulders seemed almost too heavy for her slender feet; she nervously moved her black dusty shoes, shifting her weight from one foot to the other more often than was necessary; the young man kept brushing back a few strands of hair as they fell over his forehead, and his small round mouth expressed a painful but at the same time elated determination. I could see they were deliberately avoiding each other's eyes, and they did not speak to one another, while I for my part was glad to be busily occupied with my cigar, to be able to clip it, light it, look critically at the tip, relight it, and start smoking. Every second of waiting must be agony, I knew; for the girl, no matter how unabashed and happy she might look, continued to shift her weight as she tugged at her coat, while the boy continued to pass his hand over his forehead although there were no more strands of hair to brush back. At last the woman reappeared, quietly said "Good evening," and placed the bottle of wine on the counter.

I jumped up at once, saying, "Allow me!" She looked at me in surprise, then set down the glass, handed me the corkscrew, and asked the young man, "What can I do for you?" As I put the cigar between my lips and twisted the corkscrew into the cork, I heard the young man ask, "Can you let us have two rooms?"

"Two?" asked the landlady. Just then I pulled out the cork and from the corner of my eye saw the girl flush, while the boy bit hard on his lower lip and, barely opening his mouth, said, "Yes, two."

"Oh, thank you," the landlady said, filling the glass and passing it to me. I went back to my table, began to sip the gentle wine, and could only hope that the inevitable ritual would not be dragged out even further by the arrival of my supper. But the entries in the register, the filling out of forms, and the producing of gray-blue identity cards, all took less time than I had expected; and at one point, when the boy opened the leather bag to get out the identity cards, I saw that it contained greasy paper bags, a crumpled hat, some packets of cigarettes, a beret, and a shabby old red wallet.

During all this time the girl tried to look poised and confident; with an air of nonchalance she surveyed the bottles of lemonade, the green of the hessian wall covering, and the rosette-shaped nails, but the flush never left her cheeks, and when everything was finally settled they took their keys and hurried upstairs without saying good night. A few minutes later my supper was passed through the hatch; the landlady brought me my plate, and when our eyes met she did not smile, as I had thought she would, but looked gravely past me and said, "I hope you enjoy your supper, sir."

"Thank you," I replied. She remained standing beside me.

I slowly began my meal, helping myself to bread, butter, and cheese. She still did not move. "Smile," I said.

And she did smile, but then she sighed, saying, "There's nothing I can do about it."

"Do you wish there were?"

"Oh yes," she said fervently, sitting herself down beside me, "indeed I do. I'd like to do something about a lot of things. But if he asks for two rooms. . . . If he had asked for one, now . . ." She paused.

"What then?" I asked.

"What then?" she mimicked angrily. "I would have thrown him out."

"What for?" I said wearily, putting the last piece of bread in my mouth. She said nothing. What for, I thought, what for? Doesn't the world belong to lovers, weren't the nights mild enough, weren't other doors open, dirtier ones perhaps, but doors one could close behind one? I looked into my empty glass and smiled. . . .

The landlady had risen, fetched her big book and a pile of forms, and sat down beside me again.

She watched me as I filled everything out. I paused at the column "Occupation," raised my eyes, and looked into her smiling face. "Why do you hesitate?" she asked calmly. "Have you no occupation?"

"I don't know."

"You don't know?"

"I don't know whether I am a workman, a salesman, a manufacturer, unemployed, or only an agent . . . but whose agent?" Whereupon I quickly wrote down "Agent" and gave her back the book. For a moment I considered offering her candles—twenty, if she liked, for a glass of wine, or ten for a cigar. I don't know why I didn't; perhaps I was just too tired, or too lazy, but the next morning I was glad I hadn't. I relit my dead cigar and got to my feet. The woman had shut the book, laying the forms between the pages, and was yawning.

"Would you like coffee in the morning?" she asked.

"No, thank you, I have to catch an early train. Good night."

"Good night," she said.

But next morning I slept late. The passage, which I had glimpsed the previous evening—carpeted in dark red—had remained silent throughout the night. The room was quiet too. The unaccustomed wine had made me sleepy but also happy. The window was open, and all I could see against the quiet, deep-blue summer sky was the dark roof of the church opposite; farther to the right I could see the colorful reflection of the town lights, hear the noise of the livelier district. I took my cigar with me as I got into bed so that I could read the newspaper, but fell asleep at once. . . .

It was after eight when I woke up. The train I had meant to catch had already left, and I was sorry I had not asked to be woken. I washed, decided to go out for a shave, and went downstairs. The little green room was now light and cheerful, the sun shining in through the thin curtains, and I was surprised to see tables set for breakfast, with breadcrumbs, empty jam dishes, and coffeepots. I had felt as if I were the only guest in this silent house. I paid my bill to a friendly maid and left.

Outside, I hesitated. The cool shadow of the church surrounded me. The lane was narrow and clean; to the right a baker had opened his shop, loaves and rolls shone pale brown and yellow in the glass cases, and farther on, jugs of milk stood at a door to which a thin, blue-white trail of milkdrops led. The other side of the street was entirely taken up by a high black wall built of great square blocks of stone; through a big arched gateway I saw green lawn and walked in. I was standing in a monastery garden. An old, flat-roofed building, its stone window frames touchingly whitewashed, stood in the middle of a green lawn, stone tombs in the shade of weeping willows. A monk was padding along a flagged path toward the church. In passing, he gave me a nod of greeting. I nodded back, and when he entered the church, I followed him, without knowing why.

The church was empty. It was old, devoid of decoration, and when by force of habit I dipped my hand in the stoup and bent my knee toward the altar, I saw that the candles must have just gone out: a thin black ribbon of smoke was rising from them into the clear air. There was no one in sight; Mass seemed to be over for this morning. My eyes involuntarily followed the black figure as it bobbed an awkward genuflection in front of the tabernacle and vanished into a side aisle. I went closer and came to a sudden halt. I found myself looking at a confessional. The young girl of the previous evening was kneeling in a pew in front of it, her face hidden in her hands, while at the edge of the nave, showing no apparent interest, stood the young man, the leather bag in one hand, the other hanging slackly by his side, his eyes on the altar. . . .

In the midst of this silence I could hear my heart beating, louder, stronger, strangely unquiet, and I could feel the boy looking at me: our eyes met, he recognized me and flushed. The girl was still kneeling there, her face in her hands, a thin, faint thread of smoke still rising from the candles. I sat down in a pew, placed my hat beside me, and put my suitcase on the ground. I felt as if I were waking up for the first time, as if until now I had seen everything with my eyes only, a detached spectator— church, garden, street, girl, man—it had all been like a stage set that I had brushed by as an outsider, but now, looking at the altar, I longed for the young man to go and confess too. I wondered when I had last gone to confession, found it hard to keep track of the years, roughly it would be about seven, but as I went on thinking about it, I realized something much worse: I couldn't put my finger on any sin. No matter how honestly I tried, I couldn't think of any sin worth confessing, and this made me very sad. I felt unclean, full of things that needed to be washed away, but nowhere was there actually anything that in coarse, rough, sharp, clear terms could have been called sin. My heart beat louder than ever. Last night I had not envied the young couple, but now I did envy that ardent kneeling figure, still hiding her face in her hands, waiting. The young man stood completely motionless and detached.

I was like a pail of water that has remained exposed to the air for

a long time. It looks clean, a casual glance reveals nothing in it: nobody
has thrown stones, dirt, or garbage into it, it has been standing in the
hallway or basement of a well-kept, respectable house; the bottom appears
to be immaculate; all is clear and still, yet, when you dip your hand into
the water, there runs through your fingers an intangible repulsive fine dirt
that seems to be without shape, without form, almost without dimension.
You just know it is there. And on reaching deeper into this immaculate
pail, you find at the bottom a thick indisputable layer of this fine disgusting
formless muck to which you cannot put a name; a dense, leaden sediment
made up of these infinitesimal particles of dirt abstracted from the air of
respectability.

I could not pray; I could only hear my heart beating and wait for
the girl to go into the confessional. At last she raised her hands, laid her
face against them for an instant, stood up, and entered the wooden box.

The young man kept his place. He stood there aloof, having no part
in it, unshaven, pale, his face still expressing a mild yet insistent determination. When the girl emerged, he suddenly put down the bag and stepped
into the confessional.

I still could not pray, no voice spoke to me or in me, nothing moved,
only my heart was beating, and I could not curb my impatience: I stood
up, left my suitcase where it was, and crossed over to the side aisle, where
I stood beside a pew. In the front pew the young woman was kneeling
before an old stone Madonna standing on a bare, disused altar. The Virgin's
face was coarse-featured but smiling, a piece of her nose was missing, the
blue paint of her robe had flaked off, and the gold stars on it were now
no more than lighter spots; her scepter was broken, and of the Child in
her arms only the back of the head and part of the feet were still visible.
The center part, the torso, had fallen out, and she was smilingly holding
this fragment in her arms. A poor monastic order, evidently, that owned
this church.

"Oh, if I could only pray!" I prayed. I felt hard, useless, unclean,
unrepentant; I couldn't even produce one sin; the only thing I possessed
was my pounding heart and the knowledge that I was unclean. . . .

The young man brushing past me from behind roused me from my
thoughts, and I stepped into the confessional.

By the time I had been dismissed with the sign of the cross, the young
couple had left the church. The monk pushed aside the purple curtain of
the confessional, opened the little door, and padded slowly past me; once
again he genuflected awkwardly before the altar.

I waited until I had seen him disappear, then quickly crossed the nave,
also genuflecting, carried my suitcase back to the side aisle, and opened it.

There they all lay, tied in bundles by my wife's loving hands, slim, yellow, unadorned, and I looked at the cold, bare stone plinth on which the Madonna stood and regretted for the first time that my suitcase was not heavier. I ripped open the first bundle and struck a match. . . .

Warming each candle in the flame of another, I stuck them all firmly onto the cold plinth, which quickly allowed the soft wax to harden; on they all went, until the whole surface was covered with restless flickering lights and my suitcase was empty. I left it where it was, seized my hat, genuflected once more, and left: it was as if I were running away.

And now at last, as I walked slowly toward the station, I recalled all my sins, and my heart was lighter than it had been for a long time. . . .

Across the Bridge

THE STORY I want to tell you has no particular point to it, and maybe it isn't really a story at all, but I must tell you about it. Ten years ago there was a kind of prelude, and a few days ago the circle was completed. . . .

A few days ago I was in a train crossing the bridge that once, before the war, had been strong and wide, as strong as the iron of Bismarck's chest on all those monuments, as inflexible as the rules of bureaucracy: a wide, four-track railroad bridge over the Rhine, supported by a row of massive piers. Ten years ago I used to take the same train across that bridge three times a week: Mondays, Wednesdays, and Saturdays. In those prewar days I was an employee of the Reich Gun Dog and Retriever Association— a modest position; I was a kind of errand boy, really. I knew nothing about dogs, of course; I haven't had much education. Three times a week I would take the train from Königstadt, where our head office was, to Gründerheim, where we had a branch office. There I would pick up urgent correspondence, money, and "Pending Cases." The latter were in a large manila folder. Being only a messenger, of course, I never was told what was in the folder. . . .

In the morning I would go straight from the house to the station and catch the eight o'clock train to Gründerheim. The journey took three-quarters of an hour. Even in those days, crossing the bridge scared me. All the technical assurances of well-informed people concerning the ample load capacity of the bridge were to no avail: I was just plain scared. The mere connection of train and bridge scared me; I am honest enough to admit it. The Rhine is very broad where we live. With a quaking heart I was invariably conscious of the slight swaying of the bridge, of the ominous rocking that continued for six hundred yards. At last came the reassuring, more muffled rattle as we regained the railroad embankment, and then came the vegetable plots, rows and rows of vegetable plots—and finally, just before Kahlenkatten, a house: it was to this house that I clung, so to speak, with my eyes. This house stood on solid ground; my eyes would clutch at this house.

The exterior of the house was of reddish-brown stucco, it was very clean, the window frames and ledges all picked out in dark brown. Two floors, three windows upstairs and two down, in the middle the front door with three steps leading up to it. And invariably, if it was not raining too hard, a child would be sitting on these steps, a spindly little girl of about nine or ten holding a large, clean doll and frowning up at the train. Invariably my eyes would stumble over this child, to be brought up short by the window on the left, for each time I saw a woman in there, a bucket beside her, bent double, a scrubbing cloth in her hands, laboriously washing the floor. Invariably, even when it was raining cats and dogs, even when the child was not sitting there on the steps. The woman was always there: the thin nape of her neck, betraying her as the mother of the little girl, and that movement to and fro, that typical scrubbing movement. Many a time I meant to notice the furniture, or the curtains, but my eyes were glued to this thin, eternally scrubbing woman, and before I could think about anything else the train had passed. Mondays, Wednesdays, and Saturdays, it must always have been about ten minutes past eight, for in those days the trains were nothing if not punctual. By the time the train had passed, I was left with a view of the clean rear of the house, silent and uncommunicative.

Needless to say, I began wondering about this woman and this house. All the other places we passed held little interest for me. Kahlenkatten— Bröderkotten—Suhlenheim—Gründerheim—there was nothing very interesting about these stations. My thoughts were always preoccupied with that house. Why does the woman wash and scrub three times a week? I wondered. The house didn't look at all as if there were dirty people living in it, or as if a great many visitors came and went. In fact it looked almost inhospitable, although it was clean. It was a clean and yet unwelcoming house.

But when I caught the eleven o'clock train from Gründerheim for the return trip and saw the rear of the house shortly before noon, just beyond Kahlenkatten, the woman would then be washing the panes of the end window on the right. Oddly enough, on Mondays and Saturdays she would be washing the end window on the right, and on Wednesdays the middle window. Chamois in hand, she rubbed and rubbed. Round her head she wore a scarf of a dull, reddish color. But on the way back I never saw the little girl, and now, approaching midday—it must have been a few minutes to twelve, for in those days the trains were nothing if not punctual —it was the front of the house that was silent and uncommunicative.

Although in telling my story I shall make every effort to describe only what I actually saw, presumably no one will object to the modest observation that, after three months, I permitted myself the mathematical combination that on Tuesdays, Thursdays, and Fridays the woman probably washed the other windows. This combination, modest though it was, gradually became an obsession. Sometimes, all the way from just before Kahlenkatten to Gründerheim, I would puzzle over which afternoons and mornings the other windows of the two floors were likely to get washed. In fact, I finally sat down with pencil and paper and devised a kind of cleaning timetable for myself. From what I had observed on the three mornings, I tried to figure out what was likely to get cleaned the other three afternoons and the remaining whole days. For I had the curiously fixed notion that the woman never did anything but wash and scrub. After all, I never saw her any other way, always bent double, so that I thought I could hear her labored breathing, at ten minutes past eight; and busily rubbing with the chamois, so that I thought I could see the tip of her tongue between her tightly drawn lips, shortly before twelve.

The story of this house preyed on my mind. I started daydreaming. This made me careless in my work. Yes, I became careless. I let my thoughts wander too often. One day I even forgot the "Pending Cases" folder. I drew down upon my head the wrath of the district manager of the Reich Gun Dog and Retriever Association. He sent for me; he was quivering with indignation. "Grabowski," he said to me, "I hear you forgot the 'Pending Cases.' Orders are orders, Grabowski." When I maintained a stubborn silence, the boss became more severe. "Messenger Grabowski, I'm warning you. The Reich Gun Dog and Retriever Association has no use for forgetful employees, you know. We can look elsewhere for qualified staff." He looked at me menacingly, but then he suddenly became human. "Have you got something on your mind?" I admitted in a low voice, "Yes." "What is it?" he asked kindly. I merely shook my head. "Can I help? Tell me what I can do."

"Give me a day off, sir," I asked diffidently, "that's all I ask." He nodded magnanimously. "Done! And don't take what I said too seriously. Anybody can make one mistake; we've always been quite satisfied with you. . . ."

My heart leaped with joy. This interview took place on a Wednesday. And the following day, Thursday, was to be my day off. I had it all figured out. I caught the eight o'clock train, trembling more with impatience than with fear as we crossed the bridge: there she was, washing the front steps. I caught the next train back from Kahlenkatten and passed her house just about nine: top floor, middle window, front. I rode back and forth four times that day and had the whole Thursday timetable complete: front steps, middle window top floor front, middle window top floor back, attic, front room top. As I passed the house for the last time at six o'clock, I saw a little man's stooped figure digging humbly away in the garden. The child, holding the clean doll, was watching him like a jaileress. The woman was not in sight. . . .

But all this happened ten years ago, before the war. A few days ago I crossed that bridge again by train. My God, how far away my thoughts had been when I got onto the train at Königstadt! I had forgotten the whole business. Our train was made up of boxcars, and as we approached the Rhine, a strange thing happened: one after another the boxcars ahead of us fell silent. It was quite extraordinary, as if the whole train of fifteen or twenty cars were a series of lights going out one after another. And we could hear a horrible, hollow rattle, a kind of windy rattle; and suddenly it sounded as if little hammers were being tapped against the floor of our boxcar, and we fell silent too, and there it was: nothing, nothing . . . nothing; left and right there was nothing, a ghastly void . . . in the distance the grassy banks of the Rhine . . . boats . . . water, but one didn't dare look too far out: just looking made one giddy. Nothing, nothing whatever! I could tell from the white face of a silent farmer's wife that she was praying; other people were lighting cigarettes with trembling hands; even the men playing cards in the corner had fallen silent. . . .

Then we could hear the cars up front riding over solid ground again, and we all had the same thought: They've made it. If something happens to the train, maybe those people can jump out, but we were in the last car but one, and it was almost a foregone conclusion that we would plunge into the river. The conviction was there in our eyes and in our pale faces. The temporary bridge was no wider than the tracks; in fact, the tracks themselves were the bridge, and the side of the boxcar hung out over the bridge into space, and the bridge rocked as if it were about to tip us off into space. . . .

But then all of a sudden there was a firmer rattle; we could hear it coming closer, quite distinctly, and then under our car too it became somehow deeper, more substantial, this rattle, we breathed again and dared to look out: there were vegetable plots! Oh, may God bless vegetable plots! And suddenly I realized where we were, and my heart throbbed queerly the closer we came to Kahlenkatten. For me there was but one question: would that house still be standing? And then I saw it, first from a distance through the delicate sparse green of a few trees in the vegetable plots, the red façade of the house, still very clean, coming closer and closer. I was gripped by an indefinable emotion. Everything, the past of ten years ago and everything that had happened since then, raged within me in a frenzied, uncontrollable turmoil. And then the house came right up close, with giant strides, and then I saw her, the woman: she was washing the front steps. No, it wasn't her—those legs were younger, a little heavier, but she had the same movements, those jerky, thrusting movements as she pushed the scrubbing cloth to and fro. My heart stood still, my heart marked time. Then the woman turned her face for just a moment, and instantly I recognized the little girl of ten years ago; that pinched, spidery, frowning face, and in the expression on her face something rather sour, something disagreeably sour like stale salad. . . .

As my heart slowly started beating again, it struck me that today was in fact Thursday. . . .

That Time
We Were in Odessa

THAT TIME we were in Odessa it was very cold. Every morning we drove in great rattling trucks along cobbled streets to the airfield, where we waited, shivering, for the great gray birds that came lumbering across the landing strip; but the first two days, just as we were boarding, an order came through canceling the flight due to bad weather—the fog over the Black Sea was too thick or the clouds were too low—and we climbed onto the great rattling trucks again and drove along cobbled streets back to barracks.

The barracks were huge, dirty, and louse-ridden; we sat about on the floor or sprawled over the stained tables playing cards, or sang and waited for a chance to sneak into town. There were a lot of soldiers waiting there, and the city was off limits. The first two days we tried to slip out, but they caught us, and we were given KP duty and had to carry the heavy, scalding coffee urns and unload the bread, while a paymaster, wearing a magnificent fur coat intended for the front lines, stood by counting to see that no one pinched a loaf, and to us it looked as though the paymaster was concerned less with paying than with counting. The sky was still cloudy and dark over Odessa, and the sentries sauntered up and down in front of the black, grimy barrack walls.

The third day we waited till it was quite dark and then simply walked to the gates; when the sentry stopped us, we said "Seltchini Commando," and he let us through. There were three of us, Kurt, Erich, and myself, and we walked along very slowly. It was only four o'clock and already quite dark. All we had really wanted was to get outside those great, black, grimy walls, and now that we were outside we would almost rather have been inside again. We hadn't been in the army more than eight weeks and were very scared, but we also knew that if we had been inside again we would most certainly have wanted to get out, and then it would have been impossible, and it was only four o'clock, and we couldn't sleep because of the lice and the singing, and also because we dreaded and at the same time hoped that the next morning might bring good flying weather, and they would fly us out to the Crimea, where we were supposed to die. We didn't want to die, and we didn't want to go to the Crimea, but neither did we want to spend the whole day cooped up in those grimy, black barracks that smelled of ersatz coffee and where they were forever unloading bread for the front and where paymasters in coats intended for the front lines stood around and counted to see that no one pinched a loaf.

I don't know what we wanted. We walked very slowly along that dark, uneven road on the outskirts of the city. Between unlighted, low houses, the night was contained by a few rotting fence posts, and somewhere beyond lay what seemed to be wasteland, wasteland just like at home, where people believe a road is going to be built, where they dig sewers and fiddle around with surveying instruments, and nothing ever comes of it, and they toss out rubbish, cinders, and garbage, and grass grows again, coarse, wild grass, and rank weeds, and the sign saying "No Dumping" is hidden by all the rubbish they have dumped around it. . . .

We walked along very slowly because it was still so early. In the darkness we met soldiers heading for the barracks, and there were others coming from the barracks who overtook us. We were scared of the patrols and would have liked to turn back, but we knew that once we were back in barracks we would really be desperate, and it was better to be scared than merely desperate inside those black, grimy barrack walls, where they were forever carrying coffee around and unloading bread for the front, forever unloading bread for the front, and where the paymasters got themselves up in fur coats while we shivered with cold.

Now and again a house to the left or right showed a dim yellow light, and we could hear shrill voices, high-pitched, foreign, scary. And suddenly in the darkness there was a brightly lit window, a lot of noise came from inside, and we heard soldiers' voices singing "Ah, the Sunshine of Mexico!"

We pushed open the door and went in: the air was warm and blue with smoke, and there were soldiers, eight or ten of them, some with women, and they were all drinking and singing, and one of the soldiers burst out laughing as we entered. We were young, and short, the shortest in the whole company; our uniforms were brand-new, the synthetic fibers pricked our arms and legs, and the long underwear made our bare skin itch terribly, and the sweaters were brand-new and prickly too.

Kurt, the shortest, went ahead and picked a table; he was an apprentice in a leather factory, and he had told us where the hides came from, although that was a trade secret, and he had even told us the profit they made, although that was a really strict trade secret. We sat down beside him.

A very dark, fat woman with a good-natured face came out from behind the bar and asked us what we wanted to drink; since we had heard that everything was very expensive in Odessa, we first asked how much the wine was.

"Five marks a carafe," she replied, and we ordered three carafes. We had lost a lot of money at cards and had divided up what we had left: each of us had ten marks. Some of the soldiers were eating too: roast meat, still steaming, on slices of white bread, and sausages smelling of garlic. We suddenly realized we were hungry, and when the woman brought the wine, we asked the price of the food. She told us the sausages were five marks and meat on bread eight; it was fresh pork, she said, but we ordered three sausages. Some of the soldiers were kissing the women or quite openly hugging them, and we didn't know where to look.

The sausages were hot and greasy, and the wine was very sour. When we had finished the sausages, we didn't know what to do next. We had nothing more to say to each other; for two weeks we had lain side by side in the troop train and exchanged confidences. Kurt had been in a leather factory, Erich was from a farm, and I had come straight from school. We were still scared, but we weren't cold any more. . . .

The soldiers who had been kissing the women now buckled on their belts and went out with the women—three girls with round, friendly faces, giggling and twittering, but they went off now with six soldiers, I think it was six, five anyway. The only soldiers left were the drunk ones who had been singing "Ah, the Sunshine of Mexico!" One of them, who was standing at the bar, a tall, fair-haired corporal, turned round and laughed at us again; as I remember, we were sitting there at our table, very quiet and well behaved, hands on knees, the way we did during instruction period in barracks. The corporal then said something to the woman behind the bar and she brought us some clear schnapps in quite big glasses. "We must drink to him now," said Erich, nudging us with his knees, and I kept on calling "Corporal!" until he realized I meant him; then Erich nudged us again and we stood up and shouted in unison, "*Prost,* Corporal!" The other soldiers all roared with laughter, but the corporal raised his glass and called across to us, "*Prost,* grenadiers. . . ."

The schnapps was sharp and bitter, but it warmed us, and we would have liked another.

The fair-haired corporal beckoned to Kurt, and Kurt went over to him and beckoned to us after a few words with the corporal. The corporal told us we were crazy not to have any money, we ought to sell something; and he asked us where we came from and where we were being sent, and we told him we were waiting at the barracks and were to be flown out to the Crimea. His face became serious, and he said nothing. Then I asked him what we could sell, and he said anything.

We could sell anything here, he said, coats and caps, long underwear, watches, fountain pens.

We didn't want to sell our coats, we were too scared, it was against regulations, and besides we felt the cold very much, that time we were in Odessa. We emptied out our pockets: Kurt had a fountain pen, I had a watch, and Erich a brand-new leather wallet he had won at a lottery back at barracks. The corporal took all three and asked the woman what she would give for them; she examined everything very minutely, said it was poor stuff, and offered two hundred and fifty marks, a hundred and eighty for the watch alone.

The corporal said that wasn't much, two hundred and fifty, but he also told us she wouldn't be likely to offer more, and if we had to fly to the Crimea next day, maybe it didn't make any difference, we might as well take it.

Two of the soldiers who had been singing "Ah, the Sunshine of Mexico!" came over and tapped the corporal on the shoulders; he nodded to us and they all left together.

The woman had handed all the money to me, so I ordered for each of us two portions of roast pork on bread and a large schnapps, then we each had another two portions of roast pork and another schnapps. The meat was fresh and juicy, hot and almost sweet, the bread was soaked with fat, and we had another schnapps. Then the woman told us she had no more roast pork, only sausages, so we each had a sausage and ordered some beer to go with it, thick, dark beer, and we had another schnapps and ordered cakes, flat dry cakes made of ground nuts. Then we had some more schnapps and were not drunk at all; we felt warm and snug and forgot all about our prickly long underwear and sweaters; and some more soldiers came in and we all sang "Ah, the Sunshine of Mexico!"

By six o'clock we had spent all our money, and still we weren't drunk; we went back to barracks because we had nothing else to sell. Along the dark, uneven road there were no more lights, and when we reached the gates the sentry told us to report to the guardhouse. The guardhouse was hot and dry, dirty, and smelled of tobacco, and the sergeant shouted at us and told us we needn't think we could get away with it. But that night we slept very well, and the next morning we again drove in the great rattling trucks along cobbled streets to the airfield, and it was cold there in Odessa, the weather was gloriously clear, and at last we were boarded onto the planes; and as they rose into the sky we suddenly knew that we would never come back, never. . . .

"Stranger, Bear Word
to the Spartans We . . ."

AFTER THE truck stopped, the engine kept on throbbing for a while; somewhere outside a big gate was flung open. Light fell through the shattered window into the truck, and I saw that the light in the roof was smashed too; only its metal screw was left sticking out of the socket, with a few quivering wires and shreds of glass. Then the engine stopped, and outside a voice shouted, "The dead over here—got any dead in there?"

"For Chrissake," the driver called back, "don't you bother about the blackout any more?"

"What the hell good is a blackout when the whole town's burning like a torch?" shouted the other voice. "Well? Got any dead in there?"

"Dunno."

"The dead over here, d'you hear? And the others up the stairs into the art room, right?"

"OK, OK."

But I wasn't dead yet, I was one of the others, and they carried me up the stairs. First came a long, dimly lit corridor, green oil paint on the walls; bent, black, old-fashioned clotheshooks had been let into the walls, and there were doors with little enamel plaques—VIa and VIb—and between these doors, shining softly under glass in a black frame, Feuerbach's *Medea* gazed into the distance; then came doors with Va and Vb, and between them hung a photograph of the boy plucking a thorn from his foot, its marvelous russet sheen framed in brown.

The great central column at the foot of the stairs was there too, and behind it, long and narrow, a beautiful plaster reproduction of the Parthenon frieze, creamy yellow, genuine, antique, and everything was all there just as it should be: the ancient Greek warrior, resplendent and formidable, plumed like a cock; and there along the staircase wall—yellow oil paint here—they all hung: from the Hohenzollern rulers down to Hitler. . . .

And over in the narrow passageway, where at last I could lie level on my stretcher for a few paces, there was the finest, biggest, most colorful picture of all: old Frederick the Great with his sky-blue uniform, lively eyes, and the great shining gold star on his chest.

Once again I was lying tilted on the stretcher and being carried past the racial paradigms, including the Nordic captain with the eagle eye and the stupid mouth, the Rhine maiden, a bit bony and severe, the East Prussian with his broad grin and bulbous nose, and the Alpine profile with lantern jaw and Adam's apple; then came another corridor, again I lay level on my stretcher for a few paces, and just before the stretcher bearers swung round onto the second staircase I caught a glimpse of it: the war memorial surmounted by the great gilded Iron Cross and the stone laurel wreath.

This all happened very quickly: I am not heavy, and the stretcher bearers were in a great hurry. Yet it might all be a hallucination, I was running a high fever and my whole body hurt—head, arms, and legs, and my heart was thumping like crazy. You see a lot of funny things when you're feverish.

But after the Nordic faces came all the other things: the three busts of Caesar, Cicero, and Marcus Aurelius, superb reproductions, standing sedately side by side against the wall, yellowed and genuine, antique and dignified, and then as we swung round the corner came the Hermes column, and way at the end of the corridor—painted pink here—way, way at the end of the corridor Zeus' big ugly mug hung over the entrance to the art room; but that was still a long way off. To the right, through the window, I could see fire reflected, the whole sky was red, and dense black clouds of smoke filed past in solemn procession. . . . And again my eyes turned to the left and I saw the little plaques over the doors, Ia and Ib, and between the musty brown doors I saw just the tip of Nietzsche's nose and his mustache in a gilt frame because the other half of the picture had a sign stuck over it saying "Minor Surgery."

I wonder, I thought fleetingly . . . I wonder . . . and there it was: the picture of Togoland, large, highly colored, flat as an old engraving, a thing of beauty, and in the foreground in front of the colonial houses, in front of the Africans and the soldier standing pointlessly around with his rifle, in the very foreground was the huge, lifelike bunch of bananas: one bunch on the left, one on the right, and on the middle banana in the right-hand bunch something had been scribbled, I could just make it out. I must have written it myself. . . .

But just at that moment the door to the art room was flung open, and I floated in under Zeus' whiskers and shut my eyes. I didn't want to see any more. The art room smelled of iodine, excrement, bandages, and tobacco, and it was noisy. As they set me down I asked the stretcher bearers, "Light me a cigarette, will you, top left-hand pocket."

I could feel one of them fumbling in my pocket, a match hissed, and the lighted cigarette was stuck between my lips. I took a long pull. "Thanks," I said.

All this, I thought, doesn't prove a thing. Logically speaking, every high school has an art room, corridors with bent old clotheshooks let into green- and yellow-painted walls; logically speaking, the fact that *Medea* hangs between VIa and VIb and Nietzsche's mustache between Ia and Ib is no proof that I'm in my old school. No doubt there's some regulation requiring it to hang there. Rule for Prussian High Schools: *Medea* between VIa and VIb, *Boy with a Thorn* on that wall, Caesar, Marcus Aurelius, and Cicero in the corridor, and Nietzsche upstairs where they're already taking philosophy. Parthenon frieze, colored print of Togoland. *Boy with a Thorn* and Parthenon frieze are, after all, good old stand-bys, traditional school props, and no doubt I wasn't the only boy who had been moved to write on a banana "Long live Togoland." And the jokes, too, that boys tell each other in school are always the same. Besides, maybe I'm feverish, maybe I'm dreaming.

The pain had gone now. In the truck it had still been pretty bad; I had yelled every time they drove through the small potholes, the shell craters had been better: the truck rose and sank like a ship in a wave trough. But now the injection they had stuck in my arm somewhere in the dark seemed to be working: I had felt the needle boring through the skin and my leg lower down getting all hot.

It can't be true, I thought, the truck couldn't have driven that far: nearly twenty miles. Besides, I feel nothing. Apart from my eyes, nothing tells me I'm in my school, in my old school that I left only three months ago. Eight years in the same school is a pretty long time—is it possible that after eight years only your eyes recognize the place?

Behind my closed lids I saw it all again, reeling off like a film: downstairs corridor, painted green, up the stairs, painted yellow, war memorial, corridor, up more stairs, Caesar, Cicero, Marcus Aurelius . . . Hermes, Nietzsche's mustache, Togoland, Zeus' ugly mug. . . .

I spat out my cigarette and yelled. It always felt good to yell; but you had to yell loud, it was a glorious feeling, I yelled like mad. When someone bent over me, I still didn't open my eyes; I smelled someone's breath, hot and fetid with tobacco and onions, and a quiet voice asked, "What's the matter?"

"I want a drink," I said, "and another cigarette, top pocket."

Once more someone fumbled in my pocket, once more a match hissed, and someone stuck a burning cigarette between my lips.

"Where are we?" I asked.

"In Bendorf."

"Thanks," I said, and drew on my cigarette.

So at least I really was in Bendorf, in my home town, that is, and unless I had an exceptionally high fever there seemed to be no doubt that I was in a high school with a classics department; it was certainly a school. Hadn't that voice downstairs shouted, "The others into the art room"? I was one of the others, I was alive; the living were evidently the others. The art room was there, then, and if I could hear properly why shouldn't I be able to see properly, so that it was probably true that I had recognized Caesar, Cicero, and Marcus Aurelius, and that could only happen in a classics high school. I didn't think they stood those fellows up against the wall in any other kind of school.

At last he brought me some water: again I smelled the tobacco-and-onion breath and, without wanting to, I opened my eyes. They saw a weary, elderly, unshaven face above a fireman's uniform, and an old man's voice whispered, "Drink, lad!"

I drank; it was water, but water is glorious. I could taste the tin mug against my lips, and it was wonderful to feel how much water was still waiting to be drunk, but the fireman whisked the mug from my lips and took off. I yelled, but he didn't turn round, just gave a weary shrug of the shoulders and walked on. A man lying next to me said quietly, "No use yelling, they haven't any more water. The town's burning, you can see for yourself."

I could see it through the blackout curtains: there were flares and booms behind the black material, red behind black like in a stove when you throw on fresh coal. I could see it all right: the town was burning.

"What town is it?" I asked the man lying next to me.

"Bendorf," he said.

"Thanks."

I looked straight ahead at the row of windows, and sometimes at the ceiling. The ceiling was still in perfect condition, white and smooth, with a narrow antique stucco border; but all schools have antique stucco borders on their art-room ceilings, at least the good old traditional classics high schools. No doubt about that.

I had to accept the fact that I was in the art room of a classics high school in Bendorf. Bendorf has three of these schools: the Frederick the Great School, the Albertus School, and—perhaps I need hardly add—the last, the third, was the Adolf Hitler School. Hadn't old Frederick's picture on the staircase wall at the Frederick the Great School been the biggest, the most colorful and resplendent of all? I had gone to that school for eight years, but why couldn't the same picture hang in exactly the same place in other schools, so clear and noticeable that it couldn't fail to catch your eye whenever you went up the first flight of stairs?

Outside, I could hear the heavy artillery firing now. There was hardly any other sound; just occasionally you could hear flames consuming a house and somewhere in the dark a roof would cave in. The artillery was firing quietly and regularly, and I thought: Good old artillery! I know that's a terrible thing to think, but I thought it. God, how reassuring the artillery was, how soothing: dark and rugged, a gentle, almost refined organ sound, aristocratic somehow. To me there is something aristocratic about artillery, even when it's firing. It sounds so dignified, just like war in picture books. . . . Then I thought of how many names there would be on the war memorial when they reconsecrated it and put an even bigger gilded Iron Cross on the top and an even bigger stone laurel wreath, and suddenly I realized that if I really was in my old school, my name would be on it too, engraved in stone, and in the school yearbook my name would be followed by "Went to the front straight from school and fell for . . ."

But I didn't know what for, and I didn't know yet whether I was in my old school. I felt I absolutely had to make sure. There had been nothing special about the war memorial, nothing unusual, it was like all the rest, a ready-made war memorial—in fact they got them from some central supply house. . . .

I looked round the art room, but they had removed the pictures, and what can you tell from a few benches stacked up in a corner, and from the high, narrow windows, all close together to let in a lot of light because it was a studio? My heart told me nothing. Wouldn't it have told me something if I had been in this place before, where for eight solid years I had drawn vases and practiced lettering, slender, delicate, beautiful reproductions of Roman vases that the art teacher set on a pedestal up front, and all kinds of lettering, Round, Antique, Roman, Italic? I had loathed these lessons more than anything else in school; for hours on end I had suffered unutterable boredom, and I had never been any good at drawing vases or lettering. But where were my curses, where was my loathing, in the face of these dun-colored, monotonous walls? No voice spoke within me, and I mutely shook my head.

Over and over again I had erased, sharpened my pencil, erased . . . nothing. . . .

I didn't know exactly how I had been wounded. I only knew I couldn't move my arms or my right leg, just the left one a little; I figured they had bandaged my arms so tightly to my body that I couldn't move them.

I spat the second cigarette into the aisle between the straw pallets and tried to move my arms, but it was so painful I had to yell; I kept on yelling; each time I tried it, it felt wonderful to yell. Besides, I was mad at not being able to move my arms.

Suddenly the doctor was standing in front of me. He had taken off his glasses and was peering at me. He said nothing; behind him stood the fireman who had brought me the water. He whispered something into the doctor's ear, and the doctor put on his glasses: I could distinctly see his large gray eyes with the faintly quivering pupils behind the thick lenses. He looked at me for a long time, so long that I had to look away, and he said softly, "Hold on, it'll be your turn in a minute. . . ."

Then they picked up the man lying next to me and carried him behind the blackboard. My eyes followed them: they had taken the blackboard apart and set it up crossways and hung a sheet over the gap between wall and blackboard; a lamp was glaring behind it. . . .

There was not a sound until the sheet was pushed aside and the man who had lain next to me was carried out; with tired, impassive faces the stretcher bearers carted him to the door.

I closed my eyes again and thought, I must find out how I've been wounded and whether I'm in my old school.

It all seemed so cold and remote, as if they had carried me through the museum of a city of the dead, through a world as irrelevant as it was unfamiliar, although my eyes, but only my eyes, recognized it; surely it couldn't be true that only three months ago I had sat in this room, drawn vases and practiced lettering, gone downstairs during breaks with my jam sandwich, past Nietzsche, Hermes, Togoland, Caesar, Cicero, Marcus Aurelius, taking my time as I walked to the lower corridor where *Medea* hung, then to the janitor, to Birgeler, for a glass of milk, milk in that dingy little room where you could risk a smoke although it was against the rules. They must be carrying the man who had lain next to me downstairs now, to where the dead were lying, maybe the dead were lying in Birgeler's gray little room that smelled of warm milk, dust, and Birgeler's cheap tobacco. . . .

At last the stretcher bearers came back, and now they lifted me and carried me behind the blackboard. I was floating again, passing the door now, and as I floated past I could see that was right too: in the old days, when the school had been called St. Thomas's, a cross had hung over the door, and then they had removed the cross, but a fresh deep-yellow spot in the shape of a cross had stayed behind on the wall, hard and clear, more noticeable in a way than the fragile little old cross itself, the one they had removed; the outline of the cross remained distinct and beautiful on the faded wall. At the time they were so mad they repainted the whole wall, but it hadn't made any difference. The painter hadn't got quite the right color: the cross stayed, deep yellow and clear, although the whole wall was pink. They had been furious, but it was no good: the cross stayed, deep yellow and clear on the pink wall; they must have used up their budget for paint so there wasn't a thing they could do about it. The cross was still there, and if you looked closely you could even make out a slanting line over the right arm of the cross where for years the boxwood sprig had been, the one Birgeler the janitor had stuck behind it, in the days when it was still permitted to hang crosses in schools. . . .

All this flashed through my mind during the brief second it took for me to be carried past the door to the place behind the blackboard where the glaring lamp shone.

I lay on the operating table and saw myself quite distinctly, but very small, dwarfed, up there in the clear glass of the light bulb, tiny and white, a narrow, gauze-colored little bundle looking like an unusually diminutive embryo: so that was me up there.

The doctor turned away and stood beside a table sorting his instruments; the fireman, stocky and elderly, stood in front of the blackboard and smiled at me. His smile was tired and sad, and his unshaven, dirty face was the face of someone asleep. Beyond his shoulder, on the smudged reverse side of the blackboard, I saw something that, for the first time since being in this house of the dead, made me aware of my heart—somewhere in a secret chamber of my heart I experienced a profound and terrible shock, and my heart began to pound: the handwriting on the blackboard was mine. Up at the top, on the very top line. I know my handwriting: it is worse than catching sight of oneself in a mirror, much clearer, and there was not the slightest possibility of doubting the identity of my handwriting. All the rest hadn't proved a thing, neither *Medea* nor Nietzsche, neither the Alpine profile nor the banana from Togoland, not even the outline of the cross over the door: all that was the same in every school, but I don't believe they write on blackboards in other schools in my handwriting. It was still there, the Thermopylae inscription we had had to write, in that life of despair I had known only three months ago: "Stranger, bear word to the Spartans we . . ."

Oh, I know, the board had been too short, and the art teacher had bawled me out for not spacing properly, for starting off with letters that were too big, and shaking his head he had written underneath, in letters the same size, "Stranger, bear word to the Spartans we . . ."

Seven times I had had to write it: in Antique, Gothic, Cursive, Roman, Italic, Script, and Round. Seven times, plain for all to see: "Stranger, bear word to the Spartans we . . ."

The fireman, responding to a whispered summons from the doctor, had stepped aside, so now I saw the whole quotation, only slightly truncated because I had started off too big, had used up too many dots.

A prick in my left thigh made me jerk up, I tried to prop myself on my elbows, but couldn't. I looked down at my body, and then I saw: they had undone my bandages and I had no arms, no right leg, and I fell back instantly because I had no elbows to lean on. I screamed; the doctor and fireman looked at me in alarm, but the doctor merely shrugged his shoulders, keeping his thumb on the plunger of his hypo as he pressed it slowly and gently down. I tried to look at the blackboard again, but the fireman was standing right beside me now, obscuring it. He was holding down my shoulders, and I was conscious only of the scorched, grimy smell of his stained uniform, saw only his tired, sad face, and then I recognized him: it was Birgeler.

"Milk," I whispered. . . .

Drinking in Petöcki

The soldier felt he was getting drunk at last. At the same moment it crossed his mind again, very clearly, that he hadn't a single pfennig in his pocket to pay the bill. His thoughts were as crystal-clear as his perception, he saw everything with the utmost clarity: the fat, shortsighted woman sitting in the shadows behind the bar, intent on her crocheting as she chatted quietly to a man with an unmistakably Magyar mustache—a true operetta face, straight from the puszta, while the woman looked stolid and rather German, somewhat too respectable and sedate for the soldier's image of a Hungarian woman. The language they were chatting in was as unintelligible as it was throaty, as passionate as it was strange and beautiful. The room was filled with a dense green twilight from the many close-planted chestnut trees along the avenue leading to the station: a wonderful dense twilight that reminded him of absinthe and made the room exquisitely intimate and cozy. The man with the fabulous mustache, half perched on a chair, looked relaxed and comfortable as he sprawled across the counter.

The soldier observed all this in great detail, at the same time aware that he would not have been able to walk to the counter without falling down. It'll have to settle a bit, he thought, then with a loud laugh shouted "Hey there!", raised his glass toward the woman, and said in German, *"Bitte schön!"* The woman slowly got up from her chair, put aside her crochet work equally slowly, and, carrying the carafe, came over to him with a smile, while the Hungarian also turned round and eyed the medals on the soldier's chest. The woman waddling toward him was as broad as she was tall, her face was kind, and she looked as if she had heart trouble; clumsy pince-nez, attached to a worn black string, balanced on her nose. Her feet seemed to hurt too; while she filled his glass she took the weight off one foot and leaned with one hand on the table. She said something in her dark-toned Hungarian that was doubtless the equivalent of *"Prost"* or "Your very good health," or perhaps even of some affectionate, motherly remark such as old women commonly bestow on soldiers.

The soldier lit a cigarette and drank deeply from his glass. Gradually the room began to revolve before his eyes; the fat proprietress hung somewhere at an angle in the air, the rusty old counter now stood on end, and the Hungarian, who was drinking sparingly, was cavorting about somewhere up near the ceiling like an acrobatic monkey. The next instant everything tilted the other way, the soldier gave a loud laugh, shouted *"Prost!"*, took another drink, then another, and lit a fresh cigarette.

The door opened and in came another Hungarian, fat and short, with a roguish onion face and a few dark hairs on his upper lip. He let out a gusty sigh, tossed his cap onto a table, and hoisted himself onto a chair by the counter. The woman poured him some beer. . . .

The gentle chatter of the three at the counter was wonderful, like a quiet humming at the edge of another world. The soldier took another gulp of wine, put down his empty glass, and everything resumed its proper place.

The soldier felt almost happy as he raised his glass again, repeating with a laugh, *"Bitte schön!"*

The woman refilled his glass.

I've had almost ten glasses of wine, the soldier thought. I'll stop now, I'm so gloriously drunk that I feel almost happy. The green twilight thickened, the farther corners of the bar were already filled with impenetrable deep-blue shadows. What a crime, thought the soldier, that there are no lovers here. It would be a perfect spot for lovers, in this wonderful green-and-blue twilight. What a crime, he thought, as he pictured all those lovers somewhere out there in the world who had to sit around or chase around in the bright light, while here in the bar there was a place where they could talk, drink wine, and kiss. . . .

Christ, thought the soldier, there ought to be music here now, and all these wonderful dark-green and dark-blue corners ought to be full of lovers—and I would sing a song. You bet I'd sing a song. I feel very happy, and I would sing those lovers a song, then I'd really quit thinking about the war; now I'm always thinking a little bit about this damn war. Then I'd quit thinking about it altogether.

He looked closely at his watch: seven-thirty. He still had twenty minutes. He drank long and deep of the dry, cool wine, and it was almost as if someone had given him stronger spectacles: now everything looked closer and clearer and very solid, and he felt himself becoming gloriously, beautifully, almost totally drunk. Now he saw that the two men at the counter were poor, either laborers or shepherds, in threadbare trousers, and that their faces were tired and terribly submissive in spite of the dashing mustache and the wily onion look. . . .

Christ, thought the soldier, how horrible it was back there when I had to leave, so cold, and everything bright and full of snow, and we still had a few minutes left and nowhere was there a corner, a wonderful, dark, human corner where we could have kissed and embraced. Everything had been bright and cold. . . .

"*Bitte schön!*" he shouted to the woman; then, as she approached, he looked at his watch: he still had ten minutes. When the woman started to fill his half-empty glass, he held his hand over it, shook his head with a smile, and rubbed thumb and forefinger together. "Pay," he said, "how many pengös?"

He very slowly took off his jacket, slipped off the handsome gray turtleneck sweater, and laid it beside him on the table in front of the watch. The men at the counter had stopped talking and were looking at him, the woman also seemed startled. Very carefully she wrote a 14 on the tabletop. The soldier placed his hand on her fat, warm forearm, held up the sweater with the other, and asked with a laugh, "How much?" Rubbing thumb and forefinger together again, he added, "Pengös."

The woman looked at him and shook her head, but he went on shrugging his shoulders and indicating that he had no money until she hesitantly picked up the sweater, turned it over, and carefully examined it, even sniffed it. She wrinkled her nose a little, then smiled and with a pencil quickly wrote a "30" next to the "14." The soldier let go of her warm arm, nodded, raised his glass, and took another drink.

As the woman went back to the counter and eagerly began talking to the men in her throaty voice, the soldier simply opened his mouth and sang. He sang "When the Drum Roll Sounds for Me," and suddenly realized he was singing well—singing well for the first time in his life; at the same time he realized he was drunker again, that everything was gently swaying. He took another look at his watch and saw he had three minutes in which to sing and be happy, and he started another song, "Innsbruck, I Must Leave You." Then with a smile he took the money the woman had placed in front of him and put it in his pocket. . . .

It was quite silent now in the bar. The two men with the threadbare trousers and the tired faces had turned toward him, and the woman had stopped on her way back to the counter and was listening quietly and solemnly, like a child.

The soldier finished his wine, lit another cigarette, and knew he would walk unsteadily. But before he left he put some money on the counter and, with a "*Bitte schön,*" pointed to the two men. All three stared after him as he at last opened the door and went out into the avenue of chestnut trees leading to the station, the avenue that was full of exquisite dark-green, dark-blue shadows where a fellow could have put his arms around his girl and kissed her good-bye. . . .

What a Racket

THE HALF-WOMAN, the "Woman with No Lower Half," turned out to be one of the most delightful persons I had ever met. She was wearing a charming sombrero-type straw hat, for, like any other modest housewife, she was sitting in the sun on the little raised porch that had been attached to her trailer home. Below the porch her three children were playing a very original game known to them as "The Neanderthals." The two youngest, a boy and a girl, were obliged to be the Neanderthal couple, while the oldest, a fair-haired youngster of eight who during performances was the Fat Lady's son, took the part of the modern explorer who discovers the Neanderthal couple. Right at the moment he was doing his best to wrench his younger siblings' jawbones out of their sockets so he could take them back to his museum.

The Half-Woman stamped several times on the porch floor on account of the frenzied screams that were threatening to stifle our budding conversation.

The oldest boy's head appeared above the low railing, which was adorned with red geraniums, and he asked crossly, "Yes?"

"Stop that bullying," said his mother, a suppressed amusement in her gentle gray eyes. "Why don't you play Air-Raid Shelter or Bombed Out?"

The boy grumbled something that sounded like "Nuts!", disappeared below the railing, and shouted to the others, "Fire! The whole house is on fire!" Unfortunately I was unable to follow the further course of the game known as Bombed Out, for the Half-Woman was now eyeing me somewhat more closely. In the shade of her broad-brimmed hat, with the sun shining warm and red through it, she looked much too young to be the mother of three children and to fulfill the exacting demands, five times a day, of the role of Half-Woman.

"You are . . ." she said.

"Nothing," I said, "nothing at all. Consider me nothing but a nothing. . . ."

"You are," she placidly continued, "a former black-market operator, I suppose."

"That's right," I said.

She shrugged her shoulders. "I can't really offer you anything. In any case, wherever we found a spot for you, you would have to work—work, do you know what I mean?"

"Ma'am," I replied, "possibly your idea of a black-market operator's life is a little on the rosy side. Speaking personally, I was, one might say, at the front."

"What?" She stamped her foot again on the porch floor, the children having set up a rather protracted and demented howling. Once again the boy's head appeared above the railing.

"Well?" he asked curtly.

"Play Refugees now," the woman said quietly. "You must flee from the burning city, understand?"

The boy's head vanished again, and the woman asked me, "What?" Oh, she hadn't lost the thread, not she.

"Right at the front," I said, "I was right in the front lines. Is that your idea of an easy way to make a living?"

"At the corner?"

"Well, at the station, actually; you know where I mean?"

"I do. And now?"

"I'd like some kind of a job. I'm not lazy, I assure you, ma'am, I'm not lazy."

"Excuse me," she said. Turning her delicate profile toward me, she called into the trailer, "Carlino, isn't the water boiling yet?"

"Hang on," called a bored voice. "I'm just making the coffee."

"Are you going to have some?"

"No."

"Then bring two cups, if you don't mind. You'll have a cup, won't you?"

I nodded. "And I'll invite you to a cigarette."

The screams below the porch now became so piercing that any further conversation would have been impossible. The Half-Woman leaned over the geranium box and called, "You must run for your lives, hurry, hurry —the Russians have reached the village!"

"My husband," she said, turning round, "isn't here at the moment, but when it comes to hiring I can . . ."

We were interrupted by Carlino—a slightly built, taciturn, swarthy fellow wearing a hairnet—emerging with cups and coffeepot. He looked at me suspiciously.

"Why won't you join us?" the woman asked him as he turned abruptly away.

"Not thirsty," he mumbled, disappearing inside the trailer.

"When it comes to hiring, I can act pretty well on my own. All the same, you would have to have some kind of skill. Nothing is nothing."

"Perhaps, ma'am," I said humbly, "I could grease wheels or take down the tents, drive the tractor, or be the Strong Man's knockabout."

"Driving the tractor is out," she said, "and there's quite an art to greasing wheels."

"Or operate the brakes," I continued, "on the gondola swings . . ."

She raised her eyebrows haughtily, for the first time giving me a slightly disdainful look. "Operating the brakes," she said coldly, "is a science, and it wouldn't surprise me if you broke all the customers' necks. Carlino is our brakeman."

"Or . . ." I was about to suggest diffidently, but a little dark-haired girl with a scar across her forehead came dashing up the half dozen steps that put me in mind of a gangplank.

Throwing herself into her mother's lap she sobbed indignantly, "I've got to die. . . ."

"What?" asked the Half-Woman, aghast.

"I'm supposed to be the little refugee who freezes to death, and Freddi wants to sell my shoes and everything. . . ."

"Well," said her mother, "if you will insist on playing Refugees. . . ."

"But why always me?" said the child. "It's always me who has to die. I'm always the one who's got to die. When we play Bombs or War or Tightrope Walkers, it's always me that's got to die."

"Tell Freddi he's got to die; tell him I said it's his turn to die now." The little girl ran off.

"Or?" asked the Half-Woman. Oh, she didn't lose the thread that easily, not she.

"Or straighten nails, peel potatoes, ladle out soup, anything you say," I cried in despair. "Just give me a chance!"

She stubbed out her cigarette, poured us each another cup of coffee, and gave me a long, smiling look. Then she said, "I'll give you a chance. You're good at figures, aren't you? You had to be, didn't you, in your former occupation, so"—she hesitated a second—"I'll make you cashier."

I had no words, I was literally speechless, I just got up and kissed her small hand. We said no more. It was very quiet; all we could hear was Carlino humming to himself inside the trailer, the way a man hums when he is shaving. . . .

Parting

W E WERE in that bleak, miserable mood that comes when you have already said good-bye but can't part because the train hasn't left yet. The station was like all stations, dirty and drafty, filled to its vaulted roof with vapory haze and noise, the noise of voices and railway coaches.

Charlotte was standing at the window of the long corridor, constantly jostled and shoved from behind, the object of much cursing, but during these final precious minutes, the last we would ever share, we needed more than just a wave from an overcrowded compartment. . . .

"It was nice of you," I said, for the third time, "it really was nice of you to stop by on your way to the station."

"Don't be absurd, look how long we've known each other. Fifteen years."

"That's right, we're thirty now. Still . . . you needn't have."

"Please. Yes, we're thirty now. As old as the Russian Revolution."

"As old as dirt and hunger . . ."

"A bit younger . . ."

"You're right: we're terribly young."

She laughed.

"Did you say something?" she asked nervously: she had been bumped from behind with a heavy suitcase.

"No, it was my leg."

"You must do something about it."

"Yes, I will do something about it, it really talks too much."

"Is it all right for you to stand so long?"

"Yes . . ." What I really wanted to tell her was that I loved her, but I couldn't find the words; for fifteen years I hadn't been able to find the words.

"What was that?"

"Nothing. Sweden, so you're going to Sweden."

"Yes, I feel a bit ashamed, this has become part of our life, really, the dirt and rags and ruins, and I feel a bit ashamed. I feel like a deserter. . . ."

"Nonsense, that's where you belong. Be glad you're going to Sweden."

"Sometimes I am glad, you know, the food, that must be marvelous, and no ruins, no ruins at all. His letters sound so enthusiastic. . . ."

The voice that always announces the train departures sounded out now one platform closer, and I held my breath, but it was not our platform. The voice was only announcing the arrival of an international train from Rotterdam to Basel, and as I looked at Charlotte's small, delicate face, I suddenly recalled the smell of soap and coffee, and I felt utterly wretched.

For a moment a desperate courage filled me, I wanted to drag this little person out of the window and keep her here, for she was mine, I loved her. . . .

"What's the matter?"

"Nothing," I said, "be glad you're going to Sweden."

"I am. His vitality is fantastic, don't you agree? A prisoner of war for three years in Russia, that hair-raising escape, and now he's in Sweden lecturing on Rubens."

"Fantastic, it really is."

"You must get busy too, get your degree at least. . . ."

"Oh, shut up!"

"What?" she asked, horrified. "What?" She had gone quite pale.

"Forgive me," I whispered, "I mean my leg. I talk to it sometimes. . . ."

She didn't look in the least like Rubens, she looked more like Picasso, and I kept wondering why on earth he had married her. She wasn't even pretty, and I loved her.

It was quieter now on the platform; everyone had got onto the train, a few people stood around seeing their friends off. Any moment now the voice would say the train was leaving. Any moment might be the last. . . .

"You really must do something, anything, you can't go on like this."

"No, I can't," I said.

She was the very opposite of Rubens—slim, long-legged, high-strung—and she was as old as the Russian Revolution, as old as the hunger and dirt in Europe, as old as the war.

"I can't believe it . . . Sweden . . . it's like a dream."

"It is all a dream."

"Do you think so?"

"Of course. Fifteen years. Thirty years . . . another thirty years. Why bother about a degree? It's not worth the effort. Be quiet, damn you!"

"Are you talking to your leg?"

"Yes."

"What does it say?"

"Listen."

We were quite silent, we looked at one another and smiled, and we told one another without saying a word.

She smiled at me. "Do you understand now, is it all right?"

"Yes . . . yes."

"Truly?"

"Yes, yes."

"You see," she went on softly, "it's not important to be together and all that. That's not what really matters, is it?"

The voice that announces the train departures was right above me now, official, distinct, and I winced, as if a great gray, impersonal whip had come swishing down under the vaulted roof.

"Good-bye!"

"Good-bye!"

Very slowly the train started to move, sliding away in the darkness under the great roof.

Between Trains in X

As I awoke, I was filled with a sense of almost utter isolation; I seemed to be floating in darkness on sluggish waters, borne along by aimless currents. Like a corpse that is finally washed up by the waves to the pitiless surface, I eddied this way and that, gently swaying in a dark void. I could not feel my limbs, they had ceased to be a part of me, and my senses no longer functioned. There was nothing to see, nothing to hear, no smell to cling to; only the soft touch of the pillow under my head linked me with reality, my head was the only thing I was conscious of. My thoughts were crystal-clear, barely dimmed by the racking headache that comes from bad wine.

Not even her breath was audible; she slept as lightly as a child, and yet I knew she must be lying beside me. There would have been no point in reaching out my hands to grope for her face or her soft hair, I had no hands. Memory was but a memory of the mind, a bloodless structure that had left no trace on my body.

This was how I had often felt as I walked along the brink of reality with the assurance of the drunk making his way beside the narrow edge of a precipice, lurching with an unaccountable sense of balance toward a goal whose splendor is written on his mouth. I had walked along avenues lit only by sparse gray lamps, leaden lamps that seemed only to suggest reality the better to be able to deny it. With unseeing eyes I had submerged myself in somber streets crowded with people, knowing that I was alone, alone.

Alone with my head, and not even my whole head; nose, eyes, and ears were dead. Alone with only a brain that was straining to recapture memory, as a child builds apparently meaningless objects out of apparently meaningless sticks.

She must be lying beside me, although I had no physical consciousness of her.

The previous day I had left the train that continued south toward the Balkans as far as Athens while I had to change at this little station and wait for a train that was to take me closer to the Carpathian passes. As I stumbled across the platform, uncertain even of the name of the station, a drunken soldier came reeling toward me, a lone figure in his gray uniform among the Hungarians in their colored civilian clothes. He was shouting insults that burned themselves into my brain like the slap in the face whose stinging pain one remembers all one's life.

"Bunch of whores!" he shouted. "Swine, trash—I'm sick of the whole pack!" He was shouting all this into the very faces of the foolishly smiling Hungarians, while, carrying his heavy pack, he headed for the train I had just left.

Immediately a sinister steel-helmeted head called out from a train window, "Hey you! You there!" The drunk drew his pistol, aimed at the steel helmet; people screamed. I made a dash for the soldier, put my arms around him, removed his weapon and hid it, keeping a firm grip on his flailing arms. The steel helmet shouted, people shouted, the drunk shouted, but the train moved off, and in most cases a moving train renders even a steel helmet powerless. I let go of the drunk, gave him back his pistol, and steered the dazed man to the exit.

The little place had a desolate look. The bystanders had quickly dispersed; the station square was empty. A tired and dirty railroad employee directed us to a tiny bar beneath some low trees on the other side of the dusty square.

We put down our packs, and I ordered wine, that bad wine which was responsible for my present misery. The soldier sat there mute and angry. I offered him cigarettes, we smoked, and I had a good look at him: he was wearing the usual decorations, he was young, about my age, his fair hair hanging loosely over a flat, broad forehead into dark eyes.

"The point is, chum," he said suddenly, "I'm sick of the whole business, see?"

I nodded.

"Sick to death of it, see? I'm getting out."

I looked at him.

"That's right," he said soberly, "I'm getting out, I'm heading for the puszta. I can handle horses, make a decent soup if I have to, they can kiss my ass for all I care. Want to come along?"

I shook my head.

"Scared, eh? . . . No? . . . OK, anyway I'm getting out. So long."

He got up, left his pack on the floor, put some money on the table, nodded to me again, and went out.

I waited a long time. I didn't believe he had really quit, was really heading for the puszta. I kept an eye on his pack and waited, drank the bad wine, tried without success to strike up a conversation with the landlord, and stared at the square, across which, from time to time, wreathed in clouds of dust, dashed a cart drawn by thin horses.

After a while I had a steak, went on drinking the bad wine, and smoked cigars. The light was beginning to fade, now and then a cloud of dust would be wafted into the room through the open door; the landlord yawned or chatted with Hungarians as they drank their wine.

Darkness was coming on quickly; I shall never know all the things I was thinking about as I sat there and waited, drank wine, ate steak, watched the fat landlord, stared at the square, and puffed cigars. . . .

My brain reproduced all this quite neutrally, spewing it out while I floated giddily around on those dark waters, in that hourless night, in a house I did not know, in a nameless street, beside a girl whose face I had never seen properly. . . .

Later on I had hurried across to the station, found my train gone and the next one not due till the morning. I had paid my bill, left my pack lying beside the other one, and staggered out into the twilight of the little town. Gray, dark gray, flooded in on me from all sides, and only the sparse lamps gave the faces of passers-by the look of living people.

Somewhere I drank a better wine, looked forlornly into the unsmiling face of a woman behind the bar, smelled something like vinegar through a kitchen door, paid, and disappeared again into the dusk.

This life, I thought, is not my life. I have to behave as if this were my life, but I'm no good at it. It was quite dark by now, and the mild sky of a summer evening hung over the town. Somewhere the war was going on, invisible, inaudible in these silent streets where the low houses slept beside low trees; somewhere in this absolute silence the war was going on. I was alone in this town, these people were not my people; these little trees had been unpacked from a box of toys and glued onto these soft, gray sidewalks, with the sky hovering overhead like a soundless dirigible that was about to crash. . . .

Somewhere under a tree there was a face, faintly lit from within. Sad eyes under soft hair that must be light brown although it looked gray in the night; a pale skin with a round mouth that must be red although it too looked gray in the night.

"Come along," I said to the face.

I took hold of her arm, a human arm; the palms of our hands clung together; our fingers met and interlocked as we walked along in this unknown town and turned into an unknown street.

"Don't turn the light on," I said as we entered the room I was now lying in, floating unattached in the darkness.

I had felt a weeping face in the dark and plunged into abysses, down into abysses the way you tumble down a staircase, a dizzying staircase of velvet; on and on I plunged, down one abyss after another. . . .

My memory told me all this had happened, and that I was now lying on this pillow, in this room, beside this girl, without being able to hear her breath; she sleeps as lightly as a child. My God, was my brain all that was left of me?

Often the pitch-black waters would seem to stand still, and hope would stir in me that I was going to wake up, feel my legs, hear again, smell, and not merely think; and even this modest hope was a lot, for it would gradually subside, the pitch-black waters would start eddying again, repossess my helpless corpse, and let it drift, timelessly, in total isolation.

My memory also told me that the night could not last forever. Day had to come some time. And it told me that I could drink, kiss, and weep, even pray, although you can't pray just with your brain. While I knew that I was awake, was lying awake in a Hungarian girl's bed, on her soft pillow in a dark, dark night, while I knew all this, I could not help also believing that I was dead. . . .

It was like a dawn that comes very gently and slowly, so indescribably slowly as to be barely perceptible. First you think you're mistaken; when you're standing in a foxhole on a dark night you can't believe that that's really the dawn, that soft, soft pale strip beyond the invisible horizon; you think you must be mistaken, your tired eyes are oversensitive and are probably reflecting something from some secret reserves of light. But it actually is the dawn, growing stronger now. It actually is getting light, lighter, daylight is growing stronger, the gray patch out there beyond the horizon is slowly spreading, and now you know for certain: day has come.

I suddenly realized I was cold; my feet had slipped out from under the blanket, bare and cold, and the sense of chill was real. I sighed deeply, could feel my own breath as it touched my chin; I leaned over, groped for the blanket, covered my feet. I had hands again, I had feet again, and I could feel my own breath.

Then I reached down over the precipice to my left, fished up my trousers from the floor, and heard the sound of the matchbox in the pocket.

"Don't turn on the light, please," said her voice next to me now, and she sighed too.

"Cigarette?" I whispered.

"Yes," she said.

In the light of the match she was all yellow. A dark yellow mouth, round, black, anxious eyes, skin like fine, soft, yellow sand, and hair like dark honey.

It was hard to talk, to find something to say. We could both hear time trickling away, a wonderful dark flowing sound that swallowed up the seconds.

"What are you thinking about?" she asked all of a sudden. It was as if she had fired a shot, quietly and with such perfect accuracy that a dam burst inside me, and before I had time to take another look at her face in the light of the glowing cigarette tips I found myself speaking. "I was just thinking about who will be lying in this room seventy years from now, who will be sitting or lying on these six square feet of space, and how much he will know about you and me. Nothing," I went on, "he'll only know there was a war."

We each threw our cigarette ends onto the floor to the left of the bed; they fell soundlessly onto my trousers. I shook them off, and the two little glimmering dots lay side by side.

"And then I was thinking who had been here seventy years ago, or what. Maybe there was a field, maybe corn or onions grew here, six feet over my head, with the wind blowing across, and every morning this sad dawn came up over the horizon of the puszta. Or maybe there was already a house belonging to someone."

"Yes," she said softly, "seventy years ago there was a house here."

I was silent.

"Yes," she said, "I think it was seventy years ago that my grandfather built this house. That's when they must have put the railroad through here. He worked for the railroad and built this little house with his savings. And then he went to war, ages ago, you know, in 1914, and he was killed in Russia. And then there was my father; he had some land and also worked for the railroad. He died during this war."

"Killed?"

"No, he died. My mother had died before. And now my brother lives here with his wife and children. And seventy years from now my brother's great-grandsons will be living here."

"Maybe so," I said, "but they'll know nothing about you and me."

"No, not a soul will ever know that you were here with me."

I took hold of her small hand—it was soft, so soft—and held it close to my face.

In the square patch of window a dark-gray darkness showed now, lighter than the blackness of the night.

I suddenly felt her moving past me, without touching me, and I could hear the light tread of her bare feet on the floor; then I heard her dressing. Her movements and the sounds were so light; only when she reached behind her to do up the buttons of her blouse did I hear her breath come more strongly.

"You'd better get dressed," she said.

"Let me just lie here," I said.

"I don't want to put on the light."

"Don't put on the light, let me just lie here."

"But you must have something to eat before you go."

"I'm not going."

I could hear her pause as she put on her shoes and knew she was staring in astonishment into the darkness where I was lying.

"I see," was all she said, softly, and I couldn't tell whether she was surprised or alarmed.

When I turned my head to one side I could see her figure outlined in the dark-gray dawn light. She moved very quietly about the room, found kindling and paper, and took the box of matches from my trouser pocket.

These sounds reached me almost like the thin, anxious cries of a person standing on a riverbank and calling out to someone who is being driven by the current into a great body of water; and I knew then that if I did not get up, did not decide within the next minute or so to leave this gently heaving ship of isolation, I would die in this bed as if paralyzed, or be shot to death here on this pillow by the tireless myrmidons whose eyes miss nothing.

While I listened to her humming as she stood there by the stove gazing at the fire, its warm light growing with quiet wingbeats, I felt divided from her by more than a world. There she stood, somewhere on the periphery of my life, quietly humming and enjoying the growing fire; I understood all that, I could see it, smell the singeing of scorched paper, and yet nowhere could she have been further removed from me.

"Please get up, will you?" said the girl from across the room. "You must leave now." I heard her put a saucepan on the fire and began to stir; it was a soothing sound, the gentle scraping of the wooden spoon, and the smell of browning flour filled the room.

I could see everything now. The room was very small. I was lying on a low wooden bed; next to it was a closet, brown, quite plain, that took up the whole wall as far as the door. Somewhere behind me there must be a table, chairs, and the little stove by the window. It was very quiet, and the early light still so opaque that it lay like shadows in the room.

"Please," she said in a low voice, "I have to go now."

"You have to go?"

"Yes, I have to go to work, and first you must leave, with me."

"Work?" I asked. "Why?"

"What a thing to ask!"

"But where?"

"On the railroad tracks."

"Railroad tracks?" I asked. "What do you do there?"

"We shovel stones and gravel so that nothing will happen to the trains."

"Nothing's going to happen to the trains," I said. "Where do you work? Toward Nagyvárad?"

"No, toward Szeged."

"That's good."

"Why?"

"Because then I won't have to pass you in the train."

She laughed softly. "So you're going to get up after all."

"Yes," I said. I shut my eyes again and let myself drop back into that swaying void whose breath was without smell and without trace, whose gentle rippling touched me like a quiet, barely perceptible waft of air; then I opened my eyes with a sigh and reached for my trousers, now lying neatly beside the bed on a chair.

"Yes," I repeated, and got out of bed.

She stood with her back to me while I went through the familiar motions, drew on my trousers, did up my shoes, and pulled on my gray tunic.

I stood there for a while, saying nothing, my cigarette cold between my lips, looking at her figure, small and slight and now outlined clearly against the window. Her hair was beautiful, soft as a quiet flame.

She turned round and smiled. "What are you thinking about now?" she asked.

For the first time I looked into her face. It was so simple that I could not take it in: round eyes, in which fear was fear, joy was joy.

"What are you thinking about now?" she asked again, and this time she was not smiling.

"Nothing," I said. "I can't think at all. I must go. There's no escape."

"Yes," she said and nodded. "You must go. There's no escape."

"And you must stay."

"I must stay," she said.

"You have to shovel stones and gravel so that nothing will happen and the trains can safely go where things do happen."

"Yes," she said, "that's what I have to do."

We walked down a silent street leading to the station. All streets lead to stations, and from stations you go off to war. We stepped aside into a doorway and kissed, and I could feel, as my hands lay on her shoulders, I could feel as I stood there that she was mine. And she walked away with drooping shoulders without once looking round at me.

She is all alone in this town, and although my way lies along the same street, to the station, I cannot go with her. I must wait till she has disappeared round that corner, beyond the last tree in this little avenue now lying remorselessly in full daylight. I must wait, I can only follow her at a distance, and I shall never see her again. I have to catch that train, go off to that war. . . .

I have no pack now as I walk to the station; all I have is my hands in my pockets and my last cigarette between my lips, and that I shall soon spit out. But it is easier to be carrying nothing when you are once more walking slowly but unsteadily toward the edge of an abyss over which, at a given second, you are going to plunge, down to where we shall meet again. . . .

And it was comforting when the train pulled in on time, cheerfully puffing steam between tall heads of corn and pungent tomato plants.

Reunion with Drüng

T<small>HE BURNING</small> pain in my head let me pass smoothly into the reality of time and space from a dream in which dark figures in gray-green coats had been pounding my skull with hard fists. I was lying in a low room in a farmhouse, and the ceiling seemed to be sinking down on me out of the green dimness like the lid of a tomb. The few traces of light that made the room barely discernible were green: a soft, yellow-frosted green with a black door sharply outlined by a bright band of light, a steadily deepening green that became the color of old moss in the shadows above my face.

I awoke fully as a sudden, strangling nausea made me jerk upright, lean over, and vomit onto the invisible floor. The contents of my stomach seemed to drop into unplumbed depths, a bottomless well, before eventually penetrating my senses as liquid splashing on wood. I vomited again, bent painfully over the edge of the stretcher, and as I leaned back in relief the connection with the past became so clear that I at once remembered a roll of lemon drops, left over from last night's rations, that must still be in one of my pockets. My grimy fingers groped around in my greatcoat pockets, let a few loose cartridges fall clattering into the green abyss, and turned over every item—a pack of cigarettes, pipe, matches, handkerchief, a crumpled letter—and when I couldn't find what I was looking for in my coat pockets, I undid my belt, the buckle clanking as it struck the iron stretcher bar. I found the roll at last in one of my trouser pockets, ripped off the paper, and stuck one of the tart-flavored drops into my mouth.

At certain moments, when the pain flooded every level of my consciousness, relationships between time, space, and events would become confused again: the abyss on either side seemed to fall still further away, and the stretcher I was suspended on felt like a towering pedestal rising closer and closer toward the green ceiling. There were moments when I even thought I was dead, relegated to an agonizing limbo of uncertainty, and the door—outlined by its bright band—was like a gateway to light and enlightenment that some kindly hand must surely open; for at such moments I lay motionless as a statue, dead, and the only living thing was the burning pain spreading out from the wound in my head and associated with a sickening, all-pervading nausea.

Then the pain would ebb away again, as if someone were loosening a vise, and reality would become less brutal: the various shades of green were balm to my tormented eyes, the absolute silence soothing to my racked ears, and memory unwound within me like a roll of film in which I played no part. Everything seemed to lie in an infinitely remote past, whereas in fact not more than an hour could have gone by.

I tried to revive memories from my childhood, days spent in deserted parks instead of school, and these experiences seemed closer, and to involve me more directly, than what had happened an hour ago, although the pain in my head derived from these recent events and should have made me feel otherwise.

What had happened an hour ago I was now able to see very clearly, but distantly, as if I were looking from the edge of our globe into another world divided from ours by a vast abyss of glassy clarity. There I saw someone, who must be me, creeping over churned earth in nocturnal darkness, the lonely silhouette at intervals starkly illuminated by a distant tracer bullet. I watched this stranger, who must be me, struggling on visibly sore feet over the broken ground, often on all fours, then on his feet again, then back on all fours, up on his feet again, and finally heading for a dark valley where a group of similar dark figures stood gathered round a vehicle. In this spectral corner of the globe, where all was anguish and darkness, the stranger mutely took his place in a line of men whose mugs were being filled from metal cauldrons with coffee or soup by someone they did not know, had never seen, someone hidden by dense shadows, wordlessly ladling; the owner of a scared voice, also invisible, doled out bread, cigarettes, sausage, and candies into the waiting hands. And suddenly this mute, somber spectacle on the valley floor was luridly lit up by a red flame followed by screams, whimpering, and the terrified neighing of a wounded horse; more dusky red flames kept shooting up out of the ground, stench and noise filled the air; then the horse screamed—I heard it pull away and dash off, dragging the clattering field kitchen—and a fresh burst of fierce fire covered the figure that must be me.

And now here I was, lying on my stretcher, looking at the deepening shades of green in the dimness of this Russian farmhouse room where the only brightness was the light outlining the oblong of the door.

Meanwhile the nausea had subsided, the lemon drop had spread soothingly through the horrible muck filling my mouth; the vise of pain attacked less and less often, and I dug into my greatcoat pocket, pulled out cigarettes and matches, and struck a light. The flare revealed dark, damp walls, lit here and there by the flickering sulfur-yellow flame, and as I tossed aside the dying match I saw for the first time that I was not alone.

I saw beside me the gray, green-stained folds of a carelessly drawn-up blanket, saw the peak of a cap like an intense black shadow over a pale face; then the match went out.

At the same moment it occurred to me that there was nothing wrong with my hands or feet, so I kicked my blanket aside, sat up, and was startled to see how close I was to the ground: that apparently bottomless pit was scarcely more than knee-deep. I struck another match. My neighbor lay motionless, his face the color of crepuscular light filtering through thin green glass; but before I could get any closer to have a good look at his face under the shadow of his cap, the match went out again, and I remembered that in one of my pockets there must still be a candle end.

The vise of pain made another assault, and I just managed to stagger to the edge of my stretcher in the dark. I sat down, dropping my cigarette onto the floor, and since I now had my back to the door I could see only darkness, a green opaque darkness containing just enough shadows to give me the feeling it was revolving, while the pain in my head seemed to be the motor making it revolve; the more the pain in my head swelled, the more violently did these darknesses revolve like separate disks overlapping as they revolved, until once more everything came to a standstill.

As soon as the attack was over, I fingered my bandage. My head felt bulky and swollen; there was the hard, lumpy crust of clotted blood, and the ultrasensitive spot where the splinter must be. I knew now that the stranger over there was dead. There is a kind of silence and muteness going beyond sleep or unconsciousness, something infinitely icy, hostile, contemptuous, that in the darkness seemed doubly malevolent.

I finally found the candle end and lit it. The glow was yellow and soft; it seemed to spread slowly and diffidently before unfolding its flame to its utmost limits, and when the candle had achieved its full radius I saw the beaten earth floor, the bluish whitewashed walls, a bench, and the dead stove with a pile of ashes lying in front of its sagging door.

I stuck the candle onto the edge of my stretcher so that the center of its radiance fell on the dead man's face. I was not surprised to see Drüng. Rather, I was surprised at my own lack of surprise, for it should have been a great shock: I had not seen Drüng for five years, and even then so briefly that we had exchanged only the barest civilities. We had been classmates for nine years, but there had been such a deep antipathy—not animosity, merely indifference—between us that during those nine years we had spoken to each other for a total of scarcely an hour.

It was so unmistakably Drüng's spare face, his pointed nose, thrusting upward now, still and greenish, from the spare flatness of his face, his narrow-lidded eyes, always somewhat protruding, now closed by a stranger's hand; so unquestionably was it Drüng's face that there was really no need for me to confirm it by bending down and reaching in under the blanket folds for the label tied with string to one of his greatcoat buttons. On it I read by candlelight: Drüng, Hubert, Corporal, the number of his regiment, and under the heading "Type of Injury," Multiple shell splinters, abdomen. Under this an academic hand had scrawled the word "Deceased."

So Drüng was really dead, or would I ever have doubted the hasty scrawl of an academic hand? Again I read the number of his regiment, one I had never heard of; then I took off Drüng's cap, whose black, sardonic shadow gave his face a cruel look, and there was that fairish, lackluster hair which at various times during those fluctuating nine years had been right in front of me.

I was sitting quite close to the candle as its flickering glow swung round the room, the strongest core of its yellow flame always centered on Drüng's face as its feebler offshoots roamed ceiling, walls, and floor. I was sitting so close to Drüng that my breath brushed the ashen skin on which a stubble of beard proliferated, unsightly and reddish-brown, and suddenly for the first time I saw Drüng's mouth. During our daily encounters over so many years, the rest of his appearance had become so familiar that I would have recognized him in a crowd—although probably unconsciously —but now I realized I had never really looked at his mouth. It was as if I had never seen it before: fine-drawn, narrow-lipped, pain still clinging to its pinched corners, a pain so alive that I thought I must be mistaken. This mouth seemed, even now, to be still fighting back the pent-up cries of pain to keep them from gushing out in a red spurt that would drown the world.

Beside me flickered the warm breath of the candle as it flared up, died down, then slowly fanned out, over and over again. I was looking at Drüng's face now without seeing him. I saw him alive, a sickly, shy fourth-grader, heavy satchel on thin shoulders, shivering as he waited for the school doors to open. Then he would rush past the burly janitor and, still wearing his overcoat, plant himself beside the stove, standing guard over it with a defensive look in his eyes. Drüng had always felt the cold, he was of poor physique, poor in every way, the son of a widow whose husband had been killed in the war. He had been ten at the time, and he stayed like that for nine years, shivering, of poor physique, poor in every way, the son of a widow whose husband had been killed in the war. Never once did he have time for those foolish things that memory alone makes memorable, while we often look back on humorless obsession with duty as a foolish thing; never once did he talk back to the teacher, for nine years he remained well behaved, hardworking, always "of average ability." At fourteen he developed acne, at sixteen his skin was smooth again, at eighteen he had acne again, and he always felt the cold, even in summer, for he was of poor physique, poor in every way, the son of a widow whose husband had been killed in the war. He had a few friends, also of average ability, with whom he worked hard and was well behaved. I hardly ever spoke to him, or he to me. Occasionally, as is to be expected over a period of nine years, he had sat in front of me, his lackluster, fairish hair had been in front of me, quite close, and he had always prompted me—now for the first time I realized he had always prompted me, faithfully and reliably; and when he didn't know the answer, he had his own special way of obstinately shrugging his shoulders.

I had been crying for some time, and the candle was now casting its wider light around the room, sighing gently so that the barren little room seemed to rock like the cabin of a ship on the high seas. For some time —without being conscious of it—I had felt the tears running down my face, warm and soothing on my cheeks, and lower down, on my chin, cold drops that I automatically wiped away with my hand like a tearful child. But now that I remembered how he had always loyally prompted me, with never a word of thanks, faithfully and reliably, with none of the spitefulness of others who put too high a price on their knowledge to give it away —now I sobbed aloud, and the tears dripped through my matted beard into my muddy fingers.

And then I remembered about Drüng's father. During history lessons, when the teachers told us in edifying tones about World War I—assuming the topic fell within the curriculum and that Verdun fell within the topic —then all eyes would turn toward Drüng, and at such times Drüng acquired a special, fleeting glory, for it was not often that we had history, or that World War I fell within the curriculum, and still less often was it permitted or appropriate to talk about Verdun. . . .

The candle was hissing now, hot wax bubbling in the cardboard holder; then the unsupported wick toppled over into the melted remains —but suddenly the room was filled with light and I was ashamed of my tears, a light that was cold and naked and gave the drab room a spurious clarity and cleanliness. . . .

It was not until I felt myself grasped by the shoulders that I realized the door had opened and two people had been sent to carry me into the operating room. I shot another glance at Drüng, lying there with pinched lips; then they had laid me back on the stretcher and were carrying me out.

The doctor looked tired and irritable. He watched without interest as the stretcher bearers placed me on a table under a glaring lamp; the rest of the room was shrouded in ruddy darkness. The doctor came closer, and I could see him more clearly: his coarse skin was sallow, with purple shadows, and his thick black hair covered his head like a cap. As he read the label attached to my chest, I noticed the cigarette smell on his breath, and I could see the whitish rolls of fat on his neck and the mask of weary despair over his face.

"Dina," he called softly, "take it off."

He stepped back, and from the ruddy darkness emerged a woman's figure in a white smock; her hair was all wrapped up in a pale-green cloth, and now that she was close, leaning over me and carefully cutting the bandage over my forehead, I saw from the serene, pale oval of her kindly face that she must be blonde. I was still crying, and through my tears her face appeared melting and blurred, and her great soft light-brown eyes seemed to be weeping too, while the doctor seemed hard and dry even through my tears.

With a sudden movement she tore the hard, bloody rag from my wound; I screamed and let the tears flow on. The doctor stood scowling at the edge of the circle of light, the smoke from his cigarette reaching us in sharp blue puffs. Dina's face was quiet while she bent over me, touching my head with her fingers as she began to sponge my clotted hair.

"Shave it!" said the doctor brusquely, tossing his cigarette butt angrily onto the floor.

Now the vise of pain renewed its attacks as the Russian nurse began to shave the filthy, matted hair around the gaping wound. Once again the disks started revolving and eerily overlapping. I had moments of unconsciousness, then I would come to again, and during those waking seconds I could feel the tears flowing more and more freely, running down my cheeks and collecting between shirt and collar, compulsively, as if a well had been drilled.

"Don't cry, damn it!" shouted the doctor from time to time, and because I neither could nor would stop, he shouted, "You ought to be ashamed of yourself!" But I was not ashamed, I was aware only of Dina now and again resting her hands in a caress on my neck, and I knew it was futile to try and explain to the doctor why I had to cry. What did I know of him or he of me, of filth and lice, Drüng's face, and nine school years that came punctually to an end when the war broke out?

"Damn it," he shouted, "for God's sake, shut up!"

Then he suddenly came closer, his face looming unbelievably huge, fiercely stern, as he approached, and for one second I felt the first boring of the knife, then saw nothing more and gave only one shrill scream.

They had closed the door behind me, turned the key, and I found myself back in the first room. My candle was still flickering, sending its fleeting light over everything it encountered. I walked very slowly. I was scared; it was all so quiet, and I felt no more pain. Never before had I been so entirely without pain, so empty. I recognized my stretcher by the rumpled blankets, looked at the candle, still burning just as I had left it. The wick was floating in liquid wax, one tiny tip sticking up just enough for it to burn, and any moment now it would be submerged. I patted my pockets apprehensively, but they were empty. I ran back to the door, rattled the handle, shouted, rattled, shouted. Surely they couldn't leave us in the dark! But outside no one seemed to hear; and when I went back, the candle was still burning, the wick was still floating, a tiny piece was still sticking up just enough for it to burn and produce an irregular, flickering light; this piece of wick seemed to have got smaller; in another second we would be in the dark.

"Drüng," I called, scared, "Drüng!"

"Yes?" came his voice. "What's the matter?"

I felt my heart stand still, and all about me there was no sound save the appallingly quiet consuming of this candle end, on the verge of going out.

"Yes?" he asked again. "What's the matter?"

I stepped to the left, bent down, and looked at him: he was lying there laughing. He was laughing very softly and painfully, and there was gentleness too in his smile. He had thrown back the blankets, and through a great hole in his stomach I could see the green canvas of the stretcher. He was lying there quite quietly, and seemed to be waiting. I looked at him for a long time, the laughing mouth, the hole in his stomach, the hair: it was Drüng.

"Well, what's the matter?" he asked again.

"The candle," I whispered, looking into the light. It was still burning; I saw its radiance as, yellow and fitful, forever expiring and forever burning again, it illumined the whole room. I heard Drüng sit up, the stretcher creaked softly, the corner of a blanket was pushed aside, and now I was looking at him again.

"Don't be scared," he shook his head and went on, "The light won't go out, it'll burn forever and ever, I know it will."

But the next instant his pale face seemed to disintegrate still further; trembling, he grasped my arm, I could feel his thin, hard fingers. "Look," he said in a frightened whisper, "now it's going out."

But the anchorless wick was still floating in the cardboard holder, it was still not quite submerged.

"No," I said, "it should have gone out long ago—there wasn't enough to last even two minutes."

"Oh, Christ!" he shouted, his face distorted, and he slammed his hand down onto the light, jarring the stretcher so that the iron clanged, and for one second we were enveloped in greenish darkness, but when he lifted his trembling hand the wick was still floating, it was still light, and through the hole in Drüng's stomach I was looking at a pale-yellow spot on the wall behind him.

"It's no use," he said, lying back on his stretcher, "you'd better lie down too, we'll just have to wait."

I pushed my stretcher right up close to his so that the iron bars were touching, and as I lay down the light was between us, flickering and unsteady, always certain and always uncertain, for it ought to have gone out long ago, but it did not go out; and sometimes we raised our heads at the same time and looked at one another in fear when the convulsive flame seemed to become shorter; and before our despairing eyes was the dark oblong of the door, surrounded by a bright band of shining light. . . .

. . . and so we lay there waiting, filled with fear and hope, shivering and yet warmed by the panic that seized our limbs when the flame threatened to go out and our green faces met over the cardboard holder as it stood in the midst of those moving lights that flowed around us like soundless wraiths, and suddenly we saw that the light must have gone out, for the wick was submerged, no tip stuck out over the waxen surface now, and yet it was still light—until our amazed eyes saw the figure of Dina, who had come in to us through the locked door, and we knew it was all right to smile now, and we took her outstretched hands and followed her. . . .

The Ration Runners

I N THE dark vault of the sky the stars hung like muted dots of leaden silver. Suddenly what had seemed to be random constellations began to move: the gleaming dots approached each other, grouping themselves into a pointed arch whose symmetrical curves were held together at their apex by a star that outshone all the rest. Scarcely had I taken in this minor miracle when at the lower end of each arching curve a star detached itself, and the two dots slid slowly downward to sink out of sight in the unending blackness. Fear stirred and gradually spread within me, for now, two by two, left and right, they proceeded to sink into the blackness, and from time to time I seemed to hear a hiss as their light went out. And so they all fell, one star after another, each pair gleaming softly as they sank together, until only the largest star of all remained up there, the one that had held the pointed arch together. It seemed to waver, tremble, and hesitate . . . then it sank too, slowly and solemnly, with an oppressive solemnity; and as it approached the blackness beneath, my fear swelled like some terrible travail, and at the very moment when the great star reached the bottom and, despite my fear, I waited with bated breath for total blackness to cover the vaulted sky, at that very moment the darkness exploded with an appalling detonation. . . .

. . . I woke up, I could still feel the air quivering from the real blast that had woken me. Part of the earth wall in front of our foxhole now rested on my head and shoulders, and the breath of the grenade still smoldered in the black and silent air. I brushed off the dirt, and as I leaned forward to pull the groundsheet over my head and light a cigarette, I could tell from Hans's yawn that he had been asleep too and was now awake; he held out his forearm to show me the phosphorescent dial of his watch, saying softly, "Punctual as the devil himself, on the dot of two. You'd better get going now." Our heads met under the groundsheet. As I held the match over Hans's pipe, I glanced at his thin face: it betrayed no emotion whatsoever.

We smoked in silence. In the dark there was no sound save the innocuous rumble of tractors bringing up ammunition. Silence and darkness seemed to have become one, lying like some enormous weight on the backs of our necks. . . .

When I had finished my cigarette, Hans repeated softly, "You'd better get going, and don't forget to take him with you, he's lying up there by the old flak emplacement." And when I had clambered out of my hole, he added, "There's only half of him, you know, in a groundsheet."

I crossed the torn-up earth, groping my way with my hands, until I reached the path that over the months had been trodden by dispatch runners and ration runners. I had slung my rifle over my shoulders and tucked the old cloth bag securely into one pocket. After a couple of hundred yards I could already make out darker patches in the darkness: trees, the remains of houses, and finally what was left of the shelled hut of the old flak emplacement. I listened nervously, hoping to hear the voices of the others, but even when I got closer and could clearly see the dark square pit where the antiaircraft gun had stood, I still couldn't hear anything. Then I did see them, the others, squatting on old ammunition cases like great mute birds in the night, and it struck me as unspeakably depressing that they were not exchanging a single word. At their feet lay a bundle wrapped in a groundsheet, just like those bundles we used to lug off with the rest of our equipment from the uniform stores to sort the hideous camphor-reeking stuff in our dorms and try it on for size. It was strange that on this night, in the midst of the reality of war, I should recall our old barracks life more concretely and vividly than ever before, and I shuddered to think that the fellow lying there in the groundsheet, a formless mass, had once been yelled at like the rest of us when he was issued the same kind of bundle from the uniform stores. "Evening," I said in a whisper, and I got an indistinct murmur in reply.

I squatted down beside the others on the nearest pile of 20-millimeter cardboard shell cases: they had been lying around here for months, some of them still full, just as they had been abandoned by the flak in its confused and hurried flight.

No one moved. We all sat there, our hands in our pockets, waiting and brooding, and each one of us must have glanced from time to time at the mute, dark bundle at our feet. At last the platoon dispatch runner got up, saying, "Shall we go?"

Instead of replying, we all rose; it was so futile to go on squatting there, it didn't make things any better for us. What difference did it make, after all, whether we squatted here or up front in our holes? And besides, we had heard there was a chocolate issue today, maybe even some schnapps, reason enough to get to the chow line as fast as possible.

"First group, how many?"

"Five," answered a subdued voice.

"Second?"

"Six."

"And third?"

"Four," I answered.

"There are two of us," counted the dispatch runner in an undertone. "OK, let's call it twenty-one, shall we? I hear it's hash."

"OK."

The dispatch runner was the first to go over to the bundle; we watched him bend down, then he said, "We'll each take one corner; it's a young sapper, half a sapper."

We bent down too, and each of us grasped a corner of the ground-sheet; then the dispatch runner said, "Let's go," and we lifted the bundle and trudged off toward the outskirts of the village. . . .

Every dead man is as heavy as the whole earth, but this half-a-dead-man was as heavy as the world. It was as if he had absorbed the sum of all the pain and all the burdens of the entire universe. We panted and groaned and, by tacit consent, set down our load after a couple of dozen yards.

And the distances became shorter and shorter, the half-a-sapper be-came heavier and heavier, as if he were absorbing more and more burdens. It seemed as if the earth's weak crust must collapse beneath this weight, and when in our exhaustion we lowered our bundle to the ground, I felt as if we would never manage to lift the dead man up again. At the same time I had the feeling the bundle was growing beyond all measurable limits. The three at the other corners seemed infinitely far away, so far that if I called they couldn't possibly hear me. And I was growing too, my hands became enormous, my head assumed nightmarish proportions, but the dead man, the corpse-bundle, was puffing up like some monstrous tube, as if it would never stop drinking in the blood of all battlefields of all wars.

All the laws of gravity and dimension were suspended and extended into infinity; so-called reality was inflated by the dim and shadowy laws of another reality, one that made a mockery of them.

The half-a-sapper swelled and swelled like a monstrous sponge satu-rating itself with leaden blood. Cold sweat broke out over my body, mingling with that foul dirt that had accumulated over it during the long weeks. I could smell myself, and I smelled like a corpse. . . .

As I trudged on and on, carrying the sapper, obeying that strange urge that compelled us each to take hold of one corner again at a certain instant; as we went on and on, always a dozen yards or so at a time, lugging the burden of the world toward the outskirts of the village, I almost lost consciousness under the impact of an appalling fear that flowed from that steadily growing bundle and filled my veins like poison. I saw no more, I heard nothing, and yet I was aware of every detail of what happened. . . .

I had not heard the grenade being fired or the whine of its approach; the explosion ripped apart the whole fine mesh of dreamlike, semiconscious agony. With empty hands I stared into space, while far away, somewhere along a slope, the echo of the explosion reverberated like peals of laughter; in front, behind, on both sides, I could hear that strange, laughing echo, as if I were caught in a valley between high mountains, and the sound reached my ears like the tinny jangle of those patriotic songs that used to crawl up and down the barracks walls. With an almost disembodied curiosity I waited expectantly for pain to make itself felt somewhere on my body, or for the sensation of warm, flowing blood. Nothing, nothing at all. But suddenly I realized that my feet were standing half over an empty space, that the front half of each foot was teetering over a void, and when I looked down, with the casual curiosity of someone just waking up, I saw, blacker than the surrounding blackness, a great crater at my feet. . . .

I stepped gamely forward into the crater, but I did not fall, I did not sink; on and on I walked, always on marvelously soft ground beneath the absolute darkness of the vaulted sky. I kept wondering, as I walked along, whether I should report twenty-one, seventeen, or fourteen to the quartermaster sergeant . . . until the great yellow shining star rose before me and planted itself firmly in the vault of the sky; then the other stars, softly gleaming, found their places, two by two, forming a closed triangle. I knew then that I had reached a different destination and that what I really had to report was four and a half, and as I smiled and said over to myself: Four and a half—a great kindly voice spoke: Five!

Lohengrin's Death

G OING UP the stairs, the men carrying the stretcher slowed down a bit. They were both feeling resentful; they had been on duty for over an hour and so far nobody had given them a cigarette for a tip. Besides, one of them was the ambulance driver, and drivers are not actually required to carry stretchers. But the hospital hadn't sent anyone down to help, and they couldn't very well leave the boy lying there in the ambulance; they still had an emergency pneumonia to pick up and a suicide who had been cut down at the last minute. They were feeling resentful, and suddenly they were carrying the stretcher along less slowly again: the corridor was poorly lit, and of course it smelled of hospital.

"I wonder why they cut him down?" muttered one of the men, referring to the suicide; he was the one behind, and the one in front growled over his shoulder, "Yeah, why would they do that?" But because he had turned round as he spoke, he collided with the doorpost, and the figure lying on the stretcher woke up and emitted shrill, terrible screams; they were the screams of a child.

"Easy now, easy," said the doctor, a young intern with fair hair and a tense face. He looked at the time: eight o'clock, his relief should have been here long ago. For over an hour he had been waiting for Dr. Lohmeyer: they might have arrested him, anyone could be arrested any time these days. The young doctor automatically fingered his stethoscope, his eyes fixed on the boy on the stretcher, and now for the first time he noticed the stretcher bearers standing impatiently by the door. "What's the matter, what are you waiting for?" he asked irritably.

"The stretcher," said the driver. "Can't you move him onto something else? We've got work to do."

"Oh, of course—over here!" The doctor pointed to the leather couch. At that moment the night nurse appeared, her expression unemotional but serious. She took hold of the boy by the shoulders, and one of the stretcher bearers, not the driver, grabbed him by the legs.

The boy screamed like one demented, and the doctor said hastily, "Take it easy now, it's not that bad. . . ."

The stretcher bearers were still standing there, waiting. The doctor's look of annoyance evoked a further response from one of them. "The blanket," he said stonily. The blanket wasn't his at all, a woman at the scene of the accident had let him have it, saying they couldn't drive the boy like that to the hospital with those shattered legs of his. But the stretcher bearer figured the hospital would keep it, and the hospital had plenty of blankets, and the blanket certainly wouldn't be returned to the woman, and it didn't belong to the boy any more than it did to the hospital, and the hospital had plenty. His wife would clean up the blanket all right, and blankets were worth a lot of money these days.

The child was still screaming. They had unwrapped the blanket from around his legs and passed it quickly to the driver. Doctor and nurse exchanged glances. The boy was an appalling sight: the whole lower part of his body was bathed in blood, his cotton shorts were mere shreds, and the shreds had coagulated with the blood into a revolting pulp. His feet were bare, and he screamed without pause, screamed with terrible persistence and regularity.

"Quick," whispered the doctor, "a hypo. Nurse, hurry, please!" The nurse's movements were skillful and swift, but the doctor kept whispering, "Hurry, hurry!" His mouth hung slack in his tense face. The boy kept up his incessant screaming, but the nurse was preparing the hypo as fast as she could.

The doctor felt the boy's pulse, his pale face twitching with exhaustion. "Be quiet," he whispered a few times distractedly, "be *quiet!*" But the child screamed as if he had been born for the sole purpose of screaming. At last the nurse brought the hypo, and the doctor swiftly and skillfully gave the injection.

With a sigh he drew the needle out of the tough, leathery skin, and just then the door opened and a nun burst into the room, but when she saw the accident case and the doctor she closed her mouth, which she had opened, and approached slowly and quietly. She gave the doctor and the pale lay sister a friendly nod and placed her hand on the child's forehead. The boy opened his eyes and looked straight up, in surprise, at the black figure standing behind him. It seemed almost as if the pressure of the cool hand on his brow were quieting him down, but the injection was already taking effect. The doctor was still holding the syringe, and he gave another deep sigh, for it was quiet now, blissfully quiet, so quiet that they could all hear their own breathing. They did not speak.

The boy was evidently out of pain now; he was looking quietly and interestedly around the room.

"How much?" the doctor asked the night nurse in a low voice.

"Ten," she replied, in the same tone.

The doctor shrugged his shoulders. "Quite a bit. We'll see what happens. Would you give us a hand, Sister Lioba?"

"Of course," the nun replied promptly, seeming to rouse herself from a deep reverie. It was very quiet. The nun held the boy by the head and shoulders, the night nurse took his legs, and together they pulled off the blood-soaked tatters. The blood, as they now saw, was mixed with something black. Everything was black, the boy's feet were caked with coal dust, his hands too, there was nothing but blood, shreds of cloth, and coal dust, thick oily coal dust.

"Obviously," murmured the doctor, "you fell off a moving train while pinching coal, eh?"

"Yes," said the boy in a cracked voice, "obviously."

His eyes were wide open, and there was a strange happiness in them. The injection must have been gloriously effective. The nun pulled his shirt all the way up, arranging it in a roll on the boy's chest, under his chin. His chest was scrawny, ludicrously scrawny like the breast of an elderly goose. Alongside the collarbones strangely deep shadows filled the hollows, great cavities where she could have hidden the whole of her broad white hand. Now they could see his legs too, as much of them as was still intact. They were skinny, and seemed to be fine-boned and shapely. The doctor nodded to the women, saying, "Double fracture of both legs, I imagine. We'll need an X-ray."

The night nurse wiped his legs clean with alcohol, and now they didn't look quite so bad. But the child was so appallingly thin. The doctor shook his head as he applied the bandage. He started worrying again about Lohmeyer: maybe they'd got him after all, and even if he kept his mouth shut it was still very awkward to let him take the rap for that Strophanthin business and get off scot-free himself, while if things had gone well he would have had a share in the profits. Hell, it must be eight-thirty, it was ominously quiet now, not a sound from the street. He had finished his bandaging, and the nun pulled the boy's shirt down again over his loins. Then she went to the closet, took out a white blanket, and spread it over the boy.

Her hands on the boy's forehead again, she said to the doctor as he was washing his hands, "What I really came about was the little Schranz girl, doctor, but I didn't want to worry you while you were treating this boy."

The doctor paused in his drying, made a slight grimace, and the cigarette hanging from his lower lip quivered.

"Well," he asked, "what about the Schranz child?" The pallor in his face was almost yellow now.

"I'm afraid that little heart is giving up, just giving up; it looks like the end."

The doctor took the cigarette between his fingers again and hung the towel on the nail beside the wash bowl.

"Hell," he cried helplessly, "what am I supposed to do? There's nothing I can do!"

The nun kept her hand on the boy's forehead. The night nurse dropped the blood-soaked rags into the garbage pail; its chrome lid cast flickering lights against the wall.

The doctor stood there thinking, his eyes lowered. Suddenly he raised his head, gave one more look at the boy, and dashed to the door, "I'll have a look at her."

"Do you need me?" the night nurse called out after him. He put his head in again, saying, "No, you stay here. Get the boy ready for X-rays and see if you can take down his history."

The boy was still very quiet, and the night nurse came and stood by the leather couch.

"Has your mother been told?" asked the nun.

"She's dead."

The nurse did not dare ask about his father.

"Whom should we notify?"

"My older brother, only he's not home right now. But the kids ought to be told, they're all alone now."

"What kids?"

"Hans and Adolf. They're waiting for me to come and make supper."

"And where does your older brother work?"

The boy was silent, and the nun did not pursue the question.

"Would you mind taking it down, nurse?"

The night nurse nodded and went over to the little white table which was covered with medicine bottles and test tubes. She pulled the ink toward her, dipped the pen in it, and smoothed out the sheet of white paper with her left hand.

"What's your name?" the nun asked the boy.

"Becker."

"Religion?"

"None. I was never baptized."

The nun winced; the night nurse's expression remained impassive.

"When were you born?"

"In 1933 . . . September 10."

"Still going to school, I suppose?"

"Yes."

"And his first name!" the night nurse whispered to the nun.

"Oh, yes . . . and your first name?"

"Grini."

"What?" The two women looked at each other and smiled.

"Grini," said the boy, slowly and peevishly, as anyone does who has an unusual first name.

"With an 'i'?" asked the night nurse.

"That's right, with two i's," and he repeated once more, "Grini."

His real name was Lohengrin. He had been born in 1933, just when the first photographs of Hitler at the Bayreuth Wagner Festival started flooding all the illustrated weeklies. But his mother had always called him Grini.

The doctor rushed suddenly into the room, his eyes blurred with exhaustion, his wispy fair hair hanging down into his young, deeply lined face.

"Come along, both of you, and be quick about it. I'm going to try a transfusion; hurry up!"

The nun's eyes went to the boy.

"That's all right," cried the doctor, "you can leave him alone for a moment."

The night nurse was already at the door.

"Will you lie there quietly like a good boy, Grini?" asked the nun.

"Yes," he answered.

But as soon as they had all left the room he let the tears flow unchecked. It was as if the nun's hand on his brow had held them back. He was crying not with pain but with happiness. And yet with pain and fear too. It was only when he thought about the kids that he cried with pain, and he tried not to think about them because he wanted to cry with happiness. Never in his life had he had such a wonderful feeling as now, after the injection. It flowed right through him like some wonderful, gently warmed milk, making him feel dizzy and yet awake, and there was a delicious taste on his tongue, more delicious than anything he had ever tasted, but he couldn't help it, he kept thinking about the kids. Hubert wouldn't be back before tomorrow morning, and Father, of course, wouldn't be home for another three weeks, and Mother . . . and right now the kids were waiting all alone, and he knew very well that they listened for every step, every tiny sound on the stairs, and there were so many,

many sounds on the stairs, and the kids were disappointed so many, many times. There wasn't much hope that Frau Grossmann would bother about them: she never had, why should she today. She never had, and after all she couldn't know that he . . . that he had had an accident. Hans might try to comfort Adolf, but Hans was so frail himself and the least thing made him cry. Maybe Adolf would comfort Hans, but Adolf was only five whereas Hans was eight; it was really more likely that Hans would comfort Adolf. But Hans was so terribly frail and Adolf much stronger. Probably they would both cry, for when it got close to seven o'clock they would tire of playing because they were hungry and knew he would be home at seven-thirty to give them something to eat. And they wouldn't dare take any of the bread; no, they would never dare do that again—he had forbidden them too strictly since those few times when they had eaten it all up, every bit, the whole week's rations. It wouldn't matter if they took some of the potatoes, but of course they didn't know that. If only he had told them it was all right to take some of the potatoes. Hans was already quite good at boiling them; but they wouldn't dare, he had punished them too severely, in fact he had even had to hit them, for it just wouldn't do for them to eat up all the bread; it just wouldn't do. But now he would have been glad if he hadn't punished them, for then they would take some of the bread and at least they wouldn't be hungry. So instead they were sitting there waiting, and at every sound on the stairs they were jumping up excitedly and thrusting their pale faces through the crack of the door, the way he had seen them so often, so often, a thousand times maybe. Oh, he always saw their faces first, and they were glad to see him. Yes, even after he had hit them, they were glad to see him; they had understood, he knew that. And now every sound was a disappointment, and they would be scared. Hans trembled at the very sight of a policeman; maybe they'd make such a noise crying that Frau Grossmann would be angry, for she liked peace and quiet of an evening, and then maybe they would go on crying, and Frau Grossmann would come and see what was the matter and take pity on them—she wasn't so bad, Frau Grossmann. But Hans would never go on his own to Frau Grossmann; he was so dreadfully scared of her, Hans was scared of everything. . . .

If only they would take some of the potatoes at least!

Now that he had begun thinking about the kids, he was crying with pain. He tried holding his hand in front of his eyes so as not to see the kids, but he felt his hand getting wet, and he cried even more. He tried to figure out the time. It must be nine o'clock, maybe ten, that was terrible. He had never got home later than seven-thirty, but today the train had been closely watched and they had had to keep a sharp lookout, those

Luxembourgers were so trigger-happy. Maybe during the war they hadn't been able to shoot much and they just enjoyed shooting; but they didn't get him, oh no, they'd never got him, he'd always given them the slip. Anthracite, people would pay seventy to eighty marks for anthracite and think nothing of it—and he was supposed to miss a chance like that? But those Luxembourgers had never got him; he'd managed to cope with the Russians, with the Yanks, and the Tommies, and the Belgians, was he going to let himself get caught by the Luxembourgers of all people, those clowns? He had slipped past them, up onto the train, filled his sack, tossed it down, and then thrown down whatever he still had time to lay hands on. But then, crash, the train had stopped with a sudden jolt, and he knew nothing except that he had been in the most frightful agony until he knew nothing whatever, and then there had been the pain again when he woke up in the doorway and saw the white room. And then they had given him the injection. Now he was crying with happiness again. The kids had gone; this happiness was glorious, he had never known such bliss. His tears seemed to be bliss itself, bliss was flowing out of him, and yet it didn't get any smaller, this flickering, exquisite, circling thing in his chest, this funny lump that welled up out of him in tears, didn't get any smaller. . . .

Suddenly he heard the Luxembourgers shooting. They had machine pistols, and it made a horrible racket in the cool spring evening; there was a smell of fields, smoke from the station, coal, and even a bit of real spring. Two shots barked into the sky, which was dark gray, and the echo of them returned to him a thousand times over, and there was a prickling in his chest like pins and needles. Those damned Luxembourgers weren't going to get him, they weren't going to shoot him to bits! The coal he was lying on was hard and sharp; it was anthracite, and they paid eighty marks, up to eighty marks a hundredweight for it. Should he get the kids some chocolate? No, it wouldn't be enough, for chocolate they wanted forty marks, sometimes forty-five. He couldn't carry away that much: God, he'd have to lug a whole hundredweight for two bars of chocolate; and those Luxembourgers were crazy nuts, now they'd started shooting again, and his bare feet were cold and the sharp anthracite hurt them, and they were black and dirty, he could feel it. The shots were tearing great holes in the sky, but surely they couldn't shoot the sky to bits, or maybe the Luxembourgers could shoot the sky to bits. . . .

Would he have to tell the nurse where his father was and where Hubert went at night? They hadn't asked him, and it was better not to answer unless you were asked. They'd told him in school . . . damn those Luxembourgers . . . and the kids . . . the Luxembourgers ought to stop shooting; he had to get to the kids . . . they must be crazy, completely out of their minds, those Luxembourgers. Hell, no, he wasn't going to tell the nurse where their father was and where their brother went at night, and maybe the kids would take some of the bread after all . . . or some of the potatoes . . . or maybe Frau Grossmann would notice there was something wrong: for there was something wrong; it was funny, there was always something wrong. The principal would bawl him out at school too. The injection had been wonderful, he could feel the prick, and suddenly there was that bliss! That pale-faced nurse had filled the needle with bliss, and he'd heard them all right; he'd heard that she had filled the needle with too much bliss, much too much bliss, he was no fool. Grini with two i's . . . nonsense, he's dead . . . no, missing. This bliss was glorious, one day he'd buy the bliss in the needle for the kids; you could buy anything . . . bread . . . whole mountains of bread. . . .

Hell, with two i's, don't these people know a good German name when they hear it . . . ?

"None," he shouted suddenly, "I was never baptized!"

Maybe their mother was still alive after all? No, the Luxembourgers had shot her, no the Russians . . . no, who knows, maybe the Nazis had shot her, she had got so terribly mad at them . . . no, the Yanks . . . for God's sake, what did it matter if the kids ate the bread, ate the bread . . . a whole mountain of bread, that's what he'd buy the kids . . . bread piled up to the sky . . . a whole boxcar full of bread . . . full of anthracite; and bliss in the needle.

With two i's, damn it!

The nun hurried over to him, felt at once for his pulse, and looked round in alarm. Dear God, ought she to call the doctor? But she couldn't leave the delirious child alone now. The little Schranz girl was dead, gone, thank God, that child with the Russian face! Why didn't the doctor come. She ran round behind the leather couch. . . .

"None," shouted the child, "I was never baptized!"

His pulse was getting wilder and wilder every moment. Sweat stood out on the nun's forehead. "Doctor, doctor!" she called, but she knew quite well that no sound penetrated the padded door.

The child was now whimpering pitifully.

"Bread . . . a whole mountain of bread for the kids . . . chocolate . . . anthracite . . . the Luxembourgers, those swine, they oughtn't to shoot, damn it, the potatoes, sure you can take some of the potatoes . . . go ahead, take some! Frau Grossmann . . . Father . . . Mother . . . Hubert . . . through the crack in the door, through the crack in the door."

The nun was weeping with anguish; she dared not leave. The child was beginning to thrash about and she held on to him by the shoulders. The leather couch was so horribly slippery. The little Schranz girl was dead, that little heart was in Heaven. God have mercy on her; dear God, mercy . . . she was innocent, a little angel, an ugly little Russian angel . . . but now she was pretty. . . .

"None," shouted the boy, trying to flail around with his arms. "I was never baptized!"

The nun looked up in dismay. She ran to the sink, keeping an anxious eye on the boy, but there was no glass; she ran back, stroked the feverish forehead. Then she went over to the little white table and picked up a test tube. The test tube was soon full, it doesn't take much water to fill a test tube. . . .

"Bliss," whispered the child, "fill the needle with lots of bliss, all you've got, for the kids too. . . ."

The nun crossed herself solemnly, deliberately, then sprinkled the water from the test tube over the boy's forehead, saying through her tears, "I baptize thee . . ." But the boy, suddenly sobered by the cold water, jerked up his head so violently that the tube fell from the nun's hand and smashed on the floor. The boy looked at the startled nun with a little smile and said feebly, "Baptize . . . yes . . ." Then he dropped back so abruptly that his head fell on the leather couch with a dull thud, and now his face looked narrow and old, frighteningly yellow, as he lay there motionless, his fingers spread to grasp. . . .

"Has he been X-rayed yet?" cried the doctor, chuckling as he came into the room with Dr. Lohmeyer. The nun merely shook her head. The doctor stepped closer, felt automatically for his stethoscope, but dropped it and looked at Lohmeyer. Lohmeyer removed his hat. Lohengrin was dead. . . .

A Soldier's Legacy

I

TODAY, MY dear sir, I saw a young man whose name I'm sure is familiar to you; it is Schnecker. He has been living—as far as I know—for a number of years in your neighborhood, and he was a schoolmate of your brother's, who was reported missing during the war. But that's not all. Today I also learned that for five years you have been waiting in vain to discover what actually happened to your brother, after you were informed, by way of that sinister official lie, that he had been "reported missing." Well, Schnecker could have corrected that lie. There are only two people in the world who could have told you with certainty: one is Schnecker, the other is myself. I have kept silent. After reading my report you will understand why I could not come forward and tell you what actually happened.

Forgive me if I must now inform you of something that cannot be glossed over. Your brother is dead.

Actually, when I ran across Schnecker on the terrace of an outdoor café, he appeared to be in the best of spirits. He was sitting under one of those colorful umbrellas that are surrounded by planters full of big red geraniums, where customers relax in the shade as they observe the passing scene from behind their sunglasses. Schnecker was in the company of a young lady.

The young lady was pretty, her manner lighthearted and natural. On an impulse, I stepped onto the terrace, sat down at the next table so I could overhear them, and ordered some ice cream.

The shock I felt was intensified by the fact that Schnecker hadn't changed. He was a bit plumper, seemed younger rather than older, and showed those first signs of the incipient bull neck that invariably begins to manifest itself in certain better-class Germans when they reach thirty-two and are old enough to take an active part in their father's political party. After I had thanked the waiter and seated myself so as to miss nothing, I overheard Schnecker say, "And Winnie?"

"She's married, didn't you know? She's happy—deliriously happy, in fact."

Schnecker laughed. "We'll be, too," he said gently, covering the girl's hand with his own. The way she turned her large, soft, slightly stupid eyes up at him made her look as though she would melt with happiness, leaving behind some kind of sugary mess on the graceful little terrace chair.

"Cigarette?" asked Schnecker, offering her his open case. She took one, and they smoked as they applied themselves to their ice creams. Beyond the terrace, a constant stream of perspiring, thinly clad people made their way to or from the summer clearance sales. Their faces revealed a strain similar to what one used to see, only a year ago, on the trains carrying people out into the countryside to scrounge for potatoes—fear, fatigue, greed. Deeply disturbed, I toyed with my ice cream; my cigarette didn't taste good any more.

"Come to think of it," Schnecker began again, "we have every reason to celebrate today!"

"Yes, today's a red-letter day!" said the girl.

"You're right."

"Of course I'm right! The way you got through it all! So quickly and confidently and the only one to make it with honors. But tell me" —she giggled—"are they actually going to put a doctoral cap on your head?"

"No, my dear, but listen." He paused to swallow a spoonful of ice cream. "I suggest we drive out there right away, enjoy ourselves, then change and drive to the Cosmo for a little intimate celebration, before the official stuff gets under way. . . ."

This time she placed her hand on his.

I suddenly felt so nauseated that I had to get up and do something. I left some money on the table, far too much and more than I could possibly afford. But I just didn't care. I staggered outside and let myself drift along with the perspiring, prattling crowd until I turned off onto a quiet, rubble-strewn street that was bathed in the shadow of still-standing façades. I sat down at random on what was left of a wall. The peace of rubble is the peace of graveyards. . . .

IT IS time, I think, for me to introduce myself. My name is Wenk, and I was a dispatch runner for your brother, First Lieutenant Schelling. I have already told you that he is dead. You could have found that out long ago. You needed only to enter the house of your neighbor and look closely into his eyes, those eyes that will induce such a charming, rhapsodic girl to have him father their two planned children. Oh, that sweet young thing, how she will weep when the priest joins their hands while a Bach fugue resounds from the organ, played not by the regular organist, who is much too pedestrian and inartistic, but by a specially hired musician. Don't fail to attend the wedding. Don't forget to try the cake, the wine and cigars, and make sure your mother offers appropriate congratulations and sends a gift that matches the degree of friendship. This union, from which new Schneckers will spring, must be properly celebrated. I don't know what kind of wedding presents match that degree of friendship in your circles: with us it might be an electric iron, or a punch bowl that would be used once every three years or never.

Enough of this chatter! I'm just trying to put off something I find it hard to write about because it sounds too improbable in the context of this incipiently bull-necked fledgling doctor of laws. But let me tell you: Schnecker is your brother's murderer. There it is. There you have it. And I mean it not in any figurative or allegorical sense, but baldly and simply, the way I've said it: Schnecker is your brother's murderer. . . .

You are a young man. About twenty, I would guess. I have taken the liberty of spending a few afternoons snooping around outside your house and Schnecker's, but I'm sure you won't remember that nondescript individual standing under an elderberry tree, wearing sunglasses and smoking a cigarette, a sort of amateur detective of fate who, in return for a pension of thirty marks graciously doled out to him every month at the post office, feels obliged to render the Fatherland a small service.

Well, you're twenty, I would guess. I saw you hurrying off with your book-filled briefcase at regular hours and fancied I could read something in your expression that I can only interpret as dread of your finals. Don't worry, you'll get through all right. Don't take it too seriously. We were still priding ourselves on getting a B in geography and math when we were forced to look at men who had just been neatly shot in the stomach by a machine-gun salvo. Believe me, they all looked alike, those who had a B in Latin and those who had never heard of Latin. They looked ugly; there was nothing, absolutely nothing uplifting about them. They were all alike—Poles, Germans, and Frenchmen, heroes and cowards. That's all I can tell you. They belonged to the earth, and the earth no longer belonged to them. That's all. . . .

But before I tell you how Schnecker killed your brother, I must introduce myself in greater detail. I'm not exactly a confidence-inspiring person. Most of my time is spent lying on the bed smoking cigarettes. The venetian blinds are kept closed, letting in just enough light for me to tell which side of the cigarette paper is gummed. Next to the bed is my chair, on it a great heap of loose yellow tobacco. I occupy myself by rolling a new cigarette when the butt between my lips has become damp and no longer draws. The tobacco makes my throat burn; I flick the butts out the window, and whenever I lean out I can see great quantities of them floating in the roof gutter—burst, yellowish objects like bloated maggots—from some of them the tobacco has seeped out and is floating in the greenish soupy liquid filling the gutter that slopes away from the drain. Sometimes, when this scum has grown too thick, I borrow the broom belonging to my landlord's cleaning woman and sweep all the sludge toward the drain, where with a low gurgling sound it disappears. . . .

I am very seldom persuaded to undertake any kind of activity. My one great concern is how to get hold of tobacco, which I pay for by selling my books. Even this activity is strenuous enough. Fortunately, I am fairly well informed as to the value of the books, although I must say I lack the patience to insist on getting their true value. So I reluctantly drag myself off to those dingy little second-hand bookstores that smell of the decay which only piles of books produce: dry, musty, moldy. Skinny yellow hands, whose movements remind me of the silent, repulsive haste of raccoons, assess my spiritual property according to its material value. I rarely haggle, only when the offer seems unreasonably low; otherwise I merely nod and remain adamant when the usurer thrusts his pitiful face toward me as he counts out the money, hoping to persuade me at the last moment to accept less. I have resigned myself to the fact that I can no more cope with these people than I could with the war.

II

I FIRST MET Schnecker in the summer of 1943. I had been ordered to leave an interpreter unit stationed in Paris and report to a coastal division where I was once again to partake of the joys of "real" infantry service. Leaving the last railroad station behind me, I had reached a sleepy little place that seemed to consist of long, low walls surrounding lush grass. There, in the northwestern corner of Normandy, parallel to the coast, runs a strip of land that breathes the brooding isolation of heath and marsh: here and there a few tiny hamlets, some abandoned, ruined farms, shallow streams meandering sluggishly toward the swampy arms of the Somme or petering out underground.

From the station I had laboriously asked my way to battalion head-quarters. There, predictably, I had been kept waiting a considerable time before being directed to one of the companies. The clerk, a corporal, suggested I wait for the mail orderly of my future unit and go along with him. But since that would have meant a four-hour wait outside this desolate château, I asked the corporal how to get there, saluted, and left.

As I was shouldering my pack in the dark corridor, an officer passed by, a tall slim fellow who, in spite of his youth, was wearing the insignia of a captain. I performed the infamous "salute by standing at attention": he looked at me as if I were made of glass and, without so much as a nod, walked on. It was Schnecker.

Only half a second had passed, but in that half second I felt all the humiliation forced upon us by the uniform. Every second I wore that uniform I hated it, but now I was so choked by disgust I actually felt a bitter taste on my tongue. I hurried after the officer, who was walking toward the orderly room, and planted myself in front of him, thus prevent-ing him from reaching the door handle. I stood at attention again and said, "I request the captain to acknowledge my salute." My loathing filled me with voluptuous pleasure. He looked at me as if I had gone out of my mind.

"What was that?" he asked huskily.

I repeated my words in an even tone, saluted again, looked at him, saluted again.

The battle was fought only between our eyes. He was fuming, ready to tear me to pieces, but from the ends of my coolly vibrating hair right down to my toes I was filled with a crystalline hatred. He suddenly raised his hand to his cap; I stood aside, opened the door for him, and walked away.

I passed quickly through the lethargic, sleeping village, took, as directed, the third turning on the left toward the coast, and soon found myself in a completely uninhabited area. Noonday heat quivered over the meadows; the road was dusty and stony; there were occasional little groups of trees, lots of bushes, no fields that I could see. I took advantage of the little shade there was and walked on for half an hour; then I suddenly stopped, looked up, and realized that all that time I had been staring unseeingly ahead of me. I was tired and suddenly felt quite exhausted. The roadside was covered with lush grass, but just as I was about to sit down I noticed, scarcely a hundred yards away, a larger group of trees that seemed to indicate a building. In the sultry heat the cows had sought the shade of the bushes. I walked along the flagstone path and stopped outside the building: it was very dilapidated, surrounded by tangled growth. The windows were blind, and above the door was a weathered sign, almost illegible, on which I could just make out the letters "auran" of the word "Restaurant."

The door was open. I walked into a stale-smelling passageway and opened a brown door on the right. The room was empty. I put down my pack, threw cap and belt onto a chair, pulled out my big handkerchief, and began to wipe the sweat off my face as I looked around.

In taverns like this, one automatically expects a sour old witch of a woman, mustached, dirty, who can offer only some lukewarm stuff. I was very surprised when a young girl, who was not only pretty but clean, came in and greeted me briefly but without hostility with the usual "Good morning, sir."

I returned her greeting and looked at her much too long. She was very lovely. Her brown eyes were large, slightly veiled, and seemed always to look away. Her reddish-brown hair fell loosely over her shoulders and was tied above her forehead with a blue ribbon. Her hands gave off a smell of milk and udders; her fingers were still spread, slightly curled. . . .

"What would you like?" she asked.

I wanted to say "You!" but with a gesture stopped myself and said quietly, "Something to drink; something cold perhaps."

She closed her eyes and seemed to be letting my unspoken word sink into her. Then she raised her lids again and said mockingly, "Wine or lemonade?"

"Water," I said.

"I wouldn't recommend it, sir," she said. "Our water is as foul as the Somme."

"All right," I said, "wine, then; white, if you have some."

She nodded, turned, and disappeared.

The place was furnished like most country taverns in France. It used to be customary to dismiss them as being fusty, tasteless, uninviting. True, they did contain a lot of kitsch, both old and modern, but for me every one of those taverns held something of the elusive appeal of Cézanne's cardplayers.

The girl's pale face loomed up behind the glass panel, almost like the face of a drowning person rising to the surface once more before sinking for the last time. Quickly I jumped up and opened the door for her. In her right hand she was balancing a bottle of wine and a glass, in her left a soda-water siphon. To my astonishment the siphon, which I took from her, was cool. I commented on it, and while she set down glass and bottle she explained that they always kept the siphons in the well. As she spoke she avoided looking at me and murmured, "If you need anything, just call." She was about to leave.

I said very softly, "Tell me one thing: Are you always here? Are you the owner's daughter?"

Now for the first time she turned and looked at me. I had the impression she was smiling.

"Yes," she said, "I'm always here."

"Well, then, I'd like to pay. I'll take the rest of the bottle along, if I may—who knows whether there's anything available out there?" I pointed toward the coast.

"There are some taverns there too," she said indifferently, shrugging her shoulders, "but if you like . . ."

She went to the counter, and it seemed to me she did so merely in order to avoid touching my hand, for in taverns like that the money isn't paid formally at a cash register but simply passes from hand to hand. She gave me my change and said coolly, "Good-bye, sir." I was alone. It was good to know that she had said: I'm always here. I sat down, stretched out my legs, ate, drank, and smoked. After finishing half the bottle, I stood up, adjusted my pack, called in the direction of the door leading to the rear, "Good-bye!" and left.

The road was uneven and tiring; there wasn't a soul in sight, just meadows with streams trickling away into them, shrubs, clumps of willows, until finally in the distance I made out a straight row of trees that seemed to indicate the coast road. I took another breather, smoked a cigarette under that dull gray sky, and then walked toward the pale, bluish silhouette of the row of trees. . . .

III

I PROMISE NOT to become too garrulous. Nothing of what I am telling you is irrelevant if you happen to be interested in your brother's fate, in the part played by Schnecker and, to some extent, in my person. I can no longer keep silent. Fear and dread have taken hold of me since I have had to cast a brief but enlightening glance behind the rosy façade of the German "restoration" and "restitution," a glance into Schnecker's face. The face of an average person.

I forgot to tell you that I don't care for the sun. There are times when

I believe I hate it. If I were to worship any of the idols of ancient or primitive peoples, I would choose to join those somber-minded tribes who offer tribute to the sun as a devil rather than those who venerate it as a god. I don't hate the light—I love light shining in the darkness—but that harsh summer sun, sheer light, that is something cruel.

The highway I soon reached was flanked only on the right by a row of trees whose shadow fell on open country, a meadow covered by lush, shoulder-high grass. It was only later that I discovered that all the meadows on both sides of the road were mined; left and right, grass and flowers grew with a luxuriance I had never seen before. A few fir saplings were dotted about. For three years no hand had been able to mow or care for those meadows, and no cattle had been able to browse in them.

Somewhere up ahead I had caught sight of a building at what seemed to be an intersection in the shady forest; but that bright sunshine not only dazzled me, it induced in me an almost demoralizing physical pain. The distance seemed endless, although it couldn't have been more than three hundred yards. After five minutes I reached the building. Another tavern. Scattered about the fir forest were attractive little modern houses, and along the road some other houses. At the intersection stood a little signpost that said "Blanchères." The tavern bore a newly painted sign saying "Buvette à l'Orient." I stepped inside and right away, without looking around, put down my pack and began to wipe the sweat off my face again.

As I gradually came to from my exhaustion, I found myself looking into a terrible face, which was smiling at me. I am sure you don't know about those creatures that live on the other, the seldom described side of war. Our patriotic literature has no room for reality.

The broad face was heavily coated with powder, the large, pale-blue eyes were bleary, below the eyes were terrible bags. It was the Blanchères tavern's landlady. She, too, played a major role in your brother's life: she washed his laundry, which was so important to him, and she washed it thoroughly and was cheap.

"Hello, soldier," she said to me in a surprisingly deep voice. "Have a seat," she added.

"Good afternoon, madame," I said.

"Oh," she cried, "I'm not madame, I'm mademoiselle!"

"Good afternoon, mademoiselle," I said.

"What'll you have?"

I had sat down on one of the chairs near the door.

"Beer, please, if you have any."

So far I had seen only her head, and automatically assumed her to be fat. It was a shock, when she now approached me, armed with a bottle of beer and a glass, to see that she was as skinny as an old hen, frighteningly ugly.

"*Santé!*" she said, without moving away. "You're new here?"

"Yes," I said, "I'm on my way to company headquarters."

"Oh, with that heavy pack?"

"Yes."

"Then wait a bit." She looked up at an old-fashioned clock hanging over the bar. "Just wait; the orderly from over in Larnton will be here any minute." She pointed down the road that led off to the left, whereas according to my instructions I should have walked straight on for another half mile or so. "He comes at four and has a bicycle. He'll take your pack. He's a nice fellow. You're joining the infantry, aren't you?"

"Yes," I said. I was surprised at how well informed she was. I looked at the clock: it was a few minutes to four.

Her eyes were almost bursting with curiosity. The main occupation of such creatures is to collect tidbits of news. They are just as garrulous and observant as their sisters of the other kind: the devout churchgoers. She continued the conversation as promptly as a skilled journalist embarking on an interview.

"Your sergeant is a good man," she said; "the CO is a swine. You'll see. And that one down there"—she pointed, presumably to a base—"is an angel. He is," she added firmly, as if I had been about to contradict her.

"Oh?" I merely said, dryly.

"Where've you come from?" she went on with hardly a break, the curiosity in her eyes now coupled with a kind of impertinence.

"From Paris."

"Ah," she cried again in her rough voice. "Where love reigns supreme!" I said nothing.

"Almost all of them nice fellows, your company," she prattled on. "In fact, the infantry's fine anyplace. Poor and fine, that's what I always say. . . ."

All this time my eyes had been fixed on the road, which looked to me like a haven of peace and shade. It was bordered by dense pine forests that were flecked with pale, sandy patches heralding the proximity of the dunes. On either side of the road, at irregular intervals, stood charming little houses, but it was a while before I noticed that this whole area too was marked off by mine fences and mine warnings. So that explained this graveyard silence.

"How about giving me one?" she suddenly asked, looking at my pack of cigarettes.

"Oh, excuse me!" I said.

"You're certainly generous with your tobacco—let's see what you're like in a couple of weeks!" I had said nothing although she had taken two cigarettes. "Tobacco is as scarce as hen's teeth hereabouts." To my relief I at last saw a cyclist in uniform rapidly approaching out of the shadowy depths of the avenue. He was carrying his rifle in the regulation manner, with its strap across his chest.

"Ah," she cried, "there he is! Willi!"

She stepped outside and waved to the approaching soldier, whose face I could now plainly see. He was a pale, middle-aged man; his fair mustache, narrow and sparse, looked as if it was stuck onto his upper lip. He was wearing his cap, too, like a new recruit, and there was something eager about his expression.

He dismounted, propped his bicycle outside the door, and came in. "Hello there," he said.

"Hello," I answered.

Willi looked enviously at the girl's cigarette, then at me, climbed onto a bar stool, and asked, "Did you manage to get some more cigarettes on the black market?"

"No," she said, "I'm supposed to get some tomorrow, cheap, seven francs each."

"What about that one?"

She pointed the lighted cigarette at me. I had already fished out my pack and was offering it to Willi. He gave me a surprised look, laughed shortly, and said, "Thanks a lot—you must've come straight from home, but then they don't have that much there either. . . ."

"No," I said, "but are you that short here?"

"I'll say we are," he said. "You'll find out. We wait every day with our tongues hanging out for our three rationed cigarettes, but they're gone in an hour, then the butts, and then another twenty-three hours' craving."

"Want a drink?" asked the girl.

"Yes, please, Cadette, a beer."

"Here's to you," he said. "To your cigarettes, buddy. . . ."

I paid when he did, seeing that he had quickly downed his beer and wanted to be off; I stepped up to the counter beside him as he put on his cap again. "D'you think you could take my stuff along?" I asked.

Assuming a rather ponderous expression, he looked first at my pack and bag and then said, "Mind you, it's a pretty wobbly old bike, an old rattletrap, but OK"—he made a great show of squaring his shoulders— "I wouldn't let a fellow soldier kill himself for nothing. So you're joining our outfit?"

"Yes," I said, "third company."

"Right, third, that's us. OK, let's get your stuff loaded."

Feeling very envious, I watched him sail off. Fortunately the road was shady. On the left was dense forest, starting at Cadette's house and bordering the road, and to the right side of the smooth asphalt road stood a few houses, apparently still occupied. Next to one of them some soldiers' washing was hanging on a line: shirts, underpants, and the kind of socks —gray with horizontal white stripes—that are scattered over half the world. I hurried along, for, in addition to some nervousness about my new duties, I also felt a certain curiosity. There was always something exciting about a transfer. I still hadn't caught sight of the sea, but on the map shown me by the sergeant at battalion headquarters, the dot indicating the company's orderly room had been very close to that stirring dot-and-dash line marked "Main Battle Line—High Tide Line." I was impatient to see the sea again after three years.

Five minutes later the forest came to an end. On both sides of the road, those lush meadows again, and at last, beyond a gentle rise, I saw the house beside a sandy path. It looked quite charming, like a rich man's comfortable weekend cottage. To the right of the road was another tavern, a kind of summer café built of wood with a covered veranda; in the background, more buildings; then, for the first time since noon I saw sergeants' stars again among corporals' braid—a bunch of soldiers standing around a field kitchen—and all romantic notions of a lovely summer on the Atlantic coast vanished. I saluted a few sergeants who were standing by a shed watching the food distribution, and finally I reached the orderly room.

After walking up a few steps, the first thing I saw was my pack lying on the floor. There was a pervasive, musty smell of heat and dry timbers. I heard voices, among them Willi's calling out "Here!" someplace where mail was evidently being distributed. I entered the room that had a sign saying: "Field Post Office No. ———." Well, that was the number I was to see so often on the postcards I later accepted here for your brother and took to Larnton. For you too that number must be unforgettable.

After completing the ritual of saluting at the door, I immediately heard a voice speaking in a Saxonian accent. I looked in that direction and saw a first lieutenant whose curly coal-black hair was cut in a rather fancy style, and my first impression was that the little red ribbon of his Iron Cross set off his glossy hair to a T. He looked about forty, and he too had a mustache, a black one, and at the sight of that black mustache it crossed my mind how magnificently that black in turn set off the silver of his Assault Medal.

"Aha," said this person on catching sight of me, not as if he were bawling me out but rather in a reproachful, schoolmasterly tone, and indeed half an hour later I learned that he was a schoolteacher. At the same time I became aware of the not unfriendly face of a first sergeant, still young, and the impassive countenance of a clerk who looked pleasant enough.

So, "Aha," said this person, "here we have the lord and master who feels too weak to carry his pack for a distance of half a mile—right?"

With his last words he opened his eyes wide, giving them a theatrical glint, and looked at me challengingly.

"Sir!" I said, standing to attention. "I could see no point in letting my comrade ride an empty bicycle while I carried the pack that I had already lugged all the way from Crutelles."

"All the way from Crutelles!" he repeated sarcastically. The topkick burst out laughing.

"Don't laugh, Fischer," the first lieutenant snapped at him. "These goddamn intellectual bastards who've been on special assignment for years are a cheeky bunch." Then he turned to me. "So you, a Pfc, take the liberty of thinking, using your head, if I have understood you properly—hm?"

I had become so accustomed to quasi-civilian manners that I almost nodded and said, "That's right." I suppressed it and uttered the regulation "Yessir."

"I see. And weren't you taught the opposite, that you're not supposed to use your head—hm?"

"No," I replied, "in my last unit I was sometimes required to use my head."

"Well!" he said, surprised, and for a moment he looked like a boxer on the receiving end of a well-placed blow. But suddenly he bellowed, "There'll be none of that here, d'you hear me? No more thinking, understand? No more using your head, get it?"

"Yessir," I said.

"And what's more, remember that a soldier never allows himself to be separated from his pack." He turned his cheap, fiery gaze away from me, toward the topkick, and asked brusquely, "Where'll we put him?" The topkick pulled a list out of a drawer, and the first lieutenant turned his Storm Trooper eyes back to me (I later found out that he really had been a platoon leader with the Storm Troopers in his home town). "What training have you had?" he asked me. "I mean military, of course."

"Rifleman," I said, "sir, and telephone operator."

"Balls," he said furiously, "we have enough telephone operators, never enough riflemen."

"It's Larnton's turn for replacements," said the topkick.

"Good. We'll send him to Herr Schelling. Anything else? Tomorrow's schedule is clear, ammunition to be taken to the base for live firing. OK?"

"Yessir," said the topkick.

I flung open the door, stood at attention, and stepped aside for the schoolteacher. He did not deign to look my way again.

"For Chrissake!" cried the topkick when the sound of footsteps outside had died away. "I could've hugged you when I heard you were from the Rhineland!"

He shook my hand; I looked into his face and felt glad. He pointed to the clerk, who was watching us with a smile.

"Schmidt," he said, "at least Schmidt's from Berlin. We do have a few fellows from Berlin, but otherwise they're a bunch of yokels."

I handed him the envelope containing my papers, which I had closed and sealed myself. The clerk opened it, read and sorted the papers, the topkick asked me how things were at home, when I had last seen Cologne, his home town, and when I'd been on leave.

Soon after that he left for supper, and I was alone with the pleasant clerk. I asked him about the general atmosphere, the daily routine, exchanged a few mutual, skeptical observations about the war and the company commander, and fifteen minutes later I found myself walking back along the same road. Again I stopped by Cadette's, again I had a beer and gave her a cigarette.

Then I walked down that avenue that had so fascinated me. I still hadn't caught sight of the sea—from the orderly room it had been hidden by the forest; besides, I had been looking at the first lieutenant's pale-gray uniform.

But it was bound to come soon now. The road ran like a narrow ribbon between the minefields, and I felt as if I were running straight into a trap. On both sides stood attractive little houses, their gardens run wild; then the road opened up, and on the left there appeared a fair-sized, completely pillaged building that looked like a school. At last I saw the pale strip of beach. . . . There was hardly any water to be seen, the coast being so flat at that point that at low tide the sea receded for more than half a mile. In the distance—indescribably far away, it seemed—I saw a pale, broad tongue, the narrow wave of foam that the sea pushes ahead or drags behind itself, and beyond that an equally narrow strip of gray: the water. And otherwise only sand, sand, and the pale sky that was also burned gray. I felt an uprush of disappointment at having landed in a dry infinity, for when I pulled back my gaze from the distance into which it had plunged, all I saw close by, too, was sand, dunes sparsely covered with grass, and among them the ruins of houses that had obviously been dynamited—and more sand. . . .

And nowhere was there the bunker I had expected to find. Fortunately a soldier with a rifle was standing on a dune next to a spiked barrier across the road; a concrete path led up to him. I followed it. The steel helmet and the muzzle of the rifle grew bigger and more distinct, and on reaching the top I discovered a strange little colony. It looked almost like a fishing village where the nets are hung up to dry in the evening. These were camouflage nets covering guns and barracks, and the wooden huts were part of the famous Atlantic Wall in the summer of 1943 at a strategically vulnerable point. I walked toward the sentry, and when I asked him where I could find Lieutenant Schelling, he pointed with a bored expression to a hut slightly higher up, but before I had reached it, he called after me, "By the way, it's *First* Lieutenant, bud, don't get it wrong!"

"What?" I asked.

"He's a first lieutenant—not that he cares, but that's what he is. You might as well know."

I was amazed to find a first lieutenant heading a platoon. In 1943, officers were pretty thin on the ground, and it seemed extraordinary to me that this tiny base, which could, if necessary, have been in the charge of a sergeant, should be under the command of a first lieutenant.

The first person I saw as I entered the hut was Willi. He was alone, reading a letter.

"Ah," he exclaimed, "they've sent you to us!"

"Yes."

Willi laid the letter aside, pushing it under a telephone: he had opened the window, and there was a breeze from the sea.

"Let's see," said Willi, "if the first lieutenant is available." He knocked on the door, someone called out—reluctantly, it seemed to me —"Come in!" Willi opened the door and into the darkened room announced my arrival. A croaky voice said, "Very well—show him in." I stepped inside and closed the door behind me.

The window was covered by a blanket, and I could vaguely make out a bed with a long, gray figure lying on it, a cupboard, a table, and a few unidentifiable pictures on the walls.

I felt enormously heartened by the way this man immediately stood up as I entered. That may seem trivial to you, but, believe me, when one's been a soldier in this army for many years, always having to deal with so-called superiors, one develops an infallible instinct for the forms of human relationships. If you knew how many of your friends—I need only think of my own, or take any pleasant young man who you're sure would never hurt a fly—if you knew how he used to behave toward so-called inferiors, I believe you would blush with shame on his behalf. . . .

Your brother was the first officer I ran across in five years of whom I can claim that he moved with complete confidence on the narrow borderline of simultaneous authority and humility, as befits a superior. No doubt you're familiar with the other kind, those pipsqueak lieutenants: totally ignorant, brainless, and not even competent in their military, let alone soldierly, craft, sustained solely by the authority of their two shoulder straps and, last but not least, of their elegant boots. And you may grasp the extent of the uniform's demonic power from the fact that this huge army relied exclusively on this idiotic perversion of values, for even before 1943, the original illusory conception had proven as void and insubstantial as a wizened toy balloon lying trampled on a fairground.

Try to imagine any one of your brother's many contemporaries or classmates—leaving aside Schnecker—any one of them, I say, a nice kind man whose behavior is invariably decent and blameless, and I tell you: in the barracks he's a swine! And that army carted its barracks all across Europe. . . .

That's how X and Y were: X, who today stifles his bitterness over his temporarily obsolete career with American cigarettes and vague political aspirations, meanwhile getting together regularly with his former comrades to reminisce about how they used to "show them a thing or two"; and Y, who is grimly preparing himself to become a district attorney or a high-school teacher—either of which occupations offers enough scope for bullying creatures even more defenseless than soldiers: children and the poor.

IV

YOUR BROTHER, as I said, got up from his bed for me. I need hardly describe him to you: tall and slim, with a slight stoop at that time, his blue eyes full of sadness, his uniform bare of any decorations. He was about my age, twenty-five or -six, and, although it may seem ridiculous to you, a first lieutenant's star on that figure seemed to me fraught with ominous significance. A first lieutenant on that tiny base in the dunes, with a garrison of twenty-five men, the commander of a bastion which at that stage of the war could well have been entrusted to a sergeant: there must be some story behind that.

He repeated my name in his rather husky voice.

"You will remain here," he said after looking me briefly in the eyes. "I need an orderly; my present one is going on leave tomorrow. Do you understand?"

"Yessir," I said.

"Good. Please have yourself briefed. You will share telephone duty with the stretcher bearer. In addition, you will be required to make two bicycle trips a day to company headquarters. And then"—he was silent for a moment and looked at me again—"you will have noticed on the way here that we are in a mousetrap, and no one is allowed to leave it other than on duty without my knowledge. There's no such thing as time off. Do you understand?"

"Yessir," I said.

"Good. Please have the orderly explain all practical matters to you."

His eyes met mine again. I took this for a silent dismissal, saluted, and left.

ON THIS front of the Atlantic coast, my dear sir, a very special kind of warfare was being carried on, the war against boredom. Try to imagine a front extending from Norway to the Bay of Biscay and facing no opponent other than the sea. And this front was equipped like any other where each day saw wounded and dead, men screaming and dying, men horrifyingly mute. But here everything was completely frozen. Night after night, thousands of soldiers stood on guard waiting for an enemy who never came and whose coming some of them positively craved. Year after year, night after night, thousands stood there facing the sea, that monster which is eternally the same, eternally the same, comes and goes, comes and goes, is always smiling, always smiling with a serenity fit to induce a man to plunge headlong into it. An eternal smile; the sea, even when storm-tossed, always had something like laughter about it, wild laughter devoid of mockery, but still laughter. The sea was laughing at us, that was it. There stood the guns, mortars, machine guns; rifles by the hundred thousand lay there on parapets or were lugged back and forth by plodding sentries. Nothing. Year after year the same. Every evening a password to be memorized plus the various flare signals, hand grenades placed in readiness —hand grenades against the sea! During the day, instruction in the use of guns, mortars, machine guns, and other weapons, and drill on the road behind the dunes, year after year. Year after year. During the day, almost eight hours' duty, and at night at least four hours' sentry duty. The never-ending battle against the sand that relentlessly penetrated the farthest, most inaccessible crack of every weapon and never failed to be discovered by some bored corporal's eye. And somewhere beyond the horizon, far, far, incredibly far away, there was an enemy in whom it was impossible to believe—far, far away, an enemy from whom the sea seemed to have learned its laughter. All that lay like a pall of apathy over even the most idyllic little bays, driving us to drink.

Some of the men had been at it since 1940. But even those who had known it only for a few months were beginning to show signs of despair. Despair is the hope of the flesh, my dear sir. There is a kind of despair that, even if it exists only in the mind, is a wild, sensual pleasure. Despair has something of the substance of a movie. One drinks it, it is sweet, sweet, so sweet that one wants to drink up a whole sea of it, but the more one drinks the thirstier one becomes, the more convinced that this thirst is unquenchable, that perhaps here on earth one is already in hell, for hell might somehow be that perpetual thirst. Despair is terrible, despair is the hope of the flesh, and one might feel tempted to pray: Lead us not into despair.

Even a person like your brother, who was always assured of the consolations of his faith, whose strength was such that he could have spent his whole life walking along a knife edge, ultimately to leap from its utmost point into eternal bliss—even a person like your brother was feeling the gnawings of this despair when I arrived. During the first few days I was there, I observed in the melancholy expression of his eyes a vague something that almost reminded me of a person about to go berserk. Often, while he was on the phone talking to that schoolmaster, there was a quiver in his voice as if he were at breaking point, about to cry out: Nitwit, nitwit, nitwit! Incorrigible nitwit!

Well, I was as weak as he was strong. And I was no longer accustomed to any kind of hardship. I had brought off the seemingly impossible: in the uniform of an ordinary soldier I had managed to lead a life to my own liking. My firsthand experience of the war dated from 1940, when I had felt the urge for closer acquaintance after spending two years in barracks undergoing training as an infantryman. After those six weeks of campaign, I had had enough of war. Dust and dirt and heat, permanently painful, burning feet, blood, and a lot of hysteria, and, to crown it all, the worst part: helping those repulsive banners of the Nazis to invade the garden that was France. Not for me. Just four days before the Armistice I was wounded in southern France, on the border of Burgundy. I recovered, hung around for months in a military hospital, and, by bluffing a bit with my school French, contrived to have myself transferred to Paris. In those days a wounded soldier was still a hero. Having succeeded in getting to Paris, I made the most of my illness in order, as we used to say, to maintain the position.

To some extent I had been looking forward to this new tour of duty on the coast, the way one always starts out looking forward to something new. But after a few days I was on the brink of despair.

The futility was appalling. There stood the men every morning with their machine guns or mortars, drilling, drilling, in the sand dunes, practicing the movements they had ceased to master because they had been practicing them for too long. They were personally acquainted with almost every grain of sand. And every morning the same, every night the same, and always only the one enemy, the sea; all around them, minefields, empty buildings. And not even enough to eat. Not even enough to eat to keep up their strength. Food is an essential part of war. Every sensible officer knows that. The waging of war knows no romanticism; there is no place anywhere for so-called ideas or emotions. A soldier who is permanently hungry is capable of the worst, and he is fully justified in obtaining whatever food he can. The rations were simply ridiculous, my dear sir. I know you aren't aware of that. How often have I carried postcards from the men that said, "Alive and well, thanks for the parcel. Heinrich."

Picture, if you can, a man who spends eight hours a day on duty plus four hours a night on sentry duty, living on a pound of bread, two spoonfuls of jam, an ounce of margarine and, at midday, a quart of soup made from water and cauliflower in which, for a hundred and fifty men, a quarter of a skeleton of a scrawny cow has been boiled after being stripped by the mess cook of its last vestiges of meat and fat. Maybe you think that's a lot. It's nothing when a man is fighting boredom.

Well, we found ways to help ourselves. We kept back ammunition and exchanged it for bread with overfed marines and gunners who could find the time to go rabbit-hunting. In that area the navy had its own farms, and at night, whenever we were off duty, we would sneak out onto the potato fields, eluding the sentries who were guarding the crops with cocked rifles, and in the darkness we would grub around in the soil, like wild boar, to fill up our sacks. And don't believe we had any romantic notions about exposing ourselves to the risk of being shot at, for the sentries did fire whenever they caught sight of us.

So you can add hunger to boredom, and just remember that your brother fought for three years on this front.

ON THE morning of the third day, as I awoke, the stale air fell like lead into my lungs. The room was full of smoke; the stretcher bearer had, as always, fallen asleep at the phone, his stupid head lying in a flattened tin can that we used for an ashtray. Naturally, as the latest arrival, I occupied the less desirable of the two bunks, the upper one, and, not yet used to the low ceiling, I would absent-mindedly sit up every morning and bump my head painfully against the ceiling. I looked at my watch: it was six-thirty. So once again he was an hour late for his wake-up duty.

The soldiers were stubborn, fighting tooth and nail for every minute of sleep. And they had every right, for they never had a single night of unbroken sleep, and what can be more ghastly than to be wrenched night after night out of profound sleep?

The night sentries were allowed to go off duty at 6:00 a.m., unless it happened to be high tide, which always meant an intensified state of alert. If they wanted, they could grab some extra sleep until seven-thirty before getting ready to go on duty again. In order not to leave the coast totally unguarded during the next two hours, a single so-called day sentry was posted for the entire base. This sentry had to stand on higher ground, was equipped with an alarm signal, and had to leave his post at 8:00 a.m. to take part in the day's regular duties. It was the orderly's job to wake that sentry. And you can take my word for it that not a single one of the night sentries, even if he happened to be lying in the bunk next to the day sentry, would have lifted a finger to wake him. It was the orderly's job, and if the orderly failed to do so, too bad: then the base was left unguarded, and the Tommies or the Yanks could come if they ever had a mind to do so.

So the base was left unguarded. During the first three days I took all this fairly seriously. I really did think the British were coming, and when I woke up in the morning around that hour—which was unquestionably the most favorable for a potential attack—I had a vision of landing barges gliding silently up onto the beach, their troops leaping from the bow . . . and Hurrah!

So I jumped up, poked the stretcher bearer in the ribs, and said, "Get up, you have to wake the sentry!"

That stretcher bearer was one of the stupidest fellows I have ever met. He was middle-aged, forty-two years old, with crinkly hair and a thick, impenetrable skull and tiny, drink-sodden eyes. He was almost always asleep, and not only could he hardly write German—in his mouth even the spoken language became a very limited means of communication.

"Ah," he said, rubbing his eyes, "I sleeping, I goddamn sleeping, first time happen."

"OK," I said, "first time happen, but get going now, it's time." He fumbled for a slip of paper lying under the telephone, held it up close to his eyes, and silently committed the name to memory. Then he put on his cap to leave, but I knew that he often woke up the wrong man—more than once we had barely saved him from being beaten up by his victim

—so I took the slip and repeated aloud, "Pellerig, Bunker 4, first bunk left of the door, lower."

"What?" He heaved himself around. "I thinking Brunswick."

"No," I said. "Brunswick has to go to the orderly room, he's going on leave."

"OK." He left.

I lit a cigarette, ran my fingers through my hair, and stepped out the door. It was wonderful outside. A cool, gentle wind came from the sea, whose foamy, lapping tongue had halted quite close to our hut, at the foot of a sand dune. It was high tide, the water was blue-gray, and there was a genuine smell of the sea. I stared at that endless surface, that grandiose plain of water, watched the seagulls, and shielded my eyes with my hand so as to savor the solitude. Perhaps I could make out a coast-guard vessel; it was always a pleasure to see the ocean enlivened by some rare vessel. The weather was overcast, the sun, behind me, lay wrapped up in a thick gray cloud. To the north, the view was hidden by the same pine forest that stretched from Cadette's tavern all the way to the coast. I had been told that one could see the mouth of the Somme by walking to the edge of the forest. I decided to give it a try that afternoon during a free half hour. So somewhere to the northwest was England . . . one could sail across the sea, and suddenly an island would appear—England. . . .

I kept my eye on Kandick, the stretcher bearer, and made sure he went into the correct bunker. Everything was silent; soft vaporous banks of morning fog lay above the dunes and huts. It was the only truly peaceful hour of the day here.

Suddenly a voice behind me said, "Good morning." I turned, stood at attention, and saluted.

Your brother made a wry face. "Let's not have any of that, please." I had been embarrassed too, but somehow or other I had to respond to his greeting, and I had already spent too long in the prison of my uniform to allow myself the liberty of a simple "Good morning," as one summer visitor to another. He noticed my embarrassment. "I know, that's what you were taught. But it's not appropriate here, and there's no need, is there? If you like, you can say 'Good morning' to me. I'd be sorry if I'd offended you, but I think we understand each other. . . ."

I looked aside. "The point is," he went on, "I know that you find it repugnant—so do I."

He took out a cigarette and lit it from mine, then sat down on a little bench outside the entrance to our bunker. Those first minutes in the morning, when one stepped outside, saw the sea, felt the wind and the glorious air, when everything was still silent—those first minutes were beautiful. But the specter of daily duty was too real, too deeply ingrained in our memory, for us to be able to linger over our pleasure. Monotony is the most effective weapon of modern warfare.

"You know," he began again, "I'm told there are parents who greet their sleepy children in the morning with a snappy *'Heil Hitler.'* There really are such people, just imagine." His expression was somber. "Can you imagine anything more sickening?"

As I already told you, my despair had become greater after three days than that of your brother after three years. I am a weak person, I had no prop, no religion, only a very vague, ephemeral dream of a certain beauty and order. And yet on that particular morning we two were, I believe, on the same level with our despair. For three years he had swum alone against that sluggish tide of monotony and horror, I had leaped into that mire only three days before, and, filled with the same fear, we were both struggling against being swallowed up by it. We were each like a swimmer who, believing himself alone and lost in a vast body of water, suddenly looks around and finds someone at his side.

I looked at him. That remark about the Hitler salute was so daring that it put him completely at my mercy, at a time when one could be sentenced to death for even dreaming about lèse majesté.

I said, "Sir, I believe we share the same opinion."

At that moment, Kandick's thick skull surfaced above the edge of the dune.

Your brother stood up to return to his hut because he wished to avoid rebuking Kandick for the five hundredth time for oversleeping.

I felt happy.

Until that evening we had no further conversation. I took over the phone while he and Kandick went on duty. That meant he went from one emplacement to the next, attended drill, while Kandick, on the alert for any possible injury during weapons practice, slept near the latrine—a portable outhouse standing somewhat higher up.

At 11:00 a.m. Kandick relieved me again; I had to go to company headquarters before they went off duty. In Pochelet—the hamlet where the orderly room was—I was handed instructions to go to battalion headquarters, where I was to be interrogated by a judicial officer about an incident that had taken place while I was still in Paris. I gulped down my meal in order to reach Crutelles punctually by twelve-thirty. Fortunately the sun wasn't shining. While pedaling at top speed past that lonely tavern, I cast a desperate glance into the empty garden.

The interrogation took place in a small room at battalion headquarters, conducted by a bilious second lieutenant who was a law graduate and due to be promoted to lieutenant in our regiment.

I had to watch my step very closely. I was supposed to give evidence about a comrade at my Paris headquarters who, as transpired during the liquidation of the unit, had for years been trading in blank forms for French identity documents. How much money had he spent, how many women had he had, and what purchases had he made; had anything aroused my suspicions? In answering all these questions with a quaking conscience, I tried to spare the accused as much as possible, feigning ignorance. Actually I was in extreme danger myself. I too had forged documents in order to acquire cigarettes; I had placed horse-racing bets and won, and in dingy bars I had exchanged German money for French.

For almost an hour he squeezed me from every angle, but each time I sidestepped skillfully into the inviolable naïveté of a simple mind, with the result that he got nothing out of me. He had to let me go.

"Damn it," he muttered through his teeth, "it's like wading through mud; you just don't get anywhere."

I rode back very slowly; by this time it was almost two o'clock. Three days earlier I had come past that tavern at almost the same hour. I dismounted, threw the bike against the house wall, and tried the door. It was locked.

I was aghast. Hadn't she said "I'm always here"?

But, then, what does "always" mean? What do all those words mean that we utter so thoughtlessly? I rattled the doorknob, shouted—no response. I walked around the house, climbed over a small locked gate into the yard, rattled all the doorknobs, walked into the stable, stared into the calm eyes of the cows. I called and called—there was no one about. I climbed back over the gate, walked around the entire property, but there was nothing to be seen except for those sweltering meadows with their reed-choked rivulets . . . a few sleepy cows . . . not a living soul. . . .

When would I have another chance to get out of the mousetrap? When would circumstances ever be so favorable again? Already I was making plans to sneak off at night or to invent stories that would justify another trip to battalion headquarters. My God, I simply *had* to see her!

In a fit of jealousy, I hated every stone of that bumpy courtyard where, within half an hour, her feet might be treading again; full of jealousy I hated the doorknobs she would touch with her hands that smelled of milk. I hated the whole house, and that fierce hatred was almost identical with the hope of seeing her again. The hope of the flesh is despair.

While I desperately pedaled off on my bicycle, I concocted an infallible plan for seeing her again. Our plans are always infallible. I would report sick; then I would have to go to battalion headquarters, and once I was in Crutelles, there would be nothing to stop me from seeing her again.

But there was something else in store for me.

V

I BEGAN BY deciding to get drunk at Cadette's.

Just as the *ultima ratio* of the Christian is prayer, so my last resort was drink.

Any kind of narcotic holds an irresistible attraction for me. Maybe I should have become a chemist, providing mankind with new drugs of oblivion, though I know I'd never have had the will power to study the subject in depth and face possible failures in my experiments; I am not only weak, I am also impatient. Everything has to happen immediately: I couldn't wait to see that girl and put my arms around her. . . .

Every soldier demands the solace of instant forgetfulness. Let this be your explanation for the apparently inexplicable and, for civilians, shockingly direct link between soldiers and prostitutes. The prostitute supplies instant gratification.

Every soldier permanently faces death, swaying on a gently teetering or perilously bouncing springboard that is ready to hurl him off.

While I was cycling back, the certainty that I would never see her again filled me with true despair. Never again to see that pale face, never again those compelling eyes and that darkly gleaming auburn hair above the pale-olive skin . . .

I decided to get drunk at Cadette's.

A soldier's good-bye is always, as it were, a good-bye forever. Think of that massive, insane load of pain hauled across Europe by those leave trains! Oh, if only those filthy corridors could speak, those grimy window-panes scream! If only those railroad stations, those ghastly railroad stations —if only they would at last cry out with the pain and despair they have seen! There would be no more war. But with twenty pails of whitewash one of those terrible railroad halls has been restored to a forum for cheerful idiots: six brushes and a few raptly whistling painters on scaffolding, and life goes on. Life goes on. People go on living because of their weak memory. They walk through the same barrier through which they once passed full of the fear of death; but today, only a few years later, they are laughing, on their way to help in the erection of some Potemkin façade.

Oh, if only the fallen could speak, those who were hauled away in some train or other to their death, their faces gray and sad, their pockets full of jam sandwiches. If the dead could speak, there would be no more war. But look at me: the only survivors are the glib ones, those who weaseled their way through, who were smart; there wasn't a trap in Europe that could catch them.

Oh, if only there were nothing but infantrymen, all that shouting about war or no war would be superfluous. There would be no more war. All those surviving heroes, those specialists for whom war was a game, a game that had the attraction of being a little bit risky: all those glib ones praise war and, in the boredom of their bourgeois monotony, long for the "good old days." . . . Oh, if only there were nothing but infantrymen! There used to be no need to spell out that war was despicable. Everyone knew it was gruesome, a pestilence, a horror. Just take a look today at those sentimental idiots stretching out their fancy little boots under the desks in their boring offices.

Oh, to get drunk, drunk . . .

I finished two bottles before that terrible mollusk face behind the bar ceased to disgust me. Only then did my loosened tongue give me the courage to tell her straight out that even her sweetest of sweet smiles would not seduce me. She confined herself to bringing me more bottles, carefully sorting out my butts, and sometimes throwing in a good-natured word of comfort that I couldn't take amiss.

I daresay you don't know that strange feeling of sitting on a bar stool and realizing one's consciousness is gradually growing confused. There one sits, without moving, staring into space, yet filled with adventurous life. This vibrating immobility of the drunk can only be compared to the contained confidence of a tightrope walker, swinging high up between two towers in infinity. If one were to see that man only as far down as his feet, one would think, What a cautious fellow, how slowly and cautiously he is walking! Yet in reality the man on the tightrope is being quite *un*-cautious.

The secret of blissful drunkenness is a balanced imbalance.

Take this paradox any way you like. One pours wine into one's mouth, feels it pass the critical gateway of the palate, and at first everything flows into a silent underground reservoir that must be filled—until suddenly a kind of barometer starts to rise. Invisibly and quite involuntarily, something takes shape that resembles a U-shaped tube connecting the mind to the body; happiness and well-being increase as the levels of both sides of the tube approach each other. Body and mind are brought into balance

—it is a constant interplay—like tightrope walking . . . an exquisite test of one's own equilibrium. Incredibly clear insights transfix one but leave nothing behind. How sad! But no doubt their lack of substance corresponds to their indeterminate origin.

I was also perfectly aware that Cadette was cheating me (all publicans live off drunks). Several times, after wiping away the figure indicating the bottles I had consumed, she wrote down a higher one. I said nothing. Part of that condition is a sublime sense of total indifference to material things. There is no doubt that love and drunkenness, even under the most sordid circumstances, have something sublime about them even in their final stages. So I let Cadette do as she pleased, partly because of that indifference but also from inertia. I couldn't be bothered to open my mouth merely to start a conversation, let alone an argument, with that repulsive mask. She watched me tensely, like a spider lying in wait for the fly's last drop of blood. . . .

Later one never remembers how one got home. Yet, with that deadly accuracy known only to the drunk, one has taken the safest and most direct route back.

Naturally the body has its revenge by allowing the barometer of well-being to drop far below zero. Four hours of sleep would have been enough for me, but Kandick was nothing if not petty. I had telephone duty, and I had to sit it out, even though he spent the next two hours slumped beside me. There he sat, laboriously scrawling a letter to his wife, now and then giving me a gloating poke in the ribs. Those fellows see to it that regulations are complied with!

Your brother had gone off to a staff meeting. He did not return, as I later found out, until almost eight o'clock, by which time I was asleep and Kandick had gone to bed. Your brother then sat beside me from eight until nearly midnight. I slept like a dead man; not even the shrill ringing of the phone right beside my ear wakened me. Sleep after wine is almost as delicious as the wine itself: that sinking into a blue well, into bottomless depths, with a wistful fear in one's heart, until one has sunk all the way down into a sediment of dark semiconsciousness. The man drunk on wine unconsciously performs strange embryonic gestures in his sleep; it is like a thrusting against the womb, and the awakening is like a birth: pain coupled with bliss. . . . I seemed to be clinging firmly to something, something that I wanted to pull toward me, but now it was pulling me. When I awoke, I found myself looking into your brother's smiling face and holding one of his tunic buttons in my hand.

Well, of course it was embarrassing; I didn't know where to look. But he caught my eye and asked, "Is your head reasonably clear?"

"Completely," I said, and it really was.

He stood up and looked over to the bunk where Kandick was sleeping, gently snoring. Sitting down again, he began in a low voice, "Listen, I implore you: don't drink! If you start drinking, you'll be done for. If after only three days you need this phony, short-lived consolation, you'll be finished in a month. Find your consolation in staying sober, I beg you." He fell silent. Because of the blackout, the window had to be kept closed, the door too; the air smelled stale. An uncanny silence hung heavily over the room. I stood up, turned off the light without asking, and opened door and window: a breath of mild, cool air came in, free and fresh.

"Hell," he continued, "I hate lecturing anyone. It reeks of moralism, and, no matter what, there's always that holier-than-thou echo: I'm different—me, *I'm* not like that—look at me! I implore you, come to your senses." Then he suddenly asked, his tone vehement and brusque, "What are you looking for in booze?" Startled, I had to search for words, and the only thing I could think of was the threadbare platitude, "Oblivion and happiness."

"Happiness?" he repeated. "Happiness? We weren't born to be happy. We were born to suffer, and to know why we suffer. Our suffering is the only thing we will have to show for our lives. Good deeds can be performed only by a few saints, not by us . . . and as for prayer . . . perhaps you don't understand that—or perhaps better than I . . . do you?" I was silent. Something prevented me from telling him about the girl; besides, this was my first experience of such melodramatic statements, and I was taken aback. I could only long for dawn never to come again.

"And if you can't understand that we weren't born to be happy, you will at least understand that we weren't born to forget. Oblivion and happiness! We were born to remember. Not to forget but to remember —that's what we're here for."

He spoke in a very low voice, but rarely have words had such an unforgettable impact on me. Kandick was asleep; outside in the dark the tide was rolling back, down the barely perceptible slope of the beach.

I couldn't think of any reply.

"You won't drop off again now, will you?" he finally asked quietly.

"I won't," I said.

"Good night."

"Good night."

He stood up, cautiously opened the door to his room, and I was alone. Quietly and steadily the tide rolled back, quietly and imperturbably Kandick went on snoring.

My first thought, after your brother had closed the door behind him, was: I will see her again! I can't forget that. . . .

EVERY AWAKENING was terrible, sir. Any consolation one imagined to have been gained the previous night had dissolved in the light of day, and none of the ocean's beauty, no freshness of wind or quiet gurgling of water, was of any help.

Several days passed in a strange, uneasy calm. I performed my duties methodically, and time went on like an unchanging ribbon drawn across a turbulent background. Whenever I was on telephone duty in the evening, your brother would sit beside me. Kandick had started operating a canteen in the cellar of a dynamited house behind the dunes.

In our conversations we never mentioned a name, never identified by name or title an institution or person of that foundering Reich. We played games with the language, we were like two kids playing ball, bouncing it—depending on energy or mood—fourteen times or seven times against the wall and, the moment we felt our strength giving out, quickly returning the ball to our playmate.

"Any person," your brother might say, "who is incapable of recognizing his own inadequacy is a nincompoop and essentially stupid. A vain genius is no longer a genius. Anyone who isn't aware that he is part of an unknown plan is stupid. There is no such thing as a stupid genius—ergo, he's no longer a genius. Which only leaves the inglorious possibility of being a genius of stupidity—or of crime. Do you follow me?"

"I do," I said, "and think of a blockhead who considers himself a genius, and every day he is confirmed in this by the hoarse roaring of the crowds—say, eighty million—confirming that he is a genius, and a universal genius at that—artist, statesman, strategist—all to an unprecedented degree. Every day they roar that at him. He is perfection personified. Anyone attempting to claim, for instance, 'I am like X,' would be avenged more drastically than if he were to say, 'I am like God.' Don't you agree?"

"Of course. To demand that such a person come to his senses is almost impossible. But how to render him harmless?"

"There's only one way," I said. "He must be assassinated."

"OK. Assassinated. But then come the problems. How to get at him, what route to choose? You see. . . ."

For several days that was how we discussed all the institutions of that damnable regime, reducing them to zero, blowing them up like soap bubbles, letting them collapse again, then gathering up all that was left to have a good look at whatever remained of substance.

In this way a few days passed quickly enough. One evening about five I had, as usual, ridden off to company headquarters. It was always a relief to get out of the mousetrap. I cycled slowly along that wonderful avenue leading from the beach, between the mined houses, past Cadette's tavern and onto the highway. I was always glad to see people—women, civilians. My God, the pleasure the sight of a woman can give a soldier when he spends all his time with men, with men only, their smell, their garrulousness, their dirt, all their dry gruffness. I always looked forward to those trips. And how lucky I was compared to all those others who, if they were lucky, were allowed to leave the base once a month. Of course, escapes were dreamed up with a recklessness explicable only by a desperate longing for the world—secret paths through the minefields, sudden desertion of one's post, but for most of them that world existed only in Cadette's dubious consolations.

So I always took my time, maybe stopping for a beer or a glass of wine on the way, picking up mail and passwords in the orderly room, and pedaling back just as leisurely.

By now it was September; the heat hadn't abated very much. In the evenings it lay like sultry clouds on the sandy patches among the pine groves. A hot, stifling monotony pervaded the huts, most of them wooden barracks that soaked up the heat.

That day the company commander was in a good mood. Normally he would keep pestering me about petty details: the shine on my boots or belt, the cleanliness of my bicycle. That he was in a good mood was something I noticed as soon as I came in. His eyes were shining. I was soon to learn the cause. Beautifully shaven, tanned, he was wearing a light summer tunic and carelessly flapping his cap at the flies drumming on the windowpanes of the orderly room. The topkick seemed ill at ease; the orderly was wearing his expression of Olympian indifference. That fellow Schmidt could express everything by way of indifference: contempt, friendship, pleasure, hatred.

"I leave it to you, Fischer my friend, to see how you manage it. In any event, it's time something was done to improve the company's food supplies. The ground has been laid, the practical details are up to you. *Heil Hitler!* I'm looking forward to that roast!"

As he walked past me, I flung open the door and stood at attention. Before leaving the room, he paused and said to me, "I'm very satisfied with you—a pleasant surprise, I must say!" I almost bowed before that handsome schoolmaster. He stalked out: a fine figure of a man, endowed with everything—good looks, a splendid physique, and all the decorations appropriate to evening wear neatly displayed on his chest.

"Goddamn it," exclaimed the topkick, throwing down his pen. "When he smells food there's no holding him."

The orderly laughed. "He says the calf's brain is for him, he's been hoping for some for quite a while."

"I'd rather see the brain of an old sow in his belly," cried the topkick. Then he looked at me and, his eyes lighting up, exclaimed, "Say! You can speak French, can't you?"

"Yes," I said.

"Can you handle cattle?"

"No."

He laughed. "Never mind. Listen: tonight at 0200 hours we're supposed to fetch a cow from a farmer two miles from here—d'you think you can manage that?"

I shrugged. "If I can have a horse and cart, some money, and two men to help."

"Done!" cried the topkick. "And the next Cross of Merit to be handed out in this bunch is yours."

He took the map out of the drawer; I bent over his desk and asked him to show me the place. It was a tiny hamlet, two miles northeast, toward the Somme. I was to meet the cart at the crossroads at 0200 hours, but I was also to ride over there this evening to give the farmer exact instructions. I was delighted with the assignment. Any opportunity to taste a little unscheduled freedom was more than welcome. Besides, I thought it might lead me to a cheap source of butter, for Cadette charged exorbitant prices for everything, and my money was slowly running out.

VI

Your brother was also in very good spirits that evening. During the briefing he had hinted that there was shortly to be some addition to the rations. As we went back to the bunker, I asked him, "So you know about it?" I imagined he had been referring to the scheme to buy a cow.

"No," he said in surprise. I explained my assignment. He was delighted. "Why, that's terrific! Then you'll have no trouble carrying out my plan at the same time. I was thinking of buying a sheep for our base."

I had planned to leave as soon as possible, but first there was a meeting I had to attend. We had come to the conclusion that, by extending the sentry's shift by only half an hour every night, we could ensure that each man on the base would get one night of unbroken sleep at least once every two weeks. With a garrison of twenty-eight men, this amounted to a gain of fourteen hours' extra sleep per day: i.e., for each man one night without sentry duty. I had volunteered to draw up the schedule; since we had to note down the individual sentries at each strongpoint every night in a sentry log, we were familiar with the technique of devising a sentry schedule. A meeting of all the NCOs—three corporals and a lance corporal —had been called. They brought along the results of a poll taken among their men: the plan had been rejected—the men suspected duplicity. In particular, a certain Töpfer, one of the older soldiers in the lance corporal's group, had asked what would happen if someone were suddenly transferred: if he had been doing his extra half hour for a number of days, who was going to make up for his lost sleep to him?

Your brother listened calmly, then shrugged his shoulders. "Obviously I can't force anybody. But try to explain to the men that, no matter what, *we* wouldn't benefit at all. Maybe then they'll agree." He looked at each of the four in turn. "Oh well, perhaps the men are right. Sentry duty is as ancient as playing soldiers, and sentry hours are just as ancient. And you can be sure that if it were possible to demand more from a soldier under normal circumstances, it would be demanded. Still, it might be worth a try." He paused for a moment, then said, "OK, nothing doing, gentlemen. That'll be all. And you, Nolte," he said, turning to the youngest corporal, "please have the gap in the mine fence repaired this evening, preferably with old wire so it won't show, right?"

Nolte blushed; we all saluted and left.

I followed your brother into his room. He opened the window, beckoned me to his side, and pointed toward the south, where the beach was mined down to the high-tide line—a broad stretch of coast reaching as far as the next company's sector. A wonderful, still intact children's summer camp was located there in a dense minefield close to the beach. Perhaps there had been a reluctance to blow it up because it was such a valuable piece of property. I looked in that direction but was taken aback by his question: "Haven't you noticed anything about the outgoing mail the last couple of days?"

"Yes," I said in surprise. "It contained a tremendous number of small parcels."

"Right!" he went on with a laugh. "All unawares, you have been transporting, bit by bit, that children's summer camp to Dresden, Leipzig, Glauchau, and Schneiwitzenmühl or wherever. That's right!" he said, in response to my look of amazement. "For the last few days Nolte's group has been systematically looting over there during their off-duty hours. Now Frieger's group has got into the act, and soon there's going to be a glorious free-for-all, and today or tomorrow the entire base will be sneaking through the dunes on stocking feet to make sure they're not being done out of their share."

"For God's sake!" I cried. "What about the mines?"

"That's the least of their worries; there's no danger there, although they might bump into each other. But Nolte, that ingenious fellow, has ferreted out a sapper corporal from the regiment at Geneu, a man who originally helped lay the mines, so they have an accurate chart. Besides, mines that have had three years to rust through aren't that dangerous any more. I only hope Nolte got the hint. Shortly before you arrived here, one of my corporals was court-martialed for snipping through mine fences with a wire cutter: the cows smelled the high, lush grass and, naturally, in they went. Result: two badly injured cows that had to be slaughtered on the spot." He gave another laugh. "Let's hope Nolte is sensible—I'd find it very difficult to report anything. The embarrassing thing is, you see, that I have nothing against looting."

He lit a cigarette, then slowly and happily blew the smoke out through the window; he seemed altogether very cheerful and relaxed that evening. "Listen," he said. "The way I feel, it's simply part of a soldier's job. You can't expect a soldier to behave like a chaplain on a summer vacation. Every occupation has its game rules. These laborers, shoemakers, electricians, they've been turned into soldiers, these good men have been made ferocious, proud, after having first been tamed. See what I mean?"

I saw nothing.

"OK, then, let me explain. We stick these good men into uniform and destroy what the Prussians like to call gutlessness: a sense of human dignity and the glorious freedom of a civilian. OK. So much for that. The barracks have—it is assumed—fulfilled their objective. Then the men are sent out to kill or get killed, and this activity makes them a bit wild— even here, where there's no killing. And especially when these heroes don't get enough to eat. But then they are confronted with regulations that demand more tameness from them than from a civilian, more respectability, dignity, self-sacrifice than they have ever in their lives possessed. They are forbidden to loot while at the same time they are allowed to go hungry. There you have a typical German incongruity. They rant and rave in their speeches, they want to reform the world, they call that 'revolution,' yet they're so scared for their good reputation that they wet their pants when a few soldiers happen to smash some windowpanes and grab a sausage or a couple of shirts. Do you follow me?"

I could only nod, astonished at this new, reckless frankness.

"On we go, then!" he exclaimed. "I can't wait to get this off my chest. All right, you can't have a slaughterhouse without a lot of blood, and a person who can't stand that should stop eating meat. And looting is, in my opinion, the inalienable right of every soldier. The point is not that looting should be prohibited but that we shouldn't turn these men into soldiers. The whole idiotic nonsense begins with the ill-conceived, romantic notion of a 'people's army.' Damn it all, soldiering is a profession, and it can be learned. And if they are forced—and they *are* all forced, all these good men—we shouldn't be surprised if maybe they do turn into soldiers. Well," he said as he walked over to his bed, "I hope you take my hints to heart and manage the job in such a way that I don't see anything. Now, off you go, and don't forget that sheep."

I left and got onto my bike.

The map given me by the topkick proved reliable. Beyond the crossing that led to the orderly room, I had to continue straight ahead for some distance and then make a right turn. Here some of the paths were already dangerous. They led past swampy patches sweltering away in the heat, saturated with silence. Twice I crossed a little stream, and after five minutes' pedaling I admit I felt a certain uneasiness at not having seen the slightest sign of human habitation. But immediately after passing a clump of trees I saw a solitary house. The way I read the map, that must be the spot marked "Daval." Almost every farmhouse in the world is entered from the rear, and as I turned into the yard I saw a very peaceful scene: a dark-haired woman sitting with a basket in front of her, shelling peas, a youth of about fourteen helping her, and the farmer sitting beside them smoking his pipe. I had interrupted their chat. Their laughter died away when I silently rounded the corner and stopped on the sandy ground. The woman let out a little scream; the man turned toward me without a word, and the youth looked curiously at the insignia on my sleeve.

"Good evening," I said. "Excuse me, but is this Daval?"

They exchanged glances. I had the impression they were expecting a confiscation or something of the kind, so I said, "I have to get to Tulby."

"Over there," said the man, pointing his pipe in an easterly direction.

"Is this Daval, then?"

"Yes," he said curtly.

"Do you know Monsieur Preter?"

"Yes," came the curt reply again, "he's her uncle." He pointed his pipe at his wife.

"Oh, I see," I said.

The woman glanced up briefly, and she struck me as being less hostile than the man. The farmer stared at me unabashedly. "Monsieur," I said to him, "couldn't you sell us a sheep?"

"Who wants to buy?" he asked frostily.

I tried to explain and mentioned a price of about thirty marks.

The husband and wife exchanged smiles; then the man said, "I suppose you mean twice that much, if—and I say, if," he drawled, *"if* I were to sell one."

"Perhaps we could talk about it."

"This year," he said shortly, "the weather's been too dry. I can't sell you a sheep. Not enough fodder for the animals."

"All the more reason," I said.

"What do you mean?"

"Well, if you haven't enough fodder, we'll slaughter one, and you'll have one less mouth to feed."

He laughed, no longer quite so hostile.

I felt like sitting down with them and helping with the peas; it was a wonderful evening, but standing there in that hated uniform, leaning on the crossbar of my bike, my cap in my hand, I felt very homeless.

"Well, what about it?" I asked.

"You're a very stubborn fellow."

"We're hungry."

His apathetic eyes lit up a bit. "You're hungry?" he asked, almost like a child. "Doesn't your company feed you, then?"

I was genuinely ashamed and blushed.

"OK," I said impatiently, "yes or no?"

"Claire"—he turned toward his wife—"what do you think?"

I knew I had won. The woman hesitated, without looking up. "At that price . . . ," she said.

He stood up. "Follow me."

We went into the house.

I struck a deal with him and agreed that we would come for the sheep that night. I left the equivalent of forty-five marks in francs with him. It was hard to leave the house. I stood there for a while after coming back from the stable, slowly finished my cigarette, and looked at the sky as it hung, a soft and rosy gray, over the sea. It was very quiet; there was only the distant croaking of frogs and the soft, almost musical sound of the peas as they hopped out of their shells into the tin bowl and sometimes bounced off the edge with a light ping.

I was also aware of the gentle hiss of the man's pipe as he sucked on it; and, although that icy hostility between us had been replaced by a certain good will, I could feel that I was not only intruding but unwelcome.

So I threw my butt onto the flagstones, hastily ground it out, said

"Good night," and got back onto my bike. I soon reached the neighboring farm, situated in a dense little wood, one of those silent, dilapidated places often to be found thereabouts. The terrible part about those farms is that they look deserted whereas there are actually people living in them. What's missing is something of the atmosphere that is part and parcel of rural life: everything is pervaded by a kind of idleness that to us seems totally unrural, an air of decadence, of almost literary melancholy that, in the context of a farm, seems quite horrifying.

The farmer and his wife were sitting in the dark kitchen, and the first thing I saw was the glow of a cigarette.

"Good evening," I said, instinctively keeping my voice low. "I've come about the cow."

"Cow?" a woman's voice repeated slowly and sarcastically.

"That's right," a man's hoarse voice replied, equally sarcastically, more to the woman than to me. "They want to buy a cow, but . . ."

"I thought the deal was all settled," I broke in.

"Settled!" repeated that disagreeable male voice; I couldn't make out the face that went with it. "Nothing is settled, *nothing* has been settled, d'you get me?"

I was silent. Since nobody offered me a chair, I sat down on a stool by the window and began to smoke.

"Settled!" resumed that voice, this time a little less confidently.

"I was told," I remarked, "that the purchase had been completed. The cow's supposed to be picked up tonight."

"Merde!" shouted the voice. "That's what I'd call rushing things! Nothing doing—in Paris people are paying twenty-five francs for a pound of meat, and you expect me to sell two hundred pounds for twenty-five hundred francs! I'm not crazy, not by a long shot. . . ."

"All right," I said evenly. "Put a rope around your cow's neck and take it to Paris. There you might even get forty francs a pound."

I could tell that the couple had both lifted their heads and were looking at me, but what bothered me was that I could see nothing except a pair of flashing knitting needles and the suggestion of a pale cloth cap; the cigarette had been spat out.

"After all," I said quietly, "nobody's forcing you to sell the cow, are they?"

The answer was a hostile silence.

These deals were a kind of legal black market, an infringement of a law that we had instituted ourselves and whose enforcement we should really have been safeguarding; but, as I already told you, soldiers who are permanently hungry don't give a damn about such laws. Needless to say, my question was ridiculous, since I was putting it as the delegate of an enemy company, even though, legally speaking, it was the farmer's duty to refuse the deal.

"No," came the sarcastic voice, "nobody's ever forced us, no indeed."

"Very well," I said as I stood up. "We'll be here tonight at two o'clock. I have part of the money with me." I opened my wallet and took from it three crisp, brand-new thousand-franc bills.

"Here you are," I said curtly.

There are few farmers who can resist the sight of real money. The couple were on their feet in a flash; the woman rushed to the light switch and turned it on. Now for the first time I could see them both, and immediately saw how they leaned their heads toward the money. They were old, gray-haired, with pinched faces, and for a moment I thought they were brother and sister, then I saw their worn wedding rings. The man couldn't resist; he took the bills from my hand and with a repulsive tenderness snapped them between his fingers.

We soldiers, sir, have a terrible contempt for money. Money alone is nothing. Its only value is what one can get for it at any given moment: wine, women, or tobacco. Money is no more than a means. To save it or hoard it seems to us absurd.

The deal was closed. The woman also offered me some butter and eggs; I left the house with a pound of butter, ten eggs, and a very special acquisition: a bottle of thick cream.

It was almost dark outside; a shadowy gloom hung over the meadows and bushes. Cautiously I rode back.

I was filled with a weary disgust. With complete clarity I could see everything that lay ahead: I would reach the highway, have a beer at Cadette's, then sit for four hours at the phone fighting sleep. I would smoke, although nothing tasted good; try to write a letter, without success; hear Kandick's snoring. And after two hours I would be left with nothing but fatigue, hopeless fatigue, and I would keep looking at my watch to see whether it wasn't time to waken Kandick. That's how it would be for the next four or five weeks; then we would be relieved, and in some godforsaken little place eight miles from the coast we would be drilled. I wouldn't even have any money left for booze, I'd have nothing to smoke, and after those six weeks I would once again be sitting in some other bunker night after night, at that phone that never rang, waiting for the moment when I would be allowed to sink into a leaden sleep.

At 2:00 a.m. I would be collecting the cow and the sheep, then sitting at the phone again from seven to eleven, riding off to company headquarters at eleven. . . .

I dismounted for a moment because the sound of the bicycle was getting on my nerves.

In those days, sir, I still believed in what is known as coincidence. I believed that our life was an isolated fragment surrounded by other isolated fragments, each a distinct and a more or less brilliant painting; I believed in the total lack of connection between all things and in the pale, blind futility of our existence. I had as yet no inkling of that mysterious network of innumerable knotted threads, of that vast, all-encompassing fabric into which for each one of us a particular thread has been woven. I reached the highway, got back on my bike, and rode off toward Cadette's tavern.

On opening the door, I was assailed by an unaccustomed racket. Raucous singing and caterwauling. I caught sight of naval and air-force uniforms—near our base there were a lighthouse and an air-force listening post—and the next moment I was surrounded by soldiers who directed my attention to a figure sitting slumped on a bench by the window: glassy-eyed, unseeing, and mumbling incoherent, drunken nonsense. He was from our base, a man called Wiering, normally a quite inconspicuous person who, as far as I could recall the schedule, was nowhere near due for time off. I remembered that he had been due only a few days ago and that he had sold his leave for half a packet of tobacco. I took charge of Wiering, who, without even staggering overmuch, unresistingly let himself be led away. Cadette protested her innocence and accused a few laughing antiaircraft gunners of having got him drunk.

I handed Wiering over to his squad leader, and we agreed to try to say nothing about his absence. Then I entered the bunker, reported my success to your brother, and sat down resignedly at the phone. Kandick had risen from his chair as I came in, then sunk back on his bed; he was already snoring.

I declined your brother's offer to stay awake in my place and for a while sat silently across from him. My silence contained a good deal of hostility. I hated that life, and I was transferring my hatred to your brother as the wearer of a uniform, the possessor of a rank that seemed to justify that life.

Finally he rose to head for his room, turned at the door, and said, "Don't forget that our lives can change at any minute. Nothing is unalterable. Good night." Perhaps he already knew that his words were soon to come true.

VII

Events now followed in such rapid succession that I must first sort them out in my memory if I am to keep them in the right order.

That night I got almost no sleep. Fatigue and despair filled me like an ever-recurring, evil-tasting tide that I had to keep regurgitating; back and forth it flooded, unwilling either to retreat or to utterly engulf me.

Just before two I was wakened by Kandick, who had relieved me at midnight, and I rode off to meet the cook and collect the cow and the sheep: an arduous enterprise accompanied by much frustration and cursing.

It was close to five when, totally exhausted, I was able to start on my way back, and the sky was already growing light as I turned into the avenue at Cadette's tavern. A glorious morning, no doubt, but I was too tired to notice; how pointless and totally irrelevant that grayish-pink light seemed to me as it felt its way up the gray vault of the night sky with delicate, soft rays. There is a stage of fatigue—what soldier is not familiar with it!—that is almost deadly to body and soul. One would commit murder for a single night of unbroken sleep; one is on the verge of tears from exhaustion, indifferent to everything except sleep or oblivion.

When I stepped inside the bunker, Kandick was asleep, sprawled across the table. Even my noisy entrance failed to wake him. I simply flung myself down on my bunk and instantly fell asleep, too tired even to give Kandick a poke in the ribs; besides, I was beyond caring what happened. As far as I was concerned, anybody who liked could come and capture our base.

When I awoke, it was midday: a steaming mess tin was on the table. Your brother was sitting beside it, calmly looking at me. He was about to open his mouth to say something to me when the phone rang. He lifted the receiver, spoke, and the next moment I saw an expression of utter astonishment on his face. Then he repeated several times: "Yes, I understand, yes. . . ." He put down the receiver and burst out laughing.

What had happened was this: our CO had ordered the brain of the cow that had been slaughtered that night to be fried for himself at around 11:00 a.m., had polished it off, and then suddenly been taken so violently ill that it had been necessary to rush him to the field hospital in Abbeville (incidentally, on account of chronic dyspepsia he was considered "unfit for service on the eastern front"). Your brother, being next in seniority, was put in command of the company.

Within an hour your brother and I had to move from Larnton to Pochelet. With our scanty baggage we settled into the CO's quarters, a nice little four-room house, and for the time being were happy to have escaped from Larnton. Two more hours were enough to make ourselves reasonably comfortable in our new quarters and to remove the baggage of the former CO. At four o'clock your brother went over to the orderly room to take charge.

I spent the whole afternoon sitting on our little terrace with a view of the sea, reading the Kierkegaard diaries your brother had lent me.

Since by eight o'clock he hadn't returned, I went to bed and fell asleep at once. I was worn out by the exertions of the previous night and of the day, and the prospect of sleeping the whole night through without interruption seemed irresistible.

THE NEXT morning I slept until nearly eight. I barely had time to wake your brother before hurrying off to the drill in which I now had to take part. For the first time in three years I had to endure the ordeal of foot drill. You can't imagine the horror I feel to this day at having merely to write the words "position of attention," those words that form the very foundation of Prussian drill procedure.

At about eight-thirty your brother drove off to take over the command of two bases farther north.

The morning dragged slowly on. At noon I was alone. I listlessly ate my meal, then dozed on my bunk, smoking cigarettes and drinking half a bottle of wine.

Your brother's return awakened me; I heard him come in, go to his room, throw down his belt. Shortly after that he called me in.

He seemed tired and annoyed and at once asked me for a cigarette. We sat facing each other in armchairs, and after a few puffs he surprised me by pulling out a bottle of wine from under the table. He took two glasses from a cupboard, opened the bottle, and poured. We touched glasses and drank.

"Listen," he said finally, after we had sat in silence for a few minutes. "There are people who are born to polish boots. A perfectly unobjectionable, dignified occupation. Perhaps you were not born for that, I don't know. On the other hand, I don't want anyone else around me but you. I think we will be able to talk in greater privacy and at greater length and less in innuendoes. Because I want to *do* something, understand? Not only talk. We have to do something, understand?"

I nodded, although I wasn't very clear about what he meant.

"So," he went on, "it'll be best if we share the boot polishing. Right? One day I do yours and mine, the next you do yours and mine. Is that a deal? Apart from that, you will be on duty in the mornings and have the afternoons off, to which a CO's orderly is entitled. We won't infringe on any regulations. And there's another thing you'll have to take over, something I simply can't do: the cooking."

I gave him a long look. "I have a counterproposal," I said. "Each of us will polish his own boots. I'll be glad to do the cooking and collect our rations."

"Splendid," he cried, "splendid! A good idea. Thanks very much." He shook my hand, raised his glass to me, I raised mine to him. Then he suddenly stood up, walked toward the big portrait of Hitler that hung on the end wall of the room—an ostentatious affair in a heavy gilt frame—and without a word turned it back to front. His hand was still on the frame when the door opened and Schnecker stood on the threshold.

I jumped to my feet, as stipulated. Schnecker looked first at me, then at your brother, who had meanwhile moved back to the table. Then Schnecker said to me in a low voice, "Leave us, please."

I walked to the door, saluted, and left the room.

With heavy steps I walked along the corridor, listening intently, but there was nothing to be heard yet, and I supposed he was waiting for my footsteps to die away. I left the house, but walked around to the rear and lay down in the garden under the open window. There was still no sound.

"Well, then," Captain Schnecker finally said in a calm voice—he had apparently gone over to the wall and turned the picture back to its proper position—"let's begin by correcting this childishness."

"May I ask you," said your brother, his voice just as calm, "whether this is my own living room and whether there is any regulation requiring officers to have portraits of the Führer in their home?"

"No."

I could hear your brother walking over to the wall, and I knew he was turning the picture around again.

"Good," said the captain, "excellent. But with your indisputable intelligence it must be clear to you that there is not much room for doubt when in the presence of his subordinate an officer displays loathing for the portrait of his supreme commander."

"Wrong, my friend. All I loathe is the frame. You know quite well how sensitive I am when it comes to art, and to me it is outright blasphemy to frame the portrait of our modest, simple, soldierly Führer—who has said he won't take off his soldier's tunic as long as the war lasts—to stick his portrait in such a garish frame: to me that's an insult to his person. And, after all, the Führer is also an artist."

"You're as strong as ever in syntax, it seems."

"Stronger, I hope. I've had plenty of time to practice. You fellows saw to that."

They both fell silent, and I knew that your brother was standing there, his hands clasped behind his back, calmly looking Schnecker in the eye.

"Listen to me carefully," Schnecker resumed. "I have been at great pains to clear your name with the regiment and to see that the old affair is forgotten and you're put in command here. That sissy will probably be spending six months in the hospital again and then go on leave and arrive back here with a brand-new stomach ulcer. There were some nasty types who would have liked to see you take orders from a junior lieutenant. I prevented that."

"I wouldn't have cared."

"Why do you think I did that for you?"

"To set a trap for me."

The captain gave a devilish laugh. "There couldn't have been any better trap for you than the mousetrap of Larnton! You could have grown old there. But no"—he raised his voice—"you can't think of anything better to do, on the very first day, the very first day, than to send in almost word for word the same report that was the original reason for your being found unfit to command a company. You can think of nothing better to do than worry about margarine, bread, and sugar for your men. It really does look as if you were out to create difficulties."

"I can't think of anything more important here than the bread, margarine, and sugar for my men. Unfortunately I cannot improve the fortifications at my own expense. That would probably be the next priority."

"You are simply making yourself ridiculous. And, furthermore, on the very first day, another of your requests to be transferred to Russia. Don't worry—the Russian front still needs so many officers that your turn will come."

"What are you going to do with my report about the rations?" your brother asked quietly.

"I shall tear it up."

"No, you won't!" your brother shouted, and I could hear them moving toward each other.

"Then I'll wipe my ass with it!" shouted the captain furiously.

"Here"—there was a brief pause—"here," he cried again, "look at this, read this scrap of paper. It was found yesterday on a carrier pigeon shot down in the sector of our first company. 'The morale of the troops is bad, and the troops are hungry.' Needless to say, it is extremely flattering for me as battalion commander, in the eyes of the regiment and the division, when a carrier pigeon that must have been released in my sector bears a message of that kind. That is indeed extremely flattering, and on top of that you also produce your idiotic report that"—he gave his voice a sarcastic undertone and was obviously quoting—"the troops believe they are constantly being done out of small but regular quantities of fat, sugar, and bread; that the quartermaster sergeants declared that, on the basis of the quantities they received, they were simply unable to issue the prescribed rations; and that"—his voice became shrill—"this naturally served further to undermine the low morale of the quartermaster sergeants, for where there was an actual shortage of one ounce it was easy enough to pilfer two ounces. Oh, all that's just great for me!"

"The question is whether it's untrue." Your brother's voice was calm again.

"Untrue! We're not here to seek the truth, which anyway doesn't exist. We're here to win the war."

"And apparently that can only be done by constantly gypping hungry soldiers, right?"

This was followed by a terrible silence, and they must have moved even closer together.

"I daresay you believe," came Schnecker's hoarse voice at last, "that I am eating your men's margarine and sugar myself, don't you?"

Your brother said nothing.

"Do you believe that? I said, Do you believe that?" His voice seemed to be exploding with rage.

"Not directly, of course."

"Indirectly, then—right?"

"Now you listen to me." Your brother's voice was very calm. "This paymaster is not only a fool, he's also a bastard. You wouldn't deny that?"

"Of course not. But there's no way I can get rid of the fellow."

"You don't have to. You just have to make him watch his step. And you can't do that, of course, because you depend on him for your extra supplies of booze, to which, of course, you're not entitled either. You see, you need to get drunk every day. I know—on a captain's pay one can get good and drunk three times a month at the most—I know that too. And then, of course, you need women. You're a good-looking fellow, a ladies' man, as they say. There you are, then. There's no way you can get at the paymaster. Those fellows are businessmen; in other words they've covered themselves in every possible direction. And you know I'm right, don't you?"

The terrible part was that I couldn't see anything, and now I couldn't hear anything either, and at that moment, lying out there under the window sill, I realized that eavesdropping is horrible.

What was Schnecker doing, for God's sake? Was he sitting there slumped in his chair, or was he standing, pistol in hand, ready to shoot your brother at any moment? I lay there as if dead, not daring to stir or crawl away. . . .

Again came your brother's voice. "You must try to see my point," he said. "I can't imagine anything worse than cheating a soldier out of his rations or his sleep. After all, we in our officer's uniforms represent the power that compels these men to submit to being killed or being bored to death. That burden is quite enough for me. I wouldn't like the added responsibility of making them suffer more hunger than is provided for by the system." He fell silent again; then after a while his voice continued, heavier and more somber than before. "In a way it's too bad that I'm going to die—otherwise I'd look forward to writing a philosophical treatise on the ounce after the war."

Now I realized that Schnecker had been standing there grinning all the time, his arms folded. He burst into a peal of laughter, as if a pent-up flood were being released.

"Who would have believed it?" he said in a strong, firm voice. "And from the lips of someone wearing the uniform of a German officer! Who would have believed it?" Again that ringing laughter.

"Come now"—I could tell from his voice that he was tightening his belt and straightening up—"let's get back to business. For all I care, the report can go to regimental headquarters. For all I care, make yourself ridiculous, make yourself a laughingstock for the sake of three ounces of margarine, for the sake of three ounces that has to be withheld. And another thing: did you have to pick the rudest bastard in the battalion for your orderly and sit here boozing with him in the afternoon while you were both still on duty?"

Your brother was evidently looking at him in silence; then he laughed. "Oh, of course," he said, "that's right—it was four-thirty when you arrived. I leave it to you to file a counterreport."

AFTER HEARING the captain get into his car, I crawled back into the shelter of some nearby bushes, stood up, and hurried off toward the forest that blocked the view of the sea. Leaning against the trunk of a fir tree, I looked out over the waves as they rolled slowly in. It was very quiet, the air was soft, and there was nothing in sight but the water and the stretch of sand in front of it that was slowly, very slowly being covered by the tide; the barbed wire that had been drawn along the tide line was the only reminder of the war.

A painful sadness, such as I had never known before, welled up in me. There is no justice, I thought; there is no such thing as an ounce. The ounce is a fiction, an ounce is nothing, and yet they say: It is an ounce! And on this nothing, on this ounce, they all grow rich. They all grow rich solely on the ounce, so it must be something, that ounce. That's why there have to be so many poor, victimized people, because an ounce is so little and so many ounces are needed to make a rich man rich; that's why there have to be all those millions of gray, gaunt figures obediently marching across Europe with their rifles on their backs, just so the rats can get fat on their only tasty food—the ounce. There must be vast numbers of those figures that can be stuffed into a freight car designed to hold "40 soldiers or 8 horses"—simply because the horses are bigger than the soldiers, bigger and more valuable.

I was twenty-five at the time, sir. I was no innocent, I was a trooper like all the rest; I believed in nothing but the sausage on my bread, as we used to say, in wine and tobacco. At least, I believed that was all I believed. But where did that unutterable sadness come from, weighing down my heart like lead, paralyzing me so that I felt too tired even to put my hand in my pocket to dig out matches and cigarettes?

I had been fifteen when the swastika was suspended like a huge black spider in the sky over Germany.

Now I wished I could travel across the sea, far, far away to another world where there were no uniforms, no policemen, no war; but I was trapped in this cage called Europe. There was no escape: starting from this coast I could travel eastward for thousands of miles, eastward to the end of this insane continent, all the way to Vladivostok, and there would be no life anywhere.

In that hour I would have sold all the rest of my life to sink into the arms of that girl who had said, "I'm always here"—and who hadn't been there after all.

As dusk fell, I crept back home, lay down on my bed, and abandoned myself to the sluggish tide of a leaden despair that left no room even for desire. Not a sound was to be heard in our cottage. From the barracks I could hear faint singing. I was incapable of thinking or doing anything, I was at the end of my tether.

VIII

T WO DAYS later we were already on our way to Russia.

When I woke up next morning, everything was normal. From the direction of the company kitchen I could hear the men whose job it was to take coffee to their barracks. In your brother's room all was quiet. It was seven o'clock. I got up, went into our own little kitchen, set the frying pan on the electric hotplate, put some fat in it, took the loaf of bread out of the drawer, and began to slice it. As the fat melted, I beat up the eggs in a cup with some cream and stirred them around in the pan. Then I prepared the tray, putting two plates, cups, and knives on it, and went off to the company kitchen.

The mornings were always peaceful. The whole little place had the atmosphere of a somewhat run-down summer camp. That morning the air was already warm, and the soldiers were standing outside their barracks, stripped to the waist and washing.

The topkick was sitting in the kitchen, discussing with the cook how to use up the rest of the cow. He was markedly cooler toward me.

"Please tell the CO," he called out to me while I was filling my mess tin at the coffee urn, "that church services have been scheduled for this afternoon, both denominations, here. The outposts have been notified."

"Yessir," I replied.

The cook also threw me a suspicious glance. He hadn't forgiven me for doing him out of his profit of five hundred francs on the cow, and he probably assumed I'd told your brother about it.

As I left the kitchen, Schmidt called across to me from the orderly room, "We need a dispatch runner for nine o'clock to pick up special orders from the battalion—would you be interested?"

I looked into Schmidt's placid, amiable face. "Yes," I said. All I could see was the pale face of the girl, and I imagined myself pressing my mouth onto her cheeks, her lips, and the little hollow at the base of her neck.

"Yes," I repeated.

As I approached our quarters, I could already see your brother's face, covered with shaving soap, at the window. It was seven-thirty.

Shortly after that, I carried coffee, bread, and eggs into the room and told your brother about the church services and that I had been ordered for nine o'clock to ride over to battalion headquarters.

"Yes," he said as he put on his tunic, "there's something in the air; maybe the cow will be our farewell dinner."

"Do you really think so?" I asked doubtfully.

"Things look bad in Russia."

We sat down. I poured the coffee and we spread scrambled egg on the bread, but first I lit a cigarette. It was the first real breakfast in a long time. The wide, low window toward the north was open, the air, cool yet soft, streamed into the room, and one could see far out over the water.

Your brother, like me, picked up the bread and promptly put it down again, swallowed a mouthful of coffee, and suddenly began to speak in a rapid, almost droning voice:

"I daresay you know that I was considered unfit to lead a company because the very first time I was put in charge of one, I decided to get to the bottom of all those discrepancies in the issuing of rations. You see, my first day as CO, each man was supposed to receive twenty-five ounces of butter. A straightforward calculation: ten men one package, that's all. But oddly enough there was one package for every twelve men. At the time my company, including all subordinate units, consisted of a hundred and eighty men. That meant that, at fifteen times twelve men, somewhere along the line a pound and a half had gone astray. I immediately summoned my quartermaster sergeant, and his excuse was that deliveries had been short. In his presence I phoned the fellow in charge of provisions at battalion headquarters, and he admitted that he had had to short two packages per company because that was all he had received. So my quartermaster sergeant had already kept back one package; at least I had my hands on him —it's always easy to catch the small fry. I still had to clarify how it was possible for the division to have short-shipped five pounds of butter for the five ration-drawing units of our battalion.

"I kept phoning those guys till they almost went out of their minds. I made them spend hours recalculating, and it turned out that each unit had actually had to be shorted three pounds because the butter had turned rancid. Replacements were promised. After a phone bombardment of almost two days I finally had the battalion quartermaster on the hook with a shortage of two pounds. So far so good. Now just figure out how many battalions, sections, ration-drawing units, there are to a division. Oddly enough, for the next three days full rations were issued. Butter and margarine seemed to have lost their tendency to turn rancid. But I persisted. On the fourth day, a shortage again. This time, company and battalion quartermaster sergeants had clean hands. Wherever a shell explodes close by, people are scared, but farther back . . . Well, I had a phone. You can imagine how those fellows hated me; I was relentless. If one of the men told me something had gone bad, I contacted his superiors and asked whether this had been reported and whether the facts had been investigated.

But I got nowhere. It didn't work. The soldiers never received their full rations for more than four consecutive days. The funny thing was that I also became unpopular in my own company; the topkick and the sergeant were scared and thought I was crazy. Luckily I had won a few officers over to my side. I would phone, or write a report, every day if so much as a single ounce of jam was short. Well, the upshot was that I personally punched the divisional quartermaster in the nose: I need hardly tell you that fellow was fat as a bedbug in an overcrowded barracks. The officers let me down, saying it was futile to fight the administration, it was a clique, and so on."

He swallowed some coffee, picked up the bread again, put it down again.

"Well," he went on, "I was powerless, of course. At the hearing I was accused of being senselessly fanatical, quixotic. The divisional quartermaster emerged from the battle a rosy, innocent lamb. I was duly punished, transferred, and narrowly escaped demotion. But, damn it all, I can think of no more meaningful battle than against the administration, for the administration—*any* administration—is the administration of mindlessness, the administration of the administration. Oh God! I'd like to take over the administration of life! I'd like to represent the rights of the living against those dead creatures, even if during my next attack I have to throw my insignia in the general's face. I don't want them!" he suddenly shouted, then, embarrassed, began stirring his coffee although it contained neither milk nor sugar. With a sigh he raised his head. "Now it's starting all over again," he said. "You can help me. Do you want to?"

"Sir," I said, blushing, "my conscience isn't sufficiently clear for me to accuse others of filching."

"No?" he merely asked.

I told him about my finaglings in Paris. He listened with lowered head; my confessions clearly embarrassed him.

"You see," I added, after outlining the essentials, "wherever I can cheat the state, I have no scruples. The state has stolen six years of my youth, it has prevented me from learning a trade. I would call that 'getting compensation.' "

"So," he asked quietly, "you wouldn't hesitate to sell a bicycle, for instance, and pocket the proceeds?"

"Absolutely not," I admitted, "although . . ."

"Although?"

"Although several years of concentration camp seem an excessive price to pay for a bicycle."

"So it's only the punishment that deters you?"

"Yes."

"That's interesting," he cried eagerly. "Most interesting! This is the first time I've heard that put in such classically cynical form. Nevertheless," he went on with a smile, "if you thought there was the slightest chance of somebody being personally harmed, you wouldn't take anything, would you?"

"No," I said.

"We shall see," he said. "I have to go on duty now." It was eight o'clock. He ate his scrambled eggs and bread, swallowed a few more mouthfuls of coffee, and left.

Half a minute later I left the house, without having touched my breakfast.

AT EIGHT-FIFTEEN I stopped outside the quiet tavern where, barely a week earlier, I had seen and spoken to the girl. It was so quiet all around that I had to stand still and listen. I think that for the first time in my life I could hear my heart beating—rapidly pounding away, that invisible hammer in my chest. . . .

Very quietly I propped the bicycle against the wall and walked straight through the open gate into the yard, for after dismounting I had heard the gentle sounds of milking. I saw her at once, and she too, having heard my footsteps, had risen and turned around. There she stood: milk dripping from her fingers as they hung, curved inward, by her sides, her hair tied back smooth and tight, her red lips open in surprise, her grubby gray smock slipping off her left shoulder. She recognized me immediately and stood there motionless as I walked toward her.

Without a word I put my arms around her, and for half a second I felt her hair against my cheek and her warm breath on my neck, but when I turned her head toward me to kiss her I realized that her body was cold and stiff in my arms, and her face, which I could now see, registered such resistance and fear that I was shocked.

"Angel," I whispered to her in German, mad with pain, "angel—I love you!"

Her lips grimaced. *"Laisse-moi,"* she implored, *"je ne t'aime pas."*

I released her instantly, but she did not step back: she just stood there, and I could see she was on the verge of tears. Tears over me. My face must have expressed intolerable pain.

She pitied me, and when I realized that, could see it in her face, I knew for the first time how much I loved her. Even her pity seemed like a gift.

"Angel," I stammered again, "angel!"

I turned away, but she called me back with a strange, birdlike sound. She was smiling. "Wouldn't you like something to drink?" she asked.

Without waiting for a reply she walked past me, wiped her hands on her smock and, with a gesture of extraordinary grace, pulled her smock up over her shoulder. Dazed, with drooping shoulders, I followed her into the house.

I looked at my watch: twenty past eight. Five minutes had passed, and the world had almost come to an end; a last, soft red glow hung over the horizon—for what lover will ever cease to hope?

She had uncorked a bottle and filled two glasses. "I'm thirsty," she said in a low voice. "The air's so sultry, although it's early yet."

I find it hard to describe her smile: it was affectionate and sad, leaving me no spark of hope, yet not coquettish. It was ineffably human—I know no other word. She raised her glass; I nodded and drank.

The wine was delicious, cool and dry, and her face showed that she found it refreshing.

"Yes," I finally said with an effort, my muteness weighing on me like a heavy burden. "If I could just see you occasionally . . ."

We put down our glasses, and I followed her as she led the way outside. One more nod from her, and she was gone.

AT EIGHT-FORTY-FIVE I was at battalion headquarters; the other dispatch bearers were already assembled. I sat on the steps outside, surrounded by that know-it-all chatter, and the time passed incredibly fast. Again and again I dug around into my memory, resurrecting the scene in the barn in order to find some tiny hope; but I found nothing, and yet . . .

We waited a long time. We smoked, walked up and down, sat down again, and I joined listlessly in the general scuttlebutt; it was almost eleven when we were summoned to the orderly room. We were each handed a dispatch box, flat, locked wooden boxes for each of which there was one key with the battalion and one with the company, thus ensuring that we couldn't discover the contents of the dispatches. Nevertheless, it was obvious we were going to Russia. Normally that would have struck me as the ultimate horror; that day it left me cold. I felt numb. I saw the world and didn't see it. I was aware that the weather had become even more sultry, that the sky was covered with heavy gray clouds. Somehow my will power had also ceased to function. Deep down in a layer of buried consciousness I knew that I must stop, dismount, rest, and try to come to my senses, but I believe I would have gone on riding my bike to the end of the world, on and on, obsessed by the stupefying mechanics of pedaling . . . on . . . on . . . I was dead.

A terrifying clap of thunder roused me. That same instant a warm, heavy rain started coming down in torrents. I looked about me and recognized my surroundings: there was the group of trees, *her* house, and no other shelter in sight. I raced toward the house, dismounted, left my bike lying on the ground, and, carrying the box, burst into the corridor.

I left the door open and stood there without making a sound.

Our bond with nature is closer than we realize. I don't know how long I stood there; I was barely conscious. When I came to again, I realized I was crying.

The beauty of the torrential summer rain, the cosmic power invested in all flowing water, created in my being some sort of parallel; an element of release, of flow, touched me. I wept. The unspeakable, agonizing spasm was relaxed, and I was alive again.

With trembling nostrils I breathed in that marvelous, sweetly moist fragrance that rose like clouds from the meadows.

I wept. . . .

Suddenly I heard the footsteps of two people approaching along the flagstone path that skirted the house. The rain had let up a bit. I winced, as if a long, fine needle had unerringly pierced the very core of my sensitivity: they were your brother's footsteps. We know the people we live with better than we imagine: they were his footsteps. I stood stock still, leaning against the wall in the darkness of the corridor.

With the girl beside him, he entered my field of vision, and it was no surprise to me to see her with him. He was pushing his bicycle, half leaning on it, his face turned toward me; of the girl I could see only her back, her head, slightly bent, and a narrow segment of her soft cheek, and I knew that she was smiling. His face was pale and serious, and there was a kind of blissful pain in it, but the shattering thing was the naturalness with which those two seemed to belong together: uttering not a word, merely exchanging little smiles, that gentle pair simply belonged together.

I can't say I felt jealous. I was breathing heavily, suffused with the pain of being totally excluded. They scarcely moved, they just looked at each other, and there I stood: transfixed to the damp wall of that dilapidated house, thinking that it might feel good to die.

Finally he bent down, kissed her, and said, *"Au revoir, Madeleine."* He quickly turned away and, pushing his bicycle, walked toward the gate.

"Au revoir, au revoir!" she called after him.

Then she took a few steps back, probably so as to gaze after him for as long as possible from the top step, and in doing so she bumped against the closed half of the door, turned slightly, saw me, and gave a little shriek. . . .

Your brother had not yet reached the gate. He rushed back to the door; the girl was still looking at me in horror and disbelief. Now he was quite close, saw me, and instantly grasped the situation.

"Come along," he said to me huskily. I followed him like a condemned man, the dispatch box under my arm, retrieved my bike outside the gate, mounted it, and rode off at his side.

We didn't look back.

IX

NEITHER OF us ever saw her again.

We rode in silence to company headquarters, where we parted without a word. He went to his quarters; I had to deliver the dispatch box, then go to the kitchen to collect our midday meal, having, as always, handed in our mess kits in the morning.

I put my bike in the shed and stopped by the kitchen to receive our two portions of potatoes and stew; then I followed him to our quarters.

He stood up as soon as I entered. He had already brought out the plates from the kitchenette and placed them on the table, also the cutlery, but he tended to do that a bit awkwardly, so I put our two mess kits on the tray and calmly rearranged forks, knives, and plates, straightened the loaf of bread, and removed the wilted stalks from the flowers in the vase.

All this time he was pacing up and down with folded arms.

"We can eat now," I said calmly, when everything was ready.

"All right," he said, and at that moment we looked at each other again for the first time; reluctantly I had to smile. He shook his head, his expression registering bewilderment, then shrugged his shoulders; I was still waiting for him to sit down.

"We don't want to pass over this in complete silence," he said in a low voice, "but it's up to you whether we discuss it or not."

"No," I said, my voice equally subdued, "I'd rather not discuss it."

"Fair enough," he said. We sat down, and I passed him the little ladle we used for serving ourselves from the mess kits. There was a knock at the door. Putting down his spoon, he called out, "Come in!" and the topkick entered. His normally placid face showed agitation.

BY NEXT morning we were on the train heading for Russia. The reports and orders I had picked up were already superseded, canceled by telephone instructions. The men to be transferred had to be selected and prepared for departure that same day and wait at the bases for their replacements, which were said to be on their way. The trucks bringing the replacements were then to take the transferred men to an assembly point near Abbeville, where a division had already arrived, been loaded onto the train, and left. But the train had been blown up, casualties had been heavy, and the division was a hundred and twenty men short of combat strength. Your brother and Schnecker were among the officers.

Whereas I had nothing to do but keep an eye on our two packs, your brother didn't have a minute's peace. At the last moment the transferees' clothing and equipment had to be replenished, and men who had suddenly been taken violently ill had to be persuaded that they were in fact fit; men about to go on leave had where feasible to be replaced. Above all, the transferees had to be assembled as soon as possible in Pochelet so they could attend divine service.

The Catholic divisional priest arrived by car shortly before four and, in view of the general chaos, was accommodated in our quarters. I had to endure his company for half an hour, until the arrival of the first penitents, to whom I offered the use of my room while they waited. Meanwhile your brother told me to clear the living room for the celebration of Holy Mass and the administering of the Sacraments. So I found myself alone with the priest for a while. He had the smooth, rosy skin befitting a staff officer in France, and the mild and obliging manners of a wine salesman. When I threw out a few remarks about war, corruption, and officers in general, he gently rotated one hand in the other, felt constrained to remove his cigarette from his lips, and, with a bland expression, said, "Yes, there is much wickedness in the world."

We were interrupted when the first penitent knocked at the door, saluted stiffly, and came in.

I couldn't help muttering to myself, *"Ave, Caesar, morituri. . . ."*

The priest looked at me with a smile. He finally abandoned his cigarette and said, "Well, well, a Latin scholar!"

His gentle look was a signal for me to leave the room.

Out in the garden, all was quiet. Mild autumnal warmth was interspersed with cool air, the sky was blue, and the cottages of Pochelet slept behind their high hedges and fences. Your brother had driven over to Larnton, to try to talk some sense into a young soldier apparently overcome by violent cramps.

Preparations were complete, all the other transferees were ready, and divine service was expected to begin punctually at five. The Protestant clergyman was due any minute.

I strolled slowly along behind the company buildings as far as the crossroads and for the first time entered the Pochelet tavern. It was a single-story, flat-roofed building, a typical outdoor summer restaurant, with its wooden walls and garden chairs. The big room was deserted; through the open door to the kitchen I could see the landlady and her husband at their evening meal. She was a pretty, blonde woman, with a barmaid's cold beauty. Still chewing, she emerged from the kitchen, gave me a friendly smile, and handed me the bottle of white wine I had requested and for which I didn't yet know how to pay.

"Give me another," I said with a laugh. "Then I won't have to bother you again at your supper." She gave a cautionary little smile, hesitated half teasingly, but then, having made up her mind, reached in under the bar and brought out another bottle.

I sat down at one end of the room, aware of that terrible despair in abandoned places of entertainment that creeps toward one from each corner. There was a smell of dust, of summer dust.

I couldn't possibly miss the departure: the road outside the window would bring the men from Larnton and the northern bases right past my nose.

I had a whole hour in which to forget the girl's face, to say good-bye to France, and to drown the soft, pink, well-preserved corpselike face of the priest.

That yellow wine is the most exquisite of all; it is like honey and fire, like light and silk, and it's my belief that God caused it to grow in order to keep alive the memory of Paradise in this depressing den of vice that calls itself human society. The more I drank, the more I became conscious of a serenity such as I had never known, a serenity amounting almost to wisdom. It is wonderful to drink oneself to sleep, to sink into the arms of that kindly brother of Death.

I remember being able to persuade that cool but sweetly smiling woman to let me have two more bottles in exchange for my watch.

I woke up to find myself on a foul-smelling truck, closed my eyes again in horror, and finally became fully awake at the railroad station in Abbeville, beside a troop train on the point of departure. Your brother's laughing face was bent over me.

"He looked," I said, "he looked like a wine salesman. . . ."

"Sure, sure," he said quietly. "Come on, now, get up."

I got to my feet and was assigned by him to a column of fourteen men in the process of being incorporated into a company on the troop train.

WE TRAVELED across France, past the shining vineyards of the Rhineland, through central Germany, Saxony, Silesia, Poland. The railroad stations became ever more gray and dismal, the soldiers ever more desperate and cynical. Gradually we started meeting trainloads of wounded, trainloads of prisoners; the ragged population of the occupied territories crowded around our train. The last of our French matches were bartered for eggs, blankets from French houses transformed into butter, parts of equipment exchanged in the darkness of ghostly railroad stations for bacon or tobacco, for even during the transport our rations remained miserably inadequate.

The weather had turned cold, it being now almost the middle of October, and we dragged our long greatcoats through the dirt of Ukrainian stations where tractors were being hurriedly loaded for shipment back to Germany, or where we were held up to allow a transport of severely wounded soldiers to pass along the blocked section.

I didn't see your brother that often. Sometimes, during a brief halt, he would come to our car and chat with us, and on rare occasions, during a longer stop, we found an opportunity to take a stroll together. We never spoke of the past. It was an overcrowded, inadequately locked chamber whose bolts must never be touched.

Sitting side by side next to the buffer stop of a siding or on a damp stack of railroad ties, we tried to feel our way toward the mystery that was awaiting us, that neither of us knew: the front line. For the farther we were hauled into this dark land, the clearer it became that nothing we encountered here would be comparable to the kind of war we had been experiencing in France. Here anything wearing a gray uniform was filled with a frightening urge to get as far to the rear as possible.

This army had never recovered from the shock of that first disastrous winter. The wounded with whom we spoke were waiting tensely for the train to move on, farther back, without stopping. Every minute in this country seemed wasted; all they wanted was to get farther back from the front, not only quickly but also as far back as possible. It was painful to listen to their illusions on the subject of Germany. Would that country, now also dirty, mangled, wretched, and starving, where barracks had become prisons and hospitals had become barracks—would that country live up to their dreams?

A week later we stopped at a fair-sized station said to be not far from the headquarters of Army Group South. Here, after being fed miserable rations (supplied in France) throughout the journey, we were suddenly provided with an excellent meal: there was some good soup, plenty of meat and potatoes, and at the end a distribution of candies, schnapps, and cigarettes.

There was even champagne, and I was lucky enough, when lots were drawn, to win a whole bottle that we had been meant to share. It was very cold, the stove in our car glowed, and I can well remember opening the train door a crack and, while I looked out, drinking up the bottle as I absent-mindedly filled and emptied, filled and emptied, my mug, at the same time breathing in the icy air. I felt stupefied.

Having enjoyed all those delicacies, we suddenly found ourselves being unloaded, and after lining up, we started out on a long, wearisome march to the nearest airfield. That was in the afternoon.

Next morning, while it was still dark, we launched our first attack.

What a glorious ring there is to those words: to launch an attack! It sounds like a fanfare, seems to tell of keen young warriors who—in obedience to the stratagems of war—can barely suppress the song on their lips as they attack, attack with exultant hearts.

We, by contrast, had deplaned in early-morning darkness and had to suffer grievously for our premature insobriety. Crammed tightly together in trucks, half suffocated by weapons and packs, we had been driven toward the front line and spent a further two hours in strange houses in a strange village. Each sound coming from the nearby front triggered new fears, it being impossible to relate such sounds to anything one had previously experienced. Thus I was scared over and over again by the sudden high-pitched bark of an antitank cannon that seemed to be positioned right behind our building. Each time I believed that Russian tanks were at our door, and each time I experienced mortal fear.

The light in that little room where we all huddled together had gone out, and when things finally quieted down I simply leaned back in the darkness, searching among shoulders, legs, heads, and weapons for a bit of space, and closed my eyes. A vile stench filled the room. Apparently a barrel of pickled cucumbers had begun to ferment and had burst; the floor was awash with a disgusting, reeking liquid, and our groping hands kept touching the soft, nauseating objects strewn around. I smoked incessantly, if only to keep down my nausea; no one said a word. We had imagined it all quite different, not quite so bad and not so terribly sudden.

It was still dark when we were ordered outside, where to my joy I recognized your brother's voice. The little yard was packed with soldiers, as I could see when the red flash from a cannon briefly illuminated it. A company: that word represents so many living souls, so many destinies, yet how much did a company amount to on this front!

Your brother explained, briefly and seriously, that he would be in command of us, that we had been ordered to seal off a breach. Truly a task for novices! It was appallingly difficult to organize the company in the dark, to hand over the groups and platoons to their respective leaders. I was called out by him and could tell by the grip of his trembling fingers when he grabbed me by the sleeve that he too was scared.

"You stay with me," he said huskily.

Well before dawn we left the village, guided by a sergeant from the staff of the regiment to which we had been assigned. Oh, what a long way we still had to go to reach the actual front! A relief, at least, to have earth under one's feet. In front and behind, seemingly all around us in fact, were gun flares and detonations. It would have been impossible to determine the battle line from these indications. The sergeant knew nothing for certain either. Who did! He told us in a whisper, as we marched along, that a whole battalion had been taken by surprise here, some of them killed, some taken prisoner; a few survivors had managed to escape. It was still uncertain whether the Russians had occupied the position, or whether, surprised by their own success, they had merely withdrawn with booty and prisoners to their own positions.

Strangely enough, those constant detonations didn't bother us much. What was terrible was the dark silence lying ahead of us, and we had to march into that darkness until we met resistance or reached the old positions. It was our job to determine the actual battle line, if possible to reoccupy the old positions and hold them.

There were four of us in the lead: your brother and the sergeant in front, while I followed with a corporal. Sometimes when I think back to those days, I believe that war is an element. When a man falls into water he gets wet, and when a man moves around at the front, where infantrymen and sappers dig themselves into the ground, he is in the war. That atmosphere is an acid test: there are only good fellows and bad; all intermediate categories either fail or rise to the occasion.

My instinct told me: the NCO walking beside me was a bastard. He was a coward, saturated with fear and abandoning himself to it without resistance. The way he flung himself to the ground when your brother or the sergeant softly passed on the command was enough to tell me that he would be capable of anything. There was something uncontrolled, something brutish, about the way he immediately hurled himself down and hugged the earth. The sergeant was very calm; he radiated a quality that can only be called courage, a spiritual aura stronger than fear.

Meeting no resistance, not even from rifle fire, we reached the line; on both sides was a lively exchange of fire, while ahead of us there still seemed to be that dark, silent cotton batting that was going to absorb us.

The sergeant's hearing was fantastically accurate. From among all those sounds, small and large, he pinpointed the one: that of a Very flare pistol being discharged. He dropped instantly to the ground, the signal for us to hiss the command to those behind us so we would no longer be visible in the brilliance of the silver flash.

At each flare I would try to recognize something, but there was only the dark, black earth, with many, many indistinct mounds that could just as well have been plowed furrows as crouching men.

My God, how often have I wondered at the immensity of the power that—despite cowardice and fear—induces millions of men to stagger passively on toward death, as we were doing that night.

We reached the old positions, meeting no resistance and suffering no losses. For the first time we trod in the dark on corpses; for the first time we prepared ourselves for a potential enemy lying in wait for us eighty or a hundred yards away. Everything had to be done incredibly fast. Before daybreak the platoons had to be at their battle stations, the rest of the men in their positions, and contact had to be established with the units on our left and right that had not fallen back.

Perhaps this so-called front is imagined as a straight line, drawn with a ruler on a map by a general-staff officer. Actually it is a very tortuous affair, receding and projecting, a highly irregular snake that adapts to the terrain or is forced by enemy pressure onto unfavorable ground.

How much we had to do in a single hour if daylight was to find our defenses prepared! On the right, no contact could be established. A corporal and two men sent out to look for the nearest German sentry on the right never came back: we never heard or saw anything of them again. Another patrol, accompanied by your brother, moved a bit farther back and discovered that we had advanced much too far on the right. The whole line had to shift and adjust, and all that in total silence, in the dark, in a terrain pockmarked by shell holes. Corpses lay all around—Germans and Russians; weapons, parts of equipment. . . .

The company battle station was located almost in the center of the sector, slightly to the rear. There were two bunkers, each with space for three men. Telephone communication had been cut off. Try to imagine the state of mind of a telephone operator who has been sitting for three years in a hotel room in France, connecting the banal chitchat of the various staffs: now he is in Russia, in a situation fraught with danger, and has been ordered to repair and check the telephone line, half an hour before dawn.

The sergeant was a quiet, slight man, pale and unshaven. The usual decorations dangled casually from his chest. His job done, he stayed on with our group long enough to smoke a cigarette. We hardly spoke, but when he stood up to say good-bye he said with a smile—it sounded almost like an apology—"I'm due to go on leave tonight." He slung his machine pistol on his back, shrugged his shoulders, and shook hands all around; then he drew aside the blanket that shielded the bunker toward the rear.

The next moment he lay dead at our feet.

The shell struck the escarpment of the trench; the dark sky seemed to collapse—the light had gone out. The corporal screamed like a madman; and when, covered with clods of earth and fighting down my fear, I raised myself forcibly, I touched a bleeding body, my hand sank into a foul, wet mass, and I screamed too. Meanwhile your brother had drawn the blanket across again, and switched on his flashlight, revealing a ghastly sight. The legs of the dead sergeant stuck out from under the blanket, into the bunker, and the corporal's right leg had been severed below the knee. Our cigarettes were still alight: your brother held his between his lips.

"Bandage him," he told me, his face pale. He stepped outside.

The artillery barrage continued. We became familiar with the sound of Russian mortars, the horrible whine of the heavy artillery shells that seemed to be driving death before them. While the earth trembled all around us, I bandaged the whimpering corporal. With some vague notion of making a tourniquet, I rashly tore off my suspenders—the next day I would have taken his since by then he no longer needed them, whereas for me there were occasions later when the lack of them almost cost me my life. I made a tourniquet around the stump and wrapped gauze and rags, as many as I could find, over the bleeding wound. When I tried to leave the bunker, the wounded man clung to me, but I had made up my mind to die under the open sky and I pushed him away.

Outside, the darkness was lit up by brief red flames; it looked as if fire were leaping from the earth, fire instantly to be covered by darkness again.

That short barrage seemed to go on forever. I thought the entire eastern front must be in turmoil, a giant offensive under way. Actually it lasted—your brother had checked it on his wristwatch—seven minutes and was comparatively harmless. The company's casualties were four dead and seven wounded.

We were all totally exhausted after the rigors of the train journey, the march, the flight, and again the journey by truck—and now this concentrated encounter with the front. But we were to learn that there was no longer any such thing as sleep, although there were hours when one simply sank into oblivion, slept as if dead, was dragged to one's feet, stood sentry or was sent off to one of the other platoons as a dispatch runner.

In those first nights—during the day it was hardly possible to move outside our sector—I invariably lost my sense of direction. There I would lie, stretched out on the earth, darkness all around, waiting for a flare to go up that would allow me to recognize some landmark that would tell me whether I had to crawl forward, backward, or sideways. Sometimes, when I eventually crawled off, I was aware in that singing, cold silence of something eerie, something indescribable, like an invisible, inaudible, yet palpable breath: the proximity of the enemy. I would know then that I was quite close to the Russian positions, and often a hoarse whisper or call, a terrible, alien laugh, confirmed that I was not mistaken.

Oh, that fear of being taken prisoner by the Russians! It was that fear alone that prevented the war in Russia from ending as early as 1942. Imagine, if you will, what would have happened if our soldiers had been made to fight there for years under the same inhuman conditions, the same incompetent leadership, against the Americans or the British.

We remained in that sector for one week.

X

THE ATTACK expected for the morning of the following day did not come until evening. During this attack, something occurred that I would never have believed possible: we repulsed it.

From the moment I saw the first shapeless, muffled-up figures really and truly a hundred yards away from us approaching our sector—from that moment on I stood totally prepared to flee, my whistle at my lips, braced against the rear wall of the trench, one hand poised for the leap. Your brother stood there quite calmly, giving the orders that we had to pass on. Every few seconds we had to duck when a wave of Russian fire seemed to burst right in our faces, and every time that appalling fear when one could raise one's head again: Are they here?

From time to time I would look back to make sure of a retreat under cover, for one of the old soldiers had told me, between two gulps from a bottle of schnapps, "What matters most in this whole war, kiddo, is a retreat under cover."

The Russians came surging forward, forced over and over again by the scythelike action of our machine-gun fire to fling themselves to the ground: the screams of the wounded were already filling the thick gray air. From the rear we were supported by heavy artillery, while the neighboring companies also aimed their fire in front of our sector. Still, it seemed hopeless to try to stem that relentless tide. Just then your brother suddenly gave the order, "Prepare to attack!" Hardly had he uttered the command when a heavy salvo of Russian naval guns forced us to take cover. I ducked, and it flashed through my mind: This is it, you can't go back, by now the Russians are here. But suddenly your brother's voice shouted, "Forward, charge!"

He was the first to go over the top: with a frenzied gesture and another shout, he swept the entire company after him, and charge forward we did. At first the Russians hesitated, but that moment was enough; first a few of them started running, then whole groups turned tail—we could hear the shrill yelling and cursing of their officers while the rest put up their hands. We brought back twenty prisoners, the first living Russians we had seen face to face; their eyes held only one thing—fear.

The evening of the eighth day, I was sitting, for the first time in a long while, alone with your brother in the bunker. While we waited tensely for the ration runners, we drank schnapps and smoked cigarettes. The stretcher bearer had gone back with the ration runners to pick up medicines, bandages, and antitetanus ampules, for if anyone was wounded in the daytime, we had to leave him lying where he was until nightfall. Your brother sat by the phone, and I squatted at his feet on the flattened pile of straw on which we slept.

"The whole secret of attack," he suddenly said, after we had been silent for a long time, "is to imagine how scared the enemy is. Imagine yourself crouching in your hole and you suddenly see some characters charging at you and yelling their heads off! You go crazy with fear; you saw that on Tuesday—we lost all self-control. You have to force the enemy to become passive. Then he's done for."

"You've found the secret of how to win the war," I said dryly. "Sell it for a fortune, and you've got it made."

He gave a quick laugh, then his expression grew serious again, and he lit another cigarette. "But the terrible thing is that one doesn't know which side one wants to win. . . ."

At this moment the stretcher bearer rushed in, shouting, "We're being relieved, sir, we're being relieved!"

What was happening was that the front, whose defense was demanding increasingly pointless sacrifices, was being shortened; the lines were allowed to shrink, and for several days a few units could be saved that were then sent back to the front to reinforce the shortened line. Whatever the reason, it was wonderful to go back to the rear for at least a brief respite. The ration runner hadn't bothered to bring any more rations; we were to have our meal in peace and quiet at the rear. At midnight, when darkness had become solid, we moved off, a sad procession: one week earlier we had moved into position with nearly eighty men, and we were returning with forty-eight.

In the dark it was impossible to make out whether it was the same place. When we actually did reach the village I was filled with a fantastic feeling of life.

Your brother was kept busy for a while, making sure his men were properly accommodated, supervising the distribution of rations. He gave orders that the following day the men would be off duty, attended to a pile of tiresome paperwork in the orderly room, and instructed me to heat up enough water for a thorough wash.

We were billeted in a farm cottage whose rough windows had been nailed up with cardboard and then draped with blankets. I lit four bunker lights, one in each corner, and stoked up the stove with plenty of wood. It was almost November. I had lost all desire for sleep, although an hour earlier I could have collapsed from exhaustion. Slowly savoring every mouthful, I emptied my mess kit, washed down the rich bean soup with generous swigs of schnapps, and stuffed the larger of my two pipes so full of tobacco that the pale yellow shreds hung over the edge. Drawing deeply on my pipe, I would drink another schnapps and watch the roaring flames as they devoured the wood in the stove. From time to time I would dip my hand in the bucket to test the heat of the water. With every pull on my pipe I sucked in something precious, indescribable, something that felt good even as I remembered the dead and the wounded: life.

When the water seemed hot enough, I carefully pulled out my underwear from the bag I had collected from the company baggage, chose a decent civilian shirt—light blue with a proper civilized collar—and sniffed it: it still smelled of Cadette's soap.

Slowly, with an intoxicated sensuousness, I washed myself. Imagine, if you can: you live in the ground and receive every day as much or as little liquid as you need barely to satisfy your most elementary thirst; not a single opportunity to wash even your fingertips, yet still having to spend hours crawling over the wet ground. You become matted with dirt. Fortunately, since we were all newcomers, we had been spared the otherwise inevitable lice, those demoralizing vermin that contributed significantly toward our losing the war. Later I was to become familiar with them.

I kept on washing long enough for the fresh lot of water to have heated up again; then I shaved and put on clean underwear and socks. I was filled with exaltation: never had that rotgut tasted so delicious, never had tobacco tasted so good. Just before two, your brother came back. He greeted me wearily, sat down on the bench by the stove, removed his cap, and, with a sudden gesture, flung it onto the floor in the middle of the room.

While he ate, I set the bucket of water on a low wooden stool, put soap and towel beside it, and laid out the underwear I had taken out of his pack.

Then I lay down on a bed in the corner and watched him. When he began to shave, I said, "You still owe me the solution to a riddle you asked me at the station in Abbeville. About the wine salesman . . ."

"Yes," he said with a laugh, "that was two weeks ago; it feels as if it had been in another life."

"It was in another life," I said.

"Maybe you're right—I'll give you the solution before the day is out."

The door opened, and in came Schnecker. We were surprised less at the sight of him than of a new decoration on his chest.

I had jumped to my feet and accorded him the mandatory obeisance. With a wave of the hand he said, "Lie down again."

Your brother greeted him silently and, just as silently, offered him a stool.

Schnecker seated himself astride a chair, lit a cigarette, and proceeded to watch your brother shaving.

I had ample time to observe him as he sat turned sideways toward me. He sat extraordinarily still, almost motionless, but when I looked at him more closely I realized that he was completely drunk. He was at that stage when a drunk man is filled with a leaden stability, when an almost idiotic law of gravity keeps him upright. When he started to speak, it became obvious that I had assumed correctly.

"My friend," he began; his voice, very pinched, came from high up in his throat. "I see you're up to some nice little tricks, my friend, hm?"

"What do you mean?" countered your brother, who had finished shaving. He dried his face and put on his shirt.

"I see you're up to some nice little tricks. I haven't heard a thing about there being no duty tomorrow, and you simply go ahead and order it." He laughed.

Your brother laughed too. "If you haven't heard a thing about it, so much the better."

"But now I have heard about it," said the captain, his tone sharpening as he jerked himself to his feet. "And I'm telling you that it's important for the men to go over their weapons and gear tomorrow—the day after that we're being redeployed, assigned to the Seventeenth, a bit farther south, understand?" By now he was almost shouting.

"I understand perfectly, but first I'm going to see that the men get some sleep. Besides . . ." he hesitated, slowly tied his neckband, ran his hand once more over his hair, looked at Schnecker, and was silent.

"Besides what?" asked the captain.

"Besides," your brother calmly continued, "I would have preferred it if I could have seen you now and then up at the front with me this past week."

"What's that?" A wary look came over the captain's face, and he shot a glance in my direction, but I had closed my eyes and pretended to be asleep. The two men now lowered their voices.

"I would have preferred it if I could have seen you now and then in my sector during this past week. It would have given the men quite a boost, and me too, for that matter. It's dreadful to feel all the time that one is alone. After all, orders are only paper."

"Paper?" asked Schnecker. His expression was now almost maniacal; his voice had slipped too, and he was quite hoarse.

"Yes, paper!" shouted your brother, so loud that I was really startled. "Paper! Paper! A substance inferior even to that gilt tin on your manly chest!"

"Oho!" cried the captain; now he was laughing again. Suddenly he stood stiffly to attention. "I have to inform you, First Lieutenant Schelling," he said raspingly, "that you have been awarded the Iron Cross, First and Second Class, also the Infantry Assault Medal in Silver. You fought damn well. In fifteen minutes the gentlemen of the battalion will be holding a small celebration in your honor and"—he gave a little bow to himself—"in mine too."

He put on his cap and marched out stiff as a ramrod. It was almost as if he hadn't been there at all. Your brother whistled softly as he cleaned his nails, the cigarette between his lips. I rose and put out two of the lights that had begun to flicker and threatened to burst into flames.

"I don't feel much like sleeping now—how about us looking in on the party?"

"Us?" I asked in surprise.

"Of course you're coming along—you're getting a decoration too, maybe a couple."

"What, me?" I exclaimed.

"Of course," he said, laughing. "Besides, there'll be women there. I'd like to have one more chance to see a woman."

"Girls?" I cried.

"Maybe girls too!" He laughed again. "I've no idea what kind will be there. Anyway, they'll be women, and I'd like the chance to have a glass or two of wine with one of them."

"Jesus!" I cried. "Women!"

He stood up and drew on his greatcoat. I put on my cap and slipped into a padded camouflage jacket.

WE STEPPED out together into the cold night; it was quiet, something resembling peace lay spread under the dark vault of the sky. Headquarters were in a large building, something between a palace and a manor house —I imagine it had been the administrative offices of a kolkhoz.

The sentry let us pass without hindrance, although we didn't know the password. We found ourselves walking along dark corridors and managed to rout out a telephone operator who directed us to the third floor. Raucous singing filled the corridor, which smelled of Russia. A door opened, light and noise streamed out onto the corridor, were immediately swallowed up again, and we soon came upon a figure that was staggering toward a window, apparently to throw up.

"Hello, Piester!" cried your brother. The man turned, recognized your brother, and waved. We went closer. He leaned on a window sill and groaned pitifully. It was the adjutant, an agreeable young lieutenant not much given to talking.

As we stood beside him he said, "I can't take any more, Schelling. He keeps forcing me to drink, I can't take any more, but he threatens to shoot anyone who won't drink. I can't take any more." As he leaned over the sill, I followed him with my eyes; below lay a dark, silent garden that appeared to be planted with vines.

"Where's your room?" asked your brother.

"Why do you ask?"

"Come along."

Your brother took Piester by the arm and steered him ahead down the long corridor. Each time Piester hesitated, your brother gave him another push. Piester opened a door.

"Let's have some light," your brother said to me. I fished out my box of matches, and by the light of the burning match we entered the room. Then I closed the door behind me and ran to the window to fasten the blackout curtain.

The room looked bare. On the floor lay a pack; beside the narrow wooden bed stood an officer's trunk, and on it a half-written letter and a candle stuck to the lid. A piece of broken mirror hung on the wall.

We forced Piester onto the bed; his face was yellow.

"Something terrible is going to happen," mumbled Piester, his eyes closing the moment he lay down. "He's run out of schnapps, and the paymaster won't fork out any more. Something terrible—they're expecting you . . ."

We went back onto the corridor. All this time I had been listening, almost apprehensively, for a woman's voice, but even now I could hear nothing but that stupid male yowling.

The moment we opened the door, silence fell in the room. It was a scene of utter debauchery: Schnecker was sitting on the table, his legs spread-eagled, his tunic unbuttoned and revealing curly black hair on his broad chest. Beside him stood an artillery officer holding a bottle of cognac upside down over Schnecker's gaping mouth. After a brief pause they both resumed their bestial yowling.

Over in the corner stood the battalion's medical officer, an elderly bourgeois type; beside him a young Russian woman with soft blond hair and a rosy, peasantlike face: she looked like a girl. I assumed her to be the doctor's mistress, a doctor herself, of whom I had heard a good deal when collecting our rations. She was said to be very skillful at bandaging and very kind to the wounded. Now she was watching the scene at the table with a completely dispassionate curiosity, while her lover, looking very nervous, was holding her tightly by the arm.

"Good evening, gentlemen," said your brother.

Schnecker let out a hoarse roar and tried to jump off the table, but he slipped and would have struck it head first if we hadn't caught him in time. The artillery officer smashed the empty bottle onto the floor and looked at us idiotically.

"Good evening," your brother repeated, smiling in the direction of the Russian woman, who bowed slightly and smiled back at us.

We helped Schnecker down from his wedged position on the table. "Not a drop of booze left!" he shouted. "Goddamn it, not a drop left. My good friend Karlemann has just squeezed the last drops out of the bottle for me!" He gratefully patted the artillery officer, who was still laughing idiotically.

"Well!" said your brother. "You're a fine host, I must say. When I arrive there's nothing left!"

Schnecker stared at him. Those bloodshot eyes were hot and ugly.

I could look only at the Russian woman; the mere sight of her soft, rosy skin gave me a pang of happiness, and I trembled as she approached. She kept her eyes firmly on Schnecker as she took her doddering old medical officer by the hand and walked without a sound to the door.

Meanwhile Schnecker had been having an incoherent, raucous dialogue with the artillery officer, but when the Russian woman was almost at the door—I had stepped aside and was close enough to be aware of how crisp and clean she smelled—Schnecker swung around in a flash and, his mouth agape with laughter, shouted, "Stop, my girl—not yet! You have to have another drink with me!" The medical officer had freed his hand and stepped back.

"But you've nothing more to drink!" said the woman, her voice as clear as ringing metal.

"There's more on the way!" He careened around the table, guffawed, dashed to the door, flung it open, and screamed, "Alarm! Alarm! Alarm!"

At first we didn't understand and stood rooted to the spot. Even the artillery officer seemed to have sobered up a bit. Schnecker came back and called out to us, "Now he'll have to get out of bed, that stinker—then we'll have some booze!"

Your brother sighed and took a deep breath, flung himself at Schnecker, and thrust him out into the dark corridor. I followed them, the woman screamed, the medical officer shouted, "My God . . . my God . . ." while the artillery officer tried in vain to get around the table, stammering, "Karlemann . . . Karlemann . . ."

Schnecker was now wrestling outside with your brother: he was a muscular fellow, and drunkenness must have doubled his strength. I ran to them, grabbed him from behind, and dragged him over to the window, meanwhile pummeling away at him in my towering rage. Somewhere in the dark the last of his decorations fell with a tinny sound onto the tiled floor. Schnecker groaned, spat, bit, and, whenever he managed to free his mouth, which your brother was clamping shut, screamed like a madman, "Alarm! Alarm!"

When an orderly came up from downstairs and asked what was going on, your brother called out to him, "Nothing, he's drunk." By this time we were pretty close to the window, but now the artillery officer had also slipped through the door and was attacking your brother from behind; furthermore, a staff sergeant came running along the corridor shouting, "What's going on? What is it?"

"Alarm!" yelled Schnecker. "Alarm!"

"Nothing," shouted your brother. "He's drunk!"

He now had Schnecker by the throat, while I had tripped the artillery officer and was preventing him from getting up.

Schnecker had been forced over to the window. He was groaning and seemed to be bleeding somewhere. "Don't you realize, you bastard," your brother said to him, "that the other hundred and twenty men in your battalion can use a few hours' sleep?"

Schnecker, who by this time had freed himself, yelled even louder, "Alarm! I am ordering alarm!" And when your brother, suddenly seized by a sort of frenzy, punched him right in the face, Schnecker, in a lightning move, drew his pistol, held it to your brother's temple, and pressed the trigger. Your brother was dead on the spot: he fell to the floor across the whimpering artillery officer. Schnecker had turned pale; his hand was still holding the pistol. There was an eerie silence: I was about to fling myself on him, but at that moment the first Russian tank started firing outside the building. We stared at each other. Hideous bursts of firing shattered the sky. Schnecker had already run off down the corridor. I dashed after him but on the way ran into Piester's room and shouted in his ear, "The Russians are here—move!" Then I ran down the stairs to the ground-floor corridor and jumped out the window into the garden.

I managed to escape and from a distance saw that the great building was in flames. I kept running until I was scooped up by another regiment and sent back to the front. Not one man from our unit escaped. The Russians had overrun the village from three sides and in great numerical superiority. And although I never saw Schnecker again, or was ever told, I knew he had managed to get away. He can't die. I assumed that in some way or other he would inform your mother of your brother's death. He has done nothing. He just goes on living. All this I learned during the last few days.

I PASS the truth on to you. It belongs to you. . . .

Business Is Business

M Y BLACK marketeer is an honest citizen these days; it was a long time
since I had seen him, months in fact, and today I came across him
in quite a different part of the city, at a busy intersection. He has a wooden
booth there now, all done up in the best white paint; a handsome corrugated iron roof, solid and brand-new, shields him from rain and cold, and
he sells cigarettes and all-day suckers, quite legally. At first I was pleased;
it is always nice, after all, to see someone find his way back to normal life.
For when we first met, things were going badly for him, and we were
depressed. We still went around in our old army caps, and whenever I came
by some cash I used to go and see him, and we would have a chat, about
being hungry, about the war; and now and again, when I didn't have any
money, he would give me a cigarette, or I would take along some bread-
ration coupons, as I happened to be clearing rubble for a baker at the time.

He seemed to be doing all right now. He looked the picture of health.
His cheeks had that firmness that comes only from a regular intake of fats,
his expression was self-confident, and I watched him bawl out a grubby
little girl and send her packing because she was short five pfennigs for an
all-day sucker. And all the time he kept feeling around in his mouth with
his tongue as if he were forever trying to pry shreds of meat from between
his teeth.

Business was brisk; they were buying a lot of cigarettes from him,
and all-day suckers as well.

Maybe I shouldn't have—I went up to him and said, "Ernst," intending to have a word with him.

He was very surprised, gave me an odd look, and said, "What's that?"
I could see he recognized me but that he wasn't too keen on being
recognized.

I was silent. I behaved as if I had never said "Ernst" to him, bought
some cigarettes, since I happened to have some cash, and left. I watched
him a while longer; my streetcar wasn't in sight yet, and I didn't feel in

the least like going home. At home I'm always being pestered by people wanting money—my landlady asking for the rent, and the man with the electricity bill. Besides, I'm not allowed to smoke at home; my landlady always manages to smell it, she gets mad and I'm told that I seem to have money for tobacco but none for the rent. It's a sin, you see, for the poor to smoke or drink. I know it's a sin, that's why I do it secretly, I smoke outdoors, and just occasionally when I'm lying awake and everything is quiet, when I know that by morning the smell will have disappeared, then I smoke in my room too.

The terrible thing is that I have no profession. For you have to have a profession. That's what they tell you. There was a time when they used to say it was unnecessary, all we needed was soldiers. But now they say you have to have a profession. Just like that. They say you are lazy when you don't have a profession. But that's not so. I'm not lazy, but the jobs they give me are jobs I don't want to do. Clearing rubble and carrying rocks, and things like that. After two hours I'm soaked with sweat, everything becomes a blur, and when I go to the doctors they tell me there's nothing wrong. Maybe it's nerves. Nowadays they talk a lot about nerves. But I believe it's a sin for the poor to have nerves. To be poor and to have nerves, that seems to be more than they can stand. But my nerves are all shot, I can tell you that; I was a soldier too long. Nine years, I think. Maybe more, I'm not sure. Once upon a time I would have been glad to have a profession, I wanted very much to go into business. But once upon a time —what's the use of talking about it? Now I don't even feel like going into business any more. What I like to do best is lie on my bed and daydream. I figure out how many hundreds of thousands of man-hours they need to build a bridge or a big house and then I think that in a single minute they can smash both the bridge and the house. So what's the point of working? To my mind there's no sense in working. I think that's what drives me crazy when I have to carry rocks or clear rubble so they can build another café.

A minute ago I was saying it was nerves, but I think that's the real reason: it's all so senseless.

Actually I don't care what they think. But it's terrible never to have any money. You've simply got to have money. You can't get along without it. There's a meter, and you have a lamp, naturally you need light sometimes, you switch it on, and right away the money's pouring out of the light bulb. Even when you don't need any light, you have to pay rent for the meter. That's the whole trouble: rent. It seems you've got to have a room. At first I lived in a cellar, it wasn't too bad down there—I had a stove and used to steal briquettes; but they unearthed me, they came from the newspaper, took my picture, wrote an article to go with the picture:

"Returning Veteran Lives in Poverty." I had to move, that's all there was to it. The man from the housing office said it was a matter of prestige for him and I had to take the room. Sometimes, of course, I make some money. Obviously. I run errands, deliver briquettes and stack them up nice and neatly in a corner of someone's cellar. I am very good at stacking briquettes, and I don't charge much either. Needless to say, I don't earn much; it's never enough for the rent, sometimes it's enough for the electricity, a few cigarettes and bread. . . .

I was thinking of all this as I stood at the corner.

My black marketeer, who is now an honest citizen, threw me a suspicious look from time to time. That bastard knows perfectly well who I am, people do know each other, after all, when they've spoken to one another almost every day for two years. Maybe he thought I was going to steal something. I'm not as dumb as all that, to steal something at a busy spot with streetcars stopping every minute and even a cop standing at the corner. I steal things in quite different places: naturally I steal things sometimes, things like coal. Wood too. The other day I even stole a loaf in a bakery. You wouldn't believe how quick and easy it was. I just took the loaf and walked out, I walked along quite calmly, as far as the next corner, then I started to run. I've lost the nerve I used to have, that's all.

I certainly wouldn't steal anything at a corner like that, although sometimes it's easy, but I've lost my nerve. Several streetcars stopped, including my own, and I could see Ernst looking sidelong at me when mine came up. That bastard still remembers which is my streetcar!

But I threw away the butt of my first cigarette, lit another, and stayed where I was. I've progressed that far, at least, that I throw away butts. Yet over there someone was creeping around picking up butts, and you have to think of the other fellow. There are still some people who pick up cigarette butts. They aren't always the same ones. In the POW camp I had seen colonels doing it, but this one wasn't a colonel. I watched him. He had his own system, like a spider lurking in its web he had his headquarters somewhere in a pile of rubble, and whenever a streetcar stopped or started up he would emerge and walk unhurriedly along the curb collecting the butts. I would have liked to go up to him and speak to him; I feel we are two of a kind. But I know it's no use; those fellows never say anything.

I don't know what was the matter with me, but that day I just didn't want to go home. The very word: home. . . . I was past caring now, I let one more streetcar go by and lit another cigarette. I don't know what's wrong with us. Maybe some professor will find out one day and write an article about it in the paper; they have an explanation for everything. I only wish I still had the nerve to steal things, like I did in the war. In those days I used to be quick and easy. In those days, during the war, when there was anything to be stolen, it was we who had to go out and steal it; they used to say: Don't worry, he knows how to do it, and off we would go to steal something. The others just helped eat and drink up the stuff, send it home and all that, but they didn't steal anything. Their nerves were in perfect shape, and they managed to keep their copybooks clean.

And when we came home they got out of the war as if they were getting out of a streetcar that happened to slow down just where they lived, and they jumped off without paying the fare. They turned aside, went indoors, and lo and behold: the dresser was still standing, there was a little dust on the bookshelves, your wife had potatoes stored in the cellar, and some preserves; you embraced her a bit, as was right and proper, and next morning you went off to find out whether your job was still open: the job was still open. Everything was fine, your medical insurance was still OK, you had yourself de-Nazified a bit—the way you go to the barber to get rid of that tiresome beard—you chatted about decorations, wounds, acts of heroism, and came to the conclusion you were a pretty fine fellow after all: you had simply done your duty. There were weekly streetcar passes again, the best sign that everything was back to normal.

Meanwhile the rest of us stayed on the streetcar and waited to see if somewhere there would be a stop that seemed familiar enough for us to risk getting off: it never came. Some people went on a bit farther, but they jumped off somewhere too, trying to look as if they had reached their destination.

But we went on and on. The fare went up automatically, and we had to pay for our bulky, heavy baggage as well: for the leaden mass of nothingness that we had to lug around with us. First one inspector got on, then another, and we would shrug our shoulders and show them our empty pockets. They couldn't throw us off, the streetcar was going too fast—"and we were human beings after all"—but they wrote down our names, over and over again they wrote down our names, the streetcar went faster and faster; the smart ones jumped off quickly, anywhere; fewer and fewer of us stayed on, and fewer and fewer of us had the guts or the desire to get off. At the back of our minds, we meant to leave our baggage on the streetcar, to let the Lost and Found auction it off as soon as we reached the terminus; but the terminus never came, the fare went up and up, the streetcar went faster and faster, the inspectors got more and more skeptical —we are a highly suspect lot.

I threw away the butt of my third cigarette and walked slowly across to the streetcar stop; I wanted to go home now. I felt dizzy: one shouldn't smoke so much on an empty stomach, I know that. I quit looking over to where my former black marketeer was now carrying on a legitimate business. I really have no right to be angry; he made it, he jumped off, probably at the right moment, but I don't know whether it's all right for him to bawl out kids who are short five pfennigs for an all-day sucker. Maybe that's all part of legitimate business; I wouldn't know.

Just before my streetcar arrived, the bum walked unhurriedly along the curb again, in front of the ranks of waiting people, to collect butts. They don't like to see that, I know. They would rather it wasn't that way, but that's the way it is. . . .

I didn't look at Ernst again until I was on the streetcar, but he glanced away and shouted, "Chocolate, candy, cigarettes, all ration-free!" I don't know what's wrong, but I must say I liked him better before, when he didn't need to send anyone away who was short five pfennigs; but now of course he has a proper business, and business is business.

On the Hook

I KNOW IT's stupid. I ought to stop going there; it's so senseless, yet going there is what keeps me alive. A single minute of hope and twenty-three hours and fifty-nine minutes of despair. That's what keeps me alive. It's not much; there's precious little substance to it. I ought to stop going there. It's killing me, that's what: it's killing me. But I've got to go, I've got to, I've got to. . . .

The train she's supposed to arrive on is always the same one, the 1:20 p.m. The train always pulls in on time—I keep a sharp eye on everything, they can't fool me.

The man with the baton is always ready for me when I turn up; when he comes out of his little signal house—I've already heard the signal bell ringing inside it—as I say, when he comes out, I go over to him, he knows me by this time: he puts on a sympathetic expression, sympathetic and a bit scared. Yes, the man with the baton is scared; maybe he thinks I'll go for him one day. I might at that, one of these days, I might beat him up, kill him, and dump his body between the tracks to be run over by the 1:20. You see, that man with the baton—I don't trust him. I don't know whether his pity is an act or not; maybe it's just an act. He's scared all right, that's genuine enough, and he has good reason to be: one day I'll beat his brains out with his own baton. I don't trust him; maybe he's in cahoots with them. After all, he does have a phone in his signal house—all he has to do is crank the handle and call them up—those railroad jokers get through in a second. Maybe he lifts the receiver, phones the last-but-one station, and tells them, "Take her off the train, arrest her; don't let her get back on. . . . What? . . . That's right, the woman with the brown hair and the little green hat; yes, that's the one, hold on to her"—then he laughs—"that's right, that nut's here again; we'll let him wait for nothing again. Be sure you hold on to her, now."

He hangs up and laughs; then he comes out, puts on his pitying expression when he sees me shuffling over to him, and says, as he always does even before I ask him, "Right on time again, sir, same as usual!"

This not knowing whether I can trust him is driving me crazy. Perhaps he grins the moment he turns his back on me. He always does turn his back on me and acts as if he had something important to do, like on the platform; he walks up and down, waves people back from the edge of the platform, finds all sorts of things to do that are quite superfluous, for the people step back from the edge anyway as soon as they see him coming. He's just putting on a show, pretending to be busy, and perhaps he grins the moment he turns his back. Once I wanted to test him—I darted round in front of him and looked him straight in the face. But there was nothing there to confirm my suspicions: only fear. . . .

All the same, I don't trust him, those fellows have more self-control than our sort; they're capable of anything. It's a kind of clique that's got strength and security, while we—the ones who wait—have nothing. We live on a razor's edge, balancing from one minute of hope to the next minute of hope. For twenty-three hours and fifty-nine minutes we balance on the razor's edge; one minute's respite is all we get. They have us on a tight rein, those fellows, those jokers with their batons, those stinkers, they call each other up, exchange a couple of words, and our life is down the drain again, down the drain again for twenty-three hours and fifty-nine minutes. They're the ones who run the show, those bastards. . . .

His pity is an act, I'm quite sure of that now. When I really think about it, I have to acknowledge that he's double-crossing me. They're all crooks. They're holding on to her; I know she meant to come, she told me so in a letter: "I love you, and I'm coming on the 1:20 p.m." Arriving 1:20 p.m., she wrote; that was three months ago, three months and four days exactly. They're keeping her back, they don't want us to meet, they begrudge me the chance of ever having more than one minute's hope, let alone joy. They're preventing our rendezvous; somewhere or other they're sitting and laughing, they're all in it together. They laugh and call each other up, and that stinker with the baton gets paid, and well paid too, for telling me day after day, in that mealy-mouthed way of his, "Right on time again, sir, same as usual!" Even the "sir" is an insult. No one ever calls me "sir," I'm a poor down-and-out bastard who lives on one minute of hope a day. That's all. No one ever calls me "sir," shit on his "sir." They can do it to me backwards but they've got to let her go, let her get back on that train; they've got to give her to me, she's mine; didn't she send me a telegram, "I love you, arriving there 1:20 p.m."? "There" means where I live. That's what telegrams are like: you write "there," and you mean the town where the other person lives. "Arriving there 1:20 p.m." . . .

Today I'm going to do him in. I'm about ready to blow my top. My patience is exhausted, my strength too. I'm at the end of my tether. If I see him today, he's had it. It's been going on too long. Besides, I've no more money. No more money for the streetcar. I've already sold everything I own. For three months and four days I've been living off capital. I've sold the lot, even the tablecloth. I can't kid myself any more—today there's nothing left. There's just enough for one streetcar ride. Not even enough for the return trip, I'll have to walk back . . . or . . . or . . .

In any case that bastard with the baton will be lying down there between the tracks, a bloody mess, and the 1:20 will run over him, he'll be wiped out, just as I'll be wiped out this afternoon at 1:20 . . . or . . . Christ!

It's really too much when you don't even have money for the return trip; they make things too hard for a man. The clique sticks together; they control hope, they control paradise, consolation. They've got their talons round everything. We're only allowed to nibble at it, for a single minute a day. For twenty-three hours and fifty-nine minutes we have to hanker after it, lie in wait for it; they even refuse to dole out the artificial paradises. And they don't even need them; I wonder why they hang on to everything? Is it just for the sake of the money? Why don't they ever give a man money for booze or smokes, why do they put such a terrible price on consolation? They keep us dangling on the hook, and every time we bite, every time we let ourselves be pulled up to the surface, every time we breathe light, beauty, joy for one minute, some bastard laughs, slackens the line, and there we are back in the dark. . . .

They make things too hard for us; today I'm going to get my revenge. I'm going to take that stinker with the baton, that outpost of security, and dump him between the tracks. Maybe that'll give them a fright, sitting back there by their phones—Christ, if only a fellow could frighten them, just once! But you haven't a chance, that's the trouble. They hold on to everything: bread, wine, tobacco, they've got the lot, and they've got her too: "Arriving there 1:20 p.m." No date. That's the trouble: she never writes the date.

They're jealous because I might have kissed her. No, no, no, we have to perish, suffocate, despair utterly, go without consolation, sell everything we own, and when we've nothing left we have to . . .

For that's the terrible part about it—the minute is shrinking. I've noticed it the last few days: the minute is shrinking. I think it may be only thirty seconds now, perhaps much less, I don't even dare work out how much really is left. Yesterday, anyway, I noticed it was less. Up till then, whenever the train came in sight round the curve, black and snorting against the city's spreading horizon, I was always conscious of being happy. She's coming, I used to think, she's got through, she's coming! I would go on thinking that the whole time, till the train came to a halt, the people got slowly out—the platform gradually emptied . . . and . . . nothing. . . .

No, then I wasn't thinking that any more. I must try above all to be honest with myself. When the first people got out and she wasn't among them, I wasn't thinking that any more, it was all over. That happiness—it wasn't that it stopped sooner, it began later. That's how it was. One must be honest and objective about it. It began later, that's how it was. It used to begin when the train came in sight, black and snorting against the city's spreading horizon; yesterday it didn't begin until the train had come to a halt. When it had stopped moving altogether, when it was just standing there, that's when I began to hope; and when it was standing there, the doors were already opening . . . and she didn't come. . . .

Now I'm wondering whether that lasted even thirty seconds. I haven't the nerve to be quite honest and say: It's only one second . . . and . . . twenty-three hours, fifty-nine minutes, and fifty-nine seconds of black darkness. . . .

I haven't the nerve; I can scarcely bring myself to go back there; it would be too horrible if not even this second were left. Are they going to take that away from me too?

It's too little. There are limits. A certain amount of substance is needed by even the lowliest of creatures, even the lowliest of creatures needs at least one second a day. They mustn't take this one second away from me; they're making it too short.

Their callousness is assuming terrible forms. Now I don't even have the money for the return trip. Not even for the fare straight there and back, let alone transfer, as I have to. I'm short exactly a nickel. Their callousness is cruel. They've even stopped buying. They don't even want to buy things now. Until now they've always been screaming to buy things. But now their greed has become so appalling that they're sitting on their money and devouring it. I really do believe they devour their money. I wonder what for? What do they want? They've got bread, wine, tobacco, they've got money, everything, they've got their fat women—what else do they want? Why have they stopped shelling out? No money, not an ounce of bread, no tobacco, not a drop of schnapps . . . nothing . . . nothing. They're forcing me to extreme measures.

I shall have to take up the struggle. I'm going to finish off that outpost of theirs, that bastard with his baton and his pitying expression, he screws me every time he talks to them on the phone! He's in cahoots with them, I know that now for certain, because yesterday I listened in on him! That bastard's double-crossing me, I'm sure of that now. I went much earlier yesterday, much earlier, he couldn't have known I was there; I ducked down under the window and waited, and sure enough!—he cranked the handle, the bell tinkled, and I heard his voice. "Superintendent," he said, "Superintendent, something's got to be done about it. The fellow can't be allowed to go on like that. After all, the security of a civil servant is at stake! Superintendent," his voice implored—that bastard really was scared stiff. "That's right, Platform 4b."

Very well, so now I've got proof. Now they'll take drastic measures. Now they're really going to finish me off. Now it's a fight to the finish. At least the position is clear. I'm glad of that. I shall fight like a lion. I'll run down the whole lot of them, herd them all together, and toss them in front of the 1:20. . . .

Not one thing are they willing to let me keep. They're driving me to desperation; they want to rob me of my last second. And they've even stopped buying. Not even watches—till now they've always been keen on watches. All I got for my books was three pounds of tea—two hundred pretty nice books at that. I imagine they were pretty nice. I used to be very interested in literature. But three pounds of tea for two hundred books— what a lousy deal; the bread I got for the sheets and pillow slips was hardly worth mentioning, my mother's jewelry gave me enough to live on for a month, and you need such a tremendous amount when you live on a razor's edge. Three months and four days is a long time; a fellow needs too much.

As a last resort there's always Father's watch. The watch has a certain value. No one can deny that the watch has a certain value; perhaps it's enough for the return trip; perhaps the conductor has a kind heart and will let me ride back in exchange for the watch; perhaps, perhaps I shall need two tickets for the return trip: Christ!

It's twelve-thirty and I must get ready. That doesn't involve much, nothing at all really. I just have to get out of bed, that's all there is to getting ready. The room is bare, I've sold everything. A fellow has to live, after all. The landlady has taken the mattress for a month's rent. She's a good sort, a really good sort, one of the best I've ever met. A good woman. A fellow can doss down perfectly well on the wire springs. No one knows how well you can sleep on wire springs, if you sleep at all, that is; I never sleep, I live on capital, I live on one second's hope, on the second when the doors open and no one comes. . . .

I must pull myself together; the battle's about to begin. It's a quarter to one, the streetcar passes at ten to; that'll get me to the station on the dot of quarter past, onto the platform by eighteen past; when that joker with the baton comes out of his signal house, I'll be just in time to let him tell me, "Right on time again, sir, same as usual!"

The bastard really does say "sir" to me; everyone else he just bawls out, shouting, "Hey you there—get back from the edge of the platform!" To me he says "sir"! That just shows: it's all a big fake, a horrible big fake. When you look at them, you're tempted to think they're hungry too, that they're all out of tea or tobacco or booze; the expression on their faces is enough to make you almost want to sell your last shirt for them.

A fellow could cry for years over the big fake they put on. I must try to cry; it must be wonderful to cry, a substitute for wine, tobacco, bread, and maybe even a substitute for when the single solitary second is extinct and all I have left is twenty-four naked, entire hours of despair.

I can't cry in the streetcar, of course; I must pull myself together, I really must pull myself together. They mustn't notice anything; and at the station I'll have to watch out. I'm sure they have people hidden somewhere. "After all, the security of a civil servant is at stake . . . Platform 4b." I'll have to be damn careful. It makes me nervous the way the conductress keeps looking at me. She asks several times, "Tickets?" looking only at me. And I really have one; I could pull it out and hold it under her nose, she gave it to me herself, but she's forgotten already. "Tickets?" she asks three times, looking at me. I blush, I really do have one; she moves on, and everyone thinks: He hasn't got one, he's cheating the transit company. And all the time I've given up my last twenty pfennigs, I've even got a transfer. . . .

I must watch out like hell; I very nearly ran through the barrier, like I always do; but they might be standing around anyplace. As I was just about to dash through, I realized I didn't have a platform ticket, or a nickel. It's seventeen minutes past, in three minutes the train will be in, I'm going crazy. "Take this watch," I said. The man looks insulted. "For God's sake, take this watch." He pushes me back. Their excellencies the ticket holders are staring. There's no help for it: I have to go back; it's seventeen and a half minutes past.

"A watch!" I shout. "A watch for a nickel! An honest watch, not a stolen one, a watch that belonged to my father!" Everyone takes me for a nut or a criminal. Not one of those bastards will take my watch. Perhaps they'll call the police. I must find the bums. The bums will help me at least. The bums are all down below. It's eighteen minutes past, I'm going crazy. Am I to miss the train today of all days, the very day she's going to arrive? "Arriving there 1:20 p.m."

"Hey, buddy," I say to the first bum I see, "give me a nickel for this watch, but quick, quick," I say.

He stares too—even he stares. "Listen, buddy," I tell him, "I've got one more minute, understand?"

He understands—he misunderstands, of course, but at least he tries to understand, at least it's something to be misunderstood. At least it's a kind of understanding. The others understand nothing.

He gives me a mark; he's generous. "Listen, buddy," I say, "I need a nickel, get it? Not a mark, understand?"

He misunderstands again, but it's so good to be at least misunderstood; if I get out of this alive I'll hug you, buddy.

He gives me a nickel as well, that's how the bums are, they give a bit extra and at least they misunderstand.

I manage to race up the steps at nineteen and a half minutes past one. But I still have to be on the alert, I have to watch out like crazy. There comes the train, black and snorting against the city's gray horizon. My heart is silent at the sight of it, but I am in time, that's the main thing. In spite of everything, I've managed to get here in time.

I keep well away from the joker with the baton. He is surrounded by people, and suddenly he's caught sight of me, he calls out, he's scared, he waves to the clique hiding in his signal house, waves to them to catch me. They dash out, they've almost got me, but I laugh in their faces, I laugh in their faces, for the train has pulled in and before they get to me she is in my arms, my girl, and all I own in the world is my girl and a platform ticket, my girl and a punched platform ticket. . . .

My Sad Face

WHILE I was standing on the dock watching the seagulls, my sad face attracted the attention of a policeman on his rounds. I was completely absorbed in the sight of the hovering birds as they shot up and swooped down in a vain search for something edible: the harbor was deserted, the water greenish and thick with foul oil, and on its crusty film floated all kinds of discarded junk. Not a vessel was to be seen, the cranes had rusted, the freight sheds collapsed; not even rats seemed to inhabit the black ruins along the wharf, silence reigned. It was years since all connection with the outside world had been cut off.

I had my eye on one particular seagull and was observing its flight. Uneasy as a swallow sensing thunder in the air, it usually stayed hovering just above the surface of the water, occasionally, with a shrill cry, risking an upward sweep to unite with its circling fellows. Had I been free to express a wish, I would have chosen a loaf of bread to feed to the gulls, crumbling it to pieces to provide a white fixed point for the random flutterings, to set a goal at which the birds could aim, to tauten this shrill flurry of crisscross hovering and circling by hurling a piece of bread into the mesh as if to pull together a bunch of strings. But I was as hungry as they were, and tired, yet happy in spite of my sadness because it felt good to be standing there, my hands in my pockets, watching the gulls and drinking in sadness.

Suddenly I felt an official hand on my shoulder, and a voice said, "Come along now!" The hand tugged at my shoulder, trying to pull me round, but I did not budge, shook it off, and said quietly, "You're nuts."

"Comrade," the still-invisible one told me, "I'm warning you."

"Sir," I retorted.

"What d'you mean, 'sir'?" he shouted angrily. "We're all comrades."

With that he stepped round beside me and looked at me, forcing me to bring back my contentedly roving gaze and direct it at his simple, honest face: he was as solemn as a buffalo that for twenty years has had nothing to eat but duty.

"On what grounds . . ." I began.

"Sufficient grounds," he said. "Your sad face."

I laughed.

"Don't laugh!" His rage was genuine. I had first thought he was bored, with no unlicensed whore, no staggering sailor, no thief or fugitive to arrest, but now I saw he meant it: he intended to arrest me.

"Come along now!"

"Why?" I asked quietly.

Before I realized what was happening, I found my left wrist enclosed in a thin chain, and instantly I knew that once again I had had it. I turned toward the swerving gulls for a last look, glanced at the calm gray sky, and tried with a sudden twist to plunge into the water, for it seemed more desirable to drown alone in that scummy dishwater than to be strangled by the sergeants in a backyard or to be locked up again. But the policeman suddenly jerked me so close to him that all hope of wrenching myself free was gone.

"Why?" I asked again.

"There's a law that you have to be happy."

"I am happy!" I cried.

"Your sad face . . ." He shook his head.

"But this law is new," I told him.

"It's thirty-six hours old, and I'm sure you know that every law comes into force twenty-four hours after it has been proclaimed."

"But I've never heard of it!"

"That won't save you. It was proclaimed yesterday, over all the loudspeakers, in all the papers, and anyone"—here he looked at me scornfully—"anyone who doesn't share in the blessings of press or radio was informed by leaflets scattered from the air over every street in the country. So we'll soon find out where you've been spending the last thirty-six hours, comrade."

He dragged me away. For the first time I noticed that it was cold and I had no coat; for the first time I became really aware of my hunger growling at the entrance to my stomach; for the first time I realized that I was also dirty, unshaved, and in rags, and that there were laws demanding that every comrade be clean, shaved, happy, and well fed. He pushed me in front of him like a scarecrow that has been found guilty of stealing and is compelled to abandon the place of its dreams at the edge of the field. The streets were empty, the police station was not far off, and, although I had known they would soon find a reason for arresting me, my heart was heavy, for he took me through the places of my childhood which I had intended to visit after looking at the harbor: public gardens that had been full of bushes, in glorious confusion, overgrown paths—all this was now leveled, orderly, neat, arranged in squares for the patriotic groups obliged to drill and march here on Mondays, Wednesdays, and Saturdays. Only the sky was as it used to be, the air the same as in the old days, when my heart had been full of dreams.

Here and there as we walked along I saw the government sign displayed on the walls of a number of love-barracks, indicating whose turn it was to participate in these hygienic pleasures on Wednesdays; certain taverns also were evidently authorized to hang out the drinking sign, a beer glass cut out of tin and striped diagonally with the national colors: light brown, dark brown, light brown. Joy was doubtless already filling the hearts of those whose names appeared in the official list of Wednesday drinkers and who would thus partake of the Wednesday beer.

All the people we passed were stamped with the unmistakable mark of earnest zeal, encased in an aura of tireless activity probably intensified by the sight of the policeman. They all quickened their pace, assumed expressions of perfect devotion to duty, and the women coming out of the goods depots did their best to register that joy which was expected of them, for they were required to show joy and cheerful gaiety over the duties of the housewife, whose task it was to refresh the state worker every evening with a wholesome meal.

But all these people skillfully avoided us in such a way that no one was forced to cross our path directly. Where there were signs of life on the street, they disappeared twenty paces ahead of us, each trying to dash into a goods depot or vanish round a corner, and quite a few may have slipped into a strange house and waited nervously behind the door until the sound of our footsteps had died away.

Only once, just as we were crossing an intersection, we came face to face with an elderly man, I just caught a glimpse of his schoolteacher's badge. There was no time for him to avoid us, and he strove, after first saluting the policeman in the prescribed manner (by slapping his own head three times with the flat of his hand as a sign of total abasement)—he strove, as I say, to do his duty by spitting three times into my face and bestowing upon me the compulsory epithet of "filthy traitor." His aim was good, but the day had been hot, his throat must have been dry, for I received only a few tiny, rather ineffectual flecks, which—contrary to regulations—I tried involuntarily to wipe away with my sleeve, where-upon the policeman kicked me in the backside and struck me with his fist in the small of my back, adding in a flat voice, "Phase One," meaning: first and mildest form of punishment administerable by every policeman.

The schoolteacher had hurriedly gone on his way. Everyone else managed to avoid us; except for just one woman, who happened to be taking the prescribed stroll in the fresh air in front of a love-barracks prior to the evening's pleasures, a pale, puffy blonde who blew me a furtive kiss, and I smiled gratefully while the policeman tried to pretend he hadn't noticed. They are required to permit these women liberties that for any other comrade would unquestionably result in severe punishment; for, since they contribute substantially to the general working morale, they are tacitly considered to be outside the law, a concession whose far-reaching consequences have been branded as a sign of incipient liberalization by Professor Bleigoeth, Ph.D., D.Litt., the political philosopher, in the obligatory (political) *Journal of Philosophy.* I had read this the previous day on my way to the capital when, in a farm outhouse, I came across a few sheets of the magazine that a student—probably the farmer's son—had embellished with some very witty comments.

Fortunately we now reached the police station, for at that moment the sirens sounded, a sign that the streets were about to be flooded with thousands of people wearing expressions of restrained joy (it being required at closing time to show restraint in one's expression of joy, otherwise it might look as though work were a burden; whereas rejoicing was to prevail when work began—rejoicing and singing), and all these thousands would have been compelled to spit at me. However, the siren indicated ten minutes before closing time, every worker being required to devote ten minutes to a thorough washing of his person, in accordance with the motto of the head of state: Joy and Soap.

The entrance to the local police station, a squat concrete box, was guarded by two sentries who, as I passed them, gave me the benefit of the customary "physical punitive measures," striking me hard across the temple with their rifles and cracking the muzzles of their pistols down on my collarbone, in accordance with the preamble to State Law No. 1: "Every police officer is required, when confronted by any apprehended [meaning arrested] person, to demonstrate violence *per se,* with the exception of the officer performing the arrest, the latter being privileged to participate in the pleasure of carrying out the necessary physical punitive measures during the interrogation." The actual State Law No. 1 runs as follows: "Every police officer *may* punish anyone: he *must* punish anyone who has committed a crime. For all comrades there is no such thing as exemption from punishment, only the possibility of exemption from punishment."

We now proceeded down a long, bare corridor provided with a great many large windows. Then a door opened automatically, the sentries having already announced our arrival, and in those days, when everything was joy, obedience, and order and everyone did his best to use up the

mandatory pound of soap a day—in those days the arrival of an apprehended (arrested) comrade was naturally an event.

We entered an almost empty room containing nothing but a desk
with a telephone and two chairs. I was required to remain standing in the
middle of the room; the policeman took off his helmet and sat down.

At first there was silence; nothing happened. They always do it like
that—that's the worst part. I could feel my face collapsing by degrees, I
was tired and hungry, and by now even the last vestiges of that joy of
sadness had vanished, for I knew I had had it.

After a few seconds a tall, pale-faced, silent man entered the room
wearing the light-brown uniform of the preliminary interrogator. He sat
down without a word and looked at me.

"Status?"

"Ordinary comrade."

"Date of birth?"

"1/1/1," I said.

"Last occupation?"

"Convict."

The two men exchanged glances.

"When and where discharged?"

"Yesterday, Building 12, Cell 13."

"Where to?"

"The capital."

"Certificate."

I produced the discharge certificate from my pocket and handed it
to him. He clipped it to the green card on which he had begun to enter
my particulars.

"Your former crime?"

"Happy face."

The two men exchanged glances.

"Explain," said the interrogator.

"At that time," I said, "my happy face attracted the attention of a
police officer on a day when general mourning had been decreed. It was
the anniversary of the Leader's death."

"Length of sentence?"

"Five."

"Conduct?"

"Bad."

"Reason?"

"Deficient in work enthusiasm."

"That's all."

With that the preliminary interrogator rose, walked over to me, and neatly knocked out my three front center teeth—a sign that I was to be branded as a lapsed criminal, an intensified measure I had not counted on. The preliminary interrogator then left the room, and a fat fellow in a dark-brown uniform came in: the interrogator.

I was beaten by all of them: by the interrogator, the chief interrogator, the supreme interrogator, the examiner, and the concluding examiner. In addition, the policeman carried out all the physical punitive measures demanded by law, and on account of my sad face they sentenced me to ten years, just as five years earlier they had sentenced me to five years on account of my happy face.

I must now try to make my face register nothing at all, if I can manage to survive the next ten years of Joy and Soap. . . .

Adventures
of a Haversack

IN SEPTEMBER 1914 a man by the name of Joseph Stobski was called up for military service in one of the red brick barracks at Bromberg. Although according to his papers he was a German citizen, he had only a smattering of the mother tongue of his official fatherland. Stobski was twenty-two years old, a watchmaker, and, for reasons of "constitutional debility," had not yet performed any military service. He came from a sleepy little Polish-speaking place called Niestronno, where he had spent his days working in a back room of his father's cottage, tracing designs on gold-plated bracelets—delicate designs—repairing the farmers' watches, and at intervals feeding the pig, milking the cow. In the evenings, when darkness fell over Niestronno, he hadn't gone off to the tavern, hadn't gone to a dance, but had sat stewing over an invention, his oily fingers fiddling with innumerable little wheels and rolling cigarettes— almost all of which he allowed to burn out on the edge of the table—while his mother counted the eggs and complained about the consumption of kerosene.

So now he moved with his cardboard box into the red brick barracks at Bromberg and learned German insofar as it covered the vocabulary of regulations, orders, and rifle parts; he was also familiarized with the trade of infantryman. During instruction, he said "brrett" instead of "bread," "canonn" instead of "cannon"; he cursed in Polish, prayed in Polish; and in the evening he would look gloomily into his dark-brown locker at the little package containing the oily wheels before going off into town to wash down his justified sorrows with schnapps.

He swallowed the sand of Tuchel Heath, wrote postcards to his mother, received bacon from home, managed to get out of regulation church service on Sundays, and would sneak into one of the Polish churches where he could throw himself down onto the tiled floor and weep and pray, although such fervor was ill-suited to anyone wearing the uniform of a Prussian infantryman.

By November 1914 Stobski was considered sufficiently trained to rank as fit to make the journey all across Germany to Flanders. He had thrown sufficient hand grenades into the sand of Tuchel Heath, he had banged away sufficiently often in the rifle ranges, and he sent off the little package containing the oily wheels to his mother, along with a postcard. He was then stuffed into a cattle car and started out on the journey all across his official fatherland, whose mother tongue, insofar as it covered orders, he had learned to master. He allowed rosy-cheeked German girls to pour him coffee and stick flowers into his rifle, he accepted cigarettes, was once even kissed by an elderly woman; and a man wearing a pince-nez who was leaning on a barrier at a railroad crossing called out to him in a very distinct voice a few Latin words of which Stobski understood only *tandem*. For help with this word he turned to his immediate superior, Corporal Habke, who in turn mumbled something about "bicycles," declining any further information. Thus the unwitting Stobski, kissing and being kissed, showered with flowers, chocolate, and cigarettes, crossed the Oder, Elbe, and Rhine rivers, and after ten days was unloaded in the dark at a dingy Belgian railway station. His company assembled in a farmyard, and the captain shouted something in the dark that Stobski didn't understand. Next came stew with noodles to be quickly gulped down from a field kitchen in an ill-lit barn. Sergeant Pilling once again made the rounds and took a brief roll call, and ten minutes later the company marched off in the night toward the west. From that western sky there came the notorious thunderous roar, the sky being intermittently lit up by reddish flashes, and it began to rain. The company left the road, and some hundred and fifty pairs of feet plodded along muddy cart tracks. The artificial thunderstorm came closer and closer, the voices of the officers and sergeants grew hoarse and acquired a disagreeable undertone. Stobski's feet hurt, hurt him very much; besides, he was tired, very tired, but he dragged himself on, through dark villages, along muddy paths, and the closer they came to the thunderstorm the more odious, the more artificial, it sounded. Then the voices of the officers and sergeants became strangely gentle, almost mild, and from left and right came the sound of countless feet tramping along invisible paths and roads.

Stobski realized that they were now in the very heart of that artificial thunderstorm, in fact had actually left some of it behind, for ahead as well as behind them there were reddish flashes. When the order came to fan out, he left the path and ran off to the right, keeping close to Corporal Habke. He could hear shouting, banging, shooting, and now the voices of the officers and sergeants were hoarse again. Stobski's feet still hurt, hurt him very much, and leaving Habke to his own devices he sat down in a wet meadow that smelled of cow dung and thought something that in Polish might have been an approximation of the French word *merde*. He removed his steel helmet, put down his rifle beside him in the grass, unhooked his pack, thought about his beloved oily wheels, and, surrounded by the din of battle, fell asleep. He dreamed of his Polish mother making pancakes in the little warm kitchen, and in his dream it struck him as odd that as soon as the pancakes seemed to be almost ready they exploded in the pan with a bang, and nothing was left of them. His little mother kept ladling dough into the pan, faster and faster; little pancakes would form, bursting an instant before they were ready, and in a sudden rage his little mother —in his dream Stobski had to smile, for his little mother had never really been in a rage—had poured the entire remaining contents of the mixing bowl into the frying pan. Now a great fat yellow pancake lay there, as big as the frying pan, thickened, turned crisp, swelled; Stobski's little mother was already beaming with satisfaction as she picked up the spatula, slid it under the pancake, and—boom!—there was an especially horrible bang, and Stobski had no time to be wakened by it, for he was dead.

A week later, a quarter of a mile from the spot where Stobski had been killed by a direct hit, soldiers from his company found his haversack, together with a piece of his shredded belt, in an English trench: all that was ever found of him on this earth. And when Stobski's haversack containing a piece of homemade hard sausage, his iron rations, and a Polish prayer book were found in this English trench, it was assumed that on the day of the assault Stobski had run with incredible heroism deep into the English lines and been killed there. And so the little Polish mother in Niestronno received a letter from Captain Hummel, informing her of the great heroism of Private Stobski. The little mother had the letter translated by her priest, wept, folded up the letter, laid it between the sheets in her closet, and ordered three Masses for the dead.

But quite suddenly the English reconquered this section of the trench, and Stobski's haversack fell into the hands of the English soldier Wilkins Grayhead, who ate up the sausage, looked at the Polish prayer book, and with a shake of his head threw it into the Flanders mud. Then he rolled up the haversack and stowed it away in his own pack. Two days later Grayhead lost his left leg; he was transported to London, discharged nine months later from the British army, granted a small pension, and, being no longer able to pursue the honorable occupation of tram driver, found employment as a commissionaire at a London bank.

Now, the wages of a commissionaire are not munificent, and Wilkins Grayhead had brought back two vices from the war: he drank and he smoked, and, since his income was inadequate, he began to sell articles he found superfluous, and he found almost everything superfluous. He sold his furniture, drank up the proceeds, sold his clothes except for a single shabby suit, and, when he had nothing left to sell, bethought himself of the dirty bundle he had put away in the cellar after his discharge. So now he sold the rusting army pistol he had neglected to turn in, a tarpaulin, a pair of shoes, and Stobski's haversack. (As for Wilkins Grayhead, to put it very briefly: he went to the dogs. A hopeless alcoholic, he forfeited respect and job, turned to crime, and, in spite of his lost leg that was reposing in Flanders soil, landed in prison where, corrupt to the marrow, he dragged out the rest of his life as a stool pigeon.)

Stobski's haversack, however, remained in the gloomy vaults of a Soho junk dealer for exactly ten years—until 1926. In the summer of that year, the junk dealer, Luigi Banollo by name, read with close attention a letter from a certain firm called Handsuppers Ltd. which displayed such obvious interest in war surplus of all kinds that Banollo rubbed his hands. Together with his son he searched through his entire inventory and brought to light: 27 army pistols, 58 mess kits, more than 100 tarpaulins, 35 knapsacks, 18 haversacks, and 28 pairs of shoes—all from a wide variety of European armies. For this entire consignment Banollo received a check for 810 pounds sterling drawn on one of the soundest banks in London. Banollo had made a profit of roughly five hundred percent while Banollo junior saw the disappearance of the shoes with a relief that almost defies description, for it had been his responsibility to knead, grease, in short look after those shoes, a responsibility the extent of which is obvious to anyone who has ever had to look after even a single pair of shoes.

Handsuppers Ltd. then proceeded to sell, at a profit of eight hundred and fifty percent (their normal margin), all the items they had bought from Banollo to a South American state that three weeks previously had suddenly realized that it was being threatened by a neighboring state and was now determined to forestall this threat. Private Stobski's haversack, having survived the crossing to South America in the hold of a tramp steamer (the firm of Handsuppers made use of tramp steamers only), fell into the hands of a German by the name of Reinhold von Adams, who had espoused the cause of that South American state for a bounty of forty-five pesetas. Von Adams had spent only twelve of the forty-five pesetas on drink when he was requested to live up to his commitment and, under the command of General Lalango, advance to the border of the neighboring state with the cry of "Victory and loot!" on his lips. But Adams received a bullet smack in the center of his head, and Stobski's haversack passed into the possession of a German called Wilhelm Habke, who, for a bounty of only thirty-five pesetas, had espoused the cause of the other South American state. Habke appropriated the haversack and the remaining thirty-three pesetas and found in addition a piece of bread and half an onion, which had already transferred its odor to the peseta bills. But Habke's ethical and aesthetic scruples were minimal; he added his own bounty and obtained an advance of thirty pesetas after being promoted to corporal in the victorious national army. On opening the flap of the haversack and discovering it to be stamped in black ink with the number VII/2/II, he remembered his uncle Joachim Habke, who had served in that regiment and been killed. Wilhelm Habke was overcome by violent homesickness. He retired from the army, was presented with a photograph of General Gublanez, and eventually arrived in Berlin. When he took the streetcar from the Zoo station to Spandau, he rode—unwittingly—past the army ordnance department where Stobski's haversack had lain for a week in 1914 before being sent to Bromberg.

Habke was joyously welcomed by his parents and resumed his real occupation, that of a dispatcher; but it soon became apparent that he tended toward political errors. In 1929 he joined the party, with its ugly, dung-colored uniforms, and took down the haversack that he had hung beside the picture of General Gublanez on the wall over his bed to turn it to account for practical purposes: he wore it with his dung-colored uniform when he went off to Sunday training periods on the heath. During these exercises Habke shone with his military knowledge: he boasted quite a bit, promoted himself to battalion commander in that South American war, and explained in detail where, how, and why he had deployed his heavy weapons at the time. He had totally forgotten that all he had done was shoot poor von Adams in the head, rob him of his pesetas, and appropriate his haversack. In 1929 Habke married, and in 1930 his wife bore him a son, who was given the name Walter. Walter throve, although his first two years in life were spent under the sign of the dole; but by the time he was four years old he was already being given cookies, canned milk, and oranges every morning, and when he was seven, his father presented him with the faded haversack, saying, "Treat this object with respect. It used to belong to your great-uncle Joachim Habke, who rose from the ranks to be a captain, survived eighteen battles, and was executed by Red mutineers in 1918. I myself wore it in the South American war, in which I was only a lieutenant colonel although I could have become a general if the Fatherland hadn't had need of me."

Walter venerated the haversack. He wore it with his own dung-colored uniform from 1936 to 1944, frequently recalled his heroic great-uncle and his heroic father, and, when he had to spend the night in a barn, placed the haversack carefully under his head. In it he kept bread, soft cheese, butter, and his army song book; he brushed it, washed it, and was happy to see the faded tan gradually turn to soft white. He had no idea that the legendary heroic great-uncle had died as a corporal on muddy Flanders soil, not far from the place where a direct hit had killed Private Stobski.

Walter Habke turned fifteen, laboriously studied English, math, and Latin at Spandau High School, venerated the haversack, and believed in heroes until he was forced to be one himself. His father had departed some time before for Poland, to create some kind of order somewhere, and shortly after his father had returned, fuming, from Poland, smoking cigarettes and muttering "Betrayal" as he paced up and down the cramped Spandau living room—shortly after that, Walter Habke was forced to be a hero.

One night in March 1945 he lay behind a machine gun on the outskirts of a Pomeranian village, listening to the dark, thunderous rumbling that sounded exactly as it had in the movies; he pressed the trigger of the machine gun, shot holes into the dark night, and felt an urge to weep. He heard voices in the night, unfamiliar voices, went on shooting, inserted a new belt, fired, and after emptying the second belt it struck him that everything was very quiet: he was alone. He stood up, adjusted his uniform belt, made sure he had his haversack, and walked slowly off into the night toward the west. He had started to do something that is very injurious to heroism: he had started to think—he thought of the cramped but cozy living room, without knowing that he was thinking of something that no longer existed. By this time young Banollo, who had at one time held Walter's haversack in his hand, was forty, had circled in a bomber over Spandau, opened the bomb hatch, and destroyed the cramped but cozy living room, and now Walter's father was pacing up and down in the cellar of the next-door house, smoking cigarettes, muttering "Betrayal," and feeling uncomfortable at the thought of the order he had created in Poland.

That night, Walter walked on pensively toward the west, finally found an abandoned barn, sat down, pulled the haversack around onto his stomach, opened it up, and ate some army bread, margarine, and a few candies. That was how the Russian soldiers found him: asleep, with tear-stained face, a fifteen-year-old boy, empty cartridge belts around his neck, his breath smelling sourly of candy. They shoved him into a column, and Walter Habke marched eastward. Never again was he to see Spandau.

Meanwhile, Niestronno had been German, become Polish, become German again, then Polish again, and Stobski's mother was seventy-five years old. The letter from Captain Hummel still lay in the closet that had long since ceased to contain any linen: Frau Stobski used it to store potatoes; behind the potatoes were a big ham and a china bowl full of eggs, and right at the back, in the darkness, a can of oil. Wood was stacked under the bed, and on the wall an oil lamp spread a reddish glow over the picture of the Madonna of Czestochowa. Back in the stable lolled a thin pig, there was no longer a cow, and the house was filled with the racket of the seven children of the Wolniaks, who had been bombed out of their home in Warsaw. And outside on the road they came trudging by: exhausted, footsore soldiers with pinched faces. They passed by almost every day. At first Wolniak had stood at the roadside, cursing, from time to time picking up a rock, even throwing it; but now he stayed back in his room, where Joseph Stobski had once repaired watches, engraved bracelets, and fiddled around in the evening with his little oily wheels.

In 1939 Polish prisoners of war had trudged past them toward the east, other Polish prisoners toward the west; later, Russian prisoners had trudged past them toward the west, and now for a long time German prisoners had been trudging past them toward the east, and although the nights were still cold and dark, and deep was the sleep of the people of Niestronno, they still woke up at night at the sound of the soft tramping on the roads.

Frau Stobski was one of the first to get up in the morning at Niestronno. She put a coat over her pale-green nightgown, lit the fire in the stove, poured oil into the little lamp in front of the Madonna's picture, carried the ashes to the manure pile, fed the thin pig, then went back into her room to change for Mass. And one morning in April 1945 she found lying outside her front door a very young, fair-haired man with a faded haversack clutched firmly in both hands. Frau Stobski did not scream. She put down the black string bag in which she kept a Polish prayer book, a handkerchief, and a few fragments of thyme—she put down the bag on the window sill, bent down to the young man, and saw immediately that he was dead. Even now she did not scream. It was still dark, with just a faint yellow flicker behind the church windows, and Frau Stobski carefully removed the haversack from the dead man's hands, the haversack that at one time had contained her son's prayer book and a piece of hard sausage from one of her pigs. She dragged the boy inside onto the tiled floor, went into her room, taking along—as if absent-mindedly—the haversack, threw the haversack on the table, and searched through the bundle of dirty, almost worthless zloty bills. Then she set out for the village to rouse the gravedigger.

Later, after the boy had been buried, she found the haversack on her table, picked it up, hesitated—then went to look for a hammer and two nails, banged the nails into the wall, hung up the haversack, and decided to store her onions in it.

If she had only opened the haversack a little wider and raised the flap completely, she would have discovered on it the same number stamped in black ink as had appeared at the top of Captain Hummel's letter.

But she never opened the haversack that wide.

Black Sheep

IT WOULD seem that I have been singled out to ensure that the chain of black sheep is not broken in my generation. Somebody has to be the black sheep, and it happens to be me. Nobody would ever have thought it of me, but there it is: I am the one. Wise members of our family maintain that Uncle Otto's influence on me was not good. Uncle Otto was the black sheep of the previous generation, and my godfather. It had to be somebody, and he was the one. Needless to say, he was chosen as my godfather before it became apparent that he would come to a bad end; and it was the same with me—I became godfather to a little boy who, ever since I have been regarded as black, is being kept at a safe distance from me by his anxious family. As a matter of fact, they ought to be grateful to us, for a family without a black sheep is not a typical family.

My friendship with Uncle Otto began at an early age. He used to visit us often, bringing more candies than my father thought good for us, and he would talk and talk until he finally ended up cadging a loan.

Uncle Otto knew what he was talking about. There was not a subject in which he was not well versed: sociology, literature, music, architecture, anything at all—and he knew his subject, he really did. Even specialists in their field enjoyed talking to him; they found him stimulating, intelligent, an uncommonly nice fellow, until the shock of the attendant attempt to cadge a loan sobered them up. For that was the outrageous thing about it: he did not confine his marauding to the members of the family but laid his artful traps wherever a favorable prospect seemed to present itself.

Everyone used to say he could "cash in" on his knowledge—as the older generation put it—but he didn't cash in on it, he cashed in on the nerves of his relatives.

He alone knew the secret of managing to give the impression that on this particular day he would not do it. But he did do it. Regularly, relentlessly. I fancy he could not bring himself to pass up an opportunity. His conversation was so fascinating, so full of genuine enthusiasm, clearly conceived, brilliantly witty, devastating for his opponents, uplifting for his friends: he could converse far too well on any topic for anyone to have dreamed that he would . . . ! But he did. He knew all about infant care, although he had never had any children; he would involve young mothers in irresistibly fascinating discussions on diet for this or that ailment, suggest types of baby powder, write out ointment prescriptions, decide the quantity and quality of what they were given to drink. He even knew how to hold them: a squalling infant, when put into his arms, would quiet down immediately. He radiated a kind of magic. And he was equally at home analyzing Beethoven's Ninth Symphony, composing legal opinions, citing from memory some law that happened to be under discussion. . . .

But, regardless of time and topic, as the conversation approached its end and the moment of parting drew inexorably nearer—usually in the entrance hall, with the front door already half shut—he would thrust his pale face with its lively dark eyes once more through the door and, right into the apprehension of the tensely waiting relatives, remark quite casually to the head of that particular family, "By the way, I wonder if you could . . . ?"

The amounts he demanded fluctuated between one mark and fifty marks. Fifty was the uppermost limit: over the decades it had become an unwritten law that he was never to ask for more. "Just to tide me over!" he would add. To tide him over—this was his favorite phrase. He would then come in again, replace his hat on the hall stand, unwind his muffler, and launch into an explanation of why he needed the money. He always had plans, infallible plans. He never needed it directly for himself: its sole purpose was to place his livelihood at last on a firm footing. His plans varied from a soft-drink stand, which he was confident would yield a regular steady income, to the founding of a political party which would preserve Europe from its decline and fall.

The words "By the way, I wonder if you could . . ." were apt, as the years went by, to scare the wits out of our family; there were wives, aunts, great-aunts, even nieces, whom the sound of "just to tide me over" would bring to the verge of fainting.

Uncle Otto—I assume him to have been in the best of humors as he sprinted down the stairs—then took himself off to the nearest bar to mull over his plans. He would mull over them to the tune of one schnapps or three bottles of wine, depending on the size of the loan he had been able to raise.

I will no longer conceal the fact that he drank. He drank, yet no one had ever seen him drunk. Moreover, he evidently felt a need to drink alone. To offer him alcohol in the hope of dodging the request for a loan was so much wasted effort. An entire barrel of wine would not have deterred him, at the very last minute, when he was on the point of leaving, from thrusting his head once more through the door and asking, "By the way, I wonder if you could—just to tide me over . . . ?"

But his worst trait I have so far kept to myself: sometimes he would repay a loan. Every so often he appeared to earn money in one way or another: as a former law student he occasionally, I believe, dispensed legal advice. At such times he would turn up, take a bill from his pocket, smooth it out with wistful tenderness, and say, "You were kind enough to help me out—here are your five marks!" Whereupon he would leave very quickly and return after a maximum of two days to ask for a sum slightly in excess of the one he had repaid. He alone knew the secret of managing to reach the age of almost sixty without ever having what is commonly called a regular occupation. Nor was his death in any way due to some illness he might have contracted as a result of his drinking. He was as fit as a fiddle, his heart was perfectly sound, and he slept like a healthy innocent babe full of his mother's milk that sleeps away the hours till the next meal. No, he died very suddenly: he lost his life in an accident, and what happened after his death remains the greatest mystery of all.

Uncle Otto, as I say, was killed in an accident. He was run over by a truck and trailer in heavy downtown traffic, and luckily it was an honest man who picked him up, called the police, and notified the family. In his pockets they found a wallet containing a medallion of the Virgin Mary, a weekly pass good for two more streetcar rides, and twenty-four thousand marks in cash plus the carbon copy of a receipt he had had to sign for the lottery office, and he cannot have been in possession of the money for more than a minute, probably less, because the truck ran over him scarcely fifty yards from the lottery office. What followed was rather humiliating for the family. His room bore the stamp of poverty: table, chair, bed, and closet, a few books, and a large notebook, and in this notebook an accurate list of all those to whom he owed money, including an entry for a loan that had brought him in four marks the previous evening. Also a very brief will naming me his heir.

As his executor, it was my father's job to pay the outstanding debts. Indeed, Uncle Otto's list of creditors filled an entire quarto-sized notebook, his first entry going back to the years when he had suddenly broken off his legal career to devote himself to other plans, the mulling over of which had cost him so much time and so much money. His debts totaled nearly fifteen thousand marks, the number of his creditors over seven hundred, ranging from a streetcar conductor who had advanced him thirty pfennigs for a transfer to my father, who had all together two thousand marks coming to him, probably because Uncle Otto had always found him such a soft touch.

Strangely enough, I happened to come of age on the very day of the funeral and was therefore entitled to enter upon my inheritance of ten thousand marks, so I immediately broke off my university career to devote myself to other plans. In spite of my parents' tears, I left home to move into Uncle Otto's room. It held a great attraction for me, and I am still living there, although my hair is now no longer as thick as it used to be. The contents of the room have neither increased nor decreased. Today I know that I made many mistakes in those early years. It was ridiculous to attempt to become a musician, let alone a composer; I have no talents in that direction. Today I know this, but I paid for the knowledge with three years of useless study and the inevitability of acquiring a reputation for loafing, besides which it used up my whole inheritance, but that's a long time ago.

I have forgotten the sequence of my plans: there were too many of them. Besides, the periods of time needed for me to recognize their futility became shorter and shorter. I finally reached the point where one plan managed to last just three days, a life span that even for a plan is too short. The life span of my plans dwindled so rapidly that they eventually became mere lightning flashes of ideas that I could not explain to anyone because they were not clear even to me. When I think that I devoted myself for three whole months to the science of physiognomy until I finally decided in the course of a single afternoon to become a painter, a gardener, a mechanic, and a sailor, and that I fell asleep thinking I was born to be a teacher and woke up firmly convinced that a career in the customs service was what I was cut out for . . . !

In short, I had neither Uncle Otto's charm nor his relatively great endurance. I am not a talker either: I sit silent among other people; I bore them and blurt out my attempts to extract money from them so abruptly into the silence that they sound like extortions. Only with children do I get along well. This is at least one favorable attribute that I seem to have inherited from Uncle Otto. Babies quiet down the minute I take them in my arms, and when they look at me they smile, insofar as they can smile at all, although it is said that my face scares people. Unkind people have advised me to found the profession of male kindergarten teacher as its first exponent and to put an end to my eternal planning by bringing at least this plan to fruition. But I never shall. I think this is what makes us so impossible: the fact that we cannot cash in on our real talents—or, to adopt the modern jargon, exploit them financially.

One thing is certain, though: if I am a black sheep—and personally

I am by no means convinced of this—but if I am one, it is of a different kind from Uncle Otto. I lack his light touch, his charm; besides, my debts weigh heavily on me, while obviously his scarcely bothered him at all. And I did a terrible thing: I capitulated—I asked for a job. I implored the family to help me, to find me a job, to pull strings for me, so that for once, just once, I might be assured of tangible compensation in return for the performance of clearly defined duties. And they were successful. After I had sent off my petitions, given written and verbal form to my pleas, my urgent, imploring appeals, I was horrified to find they had been taken seriously and borne fruit, and I did something which no black sheep had ever done before: I did not flinch, did not turn it down, I accepted the position they had managed to find for me. I sacrificed something that I ought never to have sacrificed: my freedom!

Each evening when I came home I could have kicked myself for letting yet another day of my life go by that had brought me nothing but fatigue, rage, and just enough money to enable me to keep on working, if one can call what I was doing work: sorting bills alphabetically, punching holes in them, and fastening them into a brand-new file where they patiently submitted to the fate of never being paid; or writing the kind of circulars that travel ineffectually out into the world and amount to nothing but a superfluous burden for the mailman; and sometimes making out bills that now and then were actually paid in cash. I had to deal with salesmen who strove in vain to palm off the rubbish manufactured by our boss. Our boss: that bustling blockhead who is forever in a hurry and never does a thing, who persistently chatters away the precious hours of the day —an existence of stultifying stupidity—who never dares admit the extent of his debts, who cheats his way from one bluff to the next, a balloon-artist who starts blowing up one balloon the very moment another one bursts, leaving behind a repulsive rubber rag that a second earlier still had sheen, life, and bounce.

Our office was right alongside the factory, where a staff of a dozen or so manufactured the kind of furniture that, once bought, is an annoyance for the rest of one's life unless one decides after three days to chop it up into kindling: occasional tables, sewing cabinets, midget chests of drawers, arty little "hand-painted" chairs that collapse under the weight of three-year-old children, little stands for vases or flowerpots, shoddy bric-à-brac that ostensibly owes its existence to the art of the cabinetmaker whereas in fact an inferior workman, using cheap paint purporting to be enamel, produces a semblance of attractiveness intended to justify the prices.

So this was how I spent my days, one after another—nearly two weeks in all—in the office of this unintelligent man who not only took himself seriously but considered himself an artist, for now and again—it happened only once while I was there—he was to be seen standing at the drawing board, shuffling pencils and paper and designing some wobbly object or other, a flower stand or a new portable bar, yet another source of annoyance for future generations.

The appalling futility of his devices never seemed to enter his head. When he had finished designing one of these gadgets—as I say, it happened only once while I was working for him—he would dash off in his car to rest up from his creative labors, a respite that lasted a week after he had worked for only fifteen minutes. The drawing was tossed in front of the foreman, who would spread it out on his bench, study it with furrowed brow, and proceed to check the lumber supplies in order to get production under way. For days I could watch the new creations piling up behind the dusty windows of the workshop—he called it a factory: wall shelves or radio stands that were hardly worth the glue being wasted on them.

The only objects of any use were those turned out by the workmen without the boss's knowledge, when they could be quite certain of his absence for a few days: little stools or jewel cases of pleasing sturdiness and simplicity—great-grandchildren will straddle them or hoard their treasures in them; sensible laundry racks on which the shirts of many a future generation will flutter. What was endearing and serviceable was thus produced illegally.

But the really memorable personality I came across during this inter-lude of business life was the streetcar conductor who invalidated each day for me with his punch. He would take the slip of paper, my weekly pass, push it into the open maw of his punch, and an invisible supply of ink would blot out half an inch of it—one day out of my life, one precious day that had brought me nothing but fatigue, rage, and just enough money to continue in this futile pursuit. A godlike authority was vested in this man wearing the unpretentious uniform of the city transit system, the man who evening after evening wielded sufficient power to declare thousands of human days null and void.

To this day I feel annoyed with myself for not giving notice before I was practically forced to give notice; for not telling the boss where to get off before I was practically forced to tell him. But one day my landlady brought a sinister-looking individual along to my office who introduced himself as a lottery-office operator and announced that I was now the owner of a fortune of fifty thousand marks, provided that I was such and such a person and that I was the holder of a certain lottery ticket. Well, I was such and such a person and I was the holder of the lottery ticket. I quit my job on the spot, without giving notice, taking it upon myself to abandon the bills unpunched, unsorted, and there was nothing left for me to do but go home, collect the cash, and, by way of money orders, acquaint my relatives with the new state of affairs.

It was evidently expected of me to die soon or become the victim of an accident. But for the time being no automobile appears to have been singled out to deprive me of my life, and my heart is as sound as a bell, although I do not spurn the bottle. So after paying my debts, I find myself the possessor of a fortune of nearly thirty thousand marks, tax-free, and a sought-after uncle who has suddenly regained access to his godchild. But then children love me anyway, as I have said, and now I am allowed to play with them, buy them balls, ice cream, sundaes; I am allowed to buy whole gigantic clusters of balloons, and to populate the roundabouts and swings with the merry little throng.

While my sister has promptly bought her son, my godchild, a lottery ticket, I now spend my time wondering, musing for hours, about who among this new generation is going to be my successor; which of these thriving, romping, lovely children begotten by my brothers and sisters will be the black sheep of the next generation? For we are a typical family, and always will be. Who will be a good boy up to that point at which he ceases to be a good boy? Who will suddenly wish to devote himself to other plans, infallible, better plans? I would like to know, I would like to warn him, for we too have learned by experience; our calling also has its rules of the game, which I could pass on to him, my successor, still unknown, still playing with the gang like a wolf in sheep's clothing. . . .

But I have a foreboding that I shan't live long enough to recognize him and initiate him into our secrets. He will come forward, reveal his true colors, when I die and it is his turn to take over. With flushed cheeks he will confront his parents and tell them he is fed up; and secretly I can only hope that when that time comes, there will still be some of my money left, because I have changed my will and left the balance of my fortune to the one who shows the first incontrovertible signs of being earmarked as my successor. . . .

The main thing is that he shouldn't let them down.

My Uncle Fred

M Y UNCLE Fred is the only person who makes my memories of the years after 1945 bearable. He came home from the war one summer afternoon, in nondescript clothes, wearing his sole possession, a tin can, on a string around his neck, and supporting the trifling weight of a few cigarette butts which he had carefully saved in a little box. He embraced my mother, kissed my sister and me, mumbled something about "Bread, sleep, tobacco," and curled himself up on our family sofa, so that I remember him as being a man who was considerably longer than our sofa, a fact which obliged him either to keep his legs drawn up or to let them simply hang over the end. Both alternatives moved him to rail bitterly against our grandparents' generation, to which we owed the acquisition of this valuable piece of furniture. He called these worthy people stuffy, constipated owls, despised their taste for the bilious pink of the upholstery, but let none of this stop him from indulging in frequent and prolonged sleep.

I for my part was performing a thankless task in our blameless family: I was fourteen at the time, and the sole contact with that memorable institution which we called the black market. My father had been killed in the war, my mother received a tiny pension, with the result that I had the almost daily job of peddling scraps of salvaged belongings or swapping them for bread, coal, and tobacco. In those days coal was the cause of considerable violation of property rights, which today we would have to bluntly call stealing. So most days saw me going out to steal or peddle, and my mother, though she realized the need for these disreputable doings, always had tears in her eyes as she watched me go off about my complicated affairs. It was my responsibility, for instance, to turn a pillow into bread, a Dresden cup into a semolina, or three volumes of Gustav Freytag into two ounces of coffee, tasks to which I devoted myself with a certain amount of sporting enthusiasm but not entirely without a sense of humiliation and fear. For values—which is what grown-ups called them at the time—had shifted substantially, and now and then I was exposed to the unfounded suspicion of dishonesty because the value of a peddled article did not correspond in the least to the one my mother thought appropriate. It was, I must say, no pleasant task to act as broker between two different worlds of values, worlds which since then seem to have converged.

Uncle Fred's arrival led us all to expect some stalwart masculine aid. But he began by disappointing us. From the very first day I was seriously worried about his appetite, and when I made no bones about telling my mother this, she suggested I let him "find his feet." It took almost eight weeks for him to find his feet. Despite his abuse of the unsatisfactory sofa, he slept there without much trouble and spent the day dozing or describing to us in a martyred voice what position he preferred to sleep in.

I think his favorite position was that of a sprinter just before the start. He loved to lie on his back after lunch, his legs drawn up, voluptuously crumbling a large piece of bread into his mouth, and then roll himself a cigarette and sleep away the day till suppertime. He was a very tall, pale man, and there was a circular scar on his chin which gave his face somewhat the look of a damaged marble statue. Although his appetite for food and sleep continued to worry me, I liked him very much. He was the only one with whom I could at least theorize about the black market without getting into an argument. He obviously knew all about the conflict between the two worlds of values.

Although we urged him to talk to us about the war, he never did; he said it wasn't worth discussing. The only thing he would do sometimes was tell us about his induction, which seemed to have consisted chiefly of a person in uniform ordering Uncle Fred in a loud voice to urinate into a test tube, an order with which Uncle Fred was not immediately able to comply, the result being that his military career was doomed from the start. He maintained that the German Reich's keen interest in his urine had filled him with considerable distrust, a distrust which he found ominously confirmed during six years of war.

He had been a bookkeeper before the war, and when the first four weeks on our sofa had gone by, my mother suggested in her gentle sisterly way that he make inquiries about his old firm. He warily passed this suggestion on to me, but all I could discover was a pile of rubble about twenty feet high, which I located in a ruined part of the city after an hour's laborious pilgrimage. Uncle Fred was much reassured by my news.

He leaned back in his chair, rolled himself a cigarette, nodded triumphantly toward my mother, and asked her to get out his old things. In one corner of our bedroom there was a carefully nailed-down crate, which we opened with hammer and pliers amid much speculation. Out of it came: twenty novels of medium size and mediocre quality, a gold pocket watch, dusty but undamaged, two pairs of suspenders, some notebooks, his Chamber of Commerce diploma, and a savings book showing a balance of twelve hundred marks. The savings book was given to me to collect the money, as well as the rest of the stuff to be peddled, including the Chamber of Commerce diploma—although this found no takers, Uncle Fred's name being inscribed on it in black India ink.

This meant that for the next four weeks we were free from worry about bread, tobacco, and coal, which was a great relief to me, especially as all the schools opened wide their doors again and I was required to complete my education.

To this day, long after my education has been completed, I have fond memories of the soups we used to get, mainly because we obtained these supplementary meals almost without a struggle, and they therefore lent a happy and contemporary note to the whole educational system.

But the outstanding event during this period was the fact that Uncle Fred finally took the initiative a good eight weeks after his safe return.

One morning in late summer he rose from his sofa, shaved so meticulously that we became apprehensive, asked for some clean underwear, borrowed my bicycle, and disappeared.

His return late that night was accompanied by a great deal of noise and a penetrating smell of wine; the smell of wine emanated from my uncle's mouth, the noise was traceable to half a dozen galvanized buckets which he had tied together with some stout rope. Our confusion did not subside till we discovered he had decided to revive the flower trade in our ravaged town. My mother, full of suspicion toward the new world of values, scorned the idea, claiming that no one would want to buy flowers. But she was wrong.

It was a memorable morning when we helped Uncle Fred take the freshly filled buckets to the streetcar stop where he set himself up in business. And I still vividly remember the sight of those red and yellow tulips, the moist carnations; nor shall I ever forget how impressive he looked as he stood there in the midst of the gray figures and piles of rubble and started calling out, "Flowers, fresh flowers—no coupons required!" I don't have to describe how his business flourished: it was a meteoric success. In a matter of four weeks he owned three dozen galvanized buckets, was the proprietor of two branches, and a month later he was paying taxes. The whole town wore a different air to me: flower stalls appeared at one street corner after another, it was impossible to keep pace with the demand; more and more buckets were procured, booths were set up, and handcarts hastily thrown together.

At any rate, we were kept supplied not only with fresh flowers but with bread and coal, and I was able to retire from the brokerage business, a fact which helped greatly to improve my moral standards. For many years now, Uncle Fred has been a man of substance: his branches are still thriving, he owns a car, he looks on me as his heir, and I have been told to study commerce so I can look after the tax end of the business even before I enter on my inheritance.

When I look at him today, a solid figure behind the wheel of his red automobile, I find it strange to recall that there was really a time in my life when his appetite caused me sleepless nights.

Christmas Not Just
Once a Year

I

Among our relatives, symptoms of disintegration are beginning to show up that for a while we tried silently to ignore but the threat of which we are now determined to face squarely. I do not yet dare use the word "collapse," but the alarming facts are accumulating to the point where they represent a threat and compel me to speak of things that may sound strange to the ears of my contemporaries but whose reality no one can dispute. The mildew of decay has obtained a foothold under the thick, hard veneer of respectability, colonies of deadly parasites heralding the end of the integrity of an entire clan. Today we must regret having ignored the voice of our cousin Franz, who long ago began to draw attention to the terrible consequences of what was on the face of it a harmless event. This event was in itself so trivial that we are now shocked by the extent of its consequences. Franz warned us long ago. Unfortunately he lacked prestige in the family. He had chosen an occupation that had never before been pursued, would never have been permitted to be pursued, by any member of our entire clan: he became a boxer. Of a brooding melancholy even in his youth, and of a piety always described as "a pose of religious zeal," he set out early on paths that caused my Uncle Franz—that kindest of men—deep concern. It was Franz's wont to stay away from school with a frequency that could no longer be described as normal. He met regularly with shady characters in remote parks and dense undergrowth on the outskirts of town, where they practiced the tough rules of fistfighting, showing no concern for the fact that their humanistic heritage was being neglected. Already these young toughs were demonstrating the bad habits of their generation—one that has, needless to say, turned out to be good for nothing. The thrilling intellectual battles of previous centuries did not interest them, so totally were they preoccupied with the dubious thrills of their own century. At first, Franz's piety struck me as being incompatible with these regular exercises in passive and active brutality. But today, certain things are beginning to dawn on me. I shall have to return to this later.

So it was Franz who issued a timely warning, who dissociated himself from certain celebrations, describing it all as affectation and a pain in the neck, above all later refusing to participate in measures deemed necessary to preserve what he called a pain in the neck. However—as I have said —his prestige was not high enough for him to find a hearing among his relatives.

But now things have got so out of hand that we are at a total loss, not knowing how to put a curb on them.

Franz has long since become a famous boxer, yet today he rejects the praise heaped upon him by the family with the same indifference with which he at one time refused to accept any criticism.

His brother, however, my cousin Johannes—a man for whom I would at any time have vouched, a successful attorney, my uncle's favorite son—is said to have become involved with the Communist Party, a rumor I obstinately refuse to believe. My cousin Lucie, until now a normal woman, is said to spend her nights in disreputable places, accompanied by her helpless spouse, at dances for which I can find no other adjective than "existentialist." Even Uncle Franz, that kindest of men, is supposed to have said that he is tired of life—a man who was regarded by the entire clan as a model of vitality and as a paragon of what we have been taught to call a Christian businessman.

Medical bills pile up; psychiatrists, psychologists, are called in. Only my Aunt Milla, who must be cited as the originator of all these phenomena, enjoys the best of health, smiles, is as well and cheerful as she has almost always been. Her bright, cheery manner is now, after our years of heartfelt concern for her well-being, slowly beginning to get on our nerves. For there was a crisis in her life that threatened to become alarming. This is where I will have to go into more detail.

II

It is simple enough with hindsight to discern the origin of a disquieting trend—and, strangely enough, it is only now, when I observe the situation pragmatically, that the things which have been occurring in the family for almost two years seem unusual.

It might have struck us earlier that something was not right. In fact, something wasn't right, and if anything at all has ever been right—which I doubt—here things are occurring that fill me with horror. Throughout the family, Aunt Milla had always been known for her particular fondness for decorating the Christmas tree, a harmless if particular weakness that is fairly widespread in our Fatherland. Her weakness met with smiles all around, and the resistance displayed by Franz from his earliest youth to this "to-do" was always the object of vehement indignation, especially since Franz cut a disquieting figure anyway. He refused to help decorate the tree. Up to a certain point, all this took a normal course. My aunt had become accustomed to Franz's staying away from the pre-Christmas preparations, even from the actual celebration, appearing only for Christmas dinner. It was no longer even discussed.

At the risk of making myself unpopular, I must now mention a fact in defense of which I can only say that it really is one. During the years 1939 to 1945 there was a war on. In wartime there is a lot of singing, shooting, talking, fighting, starving, and dying—and bombs are dropped, all disagreeable things with which I have no intention of boring my contemporaries. I must merely mention them because the war had a bearing on the story I wish to tell. For the war was registered by my Aunt Milla merely as a force that began as early as Christmas 1939 to jeopardize her Christmas tree. Admittedly, her Christmas tree was unusually vulnerable.

The main attractions on my Aunt Milla's Christmas tree were glass dwarfs holding a cork hammer in their uplifted arms with a bell-shaped anvil at their feet. Under the dwarfs' feet, candles were affixed, and upon a certain temperature being reached, a hidden mechanism was set in motion, a hectic agitation was communicated to the dwarfs' arms, with their cork hammers they flailed away like crazy at the bell-shaped anvils, thus, since they were about a dozen in number, producing a concerted elfin tinkling. Furthermore: from the tip of the Christmas tree hung a red-cheeked angel in a silvery dress, and at regular intervals the angel parted its lips to whisper "Peace," and again, "Peace." The mechanical secret of this angel, obstinately guarded, became known to me much later, although at the time I had the opportunity almost every week of admiring it. In addition, of course, my aunt's Christmas tree was also bedecked with sugar rings, cookies, angel hair, marzipan figures, and—last but not least—silver tinsel; and I can still remember that properly attaching the various ornaments took a great deal of effort, requiring the participation of the entire family, so that on Christmas Eve frayed nerves cost us all our appetite, and the mood was then—as one says—dismal, except in the case of my cousin Franz, who, of course, had taken no part in these preparations and was the only one to enjoy the roast and the asparagus, the whipped cream and ice cream.

When we duly arrived, then, for a visit the day after Christmas, and risked the bold assumption that the secret of the talking angel was based on the same mechanism that caused certain dolls to say "Mama" or "Papa," the only response was mocking laughter. Now it is easy to imagine that bombs falling close by posed an extreme hazard to such a vulnerable tree. There were terrible scenes when the dwarfs fell off the tree, and once even the angel toppled to the ground. My aunt was inconsolable. After every air raid she went to endless trouble to restore the tree completely and to maintain it at least over the Christmas holidays. But even in 1940 it was already a hopeless task. Again at the risk of making myself very unpopular, I must mention in passing that the number of air raids on our city was indeed considerable, to say nothing of their violence. At any rate, my aunt's Christmas tree fell victim—the thread of my narrative forbids my mentioning other victims—to modern warfare; foreign ballistic experts temporarily snuffed out its existence.

We were all genuinely sorry for our aunt, who was a charming, gracious woman. We felt sorry that, after bitter struggles, endless arguments, after many tears and scenes, she had to agree to renounce her tree for the duration of the war.

Fortunately—or should I say unfortunately?—that was almost the only impact the war had on her. The shelter built by my uncle was bombproof; moreover, there was always an automobile ready to whisk my Aunt Milla away to areas where nothing was to be seen of the immediate effects of the war. Everything was done to spare her the sight of the appalling destruction. My two cousins were lucky enough not to have to do their war service in its most rigorous form. Johannes quickly joined his uncle's business, which played a crucial role in supplying our city with vegetables. Moreover, he had a chronic gallbladder complaint. Franz, on the other hand, although he became a soldier, was entrusted only with guarding prisoners, an assignment he utilized to render himself unpopular with his military superiors—by treating Russians and Poles as human beings. In those days my cousin Lucie was still unmarried and helped in the business. One afternoon a week she did volunteer war work at a factory that embroidered swastikas. But this is not the place to enumerate the political sins of my relatives.

Anyway, all in all there was no lack of money or food or whatever was necessary for protection, and the only thing my aunt bitterly resented was having to give up her tree. My Uncle Franz, that kindest of men, spent almost fifty years acquiring considerable merit and profit by buying up oranges and lemons in tropical and subtropical countries and selling them with a suitable markup. During the war he expanded his business to include less valuable fruits and vegetables. But after the war the gratifying produce that was his main interest was once again available, and citrus fruit became the object of keenest interest at every level. At this point Uncle Franz succeeded in regaining his former influential position, and he was able to provide the population with the enjoyment of vitamins and himself with that of a respectable fortune.

But he was almost seventy and wanted to retire, to hand over the business to his son-in-law. That is when the event occurred which at the time we smiled at but which today seems to us to have been the cause of the whole wretched sequence of events.

My Aunt Milla started in about the Christmas tree again. That was harmless enough; even the perseverance with which she insisted that everything was to be "like in the old days" merely drew smiles from us. At first there was really no reason to take it all that seriously. Although the war had destroyed so much of which the restoration caused greater concern, why—we said to ourselves—deny a charming old lady this trifling pleasure?

Everyone knows how difficult it was at that time to obtain such things as butter and bacon. But even for my Uncle Franz, who enjoyed the best of connections, it was impossible in 1945 to obtain marzipan figures, chocolate rings, and candles. It was not until 1946 that all these things could be provided. Fortunately, a complete set of dwarfs and anvils as well as an angel had survived.

I well remember the day we were invited to my uncle's home. It was in January 1947, and bitterly cold outside. But indoors it was warm, and there was no shortage of things to eat. And when the lights were put out, the candles lit, when the dwarfs began to hammer, the angel whispered "Peace," and again, "Peace," I felt transported back into an era that I had assumed to be past.

Nevertheless, this experience, although surprising, was not extraordinary. What *was* extraordinary was the experience I had three months later. My mother—it was now the middle of March—had sent me over to find out whether there was anything my Uncle Franz "could do": she was looking for fruit. I strolled through the streets to the part of town where my uncle lived; the air was mild, it was dusk. All unsuspecting, I walked past overgrown piles of rubble and neglected parks and, opening the gate to my uncle's garden, stopped, dumbfounded. In the quiet of the evening, the sound of singing was clearly audible, coming from my uncle's living room. Singing is a good old German custom, and there are many songs about spring, but now I could clearly hear "Holy infant, so tender and mild . . ."

I must admit to being confused. Slowly I approached the house, waiting for the singing to end. The curtains were drawn shut; I bent down to the keyhole. At that moment the tinkling of the dwarfs' bells reached my ear, and I could clearly hear the whispering of the angel. I didn't have the courage to intrude, and walked slowly back home. In the family, my account produced general merriment. But it was not until Franz appeared and gave us the details that we found out what had happened.

Around Candlemas, the time when in our part of the country the Christmas trees are stripped and then thrown on the garbage pile, where they are picked up by good-for-nothing children to be dragged through ashes and other rubbish, and used for various games—it was around Candlemas that the terrible thing happened. When my cousin Johannes, on Candlemas Eve, after the tree had been lit for the last time, began to detach the dwarfs from their clips, my aunt, until then such a gentle soul, set up a pitiful wail, a wail so violent and sudden that my cousin was startled, and lost control over the gently swaying tree. Then it happened: there was a tinkling and a ringing, dwarfs and bells, anvils and all-surmounting angel—everything crashed to the floor, and my aunt screamed.

She screamed for almost a week. Neurologists were summoned by telegram, psychiatrists came racing up in taxis—but all, even the most famous of them, left the house shrugging their shoulders, although also somewhat alarmed. None of them had been able to put a stop to that shrill, discordant concert. Only the strongest medication yielded a few hours of quiet; however, the dose of Luminal that can be given daily to a sixty-year-old woman without endangering her life is unfortunately rather small. But it is torture to have in the house a woman screaming at the top of her voice; by the second day the family was already totally distraught. Even the comforting words of the priest, who always celebrated Christmas Eve with the family, had no effect: my aunt screamed.

Franz made himself especially unpopular by suggesting a regular exorcism. The priest scolded him, the family was dismayed by his medieval views, and for a few weeks his reputation for brutality outweighed his reputation as a boxer.

Meanwhile everything was being tried to relieve my aunt of her condition. She refused food, did not speak, did not sleep; they tried cold water, hot foot-baths, hot and cold compresses, and the doctors searched through their reference works looking for a name for this neurosis, but could not find it.

And my aunt screamed. She went on screaming until my Uncle Franz
—really the kindest of men—hit on the idea of setting up a new Christmas
tree.

III

THE IDEA was excellent, but its execution proved to be extremely
difficult. By this time it was almost the middle of February, and it
is fairly difficult to find an acceptable Christmas tree for sale at that time.
The entire business world has long since shifted—with gratifying speed,
by the way—to other things. Carnival is approaching: masks and pistols,
cowboy hats and crazy headdresses for Czardas princesses fill the store
windows where earlier one had been able to admire angels and angel hair,
candles and Nativity scenes. The confectionery stores have long since
moved their Christmas items back into their storerooms, whereas carnival
crackers now adorn their windows. In any event, Christmas trees are not
available at this time of year on the regular market.

Eventually an expedition of rapacious grandchildren was equipped
with pocket money and a sharp ax. These young people rode out into the
state forest and returned late that afternoon, obviously in the best of moods,
with a silver fir. But meanwhile it had been discovered that four dwarfs, six
bell-shaped anvils, and the all-surmounting angel had been completely destroyed. The marzipan figures and the cookies had fallen victim to the
greedy grandchildren. So this generation too, now growing up, is good for
nothing; and if ever a generation has been good for something—which I
doubt—I have come to the conclusion that it was the generation of our
fathers.

Although there was no lack of cash, or of the necessary contacts, it
took another four days to assemble all the accessories. Throughout this
time, my aunt screamed incessantly. Telegrams to the German toy centers,
which were just beginning to get back on their feet, were sent winging
through the ether, urgent long-distance calls were made, express packages
were delivered during the night by perspiring young postal assistants,
bribery ensured an import license from Czechoslovakia at short notice.

Those days will be remembered in the annals of my uncle's family
as days of an exceptionally high consumption of coffee, cigarettes, and
nerves. Meanwhile my aunt was wasting away: her round face became hard
and angular, her mild expression gave way to one of unyielding severity,
she did not eat, did not drink, she screamed incessantly, was watched over

by two nurses, and the dose of Luminal had to be increased every day.

Franz told us that the entire family was in the grip of a pathological tension when at last, on February 12, the Christmas tree decorations were once again complete. The candles were lit, the curtains drawn, my aunt was brought from her sickroom, and among those assembled only sobs and giggles were to be heard. My aunt's expression began to relax in the light of the candles, and, upon the right degree of warmth being reached, the little glass fellows started hammering away like crazy, and finally the angel whispered "Peace," and again, "Peace," the most beautiful smile lit up my aunt's face, and almost at once the whole family would strike up "O Christmas Tree!" In order to complete the picture, the priest had also been invited, since he normally spent Christmas Eve at Uncle Franz's. He too smiled; he too was relieved and joined in the singing.

No test, no psychologist's expertise, no specialist's disclosure of hidden traumata, had achieved it, but the sensitive heart of my uncle had hit upon the right thing. The Christmas tree therapy of that kindest of men had saved the situation.

My aunt had calmed down and was almost—it was hoped at the time —cured. After a few carols had been sung, a few dishes of cookies emptied, everyone was tired and withdrew for the night, and lo and behold: my aunt fell asleep without any tranquilizer. The two nurses were dismissed, the doctors shrugged their shoulders, everything seemed to be back to normal. My aunt was eating again, drinking again, was once again gracious and gentle. But the following evening, as the twilight hour approached, my uncle was sitting reading the paper beside his wife next to the tree, when she suddenly touched his arm gently and said, "So now let's light the candles and call in the children, I think it's time to begin." Later my uncle admitted to us that he was startled but that he got up to summon his children and grandchildren as quickly as possible and to send word to the priest. The priest arrived, somewhat out of breath and surprised, but the candles were lit, the dwarfs made to hammer, the angel was made to whisper, carols were sung, cookies were eaten—and everything seemed to be back to normal.

IV

Now, all vegetation is subject to certain biological laws, and fir trees, when uprooted from their soil, are known to have the devastating tendency to drop their needles, especially when they are standing in warm rooms, and at my uncle's it was always warm. The life span of the silver fir is somewhat longer than that of the common fir, as has been proved in the well-known treatise *Abies vulgaris and abies nobilis,* by Dr. Hergenring. However, even the life span of the silver fir is not unlimited. With the approach of the carnival season, it became apparent that an attempt must be made to subject my aunt to new distress: the tree was rapidly losing its needles, and during the evening carol singing a slight frown was noticed on my aunt's forehead. At the advice of a really outstanding psychologist, the attempt was now made to speak, in a casual conversational tone, of a possible end to the Christmas season, especially now that trees were beginning to put forth their leaves, something generally acknowledged to be an indication of approaching spring, whereas in our latitudes the word "Christmas" is unquestionably associated with conceptions of winter. My very astute uncle suggested one evening that everyone join in singing the songs "Hark, the birds have all arrived!" and "Come, Lovely May," but even at the very first line of the first of those songs my aunt put on such a grim expression that everyone immediately broke off and intoned "O Christmas Tree!" Three days later, my cousin Johannes was instructed to undertake a mild act of spoliation; but no sooner had he reached out and taken the cork hammer from one of the dwarfs than my aunt started screaming so violently that the dwarf was immediately made whole again, the candles were lit, and, somewhat hastily but very loud, the carol "Silent Night" burst forth.

However, the nights were no longer silent. Loudly singing groups of youthful drunkards roamed through the city with trumpets and drums, everything was covered with streamers and confetti, and children in fancy dress filled the streets during the day, shooting, yelling, some of them singing too. According to private statistics there were at least sixty thousand cowboys and forty thousand Czardas princesses in our city. In short, it was carnival time, a feast we are accustomed to celebrate with a vigor equal to if not surpassing that of Christmas. But my aunt seemed to be blind and deaf: she deplored the carnival costumes that inevitably turn up in the clothes closets of our homes during this time; in a sad voice she complained of the decline of morality since people seemed unable, even during Christmastime, to refrain from these immoral goings-on; and when in my cousin's bedroom she discovered a balloon that, although deflated, still clearly showed a white jester's cap painted on it, she burst into tears and begged my uncle to put a stop to these unholy goings-on.

To its consternation, the family had to conclude that my aunt actually was under the delusion that it was "Christmas Eve." At any rate, my uncle called a family conclave, pleaded for forbearance toward his wife, consid-

eration for her strange mental condition, and proceeded to organize another expedition in order at least to ensure the peace of the evening
festivities.

While my aunt was asleep, the decorations were removed from the
old tree and installed on the new one, and her condition remained gratifying.

V

BUT CARNIVAL time passed too, and spring really did arrive, and instead
of the song "Come, Lovely May," one could have already sung
"Lovely May, thou art now come." Then it was June. Four Christmas trees
had already withered, and none of the more recently consulted doctors
could promise any hope of improvement. My aunt was adamant. Even Dr.
Bless, regarded as an international authority, had withdrawn with a shrug
of his shoulders to his study after collecting his fee of 1,365 marks, thus
supplying further evidence of his unworldliness. A few further, rather
vague attempts to curtail or discontinue the celebration met with such
screams on the part of my aunt that the family had once and for all to desist
from such sacrilege.

The terrible part was that my aunt insisted on all those close to her
being present. Among these were also the priest and the grandchildren. It
was difficult enough to insist that members of the family turn up regularly,
but the case of the priest presented still greater difficulties. For a few weeks,
out of consideration for his old penitent, he had stuck it out without
grumbling, but the time finally came when, with much hemming and
hawing, he tried to explain to my uncle that the situation could not
continue. Granted the actual ceremony was brief (it lasted some thirty-
eight minutes), but in the long run even this brief ritual was becoming
insupportable, the priest maintained. He had other obligations: evening
gatherings with his confreres, parochial duties, to say nothing of taking
confessions on Saturdays. For several weeks he had put up with having to
rearrange his schedule, but toward the end of June he was making vigorous
demands for his release. Franz went on the rampage in the family, looking
for accomplices to his plan to have his mother placed in an institution, but
he was met with rejection on all sides.

In short: problems began to mount. One evening the priest didn't
show up, couldn't be reached by either telephone or messenger, and it
became apparent that his absence was deliberate. My uncle cursed mightily,

and he used the occasion to call the servants of the Church names that I must refuse to repeat. As a last resort, one of the curates, a person of humble origin, was asked to help out. He did so but behaved so appallingly that the result was almost a disaster. However, it must be borne in mind that it was June, in other words—hot; nevertheless, the curtains had been drawn shut in order at least to give the impression of winter darkness, and the candles had been lit. Then the ceremony began. Although the curate had already heard of these strange happenings, he could not really imagine them. With a good deal of trepidation, the family introduced the curate to my aunt, explaining that he was substituting for the priest. To their surprise she accepted this change in the program. So: the dwarfs hammered away, the angel whispered, "O Christmas Tree!" was sung, then cookies were eaten, the carol was sung again, and suddenly the curate was seized with uncontrollable laughter. Later he confessed that he hadn't been able to hear the line ". . . in winter too, when snowflakes fall," without laughing. He exploded with clerical foolishness, left the room, and was not seen again. Everyone looked breathlessly at my aunt, but in a resigned voice she merely said something about "yokels in priest's clothing," and popped a piece of marzipan into her mouth. At the time we too deplored the incident, but today I am inclined to call it an outburst of natural mirth.

At this point I must—if I am to do justice to the truth—insert that my uncle exploited his connections with the highest ecclesiastical authorities in order to complain about the priest as well as the curate. The matter was handled with the utmost punctiliousness; an action was brought over neglect of parochial duties and was won by both clerics. An appeal is still under consideration.

Fortunately a retired priest was found who lived in the neighborhood. This charming old gentleman graciously and unhesitatingly agreed to put himself at their disposal and complete the regular evening ritual. But I am anticipating. My Uncle Franz, who was sensible enough to realize that the situation was beyond any medical aid, and who also obstinately refused to attempt exorcism, was enough of a businessman to take the long view and to work out the most economical method. He began by putting a stop to the grandchildren's expeditions as early as mid-June, having established that they were costing too much. My ingenious cousin Johannes, who maintains excellent contacts with the business world at all levels, discovered the Fresh Christmas Tree Service provided by Söderbaum's, an efficient company that for the past two years has deserved high praise for relieving the nervous strain of my relatives. After only six months Söderbaum's converted the arrangement into an annual contract at a considerably reduced rate. Further, the company undertook to have the delivery dates precisely established by Dr. Alfast, their specialist in ever-green trees, so that now, three days before the old tree becomes unaccept-able, the new one arrives and can be decorated at leisure. Furthermore, as a precautionary measure, two dozen dwarfs are kept in stock and three angels held in reserve. To this day, the confectionery has remained a sore point. It has a devastating tendency to melt and drip down from the tree, faster and more radically than melting wax. At least during the summer months. Every attempt to preserve their seasonal crispness by skillfully camouflaged cooling devices has so far failed, as has a series of experiments designed to test the possibility of embalming the tree. Nevertheless, the family is grateful for and open to any innovative suggestion that might reduce the cost of this permanent festivity.

VI

IN THE meantime, the evening ceremonies at my uncle's home have acquired an almost professional inflexibility: the family assembles at or around the tree. My aunt comes in, the candles are lit, the dwarfs begin to hammer, and the angel whispers "Peace, peace"; then a few carols are sung, cookies are nibbled, there is some casual conversation, and everyone retires with a yawn and a "Merry Christmas, everyone!"—at which point the young people turn to seasonal diversions while my kindly uncle and Aunt Milla go to bed. Candle smoke remains behind in the room, together with the mild aroma of heated fir branches and the spicy odor of Christmas cookies. The dwarfs, slightly phosphorescent, stand stiffly in the darkness, their arms raised menacingly, and the angel glows in its silvery robe, which is apparently also phosphorescent.

It may be superfluous to remark that the whole family's pleasure in the real Christmas festivities has been greatly diminished. We can, if we so wish, admire a traditional Christmas tree at any time in our uncle's home —and it often happens, when we are sitting on the veranda on a summer evening, after the labors of the day, imbibing Uncle's mild orange punch, that the tinkling of glass bells comes from within, and in the dusk the dwarfs are to be seen hammering away like nimble little devils, while the angel whispers "Peace," and again, "Peace." And we are still taken aback when, in the middle of summer, my uncle suddenly calls out to his children: "Light the tree, please, Mother will be here any minute." At that point, usually right on time, the prelate arrives, a mild old gentleman whom we have all taken to our hearts because he plays his part so beauti-

fully, assuming he even knows he is playing a part and which part. But
never mind: he plays it, white-haired, smiling, and the patch of purple
below his collar lends the last touch of refinement to his personality. And
it is an unusual experience to hear, on warm summer nights, the anxious
cry "The candle snuffer—quick, where's the candle snuffer?" It has happened more than once that, during a violent thunderstorm, the dwarfs
suddenly felt impelled, without the effect of heat, to raise their arms and
swing them wildly, thus providing a kind of unscheduled concert, a fact
that the family tried to explain, without much imagination, by the dry
word "electricity."

One not wholly inconsiderable aspect of this arrangement is the
financial one. Even though, generally speaking, our family is not strapped
for cash, such extraordinary expenditures upset all calculations. For, despite
every precaution, the wear and tear on dwarfs, anvils, and hammers is, of
course, enormous; and the sensitive mechanism enabling the angel to speak
requires constant care and maintenance and must from time to time be
replaced. Incidentally, I have meanwhile discovered the secret: the angel
is connected by a cable to a microphone in the next room, and in front
of the mike there is a constantly rotating phonograph record that whispers
at intervals "Peace," and again, "Peace." All these items are especially costly
in that they are designed for use on only a few days in the year but now
have to stand up to hard wear all year round. I was amazed when my uncle
told me one day that the dwarfs had actually to be renewed every three
months and that a complete set cost no less than a hundred and twenty-
eight marks. He had asked an engineer friend of his to reinforce them with
a latex coating but without impairing the beauty of their sound. This
attempt failed. The consumption of candles, spekulatius, and marzipan, the
tree contract, medical bills, and the token of appreciation due every month
to the prelate: all that, said my uncle, amounts to a daily average of eleven
marks, not to mention the wear and tear on his nerves and other impair-
ments to his health that were then beginning to make themselves felt. But
that was in the fall, and these deleterious effects were ascribed to a certain
autumnal sensitivity, a matter of quite common observation.

VII

THE ACTUAL Christmas celebrations went off normally. Something like
a sigh of relief went through my uncle's family now that other
families were to be seen gathered around Christmas trees, other families

had also to sing and eat spekulatius. But the relief lasted only for the duration of the Christmas season. As early as mid-January my cousin Lucie was afflicted by a strange malady: at the sight of the Christmas trees lying around on streets and garbage piles, she would burst into hysterical sobbing. This was followed by a regular attack of madness, which the family tried to pass off as a nervous breakdown. When a friend with whom she was having afternoon coffee smilingly offered her some spekulatius, she knocked the plate out of her hand. It is true, of course, that my cousin is what is known as a temperamental woman; so she knocked the plate out of her friend's hand, walked over to the Christmas tree, ripped it from its stand, and trampled on the glass baubles, artificial mushrooms, candles, and stars, a continuous howl issuing from her lips. The assembled ladies fled, including the hostess, and Lucie was left to rampage while they waited in the hall for the doctor, listening perforce to china being smashed inside the room. I find it difficult, but I must report here that Lucie was taken away in a straitjacket.

Although repeated hypnotic treatments arrested the malady, the actual cure progressed very slowly. Above all, the release from the evening ceremony, on which the doctor insisted, seemed to have a noticeably beneficial effect; after only a few days she began to thrive. After only ten days the doctor could risk at least mentioning spekulatius, but she obstinately refused to eat any. The doctor hit on the brilliant idea of feeding her pickles, offering her salads and hearty meat dishes. That was really poor Lucie's salvation. She laughed again, and she began to spice the endless therapeutic conversations with her doctor by adding ironic comments.

Although the gap caused by Lucie's absence from the evening ceremony was painful for my aunt, it was explained by a circumstance that can be accepted as a valid excuse for all women—pregnancy.

But Lucie had created what is called a precedent: she had proved that, although our aunt suffered when someone was absent, she did not start screaming right away, and my cousin Johannes and his brother-in-law Karl now tried to break out of the strict discipline by pleading illness or business commitments, or offering other more or less transparent reasons. But here my uncle was surprisingly adamant: with relentless severity he stipulated that only in exceptional cases could doctors' certificates be submitted and the briefest of dispensations applied for. My aunt immediately noticed any additional gap and would break into quiet but persistent weeping, giving rise to the most ominous concern.

After a month, Lucie returned and expressed her willingness to rejoin the daily ritual, but her doctor has insisted that a jar of pickles and a plate of hearty sandwiches be kept in readiness for her, her spekulatius trauma having proved to be incurable. Thus for a while all disciplinary problems were resolved by my uncle, who on this point turned out to be surprisingly adamant.

VIII

SOON AFTER the first anniversary of the perpetual Christmas celebration, disturbing rumors began to circulate: my cousin Johannes was said to have obtained an expert opinion from a medical friend as to the foreseeable life span of my aunt—a truly sinister rumor that threw a disquieting light on a peaceful daily family gathering. The expert opinion was said to have been devastating for Johannes. All the vital organs of my aunt, whose life has been a model of sobriety, are completely intact; the life span of her father extended over seventy-eight years, that of her mother over eighty-six. My aunt herself is sixty-two, and there is therefore no reason to prophesy an early and blessed demise for her. Even less, in my opinion, to wish it for her. So when my aunt fell ill during the summer—vomiting and diarrhea plagued the poor woman—there were whisperings that she had been poisoned; but let me expressly declare that this rumor is nothing but a figment on the part of evil-minded relatives. It has been proved beyond a doubt that she suffered from an infection brought in by a grandson. Analyses of my aunt's feces showed not even the slightest trace of poison.

That same summer the first antisocial tendencies showed up in Johannes: he resigned from his choral society, declaring, in writing, that he no longer intended to devote himself to the cultivation of German songs. It is true, of course—if I may interject this here—that, despite his academic degree, he was an uncultured person. For the male choir Virhymnia, being deprived of his bass voice was a great loss.

Lucie's husband, Karl, began secretly to get in touch with emigration offices. The land of his dreams had to have certain qualities: no fir trees must grow there, and their import must be prohibited or made impossible by high tariffs; furthermore—this for his wife's sake—the secret of baking spekulatius must be unknown there and the singing of Christmas carols prohibited. Karl declared his willingness to accept hard manual labor.

Meanwhile his attempts have been released from the curse of secrecy because my uncle has undergone a complete and abrupt change. This took place on such a disagreeable level that we had every reason to be shocked. That respectable man, of whom I can only say that he is as stubborn as he is kind, was observed on paths that are unquestionably immoral and will remain so as long as the world continues to exist. Various things have become known about him, and attested to by witnesses, to which only the word "adultery" can be applied. And the most terrible part about it is that he no longer denies it but claims that he is living under circumstances and conditions that must justify exceptional moral standards. Awkwardly enough, this sudden change came to light at the very time when the appeal against the two clerics of his parish was due to be heard. As a witness, as a crypto-plaintiff, Uncle Franz must have made such an unprepossessing impression that he can be considered solely to blame for the fact that the appeal turned out in favor of the two clerics. But by this time all such things have ceased to interest Uncle Franz: the moral disintegration of Uncle Franz is complete, a *fait accompli.*

He was also the first to hit upon the idea of having an actor represent him at the evening ritual. He had dug up an unemployed bon vivant who imitated him for two weeks so perfectly that not even his wife was aware of the substitution. His children were not aware of it either. It was one of the grandsons who, during a short pause in the singing, suddenly called out, "Grandpa's wearing striped socks!", at the same time triumphantly raising the bon vivant's trouser leg. For the poor artist, this scene must have been terrible. The family too were aghast, and, in order to avert a disaster, they immediately—as already so often in embarrassing situations—struck up a carol. After my aunt had gone to bed, the identity of the artist was quickly established. It was the signal for an almost total collapse.

IX

STILL, ONE must bear in mind that eighteen months is a long time, and that midsummer had arrived again, the season in which my relatives find it hardest to participate in this charade. Listlessly they nibble in the heat at cinnamon stars and gingerbread, smiling fixedly while they crack dry nuts, listening to the tirelessly hammering dwarfs, and flinching when the red-cheeked angel whispers "Peace" above their heads, "Peace." But they carry on while, despite their summer clothing, the perspiration runs down their necks and cheeks and their shirts stick to their bodies. Or, rather, they used to carry on.

For the time being, money is no object—on the contrary, one might say. Now there are whispers that Uncle Franz has been resorting to business methods that virtually no longer permit the description "Christian businessman." He is determined not to allow any appreciable diminution of his fortune, a commitment that both reassures and alarms us.

The unmasking of the bon vivant led to a regular mutiny, the result of which was a compromise: Uncle Franz has undertaken to finance a small ensemble to replace himself, Johannes, my brother-in-law Karl, and Lucie; and an agreement has been reached whereby one of the four takes part in the evening ritual in person, in order to keep an eye on the children. So far the prelate has been quite unaware of this fraud, to which one can by no means apply the adjective "pious." Apart from my aunt and the children, he is the only original character in this charade.

A detailed plan has been worked out, known in the family as the "game plan"; and in view of the fact that one of them always does take part, the actors are also assured of certain free days. Meanwhile the family has noticed that the actors are not at all averse to lending themselves to the ritual and are happy to earn some extra money; consequently their fees have been successfully reduced, there being fortunately no lack of out-of-work actors. Karl has told me that there is a good chance of further reducing this item, and quite considerably, especially since the actors are offered a meal, and, as everybody knows, art doesn't put bread on the table.

X

I HAVE ALREADY hinted at the disastrous trend taking place in Lucie: she now spends almost all her time gadding about in night spots, and, especially on days when she has been forced to take part in the ceremony at home, she throws all restraint to the winds. She wears cords, gaudy sweaters, runs around in sandals, and has cut off her glorious hair in favor of a plain square-cut style which, I now learn, has been in vogue more than once as "bangs." Although I have not yet been able to observe any overt immorality on her part, merely a certain exaltation that she herself calls "existentialism," I cannot see my way toward regarding this trend as desirable. I prefer women who are gentle, who move decorously to the rhythm of a waltz, who quote pleasant poetry, and whose diet does not consist exclusively of pickles and goulash overspiced with paprika. Karl's emigration plans seem to be crystallizing: he has discovered a country, not far from the equator, that promises to live up to his conditions, and Lucie is thrilled: in that country people wear clothes not unlike her own, love pungent spices, and dance to rhythms without which she maintains she is no longer able to live. Although it is somewhat shocking that this couple do not seem to cherish the idea of "Home, sweet home," I can understand their desire to get away from it all.

The situation with Johannes is even worse. Unfortunately the nasty rumor has turned out to be true: he has become a Communist. He has broken off all connection with his family, ignores all his obligations, and attends the evening ritual only by proxy: that of his double. His eyes have acquired a fanatical expression; he acts like a dervish at the public functions of his party, neglects his practice, and writes furious articles in appropriate journals. Strangely enough, he now quite often sees Franz, who tries vainly to convert him and whom he tries just as vainly to convert. Despite all spiritual alienation, they have grown somewhat closer on a personal level.

As for Franz, I have not seen him for a long time, only heard of him. He is said to have fallen into a deep depression, spending hours in dim churches, and I believe one is justified in describing his piety as exaggerated. He began to neglect his profession after his family became engulfed in its troubles; and just the other day I saw on the wall of a demolished building a faded poster announcing "Last fight of ex-champion Lenz vs. Lecoq. Lenz retiring from the ring." The poster was dated March, and we are now well into August. Franz is said to be in very poor shape. I believe he finds himself in a situation never before experienced in our family: he is poor. Fortunately he has remained single, so the social consequences of his irresponsible piety affect only himself. With amazing persistence he has been trying to arrange for Lucie's children to be placed under protective guardianship, believing as he does that they are threatened by the evening ritual. But his efforts have been in vain: we can be thankful that the children of well-to-do couples are not exposed to the interference of social institutions.

The one who has removed himself the least from the rest of the family is, in spite of some repulsive traits, Uncle Franz, although it is true that, in spite of his advanced age, he has a mistress, and his commercial practices are of a nature of which, while we may admire them, we can by no means approve. Recently he unearthed an out-of-work stage manager who supervises the evening ritual and sees to it that everything goes like clockwork. And it really does.

XI

MEANWHILE ALMOST two years have passed: a long time. And I could not refrain, on one of my evening strolls, from walking past my uncle's house, where normal hospitality is no longer possible, now that unknown artist types are milling around in there every evening and the members of the family indulge in strange-seeming amusements. It was a warm summer's evening when I passed by there, and even as I turned the corner into the chestnut avenue I could hear the words "Christmas glitter decks the forests. . . ." A passing truck rendered the remainder inaudible. I crept slowly up to the house and looked through a gap in the curtains into the room: the resemblance of the playactors to the relatives they were representing was so startling that for a moment I could not make out who actually was in charge—as they call it—that evening. I could not see the dwarfs, but I could hear them. Their chirping tinkle is on wavelengths that penetrate every wall. The whispering of the angel was inaudible. My aunt seemed genuinely happy: she was chatting with the prelate, and it took a while for me to recognize my brother-in-law as the only, if I may so put it, real person. I recognized him by the way he puckered his lips when he blew out a match. There do seem to be unmistakable traits of individuality. It occurred to me that the actors are treated to cigars, cigarettes, and wine; moreover, asparagus is served every evening. If they take advantage of this —and which artist would not?—it means a considerable additional expense for my uncle. The children were playing with dolls and toy wagons in a corner of the room: they looked pale and wan. Perhaps something really should be done about them, after all. It occurred to me that they might be replaced by wax dummies, the kind used in drugstore windows to promote milk powder and skin cream. They always seem very lifelike to me.

So I decide to draw the attention of the family to the possible effects of this unusual daily stimulation on childish minds. Although, of course, a certain amount of discipline can do no harm, it would seem that inordinate demands are being placed upon them in this instance.

I left my observation post when they started to sing "Silent Night." I really couldn't stand that carol. The air was so mild—and for a moment I had the impression of being present at a gathering of ghosts. I was suddenly seized by a craving for pickles, which gave me an inkling of how greatly Lucie must have suffered.

XII

MEANWHILE I have been successful in having the children replaced by wax dummies. The acquisition proved to be expensive—Uncle Franz balked at it for a long time, but it would have been irresponsible to continue to allow the children to be fed marzipan every evening and make them sing carols that may eventually cause psychological damage. The acquisition of the dummies proved fortunate, since Karl and Lucie really did emigrate, and Johannes also withdrew his children from his father's household. Standing amid big steamer trunks, I said good-bye to Karl, Lucie, and the children; they seemed happy, although somewhat apprehensive. Johannes has also moved away from our city. He is busy somewhere reorganizing one of the regional branches of his party.

Uncle Franz is tired of life. In a plaintive voice he recently told me that they keep forgetting to dust the dummies. The servants are giving him enough trouble as it is, and the actors are beginning to get out of hand. They are drinking more than they are entitled to, and some of them have been caught pocketing cigars and cigarettes. I advised my uncle to serve them colored water and to obtain some cardboard cigars.

The only reliable ones are my aunt and the prelate. They chat about the good old days, titter, and seem to be having a good time, and they only break off their conversation when a carol is struck up.

In any event: the ritual is being continued.

My cousin Franz's career has taken a strange turn. He has been accepted as a lay brother in a nearby monastery. The first time I saw him in his monk's habit I got a shock: that tall figure with the broken nose and swollen lips, those brooding eyes—he reminded me more of a convict than of a monk. It almost seemed as if he had divined my thoughts. "Our life is our punishment," he said in a low voice. I followed him into the visitors' room. Our conversation was stiff and halting, and he was obviously relieved when the bell summoned him for prayers in the chapel. I stood there pensively as he left: he was hurrying, and his haste seemed to be genuine.

The Balek Scales

W HERE MY grandfather came from, most of the people lived by working in the flax sheds. For five generations they had been breathing in the dust which rose from the crushed flax stalks, letting themselves be killed off by slow degrees, a race of long-suffering, cheerful people who ate goat cheese, potatoes, and now and then a rabbit; in the evening they would sit at home spinning and knitting; they sang, drank mint tea, and were happy. During the day they would carry the flax stalks to the antiquated machines, with no protection from the dust and at the mercy of the heat which came pouring out of the drying kilns. Each cottage contained only one bed, standing against the wall like a closet and reserved for the parents, while the children slept all round the room on benches. In the morning the room would be filled with the odor of thin soup; on Sundays there was stew, and on feast days the children's faces would light up with pleasure as they watched the black acorn coffee turning paler and paler from the milk their smiling mother poured into their coffee mugs.

Since the parents went off early to the flax sheds, the housework was left to the children: they would sweep the room, tidy up, wash the dishes and peel the potatoes, precious pale-yellow fruit whose thin peel had to be produced afterward to dispel any suspicion of extravagance or carelessness.

As soon as the children were out of school, they had to go off into the woods and, depending on the season, gather mushrooms and herbs: woodruff and thyme, caraway, mint and foxglove, and in summer, when they had brought in the hay from their meager fields, they gathered hayflowers. A pound of hayflowers was worth one pfennig, and they were sold by the apothecaries in town for twenty pfennigs a pound to high-strung ladies. The mushrooms were highly prized: they fetched twenty pfennigs a pound and were sold in the shops in town for one mark twenty. The children would crawl deep into the green darkness of the forest during the autumn, when dampness drove the mushrooms out of the soil, and almost every family had its own places where it gathered mushrooms, places which were handed down in whispers from generation to generation.

The woods belonged to the Baleks, as well as the flax sheds, and in my grandfather's village the Baleks had a château, and the wife of the head of the family had a little room next to the dairy where mushrooms, herbs, and hayflowers were weighed and paid for. There on the table stood the great Balek scales, an old-fashioned, ornate bronze-gilt contraption, which my grandfather's grandparents had already faced when they were children, their grubby hands holding their little baskets of mushrooms, their paper bags of hayflowers, breathlessly watching the number of weights Frau Balek had to throw on the scale before the swinging pointer came to rest exactly over the black line, that thin line of justice which had to be redrawn every year. Then Frau Balek would take the big book covered in brown leather, write down the weight, and pay out the money: pfennigs or ten-pfennig pieces and very, very occasionally a mark. And when my grandfather was a child there was a big glass jar of lemon drops standing there, the kind that cost one mark a pound, and when Frau Balek— whichever one happened to be presiding over the little room—was in a good mood, she would put her hand into this jar and give each child a lemon drop, and the children's faces would light up with pleasure, the way they used to when on feast days their mother poured milk into their coffee mugs, milk that made the coffee turn paler and paler until it was as pale as the flaxen pigtails of the little girls.

One of the laws imposed by the Baleks on the village was that no one was permitted to have any scales in the house. The law was so ancient that nobody gave a thought as to when and how it had arisen, and it had to be obeyed, for anyone who broke it was dismissed from the flax sheds, he could not sell his mushrooms or his thyme or his hayflowers, and the power of the Baleks was so far-reaching that no one in the neighboring villages would give him work either, or buy his forest herbs. But since the days when my grandfather's parents had gone out as small children to gather mushrooms and sell them in order that they might season the meat of the rich people of Prague or be baked into game pies, it had never occurred to anyone to break this law: flour could be measured in cups, eggs could be counted, what they had spun could be measured by the yard, and besides, the old-fashioned bronze-gilt, ornate Balek scales did not look as if there was anything wrong with them, and five generations had entrusted the swinging black pointer with what they had gone out as eager children to gather from the woods.

True, there were some among these quiet people who flouted the law, poachers bent on making more money in one night than they could earn in a whole month in the flax sheds, but even these people apparently never thought of buying scales or making their own. My grandfather was the first person bold enough to test the justice of the Baleks, the family who lived in the château and drove two carriages, who always maintained one boy from the village while he studied theology at the seminary in Prague, the family with whom the priest played taroc every Wednesday, on whom the local reeve, in his carriage emblazoned with the imperial coat-of-arms, made an annual New Year's Day call and on whom the emperor conferred a title on the first day of the year 1900.

My grandfather was hardworking and smart: he crawled farther into the woods than the children of his clan had crawled before him, penetrating as far as the thicket where, according to legend, Bilgan the Giant was supposed to dwell, guarding a treasure. But my grandfather was not afraid of Bilgan: he worked his way deep into the thicket, even when he was quite little, and brought out great quantities of mushrooms; he even found truffles, for which Frau Balek paid thirty pfennigs a pound. Everything my grandfather took to the Baleks he entered on the back of a torn-off calendar page: every pound of mushrooms, every ounce of thyme, and on the right-hand side, in his childish handwriting, he entered the amount he received for each item; he scrawled in every pfennig, from the age of seven to the age of twelve; by the time he was twelve, the year 1900 had arrived, and because the Baleks had been raised to the aristocracy by the emperor, they gave every family in the village a quarter of a pound of real coffee, the Brazilian kind; there was also free beer and tobacco for the men, and at the château there was a great banquet; many carriages stood in the avenue of poplars leading from the entrance gates to the château.

But the day before the banquet the coffee was distributed in the little room which had housed the Balek scales for almost a hundred years, and the Balek family was now called Balek von Bilgan because, according to legend, Bilgan the Giant used to have a great castle on the site of the present Balek estate.

My grandfather often used to tell me how he went there after school to fetch the coffee for four families: the Cechs, the Weidlers, the Vohlas, and his own, the Brüchers. It was the afternoon of New Year's Eve: there were the front rooms to be decorated, the baking to be done, and the families did not want to spare four boys and have each of them go all the way to the château to bring back a quarter of a pound of coffee.

And so my grandfather sat on the narrow wooden bench in the little room while Gertrud the maid counted out the wrapped four-ounce packages of coffee, four of them, and he looked at the scales and saw that the pound weight was still lying on the left-hand scale; Frau Balek von Bilgan was busy with preparations for the banquet. And when Gertrud was about to put her hand into the jar with the lemon drops to give my grandfather one, she discovered it was empty: it was refilled once a year, and held one pound of the kind that cost a mark.

Gertrud laughed and said, "Wait here while I get the new lot," and my grandfather waited with the four four-ounce packages which had been wrapped and sealed in the factory, facing the scales on which someone had left the pound weight, and my grandfather took the four packages of coffee, put them on the empty scale, and his heart thudded as he watched the black finger of justice come to rest on the left of the black line: the scale with the pound weight stayed down, and the pound of coffee remained up in the air; his heart thudded more than if he had been lying behind a bush in the forest waiting for Bilgan the Giant, and he felt in his pocket for the pebbles he always carried with him so he could use his catapult to shoot the sparrows which pecked away at his mother's cabbage plants—he had to put three, four, five pebbles beside the packages of coffee before the scale with the pound weight rose and the pointer at last came to rest over the black line. My grandfather took the coffee from the scale, wrapped the five pebbles in his kerchief, and when Gertrud came back with the big pound bag of lemon drops which had to last for another whole year in order to make the children's faces light up with pleasure, when Gertrud let the lemon drops rattle into the glass jar, the pale little fellow was still standing there, and nothing seemed to have changed. My grandfather took only three of the packages; then Gertrud looked in startled surprise at the white-faced child who threw the lemon drop onto the floor, ground it under his heel, and said, "I want to see Frau Balek."

"Balek von Bilgan, if you please," said Gertrud.

"All right, Frau Balek von Bilgan," but Gertrud only laughed at him, and he walked back to the village in the dark, took the Cechs, the Weidlers, and the Vohlas their coffee, and said he had to go and see the priest.

Instead he went out into the dark night with his five pebbles in his kerchief. He had to walk a long way before he found someone who had scales, who was permitted to have them; no one in the villages of Blaugau and Bernau had any, he knew that, and he went straight through them till, after two hours' walking, he reached the little town of Dielheim, where Honig the apothecary lived. From Honig's house came the smell of fresh pancakes, and Honig's breath, when he opened the door to the half-frozen boy, already smelled of punch, there was a moist cigar between his narrow lips, and he clasped the boy's cold hands firmly for a moment, saying, "What's the matter, has your father's lung got worse?"

443

"No, I haven't come for medicine, I wanted . . ." My grandfather undid his kerchief, took out the five pebbles, held them out to Honig, and said, "I wanted to have these weighed." He glanced anxiously into Honig's face, but when Honig said nothing and did not get angry, or even ask him anything, my grandfather said, "It is the amount that is short of justice," and now, as he went into the warm room, my grandfather realized how wet his feet were. The snow had soaked through his cheap shoes, and in the forest the branches had showered him with snow which was now melting, and he was tired and hungry and suddenly began to cry because he thought of the quantities of mushrooms, the herbs, the flowers, which had been weighed on the scales that were short five pebbles' worth of justice. And when Honig, shaking his head and holding the five pebbles, called his wife, my grandfather thought of the generations of his parents, his grandparents, who had all had to have their mushrooms, their flowers, weighed on the scales, and he was overwhelmed by a great wave of injustice, and began to sob louder than ever, and, without waiting to be asked, he sat down on a chair, ignoring the pancakes, the cup of hot coffee which nice plump Frau Honig put in front of him, and did not stop crying till Honig himself came out from the shop at the back and, rattling the pebbles in his hand, said in a low voice to his wife, "Two ounces, exactly."

My grandfather walked the two hours home through the forest, got a beating at home, said nothing, not a single word, when he was asked about the coffee, spent the whole evening doing sums on the piece of paper on which he had written down everything he had sold to Frau Balek, and when midnight struck, and the cannon could be heard from the château, and the whole village rang with shouting and laughter and the noise of rattles, when the family kissed and embraced all round, he said into the New Year silence, "The Baleks owe me eighteen marks and thirty-two pfennigs." And again he thought of all the children there were in the village, of his brother Fritz, who had gathered so many mushrooms, of his sister Ludmilla; he thought of the many hundreds of children who had all gathered mushrooms for the Baleks, and herbs and flowers, and this time he did not cry but told his parents and brothers and sisters of his discovery.

When the Baleks von Bilgan went to High Mass on New Year's Day, their new coat-of-arms—a giant crouching under a fir tree—already emblazoned in blue and gold on their carriage, they saw the hard, pale faces of the people all staring at them. They had expected garlands in the village, a song in their honor, cheers and hurrahs, but the village was completely deserted as they drove through it, and in church the pale faces of the people were turned toward them, mute and hostile, and when the priest mounted the pulpit to deliver his New Year's sermon, he sensed the chill in those otherwise quiet and peaceful faces, and he stumbled painfully through his sermon and went back to the altar drenched in sweat. And as the Baleks von Bilgan left the church after Mass, they walked through a lane of mute, pale faces. But young Frau Balek von Bilgan stopped in front of the children's pews, sought out my grandfather's face, pale little Franz Brücher, and asked him, right there in the church, "Why didn't you take the coffee for your mother?" And my grandfather stood up and said, "Because you owe me as much money as five pounds of coffee would cost." And he pulled the five pebbles from his pocket, held them out to the young woman, and said, "This much, two ounces, is short in every pound of your justice"; and before the woman could say anything the men and women in the church lifted up their voices and sang: "The justice of this earth, O Lord, hath put Thee to death. . . ."

While the Baleks were at church, Wilhelm Vohla, the poacher, had broken into the little room, stolen the scales and the big fat leatherbound book in which had been entered every pound of mushrooms, every pound of hayflowers, everything bought by the Baleks in the village, and all afternoon of that New Year's Day the men of the village sat in my great-grandparents' front room and calculated, calculated one-eighth of everything that had been bought—but when they had calculated many thousands of talers and had still not come to an end, the reeve's gendarmes arrived, made their way into my great-grandfather's front room, shooting and stabbing as they came, and removed the scales and the book by force. My grandfather's little sister Ludmilla lost her life, a few men were wounded, and one of the gendarmes was stabbed to death by Wilhelm Vohla the poacher.

Our village was not the only one to rebel: Blaugau and Bernau did too, and for almost a week no work was done in the flax sheds. But a great many gendarmes appeared, and the men and women were threatened with prison, and the Baleks forced the priest to display the scales publicly in the school and demonstrate that the finger of justice swung to and fro accurately. And the men and women went back to the flax sheds—but no one went to the school to watch the priest: he stood there all alone, helpless and forlorn with his weights, scales, and packages of coffee.

And the children went back to gathering mushrooms, to gathering thyme, flowers, and foxglove; but every Sunday, as soon as the Baleks entered the church, the hymn was struck up: "The justice of this earth, O Lord, hath put Thee to death," until the reeve ordered it proclaimed in every village that the singing of this hymn was forbidden.

My grandfather's parents had to leave the village, and the new grave of their little daughter; they became basket weavers, but did not stay long anywhere because it pained them to see how everywhere the finger of justice swung falsely. They walked along behind their cart, which crept slowly over the country roads, taking their thin goat with them, and passers-by could sometimes hear a voice from the cart singing, "The justice of this earth, O Lord, hath put Thee to death." And those who wanted to listen could hear the tale of the Baleks von Bilgan, whose justice lacked an eighth part. But there were few who listened.

The Postcard

Nᴏɴᴇ ᴏꜰ my friends can understand the care with which I preserve a scrap of paper that has no value whatever. It merely keeps alive the memory of a certain day in my life, and to it I owe a reputation for sentimentality which is considered unworthy of my social position: I am the assistant manager of a textile firm. But I protest the accusation of sentimentality and am continually trying to invest this scrap of paper with some documentary value. It is a tiny, rectangular piece of ordinary paper, the size, but not the shape, of a stamp—it is narrower and longer than a stamp—and although it originated in the post office it has not the slightest collector's value. It has a bright red border and is divided by another red line into two rectangles of different sizes; in the smaller of these rectangles there is a big black R, in the larger one, in black print, "Düsseldorf" and a number—the number 634. That is all, and the bit of paper is yellow and thin with age, and now that I have described it minutely I have decided to throw it away: an ordinary registration sticker, such as every post office slaps on every day by the dozen.

And yet this scrap of paper reminds me of a day in my life which is truly unforgettable, although many attempts have been made to erase it from my memory. But my memory functions too well.

First of all, when I think of that day, I smell vanilla custard, a warm, sweet cloud creeping under my bedroom door and reminding me of my mother's goodness: I had asked her to make some vanilla ice cream for my first day of vacation, and when I woke up I could smell it.

It was half past ten. I lit a cigarette, pushed up my pillow, and considered how I would spend the afternoon. I decided to go swimming; after lunch I would take the streetcar to the beach, have a bit of a swim, read, smoke, and wait for one of the girls at the office, who had promised to come down to the beach after five.

In the kitchen my mother was pounding meat, and when she stopped for a moment I could hear her humming a tune. It was a hymn. I felt very happy. The previous day I had passed my test, I had a good job in a textile factory, a job with opportunities for advancement—but now I was on vacation, two weeks' vacation, and it was summertime. It was hot outside, but in those days I still loved hot weather: through the slits in the shutters I could see the heat haze, I could see the green of the trees in front of our house, I could hear the streetcar. And I was looking forward to breakfast. Then I heard my mother coming to listen at my door; she crossed the hall and stopped by my door; it was silent for a moment in our apartment, and I was just about to call "Mother" when the bell rang downstairs. My mother went to our front door, and I heard the funny high-pitched purring of the buzzer down below; it buzzed four, five, six times, while my mother was talking on the landing to Frau Kurz, who lived in the next apartment. Then I heard a man's voice, and I knew at once it was the mailman, although I had only seen him a few times. The mailman came into our entrance hall, Mother said, "What?" and he said, "Here sign here, please." It was very quiet for a moment, the mailman said "Thanks," my mother closed the door after him, and I heard her go back into the kitchen.

Shortly after that I got up and went into the bathroom. I shaved, had a leisurely wash, and when I turned off the faucet I could hear my mother grinding the coffee. It was like Sunday, except that I had not been to church.

Nobody will believe it, but my heart suddenly felt heavy. I don't know why, but it was heavy. I could no longer hear the coffee mill. I dried myself off, put on my shirt and trousers, socks and shoes, combed my hair, and went into the living room. There were flowers on the table, pale pink carnations, it all looked fresh and neat, and on my plate lay a red pack of cigarettes.

Then Mother came in from the kitchen carrying the coffeepot and I saw at once she had been crying. In one hand she was holding the coffeepot, in the other a little pile of mail, and her eyes were red. I went over to her, took the pot from her, kissed her cheek, and said, "Good morning." She looked at me, said, "Good morning, did you sleep well?" and tried to smile, but did not succeed.

We sat down, my mother poured the coffee, and I opened the red pack lying on my plate and lit a cigarette. I had suddenly lost my appetite. I stirred milk and sugar into my coffee, tried to look at Mother, but each time I quickly lowered my eyes. "Was there any mail?" I asked, a senseless question, since Mother's small red hand was resting on the little pile on top of which lay the newspaper.

"Yes," she said, pushing the pile toward me. I opened the newspaper while my mother began to butter some bread for me. The front page bore the headline "Outrages Continue Against Germans in the Polish Corridor!" There had been headlines like that for weeks on the front pages of the papers. Reports of "rifle fire along the Polish border and refugees escaping from the sphere of Polish harassment and fleeing to the Reich." I put the paper aside. Next I read the brochure of a wine merchant who used to supply us sometimes when Father was still alive. Various types of Riesling were being offered at exceptionally low prices. I put the brochure aside too.

Meanwhile my mother had finished buttering the slice of bread for me. She put it on my plate, saying, "Please eat something!" She burst into violent sobs. I could not bring myself to look at her. I can't look at anyone who is really suffering—but now for the first time I realized it must have something to do with the mail. It must be the mail. I stubbed out my cigarette, took a bite of the bread and butter, and picked up the next letter, and as I did so I saw there was a postcard lying underneath. But I had not noticed the registration sticker, that tiny scrap of paper I still possess and to which I owe a reputation for sentimentality. So I read the letter first. The letter was from Uncle Eddy. Uncle Eddy wrote that at last, after many years as an assistant instructor, he was now a full-fledged teacher, but it had meant being transferred to a little one-horse town; financially speaking, he was hardly any better off than before, since he was now being paid at the local scale. And his kids had had whooping cough, and the way things were going made him feel sick to his stomach, he didn't have to tell us why. No, he didn't, and it made us feel sick too. It made a lot of people feel sick.

When I reached for the postcard, I saw it had gone. My mother had picked it up, she was holding it up and looking at it, and I kept my eyes on my half-eaten slice of bread, stirred my coffee, and waited.

I shall never forget it. Only once had my mother ever cried so terribly, when my father died; and then I had not dared to look at her either. A nameless diffidence had prevented me from comforting her.

I tried to bite into the bread, but my throat closed up, for I suddenly realized that what was upsetting Mother so much could only be something to do with me. Mother said something I didn't catch and handed me the postcard, and it was then I saw the registration sticker: that red-bordered rectangle, divided by a red line into two other rectangles, of which the smaller one contained a big black R and the bigger one the word "Düsseldorf" and the number 634. Otherwise the postcard was quite normal. It was addressed to me and on the back were the words "Mr. Bruno Schneider: You are required to report to the Schlieffen Barracks in Adenbrück on August 5, 1939, for an eight-week period of military training." "Bruno Schneider," the date, and "Adenbrück" were typed, everything else was printed, and at the bottom was a vague scrawl and the printed word "Major."

Today I know that the scrawl was superfluous. A machine for printing majors' signatures would do the job just as well. The only thing that mattered was the little sticker on the front for which my mother had had to sign a receipt.

I put my hand on her arm and said, "Now, look, Mother, it's only eight weeks." And my mother said, "I know."

"Only eight weeks," I said, and I knew I was lying, and my mother dried her tears, said, "Yes, of course"; we were both lying, without knowing why we were lying, but we were and we knew we were.

I was just picking up my bread and butter again when it struck me that today was the fourth and that on the following day at ten o'clock I had to be over two hundred miles away to the east. I felt myself going pale, put down the bread and got up, ignoring my mother. I went to my room. I stood at my desk, opened the drawer, closed it again. I looked round, felt something had happened and didn't know what. The room was no longer mine. That was all. Today I know, but that day I did meaningless things to reassure myself that the room still belonged to me. It was useless to rummage around in the box containing my letters, or to straighten my books. Before I knew what I was doing, I had begun to pack my briefcase: shirt, pants, towel, and socks, and I went into the bathroom to get my shaving things. My mother was still sitting at the breakfast table. She had stopped crying. My half-eaten slice of bread was still on my plate, there was still some coffee in my cup, and I said to my mother, "I'm going over to the Giesselbachs' to phone about my train."

When I came back from the Giesselbachs' it was just striking twelve noon. Our entrance hall smelled of roast pork and cauliflower, and my mother had begun to break up ice in a bag to put into our little ice-cream machine.

My train was leaving at eight that evening, and I would be in Adenbrück next morning about six. It was only fifteen minutes' walk to the station, but I left the house at three o'clock. I lied to my mother, who did not know how long it took to get to Adenbrück.

Those last three hours I spent in the house seem, on looking back, worse and longer than the whole time I spent away, and that was a long time. I don't know what we did. We had no appetite for dinner. My mother soon took back the roast, the cauliflower, the potatoes, and the vanilla ice cream to the kitchen. Then we drank the breakfast coffee which had been kept warm under a yellow cozy, and I smoked cigarettes, and now and again we exchanged a few words. "Eight weeks," I said, and my mother said, "Yes—yes, of course," and she didn't cry any more. For three hours we lied to each other, till I couldn't stand it any longer. My mother blessed me, kissed me on both cheeks, and as I closed the front door behind me, I knew she was crying.

I walked to the station. The station was bustling with activity. It was vacation time: happy suntanned people were milling around. I had a beer in the waiting room, and about half past three decided to call up the girl from the office whom I had arranged to meet at the beach.

While I was dialing the number, and the perforated nickel dial kept clicking back into place—five times—I almost regretted it, but I dialed the sixth figure, and when her voice asked, "Who is it?" I was silent for a moment, then said slowly, "Bruno" and "Can you come? I have to go off—I've been drafted."

"Right now?" she asked.

"Yes."

She thought it over for a moment, and through the phone I could hear the voices of the others, who were apparently collecting money to buy some ice cream.

"All right," she said, "I'll come. Are you at the station?"

"Yes," I said.

She arrived at the station very quickly, and to this day I don't know, although she has been my wife now for ten years, to this day I don't know whether I ought to regret that phone call. After all, she kept my job open for me with the firm, she revived my defunct ambition when I came home, and she is actually the one I have to thank for the fact that those opportunities for advancement have now become reality.

But I didn't stay as long as I could have with her either. We went to the movies, and in the cinema, which was empty, dark, and very hot, I kissed her, though I didn't feel much like it.

I kept on kissing her, and I went to the station at six o'clock, although I need not have gone till eight. On the platform I kissed her again and boarded the first eastbound train. Ever since then I have not been able to look at a beach without a pang: the sun, the water, the cheerfulness of the people seem all wrong, and I prefer to stroll alone through the town on a rainy day and go to a movie where I don't have to kiss anybody. My opportunities for advancement with the firm are not yet exhausted. I might become a director, and I probably will, according to the law of paradoxical inertia. For people are convinced I am loyal to the firm and will do a great deal for it. But I am not loyal to it and I haven't the slightest intention of doing anything for it. . . .

Lost in thought I have often contemplated that registration sticker, which gave such a sudden twist to my life. And when the tests are held in summer and our young employees come to me afterward with beaming faces to be congratulated, it is my job to make a little speech in which the words "opportunities for advancement" play a traditional role.

Recollections
of a Young King

At the age of thirteen I was proclaimed King of Capota. I happened to be sitting in my room, busy trying to erase the "un" from the "unsatisfactory" at the bottom of one of my essays. My father, Pyg Gy the First of Capota, was off for a month's hunting in the mountains, and I had been told to forward my essay to him by royal express courier. So I was counting on the poor lighting in hunting lodges and busily erasing when I suddenly heard loud cries outside the palace: "Long live Pyg Gy the Second!"

A few minutes later my personal valet came rushing into the room, prostrated himself in the doorway, and whispered devoutly, "May it please Your Majesty not to hold it against me that I once reported Your Majesty to His Excellency the prime minister for smoking."

I found the valet's servility obnoxious, sent him away, and went on erasing. It was my tutor's custom to mark my work with a red indelible pencil. I had just rubbed a hole in the paper when I was interrupted again: the prime minister entered, knelt down by the door, and cried, "Three cheers for Pyg Gy the Second!" He added, "Your Majesty, the people wish to see you."

I was quite bewildered, put down the eraser, dusted off my hands, and asked, "Why do the people wish to see me?"

"Because you are the king."

"Since when?"

"Since half an hour ago. Your most gracious father was fatally shot by a Rasac while hunting." (Rasac is the abbreviation for "Radical Sadists of Capota.")

"Oh, those Rasacs!" I exclaimed. Then I followed the prime minister out onto the balcony and showed myself to the people. I smiled, waved my arms, and felt quite bewildered.

This spontaneous demonstration lasted two hours. It was already beginning to grow dark before the crowd dispersed; a few hours later it came past the palace again in the form of a torchlight procession.

I went back to my rooms, tore up my essays, and threw the scraps into the courtyard of the royal palace. There—as I later found out—they were gathered up by souvenir hunters and sold to foreign countries where today the evidence of my weakness in spelling is displayed under glass.

There now followed some strenuous months. The Rasacs attempted a putsch but were suppressed by the Misacs ("Mild Sadists of Capota") and the army. My father was buried, and I had to attend sessions of Parliament and sign new laws—but on the whole I enjoyed being king because I could now deal differently with my tutor.

When he asked me at lesson time, "May it please Your Majesty to recite the rules regarding improper fractions?" I would say, "No, it does not please me," and he could do nothing about it. When he said, "Would Your Majesty find it intolerable if I were to ask Your Majesty to write down, on about three pages, the motives of William Tell when he murdered Gessler?" I would say, "Yes, I would find it intolerable," and I would require him to enumerate William Tell's motives for my benefit.

Thus, almost effortlessly, I acquired a certain education, burned all my textbooks and copybooks, and devoted myself to my true passions: I played ball, threw my pocketknife at the door panel, read thrillers, and had long conferences with the manager of the royal movie theater. I gave instructions for all my favorite movies to be obtained, and in Parliament I proposed some educational reforms.

It was a glorious time, although I found the parliamentary sessions wearisome. I succeeded in giving an outward impression of the melancholy youthful king and relied entirely on Prime Minister Pelzer, who had been a friend of my father and was a cousin of my deceased mother.

But after three months Pelzer urged me to get married, saying, "You must set an example to the people, Your Majesty." Marriage as such didn't scare me: the bad part was that Pelzer offered me his eleven-year-old daughter Jadwiga, a skinny little girl whom I often saw playing ball in the courtyard. She was considered dumb, was repeating the fifth grade, was pale and looked spiteful. I asked Pelzer for time to think it over and now became genuinely melancholy, spending hours leaning on my windowsill watching Jadwiga playing ball or hopscotch. She was a little more attractively dressed now and from time to time would glance up at me and smile. But her smile seemed to me artificial.

When my decision was due, Pelzer appeared before me in gala uniform: he was a big strapping man with a sallow complexion, black beard, and flashing eyes. "May it please Your Majesty," he said, "to inform me of your decision? Has my child found favor in Your Majesty's eyes?" When I replied with a point-blank "No," something terrible happened: Pelzer ripped the epaulets from his shoulders, the decorations from his chest, threw his portfolio—it was made of synthetic leather—at my feet, tore at his beard, and shouted, "So that is the gratitude of Capotian kings!"

I was in an awkward situation. Without Pelzer, I was lost. Quickly changing my mind, I said, "May I ask you for Jadwiga's hand?"

Pelzer threw himself at my feet, fervently kissed the tips of my shoes, and picked up the epaulets, decorations, and the synthetic-leather portfolio.

We were married in Huldebach Cathedral. There was beer and sausage for the populace as well as eight cigarettes per head and, at my personal suggestion, two free tickets for the carrousel; for a whole week, noise surged around the palace. From now on I helped Jadwiga with her homework, we played ball, played hopscotch, went horseback riding together, and, whenever we felt like it, ordered marzipan from the royal confectioner's or went to the royal movie theater. I still enjoyed being a king; but a serious incident finally put paid to my career.

On reaching the age of fourteen, I was made a colonel and commander in chief of the 8th Cavalry Regiment. Jadwiga was made a major. From time to time we had to inspect the regiment, attend functions at the officers' mess, and on every high holiday pin decorations on the chests of deserving soldiers. I myself received a good many decorations. But then came the Poskopek affair.

Poskopek was a soldier in the fourth squadron of my regiment who deserted one Sunday evening to follow a female circus rider across the border. He was caught, detained, and sentenced to death by a court-martial. As regimental commander it was my job to sign the death warrant, but I simply wrote at the bottom: "Sentence commuted to two weeks' detention, Pyg Gy II."

This note had terrible consequences. The officers of my regiment all ripped their epaulets from their shoulders, the decorations from their chests, and had them scattered about my room by a young lieutenant. The entire Capotian army joined in the mutiny, and by the evening of that day my entire room was full of epaulets and decorations: it looked a mess.

True, the populace cheered me lustily, but that very night Pelzer informed me that the army had gone over in a body to the Rasacs. There was the crack of rifle shots, and the frantic hammering of machine guns rent the silence around the palace. Although the Misacs had sent me a bodyguard, Pelzer went over to the Rasacs during the night, which meant that I was forced to flee with Jadwiga.

We hastily gathered up clothing, bank notes, and jewelry, the Misacs requisitioned a taxi, and we barely made it to the railway station of the neighboring country, where we sank exhausted into a second-class sleeping compartment and moved off toward the west.

From across the border with Capota came the sound of rifle shots, frantic yelling, the whole terrible music of rebellion.

We traveled for four days and left the train at a city called Wickelheim. Wickelheim—dim memories from my geography lessons told me —was the capital of our neighboring country.

By this time Jadwiga and I had experienced things that we were beginning to appreciate: the smell of the train, acrid and pungent, the taste of sausages at railway stations of which we had never even heard. I could smoke to my heart's content, and Jadwiga began to blossom now that she was relieved of the burden of homework.

On the second day of our stay in Wickelheim, posters appeared everywhere that caught our attention: "Hunke Circus—Hula, the famous equestrienne, with her partner Jürgen Poskopek!" Jadwiga became all excited. "Pyg Gy," she said, "think of our livelihood. Poskopek will help you!"

At our hotel, telegrams were arriving hourly from Capota announcing the victory of the Misacs, the execution of Pelzer, a reorganization of the military.

The new prime minister—he was called Schmidt and was the leader of the Misacs—implored me to return and once again to accept the steel crown of the kings of Capota from the hands of the people.

For a few days I wavered, but ultimately Jadwiga's dread of homework won out. I went to the Hunke Circus, asked for Poskopek, and was welcomed by him ecstatically. "You saved my life!" he cried, standing in the doorway of his trailer. "What can I do for you?"

"Provide me with a livelihood," I said modestly.

Poskopek could not do enough for me: he interceded on my behalf with Herr Hunke, and I began by selling lemonade, then cigarettes, later goulash at the Hunke Circus. I was given a trailer and within a short time was made a cashier. I adopted the name Tückes, Wilhelm Tückes, and from then on ceased to be bothered by telegrams from Capota.

I am regarded as dead, as having disappeared without trace, whereas actually I am roaming the country in Hunke Circus's trailer with my blossoming Jadwiga. I get to sniff the air of foreign lands, to see them, I enjoy the great confidence placed in me by Herr Hunke. And if it were not for Poskopek visiting me now and then and telling me about Capota, if it were not for his wife, Hula, the beautiful equestrienne, assuring me over and over again that her husband owes his life to me, I would never give so much as a thought to having once been a king.

But the other day I came upon actual proof of my former royal life.

We were performing in Madrid, and one morning I was strolling with Jadwiga through the city when a big gray building with the inscription "National Museum" caught our eye. "Let's go in," said Jadwiga, so in we went, into one of the large, more remote rooms over whose door hung a sign saying "Holographs."

All unsuspecting, we proceeded to look at the handwritings of various heads of state and kings until we came to a glass case discreetly labeled "Kingdom of Capota—now a republic." I saw the handwriting of my grandfather Wuck the Fortieth; I saw an excerpt from the famous Capotian Manifesto written in his own hand; I found a sheet from my father's hunting diaries—and finally a scrap from one of my copybooks, a piece of soiled paper on which I read "Helth is Welth." Embarrassed, I turned toward Jadwiga, but she merely smiled and said, "That's all behind you now, forever."

We quickly left the museum, for it was now one o'clock, the performance began at three, and at two I had to open the box office.

The Death
of Elsa Baskoleit

THE BASEMENT of the house we used to live in was rented to a shop-keeper called Baskoleit; there were always orange crates standing around in the passages, it smelled of rotten fruit that Baskoleit put out for the garbage trucks, and from beyond the dim light of the frosted glass panel we could often hear his voice, with its broad East Prussian dialect, complaining about the bad times. But in his heart of hearts Baskoleit was a cheerful man: we knew, as surely as only children can know, that his grumbling was a game, even the way he used to swear at us, and he would often come up the three or four steps leading from the basement to the street with his pockets full of apples and oranges which he tossed to us like rubber balls.

But the interesting thing about Baskoleit was his daughter Elsa, of whom we knew that she wanted to be a dancer. Perhaps she already was one. In any case, she practiced a great deal, she practiced downstairs in the basement room with the yellow walls next to Baskoleit's kitchen: a slender girl with fair hair who stood on the tips of her toes, dressed in green tights, pale, hovering for minutes like a swan, whirling around, leaping, or doing handsprings. I could watch her from my bedroom window when it got dark; in the yellow rectangle of the window frame, her thin, green-clad body, her pale strained face, and her fair head that sometimes, when she jumped, touched the naked light bulb, which began to swing and for the space of a few seconds expanded the yellow circle of light on the gray courtyard. There were some people who shouted across the courtyard, "Whore!", and I didn't know what a whore was; there were others who shouted, "It's disgusting!", and although I thought I knew what disgusting was, I couldn't believe it had anything to do with Elsa. Then Baskoleit's window would be flung open, and in the steam of the kitchen his big bald head would loom up, and with the light that fell from the open kitchen window into the courtyard he would pour out into the dark courtyard a torrent of oaths of which I didn't understand a single one. At any rate, Elsa's window was soon provided with a curtain, heavy green plush, which let out hardly any light at all, but every evening I would gaze at the faintly glowing rectangle and see her, although I couldn't see her: Elsa Baskoleit in her light-green tights, thin and fair-haired, hovering for seconds on end under the naked light bulb.

But before long we moved away, I got older, found out what a whore was, thought I knew what disgusting was, saw dancers, but liked none of them as well as Elsa Baskoleit, of whom I never heard again. We moved to another town, war came, a long war, and I thought no more of Elsa Baskoleit, I didn't even think of her when we moved back to the old town. I tried my hand at all sorts of jobs, till I became a truck driver for a wholesale vegetable dealer: handling a truck was the only thing I was good at. Each morning I was given a list, cases of apples and oranges, baskets of plums, and drove into town.

One day, while I was standing on the ramp where my truck was being loaded and checking what the warehouseman was loading on the truck against my list, the bookkeeper emerged from his cubbyhole, which is plastered with banana posters, and asked the warehouseman, "Can we supply Baskoleit?"

"Has he ordered something? Purple grapes?"

"Yes." The bookkeeper removed the pencil from behind his ear and looked at the warehouseman in surprise.

"Once in a while," said the warehouseman, "he orders something— purple grapes, I don't know why—but we can't supply him. Get a move on!" he shouted to the helpers in their gray smocks. The bookkeeper went back to his cubbyhole, and I ceased to check whether they were really loading the stuff that was on my list. I saw the rectangular, brightly lit frame of the basement window, I saw Elsa Baskoleit dancing, thin and pale, dressed in bright green, and that morning I took a different route from the one I was supposed to take.

Of the lampposts we had played beside, only one was still standing, and even this one was minus its head, most of the houses were in ruins, and my truck jolted through deep potholes. There was only one child in the street, which used to swarm with children: a pale, dark-haired boy sitting on a bit of broken wall and drawing lines in the whitish dust. He looked up as I drove by, but then let his head droop again. I stopped in front of Baskoleit's house and got out.

His small windows were dusty, pyramids of packages had collapsed, and the green cardboard was black with dirt. I looked up at the patched housewall, hesitatingly opened the door, and stepped slowly down into the shop: there was an acrid smell of damp soup mix, which was stuck together in lumps in a cardboard box by the door, but then I saw Baskoleit's back, saw his gray hair below his cap, and could sense how he disliked having to fill a bottle with vinegar from a big barrel. He evidently didn't know how to manage the spigot properly, the sour fluid ran over his fingers, and down on the floor a puddle had formed, a rotting, sour-smelling place in the wood, which squeaked under his feet. A thin woman in a rust-brown coat was standing by the counter, watching him with indifference. At last he seemed to have filled the bottle, he put in the cork, and once again I said what I had already said at the door, quietly said, "Good morning," but no one answered. Baskoleit put the bottle on the counter. His face was pale and unshaven, and he looked at the woman now and said, "My daughter has died—Elsa—"

"I know," said the woman hoarsely, "I've known that for five years. I need some scouring powder too."

"My daughter has died," said Baskoleit. He looked at the woman as if it had just happened, looked at her helplessly, but the woman said, "The loose kind—a pound." And Baskoleit pulled out a black barrel from under the counter, poked around in it with a metal scoop, and with his trembling hands conveyed some yellowish lumps into a gray paper bag.

"My daughter has died," he said. The woman said nothing, and I looked around. All I could see was some dusty packages of noodles, the vinegar barrel, which had a dripping tap, and the scouring powder and an enamel sign showing a grinning fair-haired boy eating a brand of chocolate that hasn't existed for years. The woman put the bottle into her shopping bag, stuffed the scouring powder in next to it, threw a few coins onto the counter, and as she turned round and walked past me she tapped her forehead briefly with her finger and smiled at me.

I thought of a lot of things, thought of the days when I had been so small that my nose was still below the edge of the counter, but now I could look without effort over the glass showcase bearing the name of a biscuit company and now containing only dusty packets of breadcrumbs; for a few seconds I seemed to shrink, I felt my nose below the dirty edge of the counter, felt the pfennigs for candies in my hand, I saw Elsa Baskoleit dancing, heard people shouting across the courtyard, "Whore!" and "It's disgusting!" till I was roused by Baskoleit's voice.

"My daughter has died." He said it mechanically, almost without emotion, he was standing by the showcase now, looking out into the street.

"Yes," I said.

"She is dead," he said.

"Yes," I said. He turned his back to me, his hands in the pockets of his gray smock, which was stained.

"She loved grapes—the purple kind—but now she's dead." He did not say, "What would you like?" or "May I help you?", he stood near the dripping vinegar barrel beside the showcase, saying, "My daughter has died" or "She is dead," without looking at me.

I seemed to stand there for an eternity, oblivious and forgotten, while around me time trickled away. It was only when another woman came into the shop that I could rouse myself. She was short and plump, and held her shopping bag against her stomach, and Baskoleit turned to her and said, "My daughter has died," the woman said, "Yes," began suddenly to cry, and said, "Some scouring powder, please, a pound of the loose kind," and Baskoleit went behind the counter and poked around in the barrel with the metal scoop. The woman was still crying when I left.

The pale, dark-haired boy who had been sitting on the bit of broken wall was standing on the running board of my truck, looking closely at the dashboard. He reached in through the open window and raised the right, then the left indicator. The boy jumped when I suddenly stood behind him, but I grabbed him, looked into his pale frightened face, took an apple from one of the cases on my truck, and gave it to the boy. He looked at me in amazement when I let him go, in such amazement that I was startled, and I took another apple, and another, stuffed them into his pocket, shoved them under his jacket, a lot of apples, before I got in and drove off.

A Peach Tree
in His Garden Stands

SPECIAL CIRCUMSTANCES require me to reveal a secret that I had wanted to preserve to the end of my life: I belong to a club or, rather, a secret society, although I had sworn never to join such an institution. It is most embarrassing, but the problems of the younger generation, as well as the deadly seriousness with which my neighbor guards his peaches, prompt me to make this confession, which I do blushingly. I am a Ribbeckian—and, obedient to the rules of our club, I take pen, ink, and paper, open my old school copybook, and begin to write: "Herr Ribbeck of the Havel lands,/A pear tree in his garden stands. . . ." It feels good to write by hand for a change, it encourages patience, compels me to read the poem slowly and with care, and this in turn compels me to smile, and it certainly does no harm to smile once in a while.

So I slowly copy out the ballad and press down onto the paper the rubber stamp which we—the members of the Society of Ribbeckians— are obliged to keep on hand: "Join our club! Your sole obligation is to copy out the enclosed poem ten times and send it to the owners of fruit trees. You may then call yourself a Ribbeckian, a distinction we trust you will appreciate."

I write my neighbor's address on an envelope, stick on a stamp, and betake myself to the mailbox. It so happens, however, that the mailbox is attached to the garden fence of this very neighbor, and as I lift up the yellow flap of the mailbox I can see him—my neighbor—standing there on a ladder, with outstretched forefinger, lightly touching his peaches one by one. No doubt about it, he is counting them!

Next morning we are standing side by side, my neighbor and I, waiting for the mailman, that grossly underpaid cherub whom not even his obviously flat feet can rob of charm.

My neighbor's face seems even yellower than usual, his lips tremble, and his slightly bloodshot eyes seem to point to a sleepless night.

"It is indescribable," he said to me, "how moral standards are declining. Today's young people: nothing but thieves and robbers. Where is it all going to end?"

"In disaster."

"Precisely. I see you agree."

"Of course, it's inevitable. We are drifting inexorably toward the abyss. All this depravity, this dissipation!"

"No respect for the property of others! One should . . . but the police refuse to intervene. Just imagine. Yesterday evening I still had a hundred and thirty-five peaches on my tree—and this morning—care to guess?"

"A hundred and thirty-two?"

"Optimist! A hundred and thirty. Five ripe peaches! Just imagine. I shudder to think of it."

"Sackcloth and ashes—we'll have no alternative. Morality is a thing of the past. I can see there are times ahead of us . . ."

But the approaching mailman relieves me of having to complete my sentence. The letter that I threw in the mailbox yesterday has gone full circle and now, via the collector, the sorter, and the mailman, has landed in the hands of my neighbor.

There was no mail for me. Who would write to me anyway, since I am not even an active Ribbeckian but merely a passive one? I own no fruit trees, not even a currant bush, and the only person who knows my name is the corner grocer who grudgingly grants me credit and with a sorrowful eye sees gray bread, margarine, and fine-cut tobacco disappear into my shopping bag and stubbornly refuses me any credit for regular cigarettes and red wine. But it is time to observe my neighbor's expression: he has opened the letter, put on his glasses and, with a frown, started to read: he reads, reads, and I am surprised at the length of that ballad. In vain I wait for a smile on his face: nothing, there is nothing. Obviously a person who is not responsive to literature as well as devoid of humor. He takes off his glasses as if he had been reading some trivial bit of printed matter, folds up the letter, opens it again, and hands it to me across the fence, saying, "Listen, aren't you . . . er . . . what was it again?"

"A writer," I said.

"Of course. Take a look at this, what d'you make of it?"

The sudden sight of my handwriting gives me a bit of a shock. Perhaps, I think, he is a person who can only be reached acoustically, impervious to the charms of the visual. And I begin to read aloud: "Herr Ribbeck of the Havel lands,/A pear tree in his garden stands. . . ."

"Oh, I know what it says!"

"Did you see the stamp at the bottom? There is a stamp there: 'Join our club! . . .'"

"I know, I know," he says impatiently, and his sallow face turns a shade darker, "but it makes no sense to send me something like that since I only have a peach tree. It's something about pears, isn't it? The way people waste their time!"

Without so much as a nod, he shuffles off to his observation post at the back, where he can keep an eye on his peaches.

I see, I thought, as I folded up my sheet of paper, and now I am wondering whether I should apply for a change in the statutes of our club. Of course the ballad would lose its melody, for there are not that many one-syllable fruits.

Pale Anna

I DIDN'T GET home from the war till the spring of 1950, and there was nobody left in town whom I knew. Luckily for me, my parents had left me some money. I rented a room in town, and there I lay on the bed, smoking and waiting and not knowing what I was waiting for. The idea of a job didn't appeal to me. I gave my landlady money, and she bought what I needed and cooked my meals. Whenever she brought coffee or a meal to my room, she stayed longer than I liked. Her son had been killed at a place called Kalinovka, and after coming into the room she would set the tray down on the table and come over to the darkish corner where my bed was. That's where I dozed away my time, stubbing out my cigarettes against the wall so that the wallpaper around my bed was covered with black smudges. My landlady was pale and skinny, and when her face hung there in the shadows over my bed, I was scared of her. At first I thought she was queer in the head, for her eyes were very bright and large, and she kept on asking me about her son.

"Are you sure you didn't know him? The place was called Kalinovka —weren't you there?"

But I had never heard of a place called Kalinovka, and I would always turn toward the wall saying, "No, really, I can't remember him at all."

My landlady was not queer in the head, she was a very good soul, and I found her questioning painful. She questioned me very often, several times a day, and whenever I went into her kitchen I had to look at the photo of her son, a colored photo hanging over the bench. He had been a laughing, fair-haired boy, and in the photo he was wearing an infantry dress uniform.

"That was taken in the garrison town," said my landlady, "before they were sent to the front."

It was a half-length portrait: he was wearing his steel helmet, and behind him you could see some dummy castle ruins entwined with artificial creepers.

"He was a conductor," my landlady said, "a streetcar conductor. A good worker, my boy was." And then she would reach for the cardboard box of photographs that stood on her sewing table between the scraps of cloth for patching and the skeins of thread. And I had to go through piles of photos of her son: group pictures from his school days, each showing a boy seated in the middle with a slate between his knees, and on the slate a "VI," a "VII," and finally an "VIII." In a separate packet, held together by a red rubber band, were the pictures of his first communion: a smiling little boy in a formal black suit, holding an enormous candle and standing in front of a transparency painted with a golden chalice. Then came pictures of him as a mechanic's apprentice standing by a lathe, grimy-faced, his hands grasping a file.

"That wasn't the right kind of job for him," my landlady would say; "the work was too difficult." And she would show me the last photo taken before he was called up: he was wearing a streetcar conductor's uniform and standing beside a Number 9 streetcar at the terminus, where the tracks curve around in a loop, and I recognized the soda-pop stand where I had so often bought cigarettes, in the days before the war; I recognized the poplars, which are still there now, saw the villa, its gateway flanked by golden lions, which aren't there now, and I would remember the girl I used to think about so often during the war. She had been pretty, with a pale face and almond-shaped eyes, and she had always boarded the streetcar at the Number 9 terminus.

I would stare for a long time at the photo of my landlady's son at the Number 9 terminus and think of many things: of the girl, and the soap factory where I was working in those days; I could hear the screeching of the streetcar, see the pink soda pop I used to drink at the stand in summer, and the green cigarette ads, and again the girl.

"Maybe," the landlady would say, "you did know him after all." I would shake my head and put the picture back in the box: it was a shiny photo and looked like new, although by now it was eight years old.

"No, no," I would say, "and I was never in Kalinovka—really I wasn't."

I often had to go to the kitchen, and she often came to my room, and all day I would think of the thing I wanted to forget—the war—and I would toss my cigarette ash behind the bed and stub the glowing tip out against the wall.

Sometimes, as I lay there in the evening, I could hear a girl's footsteps in the next room, or the Yugoslav who had the room next to the kitchen; I could hear him swearing as he groped for the light switch before going into his room.

It wasn't till I had been living there for three weeks and was holding

Karl's picture for what must have been the fiftieth time that I noticed that the streetcar he was standing beside, laughing, with his leather pouch, wasn't empty. For the first time I looked closely at the photo and saw that a girl sitting inside the streetcar, smiling, had got into the snapshot. It was the pretty girl I used to think about so often during the war. The landlady came up to me, studied the look on my face, and said, "Now you recognize him, eh?" Then she stepped behind me and looked over my shoulder at the photo, and from close behind me rose the smell of the fresh peas she was holding in the folds of her apron.

"No," I said quietly, "but the girl."

"The girl?" she said. "That was his fiancée, but maybe it's just as well he never saw her again. . . ."

"Why?" I asked.

She didn't answer but walked away, sat down on her chair by the window, and went on shelling peas. Without looking at me, she said, "Did you know the girl?"

I kept a tight grip on the photo, looked at my landlady, and told her about the soap factory, about the Number 9 terminus, and the pretty girl who always got on there.

"Is that all?"

"Yes," I said. She tipped the peas into a sieve, turned on the faucet, and I could see her thin back.

"When you see her, you'll understand why it's a good thing he never saw her again. . . ."

"See her?" I asked.

She dried her hands on her apron, came over to me, and carefully took away the photo. Her face seemed thinner than ever, her eyes looked past me, but she gently laid her hand on my left arm. "She lives in the room next to yours, Anna does. We always call her our pale Anna because she's got such a white face. You really mean you haven't seen her yet?"

"No," I said, "I haven't, though I guess I've heard her a few times. What's wrong with her, then?"

"I hate to tell you, but it's better for you to know. Her face has been completely destroyed, it's full of scars. She was thrown into a plate-glass window by a bomb blast. You won't recognize her."

That evening I waited a long while before hearing steps in the hall, but the first time I was wrong: it was the tall Yugoslav, who looked at me in astonishment when I dashed out into the hall. Embarrassed, I said "Good evening" and went back into my room.

I tried to imagine her face with scars, but I couldn't, and whenever I saw her face, it was beautiful even with the scars. I thought about the soap factory, about my parents, and about another girl I used to go out with often at that time. Her name was Elizabeth, but she was known as Puss; when I kissed her, she always laughed, and I felt like an idiot. I had written her postcards from the front, and she used to send me little parcels of homemade cookies that were always in crumbs by the time they arrived; she sent me cigarettes and newspapers, and in one of her letters she wrote, "Our boys will win the war all right, and I'm so proud you're one of them."

But I wasn't at all proud to be one of them, and when I was due for leave I didn't write and tell her; I went out with the daughter of a tobacconist who lived in our apartment house. I gave the tobacconist's daughter soap sent me by my firm, and she gave me cigarettes, and we went to the movies together, and we went dancing, and once, when her parents were away, she took me up to her room and I pressed her down onto the couch in the dark; but when I bent over her, she switched on the light and smiled slyly up at me, and in the glare I saw Hitler on the wall, a colored photo, and all around Hitler's picture, arranged in the shape of a heart on the pink wallpaper, was a series of men wearing heroic expressions, postcards thumbtacked to the wall, and men in steel helmets cut out of illustrated weeklies. I left the girl lying there on the couch, lit a cigarette, and went away. Later on, both girls wrote postcards to me at the front telling me I had behaved badly, but I didn't answer. . . .

I waited a long time for Anna, smoked one cigarette after another in the dark, thought of many things, and when the key was thrust into the lock I was too scared to get up and see her face. I heard her open the door to her room, move around in there humming softly to herself, and after a while I got up and waited in the hall. All of a sudden there was silence in her room, she wasn't moving about now or humming, and I was afraid to knock. I could hear the tall Yugoslav walking up and down in his room, muttering to himself, could hear the water bubbling in my landlady's kitchen. But in Anna's room all was quiet, and through the open door of my own room I could see the black smudges from all those stubbed-out cigarettes on the wallpaper.

The tall Yugoslav was lying on his bed now, there were no more footsteps, I could just hear him muttering; the kettle in my landlady's kitchen had stopped bubbling, and I heard the sound of metal on metal as the landlady put the lid on the coffeepot. Anna's room was still silent, and the thought struck me that later she would tell me everything she had been thinking about while I stood outside her door, and later on she did tell me everything.

I stared at a picture hanging beside the door: the silvery sheen of a lake and a naiad with wet fair hair emerging from it to smile at a young peasant hiding among some very green bushes. I could see part of the naiad's left breast, and her neck was very white and a little too long.

I don't know when it was, but some time later I took hold of the doorknob, and before I turned the knob and slowly pushed open the door, I knew Anna was mine: her face was covered with little scars of a bluish sheen, the smell of mushrooms simmering in a pan came from her room, and I opened the door wide, laid my hand on Anna's shoulder, and tried to smile.

This Is Tibten!

SOULLESS PEOPLE cannot understand why I take such pains and humble pride in performing duties which they regard as beneath my dignity. My occupation may not correspond to my level of education, nor was it foretold by my fairy godmother at my christening, but I enjoy my work, and it provides me with a living: I tell people where they are. Passengers who in the evening at their own railway stations board trains that carry them to distant places, and who then during the night wake up at our station, peer out, confused, into the darkness, not knowing whether they have gone beyond their destination or have not yet reached it, or are possibly even at their destination (for our town contains a variety of tourist attractions and draws many visitors)—I tell all these people where they are. I switch on the loudspeaker as soon as a train arrives and the wheels of the locomotive have come to a standstill, and I say diffidently into the night, "This is Tibten! You are now in Tibten! Passengers wishing to visit the tomb of Tiburtius must alight here!", and the echo comes back to me from the platforms, right into my cubbyhole: a dark voice out of the darkness which seems to be announcing something doubtful, although actually it is speaking the plain truth.

A number of passengers then hurriedly descend onto the dimly lit platform, carrying their suitcases, for Tibten is their destination, and I watch them go down the stairs, reappear on Platform 1, and hand over their tickets to the sleepy ticket collector at the barrier. Very few people arrive on business at night—businessmen intending to fill their companies' requirements at the Tibten lead mines. The visitors are mostly tourists attracted by the tomb of Tiburtius, a young Roman boy who committed suicide eighteen hundred years ago for the sake of a Tibten beauty. "He was but a lad," is inscribed on his tombstone, which can be admired in our local museum, "yet Love was his undoing." He came here from Rome to purchase lead for his father, who was an army contractor.

Certainly I would not have had to attend five universities and obtain two doctorates in order to be able to call out night after night into the darkness, "This is Tibten! You are now in Tibten!" And yet my work fills me with satisfaction. I speak my lines softly, so that those who are asleep do not wake up but those who are awake will not fail to hear it, and I make my voice sound just enticing enough for those who are dozing to rouse themselves and wonder whether they had not meant to go to Tibten.

In the latter part of the morning, therefore, when I wake up and look out of the window, I can see the passengers who succumbed to the spell of my voice making their way through our little town, armed with the brochures which our travel bureau so generously distributes all over the world. At breakfast they have already read that the wear and tear of centuries has reduced the Latin Tiburtinum to its present form of Tibten, and they proceed to the local museum, where they admire the tombstone erected eighteen hundred years ago to the Roman Werther. A boy's profile has been chiseled out of reddish sandstone, his hands outstretched in vain toward a girl. "He was but a lad, yet Love was his undoing. . . ." His youthfulness is also attested to by the objects which were found in his grave: little figures made of some ivory-colored substance, two elephants, a horse, and a mastiff, which—as Brusler claims in his *Theory of the Tomb of Tiburtius*—were said to have been used in a kind of chess game. I doubt this theory, however. I am sure that to Tiburtius these objects were simply toys. The little ivory objects look exactly like the ones we get as a premium when we buy half a pound of margarine, and they served the same purpose: they were for children to play with. . . . Possibly it behooves me to refer here to the excellent novel written by our local author, Volker von Volkersen, entitled *Tiburtius: A Roman Destiny That Found Fulfillment in Our Town*. But I regard Volkersen's book as misleading, because he also supports Brusler's theory as to the purpose of the toys.

I myself—at this point I must at last make a confession—am in possession of the original figures contained in Tiburtius' grave; I stole them from the museum and replaced them with the ones I obtain as a premium with half a pound of margarine: two elephants, a horse, and a mastiff. They are as white as Tiburtius' animals, they are the same size, the same weight, and—what seems to me most important of all—they serve the same purpose.

So tourists come from all over the world to admire the tomb of Tiburtius and his toys. Posters saying "Come to Tibten" hang in the waiting rooms of the Anglo-Saxon world, and when at night I speak my lines—"This is Tibten! You are in Tibten! Passengers wishing to visit the tomb of Tiburtius must alight here!"—I lure out of the trains the people who at their own railway stations succumbed to the spell of our posters. To be sure, they look at the sandstone slab, the authenticity of which is unquestioned. They look at the touching profile of a Roman boy for whom Love was his undoing and who drowned himself in a flooded shaft of the lead mines. And then the visitors' eyes move to the little animals: two elephants, a horse, and a mastiff—and this is just where they could study the wisdom of the world, but they do not. Ladies from our own and other countries, deeply moved, pile roses onto the tomb of this young lad. Poems are written; even my animals, the horse and the mastiff (I had to use up two pounds of margarine to acquire them!), have already become the subject of lyrical endeavors. "Thou didst play, even as we play, with mastiff and horse . . ." goes one line in the verses written by a not unknown poet. So there they lie, free gifts from the Klüsshenn Margarine Company, on red velvet under heavy glass in our local museum: witnesses to my consumption of margarine. Often, before I go on shift in the afternoon, I visit the museum for a minute and study them. They look genuine, slightly yellowed, and are completely indistinguishable from the ones lying in my drawer, for I threw in the originals among those I got with Klüsshenn's margarine, and I try in vain to separate them again.

Deep in thought, I then go off to work, hang up my cap on the hook, take off my coat, place my sandwiches in the drawer, arrange my cigarette papers, tobacco, and newspaper, and, when a train arrives, speak the lines it is my job to speak: "This is Tibten! You are now in Tibten! Passengers wishing to visit the tomb of Tiburtius must alight here!" I speak them softly, so that those who are asleep do not wake up, and those who are awake will not fail to hear me, and I make my voice sound just enticing enough for those who are dozing to rouse themselves and wonder whether they had not meant to go to Tibten.

And I cannot understand why anyone regards this work as beneath my dignity. . . .

Daniel the Just

A s LONG as it was dark, the woman lying beside him could not see his face, and this made everything easier to bear. She had been talking away at him for an hour, and it did not take much effort to keep on saying "Yes," or "Yes, of course," or "Yes, that's right." The woman lying beside him was his wife, but when he thought of her he always thought: the woman. She was actually quite beautiful, and there were people who envied him his wife, and he might have had cause to be jealous—but he was not jealous. He was glad the darkness hid the sight of her face from him and allowed him to relax his own face; there was nothing more exhausting than to put on a face and wear it all day, as long as daylight lasted, and the face he showed in the daytime was a put-on face.

"If Uli doesn't make it," she said, "I can't bear to think what will happen. It would finish Marie, you know what she's gone through, don't you?"

"Yes, of course," he said, "I know."

"She's had to eat dry bread, she—really, I don't know how she could stand it—she's slept for weeks in beds without sheets, and when Uli was born, Erich was still listed as missing. If the boy doesn't get through his entrance exam—I just don't know what will happen. Don't you agree?"

"Yes, I agree," he said.

"Make sure you see the boy before he goes into the classroom where the exam's being given—say something to encourage him. You'll do what you can, won't you?"

"Yes, I will," he said.

One day in spring, thirty years ago, he too had come to town to take the entrance exam: that evening the red light of the sun had fallen over the street where his aunt lived, and to the eleven-year-old boy it seemed as if someone were spilling liquid fire over the roofs, and hundreds of windows caught this red light like molten metal.

Later, while they were sitting at supper, the windows were filled with greenish darkness for that half hour when women hesitate before turning on the light. His aunt hesitated too, and when she touched the switch she seemed to be giving the signal to hundreds and hundreds of women: suddenly yellow light from all the windows pierced the green darkness; the lights hung in the night like brittle fruits with long yellow spikes.

"Do you think you'll make it?" asked his aunt, and his uncle, who was sitting by the window holding the newspaper, shook his head as if the question were an insult.

His aunt proceeded to make up a bed for him on the bench in the kitchen, using a quilt for a mattress; his uncle let him have his blanket and his aunt one of their pillows. "You'll soon have your own bedding here," said his aunt, "and now sleep well. Good night."

"Good night," he said, and his aunt turned out the light and went into the bedroom.

His uncle stayed behind and tried to pretend he was looking for something; his hands groped across the boy's face toward the window sill, and the hands, which smelled of wood stain and shellac, groped back across his face; his uncle's shyness hung like lead in the air, and without saying what he wanted to say, he disappeared into the bedroom.

I'll make it all right, thought the boy when he was alone, and in his mind's eye he saw his mother, who at this moment was sitting at home by the fire knitting, from time to time letting her hands fall into her lap and sending up a prayer to one of her favorite saints: Judas Thaddeus— or was Don Bosco the proper saint for him, the farm boy who had come to town to try to get into high school?

"There are some things which simply shouldn't be allowed to happen," said the woman beside him, and as she seemed to be waiting for a reply, he wearily said "Yes," and noticed to his despair that it was already getting light; day was coming and bringing him the hardest of all his duties: that of putting on his face.

No, he thought, enough things happen which shouldn't be allowed to happen. All those years ago, in the darkness on the kitchen bench, he had been so confident: he thought of the math problem, of the essay, and he was sure everything would be all right. The essay theme would almost certainly be "A Strange Experience," and he knew exactly what he was going to describe: the visit to the institution where Uncle Thomas was confined. Green-and-white-striped chairs in the consulting room, and Uncle Thomas who—no matter what anyone said to him—always replied in the same words, "If only there were justice in this world."

"I've knitted you a lovely red pullover," said his mother, "you were always so fond of red."

"If only there were justice in this world."

They talked about the weather, about the cows and a little about politics, and Thomas always said the same thing, "If only there were justice in this world."

And later, when they walked back along the green-painted corridor, he saw at the window a thin man with narrow drooping shoulders gazing mutely out into the garden.

Just before they went out through the gate, a pleasant-looking man with a kindly smile came up to them and said, "Madame, please do not forget to address me as Your Majesty," and his mother said softly to the man, "Your Majesty." And when they were standing at the streetcar stop, he had looked across once more to the green house lying hidden among the trees, and seen the man with the drooping shoulders standing at the window, and a laugh rang out through the garden that sounded like tin being cut with blunt scissors.

"Your coffee's getting cold," said the woman who was his wife, "and do try and eat something at least."

He raised the coffee cup to his lips and ate something.

"I know," said the woman, laying her hand on his shoulder, "I know you're worrying about that justice of yours again, but can you call it unjust to lend a helping hand to a child? You're fond of Uli, aren't you?"

"Yes," he said, and this yes was sincere: he was fond of Uli. The boy was sensitive, friendly, and in his way intelligent, but it would be torture for him to go to high school: with a lot of extra coaching, spurred on by an ambitious mother, by dint of great effort and much intercession, he would never be more than a mediocre student. He would always have to carry the burden of a life, of demands, with which he could not cope.

"Promise me you'll do something for Uli, won't you?"

"Yes," he said, "I'll do something for him," and he kissed his wife's beautiful face and left the house. He walked slowly along, put a cigarette between his lips, dropped his put-on face, and enjoyed the relaxation of feeling his own face on his skin. He looked at it in the window of a fur shop; between a gray sealskin and a leopard skin, he saw his face on the black velvet draping the display: the pale, rather puffy face of a man in his mid-forties—the face of a skeptic, a cynic perhaps, the cigarette smoke wreathed in white coils around the pale puffy face. His friend Alfred, who had died the year before, used to say, "You have never got over certain feelings of hostility—and everything you do is influenced much too much by your emotions."

Alfred had meant well; in fact what he had had in mind was right, but you can't define a person with words, and for him the word "hostility" was one of the most facile, one of the most convenient.

Thirty years ago, on the bench in his aunt's kitchen, he had thought: No one will write an essay like that; no one can have had such a strange experience, and before he fell asleep he thought about other things: he was going to sleep on this bench for nine years, do his homework at this table for nine years, and throughout this eternity his mother would sit at home by the fire knitting and sending up prayers to heaven. In the next room he could hear his uncle and aunt talking, and the only word he could make out from the murmuring was his name: Daniel. So they were talking about him, and although he could not make out the words, he knew they were speaking kindly about him. They were fond of him, they had no children themselves. Then all of a sudden fear shot through him: In two years, he thought in panic, this bench will already be too short for me—where will I sleep then? For a few minutes this idea really scared him, but then he thought: Two years, what an eternity that is, such a lot of darkness, day after day it would turn into light; and quite suddenly he slipped into that little portion of darkness which lay ahead of him—the night before the exam—and in his dreams he was pursued by the picture hanging on the wall between the buffet and the window: grim-faced men standing in front of a factory gate, one holding a tattered red flag in his hand, and in his dream the boy could clearly read the words which in the semidarkness he had been barely able to make out: "On Strike."

He took leave of his face as it hung there pale and intense between the sealskin and the leopard skin in the shop window, as if drawn with a silver pencil on black cloth; he took leave reluctantly, for he saw the child he had once been, behind this face.

" 'On Strike,' " the school superintendent had said to him thirteen years later, " 'On Strike'—do you consider that a suitable essay theme to give seventeen-year-olds?" He had not given it, and by that time, in 1934, the picture had long since disappeared from his uncle's kitchen wall. It was still possible to visit Uncle Thomas in the institution, to sit on one of the green-striped chairs, smoke cigarettes, and listen to Thomas, who seemed to be replying to a litany which only he could hear. Thomas sat there listening—but he was not listening to what the visitors were saying to him, he was listening to the dirge of an invisible choir as it stood hidden in the wings of the world's stage chanting a litany to which there was but one response, Thomas's response, "If only there were justice in this world."

The man who always stood at the window looking out into the garden had one day been able—so thin had he become—to squeeze through the bars and fall headlong into the garden: his metallic laugh came crashing down with him. But His Majesty was still alive, and Heemke never failed to go up to him and whisper with a smile, "Your Majesty."

"Types like that go on forever," the keeper said to him. "It'll take a lot to finish him off."

But seven years later His Majesty was no longer alive, and Thomas was dead too: they had been murdered, and the choir standing hidden in the wings of the world's stage chanting its litany waited in vain for the response which only Thomas could give.

Heemke turned into the street where the school was, and he was startled to see all the candidates. They were standing around with mothers, with fathers, and over them all lay that spurious, hectic cheerfulness which descends like a sickness on people before an examination: desperate cheerfulness lay like makeup on the faces of the mothers, desperate indifference on those of the fathers.

His eye, however, was caught by a boy sitting alone and apart from the rest on the doorstep of a bombed house. Heemke stopped and felt fear rising in him like moisture in a sponge: I must watch out, he thought, if I'm not careful, I'll end up sitting in Uncle Thomas's place, and maybe I'll be saying the same words. The child sitting on the doorstep reminded him of himself thirty years ago, so intensely that he felt the thirty years falling away from him like dust being blown off a statue.

Noise, laughter—the sun shone on damp roofs from which the snow had melted, and only in the shadows of the ruins was the snow still lying.

His uncle had brought him here much too early, all those years ago; they had taken the streetcar over the bridge, had not exchanged a single word, and while he was looking at the boy's black stockings he thought: Shyness is a disease that deserves to be cured the way whooping cough is cured. His uncle's shyness, coupled with his own, had caught him by the throat. Mute, his red scarf round his neck, the Thermos flask in his right coat pocket, his uncle had stood beside him in the empty street, had suddenly muttered something about "go to work," and was gone. He had sat down on a doorstep. Vegetable carts rumbled over the cobbles, a baker's boy walked past with his basket of rolls, and a girl carrying a milk jug went from house to house, leaving a little blue-white spot of milk behind on every doorstep. He had been very impressed by the houses, houses in which no one seemed to be living, and today he could still see traces among the ruins of the yellow paint that had so impressed him at the time.

"Good morning, Principal," said someone walking by; he nodded briefly, and he knew that inside his colleague would say, "The old man's off his head again."

I have three alternatives, he thought. I can turn into that child sitting over there on the doorstep, I can go on being the man with the pale, puffy face, or I can become Uncle Thomas. The alternative with the least appeal was to go on being himself: the heavy burden of carrying his put-on face. There was also not much to be said for turning into the child: books he had loved, had hated, gobbled up, devoured at the kitchen table, and every week the battle for paper, for exercise books which he filled with notes, problems, draft essays; every week thirty pfennigs which he had to fight for, till it occurred to his teacher to let him tear the blank pages out of old exercise books stored in the school basement. But he also tore out the pages where only one side had been written on, and at home he sewed them with black cotton into thick notebooks—and now he sent flowers every year for the teacher's grave in the village.

No one, he thought, ever knew what it cost me, not a living soul, except perhaps Alfred, but Alfred always fell back on one very silly word, "hostility." It is useless to talk about it, to explain it to anyone—the last person to understand would be the one with the beautiful face who lies beside me in bed.

He hesitated a few moments longer, while the past lay upon him: what appealed to him most was to take over Uncle Thomas's role and spend his days reciting the one solitary response to the litany which the choir was chanting in the wings.

No, he didn't want to be that child again, it was too hard—what boy wears black stockings these days? The middle alternative was the one, to go on being the man with the pale, puffy face, and he had always chosen the middle alternative. He walked over to the boy and as his shadow fell across him, the child raised his eyes and gave him a startled look. "What's your name?" asked Heemke.

The boy got hastily to his feet and from his blushing face came the answer, "Wierzok."

"Spell it for me, please," said Heemke, reaching in his pocket for his notebook, and the child slowly spelled "W-i-e-r-z-o-k."

"And where do you come from?"

"From Wollersheim," said the child.

Thank God, thought Heemke, he's not from my village and doesn't bear my name—he's not a child of one of my many cousins.

"And where are you going to live here in town?"

"At my aunt's," said Wierzok.

"That's fine," said Heemke. "It's going to be all right with the exam. I expect you've always had good marks and a good report from your teacher, haven't you?"

"Yes, I've always had good marks."

"Don't worry," said Heemke, "it'll be all right, you will . . ." He stopped, because what Alfred would have called emotion and hostility were strangling him. "Mind you don't catch a chill on those cold stones," he said in a low voice, turned on his heel and entered the school through the janitor's premises, so as to avoid Uli and Uli's mother. Concealed behind the curtain of the hall window, he looked out once more at the children and their parents waiting outside and, as happened every year on this day, he was swept by a feeling of despondency: it seemed to him that in the faces of those ten-year-old boys he could read a bleak future. They were pressing at the school gates like cattle at the stable door. Among these seventy youngsters, two or three would be better than mediocre, and all the rest would simply form a background. Alfred's cynicism has penetrated me deeply, he thought, and he looked despairingly over to the Wierzok boy, who had sat down again and, his head bowed, seemed to be brooding.

When I did that I got a bad cold, thought Heemke. This boy will get through, and if I, if I—if I what?

Hostility and emotion, Alfred my friend, these are not the words to express what I feel.

He entered the common room, greeted the other teachers who had been waiting for him, and said to the janitor who helped him off with his coat, "Have the children come in now."

He could tell from the faces of the other teachers how strange his behavior had been. Perhaps, he thought, I was standing out there on the street for half an hour watching the Wierzok boy, and he glanced nervously at his watch: but it was only four minutes past eight.

"Gentlemen," he said aloud, "bear in mind that for many of these children, the test they are about to undergo is more crucial and decisive than university finals will be for some of them twelve years from now." They waited for more, and those who knew him were waiting for the word he was so fond of using whenever he could, the word "justice." But he said no more, merely turned to one of the teachers and quietly asked, "What is the essay theme for the candidates?"

" 'A Strange Experience.' "

Heemke stayed behind as the room emptied.

Those childish fears of his, that in two years the kitchen bench would be too short for him, had been superfluous, for he had not passed the exam, although the essay theme had been "A Strange Experience." Right up to the moment when they had been let into the school he had clung to his confidence, but as soon as he entered the school, his confidence had melted away.

When he came to write the essay, he tried in vain to grasp hold of Uncle Thomas. Thomas was suddenly very close, too close for him to be able to write an essay about him; he wrote down the title, "A Strange

Experience," and underneath he wrote, "If only there were justice in this world," but as he wrote "justice" what he really meant was "vengeance."

It had taken him more than ten years not to think of vengeance whenever he thought of justice.

The worst of those ten years had been the year after he failed his entrance exam: the people he had left behind when he embarked on what merely seemed to promise a better life could be just as unsympathetic as those who were completely unaware, completely ignorant, and whom a phone call from his father saved from becoming involved in months of pain and effort. A smile from his mother, a clasp of the hand on Sunday after Mass, and a hasty word or two: that was the justice of this world—and the other, the thing he had always wanted but had never achieved, was what Uncle Thomas had so desperately longed for. The desire to achieve that had earned him the nickname "Daniel the Just." He was roused by the door opening, and the janitor ushered in Uli's mother.

"Marie," he said, "what—why . . ."

"Daniel," she said, "I," but he interrupted her, "I've got no time now, no, not even a second," he said fiercely, and he left his room and went up to the second floor: up here the sounds of the waiting mothers were muted. He went to the window overlooking the playground, put a cigarette between his lips but forgot to light it. It has taken me thirty years to get over it and arrive at a knowledge of what it is I want. I have eliminated vengeance from my idea of justice; I make a good living, I put on my grim face, and most people believe this means I have reached my goal; but I have not reached my goal. I have only just begun—but now I can take off my grim face, as you put away a hat you no longer need. I shall wear a different face, perhaps my own. . . .

He would spare Wierzok this year; he did not want to make any child go through what he had gone through, any child at all, least of all this one—whom he had met as if it were himself.

In Search
of the Reader

MY FRIEND Witt has a strange occupation: he is not afraid of calling himself an author, simply because he has some latent knowledge of spelling, vaguely masters a few rules of grammar, and now covers one typed page after another with stylistic exercises that he calls a manuscript as soon as he has enough to make up a bundle.

For years he had to eat the sparse grass of this art on the steppes of culture, until he found a publisher. Soon after the publication of his book, I ran across him in a state of deep depression. His report was indeed depressing: according to his publisher's statement, during the first six months three hundred and fifty copies had been sent out free of charge for reviewing, a few good reviews had appeared, and thirteen copies had actually been sold—resulting in a credit of 5.46 marks for my friend. But he had received an advance of eight hundred marks, and, with sales remaining at that level, this advance would be paid off in roughly a hundred and fifty years.

Now human life expectancy is generally less than that. Disregarding a few, almost legendary Turks, it is estimated at seventy—and, taking into account the memorable hardships imposed upon our lost generation, one can confidently deduct a further ten years from our life span.

I advised my friend to write a second book. Upon publication, it received a warm welcome among experts; the number of review copies rose to more than four hundred; the number of copies sold after six months amounted to twenty-nine. I rolled two cigarettes a day for my friend, patted him on the back, and suggested he now write a third book. But, strangely enough, he took this for sarcasm and withdrew in a huff.

Meanwhile he had passed into literary history as "Standard-Bearer Witt," and a book that had been published about him sold better than his own books.

I didn't see him for almost six months, and imagined him to be puttering around again in the purlieus of a lonely genius. Then he turned up at my place and ruefully confessed that he had started a third book after all. I made the suggestion that he offer this work to the book trade in a mimeographed edition of thirty to fifty copies. But he was under the spell of genuine printer's ink; besides, he had accepted another advance, his second child was on the way, and he proclaimed his unwillingness to contribute to the unemployment of sundry compositors, printers, and packers. (His social consciousness has always been very strong!)

Meanwhile nearly a hundred good reviews of his work had appeared and more than ninety copies of his two books had been sold. His publisher had started an action that he called "In Search of the Reader." Handbills had been sent to all bookstores requesting that every Witt purchaser be identified and immediately reported to the publisher with a view to establishing contact between author and reader.

The success of this action was not long in coming. A month after it was launched, a man evidently appeared in the far north who asked for one of my friend's books, bought it, and paid for it. The owner of the bookstore immediately sent off a telegram: "Witt purchaser here—what do I do?" Meanwhile he kept the customer engaged in conversation, poured coffee, opened packs of cigarettes—behavior to which the customer, albeit astonished, was quite happy to submit himself. Then came the publisher's reply, by top-priority wire: "Send purchaser to me, all expenses paid." Fortunately the customer was a high-school teacher, it was a vacation time, and he had no objection to a free trip to southern Germany. The first day he traveled as far as Cologne, where he spent the night in a good hotel, and the next day his train took him south beside the beautiful Rhine, a journey he greatly enjoyed.

By about four o'clock of the second day he had reached his destination, took a taxi from the station to the publishing house, and spent a stimulating hour over coffee and cakes with the publisher's charming wife. Then he was supplied with additional travel funds, taken back to the station, and now traveled second class to that quiet little town where my friend serves the Muses. As the second child had been born some time before, my friend's wife had gone to a movie—a relaxation that, despite all financial embarrassment, should not be denied the wives of authors. So the purchaser happened to find my friend in the process of warming up the children's evening milk and keeping them quiet by singing them a song in which a vulgar word was prominent. This word threw an ugly light on modern German literature. . . .

My friend welcomed his reader enthusiastically, pressed the coffee grinder into his hand, and swiftly disposed of his paternal duties. Before long, the water for the coffee was boiling, and the conversation could have begun. But they were both such shy people that they first regarded each other in mutual, silent admiration for quite a while, until my friend burst out with a cry of "You are a genius—an absolute genius!"

"Oh no," the guest said diffidently, "I was thinking that of you."

"You're mistaken," said my friend, and finally poured the coffee. "The hallmark of a genius is his rarity, and you belong to a rarer class of human beings than I do."

The visitor tried to put forward some modest objections but was brusquely corrected: "Nothing doing," said my friend. "Writing a book isn't half as bad as it's made out to be. Finding a publisher is child's play, but to buy a book—that I call an act of genius. Do you take milk and sugar?"

The man helped himself, then shyly drew from the right inside pocket of his overcoat the book he had bought in the far north and asked my friend to inscribe it.

"On one condition only," my friend said sternly. "Only on condition that you inscribe my manuscript!"

From a shelf he took down a file, from it removed a stack of typed sheets, placed the stack beside his guest's coffee cup, and said, "Do me the pleasure!"

The guest, a bit flustered, drew out his fountain pen and wrote hesitatingly on the lower edge of the last manuscript page: "In sincere admiration—Günther Schlegel."

But half a minute later, while my friend was still trying to dry the ink by waving his manuscript above the stove, the guest drew from the left inside pocket of his overcoat a bundle of typed sheets and asked my friend to submit this work, which he regarded as his contribution to modern literature, to the publisher for an opinion.

My friend told me that for several minutes he had been speechless with disappointment. His concern for the fate of this man, he said, had filled him with profound bitterness.

So once again they sat silently facing one another for several minutes, until my friend said in a low voice, "I implore you, don't do it—you're forfeiting your originality!"

The guest remained stubbornly silent, clutching his manuscript.

"You will never again receive travel funds," said my friend, "you will never again be served cream cakes. The publisher's wife will put on her sourest expression. For your own sake, I implore you: forget about it!"

But the guest doggedly shook his head, and my friend, in his strenuous efforts to rescue a human being, did not shrink from bringing in his publisher's statements. But all this did not interest Schlegel.

At this point my friend usually broke off his account, and I assume that he simply got into an argument with his visitor. At any rate, a pause ensued while my friend pensively regarded his clenched fists and muttered unintelligibly to himself. But I did learn that Schlegel departed after a curt good-bye, leaving his manuscript behind.

Meanwhile Schlegel's novel, *Woe Unto You, Penelope!,* the story of a returning prisoner of war, has caused quite a stir, and rightly so, among the experts. Schlegel has given up his teaching career—in other words, abandoned a genuine profession in order to devote himself to another profession that I still do not consider to be one. . . .

The Tidings
of Bethlehem

THE DOOR was not a proper door: it was no more than a few planks loosely nailed together and closed by a wire loop hung over a nail in the doorpost. The man stopped and waited. It's really a disgrace, he thought, that a woman should have to have her child here. He carefully lifted the wire loop off the nail, pushed open the door—and was startled to see the child lying in the straw, the mother, very young, seated on the ground beside it, smiling at the child. . . . Farther back, against the wall, stood someone whom the man didn't dare look at too closely: it might be one of those whom the shepherds had taken for angels. The figure leaning against the wall was wearing a mouse-gray robe and holding flowers in each hand: slender, creamy lilies. The man felt fear mounting in him and thought: Maybe there's some truth after all in the wild tales the shepherds have been telling in town.

The young woman raised her eyes, gave him a friendly, questioning look, and the young man said softly, "Does the master carpenter live here?"

The young woman shook her head. "He's not a master carpenter—just a carpenter."

"Never mind," said the man. "I imagine he'll be able to fix a door if he's brought his tools along."

"He has," said Mary, "and he can fix doors. He used to do that in Nazareth too."

So they really were from Nazareth.

The figure holding the flowers now looked at the man and said, "There's no need to be afraid." The voice was so beautiful that again the man was startled, and he glanced up: the mouse-gray figure looked benevolent but also sad.

"He means Joseph," said the young woman. "I'll go and wake him up. Do you want him to fix a door?"

"Yes, at the inn called the Red Man, just to run the plane over the groove a bit and check the jamb. The door keeps sticking. I'll wait outside, if you wouldn't mind getting him."

"You're welcome to wait in here," said the young woman.

"No, I'd rather wait outside." He glanced across at the mouse-gray figure, who nodded at him with a smile. Then he retreated, walking backward and carefully closing the door by lifting the wire loop over the nail. Men with flowers had always struck him as comical, but the mouse-gray figure didn't look like a man, and not like a woman either, and certainly hadn't struck him as comical.

When Joseph came out with his tool box, the young man took him by the arm, saying, "This way, we have to go around to the left." They went around to the left, and now at last the young man plucked up enough courage to say what he had wanted to say to the young woman but had been afraid to because the figure with the flowers had been standing there. "The shepherds," he said, "have been telling wild tales in town about you people." But Joseph, instead of answering, merely said, "I hope at least you have a chisel—the handle of mine is broken. Is there more than one door?"

"Just the one," said the man, "and we do have a chisel. We need to fix the door in a hurry. We're having some soldiers billeted in our house."

"Billeted? Now? I haven't heard about any maneuvers."

"No, there are no maneuvers, but a whole company of soldiers is coming to Bethlehem. And our house," he said proudly, "our house is getting the captain. The shepherds . . ." But he broke off, stopped; Joseph stopped too. At the street corner stood the mouse-gray figure with an armful of flowers, white lilies, giving them away to little children who could scarcely toddle: more and more children arrived, as well as mothers with children in arms, and the man who had come for Joseph was much alarmed, for the mouse-gray figure was weeping—the voice, the eyes, had already alarmed him, but the tears were more alarming still. The figure touched the children's mouths, their foreheads, with outstretched hand, kissed their small, dirty hands, and gave each child a lily.

"I was looking for you," Joseph told the mouse-gray figure. "Just now, while I was asleep, I dreamed . . ."

"I know," said the mouse-gray figure, "we must leave at once."

He waited for a moment until a very small, dirty girl had come up to him.

"Am I not to fix the door for this captain after all?"

"No, we must leave immediately." The figure turned away from the children and took Joseph by the arm, and Joseph said to the man who had come for him, "I'm sorry, it looks as if I won't be able to do it."

"Oh, never mind," said the man. His gaze followed the other two as they walked back to the stable; then he looked down the street where the laughing children were running around with their big white lilies. At that moment he heard the clatter of horses' hooves behind him, turned around, and saw the company riding into town from the highway.

I'll catch it again, he thought, because the door hasn't been fixed.

The children stood by the roadside, waving their flowers at the soldiers. So the soldiers rode into Bethlehem between two lanes of white lilies, and the man who had come for Joseph thought: I believe the shepherds were right in everything they told us. . . .

And There Was
the Evening
and the Morning . . .

I T WAS not until noon that he thought of leaving his Christmas presents for Anna in the baggage room at the station; he was glad he had thought of it, for it meant he didn't have to go home immediately. Ever since Anna had stopped speaking to him, he was afraid of going home; her silence bore down on him like a tombstone the minute he entered the apartment. He used to look forward to going home, for two years after his wedding day: he loved having supper with Anna, talking to her, and then going to bed; best of all he loved the hour between going to bed and falling asleep. Anna fell asleep earlier than he did because nowadays she was always tired—and he would lie there in the darkness beside her, he could hear her breathing, and from the far end of the street the headlights of cars now and again threw rays of light onto the ceiling, light that curved down as the cars reached the rise in the street, bands of pale yellow light that made his sleeping wife's profile leap up for a second against the wall; then darkness would fall once more over the room, and all that remained was delicate whorls: the pattern of the curtains drawn on the ceiling by the gas lamp in the street. This was the hour he loved more than any hour of the day, because he could feel the day falling away from him, and he would slide down into sleep as into a bath.

Now he strolled hesitatingly past the baggage counter and saw his box still there at the back, between the red suitcase and the demijohn. The open elevator coming down from the platform was empty, white with snow: it descended like a piece of paper into the gray concrete of the baggage room, and the man who had been operating it walked over and said to the clerk, "Now it really feels like Christmas. It's nice when there's snow for the kids, eh?" The clerk nodded, silently impaled baggage checks on his spike, counted the money in his drawer and looked suspiciously across to Brenig, who had taken his claim check out of his pocket but folded it up and put it back again. This was the third time he had come, the third time he had taken the claim check out and put it back in his pocket again. The clerk's suspicious glances made him uncomfortable; he strolled over to the exit and stood looking out onto the empty station square. He loved the snow, loved the cold; as a boy it had intoxicated him to breathe in the cold clear air, and now he threw away his cigarette and held his face against the wind, which was driving light, profuse snowflakes toward the station. Brenig kept his eyes open, for he liked it when the flakes got caught in his eyelashes, new ones constantly replacing the old, which melted and ran down his cheeks in little drops. A girl walked quickly past him, and he saw how her green hat became white with snow while she hurried across the square, but it was only when she was standing at the streetcar stop that he recognized the little red suitcase she was carrying as the one which had stood next to his box in the baggage room.

It was a mistake to get married, thought Brenig; they congratulate you, send you flowers, have stupid telegrams delivered to your door, and then they leave you alone. They ask whether you have thought of everything: of things for the kitchen, from salt shaker to stove, and finally they make sure you even have plenty of soup seasoning on the shelf. They estimate whether you can support a family, but what it means to *be* a family is something nobody tells you. They send flowers, twenty bouquets, and it smells like a funeral; then they throw rice and leave you alone.

A man walked past him, and he could tell the man was drunk, he was singing "Oh Come All Ye Faithful," but Brenig did not shift the angle of his head, so that it was a moment or two before he noticed that the man was carrying a demijohn in his right hand and he knew the box with his Christmas presents for his wife was now standing all by itself on the top shelf of the baggage room. It contained an umbrella, two books, and a big piano made of mocha chocolate: the white keys were of marzipan, the black ones of dark brittle. The chocolate piano was as big as an encyclopedia, and the girl in the store had said the chocolate would keep for six months.

Maybe I was too young to get married, he thought, maybe I should have waited until Anna became less serious and I became more serious, but actually he knew he was serious enough and that Anna's seriousness was just right. That was what he loved about her. For the sake of the hour before falling asleep he had given up movies and dancing, and hadn't even bothered to meet his friends. At night, when he was lying in bed, he was filled with devoutness, with peace, and he would often repeat the sentence to himself, although he wasn't quite certain of the exact wording: "And God made the earth and the moon, to rule over the day and over the night, to divide the light from the darkness, and God saw that it was good, and there was the evening and the morning." He had meant to look it up in Anna's Bible again to see just how it went, but he always forgot. For God to have created day and night seemed to him every bit as wonderful as the creation of flowers, beasts, and man.

He loved this hour before falling asleep more than anything else. But now that Anna had stopped speaking to him, her silence lay on him like a weight. If she had only said, "It's colder today," or "It's going to rain," it would have put an end to his misery—if she had only said, "Yes," or "No, no," or something sillier still, he would be happy, and he would no longer dread going home. But for the space of a few seconds her face would turn to stone, and at these moments he suddenly knew what she would look like as an old woman; he was seized with fear, suddenly saw himself thrust thirty years forward into the future as onto a stony plain, saw himself old too, with the kind of face he had seen on some men: deeply lined with bitterness, strained with suppressed suffering, and tinged to the very nostrils with the pale yellow of gall. Masks scattered throughout the everyday world like death's-heads . . .

Sometimes, although he had only known her for three years, he also knew what she had looked like as a child. He could picture her as a ten-year-old girl, dreaming over a book under the lamplight, grave, her eyes dark under her light lashes, her eyelids flickering above the printed page, her lips parted. . . . Often, when he was sitting opposite her at table, her face would change like the pictures that change when you shake them, and he suddenly knew that she had sat there exactly like that as a child, carefully breaking up her potatoes with her fork and slowly dribbling the gravy over them. . . . The snow had almost stuck his eyelashes together, but he could just make out the Number 4 gliding up over the snow as if on sleds.

Maybe I should phone her, he thought, have her come to the phone at Menders'; she'd have to speak to me then. The Number 4 would be followed immediately by the 7, the last streetcar that evening, but by this time he was bitterly cold and he walked slowly across the square, saw the brightly lit blue 7 in the distance, stood undecided by the phone booth, and looked in a store window where the window dressers were exchanging Santa Clauses and angels for other dummies: ladies in décolletage, their bare shoulders sprinkled with confetti, their wrists festooned with paper streamers. Their escorts, male dummies with graying temples, were being hurriedly placed on bar stools, champagne corks scattered on the floor; one dummy was having its wings and curls taken off, and Brenig was surprised how quickly an angel could be turned into a bartender. Mustache, dark wig, and a sign swiftly nailed to the wall, saying "New Year's Eve without champagne?"

Here Christmas was over before it had begun. Maybe, he thought, Anna is too young, she was only twenty-one, and while he contemplated his reflection in the store window he noticed the snow had covered his hair like a little crown—the way he used to see it on fenceposts—and it struck him that old people were wrong to talk about the gaiety of youth: when you were young, everything was serious and difficult, and nobody helped you, and he was suddenly surprised that he did not hate Anna for her silence, that he didn't wish he had married someone else. The whole vocabulary that people offered you was meaningless: forgiveness, divorce, a fresh start, time the Great Healer—these words were all useless. You had to work it out for yourself, because you were different from other people, and because Anna was different from other people's wives.

The window dressers were deftly nailing masks onto the walls, stringing crackers on a cord: the last Number 7 had left long ago, and the box with his presents for Anna was standing all by itself up there on the shelf.

I am twenty-five, he thought, and because of a lie, one little lie, a stupid lie such as millions of men tell every week or every month, I have to endure this punishment; with my eyes staring into the stony future I have to look at Anna crouching like a sphinx on the edge of the stony desert, and at myself, my face yellowed with bitterness, an old man. Oh yes, there would always be plenty of soup seasoning on the kitchen shelf, the salt shaker would always be in its proper place, and he would have been a department head for years and well able to support his family: a stony clan, and never again would he lie in bed and in the hour before falling asleep rejoice in the creation of evening, and offer thanks to God for having created rest from the labors of the day, and he would send the same stupid telegrams to young people when they got married as he had been sent himself. . . .

Other women would have laughed over such a stupid lie about his salary, other women knew that all men lie to their wives: maybe it was a kind of instinctive self-defense, against which they invented their own lies, but Anna's face had turned to stone. There were books about marriage, and he had looked up in these books what you could do when something went wrong with your marriage, but none of the books said anything about a woman who had turned to stone. The books told you how to have children and how not to have children, and they contained a lot of big fine words, but the little words were missing.

The window dressers had finished their work: streamers were hanging over wires that were fastened out of sight, and he saw one of the men disappearing at the back of the store with two angels under his arm, while the second man emptied a bag of confetti over the dummy's bare shoulders and gave a final pat to the sign saying "New Year's Eve without champagne?"

Brenig brushed the snow from his hair, walked back across the square to the station, and when he had taken the claim check from his pocket and smoothed it out for the fourth time, ran quickly, as if he hadn't a second to lose. But the baggage room was closed, and there was a sign hanging in front of the grille: "Will open ten minutes before arrival or departure of a train." Brenig laughed, he laughed for the first time since noon and looked at his box, lying up there on the shelf behind bars as if it were in prison. The departure board was right next to the counter, and he saw the next train would not be arriving for another hour. I can't wait that long, he thought, and at this time of night I won't even be able to get flowers or chocolate, not even a little book, and the last Number 7 has gone. For the first time in his life he thought of taking a taxi, and he felt very grown-up and at the same time a bit foolish as he ran across the square to the taxi rank.

He sat in the back of the cab, clasping his money: ten marks, the last of his cash, which he had set aside to buy something special for Anna. But he hadn't found anything special, and now he was sitting there clasping his money and watching the meter jump up at short intervals—very short intervals, it seemed to him—ten pfennings at a time, and every time the meter clicked it felt like a stab in the heart, although it only showed 2.80 marks. Here I am coming home, with no flowers, no presents, hungry, tired, and stupid, and it occurred to him that he could almost certainly have got some chocolate in the waiting room at the station.

The streets were empty, the cab drove almost soundlessly through the snow, and in the lighted windows Brenig could see the Christmas trees glowing in the houses. Christmas, the way he had known it as a child and the way he had felt today, seemed very far away: the important things, the things that mattered, happened independently of the calendar, and in the stony desert Christmas would be like any other day of the year and Easter like a rainy day in November: thirty, forty torn-off calendars, metal holders with shreds of paper, that's all that would be left if you didn't watch out.

He was roused by the driver saying "Here we are. . . ." Then he was relieved to see that the meter had stopped at 3.40 marks. He waited impatiently for his change from five marks, and he felt a surge of relief when he saw a light upstairs in the room where Anna's bed stood next to his. He made up his mind never to forget this moment of relief, and as he got out his house key and put it in the door, he experienced that silly feeling again that he had had when he got into the taxi: he felt grown-up, yet at the same time a bit foolish.

In the kitchen the Christmas tree was standing on the table, with presents spread out for him: socks, cigarettes, a new fountain pen, and a gay, colorful calendar which he would be able to hang over his desk in the office. The milk was already in the saucepan on the stove, he had only to light the gas, and there were sandwiches ready for him on the plate—but that was how it had been every evening, even since Anna had stopped speaking to him, and the setting up of the Christmas tree and the laying out of the presents was like the preparing of the sandwiches, a duty; Anna would always do her duty. He didn't feel like the milk, and the appetizing sandwiches didn't appeal to him either. He went into the little hall and noticed at once that Anna had turned out the light. But the door to the bedroom was open, and without much hope he called softly into the dark rectangle, "Anna, are you asleep?" He waited, for a long time it seemed, as if his question were falling into a deep well, and the dark silence in the dark rectangle of the bedroom door contained everything that was in store for him in thirty, forty years—and when Anna said "No," he thought he must have heard wrong, perhaps it was an illusion, and he went on hurriedly in a louder voice, "I've done such a stupid thing. I checked my presents for you at the station, and when I wanted to pick them up the baggage room was closed, and I didn't want to hang around. Are you angry?"

This time he was sure he had really heard her "No," but he could also hear that this "No" did not come from the corner of the room where their beds had been. Evidently Anna had moved her bed under the window. "It's an umbrella," he said, "two books and a little piano made of chocolate; it's as big as an encyclopedia, the keys are made of marzipan and brittle." He stopped, listened for a reply, nothing came from the dark rectangle, but when he asked, "Are you pleased?" the "Yes" came quicker than the two "No's" had done. . . .

He turned out the light in the kitchen, undressed in the dark, and got into bed. Through the curtains he could see the Christmas trees in the building across the street, and downstairs there was singing, but he had regained his hour, he had two "No's" and a "Yes," and when a car came up the street, the headlights made Anna's profile leap up out of the darkness for him. . . .

The Taste of Bread

A T THE entrance to the basement he was met by stifling, sour-smelling air. He walked slowly down the slimy steps, groping his way into a yellowish darkness: from somewhere water was dripping, there must be a leak in the roof or a pipe must have burst. The water mingled with dust and rubble, making the steps as slippery as the bottom of a fish tank. He walked on. From a door at the back came some light; in the semidarkness he could make out a sign on his right saying "X-ray Room. Do Not Enter." He walked toward the light; it was yellow and soft, and the way it flickered told him that it must be a candle. As he walked on, he looked into dark rooms where he could discern a jumble of chairs, leather sofas, and collapsed cupboards.

The door from which the light came was wide open. Beside the big altar candle stood a nun in a blue habit, tossing some salad in an enamel bowl; the heap of little green leaves had a whitish coating, and he could hear the dressing gently swishing around at the bottom of the bowl. The nun's broad pink hand made the leaves go round and round, and when sometimes a few fell out over the edge, she would calmly pick them up and throw them back in again. Beside the candlestick stood a large saucepan giving off an insipid smell of soup—of hot water, onions, and some kind of bouillon cubes.

In a loud voice he said, "Good evening!"

The nun turned around, alarm on her broad, rosy face, and said softly, "Oh my goodness—what do you want?" Her hands were dripping with the milky dressing, and a few bits of lettuce leaf were clinging to her soft, childlike arms. "Oh my goodness," she said, "you did scare me! Do you want something?"

"I'm hungry," he said in a low voice.

But he was no longer looking at the nun. His gaze had shifted to the right, into an open cupboard whose door had been ripped out by air pressure; the jagged remains of the plywood door still hung in the hinges, and the floor was covered with crumbling flakes of paint. The cupboard contained loaves of bread, many loaves. They lay in a careless pile, more than a dozen wrinkled loaves. Instantly his mouth started watering, and, gulping down the surge of saliva, he thought: I'll be eating bread, whatever happens I'll be eating bread. . . . He looked at the nun: her childlike eyes showed compassion and fear. "Hungry?" she said. "You're hungry?" and looked with raised eyebrows at the bowl of salad, the pot of soup, and the pile of bread.

"Bread," he said, "some bread, please."

She went over to the cupboard, took out a loaf, put it on the table, and started looking in a drawer for a knife.

"Thanks," he said softly. "Don't bother, bread can be broken too. . . ."

The nun tucked the bowl of salad under one arm, picked up the pot of soup, and walked out past him.

He hastily broke off a hunk of bread: his chin was trembling, and he could feel the muscles of his mouth and jaws twitching. Then he dug his teeth into the soft, uneven surface of the bread where he had broken it apart. He was eating bread. The bread was stale, must have been a week old, dry rye bread with a red label from some bakery or other. He continued to dig in with his teeth, finishing off even the brown, leathery crust; then he grasped the loaf in both hands and broke off another piece. Eating with his right hand, he clasped the loaf with his left; he went on eating, sat down on the edge of a wooden crate, and, each time he broke off a piece, bit first into the soft center, feeling all around his mouth the touch of the bread like a dry caress, while his teeth went on digging.

Murke's
Collected Silences

E VERY MORNING, after entering Broadcasting House, Murke performed an existential exercise. Here in this building the elevator was the kind known as a paternoster—open cages carried on a conveyor belt, like beads on a rosary, moving slowly and continuously from bottom to top, across the top of the elevator shaft, down to the bottom again, so that passengers could step on and off at any floor. Murke would jump onto the paternoster but, instead of getting off at the second floor, where his office was, he would let himself be carried on up, past the third, fourth, fifth floors; he was seized with panic every time the cage rose above the level of the fifth floor and ground its way up into the empty space where oily chains, greasy rods, and groaning machinery pulled and pushed the elevator from an upward into a downward direction; Murke would stare in terror at the bare brick walls, and sigh with relief as the elevator passed through the lock, dropped into place, and began its slow descent, past the fifth, fourth, third floors. Murke knew his fears were unfounded: obviously nothing would ever happen, nothing could ever happen, and even if it did, it could be nothing worse than finding himself up there at the top when the elevator stopped moving and being shut in for an hour or two at the most. He was never without a book in his pocket, and cigarettes; yet as long as the building had been standing, for three years, the elevator had never once failed. On certain days it was inspected, days when Murke had to forgo those four and a half seconds of panic, and on these days he was irritable and restless, like people who had gone without breakfast. He needed this panic, the way other people need their coffee, their oatmeal, or their fruit juice.

So when he stepped off the elevator at the second floor, the home of the Cultural Department, he felt lighthearted and relaxed, as lighthearted and relaxed as anyone who loves and understands his work. He would unlock the door to his office, walk slowly over to his armchair, sit down, and light a cigarette. He was always first on the job. He was young, intelligent, and had a pleasant manner, and even his arrogance, which occasionally flashed out for a moment—even that was forgiven him, since it was known he had majored in psychology and graduated *cum laude.*

FOR TWO days now, Murke had been obliged to go without his panic-breakfast: unusual circumstances had required him to get to Broadcasting House at 8:00 a.m., dash off to a studio, and begin work right away, for he had been told by the director of broadcasting to go over the two talks on "The Nature of Art" which the great Bur-Malottke had taped and to cut them according to Bur-Malottke's instructions. Bur-Malottke, who had converted to Catholicism during the religious fervor of 1945, had suddenly, "overnight," as he put it, "felt religious qualms," he had "suddenly felt he might be blamed for contributing to the religious overtones in radio," and he had decided to omit God, who occurred frequently in both his half-hour talks on "The Nature of Art," and replace Him with a formula more in keeping with the mental outlook he had professed before 1945. Bur-Malottke had suggested to the producer that the word "God" be replaced by the formula "that higher Being Whom we revere," but he had refused to retape the talks, requesting instead that God be cut out of the tapes and replaced by "that higher Being Whom we revere." Bur-Malottke was a friend of the director, but this friendship was not the reason for the director's willingness to oblige him: Bur-Malottke was a man one simply did not contradict. He was the author of numerous books of a belletristic-philosophical-religious and art-historical nature, he was on the editorial staff of three periodicals and two newspapers, and closely connected with the largest publishing house. He had agreed to come to Broadcasting House for fifteen minutes on Wednesday and tape the words "that higher Being Whom we revere" as often as "God" was mentioned in his talks: the rest was up to the technical experts.

IT HAD not been easy for the director to find someone whom he could ask to do the job; he thought of Murke, but the suddenness with which he thought of Murke made him suspicious—he was a dynamic, robust individual—so he spent five minutes going over the problem in his mind, considered Schwendling, Humkoke, Fräulein Broldin, but he ended up with Murke. The director did not like Murke; he had, of course, taken him on as soon as his name had been put forward, the way a zoo director, whose real love is the rabbits and the deer, naturally accepts wild animals too for the simple reason that a zoo must contain wild animals—but what the director really loved was rabbits and deer, and for him Murke was an intellectual wild animal. In the end his dynamic personality triumphed, and he instructed Murke to cut Bur-Malottke's talks. The talks were to be given on Thursday and Friday, and Bur-Malottke's misgivings had come to him on Sunday night—one might just as well commit suicide as contradict Bur-Malottke, and the director was much too dynamic to think of suicide.

So Murke spent Monday afternoon and Tuesday morning listening three times to the two half-hour talks on "The Nature of Art"; he had cut out "God," and in the short breaks which he took, during which he silently smoked a cigarette with the technician, reflected on the dynamic personality of the director and the inferior Being Whom Bur-Malottke revered. He had never read a line of Bur-Malottke, never heard one of his talks before. Monday night he had dreamed of a staircase as tall and steep as the Eiffel Tower; he had climbed it but soon noticed that the stairs were slippery with soap, and the director stood down below and called out, "Go on, Murke, go on . . . show us what you can do—go on!" Tuesday night the dream had been similar: he had been at a fairground, strolled casually over to the roller coaster, paid his thirty pfennigs to a man whose face seemed familiar, and as he got on the roller coaster he saw that it was at least ten miles long, he knew there was no going back, and realized that the man who had taken his thirty pfennigs had been the director. Both mornings, after these dreams, he had not needed the harmless panic-breakfast up there in the empty space above the paternoster.

Now it was Wednesday. He was smiling as he entered the building, got into the paternoster, let himself be carried up as far as the sixth floor—four and a half seconds of panic, the grinding of the chains, the bare brick walls—he rode down as far as the fourth floor, got out, and walked toward the studio where he had an appointment with Bur-Malottke. It was two minutes to ten as he sat down in his green chair, waved to the technician, and lit his cigarette. His breathing was quiet, he took a piece of paper out of his breast pocket and glanced at the clock. Bur-Malottke was always on time, at least he had a reputation for being punctual; and as the second hand completed the sixtieth minute of the tenth hour, the minute hand slipped onto the twelve, the hour hand onto the ten, the door opened and in walked Bur-Malottke. Murke got up, and with a pleasant smile walked over to Bur-Malottke and introduced himself. Bur-Malottke shook hands, smiled, and said, "Well, let's get started!" Murke picked up the sheet of paper from the table, put his cigarette between his lips, and, reading from the list, said to Bur-Malottke:

"In the two talks, God occurs precisely twenty-seven times—so I must ask you to repeat twenty-seven times the words we are to splice. We would appreciate it if we might ask you to repeat them thirty-five times, so as to have a certain reserve when it comes to splicing."

"Granted," said Bur-Malottke with a smile, and sat down.

"There is one difficulty, however," said Murke: "where God occurs in the genitive, such as 'God's will,' 'God's love,' 'God's purpose,' He must be replaced by the noun in question followed by the words 'of that higher Being Whom we revere.' I must ask you, therefore, to repeat the words 'the will' twice, 'the love' twice, and 'the purpose' three times, followed each time by 'of that higher Being Whom we revere,' giving us a total of seven genitives. Then there is one spot where you use the vocative and say 'O God'—here I suggest you substitute 'O Thou higher Being Whom we revere.' Everywhere else only the nominative case applies."

It was clear that Bur-Malottke had not thought of these complications; he began to sweat, the grammatical transposition bothered him. Murke went on. "In all," he said, in his pleasant, friendly manner, "the twenty-seven sentences will require one minute and twenty seconds of radio time, whereas the twenty-seven times 'God' occurs require only twenty seconds. In other words, in order to take care of your alterations we shall have to cut half a minute from each talk."

Bur-Malottke sweated more heavily than ever; inwardly he cursed his sudden misgivings and asked, "I suppose you've already done the cutting, have you?"

"Yes, I have," said Murke, pulling a flat metal box out of his pocket; he opened it and held it out to Bur-Malottke. It contained some darkish sound-tape scraps, and Murke said softly, " 'God' twenty-seven times, spoken by you. Would you care to have them?"

"No, I would not," said Bur-Malottke, furious. "I'll speak to the director about the two half minutes. What comes after my talks in the program?"

"Tomorrow," said Murke, "your talk is followed by the regular program 'Neighborly News,' edited by Grehm."

"Damn," said Bur-Malottke, "it's no use asking Grehm for a favor."

"And the day after tomorrow," said Murke, "your talk is followed by 'Let's Go Dancing.' "

"Oh God, that's Huglieme," groaned Bur-Malottke. "Never yet has Light Entertainment given way to Culture by as much as a fifth of a minute."

"No," said Murke, "it never has, at least"—and his youthful face took on an expression of irreproachable modesty—"at least not since I've been working here."

"Very well," said Bur-Malottke and glanced at the clock, "we'll be through here in ten minutes, I take it, and then I'll have a word with the director about that minute. Let's go. Can you leave me your list?"

"Of course," said Murke. "I know the figures by heart."

The technician put down his newspaper as Murke entered the little glass booth. The technician was smiling. On Monday and Tuesday, during the six hours they listened to Bur-Malottke's talks and did their cutting, Murke and the technician had not exchanged a single personal word; now and again they exchanged glances, and when they stopped for a breather, the technician had passed his cigarettes to Murke and the next day Murke passed his to the technician. Now, when Murke saw the technician smiling, he thought: If there is such a thing as friendship in this world, then this man is my friend. He laid the metal box with the snippets from Bur-Malottke's talk on the table and said quietly, "Here we go." He plugged into the studio and said into the microphone, "I'm sure we can dispense with the run-through, Professor. We might as well start right away—would you please begin with the nominatives?"

Bur-Malottke nodded, Murke switched off his own microphone, pressed the button which turned on the green light in the studio, and heard Bur-Malottke's solemn, carefully articulated voice intoning, "That higher Being Whom we revere—that higher Being. . ."

Bur-Malottke pursed his lips toward the muzzle of the mike as if he wanted to kiss it, sweat ran down his face, and through the glass Murke observed with cold detachment the agony that Bur-Malottke was enduring; then he suddenly switched Bur-Malottke off, stopped the moving tape that was recording Bur-Malottke's words, and feasted his eyes on the spectacle of Bur-Malottke behind the glass, soundless, like a fat, handsome fish. He switched on his microphone and his voice came quietly into the studio, "I'm sorry, but our tape was defective, and I must ask you to begin again at the beginning, with the nominatives." Bur-Malottke swore, but his curses were silent ones which only he could hear, for Murke had disconnected him and did not switch him on again until he had begun to say, "That higher Being . . ." Murke was too young, considered himself too civilized, to approve of the word "hate." But here, behind the glass pane, while Bur-Malottke repeated his genitives, he suddenly knew the meaning of hatred: he hated this great fat, handsome creature, whose books —two million three hundred and fifty thousand copies of them—lay around in libraries, bookstores, bookshelves, and bookcases, and not for one second did he dream of suppressing this hatred. When Bur-Malottke had repeated two genitives, Murke switched on his own mike and said quietly, "Excuse me for interrupting you: the nominatives were excellent, so was the first genitive, but would you mind doing the second genitive again? Rather gentler in tone, rather more relaxed—I'll play it back to you." And although Bur-Malottke shook his head violently, he signaled to the technician to play back the tape in the studio. They saw Bur-Malottke give a start, sweat more profusely than ever, then hold his hands over his ears until the tape came to an end. He said something, swore, but Murke and the technician could not hear him; they had disconnected him. Coldly Murke waited until he could read from Bur-Malottke's lips that he had begun again with the higher Being, he turned on the mike and the tape, and Bur-Malottke continued with the genitives.

When he was through, he screwed up Murke's list into a ball, rose from his chair, drenched in sweat and fuming, and made for the door; but Murke's quiet, pleasant young voice called him back. Murke said, "But, Professor, you've forgotten the vocative." Bur-Malottke looked at him, his eyes blazing with hate, and said into the mike, "O Thou higher Being Whom we revere!"

As he turned to leave, Murke's voice called him back once more. Murke said, "I'm sorry, Professor, but, spoken like that, the words are useless."

"For God's sake," whispered the technician, "watch it!" Bur-Malottke was standing stock-still by the door, his back to the glass booth, as if transfixed by Murke's voice.

Something had happened to him that had never happened to him before: he was helpless, and this young voice, so pleasant, so remarkably intelligent, tortured him as nothing had ever tortured him before. Murke went on, "I can, of course, paste it into the talk the way it is, but I must point out to you, Professor, that it will have the wrong effect."

Bur-Malottke turned, walked back to the microphone, and said in low and solemn tones, "O Thou higher Being Whom we revere."

Without turning to look at Murke, he left the studio. It was exactly quarter past ten, and in the doorway he collided with a young, pretty woman carrying some sheet music. The girl, a vivacious redhead, walked briskly to the microphone, adjusted it, and moved the table to one side so she could stand directly in front of the mike.

In the booth Murke chatted for half a minute with Huglieme, who was in charge of Light Entertainment. Pointing to the metal container, Huglieme said, "Do you still need that?" And Murke said, "Yes, I do." In the studio the redhead was singing, "Take my lips, just as they are, they're so lovely." Huglieme switched on his microphone and said quietly, "D'you mind keeping your trap shut for another twenty seconds, I'm not quite ready." The girl laughed, made a face, and said, "OK, pansy dear." Murke said to the technician, "I'll be back at eleven; we can cut it up then and splice it all together."

"Will we have to hear it through again after that?" asked the technician. "No," said Murke, "I wouldn't listen to it again for a million marks."

The technician nodded, inserted the tape for the red-haired singer, and Murke left.

He put a cigarette between his lips, did not light it, and walked along the rear corridor toward the second paternoster, the one on the south side leading down to the coffeeshop. The rugs, the corridors, the furniture, and the pictures, everything irritated him. The rugs were impressive, the corridors were impressive, the furniture was impressive, and the pictures were in excellent taste, but he suddenly felt a desire to take the sentimental picture of the Sacred Heart which his mother had sent him and see it somewhere here on the wall. He stopped, looked round, listened, took the picture from his pocket, and stuck it between the wallpaper and the frame of the door to the assistant drama producer's office. The tawdry little print was highly colored, and beneath the picture of the Sacred Heart were the words: "I prayed for you at St. James's Church."

Murke continued along the corridor, got into the paternoster, and was carried down. On this side of the building the Schrumsnot ashtrays, which had won a Good Design Award, had already been installed. They hung next to the illuminated red figures indicating the floor: a red four, a Schrumsnot ashtray, a red three, a Schrumsnot ashtray, a red two, a Schrumsnot ashtray. They were handsome ashtrays, scallop-shaped, made of beaten copper, the copper base an exotic marine plant, nodular seaweed —and each ashtray had cost two hundred and fifty-eight marks and seventy-seven pfennigs. They were so handsome that Murke could never bring himself to soil them with cigarette ash, let alone anything as sordid as a butt. Other smokers all seemed to have had the same feeling—empty packs, butts, and ash littered the floor under the handsome ashtrays. Apparently no one had the courage to use them as ashtrays; they were copper, burnished, forever empty.

Murke saw the fifth ashtray next to the illuminated red zero rising toward him; the air was getting warmer, there was a smell of food. Murke jumped off and stumbled into the coffeeshop. Three free-lance colleagues were sitting at a table in the corner. The table was covered with used plates, cups, and saucers.

The three men were the joint authors of a radio series, "The Lung,

A Human Organ"; they had collected their fee together, breakfasted together, were having a drink together, and were now throwing dice for the expense voucher. One of them, Wendrich, Murke knew well, but just then Wendrich shouted "Art!"—"Art," he shouted again, "art, art!" and Murke felt a spasm, like the frog when Galvani discovered electricity. The last two days Murke had heard the word "art" too often, from Bur-Malottke's lips; it occurred exactly one hundred and thirty-four times in the two talks, and he had heard the talks three times, which meant he had heard the word "art" four hundred and two times, too often to feel any desire to discuss it. He squeezed past the counter toward a booth in the far corner and was relieved to find it empty. He sat down, lit his cigarette, and when Wulla, the waitress, came, he said, "Apple juice, please," and was glad when Wulla went off again at once. He closed his eyes tight, but found himself listening willy-nilly to the conversation of the free-lance writers over in the corner, who seemed to be having a heated argument about art; each time one of them shouted "Art," Murke winced. It's like being whipped, he thought.

When she brought him the apple juice, Wulla looked at him in concern. She was tall and strongly built, but not fat; she had a healthy, cheerful face. As she poured the apple juice from the jug into the glass, she said, "You ought to take a vacation, sir, and quit smoking."

She used to call herself Wilfriede-Ulla, but later, for the sake of simplicity, she combined the names into Wulla. She especially admired the people from the Cultural Department.

"Lay off, will you?" said Murke. "Please!"

"And you ought to take some nice ordinary girl to the movies one night," said Wulla.

"I'll do that this evening," said Murke, "I promise you."

"It doesn't have to be one of those dolls," said Wulla, "just some nice, quiet, ordinary girl, with a kind heart. There are still some of those around."

"Yes," said Murke, "I know they're still around, as a matter of fact I know one." Well, that's fine then, thought Wulla, and went over to the freelancers, one of whom had ordered three drinks and three coffees. Poor fellows, thought Wulla, art will be the death of them yet. She had a soft spot for the freelancers and was always trying to persuade them to economize. The minute they have any money, she thought, they blow it; she went up to the counter and, shaking her head, passed on the order for the three drinks and the three coffees.

Murke drank some of the apple juice, stubbed out his cigarette in the ashtray, and thought with apprehension of the hours from eleven to one when he had to cut up Bur-Malottke's sentences and paste them into the right places in the talks. At two o'clock the director wanted both talks played back to him in his studio. Murke thought about soap, about staircases, steep stairs, and roller coasters, he thought about the dynamic personality of the director, he thought about Bur-Malottke, and was startled by the sight of Schwendling coming into the coffeeshop.

Schwendling had on a shirt of large red and black checks and made a beeline for the booth where Murke was hiding. Schwendling was humming the tune which was very popular just then: "Take my lips, just as they are, they're so lovely. . . ." He stopped short when he saw Murke, and said, "Hello, you here? I thought you were busy carving up that crap of Bur-Malottke's."

"I'm going back at eleven," said Murke.

"Wulla, let's have some beer," shouted Schwendling over to the counter, "a pint. Well," he said to Murke, "you deserve extra time off for that, it must be a filthy job. The old man told me all about it."

Murke said nothing, and Schwendling went on, "Have you heard the latest about Muckwitz?"

Murke, not interested, first shook his head, then for politeness's sake asked, "What's he been up to?"

Wulla brought the beer. Schwendling swallowed some, paused for effect, and announced, "Muckwitz is doing a feature about the Steppes."

Murke laughed and said, "What's Fenn doing?"

"Fenn," said Schwendling, "Fenn's doing a feature about the Tundra."

"And Weggucht?"

"Weggucht is doing a feature about me, and after that I'm going to do a feature about him, you know the old saying: 'You feature me, I'll feature you. . . .'"

Just then one of the freelancers jumped up and shouted across the room, "Art—art—that's the only thing that matters!"

Murke ducked, like a soldier when he hears the mortars being fired from the enemy trenches. He swallowed another mouthful of apple juice and winced again when a voice over the loudspeaker said, "Herr Murke is wanted in Studio 13—Herr Murke is wanted in Studio 13." He looked at his watch; it was only half-past ten, but the voice went on relentlessly, "Herr Murke is wanted in Studio 13—Herr Murke is wanted in Studio 13." The loudspeaker hung above the counter, immediately below the motto the director had had painted on the wall: "Discipline Above All."

"Well," said Schwendling, "that's it, you'd better go."

"Yes," said Murke, "that's it."

He got up, put money for the apple juice on the table, pressed past the freelancers' table, got into the paternoster outside, and was carried up once more past the five Schrumsnot ashtrays. He saw his Sacred Heart picture still sticking in the assistant producer's doorframe and thought: Thank God, now there's at least one corny picture in this place.

He opened the door of the studio booth, saw the technician sitting alone and relaxed in front of three cardboard boxes, and asked wearily, "What's up?"

"They were ready sooner than expected, and we've got an extra half hour in hand," said the technician. "I thought you'd be glad of the extra time."

"I certainly am," said Murke. "I've got an appointment at one. Let's get on with it, then. What's the idea of the boxes?"

"Well," said the technician, "for each grammatical case I've got one box—the nominatives in the first, the genitives in the second, and in that one"—he pointed to the little box on the right with the words "Pure Chocolate" on it—"in that one I have the two vocatives, the good one in the right-hand corner, the bad one in the left."

"That's terrific," said Murke. "So you've already cut up the crap."

"That's right," said the technician, "and if you've made a note of the order in which the cases have to be spliced, it won't take us more than an hour. Did you write it down?"

"Yes, I did," said Murke. He pulled a piece of paper from his pocket with the numbers one to twenty-seven; each number was followed by a grammatical case.

Murke sat down, held out his cigarette pack to the technician; they both smoked while the technician laid the cut tapes with Bur-Malottke's talks on the roll.

"In the first cut," said Murke, "we have to stick in a nominative."

The technician put his hand into the first box, picked up one of the snippets, and stuck it into the space.

"Next comes a genitive," said Murke.

They worked swiftly, and Murke was relieved that it all went so fast.

"Now," he said, "comes the vocative; we'll take the bad one, of course."

The technician laughed and stuck Bur-Malottke's bad vocative into the tape.

"Next," he said, "next!"
"Genitive," said Murke.

THE DIRECTOR conscientiously read every letter from a listener. The one he was reading at this particular moment went as follows:

Dear Radio,
      I am sure you can have no more faithful listener than myself. I am an old woman, a little old lady of seventy-seven, and I have been listening to you every day for thirty years. I have never been sparing with my praise. Perhaps you remember my letter about the program "The Seven Souls of Kaweida the Cow." It was a lovely program—but now I have to be angry with you! The way the canine soul is being neglected in radio is gradually becoming a disgrace. And you call that humanism. I am sure Hitler had his bad points: if one is to believe all one hears, he was a dreadful man, but one thing he did have: a real affection for dogs, and he did a lot for them. When are dogs going to come into their own again in German radio? The way you tried to do it in the program "Like Cat and Dog" is certainly not the right one: it was an insult to every canine soul. If my little Lohengrin could only talk, he'd tell you! And the way he barked, poor darling, all through your terrible program, it almost made me die of shame. I pay my two marks a month like any other listener and stand on my rights and demand to know: When are dogs going to come into their own again in German radio?
      With kind regards—in spite of my being so cross with you,
                                        Sincerely yours,
                                        Jadwiga Herchen (retired)

P.S. In case none of those cynics of yours who run your programs should be capable of doing justice to the canine soul, I suggest you make use of my modest attempts, which are enclosed herewith. I do not wish to accept any fee. You may send it direct to the SPCA. Enclosed: 35 manuscripts.
                                        Yours,
                                        J.H.

The director sighed. He looked for the scripts, but his secretary had evidently filed them away. The director filled his pipe, lit it, ran his tongue over his dynamic lips, lifted the receiver, and asked to be put through to Krochy. Krochy had a tiny office with a tiny desk, although in the best of taste, upstairs in Culture and was in charge of a section as narrow as his desk: Animals in the World of Culture.

"Krochy speaking," he said diffidently into the telephone.

"Say, Krochy," said the director, "when was the last time we had a program about dogs?"

"Dogs, sir?" said Krochy. "I don't believe we ever have, at least not since I've been here."

"And how long have you been here, Krochy?" And upstairs in his office Krochy trembled, because the director's voice was so gentle; he knew it boded no good when that voice became gentle.

"I've been here ten years now, sir," said Krochy.

"It's a disgrace," said the director, "that you've never had a program about dogs; after all, that's your department. What was the title of your last program?"

"The title of my last program was—" stammered Krochy.

"You don't have to repeat every sentence," said the director, "we're not in the army."

" 'Owls in the Ruins,' " said Krochy timidly.

"Within the next three weeks," said the director, gentle again now, "I would like to hear a program about the canine soul."

"Certainly, sir," said Krochy. He heard the click as the director put down the receiver, sighed deeply, and said, "Oh God!"

The director picked up the next letter.

At this moment Bur-Malottke entered the room. He was always at liberty to enter unannounced, and he made frequent use of this liberty. He was still sweating as he sank wearily into a chair opposite the director and said, "Well, good morning."

"Good morning," said the director, pushing the letter aside. "What can I do for you?"

"Could you give me one minute?"

"Bur-Malottke," said the director, with a generous, dynamic gesture, "does not have to ask me for one minute; hours, days, are at your disposal."

"No," said Bur-Malottke, "I don't mean an ordinary minute, I mean one minute of radio time. Due to the changes, my talk has become one minute longer."

The director grew serious, like a satrap distributing provinces. "I hope," he said sourly, "it's not a political minute."

"No," said Bur-Malottke, "it's half a minute of 'Neighborly News' and half a minute of Light Entertainment."

"Thank God for that," said the director. "I've got a credit of seventy-nine seconds with Light Entertainment and eighty-three seconds with 'Neighborly News.' I'll be glad to let someone like Bur-Malottke have one minute."

"I am overcome," said Bur-Malottke.

"Is there anything else I can do for you?" asked the director.

"I would appreciate it," said Bur-Malottke, "if we could gradually start correcting all the tapes I have made since 1945. One day," he said—he passed his hand over his forehead and gazed wistfully at the genuine Kokoschka above the director's desk—"one day I shall"—he faltered, for the news he was about to break to the director was too painful for posterity—"one day I shall . . . die," and he paused again, giving the director a chance to look gravely shocked and raise his hand in protest, "and I cannot bear the thought that after my death, tapes may be run off on which I say things I no longer believe in. Particularly in some of my political utterances, during the fervor of 1945, I let myself be persuaded to make statements which today fill me with serious misgivings and which I can only account for on the basis of that spirit of youthfulness that has always distinguished my work. My written works are already in process of being corrected, and I would like to ask you to give me the opportunity of correcting my spoken works as well."

The director was silent; he cleared his throat slightly, and little shining beads of sweat appeared on his forehead. It occurred to him that Bur-Malottke had spoken for at least an hour every month since 1945, and he made a swift calculation while Bur-Malottke went on talking: twelve times ten hours meant one hundred and twenty hours of spoken Bur-Malottke.

"Pedantry," Bur-Malottke was saying, "is something that only impure spirits regard as unworthy of genius; we know, of course"—and the director felt flattered to be ranked by the We among the pure spirits—"that the true geniuses, the great geniuses, were pedants. Himmelsheim once had a whole printed edition of his *Seelon* rebound at his own expense because he felt that three or four sentences in the central portion of the work were no longer appropriate. The idea that some of my talks might be broadcast which no longer correspond to my convictions when I depart this earthly life—I find such an idea intolerable. How do you propose we go about it?"

The beads of sweat on the director's forehead had become larger. "First of all," he said in a subdued voice, "an exact list would have to be made of all your broadcast talks, and then we would have to check in the archives to see if all the tapes were still there."

"I should hope," said Bur-Malottke, "that none of the tapes has been erased without notifying me. I have not been notified, therefore no tapes have been erased."

"I will see to everything," said the director.

"Please do," said Bur-Malottke curtly, and rose from his chair. "Good-bye."

"Good-bye," said the director as he accompanied Bur-Malottke to the door.

THE FREELANCERS in the coffeeshop had decided to order lunch. They had had some more drinks, they were still talking about art, their conversation was quieter now but no less intense. They all jumped to their feet when Wanderburn suddenly came in. Wanderburn was a tall, despondent-looking writer with dark hair, an attractive face somewhat etched by the stigma of fame. On this particular morning he had not shaved, which made him look even more attractive. He walked over to the table where the three men were sitting, sank exhausted into a chair, and said, "For God's sake, give me a drink. I always have the feeling in this building that I'm dying of thirst."

They passed him a drink, a glass that was still standing on the table, and the remains of a bottle of soda water. Wanderburn swallowed the drink, put down his glass, looked at each of the three men in turn, and said, "I must warn you about the radio business, about this pile of junk —this immaculate, shiny, slippery pile of junk. I'm warning you. It'll destroy us all." His warning was sincere and impressed the three young men very much; but the three young men did not know that Wanderburn had just come from the accounting department, where he had picked up a nice fat fee for a quick job of editing the Book of Job.

"They cut us," said Wanderburn, "they consume our substance, splice us together again, and it'll be more than any of us can stand."

He finished the soda water, put the glass down on the table, and, his coat flapping despondently about him, strode to the door.

ON THE dot of noon Murke finished the splicing. They had just stuck in the last snippet, a genitive, when Murke got up. He already had his hand on the doorknob when the technician said, "I wish I could afford a sensitive and expensive conscience like that. What'll we do with the box?" He pointed to the flat tin lying on the shelf next to the cardboard boxes containing the new tapes.

"Just leave it there," said Murke.

"What for?"

"We might need it again."

"D'you think he might get pangs of conscience all over again?"

"He might," said Murke. "We'd better wait and see. So long." He walked to the front paternoster, rode down to the second floor, and for the first time that day entered his office. His secretary had gone to lunch; Murke's boss, Humkoke, was sitting by the phone reading a book. He smiled at Murke, got up, and said, "Well, I see you survived. Is this your book? Did you put it on the desk?" He held it out for Murke to read the title, and Murke said, "Yes, that's mine." The book had a jacket of green, gray, and orange and was called *Batley's Lyrics of the Gutter*; it was about a young English writer a hundred years ago who had drawn up a catalogue of London slang.

"It's a marvelous book," said Murke.

"Yes," said Humkoke, "it is marvelous, but you never learn."

Murke eyed him questioningly.

"You never learn that one doesn't leave marvelous books lying around when Wanderburn is liable to turn up, and Wanderburn is always liable to turn up. He saw it at once, of course, opened it, read it for five minutes, and what's the result?"

Murke said nothing.

"The result," said Humkoke, "is two hour-long broadcasts by Wanderburn on 'Lyrics of the Gutter.' One day this fellow will do a feature about his own grandmother, and the worst of it is that one of his grandmothers was one of mine too. Please, Murke, try to remember: never leave marvelous books around when Wanderburn is liable to turn up, and, I repeat, he's always liable to turn up. That's all, you can go now, you've got the afternoon off, and I'm sure you've earned it. Is the stuff ready? Did you hear it through again?"

"It's all done," said Murke, "but I can't hear the talks through again, I simply can't."

" 'I simply can't' is a very childish thing to say," said Humkoke.

"If I have to hear the word 'art' one more time today, I'll become hysterical," said Murke.

"You already are," said Humkoke, "and I must say you've every reason to be. Three hours of Bur-Malottke—that's too much for anybody, even the toughest of us, and you're not even tough." He threw the book on the table, took a step toward Murke, and said, "When I was your age I once had to cut three minutes out of a four-hour speech of Hitler's, and I had to listen to the speech three times before I was considered worthy of suggesting which three minutes should be cut. When I began listening to the tape for the first time I was still a Nazi, but by the time I had heard the speech for the third time I wasn't a Nazi any more. It was a drastic cure—a terrible one, but very effective."

"You forget," said Murke quietly, "that I had already been cured of Bur-Malottke before I had to listen to his tapes."

"You really are a vicious beast!" said Humkoke with a laugh. "That'll do for now. The director is going to hear it through again at two. Just see that you're available in case anything goes wrong."

"I'll be home from two to three," said Murke.

"One more thing," said Humkoke, pulling out a yellow biscuit tin from a shelf next to Murke's desk. "What's this scrap you've got here?"

Murke colored. "It's . . ." he stammered, "I collect a certain kind of leftovers."

"What kind of leftovers?" asked Humkoke.

"Silences," said Murke. "I collect silences."

Humkoke raised his eyebrows, and Murke went on, "When I have to cut tapes, in the places where the speakers sometimes pause for a moment —or sigh, or take a breath, or there is absolute silence—I don't throw that away, I collect it. Incidentally, there wasn't a single second of silence in Bur-Malottke's tapes."

Humkoke laughed. "Of course not, he would never be silent. And what do you do with the scrap?"

"I splice it together and play back the tape when I'm at home in the evening. There's not much yet, I only have three minutes so far—but then people aren't silent very often."

"You know, don't you, that it's against regulations to take home sections of tape?"

"Even silences?" asked Murke.

Humkoke laughed and said, "For God's sake, get out!" And Murke left.

WHEN THE director entered his studio a few minutes after two, the Bur-Malottke tape had just been turned on:

> . . . and wherever, however, why ever, and whenever we begin
> to discuss the Nature of Art, we must first look to that higher
> Being Whom we revere, we must bow in awe before that
> higher Being Whom we revere, and we must accept Art as a
> gift from that higher Being Whom we revere. Art . . .

No, thought the director, I really can't ask anyone to listen to Bur-Malottke for a hundred and twenty hours. No, he thought, there are some things one simply cannot do, things I wouldn't want to wish even on Murke. He returned to his office and switched on the loudspeaker just in time to hear Bur-Malottke say, "O Thou higher Being Whom we revere. . . ." No, thought the director, no, no.

MURKE LAY on his chesterfield at home smoking. Next to him on a chair was a cup of tea, and Murke was gazing at the white ceiling of the room. Sitting at his desk was a very pretty blonde who was staring out of the window at the street. Between Murke and the girl, on a low coffee table, stood a tape recorder, recording. Not a word was spoken, not a sound was made. The girl was pretty and silent enough for a photographer's model.

"I can't stand it," said the girl suddenly. "I can't stand it, it's inhuman, what you want me to do. There are some men who expect a girl to do immoral things, but it seems to me that what you are asking me to do is even more immoral than the things other men expect a girl to do."

Murke sighed. "Oh hell," he said, "Rina dear, now I've got to cut all that out; do be sensible, be a good girl, and put just five more minutes' silence on the tape."

"Put silence," said the girl, with what thirty years ago would have been called a pout. "Put silence, that's another of your inventions. I wouldn't mind putting words onto a tape—but putting silence. . . ."

Murke had got up and switched off the tape recorder. "Oh, Rina," he said, "if you only knew how precious your silence is to me. In the evening, when I'm tired, when I'm sitting here alone, I play back your silence. Do be a dear and put just three more minutes' silence on the tape for me and save me the cutting; you know how I feel about cutting."

"Oh, all right," said the girl, "but give me a cigarette at least."

Murke smiled, gave her a cigarette, and said, "This way I have your silence in the original and on tape, that's terrific." He switched the tape on again, and they sat facing one another in silence till the telephone rang. Murke got up, shrugged helplessly, and lifted the receiver.

"Well," said Humkoke, "the tapes ran off smoothly, the boss couldn't find a thing wrong with them. . . . You can go to the movies now. And think about snow."

"What snow?" asked Murke, looking out onto the street, which lay basking in brilliant summer sunshine.

"Come on, now," said Humkoke, "you know we have to start thinking about the winter programs. I need songs about snow, stories about snow—we can't fool around for the rest of our lives with Schubert and Stifter. No one seems to have any idea how badly we need snow songs and snow stories. Just imagine if we have a long hard winter with lots of snow and freezing temperatures: where are we going to get our snow programs from? Try to think of something snowy."

"All right," said Murke, "I'll try to think of something." Humkoke had hung up.

"Come along," he said to the girl, "we can go to the movies."

"May I speak again now?" said the girl.

"Yes," said Murke, "speak!"

IT WAS just at this time that the assistant drama producer had finished listening again to the one-act play scheduled for that evening. He liked it, only the ending did not satisfy him. He was sitting in the glass booth in Studio 13 next to the technician, chewing a match and studying the script.

> *(Sound effects of a large empty church)*
>
> ATHEIST *(in a loud clear voice):* Who will remember me when I have become the prey of worms?
>
> *(Silence)*
>
> ATHEIST *(his voice a shade louder):* Who will wait for me when I have turned into dust?
>
> *(Silence)*
>
> ATHEIST *(louder still):* And who will remember me when I have turned into leaves?
>
> *(Silence)*

There were twelve such questions called out by the atheist into the church, and each question was followed by—? Silence.

The assistant producer removed the chewed match from his lips, replaced it with a fresh one, and looked at the technician, a question in his eyes.

"Yes," said the technician, "if you ask me, I think there's a bit too much silence in it."

"That's what I thought," said the assistant producer; "the author thinks so too and he's given me leave to change it. There should just be a voice saying 'God'—but it ought to be a voice without church sound effects, it would have to be spoken somehow in a different acoustical environment. Have you any idea where I can get hold of a voice like that at this hour?"

The technician smiled, picked up the metal container which was still lying on the shelf. "Here you are," he said, "here's a voice saying 'God' without any sound effects."

The assistant producer was so surprised he almost swallowed the match, choked a little, and got it up into the front of his mouth again. "It's quite all right," the technician said with a smile. "We had to cut it out of a talk, twenty-seven times."

"I don't need it that often, just twelve times," said the assistant producer.

"It's a simple matter, of course," said the technician, "to cut out the silence and stick in 'God' twelve times—if you'll take the responsibility."

"You're a godsend," said the assistant producer, "and I'll be responsible. Come on, let's get started." He gazed happily at the tiny, lusterless tape snippets in Murke's tin box. "You really are a godsend," he said. "Come on, let's go!"

The technician smiled, for he was looking forward to being able to present Murke with the snippets of silence: it was a lot of silence, all together nearly a minute; it was more silence than he had ever been able to give Murke, and he liked the young man.

"OK," he said with a smile, "here we go."

The assistant producer put his hand in his jacket pocket, took out a pack of cigarettes; in doing so he touched a crumpled piece of paper. He smoothed it out and passed it to the technician. "Funny, isn't it, the corny stuff you can come across in this place? I found this stuck in my door."

The technician took the picture, looked at it, and said, "Yes, it's funny," and he read out the words under the picture:

"I prayed for you at St. James's Church."

Monologue
of a Waiter

I DON'T KNOW how it could have happened; after all, I'm no longer a child, I'm almost fifty and should have known what I was doing. Yet I did it, and, to top it all, when I was already off duty and actually nothing more should have happened to me. But it did happen, and so on Christmas Eve I was given notice.

Everything had gone off without a hitch: I had served the guests at dinner without knocking over a glass, without tipping over a gravy boat, without spilling any red wine, had pocketed my tips and withdrawn to my room, thrown jacket and tie onto the bed, slipped my suspenders off my shoulders, opened my bottle of beer, and I was just lifting the lid of the tureen and sniffing—pea soup. That's what I had ordered from the chef, with bacon, without onions, but thickened, well thickened. I'm sure you don't know what "well thickened" means: it would take too long to try and explain this to you—it took my mother three hours to explain what she meant by "well thickened." Well, the soup smelled glorious, and I dipped in the ladle, filled my plate, could feel and see that the soup was thoroughly well thickened—and at that moment my door opened and in came the young rascal I'd noticed at dinner. Small, pale, certainly no older than eight, he had allowed his plate to be piled high and then, without touching any of it, had it all taken away again—turkey and chestnuts, truffles and veal, and not even the dessert, which after all no child ever passes up, he had not so much as touched with a spoon; he'd allowed five pear halves and half a bucket of chocolate sauce to be tipped onto his plate, and he hadn't touched a thing, not a thing, yet all the time not looking as if he were fussy but like someone with a definite plan in mind.

He closed the door quietly behind him, looked at my plate, then at me. "What's that?" he asked.

"That's pea soup," I said.

"There's no such thing," he said with a smile. "That only exists in the fairy tale about the king who lost his way in the forest."

"Well," I said, "one thing's for sure: that's pea soup."

"May I have a taste?"

"Sure, go ahead," I said, "come and sit down."

Well, he ate three plates of pea soup while I sat beside him on my bed, drinking beer and smoking, and I could actually see his little stomach becoming rounder. While I sat on the bed, I thought about a lot of things that I have meanwhile forgotten again—ten minutes, fifteen, quite a long time, time enough to think about many things, about fairy tales, about grown-ups, parents, and suchlike. Finally the little fellow gave up. I took his place and finished off the soup, a plate and a half, while he sat on the bed beside me. Maybe I shouldn't have looked into the empty tureen, for he said, "Oh dear, I've eaten up all your soup!"

"Never mind," I said, "that was plenty for me. Did you come here to eat pea soup?"

"No, I was just looking for someone to help me find a pit. I thought you might know of one."

Pit, pit . . . then it dawned on me—you need one for playing marbles, and I said, "Well, you know, it'll be difficult to find a pit here in this building."

"Can't we make one?" he asked. "Just scoop one on the floor of the room?"

I don't know how it could have happened, but I did it, and when the boss asked me, "How could you do such a thing?" I was at a loss for an answer. Maybe I should have said: Haven't we promised to fulfill our guests' every wish in order to make sure they have a happy and harmonious Christmas? But I didn't, I said nothing. After all, I couldn't have foreseen that the child's mother would trip over the hole in the floor and break her ankle, at night, when she came back drunk from the bar. How could I know that? And that the insurance people would demand an explanation, and so on and so forth? Third-party liability, labor tribunal, and over and over again: incredible, incredible. Should I have explained to them that for three hours, three whole hours, I played marbles with the boy, that he always won, that he even drank some of my beer—until finally, dead tired, he fell into bed? I said nothing; but when they asked me if it was I who had scooped out the hole in the hardwood floor, I couldn't deny it. The pea soup was the only thing they never found out about: that will remain our secret.

Thirty-five years in my profession, always conducted myself impeccably. I don't know how it could have happened; I should have known what I was doing, yet I did it. I took the elevator down to the janitor, borrowed a hammer and chisel, took the elevator up again, chipped a hole in the hardwood floor. After all, I couldn't have foreseen that his mother would trip over it when she came home drunk at four in the morning from the bar. To be quite frank, I'm not all that upset, not even at being fired. Good waiters are always in demand.

Like a Bad Dream

THAT EVENING we had invited the Zumpens over for dinner, nice people; it was through my father-in-law that we had got to know them. Ever since we have been married he has helped me to meet people who can be useful to me in business, and Zumpen can be useful: he is chairman of a committee which places contracts for large housing projects, and I have married into the excavating business.

I was tense that evening, but Bertha, my wife, reassured me. "The fact," she said, "that he's coming at all is promising. Just try to get the conversation round to the contract. You know it's tomorrow they're going to be awarded."

I stood looking through the net curtains of the glass front door, waiting for Zumpen. I smoked, ground the cigarette butts under my foot, and shoved them under the mat. Next I took up a position at the bathroom window and stood there wondering why Zumpen had accepted the invitation; he couldn't be that interested in having dinner with us, and the fact that the big contract I was involved in was going to be awarded tomorrow must have made the whole thing as embarrassing to him as it was to me.

I thought about the contract too: it was a big one, I would make twenty thousand marks on the deal, and I wanted the money.

Bertha had decided what I was to wear: a dark jacket, trousers a shade lighter, and a conservative tie. That's the kind of thing she learned at home, and at boarding school from the nuns. Also what to offer guests: when to pass the cognac, and when the vermouth, how to arrange dessert. It is comforting to have a wife who knows all about such things.

But Bertha was tense too: as she put her hands on my shoulders, they touched my neck, and I felt her thumbs damp and cold against it.

"It's going to be all right," she said. "You'll get the contract."

"Christ," I said, "it means twenty thousand marks to me, and you know how we need the money."

"One should never," she said gently, "mention Christ's name in connection with money."

A dark car drew up in front of our house, a make I didn't recognize, but it looked Italian. "Take it easy," Bertha whispered, "wait till they've rung, let them stand there for a couple of seconds, then walk slowly to the door and open it."

I watched Herr and Frau Zumpen come up the steps: he is slender and tall, with graying temples, the kind of man who fifty years ago would have been known as a "ladies' man"; Frau Zumpen is one of those thin, dark women who always make me think of lemons. I could tell from Zumpen's face that it was a frightful bore for him to have dinner with us.

Then the doorbell rang, and I waited one second, two seconds, walked slowly to the door and opened it.

"Well," I said, "how nice of you to come!"

Cognac glasses in hand, we went from room to room in our apartment, which the Zumpens wanted to see. Bertha stayed in the kitchen to squeeze some mayonnaise out of a tube onto the appetizers; she does this very nicely: hearts, loops, little houses. The Zumpens complimented us on our apartment. They exchanged smiles when they saw the big desk in my study; at that moment it seemed a bit too big even to me.

Zumpen admired a small rococo cabinet, a wedding present from my grandmother, and a baroque Madonna in our bedroom.

By the time we got back to the dining room, Bertha had dinner on the table. She had done this very nicely too; it was all so attractive yet so natural, and dinner was pleasant and relaxed. We talked about movies and books, about the recent elections, and Zumpen praised the assortment of cheeses, and Frau Zumpen praised the coffee and the pastries. Then we showed the Zumpens our honeymoon pictures: photographs of the Breton coast, Spanish donkeys, and street scenes from Casablanca.

After that we had some more cognac, and when I stood up to get the box with the photos of the time when we were engaged, Bertha gave me a sign, so I didn't get the box. For two minutes there was absolute silence, because we had nothing more to talk about, and we all thought about the contract; I thought of the twenty thousand marks, and it struck me that I could deduct the bottle of cognac from my income tax. Zumpen looked at his watch and said, "Too bad, it's ten o'clock; we have to go. It's been such a pleasant evening!" And Frau Zumpen said, "It was really delightful, and I hope you'll come to us one evening."

"We would love to," Bertha said, and we stood around for another half minute, all thinking again about the contract, and I felt Zumpen was waiting for me to take him aside and bring up the subject. But I didn't.

Zumpen kissed Bertha's hand, and I went ahead, opened the doors, and held the car door open for Frau Zumpen down below.

"Why," said Bertha gently, "didn't you mention the contract to him? You know it's going to be awarded tomorrow."

"Well," I said, "I didn't know how to bring the conversation round to it."

"Now, look," she said in a quiet voice, "you could have used any excuse to ask him into your study, that's where you should have talked to him. You must have noticed how interested he is in art. You ought to have said: I have an eighteenth-century crucifix in there you might like to have a look at, and then . . ."

I said nothing, and she sighed and tied on her apron. I followed her into the kitchen; we put the rest of the appetizers back in the refrigerator, and I crawled about on the floor looking for the top of the mayonnaise tube. I put away the remains of the cognac, counted the cigars: Zumpen had smoked only one. I emptied the ashtrays, ate another pastry, and looked to see if there was any coffee left in the pot. When I went back to the kitchen, Bertha was standing there with the car key in her hand.

"What's up?" I asked.

"We have to go over there, of course," she said.

"Over where?"

"To the Zumpens'," she said, "where do you think?"

"It's nearly half past ten."

"I don't care if it's midnight," Bertha said, "all I know is, there's twenty thousand marks involved. Don't imagine they're squeamish."

She went into the bathroom to get ready, and I stood behind her watching her wipe her mouth and draw in new outlines, and for the first time I noticed how wide and primitive that mouth is. When she tightened the knot of my tie I could have kissed her, the way I always used to when she fixed my tie, but I didn't.

Downtown the cafés and restaurants were brightly lit. People were sitting outside on the terraces, and the light from the streetlamps was caught in the silver ice-cream dishes and ice buckets. Bertha gave me an encouraging look; but she stayed in the car when we stopped in front of the Zumpens' house, and I pressed the bell at once and was surprised how quickly the door was opened. Frau Zumpen did not seem surprised to see me; she had on some black lounging pajamas with loose full trousers embroidered with yellow flowers, and this made me think more than ever of lemons.

"I beg your pardon," I said. "I would like to speak to your husband."

"He's gone out again," she said. "He'll be back in half an hour."

In the hall I saw a lot of Madonnas, Gothic and baroque, even rococo Madonnas, if there is such a thing.

"I see," I said. "Well, then, if you don't mind, I'll come back in half an hour."

Bertha had bought an evening paper; she was reading it and smoking, and when I sat down beside her, she said, "I think you could have talked about it to her too."

"But how did you know he wasn't there?"

"Because I know he is at the Gaffel Club playing chess, as he does every Wednesday evening at this time."

"You might have told me that earlier."

"Please try to understand," said Bertha, folding the newspaper. "I am trying to help you, I want you to find out for yourself how to deal with such things. All we had to do was call up Father and he would have settled the whole thing for you with one phone call, but I want you to get the contract on your own."

"All right," I said, "then what'll we do: wait here half an hour, or go up right away and have a talk with her?"

"We'd better go up right away," said Bertha.

We got out of the car and went up in the elevator together. "Life," said Bertha, "consists of making compromises and concessions."

Frau Zumpen was no more surprised now than she had been earlier, when I had come alone. She greeted us, and we followed her into her husband's study. Frau Zumpen brought some cognac, poured it out, and before I could say anything about the contract she pushed a yellow folder toward me: "Fir Tree Haven Housing Project," I read, and looked up in alarm at Frau Zumpen, at Bertha, but they both smiled, and Frau Zumpen said, "Open the folder," and I opened it; inside was another one, pink, and on this I read: "Fir Tree Haven Housing Project—Excavation Work." I opened this too, saw my estimate lying there on top of the pile; along the upper edge someone had written in red: "Lowest bid."

I could feel myself flushing with pleasure, my heart thumping, and I thought of the twenty thousand marks.

"Christ," I said softly, and closed the file, and this time Bertha forgot to rebuke me.

Prost," said Frau Zumpen with a smile. "Let's drink to it, then."

We drank, and I stood up and said, "It may seem rude of me, but perhaps you'll understand that I would like to go home now."

"I understand perfectly," said Frau Zumpen. "There's just one small item to be taken care of." She took the file, leafed through it, and said,

"Your price per square yard is thirty pfennigs below that of the next-lowest bidder. I suggest you raise your price by fifteen pfennigs: that way you'll still be the lowest and you'll have made an extra four thousand five hundred marks. Come on, do it now!" Bertha took her pen out of her purse and offered it to me, but I was in too much of a turmoil to write; I gave the file to Bertha and watched her alter the price with a steady hand, rewrite the total, and hand the file back to Frau Zumpen.

"And now," said Frau Zumpen, "just one more little thing. Get out your checkbook and write a check for three thousand marks; it must be a cash check and endorsed by you."

She had said this to me, but it was Bertha who pulled our checkbook out of her purse and made out the check.

"It won't be covered," I said in a low voice.

"When the contract is awarded, there will be an advance, and then it will be covered," said Frau Zumpen.

Perhaps I failed to grasp what was happening at the time. As we went down in the elevator, Bertha said she was happy, but I said nothing.

Bertha chose a different way home. We drove through quiet residential districts, I saw lights in open windows, people sitting on balconies drinking wine; it was a clear, warm night.

"I suppose the check was for Zumpen?" was all I said, softly, and Bertha replied, just as softly, "Of course."

I looked at Bertha's small brown hands on the steering wheel, so confident and quiet—hands, I thought, that sign checks and squeeze mayonnaise tubes—and I looked higher, at her mouth, and still felt no desire to kiss it.

That evening I did not help Bertha put the car away in the garage, nor did I help her with the dishes. I poured myself a large cognac, went up to my study, and sat down at my desk, which was much too big for me. I was wondering about something. I got up, went into the bedroom, and looked at the baroque Madonna, but even there I couldn't put my finger on the thing I was wondering about.

The ringing of the phone interrupted my thoughts; I lifted the receiver and was not surprised to hear Zumpen's voice.

"Your wife," he said, "made a slight mistake. She raised the price by twenty-five pfennigs instead of fifteen."

I thought for a moment and then said, "That wasn't a mistake, she did it with my consent."

He was silent for a second or two, then said with a laugh, "So you had already discussed the various possibilities?"

"Yes," I said.

"All right, then, make out another check for a thousand."

"Five hundred," I said, and I thought: It's like a bad dream—that's what it's like.

"Eight hundred," he said, and I said with a laugh, "Six hundred," and I knew, although I had no experience to go on, that he would now say seven hundred and fifty, and when he did I said "Yes" and hung up.

It was not yet midnight when I went downstairs and over to the car to give Zumpen the check; he was alone and laughed as I reached in to hand him the folded check.

When I walked slowly back into the house, there was no sign of Bertha; she didn't appear when I went back into my study; she didn't appear when I went downstairs again for a glass of milk from the refrigerator, and I knew what she was thinking; she was thinking: He has to get over it, and I have to leave him alone; this is something he has to understand.

But I never did understand. It is beyond understanding.

A Case for Kop

W HEN LASNOV got back from the station, he brought a message that a case had arrived for Kop. Every day Lasnov met the train from Odessa and tried to make deals with the soldiers. During the first year he had paid for socks, saccharine, salt, matches, and lighter flints with butter and oil—and had enjoyed the generous margins that are always involved in bartering; later on the rates had become more established, and there was tough bargaining over this money that kept on decreasing in value as the fortunes of war declined. There was no more butter to trade, and no oil, and for a long time now none of those juicy hunks of bacon for which in the beginning you could get a French double-bed mattress. Trade had become acute, sour and exasperating, ever since the soldiers had begun to despise their own money. They laughed when Lasnov ran along beside the train with his bundles of notes, calling through the open windows in an agitated, singsong voice, "I pay top prices for everything. Top prices for everything."

Only occasionally did a novice turn up who let himself be talked out of a coat or an undervest, carried away by the sight of the bank notes. And the days were now few and far between when Lasnov had to negotiate so long over a more valuable article—a pistol, a watch, or a telescope—that he was obliged to bribe the stationmaster to keep the train waiting till Lasnov had finished his business. In the early days each minute had cost only a mark, but the greedy stationmaster, a heavy drinker, had long since raised the cost of one minute to six marks.

On this particular morning there had been no business at all. A gendarme paced up and down alongside the waiting train, compared his wristwatch with the stationmaster's pocketwatch, and shouted at the ragged boy who ran along by the train looking for cigarette ends. But the soldiers had stopped throwing away cigarette ends a long time ago: they would carefully scrape off the black ash and hoard their remnants of tobacco like jewels in their tobacco tins; they were no longer generous with bread either, and when the boy could not find any bits of tobacco and ran along by the train waving his arms and chanting most impressively in a howling singsong voice, "Bread, bread, bread, comrades!", all he got was a kick from the gendarme. When the train pulled out, he pressed himself against the wall, and a paper bag rolled to his feet. In it were a slice of bread and an apple. The boy grinned as Lasnov passed him on his way to the waiting room. The waiting room was empty and cold. Lasnov left the station and stood outside, hesitating. He felt as if the train had yet to arrive; it had all been over too quickly, correctly, punctually, but he could hear the rusty creak: the signal arm was slipping back into Stop.

Lasnov jumped when someone put a hand on his shoulder. The hand was too light for the stationmaster's; it was the boy's, and he was holding out the apple he had bitten into and mumbling, "It's so sour, the apple—but what'll you give me for this?" From his left pocket he pulled out a red toothbrush and held it out to Lasnov. Lasnov opened his mouth and involuntarily drew his forefinger across his strong teeth, which felt slightly furry; he shut his mouth, took the toothbrush from the boy, and studied it; its red handle was transparent, the bristles were white and firm.

"A nice Christmas present for your wife," said the boy. "She has such lovely white teeth."

"You monkey," Lasnov said softly, "what are you doing looking at my wife's teeth?"

"Or for your kids," said the boy. "You can look through it—like this." He took the toothbrush from Lasnov, held it up to his eyes, looked at Lasnov, the station, the trees, the dilapidated sugar factory, and gave the brush back to him. "You try," he said, "it looks nice." Lasnov took the brush and held it up to his eyes. On the inside of the handle the refractions were broken: the station looked like a long, long barn, the trees like broken-off brooms, the boy's face was distorted into a squat grimace, the apple he was holding up to his face looked like a red sponge. Lasnov handed the toothbrush back to the boy. "Yes," he said, "not bad at all."

"Ten," said the boy.

"Two."

"No," whimpered the boy, "no, it's so pretty." Lasnov turned away. "Give me five at least."

"All right," said Lasnov, "here's five." He took the toothbrush and gave the boy the money. The boy ran back into the waiting room, and Lasnov saw him carefully and systematically going through the ashes of the stove with a stick, looking for cigarette ends; a gray cloud of dust rose up, and the boy murmured something to himself in his singsong voice which Lasnov was unable to make out.

The stationmaster came up just when Lasnov had decided to roll a cigarette and was checking his tobacco supply in the palm of his hand, separating the dust from the shreds of tobacco. "Well, now," said the stationmaster, "that looks like enough for two." He took some, without asking permission, and the two men stood smoking at the station corner, looking out into the street where booths, stalls, and dirty tents were being set up. Everything was gray, brown, or dirt-colored; there wasn't a spot of color even on the children's carrousel.

"Someone," said the stationmaster, "once gave my kids some coloring books; on one page you could see the finished pictures, in color, and on the opposite page the outlines where you had to put in the colors. But I didn't have any paints, or any crayons either, and the kids filled it all in with pencil—I always have to think of that when I look at this market-place. I guess they ran out of colors, all they had was pencil—gray, dirty, dark . . ."

"Yes," said Lasnov, "there's no business at all; the only thing to eat is Rukhev's corn cakes, but you know how he makes those."

"Raw corncobs pressed together, I know," said the stationmaster, "then smeared with dark-colored oil to make you think they've been cooked in oil."

"Well," said Lasnov, "I'll see if I can't do something anyway."

"If you see Kop, tell him a case has arrived for him."

"A case? What's in it?"

"I don't know. It's from Odessa. I'll send the boy over to Kop with my handcart. Will you let him know?"

"Sure," said Lasnov.

As he strolled through the square, he kept looking over to the station to see if the boy was coming with the case. And he told everyone that a case had come for Kop from Odessa. The rumor spread quickly through the market, got ahead of Lasnov, and, as he slowly approached Kop's stall, came back to him on the other side of the street.

When he reached the children's carrousel, the owner was just harnessing the horse. The horse's face was thin and dark, ennobled by hunger: it reminded Lasnov of the nun of Novgorod whom he had once seen as a child. Her face had also been thin and dark, ennobled by abstinence; you could look at her in a dark-green tent at fairs, and it had cost nothing to go in; people were merely asked, when they left the tent, to make a donation.

The carrousel owner came up to Lasnov, leaned over, and whispered, "Have you heard about the case that's supposed to have come for Kop?"

"No," said Lasnov.

"They say it's got toys in it, cars you can wind up."

"No," said Lasnov, "I heard it was toothbrushes."

"No, no," said the carrousel owner, "toys."

Lasnov stroked the horse's nose affectionately, went wearily on, and thought bitterly of the deals he used to be able to make. He had bought and sold so much clothing that he could have outfitted a whole army, and now he had sunk so low that this kid had talked him into buying a toothbrush. He had sold butter and bacon and barrels of oil, and at Christmas time he had always had a stall with candy canes for the kids; the colors of the candy canes had been as piercing as the joys and sufferings of the poor—red like the love that was celebrated in doorways or beside the factory wall while the bittersweet smell of molasses came wafting over the wall; yellow like the flames in a drunk man's brain, or pale green like the pain you felt when you woke up in the morning and looked at the face of your sleeping wife, a child's face, whose sole protection from life was those frail pink lids, fragile little covers which she had to open as soon as the children began to cry. But this year there weren't even any candy canes, and they would spend Christmas sitting at home, sipping thin soup, and taking turns looking through the handle of the toothbrush.

Next to the carrousel a woman had put two old chairs side by side and opened a shop on them: she had two mattresses to sell with the words "Magasin du Louvre" still visible on them, a well-thumbed book entitled *Left and Right of the Railroad Tracks—From Gelsenkirchen to Essen,* an English magazine dating from 1938, and a little tin that had once contained a typewriter ribbon.

"Some lovely things," said the old woman when Lasnov stopped beside her.

"Very nice," he said, and was about to move on when the woman pounced on him, drew him by the sleeve, and whispered, "A case has come for Kop from Odessa. With things for Christmas."

"Has it?" he said. "What things?"

"Candy, all colored, and rubber animals that squeak. It's going to be such fun."

"Sure," said Lasnov, "it's going to be fun."

When he finally reached Kop's stall, Kop had just begun to unload his stuff and spread it out: pokers, saucepans, stoves, rusty nails which he always found himself and hammered straight. Nearly everyone had gathered around Kop's stall; they stood there speechless with excitement, looking along the street. As Lasnov went up to him, Kop was just unpacking a firescreen with a design of gold flowers and a Chinese woman.

"I've got a message for you," said Lasnov, "a case has arrived for you.

The boy who's always hanging around the station is going to bring it over."

Kop looked at him with a sigh and said quietly, "Now I'm getting it from you too."

"What d'you mean, me too?" said Lasnov. "I've come straight here from the station to give you the message."

Kop ducked nervously. He was well dressed and wore an immaculate gray fur cap; he always carried a stick, with which he made dents in the ground as he walked along, and as a sole reminder of his better days he kept a cigarette dangling nonchalantly from his lips, a cigarette that was rarely alight because he rarely had money for tobacco. Twenty-seven years ago, when Lasnov came back to the village as a deserter with the news of the revolution, Kop had been an ensign in command of the railway station, and when Lasnov had entered the station at the head of the Soldiers' Council to arrest him, Kop had been prepared to allow a movement of his lips, the angle of his cigarette, to cost him his life; in any case, they all looked at the corner of his mouth, and he realized they might shoot him, but he did not remove the cigarette from his lips when Lasnov approached him. However, Lasnov had merely slapped his face. The cigarette had fallen out of his mouth, and without it he looked like a boy who has forgotten his homework. They had left him in peace; first he had been a teacher, then a dealer, but still whenever he saw Lasnov he was afraid Lasnov would knock the cigarette out of his mouth. He raised his head apprehensively, straightened the firescreen, and said, "If you only knew how many people have told me that already."

"A firescreen," said a woman, "if only one had enough heat to shield oneself from it with a firescreen." Kop looked at her contemptuously. "You have no sense of beauty."

"No," said the woman with a laugh, "I'm beautiful myself, and look at all the nice kids I've got." She ran her hand lightly over the heads of the four children grouped around her. "You don't . . ." She looked up quickly as her children suddenly ran off toward the station, following the other children, toward the boy who was bringing Kop's case on the stationmaster's handcart.

Everyone hurried away from their stalls, the children jumped down off the carrousel.

"My God," whispered Kop to Lasnov, the only one who had stayed behind, "I could almost wish the case hadn't come. They'll tear me to pieces."

"Don't you know what's in it?"

"No idea," said Kop, "I only know it must be made of tin."

"There's a lot of things can be made of tin—cans, toys, spoons."

"Music boxes—the kind you turn with a handle."

"Yes—just imagine."

Kop and Lasnov helped the boy lift the case down off the cart; the case was white, made of fresh, smooth boards, and it was nearly as high as the table on which Kop had spread out his rusty nails, pokers, and scissors.

Everyone fell silent as Kop thrust an old poker under the lid of the case and slowly raised it up; you could hear the faint creak of the nails. Lasnov wondered where all the people had suddenly sprung from: he was startled when the boy suddenly said, "I know what's inside."

No one asked, they all looked at him in suspense, and the boy looked silently at the tense faces. He broke out in a sweat and said in a low voice, "Nothing—there's nothing inside."

If he had said that one second earlier, they would have fallen on him and beaten him up in their disappointment, but now Kop had just taken the lid off and was groping around in the shavings; he removed a whole layer of shavings, then another, then screwed-up paper—then he held up both hands filled with the things he had found in the center of the case. "Tweezers," a woman cried out, but they weren't.

"No," said the woman who had called herself beautiful, "no, they're . . ."

"What are they?" said a little boy.

"Sugar tongs, that's what they are," said the carrousel owner in a dry voice; then he suddenly let out a wild laugh, threw up his arms, and ran back to his carrousel, still roaring with laughter.

"So they are," said Kop, "they're sugar tongs—dozens of them." He threw the tongs he was holding back into the case and groped around in it, but although they could not see his face, they all knew he was not smiling. He ran his hands through the clinking metal tongs the way misers in paintings finger their treasures.

"Isn't that just like them?" said one woman. "Sugar tongs . . . I really believe if there was such a thing as sugar I could manage to pick it up in my fingers, eh?"

"I had a grandmother," said Lasnov, "who always picked sugar up in her fingers—but then she was a dirty peasant woman."

"I think I could bring myself to do that too."

"You always were a pig anyhow, picking sugar up in your fingers. Ugh."

"You could use them," said Lasnov, "to fish tomatoes out of jars."

"Provided you had any tomatoes," said the woman who had called herself beautiful. Lasnov looked at her closely. She really was beautiful; she had plentiful fair hair, a straight nose, and fine dark eyes.

"You could also use them," said Lasnov, "for pickles."

"If you had any," said the woman.

"You could use them to pinch yourself in the behind."

"If you still had one," said the woman coldly. Her expression was becoming more and more angry and beautiful.

"You could pick up coal with them too."

"If you had any."

"You could use them as a cigarette holder."

"If you had anything to smoke."

Whenever Lasnov spoke, they all turned toward him, and as soon as he had finished they all turned toward the woman, and the more ridiculous the sugar tongs became in this dialogue, the more empty and miserable became the faces of the children and their parents. I must make them laugh, thought Lasnov. I was afraid there would be toothbrushes in the case, but sugar tongs are really even worse. He blushed under the woman's triumphant gaze and said loudly, "You could use them to serve boiled fish."

"If you had any," said the woman.

"The children could play with them," said Lasnov in a low voice.

"If you . . . ," began the woman, then she suddenly laughed out loud, and everyone else laughed too, for children were something they all had plenty of.

"All right," said Lasnov to Kop. "I'll take three. How much are they?"

"Twelve," said Kop.

"Twelve," said Lasnov and threw the money down on Kop's table. "It's a real bargain."

"It's really not expensive," said Kop shyly.

Ten minutes later all the children were running about the square with their sugar tongs glittering like silver; they sat on the carrousel, pinched their noses with them, brandished them in front of the grown-ups.

The boy who had brought the case over had been given one too. He sat on the steps in front of the station and hammered his sugar tongs flat. Now at last, he thought, I've got something I can use to get in between the cracks of the floorboards. Of course he had never thought of this. He had tried with pokers, scissors, and bits of wire, but he had never been able to manage it. He was sure he would be able to now he had this tool.

Kop counted his money, stacked it, and placed it carefully in his wallet. He looked at Lasnov, who was standing beside him, gloomily watching the activity in the square.

"You could do me a favor," said Kop.

"What favor?" said Lasnov absent-mindedly, without looking at Kop.

"Slap my face," said Kop, "hard enough for the cigarette to fall out." Lasnov, still without looking at Kop, shook his head thoughtfully.

"Do that," said Kop, "please do. Don't you remember?"

"I remember," said Lasnov, "but I don't feel like doing it again."

"Are you sure?"

"Yes," said Lasnov, "I'm sure. I've never thought of doing it again."

"Damn it," said Kop, "and here I've been dreading it for twenty-seven years."

"You didn't have to," said Lasnov. He walked back to the station shaking his head. There's still a chance, he thought, that they'll run a special, a leave train or one for the wounded; specials didn't come very often, but just the same there might still be one today. He thoughtfully fingered the toothbrush and the three sugar tongs in his coat pocket. There have been times, he thought, when three special trains have arrived in one day.

He leaned against the lamppost in front of the station and scraped the last of his tobacco into a little heap. . . .

Undine's Mighty Father

I AM PREPARED to believe almost anything of the Rhine, but I have never been able to believe in its carefree summer mood; I have looked for this carefree mood but never found it. Perhaps it is a flaw in my vision or in my character that prevents me from discovering this aspect.

My Rhine is dark and brooding, it is too much a river of merchant cunning for me to be able to believe in its youthful summertime face.

I have traveled on its white ships, have walked over its bordering hills, cycled from Mainz to Cologne, from Rüdesheim to Deutz, from Cologne to Xanten, in fall, spring, and summer; in winter I have stayed at small riverside hotels, and my Rhine was never a summer Rhine.

My Rhine is the one I remember from earliest childhood: a dark, brooding river that I have always feared and loved. I was born three minutes' walk away from it. Before I could talk, when I could barely walk, I was already playing on its banks: we would wade knee-deep in the fallen leaves along the avenue, looking for the paper pinwheels we had entrusted to the east wind, the wind that, too fast for our childish legs, drove the pinwheels westward toward the old moats.

It was fall, the weather was stormy, heavy clouds and the acrid smoke from ships' funnels hung in the air; in the evenings the wind would subside, fog would lie over the Rhine valley, foghorns toot somberly, red and green signal lights at the mastheads float past as if on phantom ships, and we would lean over the bridge railings listening to the strained, high-pitched signal horns of the raftsmen as they traveled downriver.

Winter came: ice floes as big as football fields, white, covered with a thick layer of snow; on such clear days the Rhine was very quiet, the only passengers were the crows being carried by the ice floes toward Holland, calmly riding along on their huge, fantastically elegant taxis.

For many weeks the Rhine remained quiet: only a few narrow, gray channels between the big white floes. Seagulls sailed through the arches of the bridges, ice floes splintered against the piers, and in February or March we waited breathlessly for the great drifts coming down from the Upper

Rhine. Ice masses evoking the Arctic came from upriver, and it was impossible to believe that this was a river on whose banks wine grew, good wine. Layer upon layer of cracking, splintering ice drifted past villages and towns, uprooting trees, crushing houses, less compacted, already less menacing, by the time it reached Cologne.

There is no doubt at all about there being two Rhines: the Upper, the wine drinker's Rhine, and the Lower, the schnapps drinker's Rhine— less well known and on whose behalf I would put in my plea: a Rhine that to this day has never really come to terms with its east bank. Where in bygone times smoke used to rise from the sacrificial fires of Teutonic tribes, now smoke rises from chimney stacks—from Cologne downriver to well north of Duisburg: red, yellow, and green flames, the ghostly silhouette of great industries, while the western, left bank, is more reminis- cent of a pastoral riverbank: cows, willows, reeds, and the traces of the Romans' winter encampments. Here they stood, those Roman soldiers, staring at the unreconciled east bank; sacrificing to Venus, to Dionysus, celebrating the birth of Agrippina: a Rhenish girl was the daughter of Germanicus, the granddaughter of Caligula, the mother of Nero, the wife and murderess of Claudius, later murdered by her son, Nero. Rhenish blood in the veins of Nero! She was born in an area of barracks—even in those days, horsemen's barracks, sailors' barracks, legionaries' barracks —and, at the western end of Cologne, the villas of merchants, administra- tors, officers; bathhouses, swimming baths. Modern times have still not quite caught up with that luxury lying buried beneath the rubble of the centuries, thirty feet below our children's playgrounds.

This river, the old, green Rhine, has seen too many armies—Ro- mans, Teutons, Huns, Cossacks, robber barons, victors and vanquished, and, representing history's most recent heralds, those who came from farthest away: the boys from Wisconsin, Cleveland, or Manila, who car- ried on the trade started by the Roman mercenaries in the year 0. This broad, green-gray, flowing Rhine has seen too much trade, too much history, for me to be able to believe in its youthful summer face. It is easier to believe in its brooding nature, its darkness; the grim ruins of the robber-baron castles on its hills are not the relics of a very joyful inter- regnum. Here Roman frippery was bartered in the year 0 for Teutonic feminine favors, and in the year 1947 Zeiss binoculars were bartered for coffee and cigarettes, those little white incense offerings to the transitory nature of life. Not even the Nibelungs, who lived where the wine grows, were a very joyful race; blood was their coin, one side of which was loyalty, the other treachery.

The wine drinker's Rhine ends roughly at Bonn, then passes through a sort of quarantine that reaches as far as Cologne, where the schnapps drinker's Rhine begins. To many this may mean that the Rhine stops here. My Rhine starts here, switches to tranquillity and brooding without forgetting what it had learned and witnessed farther up. It becomes more and more serious toward its mouth until it dies in the North Sea, its waters mingling with those of the open sea. The Rhine of the lovely Middle Rhine madonnas flows toward Rembrandt and is swallowed up by the mists of the North Sea.

My Rhine is the winter Rhine, the Rhine of the crows traveling northwest on their ice floes toward the Lowlands, a Breughel Rhine whose colors are green-gray, black, and white, much gray, and the brown façades of the buildings that wait for the approach of summer before sprucing up again; the quiet Rhine that is still sufficiently elemental to ward off the bustling of the worshipers of Mercury for at least a few weeks, maintaining its own sovereignty, abandoning its old bed to birds, fish, and ice floes. And I am still scared of the Rhine that in spring can become vicious, when household goods come drifting down the river, drowned cattle, uprooted trees, when posters saying "Warning!" in red are fixed to the trees along its banks, when the muddy tides rise, when the chains mooring the huge, floating boathouses threaten to snap—scared of the Rhine that murmurs so eerily and so gently through the dreams of children, a dark god bent on showing that it still demands sacrifices. Heathen, pristine Nature, in no way beautiful, it widens out like a sea, thrusts itself into dwellings, rises greenly in cellars, surges out of canals, roars its way along under bridges: Undine's mighty father.

In the Valley of the
Thundering Hoofs

I

THE BOY had not noticed that it was his turn. He was staring at the tiles on the floor dividing the side nave from the center nave: they were red and white, shaped like honeycomb cells, the red ones were speckled with white, the white with red; he could no longer distinguish the white from the red, the tiles ran together, and the dark lines of the cement joins became blurred, the floor swam before his eyes like a gravel path of red and white chips; the red dazzled, the white dazzled, the joins lay indistinctly over them like a soiled net.

"It's your turn," whispered a young woman next to him; he shook his head, made a vague gesture with his thumb toward the confessional, and the woman went ahead of him; for a moment the smell of lavender became stronger; then he heard murmuring, the scuffing sound of her shoes on the wooden step as she knelt down.

Sins, he thought, death, sins; and the intensity with which he suddenly desired the woman was torture. He had not even seen her face; a faint smell of lavender, a young voice, the sound of her high heels, light yet crisp, as she walked the four steps to the confessional; this rhythm of the heels, crisp yet light, was but a fragment of the eternal refrain that seethed in his ears for days and nights on end. In the evening he would lie awake, beside the open window, and hear them walking along outside on the cobblestones, on the asphalt sidewalk: shoes, heels, crisp, light, unsuspecting; he could hear voices, whispering, laughter under the chestnut trees. There were too many of them, and they were too beautiful. Some of them opened their handbags; in the streetcar, at the movie box office, on the store counter, they would leave their handbags lying open in cars, and he could see inside: lipsticks, handkerchiefs, loose change, crumpled bus tickets, packs of cigarettes, compacts. His eyes were still moving in torment back and forth over the tiles: this was a thorny path, and never-ending.

"It's your turn, you know," said a voice beside him, and he looked up. A little girl, red-cheeked and with black hair. He smiled at the child and waved her on too with his thumb. Her flat child's shoes had no rhythm. Whispering over there to the right. What had he confessed, when he was her age? I stole some cookies. I told lies. Disobedient. Didn't do my homework. I stole from the sugar jar, cake crumbs, wineglasses with the dregs from grown-ups' parties. Cigarette butts. I stole some cookies.

"It's your turn." This time he waved mechanically. Men's shoes. Whispering and the obtrusiveness of that faint no-smell smell.

Once again his glance fell on the red and white chips of the aisle. His naked eyes hurt as acutely as his naked feet would have hurt on a rough gravel path. The feet of my eyes, he thought, wander round their mouths as if round red lakes. The hands of my eyes wander over their skin.

Sins, death, and the insolent unobtrusiveness of that no-smell smell. If only there were someone who smelled of onions, of stew, laundry soap, or engines, of pipe tobacco, lime blossom, or road dust, of the fierce sweat of summer toil, but they all smelled unobtrusive; they smelled of nothing.

He raised his eyes and looked across the aisle, letting his glance rest where those who had received absolution were kneeling and saying their prayers of penance. Over there it smelled of Saturday, of peace, bathwater, poppyseed rolls, of new tennis balls, like the ones his sisters bought on Saturdays with their pocket money; it smelled of the clear, pure oil Father cleaned his pistol with on Saturdays. It was black, his pistol, shining, unused for ten years, an immaculate souvenir of the war, discreet, useless; it merely served Father's memory, summoned a glow to his face when he took it apart and cleaned it; the glow of an erstwhile mastery over death, which a light touch on a spring could move out of the pale, gleaming magazine into the barrel. Once a week on Saturday, before he went to the club, this ritual of taking apart, caressing, oiling the black sections, which lay spread out on the blue cloth like those of a dissected animal: the rump, the great metal tongue of the trigger, the smaller innards, joints, and screws. He was permitted to look on, he would stand there spellbound, speechless before his father's enraptured face; he was witnessing the celebration of the cult of an instrument that so frankly and terrifyingly resembled his sex; the seed of death was thrust out of the magazine. Father checked that too, to see whether the magazine springs were still working. They were still working, and the safety catch held back the seed of death in the barrel; with the thumb, with a tiny delicate movement, it could be released, but

Father never released it; delicately his fingers fitted the separate parts together again before hiding the pistol under some old checkbooks and ledger sheets.

"It's your turn." He gestured again. Whispers. Whispered replies. The obtrusive smell of nothing.

Here on this side of the aisle it smelled of damnation, sins, the sticky banality of the other days of the week, the worst of which was Sunday: boredom, while the coffee percolator hummed on the terrace. Boredom in church, in the outdoor restaurant, in the boathouse, movie, or café, boredom up at the vineyards where the progress of the Zischbrunner Mönchsgarten vines was inspected, slender fingers smoothly and expertly feeling the grapes; boredom which seemed to offer no escape except sin. It was visible everywhere: green, red, brown leather of handbags. Over there in the center nave he saw the rust-colored coat of the woman he had allowed to go ahead of him. He saw her profile, the delicate nose, the light-brown skin, the dark mouth, saw her wedding ring, the high heels, those fragile instruments which harbored the deadly refrain; he listened to them going away, a long, long walk on hard asphalt, then on rough cobblestones, the crisp yet firm staccato of sin. Death, he thought, mortal sin.

Now she was actually leaving: she snapped her handbag shut, stood up, genuflected, crossed herself, and her legs passed on the rhythm to her shoes, her shoes to her heels, her heels to the tiles.

The aisle seemed to him like a river which he would never cross: he would stand forever on the banks of sin. Only four steps separated him from the voice which could release and bind, only six to the center nave, where Saturday reigned, peace, absolution—but he took only two steps as far as the aisle, slowly at first, then he ran as if fleeing from a burning house.

As he pushed open the padded door, light and heat hit him too suddenly; for a few seconds he was dazzled, his left hand struck the doorpost, the prayer book fell to the floor, he felt a jab of pain on the back of his hand, bent down, picked up the book, let the door swing back, and stopped for a moment in the porch to smooth out the crumpled page of the prayer book. "Utter repentance," he read, before shutting the book; he put it into his trouser pocket, rubbed his smarting left hand with his right, and cautiously opened the door by pushing against it with his knee. The woman was no longer in sight, the forecourt was empty, dust lay on the dark-green leaves of the chestnuts; near the lamppost stood a white ice-cream cart, from the lamppost hook hung a gray sack containing evening papers. The ice-cream man was sitting on the curb reading the evening paper, the newspaper vendor was perched on one of the shafts of the ice-cream cart licking an ice-cream cone. A passing streetcar was almost empty: there was only a boy standing on the back platform, letting his green swimming trunks flap in the air.

Slowly Paul pushed open the door, went down the steps; within a few seconds he was sweating, it was too hot and too dazzling, and he longed for darkness.

There were some days when he hated everything except himself, but today was like most days, when he hated only himself and loved everything: the open windows in the houses around the square; white curtains, the clink of coffee cups, men's laughter, blue cigar smoke puffed out by someone he could not see; thick blue clouds came out of the window over the savings bank; whiter than fresh snow was the cream on a piece of cake which a girl standing at the window next door to the pharmacy was holding; white, too, was the ring of cream around her mouth.

The clock over the savings bank showed half past five.

Paul hesitated a moment when he reached the ice-cream cart, a moment too long, so that the ice-cream man got up from the curb, folded the evening paper, and Paul could read the first line on the front page: "Khrushchev," and in the second line, "open grave"; as he walked on, the man unfolded the paper and with a shake of his head sat down again on the curb.

When Paul had passed the corner by the savings bank and turned the next corner, he could hear a voice down on the riverbank announcing the next regatta race: men's four—Ubia, Rhenus, Zischbrunn 67. It seemed to Paul that he could smell and hear the river, which was a quarter of a mile away: oil and algae, the bitter smoke of the tugs, the slapping of the waves as the paddle steamers moved downstream, the hooting of long-drawn-out sirens in the evening; lanterns in outdoor cafés, chairs so red they seemed to burn like flames in the shrubberies.

He heard the starting gun, shouts, voices chanting, at first clearly in time with the beat of the oars: "Zischbrunn, Rhe-nuss, U-bja," and then all mixed up: "Rhebrunn, Zisch-nuss, Bja-Zisch-U-nuss."

Quarter past seven, thought Paul, till quarter past seven the town will stay as deserted as it is now. There were parked cars all the way to here, empty, hot, smelling of oil and sun, parked under trees, on both sides of the street, in driveways. As he turned the next corner and had a view of the river and the hills, he saw the parked cars up on the slopes, in the schoolyard, they were even parked in the entrances to the vineyards. In the silent streets through which he was walking they were parked on both sides, they heightened the impression of loneliness. He felt a pang at the glittering beauty of the cars, shining elegance from which the owners seemed to protect themselves with hideous mascots: grotesque monkey faces, grinning hedgehogs, distorted zebras with bared teeth, dwarfs leering malevolently above tawny beards.

The chanting became clearer, the shouts louder, then the announcer's voice proclaimed the victory of the Zischbrunn four. Applause, fanfare, then the song: "Zischbrunn, high on the slopes, caressed by the river, nourished by wine, pampered by lovely women . . ." Trumpets puffed out the tedious tune like soap bubbles into the air.

As he passed through a gateway it was suddenly quiet. In this courtyard behind the Griffduhnes' house the sounds from the river were muted: filtered through the trees, caught by old sheds, swallowed up by walls, the announcer's voice was subdued: "Ladies' pairs." The starting gun sounded like the pop from a toy pistol, the chanting like school choir practice behind walls.

Now his sisters were thrusting their oars into the water, their broad faces serious, beads of sweat forming on their upper lips, their yellow headbands turning dark; now their mother was adjusting the binoculars, elbowing away Father's hands, which were trying to snatch the binoculars. "Zisch-Zisch-Brunn-Brunn" roared one chorus that drowned out the others, now and again a feeble syllable: "U-nuss, Rhe-bja," then a roaring that here in the courtyard sounded as if it came from a muffled radio. The Zischbrunn pair had won: now the sisters' faces relaxed, they tore off the sweat-darkened headbands, paddled calmly toward the judges' boat, waved to their parents. "Zisch-Zisch," shouted their friends. "Hurrah for Zisch!"

Over their tennis balls, thought Paul, red blood over the white fleecy balls.

"Griff," he called softly, "are you up there?"

"Yes," replied a languid voice, "come on up!"

The wooden staircase was saturated with summer heat; it smelled of tar, of ropes that had not been sold for the past twenty years. Griff's grandfather had owned all these sheds, buildings, and walls. Griff's father owned scarcely a tenth of them, and "As for me," Griff always said, "all I'll ever own will be the pigeon loft where Dad used to keep pigeons. You can stretch out comfortably in it, and I shall stay up there and contemplate my big right toe—but even the pigeon loft will only be mine because nobody wants it any more."

The walls upstairs were covered with old photographs. They were dark red, mahogany almost, the white had gone cloudy and yellow: picnics of the nineties, regattas of the twenties, lieutenants of the forties; young girls who had died thirty years ago as grandmothers looked soulfully across the passage at their life partners: wine merchants, rope chandlers, shipyard owners, whose Victorian melancholy had been captured and preserved by

Daguerre's early disciples; a student of the year 1910 solemnly contemplated his son, an ensign who had frozen to death near Lake Peipus in Russia. Old furniture cluttered up the passage, and there was a stylish bookcase containing fruit jars, empty ones with limp red rubber rings rolled up on the bottom, full ones whose contents were only visible here and there through the dust; dark plum jam, or cherries of anemic red, pallid as the lips of sickly young girls.

Griffduhne was lying on the bed, naked from the waist up. His white, narrow chest contrasted alarmingly with his red cheeks: he looked like a poppy whose stalk has already withered. An unbleached linen sheet hung in front of the window, there were spots on it as if it were being X-rayed by the sun; the sunlight, filtered down to a yellow dusk, penetrated the room. Schoolbooks lay on the floor, a pair of slacks hung over the bedside table, Griff's shirt over the wash basin; a green corduroy jacket hung on a nail on the wall between the crucifix and photos of Italy: donkeys, steep cliffs, cardinals. An open jar of plum jam with a kitchen spoon sticking in it stood on the floor beside the bed.

"So they're rowing again; rowing, paddling, water sports—those are their problems. Dancing, tennis, wine harvest festivals, graduation parties. Songs. Is the town hall going to have gold, silver, or copper columns? Don't tell me, Paul," he said, lowering his voice, "that you were actually down there?"

"I was."

"Well?"

"Nothing. I left again. I couldn't stand it. It's so pointless. How about you?"

"I haven't been for ages. What's the use? I've been thinking about what's the right height for our age: I'm too tall for fourteen, so they say, you're too short for fourteen. D'you know anyone who is just the right height?"

"Plokamm is the right height."

"Huh—d'you want to be like him?"

"No."

"You see," said Griff, "there are . . ." He hesitated, broke off, as he watched Paul's eyes looking intently and uneasily around the room. "What's up? Are you looking for something?"

"Yes," said Paul, "where have you put it?"

"The pistol?"

"Yes, let me have it." Over the box with the new tennis balls is where I'll do it, he thought. "Come on," he said loudly, "hand it over."

"Wait," said Griff, shaking his head. Embarrassed, he took the spoon out of the plum jam, then stuck it back in the jar, folded his hands. "No, let's smoke instead. There's lots of time before quarter past seven. Rowing, paddling, maybe it'll be even later. Outdoor reception. Lanterns. Prize-giving ceremony. Your sisters won the pairs. Zisch, zisch zisch . . ." he went under his breath.

"Show me the pistol."

"Hell, why should I?" Griff sat up, seized the jar, and threw it against the wall: broken glass flew, the spoon struck the edge of the bookshelf, from there it did a somersault in front of the bed. The jam splashed onto a book that said *Algebra I,* some of it ran in a viscous blue across the yellow of the wall, dying it a kind of green. Without moving, without saying a word, the boys looked at the wall. When the noise of the crash had died away, and the last of the pulp had trickled down, they looked at each other in amazement: the shattering of the glass had left them unmoved.

"No," said Paul, "that's no good. The pistol's better, or maybe fire, a blaze or water—the pistol's best. Kill."

"But who?" asked the boy on the bed; he leaned over, picked up the spoon, licked it, and placed it tenderly on the bedside table. "But who?"

"Me," said Paul hoarsely, "tennis balls."

"Tennis balls?"

"Oh, nothing. Give it to me. Now."

"Right," said Griff. He stripped off the sheet, jumped out of bed, kicked the broken glass aside, and took a narrow brown cardboard box from the bookshelf. The box was not much bigger than a pack of cigarettes.

"What?" said Paul. "Is that it? In there?"

"Yes," said Griff, "that's it."

"And that's what you fired eight shots at a tin can with, at a distance of thirty yards, and got seven hits?"

"That's right, seven," said Griff uncertainly. "Don't you want to look at it even?"

"No, I don't," said Paul; he looked angrily at the box, which smelled of sawdust, of the stuff blanks were packed in. "No, I don't, I don't want to look at it. Show me the ammunition."

Griff bent down. From his long, pale back the vertebrae stood out, disappeared again, and this time he quickly opened the box, which was as big as a matchbox. Paul took one of the copper cartridges, held it between two fingertips, as if to see how long it was, turned it this way and that, shook his head as he contemplated the round, blue head of the bullet. "No," he said, "that's no good. My dad has one—I'll get my dad's."

"But it's locked up," said Griff.

"I'll get hold of it. As long as I do it before half past seven. He always cleans it then, before he goes to the club. He takes it apart: it's a big one, black and smooth, heavy, and the bullets are big like this"—he showed how big with his fingers—"and . . ." He was silent, and sighed: over the tennis balls, he was thinking.

"Do you really want to shoot yourself, properly?"

"Maybe," said Paul. The feet of my eyes are sore, the hands of my eyes are sick, he thought. "Hell, you know how it is."

Griff's face suddenly turned dark and stiff; he swallowed, went to the door, only a few steps away; there he stopped.

"You're my friend," he said, "or aren't you?"

"Sure."

"Then go and get a jar too and throw it against the wall. Will you?"

"Why?"

"My mother," said Griff, "my mother told me she wants to have a look at my room when she gets back from the regatta, she wants to see whether I've improved. Tidied up and all that. She got mad at my report. Let her look at my room, then—are you going to get the jar now?"

Paul nodded, went out into the passage, and heard Griff call out, "Take the golden plum jam, if there's any left. Something yellow would look good, better than this purplish mess." Paul wiped off some of the jars outside in the semidarkness till he found a yellow one. They won't understand, he thought, nobody will understand, but I have to do it. He went back to the room, raised his right hand, and threw the jar against the wall.

"It's no good," he said quietly, while they both regarded the effect of the throw, "it's not what I want."

"What is it you want?"

"I want to destroy something," said Paul, "but not jars, or trees, or houses—and I don't want your mother to get mad, or mine; I love my mother, yours too—there's no sense to it."

Griff fell back onto the bed, covered his face with his hands, and murmured, "Kuffang has gone to that girl."

"The Prohlig girl?"

"Yes."

"I've been with her too."

"You have?"

"Yes. She's not serious. Giggles around there in the passage—stupid, she's stupid. She doesn't know it's a sin."

"Kuffang says it's great."

"No, I tell you, it's not great. Kuffang's stupid too, you know he's stupid."

"I know he is, but what are you going to do?"

"Nothing with girls—they giggle. I've tried it. They're not serious —they just giggle." He went across to the wall and smeared his forefinger through the big splash of golden plum jam.

"No," he said without turning round, "I'm going to get my dad's pistol."

Over the tennis balls, he thought. They're as white as washed lambs. The blood over the lambs.

"Women," he whispered, "not girls."

The filtered noise of the regatta came faintly into the room. Men's eights. Zischbrunn. This time Rhenus won. The jam dried slowly on the wooden wall, became as hard as cow dung, flies buzzed around the room, there was a sweetish smell, flies crawled over the schoolbooks, the clothes, flew greedily from one spot, from one pool, to another, too greedy to stay long on one pool. The two boys did not move. Griff lay on the bed, staring at the ceiling and smoking. Paul perched on the edge of the bed, bent forward like an old man; deep within him, over him, on him, lay a burden to which he couldn't put a name, a dark, heavy burden. Suddenly he stood up, ran out into the passage, snatched up one of the fruit jars, came back into the room, raised the jar—but he did not throw it; he stood there with the jar in his raised hand. Slowly his arm dropped, the boy put down the jar, on a paper bag which was lying neatly folded on the bookshelf. "Fürst Slacks," it said on the paper bag, "Fürst Slacks Are the Only Slacks."

"No," he said, "I'll go and get it."

Griff puffed his cigarette smoke at the flies, then aimed the butt at one of the pools. Flies flew up, settled hesitantly around the smoking butt, which sank slowly into the jam and fizzled out.

"Tomorrow evening," he said, "I'll be in Lübeck, at my uncle's; we'll go fishing, we'll sail and swim in the Baltic; and you, tomorrow you'll be in the Valley of the Thundering Hoofs." Tomorrow, thought Paul, who did not move, tomorrow I shall be dead. Blood over the tennis balls, dark red like in the fleece of the lamb; the Lamb will drink my blood. O Lamb. I shall never see my sisters' little laurel wreath, "Winners of the Ladies' Pairs," black on gold; they'll hang it up there between the photos of holidays in Zalligkofen, between withered bunches of flowers and pictures of cats; next to the framed graduation diploma hanging over Rosa's bed, next to the certificate for long-distance swimming hanging over Franziska's bed; between the colored prints of their patron saints, Rosa of Lima, Franziska Romana; next to the other laurel wreath, "Winners of the Ladies' Doubles"; under the crucifix. The dark-red blood will cling stiffly to the fuzz of the tennis balls, the blood of their brother, who preferred death to sin.

"I must see it one day, the Valley of the Thundering Hoofs," Griff was saying, "I must sit up there where you always sit, I must hear them, the horses charging up to the pass, galloping down to the lake, I must hear their hoofs thundering in the narrow gorge—their whinnying cries streaming out over the mountaintops—like—like a thin fluid."

Paul looked disdainfully at Griff, who had sat up and was excitedly describing something he had never seen: horses, many horses, charging up over the pass, galloping with thundering hoofs down into the valley. But there had only been *one* horse there, and only *once*: a colt, which had raced out of the paddock and cantered down to the lake, and the sound of its hoofs had not been like thunder, just a clatter, and it was such a long time ago, three years, maybe four.

"So you," he said quietly, "are going fishing; you'll go sailing and swimming, and stroll up the little streams, in wading boots, and catch fish with your hands."

"That's right," said Griff sleepily, "my uncle catches fish with his hands, even salmon, yes . . ." He sank back onto the bed with a sigh. His uncle in Lübeck had never caught a fish, not even with a rod or a net, and he, Griff, doubted whether there were any salmon at all up there on the Baltic and in the little streams. Uncle was just the owner of a small cannery; in old sheds in the backyard the fish were slit open, cleaned, salted or pickled; preserved in oil or tomato sauce; they were pressed into cans by an ancient machine which threw itself with a grunt like a tired anvil onto the tiny cans and shut the fish up in tinplate. Lumps of damp salt lay around in the yard, fish bones and skin, scales and entrails; seagulls screamed, and light-red blood splashed onto the white arms of the women workers and ran down their arms in watery trickles.

"Salmon," said Griff, "are smooth, silvery and pink, they're strong, much too beautiful to eat; when you hold them in your hand, you can feel their strong muscles."

Paul shuddered: they had once had some canned salmon for Christmas, a putty-colored mass swimming in pink fluid, full of bits of fish bone.

"And you can catch them in the air when they jump," said Griff; he sat up, knelt on the bed, threw up his hands, fingers spread wide, brought them together till they looked as if they were about to strangle something; the rigid hands, the motionless face of the boy, it all seemed to belong to someone who worshiped a stern god. The soft yellow light bathed the rigid boyish hands, lent the flushed face a dark, brownish tinge—"Like that,"

Griff whispered, snatched with his hands at the fish that wasn't there, and suddenly dropped his hands, letting them hang limp, inert, by his sides. "Come on," he said, jumped off the bed, picked up the box with the pistol from the bookshelf, opened it before Paul could turn away, and held out the open bottom half of the box containing the pistol. "Look at it now," he said, "just have a look at it." The pistol looked rather pathetic: only the firmness of the material distinguished it from a toy pistol; it was even flatter, but the solidity of the nickel gave it some glamour and a degree of seriousness. Griffduhne threw the open box containing the pistol into Paul's lap, took the closed glass jar from the bookshelf, unscrewed the lid, separated the perished rubber ring from the edge, lifted the pistol out of the box, dropped it slowly into the jam; the boys watched while the level of the jam rose slightly, scarcely beyond the narrowing of the neck. Griff put the rubber ring back around the edge, screwed on the lid, and replaced the jar on the bookshelf.

"Come on," he said, and his face was stern and dark again. "Come on, we'll go and get your dad's pistol."

"You can't come with me," said Paul. "I have to climb in through a window because they didn't give me a key—I have to get in at the back. They would notice; they didn't give me a key because they thought I was going to the regatta."

"Rowing," said Griff, "water sports, that's all they ever think about." He was silent, and they both listened for sounds from the river: they could hear the cries of the ice-cream vendors, music, fanfares, a steamer hooting.

"Intermission," said Griff. "Plenty of time still. All right, go by yourself, but promise me you'll come back with the pistol. Will you promise?"

"I promise."

"Shake."

They shook hands: they were warm and dry, and each wished the other's hand had been firmer.

"How long will you be?"

"Twenty minutes," said Paul. "I've thought it out so many times but never done it—with the screwdriver. It'll take me twenty minutes."

"Right," said Griff; he reached across the bed and took his watch from the bedside table drawer. "It's ten to six; you'll be back at quarter past."

"Quarter past," said Paul. He paused in the doorway, looked at the great splashes on the wall: yellow and purplish. Swarms of flies were sticking to the splashes, but neither of the boys moved a finger to drive them away. Laughter drifted up from the riverbank: the water clowns had begun to add zest to the intermission. An "Ah" rose up like a great soft sigh; the boys looked up at the sheet over the window as if they expected it to billow out, but it hung limp, yellowish, the dirt spots were darker now, the sun had moved farther westward.

"Water skiing," said Griff, "the women from the face-cream factory." An "Oh" came up from the river, a sigh, and again the sheet did not billow out.

"The only one," said Griff quietly, "the only one who looks like a woman is the Mirzov girl." Paul did not move. "My mother," Griff said, "found the piece of paper with those things about the Mirzov girl on it —and her picture."

"Good God," said Paul, "d'you mean to say you had one too?"

"Yes," said Griff, "I spent all my pocket money on it—I—I don't know why I did it. I didn't even read what was on the paper, I stuck it in my report envelope, and my mother found it. D'you know what was on it?"

"No," said Paul, "I don't, I bet it's all lies, and I don't want to know about it. Everything Kuffang does is a lie. I'm off now—"

"Right," said Griff firmly, "hurry up and get the pistol, and come back. You promised. Go on, go."

"OK," said Paul, "I'm going." He waited a moment, listening to the sounds from the river: he could hear laughter, fanfare. "Funny I never thought of the Mirzov girl. . . ." And he said again, "OK," and went.

II

CUTOUTS MIGHT be like that, she thought, miniatures or colored medallions: the images were sharply punched, round and clear, a whole series of them. She was looking at it from a distance of twelve hundred yards, magnified twelve times through binoculars. The church with the savings bank and pharmacy, in the center of the gray square an ice-cream cart: the first picture, detached and unreal. A section of the riverbank, above it, in a semicircle of horizon, green water with boats on it, colored pennants: the second picture, the second miniature. The series could be added to at will: hills with woods and a monument; over there—what were their names?—Rhenania and Germania, torch-bearing, stalwart female figures with stern faces, on bronze pedestals, facing each other; vineyards, with green vines—hatred welled up in her, salty, bitter and satisfying. She hated wine; they were always talking about wine, and everything they did, sang, or believed was associated ritually with wine: puffy faces, mouths emitting sour breath, hoarse gaiety, belching, shrill women, the bloated stupidity of the men who thought they resembled this —what was he called?—Bacchus. She hung on to this picture for a long time: I'll certainly stick this little picture in my album of memories, a round picture of a green vineyard with vines. Perhaps, she thought, I might be able to believe in You, their God, if it were not wine which turns into Your blood for them, is wasted for them, poured out for those useless idiots. My memory will be a clear one, as acid as the grapes taste at this time of year when you pick one the size of a pea. All the pictures were small, distinct, and ready to be stuck in; vignettes of sky blue, grass green, river green, banner red, blending with the sounds which formed the background to the pictures, as in a movie, spoken words, dubbed-in music: chanting, hurrahs, shouts of victory, fanfare, laughter, and the little white boats, as tiny as the feathers of young birds, as light too, and as quickly blown away, the white feathers scudding airily across the green water. When they reached the rim of the binoculars the noise swelled slightly. That's how I shall remember it all: just a little album of miniatures. A tiny twist of the binoculars, and already everything was blurred, red with green, blue with gray; another twist of the screw, and all that was left was a round patch of mist in which noise sounded like cries for help from a group of lost mountain climbers, like the shouts of the search party.

She swung the binoculars up and down, trailed them slowly across the sky, punching out circles of blue; just as her mother did when she was baking, punching the uniform yellow dough with the cookie cutters, that was how she punched out the uniform blue sky: round sky-cookies, blue, a great quantity of them. But where I am going there will be blue sky too, so why stick these miniatures into the album? That'll do. Slowly she let the binoculars sweep downward. Careful, she thought, I'm falling, and she felt slightly giddy as she flew from the blue of the sky onto the trees in the avenue, covering more than a mile in less than a second; past the trees, over the gray tiles of the next house. She looked into a room: a powder compact, a Madonna, a mirror, a single black shoe, a man's, on the polished floor; she flew on to the living room: a samovar, a Madonna, a large family photo, the brass strip along the carpet and the russet, warm gleam of mahogany. She stopped, but her giddiness persisted in subsiding waves. Then she saw the open box with the snow-white tennis balls in the hall —how ugly those balls are, she thought, the way women's breasts sometimes look on statues I don't like; the terrace: a garden umbrella, a table with a cloth and dirty cups and saucers, an empty wine bottle still with its white foil cap. Oh, Father, she thought, how wonderful to be going to you, and how wonderful that you don't drink wine, only schnapps.

Melting tar was dripping from the garage roof in a few places. Then she jumped as Paul's face—eighty feet away, such a long way off, but in the binoculars only six feet—came directly toward her. His pale face looked as if he were on the verge of doing something desperate: he was blinking into the sun, his arms, fists clenched, were hanging down limply as if he were holding something, but he wasn't holding anything; his fists were empty, squeezed tight. He turned the corner of the garage, sweating, his breath labored, jumped up onto the terrace. The cups and saucers clinked on the table; he rattled at the door, took two steps to the left, swung himself up onto the window sill, and jumped into the room. The samovar gave off a silvery chime as Paul bumped into the buffet: inside, the rims of the glasses passed on the vibration to each other; they were still faintly twittering as the boy ran on, across the brass strip in the doorway. When he came to the tennis balls, he paused, bent down, but did not touch them; he stood there for a long time, stretched out his hands again, almost as if in benediction or tenderness, suddenly pulled a little book out of his pocket, threw it on the floor, picked it up, kissed it, and placed it on the shelf under the hall mirror. Then all she could see was his legs as he ran upstairs, and in the center of this miniature was the carton with the tennis balls.

She sighed, lowered the binoculars, letting her eyes linger on the pattern of the carpet; it was rust red, with a black pattern of innumerable squares all joined together in labyrinths; toward the middle of each labyrinth the red got thinner and thinner, the black wider and wider, almost dazzling in its purity.

His bedroom was in the front of the house, facing the street. She remembered it from the days when he had still been allowed to play with her—it must be a year or two ago now; she had been allowed to play with him till he had begun to stare at her breasts with such a strange persistence that it interfered with their game, and she had asked: What are you looking at, do you want to see it? And he had nodded as if in a dream; she had undone her blouse, and she did not realize it was wrong till it was already too late. She saw it was wrong, not from his eyes but from the eyes of his mother, who had been in the room all the time, who came over now and screamed, while the darkness in her eyes turned to stone. That scream, that's also something I have to preserve on one of the phonograph records of my memory; that's what the screams must have sounded like at the witch burnings the man used to describe, the one who came to have discussions with Mother; he looked like a monk who no longer believes in God. And her mother looked like a nun who no longer believed in her God: home again in this place called Zischbrunn, after years of bitter disillusionment, salty error, preserved in the faith she had had and lost in something called Communism, floating in the brine of the memory of the man who was called Mirzov, drank schnapps, and had never possessed the faith which she had lost; her mother's words were as salty as her heart.

Scream across the carpet pattern, broken game on the floor: models of houses his father had been the sales agent for twenty years ago, little houses such as had not been built for twenty years; old pneumatic mail tubes from the bank, samples of rope which the other boy—that's right, Griff was his name—had contributed; corks of various sizes, various shapes; Griff had not been there that afternoon. All broken by that scream, which was to hang over her in future like a curse: she was the girl who had done what one must never do.

As she sighed, her glance lingered on the rust-red carpet, watching the sparkling threshold for his brown shoes to reappear.

Languidly she swung the binoculars back to the table: under the garden umbrella on the terrace, a basket of fruit, dark brown wickerwork full of orange peel, the wine bottle with the label "Zischbrunner Mönchsgarten"; one still life after another, with an undercurrent of noise from the regatta; dirty plates with remains of ice cream; the folded evening paper on which she could make out the second word in the headline, "Khrushchev," and in the second line, "open grave"; some cigarettes with brown filter tips, others white, stubbed out in the ashtray, a brochure from a refrigerator firm—but they had had one for ages!—a box of matches; russet mahogany, like fire in old paintings; the samovar gleaming on the buffet, silver and bright, unused for years, shining like some strange trophy. Teawagon with salt cellar and mustard pot, the big family photograph: the children sitting at table with their parents at a restaurant out in the country, in the background the pond with swans, then the waitress bringing the tray with two mugs of beer and three bottles of lemonade; in the foreground, the family seated at the table: on the right, in profile, their father, holding a fork level with his chest, a piece of meat skewered on it, noodles festooned round the meat; on the left their mother, a crumpled serviette in her left hand, a spoon in her right; in the middle the children, their heads below the edge of the waitress's tray: ice-cream dishes reached to their chins, patches of light, filtered through the leaves, lay on their cheeks; in the middle, framed by the curly heads of his sisters, the one who had stood for such a long time by the tennis balls and had then run upstairs: his brown shoes had still not returned across the brass strip.

The tennis balls again, on their right the clothes closet, straw hats, an umbrella, a linen bag with the handle of a shoebrush sticking out of it;

in the mirror the large picture that hung in the hall on the left, of a woman picking grapes, with eyes like grapes, a mouth like a grape.

Tired of looking, she put down the binoculars. Her eyes plunged across the lost distance, smarted; she closed them. Red and black circles danced behind her closed lids, she opened them again, was startled to see Paul coming through the door. He was carrying something which sparkled in the sun, and this time he did not pause when he came to the tennis balls. Now that she saw his face without the binoculars—detached from her collection of miniatures—now she was certain he was going to do something desperate. Once more the samovar chimed, once more the glasses inside the buffet passed along the vibration, twittering like women exchanging secrets; Paul knelt down on the carpet in the corner by the window. All she could see of him was his right elbow, moving back and forth like a piston, regularly disappearing in a forward drilling movement —she ransacked her memory for a clue as to where she had seen this movement, she imitated the drilling pumping movement and then she knew: he was holding a screwdriver. The red-and-yellow-checked shirt came, went, was still—Paul jerked back a little; she saw his profile, raised the binoculars to her eyes, was startled at the sudden nearness, and looked into the open drawer. It contained bundles of blue checkbooks, neatly tied with white string, and some ledger sheets, bound through the holes with blue string. Paul hastily stacked up the bundles beside him on the carpet, clutched something to his chest, something wrapped in a blue cloth, put it down on the floor, replaced the checkbooks and ledger sheets in the drawer, and again all she could see, while the bundle in the blue cloth lay beside him, was the pumping, drilling movement of his elbow.

She cried out when he unwrapped the cloth: black, smooth, glistening with oil, the pistol lay in the hand that was much too small for it. It was as if the girl had shot her cry through the binoculars at him; he turned, she lowered the binoculars, screwed up her smarting eyes, and called out, "Paul! Paul!"

He held the pistol close to his chest as he climbed slowly out of the window onto the terrace.

"Paul," she called, "come over here, through the garden."

He put the pistol in his pocket, shaded his eyes with his hand, walked slowly down the steps, across the lawn, scuffed across the gravel by the fountain, dropped his hand when he suddenly found himself in the shadow of the summerhouse.

"Oh," he said, "it's you."

"Didn't you recognize my voice?"

"No—what d'you want?"

"I'm going away," she said.

"I'm going away too," he said. "So what? Everyone's going away, almost. I'm leaving tomorrow for Zalligkofen."

"No," she said, "I'm leaving for good, I'm going to my father's in Vienna . . ." and she thought: Vienna, that has something to do with wine too, in songs anyway.

"Vienna," he said, "down there . . . and you're staying there?"

"Yes."

The look in his eyes, raised almost vertically to her, motionless, trancelike, frightened her: I am not your Jerusalem, she thought, no, I'm not, and yet your eyes have the look the eyes of pilgrims must have when they see the towers of their Holy City.

"I——" she said softly, "I saw everything."

He smiled. "Come on down," he said, "come on."

"I can't," she said, "my mother's locked me in. I'm not allowed out till the train leaves, but . . ." She suddenly stopped, her breathing was labored, shallow, excitement was choking her, and she said what she had not meant to say, "But why don't you come up here?"

I am not your Jerusalem, she thought. No, no. He did not lower his eyes as he asked, "How can I get up there?"

"If you climb up onto the roof of the summerhouse, I'll give you a hand and help you up onto the veranda."

"I——there's someone waiting for me." But he was already testing the trellis to see if it would hold; it had been recently nailed and painted, dense dark vine leaves were growing up the trellis, which formed a kind of ladder. The pistol swung heavily against his thighs; as he pulled himself up by the weathervane, he remembered Griff, lying in his room back there, flies buzzing round him, with pale chest and red cheeks, and Paul thought of the little flat nickel pistol: I must ask Griff whether nickel oxidizes. If it does, he'll have to stop them eating out of the jar.

The girl's hands were larger and firmer than Griff's hands, larger and firmer than his own too: he felt this and was ashamed when she helped him climb from the ridge of the summerhouse roof onto the veranda balustrade.

He brushed the dirt off his hands and said, without looking at the girl, "It's funny that I'm really up here."

"I'm glad you're here. I've been locked in since three." He looked warily over to her, at her hand, which was holding her coat together over her chest.

"Why've you got your coat on?"

"You know why."

"Because of that?"

"Yes."

He took a step toward her. "I expect you're glad to be going away?"

"Yes, I am."

"There was a boy in school this morning," he said in a low voice, "selling pieces of paper with things about you written on them, and a picture of you."

"I know," she said, "and he said I get part of the money he gets for the pieces of paper, and that he has seen me the way he drew me. None of it's true."

"I know it isn't," he said. "He's called Kuffang; he's stupid and tells lies, everyone knows that."

"But they believe him when he tells them *that*."

"Yes," he said, "it's strange, they do believe that."

She pulled her coat tighter around her chest. "That's why I have to leave so suddenly, quickly, before they all get back from the regatta—for a long time now they've given me no peace. You make a show of your body, they say; they say it when I wear a dress with a low neck, and they say it when I wear a dress with a high neck—and a sweater. They go crazy then—but I have to wear something, don't I?"

He watched her without emotion as she went on talking. He was thinking: Funny that I never thought of her, not once. Her hair was blond, her eyes seemed blond too, they were the color of freshly planed beechwood—blond and slightly moist.

"I don't make a show of my body at all," she said, "I just have it."

He nodded, pushed the pistol up a bit with his right hand, as it was lying heavy against his thigh. "Yes," he said, and she was afraid: he had that dream face again. You would have thought he was blind, that other time, those empty, dark eyes had seemed to fall upon her and yet past her in an unpredictable refraction, and now again he looked as if he were blind.

"The man," she went on hurriedly, "who sometimes comes to have discussions with my mother, the old man with white hair, do you know him?" There was silence, the noise from the river was too far off to disturb this silence—"Do you know him?" she asked impatiently.

"Of course I know him," he said; "that's old Dulges."

"Yes, that's the one—he's looked at me like that sometimes and said: Three hundred years ago they would have burned you as a witch. A woman's hair crackling, and the cry from a thousand unfeeling souls unable to tolerate beauty."

"Why did you make me come up?" he asked. "To tell me that?"

"Yes," she said, "and because I saw what you were doing."

He pulled the pistol out of his pocket, held it up, and waited with a smile for her to scream, but she did not scream.

"What are you going to do with it?"

"I don't know, shoot at something."

"At what?"

"Maybe at me."

"Why?"

"Why?" he said. "Why? Sins, death. Mortal sin. Do you understand that?" Slowly, without touching her, he made his way past her, in through the open kitchen door, and leaned with a sigh against the cupboard; the picture was still there on the wall, the one he had not seen for so long, the one he thought about sometimes: factory chimneys, with red smoke rising up from them, smoke pouring out and joining together in the sky to form a blood-red cloud. The girl was standing in the doorway, turned toward him. There were shadows across her face, and she looked like a woman. "Come inside," he said, "they might see us; that would be bad for you, you know."

"In an hour," she said, "I shall be sitting in the train. Here—here's my ticket—it's not a return." She held up the buff ticket, he nodded, and she put the ticket back in her coat pocket. "I shall take off my coat and be wearing a sweater, a sweater, d'you understand?"

He nodded again. "An hour's a long time. Do you know what sin is? Death. Mortal sin?"

"Once," she said, "the pharmacist wanted to—and the teacher too, your history teacher."

"Drönsch?"

"Yes, him. I know what they want, but I don't know what their words mean. I know what sin is too, but I don't understand it any more than I understand what the boys sometimes call out after me when I come home alone, in the dark; they call out after me from doorways, from windows, from cars sometimes, they called out things after me which I knew the meaning of but which I didn't understand. Do you know?"

"Yes."

"What is it?" she said. "Does it bother you terribly?"

"Yes," he said, "terribly."

"Even now?"

"Yes," he said, "doesn't it bother you?"

"No," she said, "it doesn't bother me. It just makes me unhappy that it's there and that other people want something—that they call out after me. Please tell me, why are you thinking of shooting yourself? Because of that?"

"Yes," he said, "simply because of that. Do you know what it means when it says in the Bible: Whatsoever thou shalt bind on earth shall be bound in heaven?"

"Yes, I know what that means; sometimes I stayed behind in class when they had religion."

"Well, then," he said, "maybe you also know what sin is. Death."

"I do," she said. "Do you really believe all that?"

"Yes."

"Everything?"

"Everything."

"You know I don't believe it. But I do know that the worst sin of all is to shoot yourself—at least, that's what I heard," she said, raising her voice, "with my own ears," she pulled her ear with her left hand, with her right she was still clutching her coat, "with my own ears I heard the priest say: We must not throw away the gift of life and toss it at God's feet."

"Gift of life," he said bitterly, "and God has no feet."

"Hasn't He?" she said quietly. "Hasn't He any feet, didn't they pierce them?"

He was silent, then flushed and said in a low voice, "I know."

"Yes," she said, "if you really believe everything, the way you say you do, then you have to believe that too. Do you believe that?"

"What?"

"That we mustn't throw away the gift of life?"

"Oh, I don't know," he said, and held the pistol straight up in the air.

"Come on," she said softly, "put it away. It looks so silly. Please put it away."

He placed the pistol in his right pocket, put his hand into his left pocket, and took out the three cartridge clips. The metal clips lay without luster on the palm of his hand. "That should do," he said.

"Shoot at something else," she said, "for instance, at"—she turned round and looked back at his own home, through the open window—"at the tennis balls," she said.

A deep flush enveloped him like darkness, his hands went limp, the clips fell from his hand. "How did you know . . . ?" he whispered.

"Know what?"

He bent down, picked up the clips from the floor, pushed one cartridge, which had dropped out, carefully back into the clip; he looked through the window at the house standing in full view in the sunshine: the tennis balls were lying back there white and hard in their carton.

Here, in this kitchen, it smelled of bath water, soap, of peace and fresh bread, of cake; red apples were lying on the table, a newspaper, and half a cucumber, its cut surface pale, green, and watery; closer to the peel the cucumber flesh was darker and firmer.

"I also know," said the girl, "what they used to do to fight sin. I've heard about it."

"Who?"

"Those saints of yours. The priest told us about it: they whipped themselves, they fasted and prayed, not one killed himself." She turned toward the boy, afraid again: No, no, I'm not your Jerusalem.

"They weren't fourteen," said the boy, "or fifteen."

"Some of them must have been," she said.

"No," he said, "no, it's not true, most of them weren't converted till after they'd sinned." He came closer, pushing himself along the window sill toward her.

"That's a lie," she said, "some of them didn't sin first at all—I don't believe any of that—if anything, I believe in the Mother of God."

"If *anything*," he said scornfully, "but She was the Mother of *God.*"

He looked the girl full in the face, turned aside, and said in an undertone: "Forgive me . . . yes, yes, I have tried. Prayed."

"And fasted?"

"Oh, fasting," he said. "I don't care what I eat."

"That's not fasting. And whipping. I would do that, I would whip myself, if I believed."

"Doesn't it bother you really?" he whispered.

"No," she said, "it doesn't bother me, to *do* something, to see something, to say something—but it does bother you, doesn't it?"

"Yes, it does."

"What a pity," she said, "that you're so Catholic."

"Why a pity?"

"Otherwise I'd show you my breasts. I would like so much to show them to you—to you. Everyone talks about them, the boys call out things after me, but no one has ever seen them yet."

"No one?"

"No," she said, "no one."

"Show it to me," he said.

"It won't be the same as it was last time, you know when I mean."

"I know," he said.

"Was it terrible for you?"

"Only because Mother was so terrible. She was absolutely furious and told everyone about it. It wasn't so terrible for me. I would have forgotten all about it. Come here," he said.

Her hair felt smooth and hard; that surprised him, he had thought it would be soft, but it was the way he imagined spun glass.

"Not here," she said. She pushed him along in front of her, slowly, for he did not let go of her head, he kept his eyes on her face while they moved, as if in some strange dance step invented by themselves, away from the open veranda door across the kitchen; he seemed to be standing on her feet, she seemed to be lifting him with every step.

She opened the kitchen door, pushed him slowly across the hall, opened the door to her room.

"Here," she said, "in my room, not out there."

"Mirzova," he whispered.

"Why do you call me that? My name is Mirzov, and Katharina."

"Everyone calls you that, and I can't think of you any other way. Show it to me now." He blushed, because again he had said "it" and not "them."

"It makes me sad," she said, "that for you it's a sin."

"I want to see it," he said.

"Not a soul—" she said, "you're not to talk to a soul about it."

"I won't."

"Promise?"

"I promise—but there's one person I must tell."

"Who's that?"

"Think for a moment," he said softly, "think for a minute, you should know all about that." She bit her lip, still clutching her coat tightly around her chest, looked thoughtfully at him, and said, "Of course, you can tell him, but no one else."

"All right," he said, "now show it to me."

If she laughs or giggles, he thought, I'll shoot; but she did not laugh: she was so serious she was trembling, her hands fluttered as she tried to undo the buttons, her fingers were ice-cold and stiff.

"Come here," he said gently, "I'll do it." His hands were calm, his fear lay deeper than hers; down in his ankles was where he felt it, they were like rubber and he thought he was going to fall over. He undid the buttons with his right hand, passed his left hand over the girl's hair, as if to comfort her.

Her tears came quite suddenly, silently, without warning, without fuss. They simply ran down her cheeks.

"Why are you crying?"

"I'm scared," she said, "aren't you?"

"Yes I am," he said. "I'm scared too." He was so nervous he almost tore off the last button, and he took a deep breath when he saw Mirzova's breasts; he had been scared because he was afraid of being disgusted, afraid of the moment when politeness would force him to pretend, so as to hide this disgust, but he was not disgusted and there was no need to hide anything. He sighed again. As suddenly as they had begun, the girl's tears stopped flowing. She held her breath as she looked at him: the least movement of his face, the expression in his eyes, she took in every detail, and she already knew that in years to come she would be grateful to him, because he had been the one to undo the buttons.

He looked at them closely, did not touch her, just shook his head, and laughter rose up in him.

"What is it?" she asked, "may I laugh too?"

"Go ahead, laugh," he said, and she laughed.

"It's beautiful," he said, and again he was ashamed because he had said "it" instead of "they," but he could not bring himself to say "they."

"Do it up again," she said.

"No," he said, "you do it up, but leave it for a moment." It was very quiet, the sun pierced the yellow curtains, which had dark-green stripes. Dark stripes also lay across the faces of the children. You can't have a woman, thought the boy, at fourteen.

"Let me do it up," said the girl.

"All right," he said, "do it up." But he held her hands back for a moment, and the girl looked at him and laughed aloud.

"Why are you laughing now?"

"I'm so happy, aren't you?"

"Yes I am," he said, "I'm happy because it's so beautiful."

He let go her hands, stepped back, and turned aside as she buttoned up her blouse.

He walked round the table, looked at the open suitcase lying on the bed; sweaters lay piled one on top of the other, underwear had been sorted into little heaps, the bed had already been stripped, the suitcase was lying on the blue mattress ticking.

"So you're really leaving?" he asked.

"Yes."

He moved on, looked into the open clothes closet: nothing but empty coat hangers, a red hair ribbon dangling from one of them. He shut the closet doors, glanced over to the bookshelf above her bed: empty except for some used blotting paper, and a brochure standing at an angle against the wall: "All About Winegrowing."

When he looked around, her coat was lying on the floor. He picked it up, threw it on the table, and ran out.

She was standing in the kitchen doorway, holding the binoculars. She winced when he laid his hand on her shoulder, lowered her binoculars, and gave him a frightened look.

"Please go," she said. "You must go now."

"Let me see it just once more."

"No, the regatta will be over soon, my mother's coming to take me to the train. You know what'll happen if anyone sees you here."

He said nothing, leaving his hand on her shoulder. She ran away quickly, round to the other side of the table, took a knife out of the drawer, cut off a piece of the cucumber, took a bite, put down the knife. "Please," she said, "if you stare at me like that much longer, you'll look like the pharmacist or that fellow Drönsch."

"Shut up," he said. She looked at him in astonishment as he suddenly came over to her, grasped her by the shoulder; she brought her hand up over his arm and put the piece of cucumber in her mouth, and smiled. "Don't you understand," she said. "I was so happy."

He looked at the floor, let go her shoulder, went to the veranda, jumped onto the balustrade, and called out, "Give me a hand." She laughed, ran over to him, put down the piece of cucumber, and held on to him with both hands, bracing herself against the wall while she slowly lowered him onto the roof of the summerhouse.

"I bet someone has seen us," he said.

"Probably," she said. "Can I let go?"

"Not yet. When are you coming back from Vienna?"

"Soon," she said. "D'you want me to come soon?" He already had both feet on the roof and said, "You can let go now." But she did not let go, she laughed. "I'll come back. When d'you want me to come?"

"When I can look at it again."

"That might be a long time."

"How long?"

"I don't know," she said, looking at him thoughtfully. "First you looked as if you were dreaming, then all of a sudden you looked almost like the pharmacist; I don't want you to look like that and commit mortal sins and be bound."

"Let go now," he said, "or pull me up again."

She laughed, let go his hands, picked up the piece of cucumber from the balustrade, and bit into it.

"I've got to shoot at something," he said.

"Don't shoot at anything living," she said. "Shoot at tennis balls or at—at jam jars."

"What made you think of jam jars?"

"I don't know," she said. "I could imagine it might be fun to shoot at jam jars. It's bound to make a noise, and splash all over the place—wait a minute," she said hurriedly as he turned away and started to climb down; he turned back and looked at her gravely. "And, you know," she said softly, "you could stand at the railroad crossing, by the water tower, and fire into the air when my train goes by. I'll be looking out of the window and waving."

"Good," he said. "I'll do that, when does your train go?"

"Ten past seven," she said, "at seven-thirteen it passes the crossing."

"Then I'd better get going," he said. "Good-bye. You'll be back?"

"I'll be back," she said, "for sure." And she bit her lip and repeated under her breath, "I'll be back."

She watched him as he clung to the weathervane, till his feet had reached the trellis. He ran across the lawn, onto the terrace, climbed into the house; she saw him cross the brass strip again, pick up the carton of tennis balls, turn back; she heard the gravel crunching under his feet as, with the carton under his arm, he ran past the garage and out onto the street.

I hope he doesn't forget to turn round and wave, she thought. There he was, waving, at the corner of the garage, he pulled the pistol out of his pocket, pressed the barrel against the carton, and waved once more before he ran round the corner and disappeared.

Up she went with the binoculars again, punching out circles of blue, medallions of sky; Rhenania and Germania, riverbank with regatta pennants, round horizon of river green with shreds of banner red.

My hair would crackle, she thought, it crackled even when he touched it. And in Vienna there's wine too.

Vineyard: pale-green, sour grapes, leaves which those fat slobs tied around their bald heads to make them look like Bacchus.

She looked for the streets, the ones she could see into with the binoculars. The streets were all deserted, all she could see was the parked cars; the ice-cream cart was still there, she could not find the boy. I'll be —she thought with a smile, while she swept the binoculars toward the river again—I'll be your Jerusalem after all.

SHE DID not turn round as her mother opened the front door and entered the hall. A quarter to seven already, she thought. I hope he makes it to the crossing by thirteen minutes after. She heard the suitcase being snapped shut and the tiny key being turned in the lock, heard the firm footsteps, and she winced as the coat fell over her shoulders: her mother's hands remained lying on her shoulders.

"Have you got the money?"
"Yes."
"Your ticket?"
"Yes."
"The sandwiches?"
"Yes."
"Did you pack your suitcase properly?"
"Yes."
"You haven't forgotten anything?"
"No."
"The address in Vienna?"
"Yes."
"The phone number?"
"Yes."

The brief pause was dark, frightening, her mother's hands slid down her shoulders, over her forearms. "I felt it was better not to be here during your last hours. It's easier that way, I know it is. I've said good-bye so many times—and I did right to lock you in, you know."

"You did right, I know."

"Then come along now . . ." She turned round. It was terrible to see her mother crying, it was almost as if a monument were crying: her mother was still beautiful, but it was a dark beauty, haggard. Her past hung over her like a black halo. Strange words echoed in the legend of Mother's life: Moscow—Communism—a Red nun, a Russian called Mirzov; her faith lost, escape, and the dogmas of the lost faith continuing to twist and turn in her brain. It was like a loom whose spools go on turning although there is no more yarn: gorgeous patterns woven into a void, only the sound remained, the mechanism. All she needed was an opposite pole: Dulges, the city fathers, the priest, the schoolteachers, the nuns; and if you shut your eyes you could imagine prayer wheels, the prayer wheels of the unbelieving, the restless wind-driven rattle known as discussion. Occasionally, very rarely, her mother had looked the way she looked now: when she had been drinking wine, and people would say: Ah yes, in spite of everything, she's still a true daughter of Zischbrunn.

It was a good thing her mother was smoking; trickling down toward the cigarette, wreathed in smoke, her tears looked less serious, more like pretended tears, but tears were the last thing her mother would pretend.

"I'll pay them back for this," she said. "I hate to see you go. To have to give in to them."

"Why don't you come too?"

"No, no—you'll be back, a year or two and you'll be back. Never do what they think you've been doing. Never, and now come along."

She slipped her arms into the sleeves of her coat, buttoned it up, felt for her ticket, for her purse, ran into her bedroom, but her mother shook her head as she went to pick up her suitcase. "Never mind that," she said, "and hurry—there's not much time."

Heat hung in the staircase, wine fumes rose from the cellar, where the pharmacist had been bottling wine: an acrid smell that seemed to go with the hazy magenta of the wallpaper. The narrow lanes: the dark windows, doorways, from which things had been called out after her, things she did not understand. Hurry. The noise from the riverbank was louder now, car engines were being started up: the regatta was over. Hurry.

The ticket collector called her mother by her first name, "OK, Kate, never mind about a platform ticket." A drunk staggered along the dark underpass, bawling out a tune, and hurled a full bottle of wine against the damp black wall; there was a crash of breaking glass, and once again the smell of wine rose to her nostrils. The train was already in, her mother pushed the suitcase into the corridor. "Never do what they think you've been doing, never."

How sensible to make the good-byes so short; there was only one minute left, it was long, longer than the whole afternoon. "I expect you'd have liked to take the binoculars along. Shall I send them on to you?"

"Yes, would you, please? Oh, Mother."

"What is it?"

"I hardly know him."

"Oh, he's nice, and he's looking forward to having you—and he never believed in the gods I believed in."

"And he doesn't drink wine?"

"He doesn't care for it—and he's got money, he's in business."

"What kind of business?"

"I don't know exactly: clothing, or something. You'll like him."

No kiss. Monuments must not be kissed, even when they weep. Without a backward glance her mother disappeared into the underpass: a pillar of salt, a monument to unhappiness, preserved in the bitter brine of her mistakes. That evening she would start up the prayer wheel, give a monologue while Dulges sat in the kitchen: "Aren't tears actually a remnant of bourgeois sentiment? Can there be tears in the classless society?"

Past the school, the swimming pool, under the little bridge, the long, long wall of the vineyards, the woods—and at the railroad crossing by the water tower she saw the two boys, heard the bang, saw the black pistol in Paul's hand, and shouted, "Jerusalem, Jerusalem!" and she shouted it again although she could no longer see the boys. She wiped away her tears with her sleeve, picked up her suitcase, and stumbled along the corridor. I won't take off my coat yet, she thought, not just yet.

III

"WHAT WAS it she called out?" asked Griff.
"Couldn't you hear?"
"No, could you? What was it?"
"Jerusalem," said Paul quietly. "Jerusalem. She shouted it again when the train had already gone by. Let's go." He looked disappointedly at the pistol, which he held in his lowered hand, his thumb on the safety catch. He had thought it would make more of a bang, that it would smoke; he had counted on it smoking. With a smoking pistol in his hand, that's how he had wanted to stand beside the train; but the pistol did not smoke, it was not even hot, he moved his forefinger carefully along the barrel, withdrew it. "Let's go," he said. Jerusalem, he thought, I could hear it quite plainly, but I don't know what it means.

They left the path that ran parallel to the railway tracks, Griff hugging under his arm the jar of jam he had brought from home, Paul carrying the pistol in his lowered hand; in the greenish light they turned to face each other.

"Are you really going to do it?"
"No," said Paul, "no, we must . . ." He blushed, turned his face away. "Did you put the balls on the tree trunk?"
"Yes," said Griff, "they kept rolling off, but then I found a groove in the bark."
"How far apart?"
"Four or five inches, like you said—listen," he said, lowering his voice and coming to a halt, "I can't go home, I can't. To that room. You do see, don't you, that I can't go back to that room." He moved the jam jar to his other hand, and held Paul, who wanted to go on, by the sleeve. "I just can't."
"No," said Paul, "I wouldn't go back to that room either."

"My mother would force me to clean it up. I can't, I tell you—wipe up the floor, clean the walls, the books, and everything. She would be standing there watching."

"No, you can't do that. Let's go!"

"What shall I do?"

"We'll see. Let's shoot first—come along. . . ." They walked on, from time to time turning their green faces toward one another, Griff nervously, Paul smiling.

"You've got to shoot me," said Griff, "you've got to, I tell you."

"You're crazy," said Paul; he bit his lip, raised the pistol, aimed at Griff, and Griff ducked, whimpered softly, and Paul said, "You see, you'd scream, and I haven't even moved the safety catch."

He shaded his eyes with his left hand when they reached the clearing, blinked across to the tennis balls which were lying in a row on a fallen tree: three were still spotless, white and fluffy, like the fleece of the Lamb, the others were muddy from falling on the damp ground.

"Go over there," said Paul, "put the jar between the third and fourth ball." Griff walked unsteadily across the clearing, placed the jar behind the balls so that it stood at an angle and threatened to topple over.

"There's not enough room. I can't put it in between."

"Out of my way," said Paul, "I'm going to shoot. Stand over here by me."

He waited until Griff was standing beside him in the shade, raised the pistol, took aim, pressed the trigger, and, frightened by the echo of the first bullet, he banged away till the magazine was empty—the echo of the last two shots came back clearly out of the forest long after he had stopped firing. The tennis balls were still there, not even the jam jar had been hit. It was quite silent, there was just a slight smell of powder—the boy was still standing there, the raised pistol in his hand, he stood there as if he would stay there forever. He was pale. The chill of disappointment flowed into his veins, and his ears rang with the clear echo that was no longer there: clear, staccato barking reverberated in his memory. He closed his eyes, opened them again: the tennis balls were still there, and not even the jam jar had been hit.

He pulled back his arm as if from a great distance, stroked his fingers along the barrel: at least it was a little hot. Paul ripped out the empty clip with his thumbnail, slid a new one in, and pushed the safety catch back.

"Here," he said quietly, "it's your turn."

He handed the pistol to Griff, showed him how to release the safety catch, stepped back, and thought, while he stood in the shade trying to swallow his disappointment: I hope you don't miss, at least; I hope you don't miss. Griff threw up his arm with the pistol, then lowered it slowly toward the target—he's read about that, thought Paul, read that somewhere, it looks as though he had read it—and Griff fired stutteringly. Once —then silence; there were the balls, and the jar was still standing there; then three times—and three times the echo yapped back at the two boys. The dark tree trunk lay there as peaceful as some strange still life, with its six tennis balls and the jar of plum jam.

Only an echo; there was a faint smell of powder, and, shaking his head, Griff handed the pistol back to Paul.

"I've got an extra shot coming to me," said Paul, "the one I fired in the air—that leaves two for each of us, and one left over."

This time he aimed carefully, but he knew he would miss, and he did miss: the echo of his shot came back to him thin and forlorn, the echo penetrated him like a red dot, circled around inside him, flew out of him again, and he was calm as he handed Griff the pistol.

Griff shook his head. "The targets are too small, we must pick bigger ones. How about the station clock or the Rapier Beer sign?"

"Where d'you mean?"

"At the corner, across from the station, where Drönsch lives."

"Or a windowpane, or the samovar we have at home. We've *got* to hit something. Is it really true that you fired eight times with your pistol and got seven hits? A tin can at thirty yards?"

"No," said Griff, "I didn't shoot at all, I've never shot before." He went over to the tree trunk, kicked the balls, and the jam jar, with his right foot; the balls rolled into the grass, the jar slipped off and fell over onto the soft ground in the shade of the tree trunk where no grass grew. Griff snatched up the jar and was about to throw it against the tree, but Paul held back his arm, took the jar from him, and put it on the ground. "Please, don't," he said, "don't—I can't bear to see it. Leave it where it is, let grass grow over it, lots of grass. . . ."

And he pictured the grass growing till the jar was completely covered; animals would sniff at it, mushrooms would grow in a dense colony, and years later he would go for a walk in the forest and find it: the pistol covered with rust, the jam decayed into a moldy, spongy scum. He took the jar, set it in a hollow at the edge of the clearing, and kicked some loose earth over it. "Leave it," he said softly. "Leave the balls too—we haven't hit a thing."

"Lies," said Griff, "all lies."

"Yes, all lies," said Paul, but while he was fastening the safety catch and putting the pistol in his pocket he said under his breath, "Jerusalem, Jerusalem."

"How did you know she was leaving?"

"I met her mother on my way over to you."

"But she'll be back, won't she?"

"No, she won't be back."

Griff returned to the clearing and kicked the balls; two of them rolled white and silent into the shady forest. "Come over here," he said. "Look at this—we aimed much too high."

Paul walked slowly across, saw the ragged blackberry bush, bullet holes in a fir tree, fresh resin, a snapped branch.

"Come on," he said. "Let's shoot at the Rapier Beer sign, it's as big as a cartwheel."

"I'm not going back into town," said Griff, "never again. I'm going to Lübeck. I've got the ticket right here. I'm not coming back."

They walked slowly back the way they had come, past the railroad crossing, past the long vineyard wall, past the school. The parked cars had long since left, the sound of music drifted up from the town. They climbed up onto the two pillars of the churchyard gates, sat ten feet apart at the same level, and smoked.

"Prize-giving ceremony," said Griff. "A ball. Vine leaves round their foreheads. Down there you can see the Rapier Beer sign on the wall of Drönsch's house."

"I'll hit it," said Paul. "Aren't you coming?"

"No, I'll stay here. I'm going to sit here and wait till you've shot it down. Then I'll walk slowly over to Dreschenbrunn, get on the train there, and go to Lübeck. I'll go for a swim, a long swim in the salt water, and I hope it'll be stormy, with high waves and lots of salt water."

They smoked silently, looked at each other now and then, smiled, listened to the sounds coming up from the town, which were getting louder and louder.

"Did the hoofs really thunder?" asked Griff.

"No," said Paul, "they didn't. It was only one horse, and his hoofs just clattered—how about the salmon?"

"I've never seen one." They exchanged smiles and were silent for a while.

"Now my dad's standing in front of the cupboard," Paul said then, "with his shirt sleeves rolled up, my mother's spreading the tablecloth; now he's unlocking the drawer; perhaps he can see the scratch I made when the screwdriver slipped; but he doesn't see it, it's dark now over there in the corner; he's opening the drawer, he stops in surprise, for the checkbooks and ledger sheets aren't lying the way he left them—he's got the wind up, he's calling out to my mother, he's throwing all the stuff on the floor, rummaging around in the drawer—now, right now—at this very moment." He looked at the church clock, whose big hand was just slipping onto the ten while the small one stood motionless below the eight. "At one time," said Paul, "he was champion pistol-cleaner in his division; in three minutes he could take a pistol apart, clean it, and put it together again —and at home I always had to stand beside him and check the time with a stop watch: it never took him more than three minutes."

He threw his cigarette butt onto the path, stared at the church clock. "At exactly ten to eight he was always through with the job, then he would wash his hands and still be at the club on the stroke of eight." Paul jumped down from the pillar, held his hand up to Griff, and said, "When'll I see you again?"

"Not for a long time," said Griff, "but one day I'll be back. I'll go to work for my uncle, canning fish, slitting them open. The girls are always laughing, and in the evening they go to the movies, maybe—they don't giggle, that's for sure. They've got such white arms and look so cute. They used to stuff chocolate in my mouth when I was little, but now I'm not so little any more. I can't—" he said quietly, "you do see, don't you, that I can't go back to that room. She would stand beside me till it was all cleaned up. Have you got any money?"

"Sure, I've got all my vacation money already. Do you want some?"

"Yes, let me have some. I'll send it back to you, later on."

Paul opened his wallet, counted out the coins, opened the flap for the bills. "All my money for Zalligkofen. I can let you have eighteen marks. D'you want it?"

"Yes," said Griff; he took the bill, the coins, stuck it all in his trouser pocket. "I'll wait here," he said, "till I can hear and see that you've shot down the Rapier Beer sign; fire quickly and empty the whole magazine. When I can hear it, and see it, I'll go over to Dreschenbrunn and get on the next train. But don't tell anyone you know where I've gone."

"I won't," said Paul. He ran off, kicking stones aside as he ran, letting out a shrill cry so as to hear the wild echo of his voice as he ran through the underpass; he did not slow down until he was passing the railway yard and approaching Drönsch's house; he gradually slackened speed, turned round but could not see the churchyard gates yet, only the big black cross in the middle of the churchyard and the white gravestones above the cross. The closer he came to the station, the more rows of graves he could see below the cross: two rows, three, five, then the gates, and Griff was still sitting there. Paul crossed the station square, slowly; his heart was thumping, but he knew it was not fear, it was more like joy, and he would have liked to fire off the whole magazine into the air and shout "Jerusalem";

he felt almost sorry for the big round Rapier Beer sign, on which two crossed swords seemed to protect a mug overflowing with foaming beer.

I must hit it, he thought before taking the pistol out of his pocket, I must. He walked past the houses, stepped back into the doorway of a butcher's shop, and nearly trod on the hands of a woman who was washing the tiled entrance. "Watch it, can't you?" she said out of the semidarkness. "Beat it!"

"Excuse me," he said, and took up a position outside the entrance. The soapsuds ran between his feet across the asphalt into the gutter. This is the best place, he thought, it's hanging directly in front of me, round, like a big moon, and I'm bound to hit it. He took the pistol out of his pocket, released the safety catch, and smiled before he raised it and took aim. He no longer felt something had to be destroyed, and yet he had to shoot: there were some things that had to be done, and if he didn't shoot, Griff wouldn't go to Lübeck, wouldn't see the white arms of the cute girls, and would never go with one of them to the movies. He thought: God, I hope I'm not too far away—I *must* hit it, I *must*; but he had already hit it: the crash of the falling glass was almost louder than the noise of the shots. First a round piece broke out of the sign—the beer mug; then the swords fell, he saw the plaster of the house wall jump out in little clouds of dust, saw the metal ring that had held the glass sign, splinters of glass were clinging to the edge like a fringe.

Drowning out everything else were the screams of the woman; she had rushed out of the passageway and then ran back and went on screaming inside in the dark. Men were shouting too, a few people came out of the station; a great many rushed out of the tavern. A window was opened, and for a moment Drönsch's face appeared up above. But no one came near him because he was still holding the pistol. He looked up toward the churchyard: Griff had gone.

An eternity passed before someone came and took the pistol from him. He had time to think of many things: Now, he thought, Father has been yelling all over the house for the past ten minutes, putting the blame on Mother—Mother, who found out ages ago that I climbed up to Katharina's room; everyone knows about it, and nobody will understand why I did it and why I did this, shot at the lighted sign. Maybe it would have been better if I had shot into Drönsch's window. And he thought: Maybe I ought to go and confess, but they won't let me; it was eight o'clock, and after eight you couldn't confess. The Lamb has not drunk my blood, he thought, O Lamb.

There are only a few pieces of broken glass, and I have seen Katharina's breasts. She'll come back. And for once Father has good reason to clean his pistol.

He even had time to think of Griff, now on his way to Dreschenbrunn, over the slopes, past the vineyards, and he thought of the tennis balls and the jar of jam, which he already imagined completely overgrown.

A lot of people were standing around him at some distance. Drönsch was leaning out of the window on his arms, his pipe in his mouth. Never will I look like that, he thought, never. Drönsch was always talking about Admiral Tirpitz. "Tirpitz was the victim of injustice. One day history will see that justice is done to Tirpitz. Objective scholars are at work to find out the truth about Tirpitz." Tirpitz? Oh well.

From behind, he thought, I might have known they would come from behind. Just before the policeman grabbed hold of him, he smelled his uniform: its first smell was of cleaning fluid, its second, furnace fumes, its third . . .

"Where do you live, you young punk?" asked the policeman.

"Where do I live?" He looked at the policeman. He knew him, and the policeman must know him too: he always brought round the renewal for Father's gun license, a friendly soul, always refused a cigar three times before he accepted it. Even now he was not unfriendly, and his grasp was not tight.

"That's right, where do you live?"

"I live in the Valley of the Thundering Hoofs," said Paul.

"That's not true," shouted the woman who had been scrubbing the passageway, "I know him, he's the son—"

"All right, all right," said the policeman, "I know. Come along," he said, "I'll take you home."

"I live in Jerusalem," said Paul.

"Now stop that," said the policeman. "Come along with me."

"All right," said Paul, "I'll stop."

The people were silent as he walked down the dark street just ahead of the policeman. He looked like a blind man: his eyes fixed on a certain point, and yet he seemed to be looking past everything. He saw only one thing: the policeman's folded evening paper. And in the first line he could read "Khrushchev" and in the second "open grave."

"Hell," he said to the policeman, "you know where I live."

"Of course I do," said the policeman. "Come along!"

When the War
Broke Out

I WAS LEANING out of the window, my arms resting on the sill. I had rolled up my shirt sleeves and was looking beyond the main gate and guard-room across to the divisional headquarters telephone exchange, waiting for my friend Leo to give me the prearranged signal: come to the window, take off his cap, and put it on again. Whenever I got the chance I would lean out of the window, my arms on the sill; whenever I got the chance I would call a girl in Cologne and my mother—at army expense—and when Leo came to the window, took off his cap, and put it on again, I would run down to the barrack square and wait in the public callbox till the phone rang.

The other telephone operators sat there bareheaded, in their under-shirts, and when they leaned forward to plug in or unplug, or to push up a flap, their identity disks would dangle out of their undershirts and fall back again when they straightened up. Leo was the only one wearing a cap, just so he could take it off to give me the signal. He had a heavy, pink face, very fair hair, and came from Oldenburg. The first expression you noticed on his face was guilelessness; the second was incredible guilelessness, and no one paid enough attention to Leo to notice more than those two expressions; he looked as uninteresting as the boys whose faces appear on advertisements for cheese.

It was hot, afternoon; the alert that had been going on for days had become stale, transforming all time as it passed into stillborn Sunday hours. The barrack square lay there blind and empty, and I was glad I could at least keep my head out of the camaraderie of my roommates. Over there the operators were plugging and unplugging, pushing up flaps, wiping off sweat, and Leo was sitting there among them, his cap on his thick fair hair.

All of a sudden I noticed the rhythm of plugging and unplugging had altered; arm movements were no longer routine, mechanical, they became hesitant, and Leo threw his arms up over his head three times: a signal we had not arranged but from which I could tell that something out of the ordinary had happened. Then I saw an operator take his steel helmet from the switchboard and put it on; he looked ridiculous, sitting there sweating in his undershirt, his identity disk dangling, his steel helmet on his head—but I couldn't laugh at him; I realized that putting on a steel helmet meant something like "ready for action," and I was scared.

THE ONES who had been dozing on their beds behind me in the room got up, lit cigarettes, and formed the two customary groups: three probationary teachers, who were still hoping to be discharged as being "essential to the nation's educational system," resumed their discussion of Ernst Jünger; the other two, an orderly and an office clerk, began discussing the female form; they didn't tell dirty stories, they didn't laugh, they discussed it just as two exceptionally boring geography teachers might have discussed the conceivably interesting topography of the Ruhr valley. Neither subject interested me. Psychologists, those interested in psychology, and those about to complete an adult education course in psychology may be interested to learn that my desire to call the girl in Cologne became more urgent than in previous weeks; I went to my locker, took out my cap, put it on, and leaned out of the window, my arms on the sill, wearing my cap: the signal for Leo that I had to speak to him at once. To show he understood, he waved to me, and I put on my tunic, went out of the room, down the stairs, and stood at the entrance to headquarters, waiting for Leo.

IT WAS hotter than ever, quieter than ever, the barrack squares were even emptier, and nothing has ever approximated my idea of hell as closely as hot, silent, empty barrack squares. Leo came very quickly; he was also wearing his steel helmet now, and was displaying one of his other five expressions that I knew: dangerous for everything he didn't like. This was the face he sat at the switchboard with when he was on evening or night duty, listened in on secret official calls, told me what they were about, suddenly jerked out plugs, cut off secret official calls so as to put through an urgent secret call to Cologne for me to talk to the girl; then it would be my turn to work the switchboard, and Leo would first call his girl in Oldenburg, then his father; meanwhile Leo would cut thick slices from the ham his mother had sent him, cut these into cubes, and we would eat cubes of ham. When things were slack, Leo would teach me the art of recognizing the caller's rank from the way the flaps fell; at first I thought it was

enough to be able to tell the rank simply by the force with which the flap
fell—corporal, sergeant, etc.—but Leo could tell exactly whether it was
an officious corporal or a tired colonel demanding a line; from the way
the flap fell, he could even distinguish between angry captains and annoyed
lieutenants—nuances that are very hard to tell apart, and as the evening
went on, his other expressions made their appearance: fixed hatred; primor-
dial malice. With these faces he would suddenly become pedantic, articu-
late his "Are you still talking?", his "Yessirs," with great care, and with
unnerving rapidity switch plugs so as to turn an official call about boots
into one about boots and ammunition, and the other call about ammunition into one about ammunition and boots, or the private conversation of
a sergeant major with his wife might be suddenly interrupted by a lieutenant's voice saying, "I insist the man be punished, I absolutely insist." With
lightning speed Leo would then switch the plugs over so that the boot
partners were talking about boots again and the others about ammunition,
and the sergeant major's wife could resume discussion of her stomach
trouble with her husband. When the ham was all gone, Leo's relief had
arrived, and we were walking across the silent barrack square to our room,
Leo's face would wear its final expression: foolish, innocent in a way that
had nothing to do with childlike innocence.

Any other time I would have laughed at Leo, standing there wearing his
steel helmet, that symbol of inflated importance. He looked past me, across
the first, the second barrack square, to the stables; his expressions alternated
from three to five, from five to four, and with his final expression he said,
"It's war, war, war—they finally made it." I said nothing, and he said, "I
guess you want to talk to her?"

"Yes," I said.

"I've already talked to mine," he said. "She's not pregnant. I don't
know whether to be glad or not. What d'you think?"

"You can be glad," I said. "I don't think it's a good idea to have kids
in wartime."

"General mobilization," he said, "state of alert, this place is soon
going to be swarming—and it'll be a long while before you and I can go
off on our bikes again." (When we were off duty we used to ride our bikes
out into the country, onto the moors, the farmers' wives used to fix us fried
eggs and thick slices of bread and butter.) "The first joke of the war has
already happened," said Leo. "In view of my special skills and services in
connection with the telephone system, I have been made a corporal. Now

go over to the public callbox, and if it doesn't ring in three minutes I'll demote myself for incompetence."

IN THE callbox I leaned against the Münster Area phone book, lit a cigarette, and looked out through a gap in the frosted glass across the barrack square; the only person I could see was a sergeant major's wife, in Block 4, I think. She was watering her geraniums from a yellow jug; I waited, looked at my wristwatch: one minute, two, and I was startled when it actually rang, and even more startled when I immediately heard the voice of the girl in Cologne: "Maybach's Furniture Company." And I said, "Marie, it's war, it's war"—and she said, "No." I said, "Yes it is." Then there was silence for half a minute, and she said, "Shall I come?", and before I could say spontaneously, instinctively, "Yes, please do," the voice of what was probably a fairly senior officer shouted, "We need ammunition, and we need it urgently." The girl said, "Are you still there?" The officer yelled, "God damn it!" Meanwhile I had had time to wonder about what it was in the girl's voice that had sounded unfamiliar, ominous almost: her voice had sounded like marriage, and I suddenly knew I didn't feel like marrying her. I said, "We're probably pulling out tonight." The officer yelled, "God damn it, God damn it!" (evidently he couldn't think of anything better to say), the girl said, "I could catch the four o'clock train and be there just before seven," and I said, more quickly than was polite, "It's too late, Marie, too late"—then all I heard was the officer, who seemed to be on the verge of apoplexy. He screamed, "Well, do we get the ammunition or don't we?" And I said in a steely voice (I had learned that from Leo), "No, no, you don't get any ammunition, even if it chokes you." Then I hung up.

IT WAS still daylight when we loaded boots from railway cars onto trucks, but by the time we were loading boots from trucks onto railway cars it was dark, and it was still dark when we loaded boots from railway cars onto trucks again; then it was daylight again, and we loaded bales of hay from trucks onto railway cars, and it was still daylight, and we were still loading bales of hay from trucks onto railway cars; but then it was dark again, and for exactly twice as long as we had loaded bales of hay from trucks onto railway cars, we loaded bales of hay from railway cars onto trucks. At one point a field kitchen arrived, in full combat rig. We were given large helpings of goulash and small helpings of potatoes, and we were given real coffee and cigarettes which we didn't have to pay for; that must have been at night, for I remember hearing a voice say: Real coffee and cigarettes for free, the surest sign of war. I don't remember the face belonging to this voice. It was daylight again when we marched back to barracks, and as we turned into the street leading past the barracks, we met the first battalion going off. It was headed by a marching band playing "Must I Then," followed by the first company, then their armored vehicles, then the second, third, and finally the fourth with the heavy machine guns. On not one face, not one single face, did I see the least sign of enthusiasm. Of course, there were some people standing on the sidewalks, some girls too, but not once did I see anybody stick a bunch of flowers onto a soldier's rifle; there was not even the merest trace of a sign of enthusiasm in the air.

LEO'S BED was untouched. I opened his locker (a degree of familiarity with Leo which the probationary teachers, shaking their heads, called "going too far"). Everything was in its place: the photo of the girl in Oldenburg, she was standing, leaning against her bicycle, in front of a birch tree; photos of Leo's parents; their farmhouse. Next to the ham there was a message: "Transferred to area headquarters. In touch with you soon. Take all the ham, I've taken what I need. Leo." I didn't take any of the ham, and closed the locker; I was not hungry, and the rations for two days had been stacked up on the table: bread, cans of liver sausage, butter, cheese, jam, and cigarettes. One of the probationary teachers, the one I liked least, announced that he had been promoted to Pfc and appointed room senior for the period of Leo's absence; he began to distribute the rations. It took a very long time; the only thing I was interested in was the cigarettes, and these he left to the last because he was a nonsmoker. When I finally got the cigarettes, I tore open the pack, lay down on the bed in my clothes, and smoked; I watched the others eating. They spread liver sausage an inch thick on the bread and discussed the "excellent quality of the butter," then they drew the blackout blinds and lay down on their beds. It was very hot, but I didn't feel like undressing. The sun shone into the room through a few cracks, and in one of these strips of light sat the newly promoted Pfc sewing on his Pfc's chevron. It isn't so easy to sew on a Pfc's chevron: it has to be placed at a certain prescribed distance from the seam of the sleeve; moreover, the two open sides of the chevron must be absolutely straight. The probationary teacher had to take off the chevron several times; he sat there for at least two hours, unpicking it, sewing it back on, and he did

not appear to be running out of patience. Outside, the band came marching by every forty minutes, and I heard the "Must I Then" from Block
7, Block 2, from Block 9, then from over by the stables—it would come
closer, get very loud, then softer again; it took almost exactly three
"Must I Thens" for the Pfc to sew on his chevron, and it still wasn't
quite straight. By that time I had smoked the last of my cigarettes and
fell asleep.

THAT AFTERNOON we didn't have to load either boots from trucks onto
railway cars or bales of hay from railway cars onto trucks; we had to help
the quartermaster sergeant. He considered himself a genius at organization;
he had requisitioned as many assistants as there were items of clothing and
equipment on his list, except that for the groundsheets he needed two; he
also required a clerk. The two men with the groundsheets went ahead and
laid them out, flicking the corners nice and straight, neatly on the cement
floor of the stable. As soon as the groundsheets had been spread out, the
first man started off by laying two neckties on each groundsheet; the second
man, two handkerchiefs; I came next with the mess kits. While all the
articles for which, as the sergeant said, size was not a factor were being
distributed, he was preparing, with the aid of the more intelligent members
of the detachment, the objects for which size was a factor: tunics, boots,
trousers, and so on. He had a whole pile of paybooks lying there. He
selected the tunics, trousers, and boots according to measurements and
weight, and he insisted everything would fit, "unless the bastards have got
too fat as civilians." It all had to be done at great speed, in one continuous
operation, and it was done at great speed, in one continuous operation, and
when everything had been spread out the reservists came in, were conducted to their groundsheets, tied the ends together, hoisted their bundles
onto their backs, and went to their rooms to put on their uniforms. Only
occasionally did something have to be exchanged, and then it was always
because someone had got too fat as a civilian. It was also only occasionally
that something was missing: a shoe-cleaning brush or a spoon or fork, and
it always turned out that someone else had two shoe-cleaning brushes or
two spoons or forks, a fact which confirmed the sergeant's theory that we
did not work mechanically enough, that we were "still using our brains
too much." I didn't use my brain at all, with the result that no one was
short a mess kit. While the first man of each company being equipped was
hoisting his bundle onto his shoulder, the first of our own lot had to start
spreading out the next groundsheet. Everything went smoothly. Meanwhile the newly promoted Pfc sat at the table and wrote everything down

in the paybooks; most of the time he had only to enter a one in the paybook, except with the neckties, socks, handkerchiefs, undershirts, and underpants, where he had to write a two.

In spite of everything, though, there were occasionally some dead minutes, as the quartermaster sergeant called them, and we were allowed to use these to fortify ourselves; we would sit on the bunks in the grooms' quarters and eat bread and liver sausage, sometimes bread and cheese or bread and jam, and when the sergeant had a few dead minutes himself he would come over and give us a lecture about the difference between rank and appointment. He found it tremendously interesting that he himself was a quartermaster sergeant—"that's my appointment"—and yet had the rank of a corporal, "that's my rank." In this way, so he said, there was no reason, for example, why a Pfc should not act as a quartermaster sergeant, indeed even an ordinary private might; he found the theme endlessly fascinating and kept on concocting new examples, some of which betokened a well-nigh treasonable imagination. "It can actually happen, for instance," he said, "that a Pfc is put in command of a company, of a battalion even."

For ten hours I laid mess kits on groundsheets, slept for six hours, and again for ten hours laid mess kits on groundsheets; then I slept another six hours and still had heard nothing from Leo. When the third ten hours of laying out mess kits began, the Pfc started entering a two wherever there should have been a one, and a one wherever there should have been a two. He was relieved of his post, and now had to lay out neckties, and the second probationary teacher was appointed clerk. I stayed with the mess kits during the third ten hours too. The sergeant said he thought I had done surprisingly well.

During the dead minutes, while we were sitting on the bunks eating bread and cheese, bread and jam, bread and liver sausage, strange rumors were beginning to be peddled around. A story was being told about a rather well-known retired general who received orders by phone to go to a small island in the North Sea where he was to assume a top-secret, extremely important command. The general had taken his uniform out of the closet, kissed his wife, children, and grandchildren good-bye, given his favorite horse a farewell pat, and taken the train to some station on the North Sea, and from there hired a motorboat to the island in question. He had been foolish enough to send back the motorboat before ascertaining the nature of his command; he was cut off by the rising tide and—so the story went —had forced the farmer on the island at pistol point to risk his life and row him back to the mainland. By afternoon there was already a variation to the tale: some sort of a struggle had taken place in the boat between the general and the farmer, they had both been swept overboard and drowned. What I couldn't stand was that this story—and a number of others—was considered criminal all right, but funny as well, while to me they seemed neither one nor the other. I couldn't accept the grim accusation of sabotage, which was being used like some kind of moral tuning fork, nor could I join in the laughter or grin with the others. The war seemed to deprive what was funny of its funny side.

At any other time the "Must I Thens" that ran through my dreams, my sleep, and my few waking moments, the countless men who got off the streetcars and came hurrying into the barracks with their cardboard boxes and went out again an hour later with "Must I Then"; even the speeches we sometimes listened to with half an ear, speeches in which the words "united effort" were always occurring—all this I would have found funny, but everything which would have been funny before was not funny any more, and I could no longer laugh or smile at all the things which would have seemed laughable; not even the sergeant, and not even the Pfc, whose chevron was still not quite straight and who sometimes laid out three neckties on the groundsheet instead of two.

It was still hot, still August, and the fact that three times sixteen hours are only forty-eight, two days and two nights, was something I didn't realize until I woke up about eleven on Sunday and for the first time since Leo had been transferred was able to lean out of the window, my arms on the sill. The probationary teachers, wearing their walking-out dress, were ready for church, and looked at me in a challenging kind of way, but all I said was "Go ahead, I'll follow you," and it was obvious that they were glad to be able to go without me for once. Whenever we had gone to church they had looked at me as if they would like to excommunicate me, because something or other about me or my uniform was not quite up to scratch in their eyes: the way my boots were cleaned, the way I had tied my tie, my belt or my haircut; they were indignant not as fellow soldiers (which, objectively speaking, I agree would have been justified), but as Catholics. They would rather I had not made it so unmistakably clear that we were actually going to one and the same church; it embarrassed them, but there wasn't a thing they could do about it, because my paybook is marked RC.

This Sunday there was no mistaking how glad they were to be able to go without me. I had only to watch them marching off to town, past the barracks, clean, upright, and brisk. Sometimes, when I felt bouts of pity for them, I was glad for their sakes that Leo was a Protestant: I think they simply couldn't have borne it if Leo had been a Catholic too.

The office clerk and the orderly were still asleep; we didn't have to be at the stable again till three that afternoon. I stood leaning out of the window for a while, till it was time to go, so as to get to church just in time to miss the sermon. Then, while I was dressing, I opened Leo's locker again: to my surprise it was empty, except for a piece of paper and a big chunk of ham. Leo had locked the cupboard again to be sure I would find the message and the ham. On the paper was written "This is it—I'm being sent to Poland—did you get my message?" I put the paper in my pocket, turned the key in the locker, and finished dressing; I was in a daze as I walked into town and entered the church, and even the glances of the three probationary teachers, who turned round to look at me and then back to the altar again, shaking their heads, failed to rouse me completely. Probably they wanted to make sure quickly whether I hadn't come in *after* the Elevation of the Host so they could apply for my excommunication; but I really had arrived *before* the Elevation, so there was nothing they could do; besides, I wanted to remain a Catholic. I thought of Leo and was scared, I thought too of the girl in Cologne and had a twinge of conscience, but I was sure her voice had sounded like marriage. To annoy my roommates, I undid my collar while I was still in church.

AFTER MASS I stood outside leaning against the church wall in a shady corner between the vestry and the door, took off my cap, lit a cigarette, and watched the faithful as they left the church and walked past me. I wondered how I could get hold of a girl with whom I could go for a walk, have a cup of coffee, and maybe go to a movie; I still had three hours before I had to lay out mess kits on groundsheets again. It would be nice if the girl were not too silly and reasonably pretty. I also thought about dinner at the barracks, which I was missing now, and that perhaps I ought to have told the office clerk he could have my chop and dessert.

I smoked two cigarettes while I stood there, watching the faithful standing about in twos and threes, then separating again, and just as I was lighting the third cigarette from the second a shadow fell across me from one side, and when I looked to the right I saw that the person casting the shadow was even blacker than the shadow itself: it was the chaplain who had read Mass. He looked very kind, not old, thirty perhaps, fair and just a shade too well fed. First he looked at my open collar, then at my boots, then at my bare head, and finally at my cap, which I had put next to me on a ledge from where it had slipped off onto the paving; last of all he looked at my cigarette, then into my face, and I had the feeling that he didn't like anything he saw there. "What's the matter?" he finally asked. "Are you in trouble?" And hardly had I nodded in reply to this question, when he said, "Do you wish to confess?" Damn it, I thought, all they ever think of is confession, and only a certain part of that even. "No," I said, "I don't wish to confess." "Well, then," he said, "what's on your mind?" He might just as well have been asking about my stomach as my mind. He was obviously very impatient, looked at my cap, and I felt he was annoyed that I hadn't picked it up yet. I would have liked to turn his impatience into patience, but after all it wasn't I who had spoken to him, but he who had spoken to me, so I asked—to my annoyance, somewhat falteringly—whether he knew of some nice girl who would go for a walk with me, have a cup of coffee, and maybe go to a movie in the evening; she didn't have to be a beauty queen, but she must be reasonably pretty, and if possible not from a good family, as these girls are usually so silly. I could give him the address of a chaplain in Cologne where he could make inquiries, call up if necessary, to satisfy himself I was from a good Catholic home. I talked a lot, toward the end a bit more coherently, and noticed how his face altered: at first it was almost kind, it had almost looked benign, that was in the early stage when he took me for a highly interesting, possibly even fascinating case of feeble-mindedness and found me psychologically quite amusing. The transitions from kind to almost benign, from almost benign to amused were hard to distinguish, but then all of a sudden—the moment I mentioned the physical attributes the girl was to have—he went purple with rage. I was scared, for my mother had once told me it is a sign of danger when overweight people suddenly go purple in the face. Then he began to shout at me, and shouting has always put me on edge. He shouted that I looked a mess, with my "field tunic" undone, my boots unpolished, my cap lying next to me "in the dirt, yes, in the dirt," and how undisciplined I was, smoking one cigarette after another, and whether perhaps I couldn't tell the difference between a Catholic priest and a pimp. With my nerves strung up as they were, I had stopped being scared of him, I was just plain angry. I asked him what my tie, my boots, my cap, had to do with him, whether he thought maybe he had to do my corporal's job, and "Anyway," I said, "you fellows tell us all the time to come to you with our troubles, and when someone really tells you his troubles, you get mad." "You fellows, eh?" he said, gasping with rage. "Since when are we on such familiar terms?" "We're not on any terms at all," I said. I picked up my cap, put it on without looking at it, and left, walking straight across the church square. He called after me to at least do up my tie, and I shouldn't be so stubborn; I very nearly turned round and shouted that *he* was the stubborn one, but then I remembered my mother telling me it was all right to be frank with a priest but you should try to avoid being impertinent—and so, without looking back, I went on into town. I left my tie dangling and thought about Catholics; there was a war on, but the first thing they looked at was your tie, then your boots. They said you should tell them your troubles, and when you did, they got mad.

I WALKED slowly through town, on the lookout for a café where I wouldn't have to salute anyone: this stupid saluting spoiled all cafés for me. I looked at all the girls I passed, I turned round to look at them, at their legs even, but there wasn't one whose voice would not have sounded like marriage. I was desperate. I thought of Leo, of the girl in Cologne, I was on the point of sending her a telegram; I was almost prepared to risk getting married just to be alone with a girl. I stopped in front of the window of a photographer's studio, so I could think about Leo in peace. I was scared for him. I saw my reflection in the shop window—my tie undone and my black boots unpolished. I raised my hands to button up my collar, but then it seemed too much trouble, and I dropped my hands again. The photographs in the studio window were very depressing. They were almost all of soldiers in walking-out dress; some had even had their pictures taken wearing their steel helmets, and I was wondering whether the ones in steel helmets were more depressing than the ones in peaked caps when a sergeant came out of the shop carrying a framed photograph: the photo was fairly large, at least twenty-four by thirty, the frame was painted silver, and the picture showed the sergeant in walking-out dress and steel helmet. He was quite young, not much older than I was, twenty-one at most; he was just about to walk past me, he hesitated, stopped, and I was wondering whether to raise my hand and salute him, when he said, "Forget it—but if I were you I'd do up your collar, and your tunic too. The next guy might be tougher than I am." Then he laughed and went off, and ever since then I have preferred (relatively, of course) the ones who have their pictures taken in steel helmets to the ones who have their pictures taken in peak caps.

Leo would have been just the person to stand with me in front of the photo studio and look at the pictures; there were also some bridal couples, first communicants, and students wearing colored ribbons and fancy fobs over their stomachs, and I stood there wondering why they didn't wear ribbons in their hair; some of them wouldn't have looked bad in them at all. I needed company and had none.

Probably the chaplain thought I was suffering from lust, or that I was an anticlerical Nazi; but I was neither suffering from lust nor was I anticlerical or a Nazi. I simply needed company, and not male company either, and that was so simple that it was terribly complicated; of course there were loose women in town as well as prostitutes (it was a Catholic town), but the loose women and the prostitutes were always offended if you weren't suffering from lust.

I stood for a long time in front of the photo studio. To this day I still always look at photo studios in strange cities; they are all much the same, and all equally depressing, although not everywhere do you find students with colored ribbons. It was nearly one o'clock when I finally left, on the lookout for a café where I didn't have to salute anyone, but in all the cafés they were sitting around in their uniforms, and I ended up by going to a movie anyway, to the first show at one-fifteen. All I remember was the newsreel: some very ignoble-looking Poles were maltreating some very noble-looking Germans. It was so empty in the movie that I could risk smoking during the show; it was hot that last Sunday in August 1939.

WHEN I got back to barracks, it was way past three. For some reason the order to put down groundsheets at three o'clock and spread out mess kits and neckties on them had been countermanded; I came in just in time to change, have some bread and liver sausage, lean out of the window for a few minutes, listen to snatches of the discussion about Ernst Jünger and the other one about the female form. Both discussions had become more serious, more boring; the orderly and the office clerk were now weaving Latin expressions into their remarks, and that made the whole thing even more repulsive than it was in the first place.

At four we were called out, and I had imagined we would be loading boots from trucks onto railway cars again or from railway cars onto trucks, but this time we loaded cases of soap powder, which were stacked up in the gym, onto trucks, and from the trucks we unloaded them at the parcel post office, where they were stacked up again. The cases were not heavy, the addresses were typewritten. We formed a chain, and so one case after another passed through my hands; we did this the whole of Sunday afternoon right through till late at night, and there were scarcely any dead minutes when we could have had a bite to eat. As soon as a truck was fully loaded, we drove to the main post office, formed a chain again, and unloaded the cases. Sometimes we overtook a "Must I Then" column, or met one coming the other way; by this time they had three bands, and it was all going much faster. It was late, after midnight, when we had driven off with the last of the cases, and my hands remembered the number of mess kits and decided there was very little difference between cases of soap powder and mess kits.

I WAS very tired and wanted to throw myself on the bed fully dressed, but once again there was a great stack of bread and cans of liver sausage, jam and butter, on the table, and the others insisted it be distributed; all I wanted was the cigarettes, and I had to wait till everything had been divided up exactly, for of course the Pfc left the cigarettes to the last again. He took an abnormally long time about it, perhaps to teach me moderation and discipline and to convey his contempt for my craving; when I finally got the cigarettes, I lay down on the bed in my clothes and smoked and watched them spreading their bread with liver sausage, listened to them praising the excellent quality of the butter, and arguing mildly as to whether the jam was made of strawberries, apples, and apricots, or of strawberries and apples only. They went on eating for a long time, and I couldn't fall asleep. Then I heard footsteps coming along the passage and knew they were for me: I was afraid and yet relieved, and the strange thing was that they all, the office clerk, the orderly, and the three probationary teachers who were sitting round the table, stopped their chewing and looked at me as the footsteps drew closer. Now the Pfc found it necessary to shout at me: he got up and yelled, calling me by my surname, "Damn it, take your boots off when you lie down."

There are certain things one refuses to believe, and I still don't believe it, although my ears remember quite well that all of a sudden he called me by my surname; I would have preferred it if we had used surnames all along, but coming so suddenly like that it sounded so funny that, for the first time since the war started, I had to laugh. Meanwhile the door had been flung open and the company clerk was standing by my bed; he was pretty excited, so much so that he didn't bawl me out, although he was a corporal, for lying on the bed with my boots and clothes on, smoking. He said, "You there, in twenty minutes in full marching order in Block 4, understand?" I said "Yes" and got up. He added, "Report to the sergeant major over there," and again I said "Yes" and began to clear out my locker. I hadn't realized the company clerk was still in the room. I was just putting the picture of the girl in my trouser pocket when I heard him say, "I have some bad news, it's going to be tough on you, but it should make you proud too; the first man from this regiment to be killed in action was your roommate, Corporal Leo Siemers."

I had turned round during the last half of this sentence, and they were all looking at me now, including the corporal. I had gone quite pale, and I didn't know whether to be furious or silent. Then I said in a low voice, "But war hasn't been declared yet, he can't have been killed—and he wouldn't have been killed," and I shouted suddenly, "Leo wouldn't get killed, not him . . . you know he wouldn't." No one said anything, not even the corporal, and while I cleared out my locker and crammed all the stuff we were told to take with us into my pack, I heard him leave the room. I piled up all the things on the stool so I didn't have to turn around; I couldn't hear a sound from the others, I couldn't even hear them chewing. I packed all my stuff very quickly; the bread, liver sausage, cheese, and butter I left in the locker and turned the key. When I had to turn around, I saw they had managed to get into bed without a sound; I threw my locker key onto the office clerk's bed, saying, "Clear out everything that's still in there, it's all yours." I didn't care for him much, but I liked him best of the five. Later on I was sorry I hadn't left without saying a word, but I was not yet twenty. I slammed the door, took my rifle from the rack outside, went down the stairs, and saw from the clock over the office door downstairs that it was nearly three in the morning. It was quiet and still warm that last Monday of August 1939. I threw Leo's locker key somewhere onto the barrack square as I went across to Block 4. They were all there, the band was already moving into position at the head of the company, and some officer who had given the "united effort" speech was walking across the square; he took off his cap, wiped the sweat from his forehead, and put his cap on again. He reminded me of a streetcar conductor who takes a short break at the terminus.

The sergeant major came up to me and said, "Are you the man from staff headquarters?" and I said "Yes." He nodded; he looked pale and very young, somewhat at a loss; I looked past him toward the dark, scarcely distinguishable mass. All I could make out was the gleaming trumpets of the band. "You wouldn't happen to be a telephone operator?" asked the sergeant major. "We're short one here." "As a matter of fact I am," I said quickly and with an enthusiasm that seemed to surprise him, for he looked at me doubtfully. "Yes, I'm one," I said, "I've had practical training as a telephone operator." "Good," he said, "you're just the man I need. Slip in somewhere there at the end, we'll arrange everything en route." I went over toward the right, where the dark gray was getting a little lighter; as I got closer, I even recognized some faces. I took my place at the end of the company. Someone shouted, "Right turn—forward march!" and I had hardly lifted my foot when they started playing their "Must I Then."

When the War
Was Over

IT WAS just getting light when we reached the German border: to our left, a broad river, to our right a forest; even from its edges you could tell how deep it was. Silence fell in the boxcar; the train passed slowly over patched-up rails, past shelled houses, splintered telegraph poles. The little guy sitting next to me took off his glasses and polished them carefully.

"Christ," he whispered to me, "d'you have the slightest idea where we are?"

"Yes," I said, "the river you've just seen is known here as the Rhine, the forest you see over there on the right is called the Reich Forest—and we'll soon be getting into Cleves."

"D'you come from around here?"

"No, I don't." He was a nuisance; all night long he had driven me crazy with his high-pitched schoolboy's voice. He had told me how he had secretly read Brecht, Tucholsky, and Walter Benjamin, as well as Proust and Karl Kraus; that he wanted to study sociology, and theology too, and help create a new order for Germany, and when we stopped at Nimwegen at daybreak and someone said we were just coming to the German border, he nervously asked us all if there was anyone who would trade some thread for two cigarette butts, and when no one said anything, I offered to rip off my collar tabs, known—I believe—as insignia, and turn them into dark-green thread. I took off my tunic and watched him carefully pick the things off with a bit of metal, unravel them, and then actually start using the thread to sew on his ensign's piping around his shoulder straps. I asked him whether I might attribute this sewing job to the influence of Brecht, Tucholsky, Benjamin, or Karl Kraus, or was it perhaps the subconscious influence of Jünger that made him restore his rank with Tom Thumb's weapon. He had flushed and said he was through with Jünger, he had written him off; now, as we approached Cleves, he stopped sewing and sat down on the floor beside me, still holding Tom Thumb's weapon.

"Cleves doesn't convey anything to me," he said, "not a thing. How about you?"

"Oh yes," I said, "Lohengrin, Swan margarine, and Anne of Cleves, one of Henry the Eighth's wives."

"That's right," he said, "Lohengrin—although at home we always ate Sanella. Don't you want the butts?"

"No," I said, "take them home for your father. I hope he'll punch you in the nose when you arrive with that piping on your shoulder."

"You don't understand," he said. "Prussia, Kleist, Frankfurt-on-the-Oder, Potsdam, Prince of Homburg, Berlin."

"Well," I said, "I believe it was quite a while ago that Prussia took Cleves—and somewhere over there on the other side of the Rhine there is a little town called Wesel."

"Oh, of course," he said, "that's right, Schill."

"The Prussians never really established themselves beyond the Rhine," I said, "they only had two bridgeheads: Bonn and Koblenz."

"Prussia," he said.

"Blomberg," I said. "Need any more thread?" He flushed and was silent.

THE TRAIN slowed down, everyone crowded round the open sliding door and looked at Cleves. English guards on the platform, casual and tough, bored yet alert: we were still prisoners. In the street a sign: "To Cologne." Lohengrin's castle up there among the autumn trees. October on the Lower Rhine, Dutch sky; my cousins in Xanten, aunts in Kevelaer; the broad dialect and the smugglers' whispering in the taverns; St. Martin's Day processions, gingerbread men, Breughelesque carnival, and everywhere the smell, even where there was none, of honey cakes.

"I wish you'd try to understand," said the little guy beside me.

"Leave me alone," I said; although he wasn't a man yet, no doubt he soon would be, and that was why I hated him. He was offended and sat back on his heels to add the final stitches to his braid; I didn't even feel sorry for him: clumsily, his thumb smeared with blood, he pushed the needle through the blue cloth of his air force tunic. His glasses were so misted over I couldn't make out whether he was crying or whether it just looked like it. I was close to tears myself: in two hours, three at most, we would be in Cologne, and from there it was not far to the one I had married, the one whose voice had never sounded like marriage.

THE WOMAN emerged suddenly from behind the freight shed, and before the guards knew what was happening, she was standing by our boxcar and unwrapping a blue cloth from what I first took to be a baby: a loaf of bread. She handed it to me, and I took it; it was heavy, I swayed for a moment and almost fell forward out of the train as it started moving. The bread was dark, still warm, and I wanted to call out "Thank you, thank you," but the words seemed ridiculous, and the train was moving faster now, so I stayed there on my knees with the heavy loaf in my arms. To this day all I know about the woman is that she was wearing a dark headscarf and was no longer young.

When I got up, clasping the loaf, it was quieter than ever in the boxcar; they were all looking at the bread, and under their stares it got heavier and heavier. I knew those eyes, I knew the mouths that belonged to those eyes, and for months I had been wondering where the borderline runs between hatred and contempt, and I hadn't found the borderline; for a while I had divided them up into sewers-on and non-sewers-on, when we had been transferred from an American camp (where the wearing of rank insignia was prohibited) to an English one (where the wearing of rank insignia was permitted), and I had felt a certain fellow feeling with the non-sewers-on till I found out they didn't even have any ranks whose insignia they could have sewn on. One of them, Egelhecht, had even tried to drum up a kind of court of honor that was to deny me the quality of being German (and I had wished that this court, which never convened, had actually had the power to deny me this quality). What they didn't know was that I hated them, Nazis and non-Nazis, not because of their sewing and their political views but because they were men, men of the same species as those I had had to spend the last six years with; the words "man" and "stupid" had become almost identical for me.

In the background Egelhecht's voice said, "The first German bread —and he of all people is the one to get it."

He sounded as if he was almost sobbing. I wasn't far off it myself either, but they would never understand that it wasn't just because of the bread, or because by now we had crossed the German border, it was mainly because, for the first time in eight months, I had for one moment felt a woman's hand on my arm.

"No doubt," said Egelhecht in a low voice, "you will even deny the bread the quality of being German."

"Yes, indeed," I said, "I shall employ a typical intellectual's trick and ask myself whether the flour this bread is made of doesn't perhaps come from Holland, England, or America. Here you are," I said. "Divide it up if you like."

Most of them I hated, many I didn't care about one way or the other, and Tom Thumb, who was now the last to join the ranks of the sewers-on, was beginning to be a nuisance; yet I felt it was the right thing to do, to share this loaf with them, I was sure it hadn't been meant only for me.

Egelhecht made his way slowly toward me: he was tall and thin, like me, and he was twenty-six, like me; for three months he had tried to make me see that a nationalist wasn't a Nazi, that the words "honor," "loyalty," "fatherland," "decency," could never lose their value—and I had always countered his impressive array of words with just five: Wilhelm II, Papen, Hindenburg, Blomberg, Keitel. It had infuriated him that I never mentioned Hitler, not even that May 1 when the sentry ran through the camp blaring through a megaphone, "Hitler's dead, Hitler's dead!"

"Go ahead," I said, "divide up the bread."

"Number off," said Egelhecht. I handed him the loaf, he took off his coat, laid it on the floor of the boxcar with the lining uppermost, smoothed the lining, and placed the bread on it, while the others numbered off around us. "Thirty-two," said Tom Thumb, then there was a silence. "Thirty-two," said Egelhecht, looking at me, for it was up to me to say thirty-three; but I didn't say it. I turned away and looked out at the highway with the old trees: Napoleon's poplars, Napoleon's elms, like the ones I had rested under with my brother when we rode from Weeze to the Dutch border on our bikes to buy chocolate and cigarettes cheap.

I could sense that those behind me were terribly offended; I saw the yellow road signs: "To Kalkar," "To Xanten," "To Geldern," heard behind me the sounds of Egelhecht's tin knife, felt the offendedness swelling like a thick cloud. They were always being offended for some reason or other. They were offended if an English guard offered them a cigarette, and they were offended if he did not; they were offended when I cursed Hitler, and Egelhecht was mortally offended when I did not curse Hitler; Tom Thumb had secretly read Benjamin and Brecht, Proust, Tucholsky, and Karl Kraus, and when we crossed the German border he was sewing on his ensign's piping. I took the cigarette out of my pocket I had got in exchange for my staff Pfc chevron, turned around, and sat down beside Tom Thumb. I watched Egelhecht dividing up the loaf: first he cut it in half, then the halves in quarters, then each quarter again in eight parts. This way there would be a nice fat chunk for each man, a dark cube of bread which I figured would weigh about two to three ounces.

Egelhecht was just quartering the last eighth, and each man, every one of them, knew that the ones who got the center pieces would get at least a quarter to a half ounce extra, because the loaf bulged in the middle and Egelhecht had cut the slices all the same thickness. But then he cut off the bulge of the two center slices and said, "Thirty-three—the youngest starts." Tom Thumb glanced at me, blushed, bent down, took a piece of bread, and put it directly into his mouth. Everything went smoothly till Bouvier, who had almost driven me crazy with his planes he was always talking about, had taken his piece of bread; now it should have been my turn, followed by Egelhecht, but I didn't move. I would have liked to light my cigarette, but I had no matches and nobody offered me one. Those who already had their bread were scared and stopped chewing; the ones who hadn't got their bread yet had no idea what was happening, but they understood: I didn't want to share the loaf with them. They were offended, while the others (who already had their bread) were merely embarrassed. I tried to look outside: at Napoleon's poplars, Napoleon's elms, at the tree-lined road with its gaps, with Dutch sky caught in the gaps, but my attempt to look unconcerned was not successful. I was scared of the fight that was bound to start now; I wasn't much good in a fight, and even if I had been it wouldn't have helped, they would have beaten me up the way they did in the camp near Brussels when I had said I would rather be a dead Jew than a live German. I took the cigarette out of my mouth, partly because it felt ridiculous, partly because I wanted to get it through the fight intact, and I looked at Tom Thumb, who, his face scarlet, was squatting on his heels beside me. Then Gugeler, whose turn it would have been after Egelhecht, took his piece of bread, put it directly into his mouth, and the others took theirs. There were three pieces left when the man came toward me whom I scarcely knew—he had not joined our tent till we were in the camp near Brussels. He was already old, nearly fifty, short, with a dark, scarred face, and whenever we began to quarrel he wouldn't say a word, he used to leave the tent and run along beside the barbed-wire fence like someone to whom this kind of trotting up and down is familiar. I didn't even know his first name; he wore some sort of faded tropical uniform, and civilian shoes. He came from the far end of the boxcar straight toward me, stopped in front of me, and said in a surprisingly gentle voice, "Take the bread"—and when I didn't, he shook his head and said, "You fellows have one hell of a talent for turning everything into a symbolic event. It's just bread, that's all, and the woman gave it to you, the woman—here you are." He picked up a piece of bread, pressed it into my right hand, which was hanging down helplessly, and squeezed my hand around it. His eyes were quite dark, not black, and his face wore the look of many prisons. I nodded, got my hand muscles moving so as to hold on to the bread; a deep sigh went through the car; Egelhecht took his bread, then the old man in the tropical uniform. "Damn it all," said the old fellow, "I've been away from Germany for twelve years. You're a crazy bunch, but I'm just beginning to understand you." Before I could put the bread into my mouth the train stopped, and we got out.

OPEN COUNTRY, turnip fields, no trees; a few Belgian guards with the lion of Flanders on their caps and collars ran along beside the train calling, "All out, everybody out!"

Tom Thumb remained beside me; he polished his glasses, looked at the station sign, and said, "Weeze—does this also convey something to you?"

"Yes," I said, "it lies north of Kevelaer and west of Xanten."

"Oh yes," he said, "Kevelaer—Heinrich Heine."

"And Xanten—Siegfried, in case you've forgotten."

Aunt Helen, I thought. Weeze. Why hadn't we gone straight through to Cologne? There wasn't much left of Weeze other than a spattering of red bricks showing through the treetops. Aunt Helen had owned a fair-sized shop in Weeze, a regular village store, and every morning she used to slip some money into our pockets so we could go boating on the river Niers or ride over to Kevelaer on our bikes; the sermons on Sunday in church, roundly berating the smugglers and adulterers.

"Let's go," said the Belgian guard. "Get a move on, or don't you want to get home?"

I went into the camp. First we had to file past an English officer who gave us a twenty-mark bill, for which we had to sign a receipt. Next we had to go to the doctor; he was a German, young, and grinned at us; he waited till twelve or fifteen of us were in the room, then said, "Anyone who is so sick that he can't go home today need only raise his hand." A few of us laughed at this terribly witty remark; then we filed past his table one by one, had our release papers stamped, and went out by the other door. I waited for a few moments by the open door and heard him say, "Anyone who is so sick that—," then moved on, heard the laughter when I was already at the far end of the corridor, and went to the next check point. This was an English corporal, standing out in the open next to an uncovered latrine. The corporal said, "Show me your paybooks and any papers you still have." He said this in German, and when they pulled out their paybooks, he pointed to the latrine and told them to throw the books into it, adding, "Down the hatch!" and then most of them laughed at this witticism. It had struck me anyway that Germans suddenly seemed to have a sense of humor, so long as it was foreign humor: in camp even Egelhecht had laughed at the American captain who had pointed to the barbed-wire entanglement and said, "Don't take it so hard, boys, now you're free at last."

The English corporal asked me too about my papers, but all I had was my release; I had sold my paybook to an American for two cigarettes. So I said, "No papers"—and that made him as angry as the American corporal had been when I had answered his question, "Hitler Youth, SA, or Party?" with "No." He had yelled at me and put me on KP, he had sworn at me and accused my grandmother of various sexual offenses the nature of which, due to my insufficient knowledge of the American language, I was unable to ascertain. It made them furious when something didn't fit into their stereotyped categories. The English corporal went purple with rage, stood up, and began to frisk me, and he didn't have to search long before he had found my diary. It was thick, cut from paper bags, stapled together, and in it I had written down everything that had happened to me from the middle of April till the end of September: from being taken prisoner by the American sergeant Stevenson to the final entry I had made in the train as we went through dismal Antwerp and I read on walls *"Vive le Roi!"* There were more than a hundred paper-bag pages, closely written, and the furious corporal took it from me, threw it into the latrine, and said, "Didn't I ask you for your papers?" Then I was allowed to go.

WE STOOD crowded around the camp gate waiting for the Belgian trucks which were supposed to take us to Bonn. Bonn? Why Bonn, of all places? Someone said Cologne was closed off because it was contaminated by corpses, and someone else said we would have to clear away rubble for thirty or forty years, rubble, ruins, "and they aren't even going to give us trucks, we'll have to carry away the rubble in baskets." Luckily there was no one near me who I had shared a tent or sat in the boxcar with. The drivel coming from mouths I did not know was a shade less disgusting than if it had come from mouths I knew. Someone ahead of me said, "But then he didn't mind taking the loaf of bread from the Jew," and another voice said, "Yes, they're the kind of people who are going to set the tone." Someone nudged me from behind and asked, "Four ounces of bread for a cigarette, how about it, eh?" and from behind he thrust his hand in front of my face, and I saw it was one of the pieces of bread Egelhecht had divided up in the train. I shook my head. Someone else said, "The Belgians are selling cigarettes at ten marks apiece." To me that seemed very cheap:

in camp the Germans had sold cigarettes for a hundred and twenty marks apiece. "Cigarettes, anyone?" "Yes," I said, and put my twenty-mark bill into an anonymous hand.

Everyone was trading with everyone else. It was the only thing that seriously interested them. For two thousand marks and a threadbare uniform someone got a civilian suit, the deal was concluded, and clothes were changed somewhere in the waiting crowd, and suddenly I heard someone call out, "But of *course* the underpants go with the suit—and the tie too." Someone sold his wristwatch for three thousand marks. The chief article of trade was soap. Those who had been in American camps had a lot of soap—twenty cakes, some of them—for they had been given soap every week but never any water to wash in, and the ones who had been in the English camps had no soap at all. The green and pink cakes of soap went back and forth. Some of the men had discovered their artistic aspirations and shaped the soap into little dogs, cats, and gnomes, and now it turned out that the artistic aspirations had lowered the exchange value. Unsculptured soap rated higher than sculptured, a loss of weight being suspected in the latter.

The anonymous hand into which I had placed the twenty-mark bill actually reappeared and pressed two cigarettes into my left hand, and I was almost touched by so much honesty (but I was almost touched only till I found out that the Belgians were selling cigarettes for five marks; a hundred-percent profit was evidently regarded as a fair markup, especially among "comrades"). We stood there for about two hours, jammed together, and all I remember is hands: trading hands, passing soap from right to left, from left to right, money from left to right and again from right to left; it was as if I had fallen into a snakepit; hands from all sides moved every which way, passing goods and money over my shoulders and over my head in every direction.

Tom Thumb had managed to get close to me again. He sat beside me on the floor of the Belgian truck driving to Kevelaer, through Kevelaer, to Krefeld, around Krefeld to Neuss; there was silence over the fields, in the towns, we saw hardly a soul and only a few animals, and the dark autumn sky hung low. On my left sat Tom Thumb, on my right the Belgian guard, and we looked out over the tailboard at the road I knew so well: my brother and I had often ridden our bicycles along it. Tom Thumb kept trying to justify himself, but I cut him off every time, and he kept trying to be clever; there was no stopping him. "But Neuss," he said, "that can't remind you of anything. What on earth could Neuss remind anybody of?"

"Novesia Chocolate," I said, "sauerkraut, and Quirinus, but I don't suppose you ever heard of the Thebaic Legion."

"No, I haven't," he said, and blushed again.

I asked the Belgian guard if it was true that Cologne was closed off, contaminated by corpses, and he said, "No—but it's a mess all right; is that where you're from?"

"Yes," I said.

"Be prepared for the worst . . . do you have any soap left?"

"Yes, I have," I said.

"Here," he said, pulling a pack of tobacco out of his pocket. He opened it and held out the pale-yellow, fresh, fine-cut tobacco for me to smell. "It's yours for two cakes of soap—fair enough?"

I nodded, felt around in my coat pocket for the soap, gave him two cakes, and put the tobacco in my pocket. He gave me his submachine gun to hold while he hid the soap in his pockets; he sighed as I handed it back to him. "These lousy things," he said, "we'll have to go on carrying them around for a while yet. You fellows aren't half as badly off as you think. What are you crying about?"

I pointed toward the right: the Rhine. We were approaching Dormagen. I saw that Tom Thumb was about to open his mouth and said quickly, "For God's sake shut up, can't you? Shut up." He had probably wanted to ask me whether the Rhine reminded me of anything. Thank God he was deeply offended now and said no more till we got to Bonn.

In Cologne there were actually some houses still standing; somewhere I even saw a moving streetcar, some people too, women even: one of them saved to us. From the Neuss-Strasse we turned into the Ring avenues and drove along them, and I was waiting all the time for the tears, but they didn't come; even the insurance buildings on the avenue were in ruins, and all I could see of the Hohenstaufen Baths was a few pale-blue tiles. I was hoping all the time the truck would turn off somewhere to the right, for we had lived on the Carolingian Ring; but the truck did not turn. It drove down the Rings—Barbarossa Square, Saxon Ring, Salian Ring—and I tried not to look, and I wouldn't have looked if the truck convoy had not got into a traffic jam up front at Clovis Square and we hadn't stopped in front of the house we used to live in, so I did look.

The term "totally destroyed" is misleading: only in rare cases is it possible to destroy a house totally. It has to be hit three or four times and, to make certain, it should then burn down; the house we used to live in was actually, according to official terminology, totally destroyed, but not in the technical sense. That is to say, I could still recognize it; the front door and the doorbells, and I submit that a house where it is still possible to recognize the front door and the doorbells has not, in the strict technical sense, been totally destroyed. But of the house we used to live in there was more to be recognized than the doorbells and the front door. Two rooms in the basement were almost intact, on the mezzanine, absurdly enough, even three: a fragment of wall was supporting the third room that would probably not have passed a spirit-level test; our apartment on the second floor had only one room intact, but it was gaping open in front, toward the street; above this, a high, narrow gable reared up, bare, with empty window sockets. However, the interesting thing was that two men were moving around in our living room as if their feet were on familiar ground; one of the men took a picture down from the wall, the Terborch print my father had been so fond of, walked to the front, carrying the picture, and showed it to a third man who was standing down below in front of the house. This third man shook his head like someone who is not interested in an object being auctioned, and the man up above walked back with the Terborch and hung it up again on the wall; he even straightened the picture—I was touched by this mark of neatness—stepped back to make sure the picture was really hanging straight, then nodded in a satisfied way. Meanwhile the second man took the other picture off the wall: an engraving of Lochner's painting of the cathedral, but this one also did not appear to please the third man standing down below. Finally the first man, the one who had hung the Terborch back on the wall, came to the front, formed a megaphone with his hands, and shouted, "Piano in sight!" and the man below laughed, nodded, likewise formed a megaphone with hands, and shouted, "I'll get the straps." I could not see the piano, but I knew where it stood: on the right in the corner I couldn't see into and where the man with the Lochner picture was just disappearing.

"Whereabouts in Cologne did you live?" asked the Belgian guard.

"Oh, somewhere over there," I said, gesturing vaguely in the direction of the western suburbs.

"Thank God, now we're moving again," said the guard. He picked up his submachine gun, which he had placed on the floor of the truck, and straightened his cap. The lion of Flanders on the front of his cap was rather dirty. As we turned into Clovis Square, I could see why there had been a traffic jam: some kind of raid seemed to be going on. English military police cars were all over the place, and civilians were standing in them with their hands up, surrounded by a sizable crowd, quiet yet tense. A surprisingly large number of people in such a silent, ruined city.

"That's the black market," said the Belgian guard. "Once in a while they come and clean it up."

BEFORE WE were even out of Cologne, while we were still on the Bonn-Strasse, I fell asleep and I dreamed of my mother's coffee mill: the coffee mill was being let down on a strap by the man who had offered the Terborch without success, but the man below rejected the coffee mill; the other man drew it up again, opened the hall door, and tried to screw the coffee mill back where it had hung before, immediately to the left of the kitchen door, but now there was no wall there for him to screw it onto, and still the man kept on trying (this mark of tidiness touched me even in my dream). He searched with the forefinger of his right hand for the pegs, couldn't find them, and raised his fist threateningly to the gray autumn sky which offered no support for the coffee mill. Finally he gave up, tied the strap around the mill again, went to the front, let down the coffee mill, and offered it to the third man, who again rejected it, and the other man pulled it up again, untied the strap, and hid the coffee mill under his jacket as if it were a valuable object; then he began to wind up the strap, rolled it into a coil, and threw it down into the third man's face. All this time I was worried about what could have happened to the man who had offered the Lochner without success, but I couldn't see him anywhere; something was preventing me from looking into the corner where the piano was, my father's desk, and I was upset at the thought that he might be reading my father's diaries. Now the man with the coffee mill was standing by the living-room door trying to screw the coffee mill onto the door panel; he seemed absolutely determined to give the coffee mill a permanent resting place, and I was beginning to like him, even before I discovered he was one of our many friends whom my mother had comforted while they sat on the chair beneath the coffee mill, one of those who had been killed right at the beginning of the war in an air raid.

Before we got to Bonn, the Belgian guard woke me up. "Come on," he said, "rub your eyes, freedom is at hand," and I straightened up and thought of all the people who had sat on the chair beneath my mother's coffee mill: truant schoolboys whom she helped to overcome their fear of exams, Nazis whom she tried to enlighten, non-Nazis whom she tried to fortify—they had all sat on the chair beneath the coffee mill, had received comfort and censure, defense and respite. Bitter words had destroyed their ideals and gentle words had offered them those things which would outlive the times: mercy to the weak, comfort to the persecuted.

The old cemetery, the market square, the university. Bonn. Through the Koblenz Gate and into the park. "So long," said the Belgian guard, and Tom Thumb with his tired child's face said, "Drop me a line some time."

"All right," I said, "I'll send you my complete Tucholsky."

"Wonderful," he said, "and your Kleist too?"

"No," I said, "only the ones I have duplicates of."

ON THE other side of the barricade through which we were finally released, a man was standing between two big laundry baskets; in one he had a lot of apples, in the other a few cakes of soap. He shouted, "Vitamins, my friends, one apple—one cake of soap!" And I could feel my mouth watering. I had quite forgotten what apples looked like; I gave him a cake of soap, was handed an apple, and bit into it at once. I stood there watching the others come out; there was no need for him to call out now: it was a wordless exchange. He would take an apple out of the basket, be handed a cake of soap, and throw the soap into the empty basket; there was a dull thud when the soap landed. Not everyone took an apple, not everyone had any soap, but the transaction was as swift as in a self-service store, and by the time I had just finished my apple, he already had his soap basket half full. The whole thing took place swiftly and smoothly and without a word; even the ones who were very economical and very calculating couldn't resist the sight of the apples, and I began to feel sorry for them. Home was welcoming its homecomers so warmly with vitamins.

IT TOOK me a long time to find a phone in Bonn; finally a girl in the post office told me that the only people to get phones were doctors and priests, and even then only those who hadn't been Nazis. "They're scared stiff of the Nazi Werewolf underground," she said. "I s'pose you wouldn't have a cigarette for me?" I took my pack of tobacco out of my pocket and said, "Shall I roll one for you?", but she said no, she could do it herself, and I watched her take a cigarette paper out of her coat pocket and quickly and deftly roll herself a firm cigarette. "Who do you want to call?" she said, and I said, "My wife," and she laughed and said I didn't look married at all. I also rolled myself a cigarette and asked her whether there was any chance of selling some soap: I needed money, train fare, and didn't have a pfennig. "Soap," she said, "let's have a look." I felt around in my coat lining and pulled out some soap, and she snatched it out of my hand, sniffed it, and said, "Real Palmolive! That's worth—worth—I'll give you fifty marks for it." I looked at her in amazement, and she said, "Yes, I know, you can get as much as eighty for it, but I can't afford that." I didn't want to take the fifty marks, but she insisted, she thrust the note into my coat pocket and ran out of the post office; she was quite pretty, with that hungry prettiness which lends a girl's voice a certain sharpness.

What struck me most of all, in the post office and as I walked slowly on through Bonn, was the fact that nowhere was there a student wearing colored ribbons; and the smells: everyone smelled terrible, all the rooms smelled terrible, and I could see why the girl was so crazy about the soap. I went to the station, tried to find out how I could get to Oberkerschenbach (that was where the one I married lived), but nobody could tell me; all I knew was that it was a little place somewhere in the Eifel district not too far from Bonn. There weren't any maps anywhere either, where I could have looked it up; no doubt they had been banned on account of the Nazi Werewolves. I always like to know where a place is, and it bothered me that I knew nothing definite about this place Oberkerschenbach and couldn't find out anything definite. In my mind I went over all the Bonn addresses I knew, but there wasn't a single doctor or a single priest among them; finally I remembered a professor of theology I had called on with a friend just before the war. He had had some sort of trouble with Rome and the Index, and we had gone to see him simply to give him our moral support; I couldn't remember the name of the street, but I knew where it was, and I walked along the Poppelsdorf Avenue, turned left, then left again, found the house, and was relieved to read the name on the door.

The professor came to the door himself. He had aged a great deal, he was thin and bent, his hair quite white. I said, "You won't remember me, Professor. I came to see you some years ago when you had that stink with Rome and the Index—can I speak to you for a moment?" He laughed when I said stink, and said, "Of course," when I had finished, and I followed him into his study; I noticed it no longer smelled of tobacco, otherwise it was still just the same, with all the books, files, and house plants. I told the professor I had heard that the only people who got phones were priests and doctors, and I simply had to call my wife. He heard me out—a very rare thing—then said that, although he was a priest, he was not one of those who had a phone, for "You see," he said, "I am not a pastor." "Perhaps you're a Werewolf," I said. I offered him some tobacco, and I felt sorry for him when I saw how he looked at my tobacco; I am always sorry for old people who have to go without something they like. His hands trembled as he filled his pipe, and they did not tremble just because he was old. When he had at last got it lit—I had no matches and couldn't help him—he told me that doctors and priests were not the only people with phones. "These nightclubs they're opening up everywhere for the soldiers," they had them too, and I might try in one of these nightclubs; there was one just around the corner. He wept when I put a few pipefuls of tobacco on his desk as I left, and he asked me as his tears fell whether I knew what I was doing, and I said, yes, I knew, and I suggested he accept the few pipefuls of tobacco as a belated tribute to the courage he had shown toward Rome all those years ago. I would have liked to give him some soap as well, I still had five or six pieces in my coat lining, but I was afraid his heart would burst with joy; he was so old and frail.

"NIGHTCLUB" was a nice way of putting it, but I didn't mind that so much as the English sentry at the door of this nightclub. He was very young and eyed me severely as I stopped beside him. He pointed to the notice prohibiting Germans from entering this nightclub, but I told him my sister worked there, I had just returned to my beloved fatherland, and my sister had the house key. He asked me what my sister's name was, and it seemed safest to give the most German of all German girls' names, so I said, "Gretchen." Oh yes, he said, that was the blond one, and let me go in. Instead of bothering to describe the interior, I refer the reader to the pertinent "Fräulein literature" and to movies and TV. I won't even bother to describe Gretchen (see above). The main thing was that Gretchen was surprisingly quick on the uptake and, in exchange for a cake of Palmolive, was willing to make a phone call to the priest's house in Kerschenbach (which I hoped existed) and have the one I had married called to the phone. Gretchen spoke fluent English on the phone and told me her boyfriend would try to do it through the army exchange, it would be quicker. While we were waiting, I offered her some tobacco, but she had something better; I tried to pay her the agreed fee of a cake of soap in advance, but she said no, she didn't want it after all, she would rather not take anything, and when I insisted on paying she began to cry and confided that one of her brothers was a prisoner of war, the other one dead, and I felt sorry for her, for it is not pleasant when girls like Gretchen cry. She even let on that she was a Catholic, and just as she was about to get her first communion picture out of a drawer the phone rang, and Gretchen lifted the receiver and said "Reverend," but I had already heard that it was not a man's voice. "Just a moment," Gretchen said, and handed me the receiver. I was so excited I couldn't hold the receiver; in fact, I dropped it, fortunately onto Gretchen's lap. She picked it up, held it against my ear, and I said, "Hello —is that you?"

"Yes," she said. "Darling, where are you?"

"I'm in Bonn," I said. "The war's over—for me."

"My God," she said, "I can't believe it. No—it's not true."

"It is true," I said, "it is—did you get my postcard?"

"No," she said, "what postcard?"

"When we were taken prisoner, we were allowed to write one postcard."

"No," she said, "for the last eight months I haven't had the slightest idea where you were."

"Those bastards," I said, "those dirty bastards. Listen, just tell me where Kerschenbach is."

"I"—she was crying so hard she couldn't speak, I heard her sobbing and gulping till at last she was able to whisper—"at the station in Bonn, I'll meet you," then I could no longer hear her, someone said something in English that I didn't understand.

Gretchen put the receiver to her ear, listened a moment, shook her head, and replaced it. I looked at her and knew I couldn't offer her the soap now. I couldn't even say "Thank you," the words seemed ridiculous. I lifted my arms helplessly and went out.

I walked back to the station, in my ear the woman's voice which had never sounded like marriage.

The Thrower-Away

FOR THE last few weeks I have been trying to avoid people who might ask me what I do for a living. If I really had to put a name to my occupation, I would be forced to utter a word that would alarm people. So I prefer the abstract method of putting down my confession on paper.

Until recently I would have been prepared at any time to make an oral confession. I almost insisted. I called myself an inventor, a scholar, even a student, and, in the melodramatic mood of incipient intoxication, an unrecognized genius. I basked in the cheerful fame which a frayed collar can radiate; arrogantly, as if it were mine by right, I exacted reluctant credit from suspicious shopkeepers who watched margarine, ersatz coffee, and cheap tobacco disappear into my pockets; I reveled in my unkempt appearance, and at breakfast, lunch, and dinner I drank the nectar of bohemian life: the bliss of knowing one is not conforming.

But for the past few weeks I have been boarding the streetcar every morning just before seven-thirty at the corner of the Roonstrasse; like everyone else I meekly hold out my season ticket to the conductor. I have on a gray double-breasted suit, a striped shirt, a dark-green tie, I carry my sandwiches in a flat aluminum box and hold the morning paper, lightly rolled, in my hand. I look like a citizen who has managed to avoid introspection. After the third stop I get up to offer my seat to one of the elderly working women who have got on at the housing settlement. Having sacrificed my seat on the altar of social compassion, I continue to read the newspaper standing up, now and again letting myself be heard in the capacity of arbitrator when morning irritation is inclined to make people unjust. I correct the worst political and historical errors (by explaining, for instance, that there is a certain difference between SA and USA); as soon as anyone puts a cigarette to his lips, I discreetly hold my lighter in front of his nose and, with the aid of the tiny but dependable flame, light his morning cigarette for him. Thus I complete the picture of a well-groomed fellow citizen who is still young enough for people to say he "has nice manners."

I seem to have been successful in donning the mask that makes it impossible to ask me about my occupation. I am evidently taken for an educated businessman dealing in attractively packaged and agreeably smelling articles such as coffee, tea, or spices, or in valuable small objects which are pleasing to the eye such as jewelry or watches; a man who practices his profession in a nice old-fashioned office with dark oil paintings of merchant forebears hanging on the walls, who phones his wife about ten, who knows how to imbue his apparently impassive voice with that hint of tenderness which betrays affection and concern. Since I also participate in the usual jokes and do not refrain from laughing when every morning at the Lohengrinstrasse the clerk from City Hall shouts out "When does the next swan leave?", since I do not withhold my comments concerning either the events of the day or the results of the football pools, I am obviously regarded as someone who, although prosperous (as can be seen from his suit material), has an attitude toward life that is deeply rooted in the principles of democracy. An air of integrity encases me the way the glass coffin encased Snow White.

When a passing truck provides the streetcar window with a background for a moment, I check up on the expression on my face: isn't it perhaps rather too pensive, almost verging on the sorrowful? I assiduously erase the remnants of brooding and do my best to give my face the expression I want it to wear: neither reserved nor familiar, neither superficial nor profound.

My camouflage seems to be successful, for when I get out at the Marienplatz and dive into the maze of streets in the Old Town, where there is no lack of nice old-fashioned offices, where notaries and lawyers abound, no one suspects that I pass through a rear entrance into the UBIA building—a firm that can boast of supporting three hundred fifty people and of insuring the lives of four hundred thousand. The commissionaire greets me with a smile at the delivery entrance, I walk past him, go down to the basement, and start in on my work, which has to be completed by the time the employees come pouring into the offices at eight-thirty. The activity that I pursue every morning between eight and eight-thirty in the basement of this respected establishment is devoted entirely to destruction. I throw away.

It took me years to invent my profession, to endow it with mathematical plausibility. I wrote treatises; graphs and charts covered—and still cover—the walls of my apartment. For years I climbed along abscissas and up ordinates, wallowed in theories, and savored the glacial ecstasy of solving formulas. Yet since practicing my profession and seeing my theories come to life, I am filled with a sense of sadness such as may come over a general who finds himself obliged to descend from the heights of strategy to the plains of tactics.

I enter my workroom, exchange my jacket for a gray smock, and immediately set to work. I open the mailbags which the commissionaire has already picked up earlier from the main post office, and I empty them into the two wooden bins which, constructed according to my design, hang to the right and left on the wall over my worktable. This way I only need to stretch out my hands, somewhat like a swimmer, and begin swiftly to sort the mail.

First I separate the circulars from the letters, a purely routine job, since a glance at the postage suffices. At this stage a knowledge of the postal tariff renders hesitation unnecessary. After years of practice I am able to complete this phase within half an hour, and by this time it is half past eight and I can hear the footsteps of the employees pouring into the offices overhead. I ring for the commissionaire, who takes the sorted letters to the various departments. It never fails to sadden me, the sight of the commissionaire carrying off in a metal tray the size of a briefcase the remains of what had once filled three mailbags. I might feel triumphant, for this, the vindication of my theory of throwing away, has for years been the objective of my private research; but, strangely enough, I do not feel triumphant. To have been right is by no means always a reason for rejoicing.

After the departure of the commissionaire there remains the task of examining the huge pile of printed matter to make sure it contains no letter masquerading behind the wrong postage, no bill mailed as a circular. This work is almost always superfluous, for the probity of the mailing public is nothing short of astounding. I must admit that here my calculations were incorrect: I had overestimated the number of postal defrauders.

Rarely has a postcard, a letter, or a bill sent as printed matter escaped my notice; about half past nine I ring for the commissionaire, who takes the remaining objects of my careful scrutiny to the departments.

The time has now come when I require some refreshment. The commissionaire's wife brings me my coffee, I take my sandwich out of the flat aluminum box, sit down for my break, and chat with the commissionaire's wife about her children. Is Alfred doing somewhat better in arithmetic? Has Gertrude been able to catch up in spelling? Alfred is not doing any better in arithmetic, whereas Gertrude has been able to catch up in spelling. Have the tomatoes ripened properly, are the rabbits plump, and was the experiment with the melons successful? The tomatoes have not ripened properly, but the rabbits are plump, while the experiment with the melons is still undecided. Serious problems, such as whether one should stock up on potatoes or not, matters of education, such as whether one should enlighten one's children or be enlightened by them, are the subjects of our intense consideration.

Just before eleven the commissionaire's wife leaves, and usually she asks me to let her have some travel folders. She is collecting them, and I smile at her enthusiasm, for I have retained tender memories of travel folders. As a child I also collected travel folders, I used to fish them out of my father's wastepaper basket. Even as a boy it bothered me that my father would take mail from the mailman and throw it into the wastepaper basket without looking at it. This action wounded my innate propensity for economy: there was something that had been designed, set up, printed, put in an envelope, and stamped, that had passed through the mysterious channels by which the postal service actually causes our mail to arrive at our addresses; it was weighted with the sweat of the draftsman, the writer, the printer, the office boy who had stuck on the stamps; on various levels and in various tariffs it had cost money. All this only to end—without being deemed worthy of so much as a glance—in a wastepaper basket?

At the age of eleven I had already adopted the habit of taking out of the wastepaper basket, as soon as my father had left for the office, whatever had been thrown away. I would study it, sort it, and put it away in a chest which I used to keep toys in. Thus by the time I was twelve I already possessed an imposing collection of wine-merchants' catalogues, as well as prospectuses on naturopathy and natural history. My collection of travel folders assumed the dimensions of a geographical encyclopedia —Dalmatia was as familiar to me as the Norwegian fjords, Scotland as close as Zakopane, the forests of Bohemia soothed me while the waves of the Atlantic disquieted me—hinges were offered me, houses and buttons, political parties asked for my vote, charities for my money; lotteries promised me riches, religious sects poverty. I leave it to the reader's imagination to picture what my collection was like when at the age of seventeen, suddenly bored with it all, I offered my collection to a junk dealer who paid me seven marks and sixty pfennigs for it.

Having finished school, I embarked in my father's footsteps and set my foot on the first rung of the civil service ladder. With the seven marks and sixty pfennigs I bought a package of squared paper and three colored crayons, and my attempt to gain a foothold in the civil service turned into a laborious detour, for a happy thrower-away was slumbering in me while I filled the role of an unhappy junior clerk. All my free time was devoted to intricate calculations.

Stopwatch, pencil, slide rule, graph paper, these were the props of my obsession; I calculated how long it took to open a circular of small, medium, or large size, with or without pictures, give it a quick glance, satisfy oneself of its uselessness, and then throw it in the wastepaper basket, a process requiring a minimum of five seconds and a maximum of twenty-five. If the circular is at all attractive, either the text or the pictures, several minutes, often a quarter of an hour, must be allowed for this. By conducting bogus negotiations with printing firms, I also worked out the minimum production costs for circulars. Indefatigably I checked the results of my studies and adjusted them (it did not occur to me until two years later that the time of the cleaning women who have to empty the wastepaper baskets had to be included in my calculations); I applied the results of my research to firms with ten, twenty, a hundred or more employees; and I arrived at results that an expert on economics would not have hesitated to describe as alarming.

Obeying my sense of loyalty, I began by offering my results to my superiors; although I had reckoned with the possibility of ingratitude, I was nevertheless shocked at the extent of that ingratitude. I was accused of neglecting my duties, suspected of nihilism, pronounced "a mental case," and discharged. To the great sorrow of my kind parents, I abandoned my promising career, began new ones, broke these off too, forsook the warmth of the parental hearth, and, as I have already said, eked out my existence as an unrecognized genius. I took pleasure in the humiliation of vainly peddling my invention, and spent years in a blissful state of being antisocial, so consistently that my punch card in the central files, which had long ago been punched with the symbol for "mental case," was now stamped with the confidential symbol for "antisocial."

In view of these circumstances, it can readily be imagined what a shock it was when the obviousness of my results at last became obvious to someone else—the manager of UBIA—how deeply humiliated I was to have to wear a dark-green tie, yet I must continue to go around in disguise as I am terrified of being found out. I try anxiously to give my face the proper expression when I laugh at the Lohengrin joke, since there is no greater vanity than that of the wags who populate the streetcar every morning. Sometimes too I am afraid the streetcar may be full of people who the previous day have done work I am about to destroy that very morning: printers, typesetters, draftsmen, writers who compose the wording of advertisements, commercial artists, envelope stuffers, packers, apprentices of all kinds. From eight to eight-thirty every morning I ruthlessly destroy the products of respected paper mills, worthy printing establishments, brilliant commercial artists, the texts of talented writers; coated paper, glossy paper, copperplate, I take it all, just as it comes from the mailbag, and without the faintest sentimentality tie it up into handy bundles for the wastepaper dealer. In the space of one hour I destroy the output of two hundred man-hours and save UBIA a further one hundred hours, so that altogether (here I must lapse into my own jargon) I achieve a concentrate of 1:300.

When the commissionaire's wife leaves with the empty coffeepot and the travel folders, I knock off. I wash my hands, exchange my smock for my jacket, pick up the morning paper, and leave the UBIA building by the rear entrance. I stroll through the town and wonder how I can escape from tactics and get back into strategy. What intoxicated me as a formula I find disappointing, since it can be performed so easily. Strategy translated into action can be carried out by hacks. I shall probably establish schools for throwers-away. I may possibly also attempt to have throwers-away placed in post offices, perhaps even in printing establishments; an enormous amount of energy, valuable commodities, and intelligence could be utilized, as well as postage saved; it might even be feasible to conceive, compose, and set brochures up in type but not print them. These are all problems still requiring a lot of study.

However, the mere throwing away of mail as such has almost ceased to interest me; any improvements on that level can be worked out by means of the basic formula. For a long time now I have been devoting my attention to calculations concerning wrapping paper and the process of wrapping: this is virgin territory, where nothing has been done, here one can strive to spare humanity those unprofitable efforts under the burden of which it is groaning. Every day billions of throwing-away movements are made, energies are dissipated which, could they but be utilized, would suffice to change the face of the earth. It would be a great advantage if one were permitted to undertake experiments in department stores; should one dispense with the wrapping process altogether, or should one post an expert thrower-away right next to the wrapping table who unwraps what has just been wrapped and immediately ties the wrapping paper into bundles for the wastepaper dealer? These are problems meriting some thought. In any case it has struck me that in many shops the customers implore the clerk not to wrap the purchased article, but that they have to submit to having it wrapped. Clinics for nervous diseases are rapidly filling with patients who complain of an attack of nerves whenever they unwrap a bottle of perfume or a box of chocolates, or open a pack of cigarettes, and at the moment I am making an intensive study of a young man from my neighborhood who earned his living as a book reviewer but at times was unable to practice his profession because he found it impossible to undo the twisted wire tied around the parcel, and even when he did find himself equal to this physical exertion, he was incapable of penetrating the massive layer of gummed paper with which the corrugated paper is stuck together. The man appears deeply disturbed and has now gone over to reviewing the books unread and placing the parcels on his bookshelves without unwrapping them. I leave it to the reader's imagination to depict for himself the effect of such a case on our intellectual life.

While walking through the town between eleven and one, I observe all sorts of details: I spend some time unobtrusively in the department stores, hovering around the wrapping tables; I stand in front of tobacco shops and pharmacies and note down minor statistics; now and again I even purchase something, so as to allow the senseless procedure to be performed on myself and to discover how much effort is required actually to take possession of the article one wishes to own.

So between eleven and one in my impeccable suit I complete the picture of a man who is sufficiently prosperous to afford a bit of leisure —who at about one o'clock enters a sophisticated little restaurant, casually chooses the most expensive meal, and scribbles some hieroglyphics on his beer coaster which could equally well be stock quotations or flights of poetry; who knows how to praise or decry the quality of the meat with arguments which betray the connoisseur to even the most blasé waiter; who, when it comes to choosing dessert, hesitates with a knowing air between cake, ice cream, and cheese; and who finishes off his scribblings with a flourish which proves that they were stock quotations after all.

Shocked at the results of my calculations, I leave the little restaurant. My expression becomes more and more thoughtful while I search for a small café where I can pass the time till three o'clock and read the evening paper. At three I reenter the UBIA building by the rear door to take care of the afternoon mail, which consists almost exclusively of circulars. It is a matter of scarcely fifteen minutes to pick out the ten or twelve letters; I don't even have to wash my hands after this; I just brush them off, take the letters to the commissionaire, leave the building, and at the Marienplatz board the streetcar, glad that on the way home I do not need to laugh at the Lohengrin joke. When the dark tarpaulin of a passing truck makes a background for the streetcar window, I can see my face. It is relaxed; that is to say, pensive, almost brooding, and I relish the fact that I do not have to put on any other face, for at this hour none of my morning fellow travelers has finished work. I get out at the Roonstrasse, buy some fresh rolls, a piece of cheese or sausage, some ground coffee, and walk up to my little apartment, the walls of which are hung with graphs and charts, with hectic curves: between the abscissas and ordinates I capture the lines of a fever going up and up; not a single one of my curves goes down, not a single one of my formulas has the power to soothe me. I groan under the burden of my vision of economics, and while the water is boiling for the coffee I place my slide rule, my notes, pencil, and paper in readiness.

My apartment is sparsely furnished, it looks more like a laboratory. I drink my coffee standing up and hastily swallow a sandwich, the epicure I was at noon is now a thing of the past. Wash hands, light a cigarette, then I set my stopwatch and unwrap the nerve tonic I bought that morning on my stroll through the town—outer wrapping paper, cellophane covering, carton, inside wrapping paper, directions for use secured by a rubber band: thirty-seven seconds. The nervous energy consumed in unwrapping exceeds the nervous energy which the tonic promises to impart to me, but there may be subjective reasons for this which I shall disregard in my calculations. One thing is certain: the wrapping is worth more than the contents, and the cost of the twenty-five yellow tablets is out of all proportion to their value. But these are considerations verging on the moral aspect, and I would prefer to keep away from morality altogether. My field of speculation is one of pure economics.

Numerous articles are waiting to be unwrapped by me, many slips of paper are waiting to be evaluated; green, red, blue ink, everything is ready. It is usually late by the time I get to bed, and as I fall asleep I am haunted by my formulas, whole worlds of useless paper roll over me; some formulas explode like dynamite, the noise of the explosion sounds like a burst of laughter: it is my own, my laughter at the Lohengrin joke originating in my fear of the clerk from City Hall. Perhaps he has access to the punch-card file, has picked out my card, discovered that it contains not only the symbol for "mental case" but the second, more dangerous one for "antisocial." There is nothing more difficult to fill than a tiny hole like that in a punch card; perhaps my laughter at the Lohengrin joke is the price I have to pay for my anonymity. I would not like to admit face to face what I find easier to do in writing: that I am a thrower-away.

Unexpected Guests

I HAVE NOTHING against animals; on the contrary, I like them, and I enjoy caressing our dog's coat in the evening while the cat sits on my lap. It gives me pleasure to watch the children feeding the tortoise in the corner of the living room. I have even grown fond of the baby hippopotamus we keep in our bathtub, and the rabbits running around loose in our apartment have long ceased to worry me. Besides, I am used to coming home in the evening and finding an unexpected visitor: a cheeping baby chick, or a stray dog my wife has taken in. For my wife is a good woman, she never turns anyone away from the door, neither man nor beast, and for many years now our children's evening prayers have wound up with the words: O Lord, please send us beggars and animals.

What is really worse is that my wife cannot say no to hawkers and peddlers, with the result that things accumulate in our home which I regard as superfluous—soap, razor blades, brushes, and darning wool—and lying around in drawers are documents which cause me some concern: an assortment of insurance policies and purchase agreements. My sons are insured for their education, my daughters for their trousseaux, but we cannot feed them with either darning wool or soap until they get married or graduate, and it is only in exceptional cases that razor blades are beneficial to the human system.

It will be readily understood, therefore, that now and again I show signs of slight impatience, although generally speaking I am known to be a quiet man. I often catch myself looking enviously at the rabbits who have made themselves at home under the table, munching away peacefully at their carrots, and the stupid gaze of the hippopotamus, who is hastening the accumulation of silt in our bathtub, causes me at times to stick out my tongue at him. And the tortoise stoically eating its way through lettuce leaves has not the slightest notion of the anxieties that swell my breast: the longing for some fresh, fragrant coffee, for tobacco, bread, and eggs, and the comforting warmth engendered by a schnapps in the throats of careworn men. My sole comfort at such times is Billy, our dog, who, like me, is yawning with hunger. If, on top of all this, unexpected guests arrive—men unshaven like myself, or mothers with babies who get fed warm milk and moistened zwieback—I have to get a grip on myself if I am to keep my temper. But I do keep it, because by this time it is practically the only thing I have left.

There are days when the mere sight of freshly boiled, snowy potatoes makes my mouth water; for—although I confess this reluctantly and with deep embarrassment—it is a long time since we have enjoyed "good home cooking." Our only meals are improvised ones of which we partake from time to time, standing up, surrounded by animals and human guests.

Fortunately it will be a while before my wife can buy useless articles again, for we have no more cash, my wages have been attached for an indefinite period, and I myself am reduced to spending the evenings going around the distant suburbs, in clothing that makes me unrecognizable, selling razor blades, soap, and buttons far below cost; for our situation has become grave. Nevertheless, we own several hundredweight of soap, thousands of razor blades, and buttons of every description, and toward midnight I stagger into the house and go through my pockets for money; my children, my animals, my wife stand around me with shining eyes, for I have usually bought some things on the way home: bread, apples, lard, coffee, and potatoes—the latter, by the way, in great demand among the children as well as the animals—and during the nocturnal hours we gather together for a cheerful meal. Contented animals, contented children are all about me, my wife smiles at me, and we leave the living-room door open so the hippopotamus will not feel left out, his joyful grunts resounding from the bathroom. At that point my wife usually confesses to me that she has an extra guest hidden in the storeroom, who is only brought out when my nerves have been fortified by food: shy, unshaven men, rubbing their hands, take their place at table, women squeeze in between our children on the bench, milk is warmed up for crying babies. In this way I also make the acquaintance of animals that are new to me: seagulls, foxes, and pigs, although once it was a small dromedary.

"Isn't it cute?" asked my wife, and I was obliged to say yes, it was, while I anxiously watched the tireless munching of this duffel-colored creature which looked at us out of slate-gray eyes. Fortunately the dromedary only stayed a week, and business was brisk: word had got round of the quality of my merchandise, my reduced prices, and now and again I was even able to sell shoelaces and brushes, articles otherwise not much in demand. As a result, we experienced a period of false prosperity, and my wife, completely blind to the economic facts, produced a remark that worried me, "Things are looking up!" But I saw our stocks of soap shrinking, the razor blades dwindling, and even the supply of brushes and darning wool was no longer substantial.

Just about this time, when I could have used some spiritual sustenance, our house was shaken one evening, while we were all sitting peacefully together, by a tremor resembling a fair-sized earthquake: the pictures rattled, the table rocked, and a ring of fried sausage rolled off my plate. I was about to jump up and see what the matter was when I noticed suppressed laughter on the faces of my children. "What's going on here?" I shouted, and for the first time in all my checkered experience I was really beside myself.

"Wilfred," said my wife quietly, and put down her fork, "it's only Wally." She began to cry, and against her tears I have no defense, for she has borne me seven children.

"Who is Wally?" I asked wearily, and at that moment the house was rocked by another tremor. "Wally," said my youngest daughter, "is the elephant we've got in the basement."

I must admit I was at a loss, which is not really surprising. The largest animal we had housed so far had been the dromedary, and I considered an elephant too big for our apartment.

My wife and children, not in the least at a loss, supplied the facts: the animal had been brought to us for safekeeping by a bankrupt circus owner. Sliding down the chute which we otherwise use for our coal, it had had no trouble entering the basement. "He rolled himself up into a ball," said my oldest son, "really an intelligent animal." I did not doubt it, accepted the fact of Wally's presence, and was led down in triumph into the basement. The animal was not as large as all that; he waggled his ears and seemed quite at home with us, especially as he had a bale of hay at his disposal. "Isn't he cute?" asked my wife, but I refused to agree. Cute did not seem to be the right word. Anyway, the family appeared disappointed at the limited extent of my enthusiasm, and my wife said, as we left the basement, "How cruel you are, do you want him to be put up for auction?"

"What d'you mean, auction," I said, "and why cruel? Besides, it's against the law to conceal bankruptcy assets."

"I don't care," said my wife. "Nothing must happen to the animal."

In the middle of the night we were awakened by the circus owner, a diffident, dark-haired man, who asked us whether we had room for one more animal. "It's my sole possession, all I have left in the world. Only for a night. How is the elephant, by the way?"

"He's fine," said my wife, "only I'm a bit worried about his bowels."

"That'll soon settle down," said the circus owner. "It's just the new surroundings. Animals are so sensitive. How about it, then: will you take the cat too—just for the night?" He looked at me, and my wife nudged me and said, "Don't be so unkind."

"Unkind," I said, "no, I certainly don't want to be that. If you like, you can put the cat in the kitchen."

"I've got it outside in the car," said the man.

I left my wife to look after the cat and crawled back into bed. My wife was a bit pale when she came to bed, and she seemed to be trembling. "Are you cold?" I asked.

"Yes," she said, "I've got such funny chills."

"You're just tired."

"Maybe," said my wife, but she gave me a queer look as she said it. We slept quietly, but in my dreams I still saw that queer look of my wife's, and a strange compulsion made me wake up earlier than usual. I decided to shave for once.

Lying under our kitchen table was a medium-sized lion; he was sleeping peacefully, only his tail moved gently and made a sound like someone playing with a very light ball.

I carefully lathered my face and tried not to make any noise, but when I turned my chin to the right to shave my left cheek I saw that the lion had his eyes open and was watching me. They really do look like cats, I thought. What the lion was thinking I don't know; he went on watching me, and I shaved, without cutting myself, but I must admit it is a strange feeling to shave with a lion looking on. My experience of handling wild beasts was practically nonexistent, so I confined myself to looking sternly at the lion, then I dried my face and went back to the bedroom. My wife was already awake, she was just about to say something, but I cut her short and exclaimed, "What's the use of talking about it!" My wife began to cry, and I put my hand on her head and said, "It's unusual, to say the least, you must admit that."

"What isn't unusual?" said my wife, and I had no answer.

Meanwhile the rabbits had awakened, the children were making a racket in the bathroom, the hippopotamus—his name was Gottlieb—was already trumpeting away, Billy was stretching and yawning; only the tortoise was still asleep, but it sleeps most of the time anyway.

I let the rabbits into the kitchen, where their feed box is kept under the cupboard; the rabbits sniffed at the lion, the lion at the rabbits, and my children—uninhibited and used to animals as they are—were already in the kitchen. I almost had the feeling the lion was smiling; my third-youngest son immediately found a name for him: Bombilus. And Bombilus he remained.

A few days later someone came to take away the elephant and the lion. I must confess I saw the last of the elephant without regret; he seemed silly to me, while the lion's quiet, friendly dignity had endeared him to me. I felt a pang at Bombilus's departure. I had grown so used to him; he was really the first animal to enjoy my wholehearted affection.

No Tears for Schmeck

I

As Müller's nausea approached the point at which voiding was inevitable, a solemn, reverent silence filled the lecture hall. Professor Schmeck's voice, deliberately unaccentuated, cultured, slightly husky, had now (seventeen minutes before the end of the lecture) advanced to that gentle chant, soothing yet stimulating, which transports a certain type of female student (the hyperintellectual, the kind that used to be known as a bluestocking) to a pitch of excitement bordering on the sexual; at this moment they would have died for him. As for Schmeck, he used—when speaking confidentially—to describe this stage of his lecture as the point at which "the rational element, driven to its outer limits, to the very furthest edge of its possibilities, begins to seem irrational, and," he would add, "my friends, when you consider that any decent church service lasts forty-five minutes, like the sex act—well then, my friends, you'll understand that rhythm and monotony, acceleration and retardation, climax—and relaxation—are an integral part of a church service, the sex act, and —in my opinion, at least—the academic lecture."

At this point, somewhere about the thirty-third minute of the lecture, all indifference vanished from the hall, leaving only adoration and hostility; the adoring listeners could have exploded any minute into inarticulate rhythmic screams, and this would have incited the hostile listeners (who were in the minority) to screams of provocation. But at the very instant when such unacademic behavior appeared imminent, Schmeck broke off in the middle of a sentence and with a prosaic gesture introduced that sobering note which he needed to bring the lecture to a controlled conclusion: he blew his nose with a brightly colored checkered handkerchief, and the compulsive glance with which he briefly inspected it before replacing it in his pocket had a sobering effect on every last female student whose lips may already have been showing traces of light foam. "I need adoration," Schmeck used to say, "but when I get it, I can't take it."

A deep sigh went through the lecture hall, hundreds swore never again to attend a Schmeck lecture—and on Tuesday afternoon they would be crowding round the door, they would stand in line for half an hour, they would miss the lecture given by Livorno, Schmeck's rival, so as to hear Schmeck (who never announced the times of his lectures until Livorno had settled on his; whenever Schmeck was supposed to announce his lecture schedule for the university timetable, he had no compunction about going off to places so remote that he could not be reached even by cable; last semester he had gone on an expedition to the Warrau Indians; for weeks he was hidden in the Orinoco delta, and when his expedition was over, he cabled his lecture schedule from Caracas, and it had been identical with Livorno's—a fact that led someone in the registrar's office to remark, "Obviously he has his spies in Venezuela too").

The deep sigh seemed to Müller to indicate the right moment to do what he ought to have done a quarter of an hour earlier but hadn't had the nerve to: go out and get rid of the contents of his stomach. When he stood up in the front row, his briefcase tucked under his arm, and made his way through the closely packed rows, he was fleetingly aware of the look of indignation, of surprise, on the faces of the students who grudgingly made room for him: even the Schmeck opponents seemed to find it inconceivable that there could be anybody—and an out-and-out Schmeck supporter at that, of whom it was rumored that he was angling for the post of chief assistant lecturer—who would deprive himself even partially of this perfidious brilliance. When Müller at last reached the exit, he heard with half an ear the remainder of the sentence which Schmeck had broken off to blow his nose—"to the heart of the problem: is the mackintosh an accidental or typical manifestation? Is it sociologically significant?"

II

MÜLLER REACHED the toilet just in time, loosened his tie, ripped open his shirt, heard a shirt button tinkle as it rolled away into the next cubicle, let his briefcase drop to the tiled floor—and vomited. He felt the cold sweat getting even colder on the gradually returning warmth of his face. Keeping his eyes closed, he flushed the toilet by groping for the lever, and was surprised to feel in some definitive way not only liberated but cleansed: what had been flushed away was more than vomit; it was a whole philosophy, a suspicion confirmed, rage—he laughed with relief, wiped his mouth with his handkerchief, hastily pushed up the knot of his tie, picked up his briefcase, and left the cubicle. They had teased him a hundred times, but here was proof of how useful it was always to carry along a towel and soap, a hundred times they had made fun of his "plebeian" soap container. As he opened it now, he could have kissed his mother, for she had urged him to take it with him when he started university three years ago: soap was the very thing he needed now. He pulled uncertainly at his tie, left it the way it was, hung his jacket up on the doorknob, washed his face and hands thoroughly, wiped his neck briefly, and left the washroom as quickly as he could. The corridors were still empty, and if he hurried he could be in his room before Marie. I'll ask her, he thought, whether disgust, which we all know originates in the mind, can have such a drastic effect on the stomach.

III

IT WAS a mild, damp day in early spring. For the first time in three years of university he missed the last, the third, step at the main entrance—he had only reckoned with two—stumbled, and, in catching himself and trying to get back into step, he was conscious of the aftereffects of the appalling quarter of an hour he had just been through. He felt giddy, and he was aware of his surroundings as a pleasant, dreamy blur. The faces of the college girls—majoring in literature, he would imagine—wore a look of impressionistic sensuality; they strolled languidly about under the green trees, carrying their books, and even the Catholic students with their colored caps, who appeared to be holding some kind of meeting in front of the main building, seemed less objectionable than usual: their colored ribbons and caps might have been wisps of a dissolving rainbow. Müller stumbled along, returning greetings mechanically, fighting his way against the stream which now, at half past twelve, was pouring into the university, like a stream of workers at change of shift.

IV

NOT UNTIL he was in the streetcar, three stops farther on, did he begin to see properly again, as if he had put on glasses which corrected his vision. From one suburb to the city center, from the center out again to another suburb: almost an hour to think things out and "get everything into proper perspective." It just couldn't be true! Surely Schmeck was the last man to have to steal from him—Rudolf Müller, third-year student? Hadn't he told Schmeck he was considering writing a series of essays to demonstrate "The Sociology of Dress," taking as his first title "On the Sociology of the Mackintosh," and hadn't Schmeck enthusiastically agreed, congratulated him, and offered to supervise the whole series? And hadn't he read the first pages of his "Sociology of the Mackintosh" aloud to Schmeck in his study, sentences which today he had heard coming word for word from Schmeck's lips? Müller turned pale again, tore open his briefcase, and rummaged through it. The soap container fell to the floor, then a book by Schmeck: *First Principles of Sociology*. Where was his manuscript? Was it a dream, a memory, or a hallucination that he suddenly found himself looking at—Schmeck's smile as he stood in the doorway of his study, the white pages of manuscript in his hand? "Of course, I'll be glad to have a look at your work!" Then the Easter vacation—first at home, then three weeks in London with a study group—and today Schmeck's lecture, "Rudiments of a Sociology of Dress, Part One: On the Sociology of the Mackintosh."

V

TRANSFER. He automatically got off, on again when his streetcar arrived, gave a troubled sigh as the elderly conductress sitting on her throne recognized him. Would she make the same joke she had been making ever since she had seen his student's pass? She made the joke: "Well, well—if it isn't our gentleman of leisure, all through by eleven-thirty— and now it's off to the girls, eh?" The passengers laughed, Müller blushed, made his way to the front, wished he could get out, run faster than the streetcar, and get home and into his room at last, to find out for sure. His diary would be proof—or would it help to have Marie as a witness? She had typed his paper for him; he remembered her suggesting she make a carbon copy, he could see her hand holding up the carbon paper, but he had waved it aside, pointing out that it was only a draft, an outline—and he could see Marie's hand putting the carbon paper back into the drawer and starting to type. "Rudolf Müller, philosophy student, 17 Buckwheat Street" . . . While he was dictating the heading it struck him one could also write a sociology of food. Buckwheat flour, pancakes, roast beef—in the working-class district where he had grown up this was considered the pinnacle of epicurean delight, on a par in the scale of bliss with sexual pleasures—rice pudding, lentil soup; and before he had even begun dictating his essay to Marie, he already had visions of following up the sociology of the mackintosh with a sociology of french fries. Ideas, ideas, all kinds, in fact—and he knew he had what it took to put these ideas into words.

VI

THESE ENDLESS streets leading out of the city, Roman, Napoleonic—the house numbers were already in the 900s. Fragmented memories: Schmeck's voice—the sudden nausea on first hearing the word "mackintosh"—eight or nine minutes up there in the front row—the urge to vomit—then the thirty-third minute, Schmeck's handkerchief, his glance at the results of his noisy exertions—at long last the toilet—misty dampness in front of the university—the girls' faces, sensual, blurred—the colored ribbons of the Catholic students like remnants of a dying rainbow—getting onto the Number 12, transferring to the Number 18—the conductress's joke—and already the house numbers on Mainz Street were up to 980, 981. He pulled out one of the three cigarettes he had taken along in his breast pocket as his morning ration, groped for the match.

"Here, son, give us a light too." He stood up, and with a wan smile walked to where the old conductress was squeezing herself down off her throne. He held the burning match to her cigarette butt, then lit his own cigarette, and was pleasantly surprised to find he felt no nausea. "Troubles, son?" He nodded, looked hard at her coarse, red-veined face, dreading the obscenity she might offer as consolation, but she merely nodded and said, "Thank you kindly," clasped his shoulder as the streetcar swung into the terminus loop, got out ahead of him when the streetcar stopped, and waddled along to the front car, where the driver was already unscrewing his Thermos flask.

VII

How small these gray houses were, how narrow the streets. A parked motorcycle was enough to block them; thirty years ago the apostles of progress had not believed that cars would ever become a commonplace. Here visions of the future had become the present, and died; everything that would later claim to be progressive and advanced was regarded with hostility. All the streets were alike, from Acanthus Avenue to Zinnia Road, wintergreen and leek, monkshood (first rejected because it smacked of clericalism but later approved by the Board as being strictly botanical and free of any clericalist taint) and privet—"all growing things" were to be found here in street names, surrounded by a Marx Avenue, at the center an Engels Square (Marx Street and Engels Street had already been appropriated by older working-class districts). The little church had been built later, when it was discovered that the declared atheists were all married to devout wives—when one day (by this time the devout mothers had their grown-up sons and daughters on their side) the polling district had to report more votes for the Catholic Center Party than for the Socialist Party, when old Socialists, crimson with embarrassment, drowned their sorrows in drink and went over in a body to the Communist Party. For years now the little church had been much too small: on Sundays it overflowed, and the model for the new one could be admired at the rectory. Very modern. Beyond Marx Avenue, the neighboring parish of St. Boniface had donated land for the new church of St. Joseph, patron saint of the working class. Construction cranes were already reaching triumphantly into the spring sky.

Müller tried to smile, but couldn't quite, when he thought of his father; it always seemed to him as if the aura of the twenties, that ardent spirit of atheism and enlightenment, still hung in the air here, as if the climate of free love were still present, and, although it was never heard any more, he seemed to hear echoes in these streets of "Brothers, toward sunlight, toward freedom"; his smile miscarried. Rosemary Street, Tulip Street, Maple Grove—and another cycle of streets in alphabetical order: Acacia Way, and finally Buckwheat Street—"all growing things." There was Number 17; now he could smile as he caught sight of Marie's bicycle: it was propped against the iron railing that Uncle Will had built around the garbage can, the none-too-clean, wobbly bicycle belonging to Baroness von Schlimm (younger branch). His desire to show affection even to the bicycle was manifested in a gentle kick against the back tire. He opened the door, called "Hello, Auntie" into the narrow passageway, which smelled of french fries, picked up the parcel lying on the bottom stair, and rushed upstairs. The staircase was so narrow that his elbow always brushed the reddish-brown hessian wall covering, and Aunt Kate claimed to be able to determine the vehemence and frequency of his ascents from the traces of wear—in the course of the three years a strip had been rubbed almost bare, to a shade resembling a bald head.

VIII

MARIE. He never failed to be moved by the intensity of his feelings for her, and each time (by now they had met more than three hundred times; he kept track, so to speak, in his diary), each time she seemed thinner than he remembered her. During the time they were together she seemed to fill out—when he thought of her afterward he remembered her as full—and he was consistently surprised when he saw her again in her original, unaltered thinness. She had taken off her shoes and stockings and was lying on his bed, dark-haired and pale, with a pallor which he still could not help feeling was a sign of consumption.

"Please," she said gently, "don't kiss me. All morning I've been listening to dirty stories about various kinds of love. If you want to be nice, rub my feet." He threw down his briefcase and the parcel, knelt down by the bed, and took her feet in his hands. "How sweet you are," she said. "I only hope you don't get a male-nurse complex—with your kind one has to be so careful—and please," she said, lowering her voice, "let's stay here, I'm too tired to go out to eat. Anyway, our social worker, who looks after employee relations, always regards my absence at lunchtime as antisocial."

"For God's sake," he said, "why don't you quit the whole ghastly business? Those swine."

"Which ones do you mean? My bosses or the other girls?"

"Your bosses," he said, "what you call dirty stories are the outward expression of the only pleasures those girls have; your bourgeois ears . . ."

"I have feudal ears, in case my ears require a sociological epithet."

"Feudalism succumbed to the bourgeoisie: it married into industry, thereby becoming bourgeois. You are confusing what is accidental in you with what is typical; to attach so much importance to a name by regarding it as valueless as you regard yours is a form of late-bourgeois idealism. Isn't it enough for you that soon—before God and man, as your kind would put it—your name will be Marie Müller?"

"Your hands do feel nice," she said. "When will you be in a position to support a wife and children with them?"

"As soon as you take the trouble to work out how much we'll have to live on when we're married and you go on working."

She sat up and recited in a schoolgirl singsong: "You get two hundred forty-three a month, that's the highest category; as an assistant lecturer you earn two hundred, of which one hundred twenty-five is available because it's earned in conjunction with your university training. That makes three hundred sixty-eight—but your father earns seven hundred ten net, i.e., two hundred sixty more than the free limit, which means that you, since you're an only child, have your income reduced by one hundred thirty. In other words, you're working as an assistant lecturer for nothing—net balance: two hundred thirty-eight. As soon as we get married, half of what I earn above three hundred—i.e., exactly two marks and fifteen pfennigs—will be deducted, so that your total net income will amount to two hundred thirty-five marks and eighty-five pfennigs."

"Congratulations," he said. "So you really got down to it?"

"Yes," she said, "and the most important thing I worked out is that you're working for precisely nothing for this Schmeck-bastard. . . ."

He took his hands off her legs. "Schmeck-bastard—what makes you say that?"

She looked at him, swung her legs round, sat up on the edge of the bed; he pushed his slippers toward her. "What's Schmeck been up to? Something new? Tell me—never mind my feet now—go on, tell me, what's he been up to?"

"Can you wait a moment?" he said; he picked up his briefcase and the parcel from the floor, took the two remaining cigarettes from his breast pocket, lit them both, gave one to Marie, threw briefcase and parcel down beside Marie on the bed, went over to the bookshelf, and pulled out his diary, a fat exercise book standing between Kierkegaard and Kotzebue, sat down at Marie's feet beside the bed.

"Listen," he said. "Here. 'December 13. During a walk with Marie through the park, suddenly struck by the idea of a "Sociology of the Mackintosh." ' "

"That's right," said Marie, "you told me about it at the time. Remember my objections?"

"Sure." He turned some more pages. "Here. 'January 2. Began work on it. Outlines, ideas—also viewed material. Went to Meier's Menswear and tried to get a look at their customer list, but no luck. . . .' It goes on —January, February, daily entries about the progress of the work."

"Yes, of course," said Marie, "and at the end of February you dictated the first thirty pages to me."

"Yes, and here, this is what I was looking for: 'March 1. Went to see Schmeck, showed him the first pages of my draft, read parts of it aloud to him. Schmeck asked me to leave the manuscript with him so he could look through it. . . .' "

"That's right, and the next day you went home to your parents."

"And then to England. Came back yesterday—and today was Schmeck's first lecture, and the audience was more interested, more enthralled, more ecstatic than ever, because the subject was so new, so thrilling—at least for the audience. I'll let you guess what Schmeck's lecture was about. Try and guess, my dear baroness."

"If you call me 'baroness' once more, I'll call you—no"—she smiled —"don't worry, I won't call you that, even if you do call me 'baroness.' Would it hurt your feelings if I called you that?"

"If you called me that, no," he said gently. "You can call me what you like. But you have no idea how wonderful it is when they call out after you, whisper as you go by, when they write it after your name on the bulletin board—'Rudolf, Son of the Working Class.' I'm a freak, you see, I'm the great phenomenon, I'm one of those of whom there are only five in every hundred, only fifty in every thousand, and—the higher you go, the more fantastic the ratio—I'm one of those of whom there are only five thousand in every hundred thousand. I am really and truly the son of a working man who is studying at a West German university."

"At the East German universities I guess it's the other way round; ninety-five percent are from working-class families."

"Over there I'd be something absurdly ordinary; here I'm the famous example in discussions, arguments, counterarguments, a real live unadulterated Son of the Working Class—and talented too, very talented. But you still haven't tried to guess what Schmeck was paying homage to today."

"Television, perhaps."

Müller laughed. "No, the big snobs are now in *favor* of television."

"Not"—Marie stubbed out her cigarette in the ashtray Müller was holding—"not the sociology of the mackintosh?"

"What else," said Rudolf in a low voice, "what else?"

"No," said Marie, "he *can't* do that."

"But he has done it, and there were sentences in his lecture that I recognized and remembered how much fun I had had formulating . . ."

"Too much fun, it seems . . ."

"Yes, I know—he quoted whole paragraphs."

He got up off the floor and began pacing up and down in the room. "You know how it is when you try to figure out whether you're quoting yourself or someone else—when you hear something you think you've heard or said before, and you try to figure out whether you said it before yourself or whether you only thought it, whether you recognize it or read it—and you go crazy because your memory's not functioning properly?"

"Yes," said Marie, "I always used to worry about whether or not I'd had anything to drink before holy communion. You think you've had a drink of water because so often, so many thousands of times, you have had a drink of water on an empty stomach—but actually you haven't had anything to drink. . . ."

"And yet you can't come up with any convincing proof—that's where a diary is so important."

"You needn't have worried about this particular question: it's obvious that Schmeck's robbed you."

"And done me out of my thesis."

"Oh my God," said Marie—she stood up next to the bed, put her hand on Rudolf's shoulder, kissed his neck—"oh my God, you're right, that's true. He's cut the ground from under your feet. Can't you sue him?"

Müller laughed. "Every university on the face of the earth, from Massachusetts to Göttingen to Lima, from Oxford to Nagasaki, will burst out in one united, crazy laugh when a person by the name of Rudolf Müller, Son of the Working Class, gets up and claims to have been robbed by Schmeck. Even the Warraus will join in the derisive laughter, for they know too that the wise white man Schmeck is omniscient in the ways of mankind. But—and this is what would happen if I sued him—if Schmeck got up and said he had been robbed by a person by the name of Müller, they would all nod their heads, even the Hottentots."

"He ought to be exterminated," said Marie.

"At last you're beginning to think in nonbourgeois terms."

"I don't understand how you can still laugh," said Marie.

"There's a very good reason for the fact that I can still laugh," said Müller. He went over to the bed, picked up the parcel, took it over to the table, and began to undo the string. He patiently untied all the knots, so slowly that Marie jerked open the drawer, took out a penknife, and silently held it out to him.

"Exterminated, yes," said Müller, "that might be an idea, but not for anything in the world would I cut this string: that would be cutting right into my mother's heart. When she opens a parcel she carefully unties the string, rolls it up, and puts it aside for future use—the next time she comes here she'll ask me about the string, and if I can't produce it she will predict the imminent end of the world."

Marie snapped the knife ʾhut again, put it back in the drawer, leaned against Müller while he unwrapped the paper from his parcel and carefully folded it up. "You haven't told me yet why you can still laugh," she said. "After all, that was the vilest, filthiest, most disgusting trick that Schmeck could play on you—when you think how he wanted to make you his chief assistant and how he's prophesied a brilliant future for you."

"Well," said Müller, "do you really want to know why?"

She nodded. "Tell me," she said.

He put down the parcel, kissed her. "Damn it all," he murmured, "if it weren't for you I would have done something desperate."

"Do it anyway," she said quietly.

"What?"

"Do something desperate to him," said Marie, "I'll help you."

"What do you want me to do, really kill him?"

"Do something physical to him, not mental—half kill him."

"How?"

"Maybe beat him up—but let's have something to eat first. I'm hungry and I have to go off again in thirty-five minutes."

"I'm not so sure you will go off again."

He carefully folded up a second layer of paper, undid a piece of thinner string tied round the core of the parcel, a shoebox, removed the sheet of notepaper stuck between string and box lid ("Every parcel should contain the address inside as well as out"), and at last, as Marie sighed, he took off the lid of the shoebox: salami, ham, cake, cigarettes, and a package of glutamate. Marie picked up the notepaper from the table and read in a low voice, "My dear boy, I am glad you could make the long journey to England so cheaply. It is wonderful what they are doing these days at the universities. Tell us about London when you come home. Remember how proud we are of you. Now you are really working on your Ph.D. thesis—I just can't believe it. Your loving Mother."

"They really are proud of me," said Müller.

"And they have every reason to be," said Marie. She put away the contents of the parcel in a little cupboard below the bookshelves, took out an opened package of tea. "I'll run down and make us some tea."

IX

"IT'S FUNNY," said Marie, "but when I propped my bike up against the railing today at noon, I knew that I wouldn't be going back after lunch to that plastics nightmare. One does have premonitions like that. Once when I came home from school I threw my bike against the hedge just like I used to every day; it always sank halfway in, tipped over, the handlebars would get caught in a branch and the front wheel would stick up in the air—and as I threw my bike in there, I knew I wouldn't be going back to school next day, that I would never be going back to any school. It wasn't just that I was fed up with it—there was much more to it than that. I simply knew that it would be wicked for me to go to school for even one more day. Father couldn't get over it; you see, it was exactly four weeks before my graduation, but I said to him: 'Have you ever heard of the sin of gluttony?' 'Yes,' he said, 'I have, but you haven't been guilty of gluttony as far as school's concerned.' 'No,' I said, 'it's just an example —but when you swallow one more mouthful of coffee or one more piece of cake than at a given point you ought to drink or eat, isn't that gluttony?' 'It is,' he said, 'and I can imagine such a thing as spiritual gluttony, only—' but I interrupted him and said, 'There's not room for another thing in me, I already feel like a stuffed goose.' 'It's a pity,' said Father, 'that this has to happen to you four weeks before your graduation. It's such a useful thing to have.' 'Useful for what?' I asked. 'You mean university?' 'Yes,' he said, and I said, 'No, if I'm going to work in a factory, then it's going to be a real one'—and that's what I did. Does it hurt you when I tell you things like this?"

"Yes," said Müller, "it hurts very much to see someone throwing away something that for countless people is the object of all their dreams and aspirations. It's also possible to laugh about clothes, or to despise them, when one has them hanging in the closet or is in a position to buy them any time—it's possible to laugh about anything one has always taken for granted."

"But I didn't laugh about it, and I didn't despise it, and it's true that I preferred to work in a real factory rather than in a university."

"Oh, I believe you," he said. "I do, just as I believe you're really a Catholic."

"By the way, I got a parcel from home yesterday too," said Marie. "Guess what was in it."

"Salami, ham, cake, cigarettes," said Müller, "and no glutamate—

and, needless to say, you cut the string with scissors, screwed the paper up into a ball and . . ."

"Exactly," said Marie, "exactly, only you've forgotten something . . ."

"No, I haven't," said Müller. "I haven't forgotten anything, you interrupted me, that's all. Then you immediately bit into the salami, then the cake, and right after that you lit a cigarette."

"Come on, let's go to the movies, and then we'll half kill Schmeck this evening."

"Today?" said Müller.

"Of course today," said Marie. "Whenever you think something is right, you should do it at once—and a woman should fight at her man's side."

X

IT WAS dark by the time they came out of the movie, and they found the bicycle-parking attendant in a state of sullen resentment; Marie's ramshackle bicycle was the sole remaining one in his charge. An old man, his coat almost trailing on the ground, rubbing his hands to warm them, walking up and down muttering curses under his breath.

"Give him a tip," whispered Marie. She remained nervously by the chain separating the parking lot from the square in front of the opera house.

"My principles forbid me to give tips except where they form part of the wages. It's an offense against human dignity."

"Perhaps you've got a mistaken idea of human dignity: seven hundred years ago my ancestor, the first Schlimm, was given a whole barony as a tip."

"And maybe that's why you have so little sense of human dignity. Christ," he said, lowering his voice, "what do you give in a case like this?"

"Twenty or thirty pfennigs, I should think, or about the same in cigarettes. Go on, please, you go first. Help your assistant. I'm so embarrassed."

Müller hesitantly approached the attendant, holding out the stub as if it were a pass he didn't quite trust, then, when the old man's furious face was turned toward him, quickly drew the cigarette pack from his pocket, saying, "Sorry, I'm afraid we're a bit late." The old man took the whole pack, stuck it into his coat pocket, gestured in wordless contempt toward the bicycle, and walked past Marie in the direction of the streetcar stop.

"When you're in love with lightweight men," said Marie, "you have the advantage of being able to take them on the luggage carrier." She rode in and out between waiting cars till they got to the front at the red light. "Look out, Müller," she said, "see you don't scratch their paint with your feet, they're very touchy about that, they worry about it more than if their wives get a scratch." And when the driver of the car waiting beside her rolled down his window, she said in a loud voice, "If I were you, I would write a sociology of the various makes of cars. Driving is the training ground of one-upmanship—and the worst ones are the so-called gentlemen behind the wheel. Their false democratic courtesy is positively nauseating; it is hypocrisy par excellence, because it means they expect a medal for something that should be taken for granted."

"Right," said Müller, "and the worst thing about them is, they all think *they* look different from the others, while actually . . ."

The driver quickly wound up his window again.

"Yellow, Marie," he said.

Marie pushed off, going straight across in front of the cars to the right-hand lane, while Müller conscientiously stuck out his right arm.

"I see I've found a good assistant," he said, as they turned into a dark side street.

"Assistant," said Marie, over her shoulder, "is a weak translation of *adjutorium*—which contains much more: counsel, and some pleasure too. Where does he live?"

"Mommsen Street," said Müller, "Number 37."

"That's wonderful—he's stuck with a street name that must annoy him every time he reads it, says it, writes it—and I hope he has to do each of those things three times a day. I'm sure he hates a classicist like Mommsen."

"He hates him like poison."

"Serves him right that he has to live on Mommsen Street. What's the time?"

"Half past seven."

"A quarter of an hour to go."

She turned into a still darker side street leading to the park, and stopped; Müller jumped off and helped her to guide the bicycle through the barrier. They walked a few yards along the dark path, stopped beside a bush, and Marie threw her bicycle against a shrub; it sank halfway in, got caught on a twig. "Almost like home," said Marie. "There's nothing like shrubbery for bikes."

Müller put his arms around her, kissed her neck, and Marie whispered, "Don't you think I'm a bit too skinny for a woman?"

"Be quiet, assistant," he said.

"You're terribly scared," she said. "I didn't know one could actually feel a person's heart beating—tell me, are you scared?"

"Of course I am," he said. "It's my first assault—and I find it quite incredible that we're really standing here for the purpose of luring Schmeck into a trap, to beat him up. I just can't believe it."

"You see, you have faith in intellectual weapons, in progress and so on, and one has to pay for such mistakes; if there ever were such things as intellectual weapons, they're no use nowadays."

"Try to understand," he whispered, "the mental process: here I am . . ."

"You poor fellows, you must be schizophrenics. I do wish I weren't so thin. I read somewhere that thin women aren't good for schizoids."

"Your hair actually smells of that filthy plastic, and your hands are quite rough."

"Yes," she whispered. "You see, I'm one of those girls you come across in modern novels. Heading: 'Baroness turns her back on her own class, decides she is really going to *live.*' What's the time now?"

"Almost quarter to."

"He's bound to come soon. It's so satisfactory to be going to trap him in his own vanity. You ought to have heard his voice when he was talking to that radio reporter, 'Regularity, rhythm, that is my principle. A light meal—just a snack, actually, at seven-fifteen—and some strong tea; and at a quarter to eight my evening walk through the park.' You're sure you know what we're going to do?"

"Yes," said Müller. "As soon as he comes round the corner, you lay your bike down right across the path, and when I go 'Psst,' you run and lie down beside it. He'll come running over to you."

"And you come from behind, beat him up thoroughly, hard enough so he needs some time to come to, and we clear off. . . ."

"That doesn't sound quite fair."

" 'Fair,' " she said, "that's just one of those mental images."

"And what if he calls for help? Or if he manages to get the upper hand? He weighs at least a hundred pounds more than I do! And, as I say, I don't like the sound of 'from behind.' "

"Of course, people like you always have your mental images. Fair election campaign, and so on—and obviously you always get defeated. Remember I'm coming to help you, that I'll hit him good and hard too —and if we have to we'll just abandon the bike."

"As a *corpus delicti?* It must be the only bike in town whose appearance is unmistakable."

"Your heart's beating stronger and stronger, faster and faster—you really must be dreadfully scared."

"Aren't you?"

"Sure I am," she said, "but I know we're in the right, and that this is the only way of seeing some kind of justice done, considering the whole world's on his side, including the Hottentots."

"Christ," whispered Müller, "there he is now."

Marie jumped onto the path, snatched her bicycle from the bushes, laid it down in the middle of the damp path. Müller watched Schmeck walking along the lane, hatless, his coat open and flapping. "Damn," he whispered to Marie, "we forgot the dog. Look at that creature, a German shepherd, almost as big as a calf." Marie was standing beside him again, looking over his shoulder toward Schmeck. "Solveig, Solveig," he called hoarsely, fending off the dog who was leaping joyously up at him; then he picked up a stone from the path and threw it toward the bushes, where it dropped scarcely ten yards from Müller.

"Damn," said Marie, "it's useless trying anything with that dog; he's vicious, and trained to attack people—I can tell. We'll get complexes because we didn't do it after all, but it's quite useless." She walked over to the path, picked up her bicycle, nudged Müller, and said softly, "Well, come on, we have to leave, what's the matter?"

"Nothing," said Müller. He took Marie's arm. "I had just forgotten how much I loathe him."

Schmeck was standing under the streetlight stroking the dog, who had laid the stone at his feet; he looked up as the couple entered the circle of light, glanced once more at the dog, then suddenly up again, and walked toward Müller with outstretched hands. "Müller," he said warmly, "my dear Müller, fancy meeting you here"—but Müller succeeded in looking at and yet through Schmeck. Mustn't meet Schmeck's eyes; if I meet them, he thought, I'm lost; I mustn't behave as if he isn't there—he is there, and I'll extinguish him with my eyes—one step, two, three—he felt Marie's firm grasp on his arm, he was panting as if after some enormous exertion.

"Müller," called Schmeck, "it *is* you—can't you take a joke?"

The rest was easy: just keep walking, fast and yet not too fast. . . . They heard Schmeck calling again, "Müller," first loud, then softer, "Müller, Müller, Müller"—and at last they had turned the corner.

Marie's deep sigh startled him; when he turned to her he saw she was crying. He took the bicycle from her, leaned it against a garden fence, wiped her tears away with his finger, put his free hand on her shoulder. "Marie," he said softly, "what's the matter?"

"You scare me," she said, "that wasn't an assault, that was murder.

I'm scared he's going to wander around for all eternity in this wretched little park whispering 'Müller, Müller, Müller.' It's like a nightmare: Schmeck's ghost with the dog, in the damp bushes, his beard growing, getting so long that it drags behind him like a frayed belt—and all the time he's whispering 'Müller, Müller, Müller.' Oughtn't I to see if he's all right?"

"No," said Müller, "no, don't, just leave him alone, he's perfectly all right. If you feel sorry for him, give him a mackintosh for his birthday. You can't even begin to think what he's done to me; he turned me into the miracle Son of the Working Class. I was his protégé, as they call it —and no doubt he expects the mackintoshes as a form of tribute—but I'm not going to pay him this tribute, not if I can help it. Tomorrow morning he's going to say casually to Wegelot, his chief assistant, just as he's leaving the room, 'By the way, Müller's gone over into the reactionary camp after all: he's transferred to Livorno. He called me up yesterday saying he wanted to leave the seminar,' and then he'll close the door again, go over to Wegelot, and say, 'Pity about Müller, very talented, but his draft thesis was simply terrible, quite hopeless. I suppose it's difficult for these people who have to fight not only the world around them but their own milieu as well. Pity'—then he'll bite his lip again and leave the room."

"Are you quite sure that's how it's going to be?"

"Quite sure," said Müller. "Come on, let's go home. No tears for Schmeck, Marie."

"The tears weren't for Schmeck," said Marie.

"For me, then?"

"Yes—you're so terribly brave."

"Now that really does sound like a modern novel. Are we going home?"

"Would you think it terrible if I said I would like one (in a word, one) hot meal?"

"All right," Müller said, laughing. "Let's ride to the nearest restaurant."

"We'd better walk. There are a lot of policemen around at this hour —the park, not many lights, spring in the air—attempted rapes—and a summons would cost us as much as two bowls of soup."

Müller wheeled the bicycle. They walked slowly along the lane beside the park; as they stepped out of the light from the next streetlamp they saw a policeman in deep shadow beyond the barrier, leaning against a tree.

"You see," said Marie, loud enough for the policeman to hear, "we've already saved two marks for the summons, but as soon as we get out of sight you can hop up again."

When they had turned the next corner, Marie got up on her bicycle, propping herself against the curb to let Müller get on. She pushed off quickly, leaned back, and called out: "What do you want to do now?"

"How do you mean?"

"I mean, what d'you want to do."

"Now, or generally speaking?"

"Now *and* generally speaking."

"Now I'm going to have something to eat with you, and generally speaking I'm going to see Livorno tomorrow, register for his course, ask for an interview, and offer a suggestion for a thesis."

"On what?"

" 'Critical Appreciation of the Collected Works of Schmeck.' "

Marie rode up to the curb, stopped, turned round in the saddle. "On what?"

"I just told you: 'Critical Appreciation of the Collected Works of Schmeck.' I know them almost by heart—and hatred makes good ink."

"Doesn't love?"

"No," said Müller, "love makes the worst ink in the world. Ride on, assistant."

Anecdote Concerning the Lowering of Productivity

IN A harbor on the west coast of Europe, a shabbily dressed man lies dozing in his fishing boat. A smartly dressed tourist is just putting a new roll of color film into his camera to photograph the idyllic picture: blue sky, green sea with peaceful, snowy whitecaps, black boat, red woolen fisherman's cap. Click. Once more: click and, since all good things come in threes and it's better to be safe than sorry, a third time: click. The snapping, almost hostile sound awakens the dozing fisherman, who sleepily sits up, sleepily gropes for his cigarettes, but before he has found what he is looking for the eager tourist is already holding a pack under his nose, not exactly sticking a cigarette between his lips but putting one into his hand, and a fourth click, that of the lighter, completes the overeager courtesy. As a result of that excess of nimble courtesy—scarcely measurable, never verifiable—a certain awkwardness has arisen that the tourist, who speaks the language of the country, tries to bridge by striking up a conversation.

"You'll have a good catch today."

The fisherman shakes his head.

"But I've been told the weather's favorable!"

The fisherman nods.

"So you won't be putting out?"

The fisherman shakes his head, the tourist grows more and more uncomfortable. It is clear that he has the welfare of the shabbily dressed man at heart and that disappointment over the lost opportunity is gnawing at him.

"Oh, I'm sorry—aren't you feeling well?"

At last the fisherman switches from sign language to the spoken word. "I feel fine," he says. "I've never felt better." He stands up, stretches as if to demonstrate his athletic build. "I feel terrific."

The tourist's expression grows steadily more unhappy, and he can no longer suppress the question that threatens, so to speak, to burst his heart: "So why aren't you putting out?"

The reply comes promptly and succinctly. "Because I was already out this morning."

"Was it a good catch?"

"It was so good that I don't need to go out again—I had four lobsters in my traps, and I caught almost two dozen mackerel. . . ."

The fisherman, finally wide awake, now thaws and gives the tourist a reassuring pat on the back. The latter's worried expression strikes him as a sign of touching although unwarranted concern.

"I even have enough for tomorrow and the day after," he says, to put the stranger's mind at rest. "Will you have one of my cigarettes?"

"Thanks, I will."

Cigarettes are placed between lips—a fifth click—the stranger sits down on the edge of the boat, shaking his head, and puts down his camera, for he now needs both hands to give emphasis to his words.

"I don't wish to interfere in your personal affairs," he says, "but just imagine if you were to go out a second, a third, maybe even a fourth time today, and you were to catch three, four, five, maybe even ten dozen mackerel . . . just imagine that!"

The fisherman nods.

"You would," the tourist continues, "go out not only today but tomorrow, the day after tomorrow, indeed on every favorable day, two, three, maybe four times. Do you know what would happen?"

The fisherman shakes his head.

"In less than a year you would be able to buy a motor, in two years a second boat, in three or four years you might have a small cutter, and with two boats or the cutter you would obviously catch much more. One day you would have two cutters, you would"—from sheer enthusiasm his voice cracks for a few seconds—"you would build a small cold-storage plant, maybe a smokehouse, later a pickling factory, you would fly around in your own helicopter, spot schools of fish, and direct your cutters by radio. You could acquire the salmon rights, open up a fish restaurant, export lobster direct to Paris without a middleman—and then . . ." Once again words fail the stranger in his enthusiasm. Shaking his head, grieved to the very core of his being, and having lost almost all pleasure in his vacation, he looks out onto the peacefully advancing tide where the uncaught fish are happily leaping around.

"And then . . ." he says, but again he is speechless in his agitation. The fisherman pats him on the back as if he were a child with a fit of choking. "Then what?" he asks softly.

"Then," says the stranger with restrained enthusiasm, "then, without a care in the world, you could sit here in the harbor, doze in the sun—and look at the glorious sea."

"But I'm already doing that," says the fisherman. "I sit here in the harbor without a care in the world and doze—it was only your clicking that disturbed me."

And so the thus enlightened tourist walked pensively away, for at one time he had believed that he too was working so as someday not to have to work any more, and no trace of pity for the shabbily dressed fisherman remained in him, only a little envy.

He Came as a
Beer-Truck Driver

I

WHAT HE liked best were the slender wine bottles; they fitted so neatly into his coat pocket. He never carried around more than would fit into his coat pockets: a bottle of wine and a piece of cheese in one; bread, tobacco, cigarette papers, matches in the other. No handkerchief, no toothbrush. What soap he needed he found in the toilets on the trains, where he also blew his nose with his fingers and washed his shirts and socks, letting them dry on his warm body. The maximum he would carry in his hands was a paper bag containing some fried chicken, bread, and fruit: after a meal he could toss the remains out the train window.

Whenever he entered a first-class compartment he was aware of that brief hesitation, as if one of the passengers were about to say: Excuse me, but this is first class. He killed this brief hesitation with a laugh. Then, whenever the conductor came along and tickets had to be produced, there was that slight tension followed by two things: surprise and relief when he produced the green-and-white piece of cardboard from his pocket. They didn't even dare look up when he belched. The women either moved away from him or too close to him, neither of which he liked.

What surprised him most was the lipsticks. Whenever a woman took one out of her handbag and put it to her lips, he laughed aloud: he hadn't imagined that this cult had penetrated so far north and become so widespread. This lack of embarrassment on the part of the women and innocence of the men, who failed to recognize their own symbol, amused him. In the course of his long journey he realized that the women made equally innocent use of this obvious symbol, and he laughed even louder. No feeling for signs and wonders. Only the waiters seemed aware of something: they served him without venomous servility and, without his having to ask, brought him only food he could eat with his fingers—chicken, bread, fruit—and they weren't even surprised at the generosity of his tips.

Twice, in Vienna and Munich, there had been a lengthy stop during which he had walked to the nearest tavern, sat down at the bar, ordered a beer, kissed the palm of the woman who served him, and stroked her forearms, and each woman had ruffled his hair with her free hand, murmuring, "What are you looking for here?", and each time he had replied, "Europa." One of them—he couldn't remember whether in Vienna or Munich—had murmured, "Europa? Not here!"; the other, "Europa? But surely not here?" And one of them had said when he kissed her palm, "God!", and the other, "Bull!"

He tried out the strange place names as if tasting wine: Munich unpleasant, Ulm pleasant; Stuttgart and Frankfurt unpleasant; Mainz—he nodded. The Rhine was good, very good; he stood at the window while the train traveled beside it; good, he nodded to himself as he smoked. At Koblenz (unpleasant) darkness fell, so he went back into the compartment and slept until he was awakened by a shout that sounded like a shot: Bonn! He laughed and took a long swig from his bottle of wine.

Cologne tasted unpleasant; he had to change trains there. On the train to Ostend he sat across from a white-haired gentleman who smiled at him over newspaper, spectacles, and a purple ascot, put aside the newspaper, and removed his spectacles; then he heard in his own language, "Tell me, where are you from?"

"Don't you know?" he said, and his mouth was filled with a wonderful taste when he could speak his own language.

The old gentleman nodded, no longer smiling. "What are you looking for here?"

"Europa."

"And where are you going?"

"To London."

The old gentleman laughed and shook his head. "But Europa isn't in London."

"Where, then—where is she?"

"Not too far from Aachen."

"And where is Aachen?"

"Next stop but one."

The old gentleman was the first person to accept the proffered bottle of wine and drink from it. "God!" he said, as he lowered it from his lips. "That's some wine." And as he handed back the bottle he asked quietly, "Why are you sad? You'll find her all right."

"It's not sadness you see in my eyes, it's envy."

"Envy? Of what?"

"Of you, because you're all mortal."

"You're mortal, too," said the old gentleman as he tucked his newspaper under his arm, stood up, and lifted a bag down from the rack. The train came to a halt. "Don't forget—the next stop's Aachen."

He stayed out in the corridor, smoking and musing: Had the old gentleman been Death? Purple and white, and spoke his language so beautifully. A young woman with a twitching face hobbled toward him with a cane, tried to pass him; he took her twitching face in his hands like a fruit, it became smooth and soft; passed his hands two or three times along her crooked spine as if it were a musical instrument. He took away her cane and tossed it into the corridor; she groaned, "God, oh God!", tried to kiss his hands. He disengaged himself, ran into the next car, pulled the emergency brake, and jumped off the train before it jerked to a halt.

He lay smiling on his back among beanstalks, heard shouting, saw lanterns swinging; a voice called out, "It was that Greek, that foreign worker!" He tore off a few bean pods, ate the young beans out of their downy shells, drank some wine, waited until the train moved off after much swinging of lanterns. He stood up and, without waiting to brush the earth off his coat and trousers, walked across to the road, toward the next village. What he read on the signpost pleased him greatly: "Langerwehe = Longborn." At the next tavern he saw behind the glass door the shadow of the landlady, who was about to lock up; he gently pushed open the door, looked into her broad, tired face, and said, "Give me a quick beer, will you?" She locked the door behind him, went to the bar, took a glass from the shelf, and held it under the beer tap.

"You don't happen to be able to drive a car, do you?" she asked.

"Of course I can," he said.

"How about a truck?"

"Sure."

"D'you have a license?"

He fished it out of his pocket, handed it to her, and she studied it carefully.

"Tauros?" she said. "Doesn't that mean 'bull'?"

"My, my!" he said. "Such erudition!"

"I went to a convent school," she said, "you learn a lot there. OK. You're hired. Let's give it a try."

And that's how he became a beer-truck driver.

II

NOT ONLY was her first name unusual; even more so was the fact that she moved in with that fellow Schmitz, an electrician at a paper mill who had inherited a cottage with stable and barn, plus a few acres of land; a bit of a dreamer who to some people seemed morose and somewhat straitlaced because he maintained a stubborn silence in the taverns while others—salesmen, house painters, mailmen—talked about women and sex. He was thought to be a "queer" because he never had anything to do with women or girls, never went to dances—except for that one time with a cousin from Langerwehe who simply dragged him off in her car because she had no escort for the evening. That night at the dance he met her school friend with the unusual name. Suddenly he could actually dance; he danced many times with her, later drew her by the hand through the gaily lit beer garden to the edge of the field, tried to embrace her among the parked cars. "Not here," she said softly.

"Where, then?" he asked.

"In the forest," she said, "far, far away from all these cars. Not where there are cars around."

She drew him away by the hand, deep into the forest.

She gave up her study of engineering and moved in with him in the hamlet of Frauenbroich.

The nuns at the school had expected more of her. "Europa," so her final report had read, "combines intuition and intellectuality in a manner that warrants the expectation of great things from her." The nuns had expected not piety from her but boldness: "The new architectural dimension of a renewed Christian spirit," was how the principal had expressed it. Their annoyance with her was forgotten: that she had usually hidden in the garden to get out of church and prayers, preferring to weed or help with the fruit harvest, and then that affair with the elderly gardener, confessed to not by her but by him. He claimed that she—she was fifteen —had seduced him. She answered all reproaches with the single sentence, "I am a woman, I am a woman, I am a woman." Later with a truck driver who was delivering cement for the new gymnasium, and again the single sentence from her, "I am a woman." Both men were married, scandals just barely avoided. The comment of her home-room teacher, "It is her lack of conscience that makes her so beautiful." High point of her school fame: her meditation on the word "vanish" with its associations of evanescence, thin air, evaporation. The school inspector's comment, "Really worthy of publication." At the same time her astonishing insight into mathematical problems. She did everything "effortlessly": picking fruit, athletics, physics.

Now she was living with that electrician Schmitz, looking after his house, the cow, the chickens, spending days wandering about in the forests collecting berries and mushrooms; putting up preserves, mowing the hay. In Frauenbroich and the surrounding hamlets, people said she also carried on with men in the forest, but no man was ever found who boasted of having carried on with her.

Schmitz was good to her, she was good to him; her origins remained as obscure to him as they had always been to the nuns. Foundling, orphan. Whenever Schmitz asked her about it, she would murmur, "I don't know where I come from." When Schmitz came home and asked her how she was feeling, she would answer as she had answered the nuns when they had asked her the same question, "Like a stranger, but fine."

At night she would often place her right arm under his neck, draw his left arm under her own neck, hum to herself, and say things that to Schmitz's ears sounded odd.

"The loveliest word in your language—vanish."

"Why do you say 'your language'—isn't it yours too?"

He could feel on his arm that she shook her head.

"You know, don't you," she said one night, "that I'm not going to stay with you?"

She could feel in the dark on her arm that he nodded his head.

Schmitz was never afraid, yet he was apprehensive. It seemed to him that she had been with him forever, as if she had always been with him. "Eternity"—the word became for him as long and as broad as it was; time lost its meaning for him: one July morning they had emerged from the forest together, and she had stayed with him; he had taken his vacation, plus some unpaid weeks, and it was early September before he took on the sales depot for bottled beer. He felt as if eternity lay behind him and time lay ahead of him. Even words dropped away, became unfamiliar. "Marry" —he felt as if he had never heard the word; cars—he saw them, yet knew they didn't exist. Europa's presence extinguished words and realities.

"When I have vanished from you," she told him early in September, "take Trude Weihrauch. She is a woman."

III

NEXT MORNING at breakfast the landlady scolded him for his manners —for refusing to use a knife, simply tearing the bread into pieces and dipping them into the butter, then into the salt. With a scornful laugh he deigned to use a spoon to scrape the eggs out of their shells. Bread, butter, eggs, salt, and coffee: he enjoyed them all. He studied his route on the map, had her explain the list of agencies to him, where they were located in the hamlets; problems of bottle deposits, and the main principle of the business: "Cash only. After all, they've sold the beer, made their profit, and can pay cash for their new supplies. Only that new fellow, Schmitz in Frauenbroich, you can give him credit for a while." Luckily the truck had already been loaded by his predecessor. "You'll be late getting back," she said as he sat down behind the wheel, "and don't get lost, Bull!"

"Yes," he said, "I'll be late getting back," and drove off with a laugh.

He liked those sleepy hamlets, too small for a tavern or too far away from the next tavern, weary cattle among the fruit trees; unloading full beer crates, loading empty ones, money into the big leather bag; lethargic women with whom he negotiated, lively ones who usually became over-familiar. Toward two in the afternoon, just outside Frauenbroich, he drove off onto a forest path, drank some wine from his bottle, ate some bread and cheese, smoked a cigarette, switched on the motor to back out. He saw her coming along the path toward the truck, put on the brake, let the motor idle in neutral, jumped off, and ran toward her. Brief shyness before he took her in his arms; he was surprised to find that her hair was dark, he had imagined her blond. It bothered her that he smelled of car. "Come," he said softly, "let us vanish."

The truck was found by a pair of lovers that night, the motor still running. Schmitz came back into time, all apprehension fell away from him. No trace of those two. They had vanished in the forests.

The Staech Affair

T HE "AE" in Staech is pronounced like a long, faintly aspirated "a," as in Bach. It bothers the inhabitants of the place—consisting almost entirely of Benedictine monks—to hear the "ae" pronounced as in aerobatics. Hence this preamble. There are some further antagonisms associated with the name "Staech" which I can only mention in passing: a heated dispute among onomatologists, for instance, some maintaining that the "ae" is an unmistakable sign of Germanic origin, while their opponents claim that the final "ch" is an unmistakable sign of Celtic origin. I plead the Celtic cause, knowing only too well how corruptible vowels are; and besides, there is the telltale dialect in and around Staech. Staech is located in the Rhineland. I must dispense with a definition of what constitutes Rhenish, restricting myself to the line of demarcation given to the Rhineland at the time of the Prussian occupation, which has persisted since 1815, and according to this line of demarcation Staech is located in the Rhineland. It is ancient, renowned, beautiful, idyllic; in the midst of tall trees, the incomparable gray of medieval Rhenish romanesque; a robust little river by the name of Brülle provides the landscape's essential ingredient of water. (Brülle is in no way related to the German verb *brüllen,* to roar. Beware of jumping to false etymological conclusions! The name probably derives from *bruhlen,* in turn a local corruption of the amply familiar *buhlen,* to consort illicitly: it has *almost* been established that here, in the midst of these venerable forests, a medieval prelate built an abode for his concubine.)

Staech has two hotels—one luxury, one modest—a youth camp, and a hostel that is used for conferences. The most important feature is the Benedictine abbey. There one can play at being a temporary monk. Tranquillity, Gregorian chants, peace within and without. And then there are the monks in their noble garb, one or other of whom, at any given moment, either at prayer or meditation or in conversation with a guest, embellishes landscape or garden. Everything extremely simple, almost austere; the soil is tilled, orchards are tended. The climate is too harsh for wine.

I CAN forgo further details and merely point out that Staech is extolled by the protocol officials of the nearby capital as being "a sheer delight." A high-ranking—perhaps even the highest-ranking—official of the protocol department is said to have remarked, "What more can we ask for? The Occident in one of its most cultivated articulations is only fifty Mercedes-minutes away."

Indeed, Staech is virtually irreplaceable. Eleventh (possibly tenth or twelfth) century, gray Rhenish romanesque, Gregorian chants, the opportunity to become a temporary monk or to stay in a luxury hotel and at the same time participate in all the delights of the liturgy and the consolations of *almost* all the sacraments. An area—again I quote a protocol official —abounding in "positively unique opportunities for country rambles" in which, depending on the condition of the heart, lungs, or glands, one can spend half an hour, an entire hour, an hour and a half, three hours, in fact a whole day walking or hiking, equipped with a handy foolproof local map obtainable *free of charge* from the hall porter at the luxury hotel. The fact that in the luxury hotel one can also be a temporary husband or wife is familiar to cynics, who know that the management there is both discreet and broad-minded.

Only the protocol department is in a position to appreciate the invaluable role Staech performs for the benefit of wives of prominent visitors to the nation's capital. While their husbands get down to the nitty-gritty in the capital, the ladies enjoy being driven out to Staech in the protocol Mercedes. Departure is timed for the visitor to arrive in the morning for the Terce or Sext services and thus admire the nobly clad monks both aurally and visually (it is said that there have even been attempts at tactile perception). This is followed by light refreshments or lunch, and then, depending on time, mood, and stamina, a stroll through the truly magnificent woods, and in the afternoon attendance at Nones or Vespers, followed by tea and a drive back, filled with a deep spiritual peace, to the capital. And German as well as foreign politicians find Staech unique as a place of meditation and purification; some very strong-minded men have been seen humbly and tearfully kneeling there. Guests from the United States and Africa are particularly enchanted with Staech, it has even been claimed that spontaneous conversions have taken place there. And, needless to say, where *Ora* is demonstrated with such credibility, *Labora* is not forgotten either: brothers with rough hands, mud on their hands and feet, their habits sometimes even bespattered with cow dung, are to be seen from time to time, and the strange part about it is: these working monks are not merely on show, they are genuine.

ONE SURPRISING aspect is that the monks are always so willing to leave this idyllic spot. The travel itch of the monks of Staech has not escaped the affectionate mockery of the good Rhenish people in the neighborhood: a well-to-do local wag with an unpaid debt of gratitude to the monks is said to have once presented them with a whole collection of suitcases for Christmas. The monks really do love to travel; they lecture, with and without slides, participate in conferences, seminars, panel discussions; some of them contribute as free-lance writers to the supplements of serious national journals, discussing matters of theology, religion, and Christianity; and they seize every opportunity of going off to Hamburg, Munich, or Frankfurt. Yes, they love to go away, these monks, and they are not always happy to come back. Some are motorized, most are not. Hence the nominal full strength, amounting at present to forty-seven monks and brothers, is seldom achieved.

There have been occasions when only eleven, and once only nine, were present at afternoon Nones. After one such service a very prominent lady from Thailand apprehensively asked the protocol official whether there was some contagion in the air and whether—she had been nourished on early nineteenth-century literature—the reverend gentlemen were "stricken." The official found himself obliged to seek an explanation from the abbot and was given the devastating information that only one was sick, the others were all away on their travels.

Since in this age of technology the number of salaried workers is perforce steadily increasing (farming, hotel staff, administration), Staech is not financially self-supporting. It is liberally subsidized by state and diocese; and, moreover, the fact *that* it is supported is taken for granted. Not once has this fact been challenged in the finance committee, not even by the most religiously emancipated of its members. Who would want to see Staech deprived of its subsidies? That would be like suggesting that Cologne Cathedral be sold as a quarry. Even rabid freethinkers, irreligious Socialists (there are still some of those about), have never thought of withholding approval of the funds earmarked for Staech. Paradoxically enough, in latter years a contrary trend has become noticeable: the representatives of the classic Christian parties are hesitating somewhat longer, whereas the others are consenting with almost embarrassing alacrity. Of one thing there can be no doubt: even the most pettifogging atheist in the capital would not refuse Staech his support. Staech is something it ought not to be: dependent on the state and on the diocese in whose territory it is located. Of course, state and diocese are in a way dependent on Staech, but who could ever plumb the depths of such dialectics of varying inter-dependence?

One thing is certain: the abbot collects, and not too badly either. But in return state and diocese want to *see* something, or rather: they feel there should *be* something to see and hear. What, after all, is the use of a vast abbey like that, with all its complex economy (which is more complex than its tradition), if, as happened one foggy autumn day during the visit of a (non-Catholic) queen, only fifteen nobly garbed monks were present and the choral singing, even though each one "gave it all he had," sounded thin? Moreover, the participants included two aged bedridden monks who had been pressed somewhat forcibly into service. The queen was disap-pointed, *very* disappointed. During the ensuing informal lunch at the hotel she looked almost miffed, like a girl who has been done out of a date. After all, Staech *stands* for something. At home the queen had requested a thorough briefing on the history, tradition, and function of Staech.

As was inevitable, the news of the choir's poor numerical showing reached the ears of the head of state. He—the head of state—was most annoyed and passed on his annoyance to the archbishop, who com-municated the incident in a handwritten document beginning *"Scandalum fuisse . . ."* to the order's abbot general in Rome: the latter took up the matter with Staech and insisted on a list of those present and those absent, with detailed information on the absent monks' reasons for travel. The inquiries were, naturally, somewhat protracted, and even after some pretty massive interpolations the results were meager. Only sixteen of the absent monks could come up with an adequate alibi: eight had been occupied in a completely bona fide pursuit—conducting religious exercises in a con-vent—and eight had been away on lecture tours for Christian educational projects, some with, some without, colored slides. Five of the younger monks had left to attend a writers' conference ("We must seek contacts with the progressive elements of our own country"), the topic of which had caused both head of state and bishop considerable raising of eyebrows: "Orgasm as Depicted in Contemporary German Literature." It turned out later that four of these young monks had found the topic boring and spent most of their time at the movies, and in the balcony at that, where they could smoke. The alibis for the remaining eleven monks remained obscure. Two had ostensibly gone off to another monastery with which Staech was on friendly terms, to consult some volumes of the *Acta Sanctorum,* those in the Staech library having been stolen during the years of postwar confusion; the two monks had never arrived at the other monastery and, what was more, stubbornly refused to say where they had actually been (as yet unclarified). One monk had gone to Holland, with a purpose but no destination: purpose—to study the changes in Dutch Catholicism. This objective was termed by the bishop "rather vague." The objective of four other monks was given as: the study of Bavarian and Austrian baroque; they may have been traipsing around anywhere between Würzburg and the Hungarian border, but they did bring back an alibi in the form of a pretty good crop of colored slides. One monk had gone to a North German university town ostensibly to encourage an eminent physicist in his desire to convert to Catholicism; what had actually happened (as the physicist himself subsequently told the head of state at a reception) was that the monk tried to prevent the conversion.

WELL, THERE was trouble. The abbot could not be deposed, only voted out of office, and this was something the monks refused to do. They liked their abbot. For a while the abbot managed to curb the monks' travel itch. The next state visitor was a president from Africa, who turned out to be an expert, having been educated by Benedictines. There were thirty-two monks present, but even thirty-two monks do not make the Staech choir seem exactly overcrowded. The effect is roughly that of a hundred and fifty bishops inside St. Peter's: something like a sightseeing group of elderly sacristans. The head of state, amazed at the African guest's fund of knowledge about the order, expressed distinct annoyance to the head of protocol and raised the question of whether Staech was still fulfilling its function. . . . The result was a verbal confrontation between protocol officials and the diocesan secretariat.

The topic remained a secret, but some things inevitably leaked out: the curbing of travel itch at Staech had been followed by accesses of kleptomania and exhibitionism. Eleven of the younger monks had had to be consigned to a private psychiatric clinic. The abbot's request that notice of important state visits be given well in advance, in order that he might adjust the monks' travel movements accordingly, was refused. He was tersely informed that it was up to Staech to be "ready for action" at all times, since guests, such as journalists from the Eastern European bloc, often turned up at short notice, eager to see the sights.

WHAT MIGHT be called the "Staech affair" ran on for about a year, when suddenly, one crisp but sunny spring day, head of state *and* bishop made an unannounced appearance. How these two old codgers had managed to keep their arrangements a secret was never divulged. Well-informed circles assume these must have been made during the solemn reading of the petition for beatification of the nun Huberta Dörffler; the two men had been seen whispering together. Both men had simply given orders after breakfast to "harness" their Mercedes 600s and be driven to Staech, where they had met, and, without first calling on the abbot, immediately entered the church, Terce having just begun. Present in the church were fourteen monks.

During the subsequent serving of light refreshments (bread, wine, olives), the abbot not only seemed relaxed, he *was* relaxed. He said that, after having managed to achieve almost a full complement during the visit of an eminent Scandinavian guest—forty-three monks in the choir!—he had been obliged to reopen the "safety valve." In reply to the bishop's sarcastic question as to what relevance the words "safety valve" had to the monastic rule, the abbot responded with a cordial invitation to have a look at the medical reports of the psychiatric clinic. The two gentlemen who had come to inflict a defeat on the abbot suffered one themselves. The abbot declared that he for his part couldn't care less about state visits, and that he found the politicians who from time to time fled to Staech in search of consolation and tranquillity a nuisance. He expressed his willingness, in the case of state visits of special importance, to allow alumni and minor orders to take part in choral prayer as guests dressed in monks' habits. Transportation for such auxiliary personnel, as well as the procurement of monks' habits, would be a matter for the Most Reverend Lord Bishop and/or the Right Honorable Herr President to arrange. "And should you wish," he added, with irreverent frankness, "to resort to actors, by all means do so! I decline any further responsibility."

At the next state visit (a Catholic dictator from southwestern Europe), seventy-eight monks could be counted in the Staech choir, by far the majority youthful. In the car, on his way back to the capital, the dictator remarked to his escort, "These Germans! There's no one like them! Even their new generation of ascetic young monks can't be beaten." What he never found out, and what could never be confirmed in the capital, was that sixty of the young monks had been students who had demonstrated there in protest against the dictator's visit and had been arrested; they had been promised release and, in return for a honorarium of forty marks (they had first demanded seventy but finally consented to forty), had been persuaded to have their hair cut.

. . .

MEANWHILE people have been saying in the capital that the chief of protocol came to a verbal agreement with the chief of police: to be more generous in the arrest of student demonstrators during state visits *and* more generous in their release. Since a relationship exists between state visits and student demonstrations analogous to that between state visits and sightseeing tours of Staech, the Staech problem is regarded as solved. On the occasion of a visit of an Asian statesman, who then evinced an almost churlish lack of interest in monks, eighty-two monks could be counted. It seems there are now also some freeloaders, who obtain more accurate information on the dates of pending state visits than the abbot has as yet been able to do, and who then proceed to demonstrate rather too demonstratively (in the opinion of objective observers)—even investing now and again in a few tomatoes or eggs—in order to be arrested, then released, and acquire a free haircut plus forty marks and a copious lunch at Staech which, at the express wish of the abbot, is charged to diocesan rather than state funds.

Musically speaking, neither freeloaders nor students have so far presented any problem. Gregorian chants seem to come naturally to them. The only problems are those arising between the demonstrating groups, one group denouncing the other as "mercenary consumer-opportunists" and the latter denouncing the former as "abstract fantasists." The abbot of Staech gets along well with both groups, some of the young men—seven so far, apparently—have already entered the monastery as novices, and the fact that now and again during choir practice they slip a Ho Chi Minh into the Gregorian rhythm has so far gone unnoticed, even by a recently converted American statesman who, weary of NATO talk, spent a longer period at Staech than had been provided for by the protocol department. In a farewell communiqué he intimated that his visit to Staech had enriched his image of Germany by an important facet.

Till Death Us Do Part

I N THE draft from the swing door her first match went out, a second one broke on the striking surface, and it was nice of her attorney to offer her his lighter, shielding the flame with his hand. Now at last she could smoke—both felt good, the cigarette and the sunshine. It had taken barely ten minutes, an eternity, and perhaps it was that eternity as well as the permanence of those endless corridors that put the hands of the clock out of action. And the crowds, all those people looking for room numbers, reminded her of a summer clearance sale at Strössel's. What was the difference between divorces and bath towels at a clearance sale? Lineups for both, only that—so it seemed to her—in divorces the final decision was announced more speedily, and speed, after all, was what she had been after. *Schröder* vs. *Schröder.* Divorced. *Naumann* vs. *Naumann.* Divorced. *Blutzger* vs. *Blutzger.* Divorced.

Was the nice lawyer really going to say at this point what he was obliged to say? The only thing he could say? He said it: "Don't take it so hard." Said it although he knew she wasn't taking it hard at all, yet he had to say it, he said it nicely, and it was nice that he said it nicely. And naturally he didn't have much time, had to hurry off to the next case, appear again in court, line up again. *Klotz* vs. *Klotz.* Divorced.

Things had been much the same at the clearance sale: waiting politely, never impatient yet ever attentive until the woman who was too old to wear out even a single new bath towel had decided to take a whole dozen; then on to the next customer, who was clutching three swimsuits. After all, even at Strössel's there was still such a thing as personal service, not like at those discount stores where they unload junk on the customers. After all, the attorney couldn't go on standing beside her forever, there really not being much more to say than "Don't take it so hard." Her position at the top of the steps reminded her acutely of another occasion, seven years ago, when she had stood at the top of the steps leading up to City Hall: parents, witnesses, parents-in-law, photographer, cute little trainbearers—Irmgard's, Ute's, and Oliver's kids; bouquets, the taxi decorated with white roses, the "Till death us do part" still ringing in her ears, and on by taxi to the second ceremony, and once again, this time in church, "Till death us do part."

And here was the bridegroom waiting for her again at the foot of these steps, elated at the successful outcome and a bit embarrassed but also visibly proud of his second success of the day: having managed to find, here at the very foot of the steps, in one of the most hopeless parking areas in town, a spot for his car. Successes of various kinds had played quite a role in the divorce proceedings.

Now it wasn't death but the court that had separated them, and the occasion had lacked all dignity. And if the court, in pronouncing the divorce, had established death, why then wasn't there a funeral? Catafalque, mourners, candles, funeral oration? Or at least the wedding in reverse? Cute little kids, this time maybe Herbert's—Gregor and Marika—who would unfasten her train, lift the bridal wreath off her head, exchange her white dress for a suit: a kind of nuptial striptease performed in public on the steps if there wasn't going to be a funeral?

She had known, of course, that he would be waiting for her here, to start another of those futile discussions, since death had now been established—futile because he couldn't grasp the fact that there was nothing more she wanted from him now that she had moved with their son into a small apartment, neither money, nor her share in the "jointly acquired assets," nor even those six Louis—the how-many-th was it again? —chairs that were indisputably hers, inherited from her grandmother. One day he would probably unload them outside her door because he "simply couldn't stand disputed ownership." She wanted neither the chairs nor the set of Meissen porcelain (thirty-six pieces), nor any kind of a "property settlement." Nothing. After all, she had the boy, for the time being, since he was still living, unmarried, with that other woman—which one was it now, Lotte or Gaby? Not until he married Lotte or Gaby (or was it Connie?) would they have to "share" the boy (and there was no Solomon holding the sword over the child to be shared); all those nasty details about custody had been agreed upon, settled, and so there would be visiting rights, she would hand over the child to be stuffed and spoiled. ("Are you sure you don't want any more whipped cream?" and "Do you really like your new parka?" and "Of course I'll get you the model airplane.") For one day, for two, or a day and a half, and she would pick him up again. ("No, I really can't buy you a new parka, and I can't buy you a color TV for your first communion"—or was it confirmation? "No.")

Another cigarette? Better not. Now that the nice attorney with the chic little lighter no longer stood at her side, that draft from the swing door would force her to light the new cigarette from the old, and little things like that would make her look more of a slut than ever and, when it came to the final decision about the child, would certainly count as a black mark against her. This habit of smoking on the street had already been noted in the divorce files; besides, since she had admitted to being guilty of adultery (before he had, which also had to be admitted), she had anyway been recorded in the court documents as a kind of slut. All that nattering about whether or why women shouldn't, couldn't, mightn't smoke on the street had been described by the opposing attorney as a "pseudo-emancipatory" affectation not appropriate to her "educational level."

A good thing he didn't come up the steps, that he restricted himself to beckoning gestures; a good thing, too, that he shook his head in disapproval when she did, after all, light that second cigarette—not from the first one but with a match that didn't go out, although the clearance sale kept the swing door in constant motion.

Despite the absence of either priest or registry official, of tearful mothers and mothers-in-law, of photographer and cute little kids, at least there might have been an undertaker who would have driven off with something—what?—in a coffin, cremated it, and somewhere—where?—secretly buried it.

Probably he was even missing an appointment for her sake (the merger negotiations with Hocker & Hocker, perhaps, where he had been appointed to solve personnel problems); but would he really miss the Hocker & Hocker negotiations for the sake of a few chairs? He couldn't grasp, simply couldn't, that she didn't hate him at all, that she wanted nothing from him, that he had not merely ceased to matter to her but had become a stranger, someone she had once known, once married, who had become someone else. They had been successful in everything: building a career and building a house. They had failed in only one thing: keeping death at bay. Nor was it only he who had died—she had died too; even her memory of him failed her. And perhaps the clerics and bureaucrats couldn't and wouldn't grasp the fact that this "Till death us do part" didn't mean physical death at all, much less a death before a physical death, that it meant only the entry of a total stranger into the conjugal bedroom insisting on rights he no longer possessed. The role of the court that issued this death certificate and called it a divorce was as irrelevant as that of the priest and the registry official: no one could revive the dead or make death reversible.

She threw down the cigarette, ground it out, and waved him away, finally and firmly. There was nothing further to discuss, and she knew exactly where he was intending to drive her: to the café out in Haydn Park, where at this hour the Turkish waitress would be placing miniature copper vases, each containing one tulip and one hyacinth, on the tables, and straightening the tablecloths; where—at this hour—somewhere in the background a vacuum cleaner was still being used. He had always called it the "Café of Memories," condescendingly pronouncing it "quite good, not high class, certainly not smart." No, she repeated her final dismissive gesture, once, twice, until, shaking his head, he finally did get into his red car, maneuver out of his parking slot and, without waving to her again, drive off, "carefully but self-confidently," in his customary manner.

It was not yet nine-thirty, and now at last she could walk down the steps, buy a newspaper, and enter the café across the street. What a relief that he no longer barred her way down the steps! She was in no hurry, and there were a few things she wanted to think about. At twelve, when her son came home from school, she would give him a big pancake with some canned cherries, and some grilled tomatoes, he loved that. She would play with him, help him with his homework, and maybe go to a movie, maybe even to Haydn Park, to establish the final death of memory. Over canned cherries, pancake, and grilled tomatoes he would naturally ask her whether she was going to get married again. No, she would say, no. One death was enough for her. And would she be going back to work at Strössel's, where he was allowed to sit in the back room, do his homework, play with fabric swatches, and where that nice Mr. Strössel sometimes stroked his head in a friendly way? No. No.

The tablecloth at the café pleased her, felt good under her hands; it actually was pure cotton, old rose with silver stripes, and she thought of the tablecloths at the café in Haydn Park: maize-yellow, coarsely woven, those first ones had been, seven years ago: later came the green ones, with a printed daisy pattern, and finally the bright yellow ones, with no pattern at all but a fringed border, and he had always (and would have done so today) fidgeted with the fringe and tried to persuade her that she really did have a right to some kind of compensation, at least fifteen—maybe twenty—thousand marks that he could (and would) easily raise with a mortgage on the unencumbered house—after all, she had always been a "good although unfaithful spouse, careful and thrifty without being stingy" and had participated "quite positively and productively in the enhancement of their standard of living." As for those Louis chairs and the Meissen porcelain, she really was entitled to those. His fury at her refusal to take any of that had exceeded his fury over her lapse with Strösser; and finally he had (and would have done so today) ripped off some of the cheap fringe and thrown it on the floor—disapproving looks from the Turkish waitress, who was just arriving with tea and coffee, tea for him, coffee for her—further grounds for ominous remarks about her health and a scornful gesture toward the ashtray (which, incidentally, was ugly, dark brown, floor-colored—and which, she must admit, already contained three butts!).

Yes, coffee. Here she was, drinking coffee again, turning over the pages of the newspaper. Here in the café she could also smoke undisturbed, without inviting annoying glances or snide remarks. She thought of the shoving and chasing in the endless corridors of the courthouse, with all those hurrying people who had a sense of injury or had inflicted injury, who were owed rent or hadn't paid rent, where everything was decided and nothing clarified, by nice attorneys and nice judges who couldn't keep death at bay.

Again and again she caught herself smiling at the thought of the timing of the death that had separated them. It had started a year ago, when they were having dinner at the home of his boss, and he suddenly remarked that she was "involved in textiles," which sounded as if she were a carpet or fabric weaver or designer, whereas she had simply been a saleswoman in a dry-goods store—and how happy she had been there, her hands unfolding, refolding, everything pleasing to the hands, the eyes and, when business was quiet, tidying everything up, putting things back into drawers, onto shelves and racks: towels, sheets, handkerchiefs, shirts, and socks, and then one day that nice young man had turned up, the one who had just died, and had asked to see some shirts, although he had no intention of buying one or the money to do so—turned up simply because he was looking for someone to whom he could spill out his excitement over his success: three years after graduating from night school ("I'm involved in electrotechnology," and all he'd been was an electrician) he already had his degree and had been given a subject for his doctoral thesis. And now that phrase, "my wife's involved in textiles," which was supposed to sound at least like applied arts if not art, and how angry, almost sick with rage, it had made him when she said, "Yes, I was a saleswoman in a dry-goods store, and I still help them out sometimes." In the car on the way home not a word, not a syllable, icy silence, hands gripping the steering wheel.

The coffee was surprisingly good, the newspaper boring ("industrial profits too low, wages too high"), and what she picked up from the conversations around her all seemed to be about court cases. ("Facts twisted." "I can prove that the sofa belongs to me." "I'm not going to let them take away my son."). Attorneys' gowns, attorneys' briefcases. An office messenger brought some files that were solemnly opened, carefully scrutinized. And then the young waitress bringing her a second cup of coffee actually put a hand on her shoulder and said, "Don't take it too hard.

It'll pass. I cried my eyes out for weeks—weeks, I tell you." She was ready to be angry, but then she smiled and said, "It's already passed." And the waitress went on, "And I was the guilty party too." Too? she thought. Am I the guilty party, and if so how do I show it—because I smoke, maybe? Drink coffee, read the paper, and smile? Yes, of course she was guilty, she had refused to acknowledge the death soon enough and had continued to live out those deadly months with him. Until one day he brought home a new evening dress, bright red, very low-cut, saying, "Wear this to the company dance tonight—I'd like you to dance with my boss and show him everything you've got," but she had worn her old silver-gray with the bead pattern she liked. A month later, when he found out about the affair with Strössel, she remembered his fury when he said, "What you refused to show my boss you've now shown to yours."

Yes, so she had—not long after he had moved out of the bedroom into the guest room, and the next morning had come back into the bedroom with all that porn stuff and a whip and had started a terrible row about his sexual achievements, which she was denying him but which he urgently needed; they were in such stark contrast to his professional achievements that he was developing a neurosis, almost a psychosis; there was no way she could offer him this satisfaction, she had taken away the whip and locked the door after him. The stuff had turned her ice cold, and she blamed herself for still not acknowledging the death, taking the child, ordering a taxi, and driving away. In actual fact she had gone on to share in the remodeling of the house—guest room, guest bathroom, TV room, study, sauna, children's room—and it had been her idea to go to Strössel and ask for a discount, for bath and hand towels, sheets and pillowcases, drapery fabrics. Naturally she had felt a bit uneasy when Strössel looked deep into her eyes and increased the discount from twenty to forty percent; and when his eyes grew misty and he tried to grab her across the counter, she had murmured, "For heaven's sake, not here, not here," and Strössel got the wrong (or right) idea and thought that somewhere else she would be willing. She had actually gone upstairs with him, with that pudgy, bald bachelor who was twenty years older than she and blissful when she lay down with him. And meanwhile he had left the store open and the cash register unattended, and not even the unavoidable unbuttoning and buttoning of clothing had embarrassed her. And later when he packed up her purchases downstairs at the cash desk, he hadn't given her a discount but had made her pay the full retail price, and when he held the door open for her, he hadn't tried to kiss her. The opposing attorney had actually tried to have Strössel attest to her claim of "discount withheld after favors granted," but then her nice attorney had succeeded in keeping Strössel out of it. Yes, she had gone back to Strössel several times. "Not to make purchases?" "No." "How often?" She didn't know, really she didn't. She hadn't counted. Marriage had never been spoken of, the word "love" never mentioned. It was that soft, deeply moved and moving bliss of Strössel's that made her afraid of sinking back onto a rose-colored pillow.

No, she couldn't go back to him, and his old-fashioned store would have been the right place for her, where she knew every case and box, every shelf and drawer, knew the stocks that genuinely did consist of only wool and cotton; she and her hands, that were infallible when it came to spotting any adulteration by even the tiniest synthetic thread. No, she couldn't work in one of those "cheap and nasty" stores either, as Strössel always called them. No, she wouldn't marry again, be present again when a living person died and once again a death separated her. She supposed the time had come when husbands became brutally obscene, and lovers, in an old-fashioned way that was almost too rose-colored, became tender and blissful.

"See?" said the waitress when she paid her bill. "Now we're feeling a bit better, aren't we? After all, you're still a young woman, nice-looking too, and"—here it came—"you've got all your life before you and your son'll stick by you!" She smiled at the waitress again as she left the café.

She would bake her son a hazelnut cake, buy the ingredients on the way home, and if he asked her, "Do I really have to go to that woman?" (Connie, Gaby, Lotte?), she would say, "No." And then there was still the firm of Haunschüder, Kremm & Co., Strössel's old competitors, where the infallibility of her hands would be equally in demand. Only that it was more of a mail-order house, and she wouldn't so often be able to unfold a shirt and smooth it out, as she had done for that attractive young man who had just received his degree and been given the subject for his doctoral thesis. Perhaps instead of cherries she would buy some smoked herring, he liked that just as much, and he would stand beside her while it turned crisp in the pan, while the pancake dough enfolded it and turned golden-brown. She could probably become a buyer at Haunschüder, Kremm & Co.; she knew she could rely on her hands, no adulterating thread would get past them.

On Being Courteous
When Compelled
to Break the Law

I‌T WOULD seem idle to extol the obvious forms of courtesy:
that naturally one holds the front door open for a child;
that one not only refrains from pushing ahead of a child when shopping
but steps back for him;

that one allows a tired, stress-ridden schoolchild traveling home on
the streetcar, bus, or train to enjoy his seat in peace without disturbing that
well-earned peace either verbally or even by so much as staring at him with
an expression of moral disapproval.

Further, I take it for granted that one does not allow one's child, one's
cat, dog, or bird, to go hungry, that one is prepared, if need be, to go out
and steal food for them, and it goes without saying that one must not let
one's wife or girlfriend hunger or thirst either;

that none of them should be beaten, even when they ask for it, the
courtesy of hands being one of the principal courtesies;

and that one should not pour the honored guest the first, second, or,
if at all possible, even the third, but the fourth cup from the teapot, bearing
in mind the Chinese proverb: Courtesy lies close to the bottom of the
teapot.

Among those courtesies we take for granted is that when dealing with
people of either sex who regard themselves as our inferiors—for ESSEN-
TIALLY the concept of "inferior" is, obviously, unacceptable—one must use
a slightly more subdued, more restrained tone of voice than when dealing
with those who regard themselves as our superiors; of course, the concept
of "superior" is also ESSENTIALLY unacceptable, since you cannot simply
have a superior served up to you like a bowl of soup, and in dealing with
these superiors one should not, need I say, be loud and rude but merely
a shade less subdued and a shade less courteous; this behavior might slightly
modify the structures.

Moreover, when confronted by a person one dislikes one should not simply make remarks to his face such as "I don't like your mug!" It is possible to express one's aversion courteously, perhaps as follows, and preferably in writing, since the spoken word always carries with it the risk of rudeness:

"By reason of unfathomable, inscrutable, I will not say cosmic constellations, not wishing to make the stars and their ascendants solely responsible—by reason, therefore, of circumstances that are neither solely responsible nor solely predestined, the—shall we say—strands of sympathetic response between us have unfortunately (I would ask you to interpret this 'unfortunately' as an expression of my regret as well as of my abstract respect for your person) proved incapable of animation. Hence, although 'essentially' you are a most pleasant person and figure, I deem it advisable, indeed necessary, to restrict the number of our encounters to a minimum, to that minimum which compels us, for professional reasons, from time to time to shake hands, discuss details—encounters that are unavoidable in view of the increasing importance of the production of [here the product in question may be inserted, e.g.: novels, bolts, herrings in aspic]. Beyond this necessary minimum I suggest that we eschew the sound of each other's voices, the sight of our skin and hair, the perception of the odors we emanate. It is with some regret that I advise you of this, in the hope that these unfathomable constellations and combinations may change, that the strands of sympathetic response between us may become animated, and that an altered overall situation of sympathetic exchange may possibly enable us to extend the necessary professional contacts to the private domain. Yours most respectfully. . . ."

Such forms of courtesy appear to me too obvious to require more than a passing allusion.

By CONTRAST, however, it seems to me as difficult as it is necessary to point to courtesy in unconventional, indeed illegal, situations. It must be emphasized that ESSENTIALLY the actions I should like to enlarge upon are not merely unconventional or immoral but downright criminal. Let us take, for example, a crime that ESSENTIALLY is as criminal as it is discourteous, such as a bank robbery or a bank holdup, and let us consider that lady, heretofore so law-abiding, respectable, and honorable, who in broad daylight—more precisely, at about 3:29 p.m.—relieved a savings bank in the suburb of a large German city of seven thousand marks. Try to imagine the scene: a sixty-one-year-old lady of the type known as frail, whose appearance calls to mind solitaire or bridge, the widow of a lieutenant colonel, enters the branch of a savings bank in order to appropriate a sum of money by illegal means! If this lady became known as the "courteous bank robber," was in fact described as such in the police files, the use of the adjective "courteous" was intended to convey her particularly dangerous quality. This lady did instinctively what the courteous bank robber must do: not even think of weapons, of violence, or shouting, not even consider such clumsy methods. After all, it is not merely discourteous, it is positively dangerous to brandish pistols or machine guns and shout, "Hand over the dough, or I'll shoot!" And of course a lady such as ours does not enter just any old bank simply out of abstract greed, or because she has suddenly become unbalanced, but because in her extremity she has regained her balance. She has carefully considered this action and has her motives!

The dire plight that forces this lady to this, to put it mildly, unconventional act must be briefly outlined. She has a son who, having taken the wrong turn, has served a few minor prison sentences but has now, discharged once again from jail, found a girlfriend who exerts a stabilizing influence on him. He has a chance of being employed as a pharmaceuticals salesman—his mother has spent a small fortune on telephone calls and postage, has made use of all her connections (among them two generals still on active duty) to obtain this chance for him. And now, like a bolt from the blue and at the last moment, comes the company's demand: a five-thousand-mark bond! His mother—that very lady who became known as the courteous bank robber—has found him a small apartment, developed an affection for his girlfriend, everything is going splendidly, and now that bombshell: a five-thousand-mark bond! Try to imagine the scene: the lady's bank credit has already been strained to the utmost; her pension has shrunk to a bare subsistence level, the greater part going to pay off the bank; she has borrowed wherever she could—from bridge friends, her husband's old fellow officers (among them two colonels and a general), all nice people; she has already eliminated the egg from her breakfast menu, and as she stands there in her apartment all she can think of is: "Beg, borrow, or steal!" and this popular saying turns out to be relatively disastrous for the savings bank.

"Beg, borrow, or steal!"—stealing seems to be the obvious remedy. I should add that the lady is not only frail but proud. Over and over again she has been humiliated, lectured, forced to submit to several thousand well-meant pieces of advice, swallow snide remarks about her beloved son; she has sold most of her furniture, disposed of her collie, to whom she was very attached, and quarreled about this with her best friend, who actually said, "A dog for a dog—that's no bargain!" She has visited her son in a number of jails, paid legal fees, incurred traveling expenses. The only luxury she still permits herself is the telephone: in order that her son can call her at any time, and she him, if he happens to have access to a telephone. There are even moments when she not only *believes* she understands him but actually does. The social experiences of the past four years have pushed her *inwardly* to the verge of becoming a social dropout, but not outwardly: she is always well groomed, looks younger than she is, and now, after her son has raised the alarm over the telephone, the fateful phrase occurs to her: "Beg, borrow, or steal!" and its implications take root in her mind in a manner unforeseen by those who spread such sayings. Steal, she thinks, that's the solution, when around two o'clock she remembers that spruce little savings-bank branch situated at the edge of a park in a nearby suburb. Before leaving her apartment she feeds her pretty dwarf finches, tiny birds half the size of a thumb, which she can still afford. The word "steal," so foreign to her, becomes increasingly familiar as she approaches the park in the adjacent suburb, which she reaches by about 3:05. Steal, she thinks, where does one steal bread? In a bakery. Where does one steal sausage? At a butcher's. Where does one steal money? From a till or a bank. The till is immediately rejected, she finds that too *personal,* she does not wish to rob anyone directly; besides, what till would ever contain five thousand marks? And robbing a till seems to her too much of an imposition, almost an importunity.

HER CONSCIENCE has long since ceased to bother her, she is already preoccupied with tactical and strategic deliberations. Hidden in some bushes, she looks across to the smart little savings bank, knowing that it closes at two-thirty. The bank is empty of customers, and strange things shoot through her mind: naturally she sometimes watches television, she also occasionally goes to the movies, and she thinks—not of weapons, not even of toy weapons, but of the stocking pulled over the face: which had always made her shudder because it was an affront to her aesthetic sense, that deformation of a human face. Moreover, she feels it is beneath her dignity here in the bushes to deprive one of her legs of its stocking; besides, it would provide a clue for possible pursuers. In these deliberations—as the indulgent reader will immediately discern—aesthetics, morals, and tactics come together in unique fashion!

In her handbag is a pair of oversized dark glasses—a gift from her son, who thought they would suit her. She puts on the glasses, ruffles her normally neatly coiffed hair, steps out from the bushes, crosses the street, enters the savings bank: behind the window on the right, a young lady sorting vouchers gives her a polite, slightly forced smile because closing time is only a few minutes away; the center window is closed; behind the one on the left stands a young man of about thirty-four, counting the contents of the cash drawer. He looks up, smiles at her politely, and says the usual, "Can I help you, madam?" At that moment she puts her hand into her bag, pulls it out as a clenched fist, steps closer to the window, and whispers, "Unusually compelling circumstances force me to this, I am sorry to say, unavoidable holdup. My right hand contains a nitrite capsule that can cause great havoc. I very much regret having to threaten you, but I need five thousand marks immediately. Give them to me. Or else . . ."

The tragic drama of the situation is enhanced by the fact that the teller —like most of his colleagues—is also a courteous person who is not in the least alarmed by the "or else" but instantly grasps the lady's quandary. Furthermore, professional bank robbers never ask for specific amounts, they demand the whole lot. He pauses in his counting—he happens to have just reached the five-hundred-mark bills!—and whispers, "You are putting me in an embarrassing position if you don't use more force. Nobody will ever believe me about the explosive capsule if you don't shout, threaten, put on a convincing scene. After all, there are rules for bank holdups too. You are doing it all wrong."

At that moment the young lady leaves her window, locks the bank from the inside, but leaves the key in the lock. The old lady, no less determined, in fact more determined than ever, recognizes her opportunity. "This capsule," she whispers threateningly. "Nitrite," says the teller, "is not explosive, merely poisonous. Probably you mean nitroglycerine." "Not only do I mean it, I have it." It is already clear that the teller, or rather his money, is doomed. Instead of simply pressing the alarm button, he allows himself to be drawn into an argument; moreover, he already has little beads of perspiration on his forehead and upper lip and is puzzling over what the lady might need the money for: Does she drink? Take dope? Has she gambling debts? A rebellious lover? He puzzles too much, fails to make use of his rights, and in this—it is fair to say *strongly* meditative— intermezzo, the old lady simply thrusts her hand through the window (she is smart enough to use her left hand), grabs as many five-hundred-mark bills as she can, runs to the door, unlocks it, crosses the street, disappears into the bushes—and only when she is long out of sight does the teller raise the alarm. It is fairly certain that *this* teller would have confronted a discourteous bank robber with far greater vigor: would have struck the clenched fist, raised the alarm.

Needless to say, the affair had a variety of sequels. Let me allude to the principal ones: the lady was never caught, the teller was not dismissed, merely transferred to a position where he had no direct contact with either cash or the public. When the lady discovered that instead of five thousand marks she had picked up seven thousand marks, she remitted one thousand nine hundred back to the bank and was clever enough not to do this by telegram since that might have led to her identification. She permitted herself a taxi, drove to the railway station, took the next train to her son: that cost her some ninety marks, the remaining ten she spent on coffee and a brandy, which she consumed in the dining car—and felt she had earned. When handing the money over to her son, she placed her hand over his mouth and said: "Don't *ever* ask me where I got it from." Then she phoned her neighbor and asked her to feed her pretty dwarf finches. Almost superfluous to add that things turned out well for her son: of course he read in the newspaper about the strange holdup by the "courteous bank robber," and this act of solidarization by a criminal action on the part of his mother had a morally stabilizing effect on him, more than several thousand pieces of good advice, more than his stabilizing girlfriend. He became a reliable pharmaceuticals salesman with opportunities for advancement, although it must be added that he could not resist saying to his mother on more than one occasion: "Imagine you doing *that* for me!" *What* was never put into words. After much cogitation, the lady fixed the rate of repayment to the bank at one mark a month, her rationale for this low rate being: "Banks can wait." From time to time she sent the teller some flowers, a book, or a theater ticket, and bequeathed him the only valuable piece of furniture she still possessed: a carved medicine chest in neo-Gothic style.

As we see: courtesy pays, for bank employees and bank robbers; and if bank robbers were completely to exclude weapons or explosive capsules, rude language, and rude behavior from their strategy, the day might come when we would no longer speak of bank holdups but only of forced loans, which will merely be a matter of a nonviolent duel between two different manifestations of courtesy.

I must add that bank robbery, when it takes place without violence or physical injury, is quite a popular offense. Every successful bank robbery in which no one is injured releases feelings of joy and even envy among those who would at any time carry out a successful and nonviolent bank robbery if they had the courage.

It is far more difficult even so much as to mention courtesy in the case of an equally punishable offense such as *desertion*. Strangely enough, deserters are considered to be cowardly, an opinion that on closer inspection fails to hold water. The deserter in wartime risks being shot—by either friend or foe, since he never knows into whose hands he will fall, although he thinks he knows from whose hands he is escaping. Whatever national yardsticks one wishes to apply—and oddly enough all nations are agreed on this—the deserter in wartime risks something, and one should respect his risk. But here I wish to speak about the *courteous* deserter *in peacetime,* about that unknown young man who leaves military service without making use of his rights—for instance, the right to conscientious objection; the young man who clears out, disappears—if possible in a foreign country —simply because he has had enough and is fed up with the main burden of a soldier's life—boredom; the man who is not attracted by the more or less enforced camaraderie or by the service as such; who is left cold by money, food, driver's license, educational opportunities, chances of promotion; a nice German boy who—let us say—has read his Eichendorff in school and found him "overwhelming"; a pleasant youth who never finished school because he found it too boring; who became a carpenter, something he enjoyed; who shortly after passing his apprenticeship test was called up for military service, with a total lack of interest in armored vehicles or weapons of any kind, also with no interest in politics but profoundly, although not exclusively, interested in the manufacture of furniture such as he has observed on a number of visits to Italy in the street-level workshops of Rome and Florence, perhaps also of Siena. Moral problems, such as the occasional out-and-out faking of furniture, do not interest him: he wants—he wanted—to go there, and instead now suddenly finds himself in an infantry barracks in—let us say—Neu-Offenbach. Of course, this young man can be seriously reproached on a number of counts: that he lacks civic consciousness, that he should have cleared out to—let us say—Bologna before, rather than after, being called up. He can be reproached for lacking a sense of duty, although this is not the case, since the master carpenter under whom he served his apprenticeship and who has meanwhile fallen victim to structural changes in the economy, gave him an excellent reference. His parents, his teachers, even his friend, have repeatedly tried to persuade him that one must think *realistically*; yet this pleasant young man does think *realistically*, he thinks about seasoned wood, about glue and screws, about workbenches and curved chair legs, and of course he also thinks about girls and wine and things like that. The point is: the army means nothing to him, it says nothing to him, gives nothing to him. There are such cases. It is useless to deplore it, although ESSENTIALLY it is deplorable. That is the way the boy happens to be, and to his credit he did behave in a reasonably fair manner, having faithfully completed his so-called basic training: not that he conceded its necessity, it merely aroused his curiosity. But now he has simply had enough, and he does not turn to some counseling service or other—church, government, nonpartisan— no, he simply clears out; yet, being a courteous person, he does not just sneak off without a word, he writes (from a safe distance and using misleading, i.e., Swiss, stamps) a letter to his captain:

"Dear Sir: The fact that I can find no satisfaction in your profession, which I would have to practice for another year, does not, I trust, hurt your feelings, in the same way that I ask you not to take my desertion personally and certainly not as an insult. It so happens that I am not a soldier and never will be, and nothing could be farther from my mind than to reproach you for not being a carpenter and probably not knowing what a tenon is, let alone how it is made. Of course I am aware—and I would ask you always to bear this in mind—that, although there are laws to force a man to be a soldier for fifteen months, there are no laws to force him to know anything about tenons, and I realize therefore that my comparison of soldier/carpenter is a lame one. So be it, and since there is this law that forces me to spend another year of atrocious boredom, I wish to inform you herewith that I am breaking that law.

"What pains me is the fact that you were such a nice, agreeable, understanding superior, and that naturally I would prefer to inflict on a lousy, beastly officer the pain I may be inflicting on you. More than once you have protected me, who has so little comprehension of absurd army regulations, from punishment; you have smiled understandingly at many a foolishness that aroused the ire of my corporal and even of my comrades —so understandingly that I suspect a crypto-deserter in you, and again you should take that not as an insult but as a compliment. In short: *as* my superior you were even better than my master carpenter, but *what* you— or rather, the army—doled out to me was, quite simply, intolerable, and this does not apply to the food or the allowance but merely to that appalling activity known as 'killing time.' The simple fact is that I do not want to go on killing my time; I want to make it come alive—no more, but no less.

"The only sensible activity, the only one I enjoyed, was the four-day disaster-relief deployment during the floods in Oberduffendorf: it was most enjoyable paddling the rubber dinghy from house to house and bringing the marooned inhabitants of Oberduffendorf hot soup, coffee, bread, and the tabloid—many a face lit up in gratitude! But I ask you, sir, would it not be positively macabre, even wicked, to wait for further disasters in order to find meaning in military service?

"Hoping that you will understand some of my thoughts and not despise my motives, I remain, respectfully yours. . . ."

Too Many Trips
to Heidelberg

For Klaus Staeck, who knows that the story
is invented from beginning to end, yet true

THAT EVENING, as he sat on the edge of the bed in his pajamas, waiting for the midnight news and smoking one last cigarette, he tried in retrospect to pinpoint the moment at which this pleasant Sunday had slipped away from him. The morning had been sunny, fresh, a coolness of May although it was June, yet the warmth to be expected at noon was already perceptible: light and temperature had reminded him of the old days when he had been out training from six to eight before going to work.

For an hour and a half that morning he had cycled along back roads between suburbs, between allotment gardens and industrial areas, past green fields, toolsheds, gardens, the big cemetery, out to where the forest began far beyond the city limits. On the asphalt stretches he had speeded up, timing himself and testing his acceleration; he had put on spurts and found that he was still in good form, might even risk entering an amateur race again, his legs responding to the joy of having passed his exam and to his intention of taking up regular training again. What with his job, night school, earning a living, studying, he hadn't been able to do much about it these last three years. He would need a new bike, but that would be no problem provided he could come to terms with Kronsorgeler tomorrow, and there was no doubt that he would.

After his training spin, a few exercises on the rug in his rented room, a shower, clean underwear, then by car out to his parents for breakfast: coffee and toast, fresh eggs and honey, on the terrace Father had built onto the house; the bright awning—a gift from Karl—and, as the morning warmed up, the reassuring stereotype utterance of his parents, "Well, you've almost made it now, you'll soon have made it now." His mother had said "soon," his father "almost," and always the pleasurable harking back to the fear of the last few years, a fear they had never blamed each other for, a fear they had shared: from amateur regional champion and electrician to passing his exam yesterday, erstwhile fear that was beginning to turn into veteran's pride. And they kept asking him what this or that word was in Spanish: carrot or motorcar, Queen of Heaven, bee and busy, breakfast, supper and sundown, and how happy they were when he stayed on for lunch and invited them over to his place next Tuesday to celebrate his success. Father went off to pick up some ice cream for dessert, and he accepted a cup of coffee although an hour later he would have to have coffee again at Carola's parents'. He even had a kirsch and chatted with them about his brother Karl, his sister-in-law Hilda, about Elke and Klaus, the two kids who, they all agreed, were being spoiled, what with their jeans and fringed jackets and cassettes and all that, and constantly there would be those pleasurable sighs: "Well, you'll soon have made it now, you've almost made it now!" That "almost," that "soon," had made him uneasy. He *had* made it! All that remained was the interview with Kronsorgeler, who had been favorably disposed toward him right from the start. Hadn't he done a good job teaching Spanish at the adult education center and German at those evening classes for Spaniards?

Later he helped his father wash the car and his mother weed the garden, and as he was about to leave she brought carrots, spinach, and a bag of cherries from the freezer, packed them in an insulated bag, and insisted that he wait until she had picked some tulips for Carola's mother. Meanwhile his father checked the tires, asked him to start the motor, listened to it suspiciously, then stepped up to the lowered window and asked, "Still making all those trips to Heidelberg—on the autobahn?" It was meant to sound as if he were querying the capability of his old, somewhat decrepit car to cover those fifty miles twice, sometimes three times a week.

"Heidelberg? Yes, I still drive there two or three times a week—it'll be some time before I can afford a Mercedes."

"Oh yes, Mercedes," said his father. "There's that fellow from the government, the Department of Education, I believe—yesterday he brought in his Mercedes again for a checkup. Insists on my doing the job personally. What's his name again?"

"Kronsorgeler?"

"Yes, that's the one. A very nice fellow. I'd even call him a gentleman, no irony intended."

Just then his mother brought the flowers, saying, "Remember us to Carola, and her parents too, of course. We'll be seeing them on Tuesday anyway." As he was about to drive off, his father came up once more and said, "Don't make too many trips to Heidelberg—with this wreck!"

On his arrival at the Schulte-Bebrungs', Carola hadn't come home yet. She had phoned and left a message that she wasn't quite through with her reports but would come as soon as she could; they were to go ahead with their afternoon coffee.

The terrace was larger, the awning, though faded, more generous, everything more elegant, and even in the barely perceptible shabbiness of the garden furniture, in the grass growing in the cracks between the red tiles, there was something that irritated him like some of those harangues at student demonstrations; things like that, and clothing, were sources of irritation between Carola and himself since she always complained that his clothes were too formal, too bourgeois. With Carola's mother he chatted about growing vegetables, with her father about bicycle races, found the coffee not as good as at his parents', and tried not to let his tension turn into irritation. After all, these were really nice, progressive people who had accepted him without prejudice, officially, even, by sending out engagement announcements. By this time he had become genuinely fond of them, including Carola's mother, whose frequent "charming" had at first got on his nerves.

Eventually Dr. Schulte-Bebrung—a bit embarrassed, so it seemed to him—asked him to come into the garage, where he showed him the newly acquired bicycle that he rode every morning for "a few turns" around the park and the Old Cemetery—a magnificent specimen of a bike. He praised it enthusiastically, quite without envy, mounted it for a test ride around the garden, explained the workings of leg muscles to Schulte-Bebrung (remembering that the senior members of the club had always suffered from cramps!); and after he had dismounted and propped the bike against the wall inside the garage, Schulte-Bebrung asked him, "What do you think—how long would it take me on this magnificent specimen of a bike, as you call it, to get from here to, say, Heidelberg?" It sounded casual enough, innocent, especially as Schulte-Bebrung went on, "You see, I was at university in Heidelberg, had a bike in those days too, and from there to here used to take me—young and strong as I was then—two and a half hours."

He smiled, obviously with no ulterior motive, talked about traffic lights, traffic jams, all the cars that in those days hadn't existed; by car— he'd already tried it out—it took him thirty-five minutes to get to his office, by bicycle only thirty minutes. "And how long does it take you by car to Heidelberg?"

"Half an hour."

The fact that he mentioned the car took away some of the casualness of mentioning Heidelberg, but at that moment Carola arrived, and she was as sweet as ever, as pretty as ever, a bit disheveled, and you could tell she really was dead tired; and now, as he sat on the edge of the bed, a second cigarette still unlit between his fingers, he simply didn't know whether his tension had already turned into irritation and been transferred from him to her, or whether she had been tense and irritable—and this had been transferred from her to him. She kissed him, of course, but whispered in his ear that she wouldn't be going with him today. Then they talked about Kronsorgeler, who had spoken so highly of him, about getting into the civil service, about the boundaries of the regional district, about cycling, tennis, Spanish, and whether he would get an A or only a B. She herself had only scraped through with a C. When invited to stay for supper he pleaded tiredness and work, and no one had particularly urged him to change his mind. The air quickly cooled off again on the terrace; he helped carry chairs and dishes into the house, and when Carola walked with him to the car she kissed him with surprising ardor, put her arms around him, leaned against him, and said, "You know I love you very, very much, and I know you're a splendid fellow, but you do have one little fault: you make too many trips to Heidelberg."

She had run quickly into the house, waved, smiled, blown him kisses, and he could still see her in the rear-view mirror, standing there waving vigorously.

Surely it couldn't be jealousy. After all, she knew he went there to see Diego and Teresa, to help them translate applications, fill out forms and questionnaires; that he drew up petitions, typed the final versions—for the department of aliens, the bureau of social services, the union, the university, the employment office—concerning placing children in schools and kindergartens, bursaries, grants, clothing, holiday camps. She knew what he was doing in Heidelberg, had gone there with him a few times, had done more than her share of typing, and displayed a surprising knowledge of officialese. Once or twice she had even taken Teresa along to a movie and a café, and her father had given her money for a Chilean fund.

Instead of driving home, he had gone to Heidelberg; Diego and Teresa had been out, as had Raoul, Diego's friend. On the way back he had got into a traffic jam, and around nine had looked in on his brother Karl, who went to the fridge for some beer while Hilda fried him some eggs. Together they had watched the Tour de Suisse on TV, in which Eddy

Merckx hadn't shown up too well, and, when he left, Hilda had given him a paper bag full of used children's clothing for "that nice gutsy Chilean and his wife."

Now AT last the news came on, and he listened with only half an ear: he was thinking of the carrots, the spinach, and the cherries that he still had to put away in the freezer compartment; he lit a second cigarette after all: somewhere—was it in Ireland? there had been an election, a landslide; someone—was it really the Federal President?—had said something very positive about neckties; someone was issuing a denial about something; the stock market was up; still no trace of Idi Amin.

He didn't finish his second cigarette and stubbed it out in a half-empty yogurt tub; he really was dead tired and soon fell asleep, though the word "Heidelberg" kept reverberating in his mind.

HE HAD a frugal breakfast, just milk and bread, tidied up, took a shower, and dressed with care. Putting on his tie he thought of the Federal President —or had it been the Federal Chancellor? Fifteen minutes early for his appointment, he sat on the bench outside Kronsorgeler's outer office, next to him a fat man in trendy, casual clothes; he recognized him from the teacher-training courses but didn't know his name. The fat man whispered, "I'm a Communist, you too?"

"No," he said. "No, I'm not—I hope you don't mind."

The fat man didn't spend long with Kronsorgeler; as he came out he made a gesture that was probably supposed to convey "no dice." Then the secretary asked him to go in; she was pleasant, not exactly young, had always been nice to him—he was surprised when she gave him an encouraging nudge, having always regarded her as too prim for that kind of thing.

Kronsorgeler received him with a smile. He was nice, conservative but nice; objective; not old, in his early forties at most. A bicycle-racing fan, he had given him a lot of encouragement, and they began by discussing the Tour de Suisse: whether Merckx had been bluffing so as to be underrated in the Tour de France or whether he had really lost his form. In Kronsorgeler's opinion, Merckx had been bluffing; he disagreed, feeling that Merckx really was almost finished, there were certain signs of exhaustion that couldn't be faked. Then came the exam: that they had wondered for a long time whether they couldn't give him straight As, the snag had been philosophy. But otherwise: his excellent work at the adult education center, at those evening classes, never taking part in demonstrations . . . there was just—Kronsorgeler gave a genuinely warm smile—one tiny little blot.

"Yes, I know," he said. "I make too many trips to Heidelberg."

Kronsorgeler almost blushed; at any rate his embarrassment was obvious. He was a sensitive, reserved person, almost shy; bluntness was not in his nature.

"How do you know?"

"I've been hearing it from all sides. Wherever I go, whoever I talk to. My father, Carola, her father, all I hear is: Heidelberg. Loud and clear, and I wonder whether, if I were to dial the weather bureau or bus information I wouldn't hear: Heidelberg."

For a moment it looked as though Kronsorgeler would rise and place his hands soothingly on his shoulders. He had already risen, then he lowered his hands again, placed them flat on his desk, and said, "I can't tell you how awkward this is for me. I have followed your path, a difficult path, with much sympathy—but there's a report on that Chilean that isn't very favorable. I can't ignore that report, I simply can't. I have not only rules to follow but also instructions, I've been given not only guidelines but also advice over the phone. Your friend—I take it he is your friend?"

"Yes."

"You'll have plenty of time on your hands during the next few weeks. What are your plans?"

"I'll be training a lot—cycling again, and I'll make lots of trips to Heidelberg."

"By bike?"

"No, by car."

Kronsorgeler sighed. It was obvious he was suffering, genuinely suffering. When he shook hands he whispered, "Don't go to Heidelberg, that's all I can say." Then he smiled and said, "Remember Eddy Merckx."

Even as he closed the door behind him and walked through the outer office, he was thinking of alternatives: translator, interpreter, tour guide, Spanish correspondent for a trading company. He was too old to become a pro, and there were already more than enough electricians. He had forgotten to say good-bye to the secretary, so he turned back and waved to her.

My Father's Cough

WHEN MY father reached the same age as I am now approaching, he (naturally?) seemed older to me than I feel. Birthdays were not celebrated in our family, that was considered a "Protestant aberration," so I cannot recall any celebration, only a few details of the mood prevailing that October 1930. (My father shared his year of birth, 1870, with Lenin, but that, I believe, was all.)

It was a dismal year. Total financial collapse, not exactly a classic "failure," merely a "compromise with creditors," a procedure I didn't understand, but at any rate it sounded more dignified than "bankruptcy." It was somehow connected with the collapse of an artisans' bank whose manager, if I remember correctly, ended up behind bars. Abuse of confidence, forfeited guarantees, unwise speculations. Our house in the suburbs had to be sold, and not a penny remained of the sales price. Upset and confused, we moved into a large—too large—apartment on Ubier-Ring in Cologne, across from what was then the vocational school.

Bailiffs, bailiffs, affixing seal after seal. We pulled these off while they were still fresh, ignoring this preliminary step to seizure; later we became indifferent and left them in place, and eventually some pieces of furniture (the piano, for instance) bore whole accumulations of seals. We got along fine with the bailiffs. There was irony on both sides, rudeness on neither.

I can remember the appearance of that four-pfennig piece, something to do with political emergency regulations, and the tobacco tax. This four-pfennig piece was a large, attractively designed copper coin, but it may not have appeared until a year or so later, perhaps 1931–32. The Nazis marched triumphantly into the Reichstag. Brüning was chancellor. We read the *Kölnische Volkszeitung.* My older brothers and sisters swore by the *RMV (Rhein-Mainische-Volkszeitung).*

I said good-bye to outdoor games. Sadly. Out in the suburb of Raderberg we had still been able to play hockey on the streets (with old umbrella handles and empty condensed-milk cans); rounders often, soccer less often, in Vorgebirg Park. We used to decapitate roses in the park with our "tweakers," known elsewhere in Germany as slings. Our hoop-tossing consisted of flinging old bicycle-wheel rims down a gentle grassy slope; the one whose hoop rolled the farthest was the winner. Records were established, and we rolled our hoops all the way around the block: it wasn't "done" to use bought, wooden hoops. Ping-Pong on the terrace, the swing in the garden; target practice with air rifles on burned-out light bulbs, which in those days were still of the bayonet type. We never found anything military, let alone militaristic, about this target practice. Ten years of freedom and many free games, too numerous for me to list. (St. Martin's torches, building and flying paper kites, marbles.)

In the long corridor of the apartment on Ubier-Ring we continued our target practice, now with regulation targets and bolts that we called "plumets" (the dictionary tells me this comes from the Latin *pluma:* the bolts had little colored tufts attached to them). During target practice, of course, whoever wanted to go into the bathroom, the kitchen, or the bedroom, or happened to be in there, had to be warned. Overall mood: recklessness and fear, not mutually exclusive. Needless to say, not all our income was revealed to the bailiff. There was moonlighting, income from renting out woodworking machinery. Recently I read in Isaac Bashevis Singer's *Enemies, a Love Story,* "If one wanted to live, one had to break the law, because all laws condemned one to death." We wanted to live.

We lived on a modest scale, yet modesty did not become our guiding principle. We had more than enough worries and debts. The rent, food, clothing, books, heating, electricity. The only thing that kept us going was a temporary lightheartedness which, of course, we only achieved temporarily. Somehow, after all, money had also to be found for movies, for cigarettes, for the indispensable coffee: something we didn't always, but did sometimes, achieve. We discovered pawnshops.

It wasn't all as carefree as it may sound. The more modest the scale, the less did modesty become our guiding principle. I gratefully remember the devotion of my older brothers and sisters, who must have made life easier for me, the youngest, by letting me have a little something from time to time. What scared me most during that period was my father's cough. He was of slight build (between the ages of twenty and eighty-five his weight varied by only two or three pounds; only after the age of eighty-five did he start to lose weight). He was moderate in his habits but liked to smoke, never inhaled, and he refused to do without (or at least entirely without!) his "Lundi"—those thin, pungent cigarillos packed in round cans. He was sad in these circumstances, and also powerless against conditions, and I sometimes think that we children never paid enough attention to his sadness.

His cough drowned out even the roar of streetcar Number 16, and we could hear his cough from far away. But the place where I was most worried by his cough was crowded St. Severin's Church on Sundays. We never went to Mass *en bloc,* always individually, rarely did two or three of us youngsters sit together in one pew, so we waited, each in his own seat, full of nervous tension, for our father's cough, knowing it would start up, increase almost to the point of suffocation, and then, as my father left the church, subside. He would then probably stand outside and smoke a "Lundi" for his cough.

Now the same age as my father was then, I find that I (and I am not the only one) have apparently inherited his cough. There are some people in our household who, as I park outside amid heavy traffic, recognize me through the noise of all those cars by my cough. I hardly ever have to ring the bell or use my key: someone is opening the front door before I do either.

My cough must be on a wavelength that penetrates not only traffic noises and screeching brakes but even police sirens, yet I don't believe that my cough can be called "penetrating." It consists of variations on differing forms of hoarseness, usually denotes embarrassment, is seldom a sign of a cold; and there are some people who know that it is more than a cough —and less. A granddaughter, for example, who is a year old, apparently regards it as a form of speech or address; she imitates it, coughing dialogues develop between us of an ironically amused nature, dialogues in which we apparently both have something to communicate. I am reminded of Beuys, who once made a speech consisting only of harrumphings and little coughs —and a very clever speech it was, by the way.

Perhaps one should establish harrumphing schools, at least consider harrumphing as a school subject; anyway, rid it of its silly admonitory function—to stop someone from making that tactless remark, for instance. *L'art pour l'art* as applied to coughing and harrumphing.

It might also be worth considering whether clever heads shouldn't invent the harrumphing letter-to-the-editor.

Rendezvous with Margret or: Happy Ending

T HE JOURNEY there was pleasant: the Rhine still under early-morning mist; weeping willows, barges, sirens, the trip taking precisely as long as I needed for my breakfast. Coffee and rolls acceptable, eggs fried; no baggage, just cigarettes, newspaper, matches, return ticket, ballpoint pen, wallet, and handkerchief, and the certainty of seeing Margret again. After so many years, after several abortive meetings, after knowing her for more than forty years, I had been surprised and stirred by something I had never seen before: her handwriting, strong yet graceful, and the words, written on the death announcement with surprising firmness: "do come—it would give me so much pleasure to see you again." The small "d" in "do" made me suspect that she had never come to terms with the capital "D"; we all have a letter or two that we stumble over.

On arrival I got rid of my largest piece of baggage, the newspaper. I left it behind in the dining car and reached the cemetery in good time after my own fashion: too late for the *Largo,* the *De Profundis,* and the incense in the chapel, too late also to join the cortège. I was just in time to see the acolytes taking off their vestments and bundling them under their arms as they walked away. The taller one unscrewed the processional cross into three sections, packing it away in a case obviously designed for that purpose, and as they got into the waiting taxi they all lit cigarettes: priest, driver, and acolytes. The driver offered the priest a light, the younger acolyte did the same for the older one, and at that point one of them must have made a joke: I saw them all laugh, saw the older acolyte coughing with laughter and cigarette smoke, and I had to laugh too, when I thought of the sacristy cupboards where in another five minutes they would be putting away their paraphernalia: oak, baroque, three hundred years old, the pride of the parish of St. Francis Xavier, which in 1925 had been renamed St. Peter Canisius; and it wasn't I, it was the deceased who had

just been buried, on whose coffin clods of earth were still falling, he who
had saved the day in 1945 by his inspired recollection of the depth of those
cupboards where, behind the neat piles of altar linen and various sacred
utensils, we had hidden cigarettes and coffee stolen from the Americans
when they left their Jeeps unattended or invited us in groups to a kind of
Werewolf-reeducation. It was he, not I, who, with the corrupt cunning
of the European, had correctly sized up the Americans' naïve awe of
ecclesiastical institutions, and for years I had wondered why, instead of
claiming credit for this inspiration, he had always ascribed it to me. Much
later, long after I had left home, it dawned on me that a story of that kind
would have done no service to his respectability, whereas it "fitted" me,
although I never really had that idea nor ever would have.

I APPROACHED the Zerhoff family grave with circumspection, avoiding the
paths on which I would have encountered men with and without top hats,
ladies with and without Persian lamb coats, former schoolmates and
knights of Catholic orders, schoolmates *as* knights of Catholic orders. I
walked along the familiar path between the rows of graves to our own
family grave, where the last burial—my father's—had taken place five
years ago; it had been insinuated that he had died brokenhearted because
neither of his two sons had begotten a male heir in any woman's womb;
well, he had no female heir either. The burial plot was well cared for, the
lease paid; the gravel was truly snow-white, the beds of pansies heartshaped, the pansies in turn—nine or eleven to a bed—planted in the shape
of a heart. The names of Mother, Father, and Josef on the lectern-shaped
marble gravestones; above Josef's name, the inevitable iron cross; the
gravestones of long-dead ancestors overgrown with ivy and, rising above
all the graves, the simple, classicistic, vaguely Puritan cross, to which had
later been added a scroll proclaiming in neo-Gothic script: "Love never
endeth." A gravestone was ready for me, too, the last bearer of the name;
the dash after my name and birth date, that graphic "to," had something
ominous about it. Who would continue to pay the (not inconsiderable)
lease when my earthly days were done? Margret, probably. She was a
woman in good health, well off, childless, a tea drinker, a moderate smoker,
and in the melody of her handwriting, particularly in the small "d," I could
perceive a long life for her.

I stood behind the tamarisk hedge, now grown quite dense, that
separated the Zerhoff burial plot from ours, and then I saw her: she seemed
more attractive than ever, more so than the girl of fifteen with whom I
had lain in the grass, more so than the woman of twenty, thirty, and

thirty-five with whom I had had those embarrassing and abortive reunions, the last one fifteen years ago in Sinzig when she turned on her heel outside the hotel room and drove away; she hadn't even allowed me to take her to the station. She must be close to fifty now, her thick, rather coarse blond hair had turned an attractive gray, and black suited her.

As children we had often had to come out here on summer evenings to water the flowers: my brother Josef, Margret, myself, and her brother Franzi, into whose grave the last members of the cortège were just then throwing their flowers or their shovelfuls of earth; the familiar drumming of earth on wood, the impact of the bunches of mimosa like the alighting of a bird. Often we had spent our streetcar money on ice cream, setting out on the long homeward journey on foot and, in the summer heat, soon regretting our recklessness, but invariably Josef had produced some hidden "reserves" and paid our fares home, and on the streetcar, relieved and tired, we would argue about whether he had paid for our ice cream or our fares.

I still had to fight back my tears when I thought of Josef, and I still didn't know, after thirty-four years I didn't know, whether it was his death or his last wish that brought tears to my eyes. At the very end of the platform, beyond the station roof, before the arrival of the leave train, we had once again discussed ways and means of not returning to the front, fever, accident, medical certificates—and in the end it was Margret who broke the taboo and spoke of—what do they call it?—"desertion," and Father had stamped his foot in rage and said, "There is no such thing as desertion in our family!" and Josef had laughed and said, "Where to? Am I supposed to swim across the Channel or to Sweden, or across Lake Constance to Switzerland—and Vladivostok, you know, is a pretty long way off," and he was already standing on the steps, the stationmaster had blown his whistle, when he leaned down once more and said clearly, more to me than to my father, "Please, no priests at my grave, no mumbo jumbo at any memorial service." He was nineteen, had given up the study of theology, and Margret was at that time considered almost his fiancée. We never saw him again. We winced, I more than my father, Margret less, as if whipped by his last words; and of course, when the news of his death arrived, I reminded Father of Josef's last wish, not repeating his words, I was too scared to do that, but simply saying, "You know what he asked for, what his last wish was." But Father had waved me away and, I need hardly say, not done as Josef had asked. They had indeed had their memorial service, with incense, Latin, and catafalque; in solemn pomp they had executed their precise choreography, in their black, gold-embroidered brocade robes, and they had even rounded up a choir of theology students who sang something in Greek. The Eastern Churches were already becoming very fashionable. I have never entered a church since, except as an acolyte and in my later capacity as salesman of devotional supplies; and when Franzi Zerhoff and I had assisted at solemn requiems, they had sometimes reminded me, in their heavy, gold-embroidered brocade robes, of Soviet marshals with their bulky gold shoulder pieces and their chests covered with about a hundred and fifty decorations. Always plenty of Latin, male choir in red-and-white sashes, top hats trembling in their hands, and the air trembling with the vehemence of their chest tones.

MARGRET'S mouth was surprisingly small and still not hard under her austere nose; she was slimmer, only her wrists revealed traces of plumpness. There she stood, dignified, erect, shaking hands, nodding, yet she had kept that swift, ephemeral, springy quality. The gray around her head reminded me of the whitish-gray dust in her hair when we staggered out of the burning house and lay down in the garden on the grass, came together on that June night after saying good-bye to Josef, when so many values and so much that was valuable had been destroyed; and I thought of the dust in her kisses, in her tears, of our irresponsible laughter when Father also came staggering out of the house and saw us lying there, and how our dust-powdered faces screwed up with laughter when he twisted the key to his safe in the air as if it, the air, contained his securities and all that notarized stuff; and of course he didn't know, none of us knew, that in this so charmingly conventional war degrees of heat would build up that venerable safes could not withstand. And in the end, when later they were poking through the debris, he had found nothing but ashes in his molten safe, and it had been Margret, not I (who was of course familiar with such sayings), who told him, *"Memento, quia pulvis es et . . . "*, but she did not complete the sentence. For a time we were inseparable, but we never came together again, not even with a kiss, not even with a handclasp.

Margret turned toward me and, in a kind of bitter joy, her woman's face changed to the face of that girl who, with me, had scorned accepted values on that June night—or had I then embraced the Margret of today, had I at last caught up with her, she with me? Had Josef's curse at last truly united us? I thought of him, of the whiplash with which he had changed the course of my life, and I realized here, at last, that that was what he had wanted: to change the course of my life, away from gold brocade, male choirs, family graves, real and potential knights of Catholic orders. Perhaps that was the only thing he had learned in that gloriously conventional war, and today, here, facing Margret, I had no reason to bear a grudge against him on that score. I bore no grudge against anyone, not even against my father, who later became very silent, almost humble, and who always looked so expectantly at me when Margret came over from next door. We used to go to the movies, to the theater, for walks, we had long discussions—but we never got as far as even a handclasp, even a flicker of memory. I carried on as an acolyte, regarding it as a job (tips and free meals); I got into the black market, finished high school, left home, and, via the black market, ended up in the devotional-supplies business when I was asked to get hold of a Leonardo da Vinci print for a Moselle vintner's first communion in exchange for butter, and did so. I had a few affairs, and I imagine Margret did, too.

I WAS standing close enough to be able to read the word "Blackbird," from Margret's lips. I nodded, withdrew, and headed for the "Blackbird," where funeral receptions have been held since time immemorial. I only had to go back to the exit, cross the street, and walk for five minutes through Douglas firs. At the "Blackbird" they were already busy cutting up limp rolls, spreading them with butter, adding slices of sausage or cheese, and decorating them with mayonnaise. I wondered whether Aunt Marga was still alive, she had always insisted on having blood sausage with onion rings, as greedily as if she were starving, although everyone knew that not even she had any idea of the extent of her fortune. The coffee machine was steaming, brandy snifters were being placed on trays, freshly opened bottles beside them (Margret was sure to have firmly insisted on a price "by the bottle"), bottles of mineral water were being snapped open, flowers stuck in little vases. Still the same old, old-fashioned routine.

I recognized the priest, who had arrived without the acolytes and was sitting in a corner smoking a cigar with a contented, off-duty expression. He nodded at me. Not because he recognized me, we had never met. He looked like a nice fellow, I sat down at his table and asked him about the special carrying case for the collapsible cross: in my days as an acolyte we used to have to lug the whole cross around, and it had always been a problem getting it into a car without smashing a window or knocking top hats off heads. And I knew of a few rural communities where the old processional cross was still in use. He told me the name of the company, I jotted it down on my return ticket, then we both speculated as to why people continued to put up with those limp rolls. I told him that even as children we had called those sandwiches "Blackbird pasteboard with mayonnaise," whether we were present as mourners or acolytes or—as frequently happened—as mourning acolytes. They were behind the times, there should be "Hawaiian Toast" or something, and sherry, not brandy, and not Persian lamb coats but mink, and instead of the lousy coffee—why did it always have to be so lousy everywhere?—they should have ordered mocha, which did sometimes turn out like reasonably good coffee.

I glanced at my return ticket, where I had noted the trains: 14:22, 15:17, then none till 17:03; it was now just on eleven, and if I wanted to take Margret along, if I wanted, after thirty-four years, to touch her hair that evening, I supposed I would have to stay on a while and run the risk of encountering a former schoolmate or two among the red-and-white sashes, maybe even among the Catholic knights: one of them was sure to shout the opening lines of *The Odyssey*—in Greek, of course—into my ear, to prove that his classical education had not failed to leave its mark on him. Another, although we had graduated from high school more than thirty years ago and not seen each other since, taking it for granted that I would fully agree, would start moaning about modern times, about his spoiled brats, the Socialists, the general moral decline, and how he was working himself to death in his practice while his third or fourth apartment building was costing him more and more due to this damned inflation. I was prepared to endure this; I knew this kind of talk from funerals I had attended not as a mourner but professionally: I also have an agency for gravestones, and my top hat counts as professional clothing and is tax-deductible. It couldn't take all that long: if we missed the 14:22 we would certainly catch the 15:17.

I WAS in luck, it was Bertholdi who sat down beside me. I recalled that in eight years of school I hadn't exchanged so much as forty words with him. There had been simply no occasion to do so, and I had reason to regret this now. He was a very nice fellow, without that bitter-sour expression that seems inevitable with successful as well as unsuccessful men at the start of the last third of their lives. Bertholdi asked how my business was going, and when I told him that I had been selling devotional supplies for some years now, he remarked that it must be hard going in this post–Vatican Council era. I agreed that business had taken a beating, but I could also report a certain upswing, and when he mentioned "Lefebvre?" I nodded but also shook my head. His shrewd question could be answered only partially in the affirmative: there was also, I said, independently of the person he had named, a return to the traditional that expressed itself in top hats, bridal trains, elaborate celebrations of first communions, confirmations, and weddings, and in its wake helped the sale of modern devotional supplies, well-crafted icon copies, for instance, in fact anything smacking of the Eastern Churches.

Because he spoke so nicely about his wife and children, I volunteered the information that, together with some business associates, I was engaged in opening up a new market for good icon reproductions: the Soviet Union, which we were supplying—illegally, of course—with excellent reproductions that were mounted over there on old wood panels, preferably worm-eaten, and painted over by skilled craftsmen, and for which there was a good demand. Since artists, craftsmen, and dealers naturally preferred foreign currency, quite a few of these reproductions were finding their way back via the tourist black market. Not exactly sharing in the profits, but doing its best to help, was an organization calling itself "Pictures for the Eastern Churches"; too many Soviet citizens in all the republics had sold off their family icons and now, caught up in the religious wave, found themselves without images. And, inwardly uneasy because Margret was still moving around and had not yet sat down, I went on to tell Bertholdi the trade's classic story of that long-dead colleague who, putting his trust in the religious currents prevalent during World War I, found himself stuck with some 10,000 portraits of Pope Benedict XV and lacked the financial and mental resources to save his business by profiting from the long reigns of the two Piuses. When asked by Bertholdi whether I would still invest much in Paul VI, I said, "As a contemporary, perhaps; as a dealer in devotional supplies, no," adding that the only pope who had remained in demand after his death was John XXIII.

Bertholdi thanked me for this insight into the "subtleties" of my business and returned the compliment with an autobiographical sketch: he was a senior official in the educational system, complained neither of his children nor of the youth of today, spoke affectionately of his wife, laughingly discussed his pension with all its probable progressions and deductions; he hoped, he was confident, that he would be able to take early retirement so that he would finally have time to read Proust and Henry James. At last Margret came and sat down beside me, beckoned to a waitress to bring me a little pot of mocha, placed her hand on my arm, and said, "I remember how you hate bad coffee, and"—she didn't take away her hand—"just now, when I saw you standing there, it occurred to me, after all these years it occurred to me, that he didn't curse God at all."

"No," I said, "it was only those cursed by God whom he cursed. And that curse was the blessing that he gave us."

Willi Offermann, seated across from us next to the priest, tried to bait me by speaking of Jerusalem and the Holy Sepulcher, and of people who had no religion yet lived very well off it. Did he mean me, or the dealers in devotional supplies in Jerusalem? Do I have no religion and live very well off it? Both questions filled me with doubts. True, I did live off it, but not as well as he seemed to believe, not even my gravestone agency brought in as much, although I can offer the latest designs and good African stones; and sometimes when I was checking a new shipment of rosaries (for which there was no longer much demand, at least not at the moment, in spite of Lefebvre), I would grasp one and recite the entire rosary. So as not to be looking constantly at Margret, who had got up again to tell a waiter carrying a plate of onion rings and slices of blood sausage to take it over to where Aunt Marga was indeed sitting, I looked at Offermann's wife: she was next to the priest and leaning across him in an effort to calm down her husband on the other side when Offermann suddenly raised his voice and started abusing the "Red scum!"—which was nonsense, because he hadn't seen me for thirty-one years and could have no idea whether I was red or green; besides, a minimum of logic should have told him that no sensible dealer in devotional supplies—and that's what I was—would ever vote for any party without the prefix "Christian." This was so obvious that he could have saved himself his uninformed provocation; I behaved as if he certainly couldn't mean me and smiled at his wife, who looked so nice that he couldn't possibly have deserved her.

THEN MARGRET was beside me again, pouring mocha and remembering that I took whipped cream with it; she had brought over a little dish of it. She smelled of soap, toilet water, and perspiration, a smell that I perceived as familiar—yet it couldn't possibly be familiar to me. It was as if we had spent these thirty-four years together, her years becoming mine, a common tally of the years: some things neglected but nothing missed. I found her much more beautiful than on that June night; actually she had never been a beauty, she had always seemed like a girl who had been bicycling too fast and broken into a sweat, yet she had never been on a bicycle. As I looked at her she became younger and younger, until I could see her playing ball on the path between our two houses, flushed, eager, yet quiet, and she was, after all, the first and only woman from whose lips I had heard the word "desertion."

She kept her hand on my arm, and Offermann grew even angrier, prophesying doom, and seeming to hold me, me personally, responsible for the simultaneous decline in morals and faith; and not even when he spoke of my brother Josef ("Of course, if your brother Josef were still alive, but then the best always get killed!") did I allow myself to be provoked into saying something like You didn't get killed either, nor did Margret—who turned pale and whose hand on my arm was trembling. Finally Offermann attacked the priest, whom he accused of being too passive, and it was I who, in order to calm him down, whispered the opening lines of *The Odyssey* to him across the table. That actually had an effect: his face relaxed, and his wife smiled at me gratefully; the priest was relieved. I had looked at the time and found it was only twelve o'clock and that we would be able to catch the 14:22, and during my Homer recitation I thought of coffee and cakes on the train, thought of the crowded dining car, which was now moving beside the Rhine toward the Lorelei rock, and that probably they still served nothing but that seed cake that was enough to choke a person. But it was a long time since I had last ridden in the dining car in the afternoon, I merely remembered that Margret liked that damn cake. Once, on the train to Sinzig, she had told me it reminded her of a deceased aunt of whom she had been very fond. I beckoned to the waitress and asked her to order me a taxi for a quarter to two.

Nostalgia

or: Grease Spots

THE NIGHT before Erica's wedding I changed my mind and did drive to the hotel to have another talk with Walter. I had known both him and Erica, his fiancée, for a long time; after all, I had lived with Erica for four years, in Mainz, while working on a construction job and at the same time going to night school. Walter had been working on the same construction site and also going to night school. It wasn't a pleasant period. I recall it without nostalgia: the arrogance of our teachers, who were more critical of our accents than of our performance, was so insidious that it was more painful than wordy abuse would have been. Apparently most of them couldn't bear the idea that, with our unabashed dialect, we might eventually acquire a university degree, and they forced us to speak in a way that we used to call "night-school German."

When I came off shift—sometimes at the same time as Walter—the first thing was always a shower, then fresh clothes and a general sprucing up, yet we still had lime under our fingernails, traces of cement in our eyelashes. We slogged away at math, history, Latin even, and when we actually did pass our exams, our teachers behaved as if it were some sort of canonization. After we'd gone on to university there were still—for a while—traces of lime in our hair, of cement behind our ears, sometimes in our nostrils, in spite of Erica's careful inspection of me, after which she would shake her head and whisper in my ear, "You'll never get rid of it, that proletarian background of yours." I felt no regret for my construction job when I won a scholarship and eventually obtained a degree, a B.Comm., with a correct accent, quite good manners, a reasonably decent job in Koblenz, and the prospect of being granted leave of absence to work toward my master's degree.

I was never quite sure whether Erica had left me or I her: I couldn't even remember whether it had been before or after I got my B.Comm. I only remember the bitter half sentences with which she reproached me for having become too stuck up for her, and I reproached her for having remained too vulgar, a word I still regret; over the years her vulgarity had lost its naturalness, it had become deliberate, especially when she came out with details about her job in a lingerie shop, or teased me when I asked her to help me look for traces of cement behind my ears long after I had given up my construction job. To this day, although I haven't set foot on a construction site for eight years (not even on my own—we're building a house, Franziska and I), I sometimes catch myself carefully inspecting my eyelashes and eyebrows in the mirror. This prompts a gentle headshake from Franziska: not knowing the reason for my concern, she ascribes this behavior to an excess of vanity.

In Mainz, Walter had often joined us for supper in our cramming days: on the table a package of margarine, hastily ripped open, potato salad or chips from the store, mayonnaise in a cardboard container; if we were lucky, two fried eggs prepared on the hotplate that never worked properly (Erica was genuinely scared of that hotplate: a thread of egg white had once given her an electric shock); also a loaf of bread from which we hacked off thick slabs—and my perpetual fear of grease spots on books and notebooks lying on the table between mayonnaise and margarine. And I was constantly confusing Ovid with Horace, and of course grease spots did appear on the books, and I happen to loathe grease spots on printed paper, even on newspapers. Even as a child I used to be disgusted when I had to take home pickled or kippered herrings wrapped in newspaper. My father would turn to my mother and say with a note of mockery, "What makes him so fastidious, I wonder? He doesn't get it from me, and certainly not from your family."

It was already quite late, nearly ten, when I reached the hotel. On the eighth floor, as I walked along the corridor looking for Walter's room, I tried to estimate from the distances between doors whether he had a single or a double room: I couldn't face an encounter with Erica. In those seven years I had heard from her only once, a postcard from Marbella on which all she had written was "Boring, boring, boring—and not even any grease spots!"

It was a single room; even before I saw Walter I saw his dark suit on a hanger outside the clothes closet, black shoes underneath, a silver-gray tie on the crossbar of the hanger. My next glance was through the open bathroom door and took in a wet cigarette in a puddle of bathwater: the shreds of tobacco dyed the puddle yellow. Walter had evidently misjudged the size of hotel bathtubs and put in too much bath oil. I saw the glass of whiskey and soda on the plastic stool before I discovered him behind clouds of foam.

"Come right in!" he said. "I imagine you've come to warn me." He wiped the foam from his face and neck and laughed at me.

"Only don't forget our difference in rank: after all, I do have my Ph.D., and you don't—I wonder whether, if it came to a duel, you'd be qualified to challenge me—and don't kid yourself that you can talk me out of marrying her! There's just one thing you should know, just one: in Mainz there was never anything between us, never."

I was glad he didn't laugh as he said that. I closed the bathroom door, sat down on his bed, and looked at the dark suit: that was how, the night before our wedding, my own suit had hung outside a hotel clothes closet in Koblenz, and my tie had also been silver-gray.

I watched Walter come out of the bathroom, rub himself down in his bathrobe, put on his pajamas, throw the bathrobe onto the floor, and, with a laugh, run the silver-gray tie through his hand. "Believe me," he said, "I only met her again a year ago, quite by chance, and—well, now we're getting married. Will you be there tomorrow?"

I shook my head and asked, "In church too?"

"Yes, in church too, because of her parents, who love a good cry at weddings. The civil ceremony alone isn't enough for the tear ducts—and she's still vulgar, but already we're using a butter dish."

"Cut it out," I said, taking the glass of whiskey he held out to me.

"I'm sorry," he said, "I really am. Let's have no old-timers' reminiscences, no explanations, no confessions—and no warnings."

I thought of what I had intended to tell him: what a tramp she really was; that she couldn't handle money; that sometimes I had found hairs in the margarine and always those goddamn grease spots, on books, newspapers, even on photos; how hard it had been to get her out of bed in the morning, and her naïve/proletarian ideas of breakfast-in-bed being the acme of luxury, and the resulting jam spots on the sheets and brown coffee stains on the quilt; yes, and she was lazy, too, and not even clean, I had literally had to force her to wash: sometimes I had actually grabbed hold of her and dumped her in the tub, bathed her the way one bathes a child, with much screaming and spluttering; yes, and that sometimes she had got mad yet had never been in a bad mood, no, never in a bad mood. At that point I remembered the house we were building, to which I never went, leaving it all to Franziska and the architect.

"And just imagine," said Walter, "she doesn't want us to start building a house, and I've always looked for a wife who didn't want that. Now I've found her, at last—she hates building and construction."

I was just about to say, "So do I," but all I said was, "Give her my regards. I suppose it's quite final, is it?"

"Final," he said, "in fact, irrevocable if only because of those parental tears. We can't do that to them, we can't deprive them of that."

"As for tears," I said, "they could also shed those if it didn't come off."

"But those wouldn't be the kind of tears they're after, they want the genuine kind, the real kind, with organ music and candles and all that—and they want the barely audible 'I do.' No. And the honeymoon—where d'you think we're going?"

"Venice?"

"Right—gondolas and color photos. Go ahead and cry a bit on your way down in the elevator."

I finished my whiskey, shook his hand, and left, and on my way down in the elevator I cried a bit more than a bit, and I didn't bother to dry my tears as I walked past the concierge out to my car. I had told Franziska I wanted to say hello to an old friend, and that was really all it had been.

In Which Language
Is One Called
Schneckenröder?

IT WASN'T at all the way he had imagined it: at worst the white van with the red thing—what was it called?—on it. From the white van into the white bed, from the white bed into the white engine room; green caps, surgical masks, lonely eyes above, red blood in plastic tubes, hurriedly whispered orders, before one was far, far, very far away. Bed? White? Van? Imagined? Ear? Ear? So he did remember something, and he tried to touch them, realized he couldn't find them, couldn't touch them, his ears, yet he could hear: female giggles, male groans, behind a—whatever was it called, what was the word for it?—rectangular, painted sky-blue with a pink border, a bluish light bulb above it, like in an air-raid shelter? Damn it, he knew that all right: air-raid shelter, knew bed, van, white, but what was the word for that rectangular, sky-blue thing with a pink border? Entrance wasn't right, that much he knew, entrance was something that led from the outside to the inside, and this one led from the inside to a still further inside. Could it be *"in*trance"? In this inside there was male laughter now, and female groaning, and damn it, someone was whispering "Paternoster," and clearly, unmistakably, someone else was whispering "Ave Maria." They must be Catholics, that much was certain. Catholics, Protestants, Jews; now he found his ears, they were still there, even his nose, he could feel it as well as his ears, but not his—what were those things called that one used for touching, grasping? He couldn't feel them, didn't know what the red thing on the white van was called. Van. Car. There had been something about a car. His nose even became aware of smells: soups, sauces, he could even hear them gently bubbling, a woman's voice saying *"Los!"*, the "o" in *"Los!"* sounded strange, he had heard that "o" before, it wasn't Russian, or French, or Italian, wasn't—what was the language he couldn't remember?—wasn't English, wasn't Swedish, or Danish, or Dutch—he could think of all the languages, even Arabic—just that one, the one whose name he was looking for, he couldn't think of that, only the word with that "o" he had heard before popped into his mind—*olvidados*—and that was Spanish. Was he in Spain? The rectangular thing that wasn't an entrance yet led somewhere, the things one grasped with, the red thing on the white van, the language, the language he thought and cursed in—he couldn't think of its name; those other things, the ones one saw with, those he could think of right away: eyes. They wouldn't open, he couldn't raise his—and he even knew that word—eyelids! He couldn't raise his eyelids, he touched them, pushed as he had pushed when trying to lift that damn heavy garage shutter in the house he had once lived in, that damn shutter that always seemed as heavy as lead. Shutter? No, it wasn't a shutter, that sky-blue, rectangular thing with a pink border, it was something one opened yet not a shutter, and not an entrance either. The things one grasped with were finding it hard to hold up his eyelids. And, true enough, he could see: aluminum pans with that pungent brew bubbling in them, spoons, plates, cold stuff beside them: cucumbers, tomatoes, mustard. Yes, it was called mustard, that yellow stuff in the smeared jar with the wooden spatula, all words he knew: soup, mustard, sauce, cucumber—he knew all those words and couldn't remember the things one grasped with and that red thing on the white van he hadn't wanted to be put into; those were spoons, or ladles actually, and a woman, nice, not thin, not old, her hair not smart at all, she was the one who had pronounced the "o" in such a Spanish way. There was also a pot of steaming noodles; did the Spanish eat noodles? The Mexicans—do *they* eat noodles? Whatever were they called, those people who ate such a lot of noodles? Paternoster, Ave Maria —damn it, whatever was going on behind that rectangular sky-blue thing had nothing to do with praying, or were they praying at the same time? Catholics, of course—obviously—how wonderful that he could remember a word like "obviously"!—obviously this was a snack bar—yes, that's what they were called!—and simultaneously—fancy his remembering the word "simultaneously"!—simultaneously one of those places where the same thing went on as behind the entrance that wasn't an entrance. One thing he couldn't do, and that was what the woman was doing when she said *"Los!"*—speak, that's what it was, he couldn't speak—or did the groaning, the giggling, the laughing, the praying have nothing to do with that? Was it a kind of prayer hall or room for confession? Yes, it was called speaking, what the woman did when she said *"Los!"*—he couldn't speak; he had to lower the things one grasps with, his eyelids were growing too heavy, leaden shutters, and on bottles and posters he read those damned "os," so many "os"—and how had he managed to see the sky-blue thing before he pushed up his eyelids? He had seen it before, and the thing one spoke with was called mouth, in the mouth was the tongue: he tried to touch it—nothing, there was nothing to touch, to feel—but smell, hear, see, he could do all that, yet he couldn't speak, and the language spoken by the people who also ate noodles, whatever was that called? Of course: the super-noodle-eaters were the Italians, but the people whose language he spoke, when he could speak, also ate noodles: white noodles, he'd eaten those at home too, white van, white bed, white engine room, green caps, skullcaps actually, lonely eyes; bluish light beyond the sky-blue rectangle, before—before the thing happened that he had imagined so differently. He knew that, before his eyelids fell and his mouth disappeared, he had gone through that sky-blue rectangle—bluish light from loose bulbs, intermittent contacts, that much he knew: intermittent contacts—smiling corpses in bluish intermittent light. He wished he were home in bed—bed? Yellow sheets, blue pillows, the orange reading lamp, and around the bed, who would be standing there? A woman, his wife? Did he have one? He must have one, since there were those whom one had together with a wife, children, so he did have a wife, and children with her, and he also had a —what was it called, what one did when busy earning a living? How did he earn his living? Traveling, a lot of traveling in his—he had just had it, the word for what was revealed on opening the garage; red cross? No, white car, no red cross on it. How had he got to Mexico by car? To this snack bar? Garage shutter—no, not shutter, door, now at last he had it, now he wouldn't have to keep thinking laboriously of the "sky-blue rectangle with a pink border." Door was easier. Here by the door soups and sauces were being ladled out of pans, and all the words on bottles and posters ended in "os." Was he a Spaniard, a Mexican? Then how come the noodles, and what was the name of the woman with whom he had those children? What was she called? He had been with her a long time, after all. One thing was certain: the things one grasped with were fingers, and the fingers were attached to hands. Door, fingers, hands, the red thing on the white van was a cross, and of course he had been beyond that door, someone had pushed him in, someone else had pushed him out. Far away a fragmented word was hovering as if on a celestial course, in lunar spheres, torn shreds flew toward him: Otte-lie-les, that "les" must somehow be related to the "os." Related? That made him laugh, and laughing hurt him around his mouth, the mouth that was no longer there; gone was the mouth along with everything in it, yet it hurt inside and out. Hurt? Everything hurt, everything, his ears, his eyes, his nose, and—what were they called? —his fingers, only his mouth didn't hurt, it wasn't there and only hurt when he laughed about "related"; he could even reverse the "les" and turn it into "sel"—Lie-otte-sel, everything was turning, not turning around, just turning: far, far away everything was rampaging among the pathways of the stars, the glitter of the universe, the shimmer of the moon—the soups and sauces were too spicy, spices, pungent, pathways of the heavens, glitter of the universe, shimmer of the moon, and when he pushed his eyelids up again, with an effort, such an effort, like that damn garage shutter he had once had, he saw the nice woman behind the pans of soups and sauces pushing back one breast into her blue blouse. No more Paternoster, no more Ave Maria, beyond the door, silence, garage, Otte? Clot? Spot? Charlotte? Gavotte? Knot? Charlotte? And then the shreds flew together, linking up like space shuttles, and there it was LIESELOTTE, that was his wife's name; not Spanish, or Mexican, but in a language that contained hardly any words ending in "os." Carlos. *Olvidados.*

WHAT WAS that language called? What were his children called? Lieselotte was better than the woman behind the counter, and the woman behind the counter was better than the woman beyond the door. Was he soiled, had he soiled himself? With what? With vomit? And the fingers that were attached to his hands couldn't thrust into the inside pocket of his soiled jacket, it was more than his fingers could manage, they couldn't thrust deeply, grasp firmly enough, at where his money and papers and checks had been. Lieselotte, so he had imagined, would have held his hand, and the other younger Lieselotte, his daughter, would have placed her hand on his forehead; it was a good thing to give one's children the names of their parents, two Lieselottes, the older one had black hair but wasn't Spanish, the younger Lieselotte had fair hair, beautiful, yes, with a real golden sheen to it—one Lieselotte should have placed her hand on his forehead, the other should have grasped his hand, or rather his wrist, with one of hers. That was how he had imagined it, if—if—but there were more children there, two more. They were standing around the bed, four of them, two Lieselottes and the boys, young men. What the devil was that language called that he couldn't remember, a language in which there were noodles in a country where noodles were also eaten yet wasn't Italy? No, he wasn't an Italian, nor was he an Austrian, although Austrians ate noodles.

THE THINGS you grasped with were fingers; the sky-blue rectangle was a door; the red thing on the white van was a cross. What was revealed behind the garage shutter when you pushed it up was a car. The older Lieselotte had black hair, the younger one fair—she had grown a bit lanky; one boy stood to the left of the older Lieselotte, the other to the right of the younger. Yellow sheets, blue pillows, the reading lamp orange—and on the opposite wall hung the thing that had been red on the white van, hanging there black, plain, crossed at right angles, a cross—and again they came from the glitter of the universe and the shimmer of the moon, came from that crossroads of celestial pathways, the names of the boys: Richard was the one to the left of the older Lieselotte, Heinrich was the one to the right of the younger Lieselotte. Damn it, in which language were you called Heinrich? Chill of the moon, heat of the sun, a circling, or rather a wheeling as with aircraft coming in to land. Aircraft? Surely he'd had his car in the aircraft? Richard was dark-haired and serious, Heinrich blond and cheerful. In which language did that name occur? Veins of the earth —rigid, deep, hard—yet also lava, hot, flowing, rampaging inside and out. As for the younger Lieselotte, she would fill out, that lanky figure, those prominent collarbones, all that would fill out, and one day she would be a stately blonde without hollows; the older Lieselotte was quite a different type, slight yet sturdy, a sturdy woman, with a surprising fullness behind the slightness, a good wife in every situation in life. Not a sturdy fortress, a sturdy wife, not athletic, not the gymnast type—no. Beyond the door it was quiet, as if someone in there were breathing with a gigantic chest. Sturdy fortress, sturdy woman—his laughter brought on a surge of pain, from ear to abdomen, from eye to knee. Everything sore and painful, painful and sore, and nothing below the knee; was there anything below the knee? Knee, that was almost a word like Heinrich. Eyelids pushed up again, heavier than ever, what an effort, how he could see the words on the posters: cigarillos, color photos, corphotolos, Carlos, that was a fellow behind a bull. Was he in Mexico after all, was he a Mexican? Could one be called Heinrich in Mexico? On Sundays, when he had to push up the garage door without help, it had been as heavy as lead and kept sliding down again until finally, with an effort, such an effort, he had pushed it into its catch at the top. The car. He had seldom driven himself, had usually sat in the back, and up front was Schneckenröder, who had an inspired way of driving fast yet phlegmatically. In which language was one called Schneckenröder, who could crawl and race at the same time? Schneckenröder hadn't been driving, nor had he; as usual he had sat in the back. What were those things called that one was driven in but not by Schneckenröder? No, not rental cars, no more than a door could be called a shutter. Those things he had seldom sat in were used only for short distances, from airport to hotel, from hotel to restaurant or movie theater, or to keep appointments. Now he had to laugh again about the sturdy fortress, sturdy woman —he had never called her that, but that's what she was, it had just occurred to him—and he certainly had been in a car, not with Schneckenröder but not driving himself either. Taxis, that's what those things were called, not rental cars, and the fellow had himself taken the money from his pocketbook. Pocket? Jacket pocket? Pocketbook? The fingers refused to go in that far. Color photos, cigarillos, Carlos, *olvidados,* on their way into the pocket the fingers went limp. Laughing was the worst, it hurt, felt sore, made that sloshing lava surge up between the stiff and stony asphalt veins. There was no white, and there was no orange reading lamp, no fair-haired girl with prominent collarbones, no sturdy wife, no mahogany-brown cross on the wall, no serious Richard or cheerful Heinrich; a bit, just a bit of white would have been good, not too much, just a bit, nothing was white here, nothing, not even the breast of the nice woman who had pushed it back into her blouse had been white. There was another "os" on one of the bottles behind the counter, and now, quite clear, quite near, the whispered Paternoster in his ear, with all the rest of it, all that he supposed went with it, and that Ave Maria too, that wasn't Spanish, that was Latin, and in the sturdy fortress—in his, anyway—he hadn't picked up all that much, no, that really was papist gabble, maybe even combined with a whole lot of superstitious mumblings. Not a bit of white, not a scrap. Where was Schneckenröder? Taxis, that's what those things were called, not rental cars. This lava that was sloshing around in him, this hot, painful, sore infinity, thinly encased as if in a toy balloon—surely it must soon burst, pour out, sore, painful, hot? What were corpholotos? And who was that saying in his ear: "Too late for the doctor, never too late for the priest"? Surely that was the language in which one was called Heinrich! He had imagined how it might happen, the best way it would happen or would have happened; how it might have happened and hadn't happened—not, oh, not like this! Someone reached into the inside pocket of his jacket, which was more than his fingers had managed, saying, "We'll find out all right," and that was the language in which one was called Schneckenröder, and Heinrich, like himself, spoken by someone who would pronounce the "os" as the woman had in *"Los!",* and it was someone else who pushed up his eyelids, and now he could clearly read what was printed on the bottle—"Calvados"—and was mystified: since when did anyone drink Calvados in these grubby snack bars with sky-blue, pink-bordered doors leading to the rear? And still he didn't know what language it was in which one was called Schneckenröder, or Heinrich, like himself.

European Classics

Honoré de Balzac
The Bureaucrats

Heinrich Böll
Absent without Leave
And Never Said a Word
And Where Were You, Adam?
The Bread of Those Early Years
End of a Mission
Irish Journal
Missing Persons and Other Essays
The Safety Net
A Soldier's Legacy
The Stories of Heinrich Böll
The Train Was on Time
Women in a River Landscape

Madeleine Bourdouxhe
La Femme de Gilles

Lydia Chukovskaya
Sofia Petrovna

Grazia Deledda
After the Divorce
Elias Portolu

Yury Dombrovsky
The Keeper of Antiquities

Aleksandr Druzhinin
Polinka Saks • The Story of Aleksei Dmitrich

Venedikt Erofeev
Moscow to the End of the Line

Konstantin Fedin
Cities and Years

Fyodor Vasilievich Gladkov
Cement

I. Grekova
The Ship of Widows

Marek Hlasko
The Eighth Day of the Week

Bohumil Hrabal
Closely Watched Trains

Erich Kästner
Fabian: The Story of a Moralist

Valentine Kataev
Time, Forward!

Ignacy Krasicki
The Adventures of Mr. Nicholas Wisdom

Miroslav Krleza
The Return of Philip Latinowicz

Curzio Malaparte
Kaputt

Karin Michaëlis
The Dangerous Age

Andrey Platonov
The Foundation Pit

Valentin Rasputin
Farewell to Matyora

Alain Robbe-Grillet
Snapshots

Arthur Schnitzler
The Road to the Open

Ludvík Vaculík
The Axe

Vladimir Voinovich
The Life and Extraordinary Adventures of
*   Private Ivan Chonkin*
Pretender to the Throne

Stefan Zweig
Beware of Pity